MANKOFF'S LUSTY EUROP

Mankoff's LUSTY EUROPE

THE FIRST ALL-PURPOSE EUROPEAN

GUIDE TO SEX, LOVE, AND ROMANCE

by Allan H. Mankoff

A RICHARD SEAVER BOOK

The Viking Press / New York

A Richard Seaver Book/The Viking Press
First published in 1972 by The Viking Press, Inc.
625 Madison Avenue, New York, N.Y. 10022
Published simultaneously in Canada by
The Macmillan Company of Canada Limited
SBN 670-45291-2
Library of Congress catalog card number: 70-189848
First Printing
Manufactured in the United States of America

Acknowledgment is made to:
A. M. Heath & Company Ltd.:
From *Doing It in Style: The Proper Affaire* by Donald Wiedenman;
The World Publishing Company:
"Lusty" from *Webster's New World Dictionary
of the American Language,* College Edition,
Copyright © 1968 by The World Publishing Co.

*This book is dedicated to
the memory of
my parents*

"Allons! Whoever you are, come travel with me!"
—WALT WHITMAN

"lusty (lus/ti), *adj.* [LUSTIER (-ti-er), LUSTIEST (-ti-ist)],
[see LUST & -Y], full of youthful vigor; strong; robust."
—*Webster's New World Dictionary of the American Language*

"Lusty as nature."
—WALT WHITMAN

CONTENTS

FOREWORD

This is an explicit narrative journey and practical guide to the sexual, the sensual, the raffish and the ribald, and the romantic and loving pleasures of eighteen representative European cities: Paris, London, Amsterdam, Rome, Copenhagen, Hamburg, Stockholm, Prague, Munich, Barcelona, Vienna, West Berlin, Madrid, The Hague, Salzburg, Frankfurt, Hanover, and East Berlin—with tangential references to many other European cities and resort areas. It is intended to transport the reader either vicariously or literally; I hope the former may lead to the latter.

The book is addressed to travelers of all ages (above the legal minimum), regardless of sex, background, lifestyle, or proclivity. It deals specifically with what you can do and where (addresses and phone numbers wherever possible), and generally with whom: the French; the English; the West Germans; the Italians; the Dutch; the Danes; the Swedes; the Austrians; the Czechoslovakians; the Spanish; and the East Germans.

How, you may reasonably ask, can someone research such a book and then presume to lead others to its secrets without the benefit of all-embracing, total-immersion participatory personal experience? Much as a play-by-play announcer describes a sporting event. I presume the reader to be far more interested in his own preferences and those of the Europeans than in my own; hence the wide-ranging offerings (admittedly highly subjective) of background and performance notes, and some statistics, on the overseas players (both professional and amateur); comprehensive descriptions and locations of the various playing fields and arenas; and the basic ground rules and tactics. While some international regulations prevail, others do not.

Consider pure practicalities: From my hard-won experience, the surest way to research a brothel is to be presented to the madam by one of her best clients (a duke is best, a retired matador is good, a picador, sales manager, or expatriate American newsman will do). Have the dear woman trot out all the fillies and mares in the stable (or stallions, as the case may be—geldings too, for you never know what people will be wanting in this, the Age of

Consent). Feign polite but credible dissatisfaction ("allergic to brunettes") with each in order to see the next. Show your letter from the government tourist office which proclaims you are writing a book about "nightlife." Request a tour of the entire premises, being careful to note such amenities as ceiling mirrors, silken sheets, sunken tubs. Tip the hostess frugally (or host, as is far less often the case), and proceed immediately to the next house on your list. In this game if you pause to pass Go, you will lose the $200 and that can add up. (Make that from about $3 to $80—nothing in this book is the exclusive province of millionaires.)

Why the guidebooks have largely neglected the following important matters or treated them at best with smug ignorance, or at worst with suspiciously Freudian disdain, is beyond the wisdom of this book—and among the reasons it was written: surely there was a vacuum to be filled.

While we are here devoted to What, When, small measures of What Was, and, when necessary, How, there is also plenty of How Much. And, of course, Where—more than 1500 places and situations, the great majority with addresses and/or telephone numbers. For the budget-minded, that's less than a cent per address. But please do not waste time counting them; a very few are "double-ups," and in rare cases it would have been imprudent to be more specific. The resourceful reader may expand the information here manyfold. One café can lead to two discothèques, then three group sex houses, four lovers' hotels, and so forth.

This book has as much respect for the law as it has for the past; thus age of consent and other statutory necessaries, as well as anecdotal or pertinent history, are duly noted. But one must bear in mind that I am far from a legal authority and statements of the law or speculations on the interpretation of it are merely those of a traveling layman.

This is as much a guide to people as it is to places. In these pages you will meet some of the real stars—a German brothel tycoon; the distinguished inventor of the electronic penis; Baroness Monique von Cleef and other Hall of Fame governesses; Hildebrand, a Cambridge engineer who creates electrical sexual flying machines; curators of museums that house exhibits commemorating bizarre and whimsical sexual activities and crimes; a gentleman who operates a master/slave marriage bureau as a hobby and respite from his even more baroque profession; the proprietor of a dance hall where the girls ask the boys; and the head of a call-girl, call-boy service.

Moreover, it is not impossible that in one of the hundreds of heterosexual rendezvous described or cited herein—which include selected cafés, clubs, discothèques, pubs, *boîtes,* museums, intro bureaus, *dansants,* escort services, university and other student meeting places, nudist clubs, mixed saunas, etc.—you may meet the future bone of your bone, flesh of your flesh. Or if your helpmate–spouse–lover is already chosen, go with him or her to one of the approximately one hundred lovers' hotels (some with light shows, many with mirrors, all with discretion), or twelve lovers' restaurants (a few where you can lock your private dining chamber and therein spoon, canoodle, and all the rest of it between coffee and crêpes).

Outdoors, *Lusty Europe* leads you to many other purely romantic situations: parks, gardens, zoos, rivers, vistas, lovers' leaps. Fortune tellers, ghosts, witches, and a séance in a Roman cave, too. Even a dolphinarium.

Alone or accompanied (by another adult) you're welcome at any of fifty-seven varieties of hard-core sex shows and somewhat softer erotic efforts (most of which, like so much in this book, would be banned, or prohibitively expensive, in the U.S.A.), and the twenty-three or so unisex saunas and mixed nudist situations. And there's an alpine club that invites you to ski in the nude with them, if you're so inclined. And a nudist restaurant too.

Likewise small groups, couples, single males, lone females, young Republicans, and old Roumanians are directed to no less than threescore specialized purveyors and/or craftsmen (and women) of sexual and/or sadomasochistic appliances, apparel, and hardware (from soft to very hard). And also beyond the tour bus pale, on to the two dozen or so sex museums, galleries, and other incidents of erotic curiosa.

Then there are the group sex houses. It might be best to go with a casual friend (some suggestions are offered as to how and where to find one), as most Europeans do, not with your spouse, or anyone else you love. Comparatively few Europeans comprehend "wife-swapping": they regard it as a game peculiar to America. (Perhaps the variety of sexual safety valves and outlets contributes to the comparatively low Continental divorce rates.)

For other sexual athletes and fresh-air lovers, there are walking tours or references to over eighty heterosexual street prostitute venues and other raffish quarters, plus perhaps thirty corresponding homosexual ones. (And several social disease and abortion clinics too; and many purveyors of birth-control equipment, some in Spain like none you or most Spaniards may have ever seen.)

Speaking of homosexuals, few general guidebooks do, other than vaguely or pejoratively. Some American publications travel rather far afield to make fun of our gay sisters and brothers, obliquely equating them, some young people, and all long-haired males (thus embracing nearly half the population) with the patrons or employees of Europe's purportedly terrible Temples of Iniquity. To restore some balance, then, you'll find descriptions or citations of many male and/or female or mélange *boîtes,* cabarets, bars, saunas, clubs, pubs, hotels, toilets, and outdoor rendezvous where homosexuals, among other good people, do not feel unwelcome. Whoever you are, many of these situations will treat you like a king. Or a queen, if you prefer. As with all references in this book, these are set forth to guide the dispassionate but interested nonparticipant as well as the bona fide connoisseur.

As to the scores of *heterosexual* bordellos, madams, governesses, call girls, and mixed-media flagellation parlors, and the demi whore and semi-pro cafés, bars, and *boîtes* . . . this book records what exists. (It also makes some highly subjective generalizations about national characteristics.) It does not counsel that travelers seek mercenary sex to the exclusion of the gifts of love. The fact that so much coverage is given to "special" matters is not only because Temple Fielding's guide often segregates them to the back of the tour bus, or because Arthur Frommer has so avoided them. (However, *Europe on $5* remains, in concept, the most revolutionary and humanistic travel guide of our time. And Fielding's the most exhaustive. By all means use either concurrently with this one.) The very fact that these gray and scarlet areas may be outside the experience of the average traveler is all the more reason he or she may wish to read about them, if not participate.

I happen to be a man and therefore write from that bias, or point of view, though not without awareness of it. Thus it appears to me that, even in these permissive and revolutionary times, rarely do women pursue men *(in public)* as avidly as men pursue women. Apparently most men like it that way. Some women don't; but it is simply the custom of humans (though, according to anthropologists, before the advent of the family structure it wasn't necessarily so; and patterns may change in the near future). However, in certain European establishments, female patrons (we are not speaking here of prostitutes) are particularly numerous and/or attractive, and these places are a focus of the book. It is axiomatic that they are also well stocked with men. So female readers are not at all ignored when a discothèque, café, or pub is noted as having a plethora of attractive girls. If you want to find the bear, go where the honey is.

The fact that most bordellos cater exclusively to men (including those staffed by men) has something to do with biology and the law of demand, not supply. And is not my fault. However, there is nothing to prevent female travelers from standing outside these establishments to offer gratuitously what the incoming gentlemen might otherwise purchase from the professionals.

Curiously, though flagellation parlors and attendant governesses are among the most male-oriented situations the book encounters, they represent the most extreme form of female domination of males—physical, financial, and emotional.

Well over half the situations cited are applicable to both sexes. And not a few are female-oriented or exclusively for women: the *bal carré* dance halls of Germany, or assorted masseurs, for example; the Love Doctor of the Black Forest; nearly every Roman male; most establishments covered in the "London and the Single Girl" section; and, happily, one of the most spectacular scenes encountered—the group sex *boîte* near Paris which, for over a decade, has functioned as a veritable ladies' bordello. There's much more to it, not the least of which are the "Magnificent Seven" highly skilled gentlemen available to service each female. Straightforward houses run by women for women, staffed by men, are hard to come by (however, free-lance volunteers are not). And difficult for nonprofessional males to research, even in drag. But we do have a bona fide brothel catering to women in Hamburg, and a call-boy service in Holland.

Tradition in Europe is not confined to architecture and museums. Often the most obvious dance halls, cafés, and pubs are the most fruitful, for the simple reason that natives and visitors have had such good luck there in the past they keep returning well into middle age. And they bring their younger sisters and brothers, too. This is not to ignore that new fields are constantly evolving. The best way to keep track of them is to consult the weekly entertainment guides available in all major cities, or the gratis government-issued brochures. Or simply go to the neighborhoods and have a look around. (Talk to strangers. You may be delighted and amazed at the results.) Names of clubs may change, discothèques may open, close, and reopen with new names, but European neighborhoods basically retain their character for relatively long periods.

Whorehouses are apt to die even harder than discothèques, which may come as a surprise to some. But not if you think about it. Once a house is no longer a home, it may acquire a certain reputation, a "good will" that it covets as much as any other business enterprise would. Management (and, of course, personnel) may be more ephemeral than general policy, standards, and price structure—and local clientele, who are apt to be even more loyal to a house than to the town football team. However, such operations are also subject to periodic closings for varying reasons (and not just Lent). Don't be too angry if that should happen; for every address given in these pages I chased down my share of blind alleys (and many dark ones), some of which are noted so that you, I hope, may avoid them. Consider some of what you read as recent history, and bear in mind that the general information gained may lead you to a wide-open establishment in another neighborhood, if not just around the corner.

Happily, however, social patterns do not change as swiftly in Europe as they do in the United States. For example, I made the first of five research trips for this book back in 1966. A lot has happened in the world since that time, but virtually all the Parisian group sex houses, lovers' hotels and restaurants, and bordels which I found on that first journey were still doing business at the same locations (some refurbished, however) through all my subsequent visits. The same can be said, by way of example, for most of the lovers' hotels in Vienna and Prague. Hundreds of similar examples—many noted in the text —could be cited.

Of course prices move. Mostly up. Curiously, however, the price of "vice" (the word is used here only because it rhymes) in Europe does not generally rise quite in proportion to the cost of other goods and services. (It was said in London that when the pound was last devalued—causing an overall increase in the British cost of living—the tarts neither raised nor lowered their prices; they raised their skirts.) *The currency equivalents used throughout the book reflect the 1972 devaluation of the dollar. The current international money market floats like a Damon Runyon crap game, with dollar equivalents fluctuating as much as two or three percent from day to day. Thus all equivalents given should be taken as "approximate" rates.*

But transatlantic airfares are a bargain!

This book is not infallible on other counts besides prices. Because it deals with customs and practices which are in the shadows, if not the obliquities (only in the sense of being obscure), of the mainstream of life, addresses, phone numbers, and general policies, not to mention clientele, persons living or working at or managing or owning the various situations, are liable to change without notice.

If you come upon a situation in your travels which you feel has been overlooked, or a new one, I'd be grateful if you'd send its address to me care of The Viking Press, 625 Madison Avenue, New York, N.Y. 10022. To all whose comments are printed in a planned "Readers' Choice" section (earliest postmark will govern), I'll send a free copy of the next edition. And if you've any questions, problems, suggestions, complaints, by all means write. Enclose a stamped, self-addressed envelope if you'd like a reply.

Similarly, the management of any European establishment or institution which has not been cited and would like to be should write to me care of the above address (practitioners please write as well). I'll do my best to have a look at your enterprise.

If some readers are inspired to demand or create a few bona fide lovers' hotels (and I don't mean motels, which are not at all the same thing), mixed saunas open to all the public and not prohibitively expensive, etc., in America's needy cities, what could be bad? Write your Congressman or -woman. Tell her or him that it is not merely the quantity of "high life" available throughout Western Europe (and sometimes behind the so-called Iron Curtain as well), it is the quality, the diversity, and the comparative longevity that make it so attractive and interesting. And exciting.

There is no suggestion that *any* situation described or noted is inhabited or visited or staffed exclusively or essentially by any particular persons or categories of people except where explicitly and unreservedly stated in the text; and even then consider that modern Europe is a very free-wheeling place and almost anyone may wander in, including you.

Opportunities for encountering particular varieties of people depend on many factors: some of these, such as time, an important factor here and an aspect of the European reverence for tradition, will be noted. However, this book is not responsible for changes in the weather, the political situation, the law (or its interpretation), or the attitudes of the police. Because we are often dealing with customs and practices that may be governed by laws that are often vague at best, consider any statements of the law to be no more or less valuable than the opinions and advice offered by a friend and layman—not an attorney or legal scholar—who has recently returned from a European trip, albeit an extensive one.

Unless explicitly and unqualifiedly stated in the text, there is no suggestion that any management, personnel, ownership, or clientele relating to any establishment cited or alluded to in this book are engaged in, or have any knowledge of any illegal or immoral activities on the premises or anywhere else, nor that they make any financial or other gains from such activities. The absence of a disclaimer in the text in no way connotes any illegal or immoral practices.

The material in this book is documented with some 150 hours of cassette tape recordings, hundreds of photographs, files of notes, newspaper and periodical clippings, and corroborative witnesses. I should here acknowledge Zeiss-Ikon of West Germany, Sony Corporation, and Eastman Kodak films for the excellence of their equipment. And my thanks to the government tourism personnel and the police and other civil authorities in all the cities covered, particularly those of London and Paris. And thanks, for their help and counsel, to various news correspondents of *Time, The New York Times, NBC, CBS, The* (London) *Times, Le Figaro, Ekstra Bladet, Il Messaggero, Bild Zeitung, Queen* magazine, *AFN, Momento Sera,* and *The News of the World.*

Although I share the blame with no one for the writing and creation of *Mankoff's Lusty Europe,* a lot of people helped make this book—literally thousands throughout Europe as well as the United States. To name them all would fill another book; to name some would be to slight others. And perhaps some do not wish to be named. But you all know who you are, and you have my gratitude.

And you too M.F. of L.A. (and South Dakota). And R.J.S. Jr., E., J., C.G.H., M., S., Serges, Vikings, H. & M., Flo, B. & Z., B.M., I.B., B.W., H.J.

And thank you, Dick Seaver—friend, editor, publisher.

A.H.M.

PARIS

France

The basic unit of currency is the franc, which can be divided into 100 centimes. At this writing you'll get about 5.07 francs for each floating dollar. Thus each franc equals about 19 U.S. cents. French law forbids you to take more than 500 francs out of the country, but you may bring in as many as you like.

THE FRENCH

The French need no introduction. Everything you have heard about them is true.

HOTELS FOR LOVERS

It says a great deal about the comparative cultures that there are probably more hotels for lovers per se in any of several European cities than in all the United States, where they are so badly needed. The American motel roughly corresponds, but generally speaking, there is really no comparison in terms of atmosphere, discretion, convenience, and even price range. As we shall see, Barcelona offers some of the most romantic and inventive lovers' hotels on the Continent, particularly if one is arriving by automobile. A connoisseur could argue that these days Prague's are the most exciting. And a few Vienna *"Stunden"* hotels (literally, "hotels rented by the hour") evoke a delicious flavor of those thrilling days of the *Belle Époque.*

But today no city has more of these establishments than Paris. No city even comes close. And that fact, together with the knowledge that you find *résidences meublées* (literally, "furnished rooms") or *hôtels particuliers* ("private hotels") strategically located throughout the city—offering a wide range of prices, conveniences, and luxuries—says more about Paris and the Parisians than all the *chansons, poèmes,* and travel brochures ever written.

Let us assume that you are not French and have recently arrived in Paris for the first time. You're strolling the Champs-Élysées with a new friend. You met her at the Dôme this afternoon, closed Fouquet's an hour ago, and you're both tired. Of strolling. She lives at home with her parents and you are traveling with your maiden aunt. What to do? What the Frenchman does whenever it would be inconvenient, indiscreet, or out of the question to make love in his own bed or in his partner's. (Or simply when he and his wife would together like a nice change of pace.)

Walk two long blocks from the Étoile, or take a cab, to 46 rue Paul-Valéry in one of Paris' most desirable residential *arrondissements* (districts), the 16th. The handsome multistoried graystone contains one of the most fashionable *meublés* in town. A small bronze plaque whispers "PAVILLON VILLEJUST, RÉSIDENCE MEUBLÉE." You ring.

Don't expect a flashing neon sign. Remember that discretion is the quintessence of the *meublé* or *hôtel particulier*. (The words will henceforth be used interchangeably.) In fact, the word *"particulier"* is translated variously as "private," "personal," "special," and even "peculiar." But more about the special and peculiar in sections to follow.

During this time you've been musing about nomenclature. Presently the Management of Pavillon Villejust arrives. She is a nice little old lady who has been showing another couple to their room. The rule here appears to be: *Never check in more than one couple at a time.* Thus there is no risk of an embarrassing meeting with friends, relatives—or co-rivals. Actually no one sees you; the aged custodians seem trained never to look a guest in the eye.

You rent the room for a short time, though the price does not vary whether you linger an hour or two or stay the night. Forty-eight francs for a large room (one franc equals about 19¢, 5.07 francs roughly equal one floating dollar), huge double bed, shower, and bidet; or 58F for a sumptuous semisuite that includes a small sitting room. You're led to No. 6, the "Venise."

It's the Venice all right. On the wall behind the headboard is an enormous mural depicting a rakish southern European gentleman wooing a very young lady in a gondola. The bed linens are freshly changed and crisp percale—none of your *Europe on $5 a Day* black muslins here. The plumbing is worthy of a Shaker Heights contractor. There are no walk-in closets, but the wall hooks and hangers are adequate for the clothes you have on, which is all the apparel any civilized person brings to a *hôtel particulier*. A small overnight bag is acceptable, but *never* bring luggage—you may frighten the management. Luggage here is as suspicious as no luggage in the Albert Pick Hotel in Akron.

You are breathing the purest air in France, according to the sign next to the air-control switch which proclaims: *"Ici comme à Mégève, l'air de cet appartement est conditionné, stérilisé, purifié, sans microbe, sans odeur."* Options for four channels of hi-fi music are controlled by bedside switches, as are the various colored lighting effects.

The rooms of the Pavillon Villejust are equivalent or superior in comfort to those found in many de-luxe Paris hotels charging up to 250F a night; some have evocative names and murals to match. (Including No. 1, Capucin; No. 3, Impératrice; No. 5, Pompadour; No. 11, Louis XVI; and No. 13, Longchamp.) Twenty-four-hour room service offers Veuve Clicquot Brut at 40F; whiskey, 7F; Mirabelle or Armagnac 1920, 5F; and breakfast of chocolate, tea, or coffee, and croissant and butter, 6F. All prices and room charges include service.

To leave, one merely presses the buzzer. The nice little old lady first checks the halls to insure that they do not contain your father-in-law, then arrives at your door with a soft knock to lead you out. But you must open the door for her, because there are no handles on the outside. Like most *meublés,*

Pavillon Villejust is open twenty-four hours a day, seven days a week. Though they are rarely necessary, reservations may be secured by telephoning 727-68-08 or 727-62-14. Convenient parking is available at Garage Foch, 35 rue Paul-Valéry, according to the Villejust's business card.

To say that all *résidences meublées* or *hôtels particuliers* with mirrored headboards are designed for and patronized almost exclusively by "lovers" (however loosely you define the term) may not be overstating the situation. However, one could do most anything in such a *meublé,* including sleep or even hold a quiet business conference, though it is difficult to imagine why anyone would want to do anything less than make love in such a place. (Some local onanists even prefer masturbation amid the mirrors of the *meublés* to their own more pedestrian bedrooms. "Portnoy's Paradises," one might call *meublés* if they existed in Newark.) Conversely, New York City's Hilton Hotel recently announced that it has commenced renting some of its rooms by the hour for the convenience of those businessmen who wish to hold "meetings and conferences." One supposes there is nothing to prevent a couple from using the Hilton rooms for other purposes, particularly during the hectic lunch hour, rather than going through the tired Jack Lemmon *Apartment* nonsense that is such a dreary aspect of New York life. In the last analysis, however, the New York Hilton is as suitable for seductions as the Parisian lovers' hotels (at least the ones with strategic mirrors) are for executive conferences.

For example, try holding a corporate meeting in the rooms of the HÔTEL PARTICULIER VILLA CAROLINE (85 rue de la Pompe, 16th *arrondissement,* tel. 504-67-38), perhaps the most precious *meublé* in Paris. Open day and night, with parking at 181–183 avenue Victor-Hugo, the Caroline charges between 45 and 55F for its rooms, most of which are in the style of Margaret O'Brien's bedroom. When she was twelve.

A sweet delicate riot of lavender and lilac is the Caroline, with its flowered pastel sheets, silk-papered walls, and silk-papered ceilings. Room 2, enhanced by a small private garden and side-wall mirrors, is well worth the 55F. Room 1, with its imitation-Louis XIV decor, demirecessed canopied bed, silk-papered walls, and three mirrored side walls is a steal at 45F. The bathroom is papered in Louis XIII, but the very efficient plumbing is unequivocally late Charles De Gaulle. (Rooms for all night from 60F.)

The beds and the rooms are a bit small, but this aspect only seems to add to the Caroline's charm. Ladies love it here because the atmosphere makes them feel so girlish. And an old Parisian friend—as a matter of fact he is seventy-three—says that every time he has a woman in this place, he feels like he is deflowering an eleven-year-old virgin princess. (Frenchmen have a special interest in very young girls; they are the pedophiles of Europe. But more about that later. All *meublés* scrupulously refuse to register minors.)

Those who are genuinely interested in mirrors should try the narcissists' paradise in rue Godot-de-Mauroy (9th; for more about this one see "A–Z" item "Mirrors"). Several rooms are a veritable Coney Island funhouse of mirrors. While this house may be the "Palace of Versailles" of *meublés*, it's a bit hectic. They do change the sheets, but apparently only from one room to the next. Crowded in the evening, and with a loyal female clientele—some of whom seem well known to the management—the place has the advantages of being cheap and remarkably quick in turnover, so reservations are never a problem.

Mum's the word at RÉSIDENCE DE LA MUETTE ("House of the Mute," or the "dumb" or "silent"), 32 rue de Boulainvilliers (16th; tel. 525–13–08), where one enjoys *every* comfort and convenience in exquisite *"fin* XVIIIe*"* 60-to-75F rooms; 120–150F for the whole night.

It should be clear that whomever a man brings to any *meublé* is his own business, not the management's (but no minors allowed). Their business is rooms. *Meublés* are not brothels—at least none of those described in this section of this book. However, the Muette once had a certain association with Claude, the celebrated madam, of whom more later. Sleeping partners of the very highest quality were available here (among other contact points) for 300F an hour, or 2000F for the weekend. Madame Claude has, from time to time, been known to take "vacations." At this writing all seems to be going quite well for her. However any connection with the Muette has been permanently severed.

While such extras as high-quality partners are not characteristic of most *meublés* (and certainly not of any mentioned here) Paris's madams will dispatch call girls to certain houses at a client's request.[1]

A highly recommended de-luxe *meublé* is the RÉSIDENCE CARDINET, 52 rue Cardinet (17th; WAG 80–91), whose attractive 40F rooms feature six-panel movable screens that virtually surround the beds. RÉSIDENCE OFFEMONT serves full meals, charges 35F for any of its nearly one hundred rooms, and is located nearby at 23 rue Henri-Rochefort (17th; CAR 64–84). Mayhap the most romantic and flaunty houses in the saturated 17th *arrondissement* are those side-by-side froufrous in rue Henri-Rochefort, MONCEAU HOUSE (No. 8; 924–50–46; 40F for two hours), and VILLA ROCHEFORT (No. 10; WAG 05–86; 40 or 45F the night; swell wall mirrors, especially in room No. 8). If one is driving, he should be advised of the HÔTEL LAUGIER, 75 rue Laugier (17th; 754–78–91), which offers entrance "directly from the garage" in the fashion of the better Barcelona *meublés*.

---

[1]These situations will be examined extensively in the section "Love for Sale"; as will those *meublés* that offer opportunities for group sex in "Lovers for Lovers." And there is a particular house—described in the section *"Spé"*—where you may enjoy virtually anything your libido craves, if your heart and expense account are up to it.

Flèches d'amour are flying on the Left Bank, albeit in fewer *meublés*. LES HORTENSIAS (4 rue Jules Chaplain, 6th; DAN 94–92), an exquisite *Belle Époque* villa, has a lovely garden, asks 30F for two hours, 55F the night. More basic is the nearby LE STANISLAS (5 rue du Montparnasse, 6th; 548–37–05). Pause between the Louvre and the Opéra at STUDIOS MAINTENON (36 rue Sainte-Anne, 1st; 742–13–61), 30F for two hours; 45F the night. *All* hotels cited welcome ordinary overnight guests as well as short-timers, though some have but one ratecard. *"Calme"* is LES PANORAMAS (3 rue des Panoramas, 2nd; 236–12–74). Popular with fiduciaries and their interests for it abuts the Bourse.

There are many more houses, including a fair selection just off the Champs-Élysées as you'd expect. Number 3 rue de Ponthieu (8th) apparently has no name other than *Maison Meublée*. "We speak English and German" brag their cards, which, according to the custom of many establishments, are perforated so you can tear off the address and phone number (ELY 32–21) and pass it along to a friend. The 30-to-40F rooms may have some good mirrorwork, but the decor is plain and the ambiance that of a private hospital run by Jesuits. Nice businessman's lunch served in bed. If they're full, one could try next door at number 5, where the HÔTEL DE PONTHIEU (ELY 70–36) boasts an elevator, telephones in all rooms, and "parking assured at 12 and 25 rue de Ponthieu." Air-conditioned rooms, 30F; 33F with large bath. Just round the corner, at 97 rue La Boëtie, CHAMPS-ÉLYSÉES STUDIOS (ELY 09–62) offers a wide range of 26-to-56F doubles, and features an exciting *"Repas à la Russe"*: salmon, caviar, and vodka served any hour, 145F for two.

Considering the neighborhood, these last three cater to closely scheduled businessmen, what with the elevators, phones in the rooms, and substantial lunches—features not found in some of the more glamorous *meublés*. They are especially crowded from 2 to 4 P.M., the new hours for Parisian love in the afternoon, the exigencies of modern living and heavy auto traffic making it difficult for the suburban Frenchman to maintain his traditional *"cinq-à-sept"* hours for love in the afternoon and still get home in time for dinner. Obviously one is paying a price for expediency and location if he books a Champs *meublé* during the day. So those who prefer *ambiance, éclairage,* and opportunities for reflection should confine themselves to the mirrored gems of the 16th and 17th *arrondissements* and restrict their visits to the evenings. If one must go completely native and make lunchtime love, he is advised to book a bed ahead.

LOVERS FOR LOVERS: LES PARTOUZES

Les Partouzes: "Sexual sharing," or a party devoted to these activities. Probably from *partie,* a "party," and/or the verb *partager,* "to share." See

Heath's New French Dictionary: "*partageur*—sharer . . . communist." (?)

The fact that sexual sharing occurs at private parties and gatherings is of no more than academic interest to most Paris visitors. Unless they have been invited. Though group sex has had a certain recent vogue in America, largely inspired by the mass media, the French lay some justifiable claim to having started the whole business, at least in modern times.

Some Americans, especially Southern Californians, may be interested to know that in Paris there have existed for decades—and exist now, right this minute—public houses where couples seeking random sexual and/or social intercourse with like-minded couples can easily find it at virtually any hour. (Except in the morning. Even the French won't do this sort of thing in the morning.) The principal appeal seems to be the excitement of making love with a stranger—someone you have never seen before and may never see again—and the anonymity afforded by such liaisons. At last one has the answer to the question posed in *Alice in Wonderland:* "What's the French for fiddle-de-dee?"

The word is *"partouzes"* (rhymes with "car shoes"). The practice reached its zenith during the 1920s, when the French discovered the motorcar to be an ideal vehicle for promoting chance meetings of couples. *It is not an orgy,* at least not an orgy "American-style." There is comparatively little drinking, no drugs, and usually no complicated sex mélanges; homosexuals, for example, have their own *partouzes.* In France one does not mix his pleasures.

Three Public Houses: rues Boursault, de Chazelles, and Le Châtelier

These are orderly, reasonably discreet *résidences meublées* where you pay a fee of between 90 and 100F per couple, ostensibly the price of two drinks. Unofficially this grants you the option, or at least the opportunity, to do anything sexual with anybody in the place (excluding the help) provided they are willing. They usually are. As a *"partouzeur"* one is presumed gamey for anything. (Apparently there is no illegality involved here; the following locations were secured with the aid of the police.)

Nonetheless a certain decorum is preserved, calculated to respect the rights of the individual, and it is perfectly acceptable for one to spend the entire afternoon and/or evening watching. Some do, most voyeurs being men. But very few women walk out of a *partouze* without having had at least one sexual experience, though it is entirely possible for any female to abstain completely. Nobody forces.

The Place in the rue Boursault

Somewhere near the midpoint of the long, narrow, dark rue Boursault, in a middle-class residential section of the 17th *arrondissement,* you enter a courtyard and approach the lighted doorway of a well-kept *résidence meu-blée.*

You ring, hand in hand with a nervous but determined American executive secretary who has lived in Paris for two years and who, like yourself, has "never been to such a place in my life! I always wanted to try it once . . ." she told you when you met earlier today, "but never had the nerve to do it with a *partouze* addict like my boss. He's English. Always trying to persuade me to go with him, just to see my reaction, he says."

A dowdy maid answers, gives you the familiar " 'soirm'ssieu'dame," lets you in quickly, takes your drink order and your 100 francs, and shows you the stairs.

First floor: There are four doors, each slightly ajar. You enter the first because the room is empty. Ordinary cheap but serviceable room—clean, bed made, metallic furniture. But wait . . . the proportions of that bed! It is twice as wide as it is long. And there is clothing hanging all over the walls on hooks—panties, ties, shirts, shorts, suits, and dresses. And the window curtains are tightly drawn. Behind the plastic drape is a bidet, toilet, stall shower, and sink with mirror. Also plenty of clean towels and an open bottle of red mouthwash on the sink.

You undress nervously, trying to avoid looking at each other. Soon you are naked. The girl keeps her panties and bra on. Sexual revolution or not (or is it evolution?), you have only just met. A thrill of expectation as feminine giggles sound from another room. Just then the maid enters with two large Scotches, and promptly leaves. That rather breaks the ice—a third person. You both laugh, relax on the bed, sip your drinks, and wait. But not for long.

The door swings open and a naked couple enters, laughing in French. They make right for *your* bed and, ignoring the two of you, lie down and begin to fondle each other. You scrunch up against the mirrored wall, thinking, "If I don't notice them, they will go away." But, in spite of yourself, the corner of your eye records the most minute details.

He is balding, dark, fiftyish; has Patek Philippe platinum watch, no wedding band, and big scar on shoulder. War? *Résistance?* Very hairy big stomach, strong calves. Tennis-player? She is vivacious, thirty-five or so, with medium build, good legs, smallish bosom, and scar on tummy. Children? Big diamond ring and wedding band; no makeup, red hair, very intelligent face. Thus far it's like your first time in an indoor nudist colony. You reach for your cigarettes in your breast pocket and discover . . . your breast.

Another couple wander in. He's about forty and well-built. Could be a cabinet minister or a cabinetmaker. Who knows? When people are naked they're just . . . naked people. His partner is a knockout: pouty pretty face, about twenty-five, sun-bronzed with no bikini marks. Your secretary feels a bit foolish and embarrassed. She's the only one in the room with clothes on.

She climbs out of her panties, yanks off her bra, and hangs them on the wall.

And you find Balding resting his right hand on her knee. Now's he's stroking her thigh, while maintaining contact with Vivacious with his left hand. And in this instance the right hand *does* know what the left hand is doing.

"What do I do?" pleads Secretary, who is the only one in the room who has no French.

"Do you like him?"

"That's not the point," she snaps.

"Try getting up and walking around the room."

Secretary does, and Balding goes right on stroking Vivacious. He is *sans souci,* shows no offense. Two expectant couples enter the room, followed by an interested voyeur. You and Secretary wander out to do a bit of exploring. What you're really seeking is an empty room to digest the first shock of the place.

Room two: A youngish couple beckon from their bed. Airline stewardess? Sorbonne professor?

Room three: Four couples chatting. *Médecin? Avocat? Chef?* Four nurses? *Avocat* and one of the nurses begin to . . .

. . . Exciting noises coming from the hall! Something is going on upstairs. People are running up there. You dash out and up the stairway. On the way you jostle two wary American gentlemen in topcoats. CIA? Delegates to the Vietnam Peace Conference? They've just arrived, accompanied by two expensively dressed but obvious tarts.

Top Floor: Huge crowd in one bedroom. The other three are empty. Push your way through the staring bodies. About ten couples ring the bed in respectful silence. On the bed a very athletic couple engage in complicated intercourse for what seems an eternity.

A few whispered comments: "He must be faking" . . . "It's impossible" . . . "Show-off!"

The man, aware of his audience, is performing as if auditioning for some grand sexual circus, changing positions every so often with much bravado. (You have a bizarre thought: Should one applaud when the gentleman is finished?) The woman—in some other world—is gasping, squealing, mooing French expletives. Two elderly gentlemen peer over the bed, getting as close to the action as possible, but careful not to interfere.

One voyeur wears an enormous pocketwatch suspended from his wrist and thin wire-rimmed glasses perched on a large De Gaullic nose. His attitude is entirely clinical. No real facial expression. The man resembles a huge inquisitive rabbit as he peers down at the loving couple on the bed.

All becomes a montage now. Naked bodies. Musky smell of sweat. Legs become bosoms become hair. A few jokes, mostly double-entendres. New arrivals. "Old guests" rush to watch the new ones. Pretty women. Matrons.

Semipros? Some pros? Not too many younger men. It is easy to spot the couples who have regard for each other: they split apart from time to time, but always return to each other. Not too many married couples here. Perhaps eighty people pass through from 7 P.M. to 2 A.M. Some nights less, some nights more.

Inquisitive Rabbit and his fellow voyeurs wander from room to room. Many women wander alone. "Don't use the mouthwash, *chéri,*" one calls to her friend. "People play tricks with it in these places."

Hours later you and Secretary relax on "your" bed, chatting with Well-Built and his Knockout. He is not a Cabinet minister, but rather a hydraulic engineer, married with two children. She is a bank clerk, separated, with no children. Most everyone else seems to have left as she begins a discourse on *partouzes.*

"Of course, *partouzes* have been practiced by the upper classes for some time, mostly at private parties. An important Paris recording producer gives two large *partouzes* a year. Fashionable guest list, discothèque dancing . . . and films. You leave your clothes at the door, or perhaps the host and hostess rise at the conclusion of dinner, disrobe, and the guests follow suit. Everything can happen. His latest had everyone in full face masks and no clothing.

"Our middle class discovered *partouzes* while yours was exploring simple adultery. It has become the national sport of France, becoming particularly modish because of the activities of X— [a well-known film director] whose whole life, considering his marriages, has been one *grande partouze.* They say he once sent out a casting call for two hundred 'soldiers' and two hundred 'peasant girls.' Each girl was told it was to be a *partouze.* They completed casting in three days. Of course, the scene had to be shot on location in the French Alps. Thirteen days they were out there making the *partouze.* It took eight minutes to shoot the scene. Of course, the film was never made.

"The essence of proper conduct in a *partouze* is respect. And laissez-faire. You do as you please, but never infringe on another's rights. She cannot withhold your freedom, nor you hers. But no man may have her if she is not willing. And no one should be insulted to be refused. The women are usually more active than the men, if only for physiological reasons. Many of the men come only to watch.

"There is a Swiss organization, headquartered in Zurich, which is dedicated to *partouzes.* People of great wealth and high birth belong. People who are interested in free sexual experience—and in finding out about the special desires of others and fulfilling them. And of course their own. Some *partouze* houses in Paris have special voyeur rooms with peepholes. . . .

"Sometimes a French girl whom you have just met, and who would not think of making the bed with you so quickly under ordinary circumstances, might go right away with you to *partouze*. To do the crazy. As a girl in America might smoke pot with the boy, but not make love so quickly.

"This place [rue Boursault] and the one in the rue Le Châtelier [discussed later] are the most civilized of the public *partouze* houses. Some very good people come here. Of course, the private *partouzes* are the best of all— among friends and carefully selected guests. It is very difficult to succeed in *partouzes*. Everyone must be beautiful, clever, and sensitive, or at least two of the three."

Well-Built interrupts: "Many people I know have been to *partouzes* at least once. I go perhaps once every three months. Foreigners are welcome as long as they obey the rules. Of course, you must always come as a couple. The essence of the thing is the sharing. *You* bring something, and *I* bring something. Like a good discothèque: as a stranger you could not get into some of the best discothèques. But bring a provocative woman and you are free to wander.

"A friend of mine came here to the rue Boursault with an English girl. After an hour she had had enough. But the maid would not let her leave without Monsieur. It would destroy the balance."

The door bursts open and a large blonde, not unattractive, leaps onto the bed as you four scatter. She's on her back, legs askew. . . . So, at last, is Inquisitive Rabbit, who arrives instants later in a breathless frenzy, having spent the entire evening building to this instant. It is over in less than a minute and they leave.

"She may have been a cheap *putain* . . . but she honored his moment," observes Well-Built, not without compassion.

On the way out you observe that the place has a liquor license. Added information: Hours 3 P.M. to 2 A.M., open seven days a week; most activity between 5 and 10 P.M. Additional drinks are 10F each, after you pay the 100F charge at the door. The business cards are perforated at one corner with the address and telephone number printed twice so that one can pass it along to a friend. After all, the essence of *partouzes* (aside from respect, laissez-faire and so forth) is new blood. One tires of the same old . . . faces.

As you part, Well-Built offers one final, timely note:

"Because of the Markovitch scandal,[2] which involved many important people including, perhaps, members of the government, lately there has been some caution observed among people who enjoy *partouzes*. However, nothing will really change, neither the private parties nor the public houses. For example, at least one of the houses survived the Germans and *Les Ballets Roses* [a Profumo scandal of the late 1950s involving young girls and promi-

[2]See pp. 30–34.

nent old men that helped topple a government and bring De Gaulle to power]
and it will survive Markovitch."

The Place in the rue de Chazelles

Though they have had some highly complex and exciting *affaires* here in
this extremely well-known swap shop—easily found just down the street from
the Ministry of War and Pensions—this house is decidedly bourgeois. The
French call it "the place where you lose your shoes." You may also lose your
courage. The entranceway has been recently remodeled to resemble the last
mile of a penitentiary death house. But though the claustrophobic 25-yard
tunnel is compartmentalized at two points by "prison-bar" gates, it eventually
looks onto a charming garden.

Through a peephole in the villa's front door the female custodian inspects
you and your companion, making sure you are respectably dressed and
sober. Pay the 100F for the two drinks and you are immediatedly offered
options:

"Do you wish to be alone, m'ssieu'dame, or with others?"

If you choose "alone," you will be shown upstairs to one of several small
private bedrooms. Here you can receive occasional couples who knock first,
or you may play *cache-cache* (hide and seek) in the halls and knock on any
door. Or you can remain completely alone with your partner, as in any other
résidence meublée.

If you seek "others," you are shown straight through the kitchen, passing
the liquor license hanging on the wall and the accompanying official notice:
"For the protection of minors and to discourage public drunkenness and to
help reduce alcoholism, minors under twenty-one years are not permitted on
these premises."

The door at the back of the kitchen opens into a small hall, which leads
to two wide-open doors, which in turn lead to the two large public bedrooms.

Even if there were not five couples frolicking from room to room, even if
you had never heard of the word *"partouzes"* or its meaning, you might still
have a good idea of what goes on here, just from the furnishings.

The walls are covered by large mirrors, the "beds" are roughly the size of
helicopter launch pads. Housewares and decor are comparable to that of a
1940s Midwestern America motel, with some important additions: additional
"bed" with proportions and height similar to that of a hospital operating table.
Adjustable height. Several stall showers with bidet and sink. Two plain pipe
clothesracks, each with a capacity sufficient to hold Scaramouche's entire
wardrobe. Original nudes by unknown artist.

There is an ample supply of soap and clean towels, but considering the very
heavy action, it is a tribute of sorts to say that Chazelles has not nearly the
time to be as well groomed as the house in the rue Boursault. Nor is the

clientele generally as select.[3] (But you'd be surprised to know how many important people have come here just once, they've heard so much about it.) However, considering that Chazelles has accommodated ten or more couples in each of its two downstairs rooms, whose thresholds are raised to assure that the doors cannot be fully closed, what can one expect?

Anything.

Open from 2 P.M. to 3 A.M., weekends to 4 A.M., Chazelles makes the gatherings held at New York City's "swingers' bars" look like nursery school socials.

The Place in rue Le Châtelier

A third establishment where one may find public *partouzes* has thrived for the past several years in rue Le Châtelier (17th); open from 3 P.M. to 2 A.M. The clientele is comparable, if not often superior, to that of the house in rue Boursault, undoubtedly attracted by the *fin-de-siècle* garnishings—some lovely rural prints and tasteful nudes, all handsomely framed; delightful glass-encased doll collection in the sumptuous, highly polished ground-floor parlor. The maroon carpeting, which exactly matches the walls' hue, is properly thick and soft. And the service is fantastic. Three uniformed maids are in constant attendance on the twenty to forty gamboling couples who may visit Le Châtelier in the course of an evening.

The first floor contains five bedrooms, unmirrored and unoccupied this evening but always available to individuals and couples who seek privacy, as are specified rooms in the rue de Chazelles and rue Boursault houses. The second floor also comprises five bedrooms, three quite large with mirrored walls, bidets, and toilets, and, this night, some fifteen frisky unclad couples whose collective mood resembles that of a pillow fight after lights out at a Pocono Mountain summer camp.

This is an amiable place . . . lots of conversation and giggling among the *partouzeurs,* who include a lovely blond antique dealer, about thirty; three fortyish insurance executives; four attractive brunettes, aged twenty-five to thirty-five; and a couple of frumpy but pleasant matrons. The sexual activity is basic enough, unless one considers extraordinary three couples balling on the same bed with occasional peeks at their neighbors' progress.

The courtesy and informality of Le Châtelier's management and guests cannot be overemphasized. For example, during the evening a number of fully clothed teams—having paid the 90F for their two drinks—wander the halls and bedrooms, timidly or calculatingly evaluating the participants. Those newcomers who like what they see will eventually disrobe—to a small crowd, for new arrivals are always greeted with enthusiasm—and join the activities.

---

[3]Several men have been observed making love with their socks on here.

And those who choose to stand and stare, for five minutes or five hours, are politely ignored and made to feel no remorse should they leave uninitiated.

Oysters

Is it a coincidence that the practical French have located the three previously discussed houses where one may experience *partouzes* near two *places,* several of whose many restaurants specialize in *fruits de mers?* In the Place de Clichy—a five minute walk from rue Boursault, a three-minute drive from rue de Chazelles—perhaps a half dozen seafood restaurants are open twenty-four hours. And in the Place Péreire—just around the corner from the rue Le Châtelier—one can enjoy oysters at any of four charming restaurants with terraces. Strictly speaking, the French choose "steak before, for power, and oysters after, to replenish."

Partouzes and the Law

"Love is legal in France, therefore *partouzes* are legal," observed a Paris vice squad inspector. "*Partouzes* are not harmful to the community or human life as are certain other group activities: LSD gatherings, narcotics orgies, or parties where excessive amounts of hard spirits are consumed. Whether the *partouze* is psychologically harmful to the individual is a matter for your psychiatrists to play their games with. No matter. Our law does not normally concern itself with such activities, carried on in private by consenting adults."

The police know the location of all public accommodations that offer opportunities for *partouzes;* indeed, they keep floor plans of each on file. All have liquor licenses and, of course, all keep rooms available for people who desire strict privacy as in any other *meublé.* As long as the guest pays for "liquor" and not for sexual services or opportunities, apparently no illegality is involved. Liquor licenses are suspended for the same reasons they would be in a bar or nightclub: service to minors under eighteen, disturbing the peace, etc. The police do make periodic checks, of course; recently they closed a place for concealing a movie camera behind one of its mirrors.

The three previously described houses have all enjoyed a continuous prosperity for a decade or so, but several other *boîtes* and houses operate more clandestinely, as well as sporadically. As in the case of other "special" activities and institutions found throughout Europe, the fact that you know of the existence of a thing can be 75 percent of finding it. With a little bit of help, of course.

Public *partouzes* are usually found in a *résidence meublée* or *hôtel particulier,* that classification of establishment which also includes the houses described in the section "Hotels for Lovers." (As far as this book is concerned, *none* of the places mentioned in that section has *partouzes.* They all specialize in "privacy.") However, if one politely inquires of any *meublé* maid whether the establishment offers *partouzes,* she'll let you know soon enough. And if one just happens to be passing a *meublé* and sees six couples going in at once, one has a right to be slightly suspicious. As you recall, the more discreet of the so-called "lovers' hotels" admit only one couple at a time. When you consider the possibilities any hotel could have *partouzes.* All it takes is two couples and a knock at a bedroom door.

Certain bars, cafés, restaurants, or gas stations in the 16th or 17th *arrondissement* can tell one exactly where the places of the moment are. A good way to begin the quest might be to order a Pernod or a few francs worth of gas. But of course a "Hey, Mac, where's the nearest *partouze?*" would doubtless lead nowhere. Gently. Gently.

If a place is clean, well run, and attracts a good clientele, word gets around quickly. Hairdressers, male and female, are second only to bartenders as the best sources of gossip and information in any city. In Paris they seem to know everything, frequently before it happens. Barbers, manicurists, and concierges are standard sources in any town. And if one were to inquire of a policeman in the proper *arrondissement*—17th is best—he *might* offer the information. One wouldn't, however, approach the gentlemen guarding the President's residence on the rue Saint-Honoré.

To plead complete ignorance is to get nowhere, but this is the case no matter what one seeks in Paris. Asking the *sommelier* for a "bottle of red wine" is like ordering a can of Fresca. But mumble something about a Latour or even a Châteauneuf du Pape (no matter how you pronounce them) and he will discuss these, plus half a dozen others equally appropriate and perhaps less expensive. And so it is with the Parisian cab driver, who is much better informed than his New York City counterpart—though capable of equal surliness.

"Où est une partouze agréable?" one should ask the cab driver no matter how bad your accent. *"Une partouze, peut-être, comme celle dans la rue de Chazelles?"*

"Ah, non, monsieur, I know another one." And he begins writing a list of addresses that includes, in addition to four public houses, a *partouze boîte* near Versailles, another near the suburb Boulogne-Billancourt; and two flagellation houses, one on the Left Bank, the other on the Right.

Finding a private *partouze* is, of course, a bit trickier than finding a public one. If one is associated with the embassy crowd or a Jet-Set regular, there should be no problem. But some quite civilized private soirées are available to the public. For example, in the rue Godot-de-Mauroy (9th), among the cruising motorized prostitutes are a few women who, as a sideline, organize and cater private *partouzes.* They are far more discriminating about whom they invite to these dos than whom they allow *se faire tromboner* (to make like a trombone-player, *i.e.,* to copulate very hard) during regular business hours. (Those who require specific addresses and telephone numbers of swap shops are referred to the "Amsterdam" chapter.)

Your French connection will give you an embossed calling card with the telephone number and address of a villa, usually on the outskirts of Paris. The charge is about 100F and this often includes a buffet dinner for two. The party comprises twenty couples this night—physicians, attorneys, brokers, businessmen, and their wives, girlfriends, or mistresses—a group quite comparable to any you'd meet at a New York City Upper East Side or Central Park West cocktail party. Except that, for dessert, everyone takes his and her clothes off.

One's own business and social contacts, native Parisians or expatriate Americans who have lived in Paris for any length of time, often know of *partouzes*—public and private. Transplanted Englishmen seem particularly well informed. Many people whom you ask such things really don't know or don't want you to know that they know. But they'll invariably know of someone who can be helpful.

Nobody on the Left Bank knows. "On the Left Bank you make your own *partouzes.*"

Next-to-last resorts for finding public *partouzes* are the semiprofessional good-time girls who café-sit along the Champs-Élysées and near the Opéra. Smartly dressed, but rarely ostentatiously, and ranging in age from twenty-five to forty-five, many are not, strictly speaking, prostitutes. Some are somebody's wife or lover. They'd like a nice meal or an apéritif. One could easily wind up in their little beds, or in a big one built for three couples.

Last resort: the rues de Tilsitt, and de Presbourg form a perfect circle around place de l'Étoile (renamed for De Gaulle). Standing at corners on the circle between avenues Victor-Hugo and Marceau and zooming round and round in a procession of white cars—mostly expensive Peugeots, Citroëns, and Panhards—are some of the most beautiful young girls in France. For 100 to 150F plus 20F for the room in a nearby *hôtel particulier* they will remove their casually elegant tweed or camel hair ensembles, maxis or minis, and for twenty minutes provide the same services as any other prostitutes in the city. (More about this outdoor auto show and others like it in the section "Love for Sale.") And for 200F they will transport and accompany a gentleman—or any man who resembles one—to a relatively nearby *partouze* and remain in his company there for about an hour. Of course, the client must also pay the 100F fee for the "drinks." Some public *partouze* houses have, on call, partners to accompany unescorted guests—about 200F.

Though it is rather bad form to bring a prostitute to a respectable public *partouze*—certainly never to a sophisticated private one—some men do, of course. If she is young and pretty, there is rarely a problem if she keeps her occupation to herself; and in Paris so many prostitutes are part-timers and look like anything but professionals that even the French have difficulty distinguishing them from other girls.

Rural *Partouzes*

A nondescript bar in a village near Versailles, a few kilometers outside Paris. You are perched on one of the ten stools, a trifle put out with your Parisian friend, a middle-echelon diplomat, who has insistently dragged you out to this place. It looks like nothing more than a rural American roadhouse.

Nothing unusual about this bar except the unexplained half dozen ladies' handbags behind it and the cloak-and-dagger nonsense at the front gate. Peephole at the door. Passport check! All right, it seems impossible for a man *(but not a woman)* to gain entrance if he is unknown or unaccompanied by a regular patron. So what?

"Go to the toilet," orders your friend.

Now we're getting somehwere.

But when you do, you see nothing unusual. Just a toilet bowl. You return. "Typical French toilet. Just the one room for boys and girls. No paper. Enough space for a man on the pot and a lady midget to stand in line. So?"

"Good. Now watch the bar."

Some minutes pass. Three rather sophisticated-looking couples drink Scotch and chat at the bar. Several others dance to the jukebox. A number of men stand apart from the couples, drinking wine. Swarthy, rather tough-looking Frenchmen who all seem to know each other. Truck drivers, or perhaps farmers? Six-day bike riders? No, they appear to be local.

From time to time one of the women has a private whisper with the barman. Now she pays her bill and goes to the toilet.

One of the single men leaves the bar. He goes to the toilet.

Another man leaves the bar and goes into the toilet. It is crowding up in there. You've seen this act before. Hunt's Three-Ring Circus, 1947. Eighteen clowns and Uncle Don in a Model-T Ford. Never could figure out how they did it. Three more men go into that little toilet. And then it is finished.

What has happened?

With an affirmative nod from the barman, your friend leads you to the back of the house.

A bedroom. The seven swarthies and that nice chic lady. They've got her down on the big bed. And they are pulling off her Balenciaga.

"A sliding panel in the back wall of the toilet opens to this bedroom," explains your French guide. But you are too engrossed to listen.

No, they are not *pulling off* her clothing: they separate her from her garments with precision and care. Complete division of labor. One man to each stocking. A big hairy gentleman making off with her lime-green panties. The stocking-rollers pause as the panties pass by. Meanwhile the other men are undressing themselves. When naked, these fellows move to the woman.

So everyone is naked.

And they begin to stroke her. Tenderly at first. Each man gradually increasing his tempo and ardor in complete sync with the others. Superb teamwork. As skilled as a team of crack mechanics in the pits at Le Mans. No two men to a thigh. No confusion over who gets the left breast. These are professionals.

"The classic *partouze*. Seven men and one woman. You see . . ."

"Shut up. I'm watching."

And it begins. For real. She is spreadeagled on the bed. Two men to her hands. Two breast-strokers. Two body masseurs. After a time, the seventh gentleman mounts her.

All goes off silently, like a ballet. No man speaks a word or appears to be aware of his associates. The woman moans, sighs, screams softly.

The men change positions now, like players rotating positions after the serve in a volleyball game. Right thigh moves to right breast. Right breast to right arm and face. Right arm and face to left arm. Left arm to left breast. Left breast to left thigh. Left thigh becomes new server. Old server to right thigh. New server . . . serves.

Later, done on one side, they flip her over gently so that she lies on her stomach. Still later two men hold her in the air for a standing third man.

As Napoleon once remarked, in a letter to General Lemarois: "You write to me that it is impossible; the word is not French." One begins to understand Napoleon. And the French.

This was a "special," a well-planned event held perhaps only once a month, with enough notice to attract particularly experienced players. The more ordinary activities, the kind that may occur here every night of the year, take place in the "Red Room" and the "Operating Room." In these the participants are quite ordinary people, at least by French standards.

By the very subdued maroon lighting of the "Red Room" you discern what appears to be a clump of religious mourners, swaying soundlessly in their dark business suits. No. As you move closer you see it's more like a rugby scrum, for the players are reaching, groping for something at the core of their huddle. They want to touch her in the act . . . this tiny young blonde standing naked and glistening, sobbing gratefully at each thrust she receives directly from the open fly of a fellow who, in other circumstances, probably sells securities. One man pats her head with a cool cloth, others reach in to fondle and buss whatever's available. At the back walls, on padded banquettes, several couples—the men fully clothed, the women naked—watch silently, one man idly dildoing his matron-partner.

Yet another room, this one well-lighted and air-conditioned, contains at its center one of those adjustable padded rectangular tables that, in other lands, are commonly found in hospitals, but here are so indispensable to modern

French culture that they are liable to turn up anywhere. On it writhes a handsome red-haired woman of about thirty, biting down on the minishift drawn above her breasts, her Sète-tanned golden thighs held apart by two modish executive types while a fat man in an expensive blue Cubavera and Sulka cravat salivas—resembling nothing so much as a cow licking an ice-cream cone—*la chatte.* Or *la minouche,* if you prefer.

From the assembly of twenty-odd serious and concerned spectators who hover about the table, one man is selected by the young manager of this *boîte* (he directs and supervises all proceedings) to administer the grand coup. The table is adjusted to the lucky Pierre's exact penis height and, standing there in his banker-cut three-piece suit, he simply unzips and thrusts his *queue* into her. During service the congregation may massage, fondle, or kiss the young woman, but the operose young manager is always close at hand to assure moderation and that, for example, no one climaxes into her face. (This happened once, and the offending *rustre* was barred for life.) Seconds after her orgasm the lady fairly leaps off the table, smooths down her shift (like most female regulars, she is not wearing panties), and, hand-in-hand with the fortyish gentleman who escorted her out here (he has done no more than observe her ecstasy from a far corner), resumes dancing back out by the bar.

On the drive back to Paris your diplomat friend fills in some important details:

"There are several places where such things have occurred nightly for decades. They are mostly in nearby villages and western suburbs of Paris—though of course you find them in various parts of the country, particularly the Riviera in summer, the ski resorts in winter—and are not so subject to control of the city police. But sometimes the police come out to record license-plate numbers. Though well-informed people know their location, to print their exact addresses might result in some embarrassments.

"The charge in these *partouzes boîtes*—which one might truly say are simply bordels for women—is twenty to thirty francs for your drink and nothing more. You will not find prostitutes here, but some of the best French bourgeoises come, and couples from all over Europe. I know a Swedish couple who spend two weeks of their vacation in Versailles every year just so they can come nightly to this place.

"Most women do not request particular men through the manager or the bargirl, though of course they may. (By the way sometimes the bargirl takes a turn herself, but not often. She is such a beautiful blonde, yes?) Usually they simply go to the back rooms and receive whoever comes. Sometimes the woman will wear a mask obscuring her vision, enjoying the whole affair while never setting eyes on her lovers. And some women wear masks to hide their identities.

"Some people drive out from the city simply to sit at the bar and watch the activity, hoping to see a special show as we saw tonight. Magnificent, those seven, eh?"

Mélange à Bois: Partouzes and *"La Pipe"* in the Park

By day the Bois de Boulogne is surely one of the most idyllic municipal parks in the world. The lawns, verdant the year round, are rolled to pool-table perfection. The lush, dense growths of trees offer a veritable forest of tranquillity in the midst of a great city.

A little girl, nostalgia in a sailor suit, both hands stretching a badminton racket to the sky, floats the shuttlecock to her governess. Giant comic poodles gavotte in pursuit of dragonflies. Old nuns shmooze and snooze in the sun. Here one feels an exhilarating sense of peace and freedom, and time stopped still; a rural elegance and upper-middle-class well-being.

And then the sun goes down and the big people come out to play.

Take a drive to the park, about an hour after dark. Enter the Porte Maillot and proceed very slowly along Route de la Porte des Sablons. Observe the scores of parked cars along the shoulders of the road, parking lights on, couples inside . . . waiting.

Funeral procession formation? Midnight auto rallye? Hardly. This is *partouzes* in the park.

Turn left on Allée de la Reine Marguerite. More couples in cars. And see those men walking from one car to another, having short discussions with each driver? Well, they are not selling tickets for the national lottery. These men are the organizers—the nexus arrangers. That man talking to the Peugeot, for instance: he represents a "nice refined couple from Neuilly, a pharmacist and his wife. And also a very handsome pair, quite young, just in from Lyons."

Many of the arrangers offer their own comfortable, often lavish apartments to interested couples. The price—for arranging the *partouze,* providing the place, the food, drinks, and linens—to watch. Other arrangers offer merely to present one couple to others. "Have your own *partouze* deep in the woods. I know a lovely quiet spot. No police. I'll stand guard." No charge for the introductions as long as M. Voyeur can watch. Or perhaps join in. Some couples, as well as many single individuals, most of whom are men, make their own arrangements, propositioning others who drive by or park along the Bois' many secluded byways. Making a *partouze* in the Bois de Boulogne is not much more difficult than making a *minyan* in Tel Aviv.

A summer night's stroll in the Bois offers some interesting sights and opportunities. Sometimes people lurk among the trees, wearing rubber animal masks that cover the wearer's face and head. It is said that this practice was inspired by an elegant Right Bank private *partouze.* The rules of the game in the woods—"anonymate," one might call it—are simple. When a rabbit mask meets a chimpanzee mask, nothing happens. (Unless the rabbit has a thing for monkeys.) But when two rabbits meet in the moonlight, everything goes. Everything but the masks. When it's over, they wander off separately. Mysterious, exciting, anonymous—to a purist, perhaps the ultimate in *partouzes.* The thing has interesting ramifications: a fellow could even have his own wife.

The heaviest traffic in *partouze*-arranging occurs along the major arteries of the Bois. One of the busiest areas is near the traffic circle at Porte Dauphine, foot of avenue Foch. This circle is hard to miss, for it's the scene of the hottest all-night *bocce* game in town.

Though many other "special" institutions taper off and move from Paris to the Riviera during July and especially August, the greatest *partouze* activity in the Bois occurs during the warmer months. But there is considerable action the year round. This is not a transitory scene. To say one *might* find something happening here would be exaggerated understatement. People have as much chance of being a party to a *partouze* in the Bois de Boulogne as they have of being mugged in Central Park after dark. (New Yorkers and their police have one kind of tolerance, Parisians another.)

From time to time—as at this writing—the police make extra-heavy patrols in the area, trying to discourage or even curtail these nocturnal happenings. But *partouzes* have been a feature of the Bois for many years, and there is no reason to expect they will suddenly disappear because of sporadic pressure from the authorities.

It is difficult for Americans to believe that an outdoor scene can last for any length of time. But in Europe traditions—whether architectural or sexual—die hard. There is no better example of this than *partouzes* in the Bois. ". . . the *partouzes* are the most recent chapter of Paris by night. They capture the feverish, restless, jaded—and somewhat morbid—character of this great city of today, which seeks the impossible in its pleasure as in its work," wrote Jules Bertaut in 1927 in *Les Belles Nuits de Paris.*

Though oral sex is not exactly new to the French, at the beginning of the 1970s, when some attractive young daughters of "very good families" began administering *"La Pipe"* (which in everyday usage means "pipe" or "tube," but caution, the verb *"piper"* means "to lure or decoy") at or near the Porte Dauphine entrance to the Bois, the event was as enthusiastically received in some circles as if a new cinema or amusement park had opened. So much so that if *"La Pipe"* has not yet been franglicized as *"Le Blow-Job,"* it has at least been swiftly overcommercialized by professionals, though the amateurs still service long lines of their schoolmates, particularly on weekends when even the daughter of a wealthy merchant needs some extra cash. Procedures are so strict and so uniformly adhered to that one can only imagine that some trade association governing body has met, voted, and duly agreed to enforce certain standards and practices. All practitioners charge 20F, carry tissues or a large towel, and none have the time or inclination to copulate. Indeed, some couldn't if they wanted to.

Follow the scent of mud, sweat, beers, and synthetic "Joy"—but beware the protectors watching from fold-up chairs back in the bushes—along Route des Poteaux from sundown to 2 A.M. and you will encounter several big transvestites in wigs, leather minijupes, and boots. Obviously these fellows are outside the pale of any respectable guild: for a paltry 10F they offer a full curb-service lubrication of your *"joyeuses"* not to mention your *"tendue."*

Partouzes at the movies

Movies were made for *partouzes.* Dark, anonymous places where you never know whom you'll meet. The well-established custom of tipping usherettes in French movie houses will never die as long as couples and single patrons persist in tipping that extra franc or two to sit next to those attractive people in the back row ("Not those . . . the ones *next* to them!"). And people seeking *partouzes* are *always* in the back rows. Coincidentally, many French cinemas charge considerably more for seats in the back of the house than in the front or the middle.

While *partouze* arrangements might be made in any Paris cinema, one would be most likely to succeed in certain houses somewhere in the vicinity of the Bastille. If one has no luck here, he might try the Cannes Film Festival.

And if that fails, chalk it up to the eternal, but clearly worsening, *crise du cinéma,* and head back to the Bois.

RESTAURANTS FOR LOVERS

"Appetite comes with eating."
—RABELAIS

Paris is a man's city—a man's city because its romance attracts so many women. Though the French are neither a romantic nor a sentimental people,[4] they do many romantic things in their pragmatic, clear-thinking way. No one knows better than the decadent French that discretion is essential to the successful continuation, or initiation, of a love affair. Privacy is surely most important in a hotel—hence the large numbers of *hôtels particuliers,*—but

[4]In a 1972 survey conducted by the magazine *European Business,* 57 percent of French chief executives interviewed were found to have married executives' daughters (and 61 percent of the Dutch, and 65 percent of the Belgian bosses in their climb for room at the top). "By contrast," the magazine notes, "the Scandinavian president seems to marry for love." Only 30 percent of Danish chief executives married executives' daughters.

the French also enjoy it in their restaurants, though not to such a degree.

Hundreds of Parisian restaurants have atmosphere and service, not to mention kitchens and cellars, which are more than satisfactory to lovers—of food or each other. But of special note here are some of those few that still preserve the charming French tradition of the *salon particulier*—the private dining room *à deux* where there is nothing between you and your lady but the waiter's bell.

Of these none is more hallowed and *particulier* than LAPÉROUSE, 51 quai des Grands-Augustins (6th; 326–68–04). A restaurant has occupied this 1708 building since 1768, and everyone from La Belle Otéro and Lola Montez to the late Aly and the late Aga Kahn have savored its several *salons particuliers.* Nowadays the private dining rooms are given over to the intrigues of government, to quiet luncheon conferences frequently attended by high-ranking officials.

But the discreet, aging waiters, in their properly musty tuxedos, cater to the whims of lovers as well. Cozily nestled in the red velvet sofa of Salon la Fontaine beneath a large 150-year-old mirror whose surface bears the diamond-scratched initials of tenscore or more *belles,* you have purposely dallied over the meal for two and a half hours or more. Yet no waiter has entered your dark-wooded fortress, except in response to your ring. This, in spite of the fact that you have neglected to slide the lock on the door. In fact the only being who stands between you and complete indulgence is the lady's poodle.

It goes without saying that its eloquently faded charm has made Lapérouse a favorite with generations of Americans, a people who for the past sixty or more years have savored the sensual pleasures of Paris with more relish than any other, save the French themselves. And *le patron,* Roger Topolinski— who succeeded his father in 1924, and is at present aided by his capable son —assures you that it is almost as popular among the Japanese. According to M. Topolinski—whose white Van Dyke, merry blue eyes, and plentiful figure suggest a Gallic Burl Ives—it is the custom in Japan that when an aged ambassador or company director retires, he is sent around the world on vacation; Lapérouse is among the first Paris stops on this one last fling.

For whatever reason (surely not a lack of discretion) a recent *Guide Michelin* removed one of Lapérouse's coveted three stars. M. Topolinski was properly shaken. *Michelin* customarily lists only twelve three-star restaurants in all of France, and Lapérouse had been among these since the *Guide* first appeared in the early twentieth century. Of the current twelve—four are Parisian: Maxim's, La Tour d'Argent, Le Grand Véfour, and Lasserre. It is hoped that the open place is being reserved for the return of Lapérouse, whose *timbale des Augustins, caneton de Colette, caviar Petrossian,* and general ambiance are a voluptuary's dream. Dinners for two from about 120F. (Brussels' three-star restaurant has no *cabinet particulier.*)

Other restaurants with *salons particuliers* include LA CROIX CATELAN in the Bois de Boulogne AUT 08–43; DROUANT, place Gaillon (2nd; 073 53–72); LASSERRE, 17 avenue Franklin Roosevelt (8th; 359–53–43); LUCAS-CARTON, 9 place de la Madeleine (8th; ANJ 22–90); and RELAIS LOUIS XIII, 8 rue des Grands-Augustins (6th; DAN 75–96). And, finally, the recently renovated L'HÔTEL, 13 rue des Beaux-Arts (6th; MED 89–20).

"Recently renovated" is accurate but hardly appropriate for the precious elegance of Guy Louis Duboucheron's eighteenth-century garden house, which had been the Hôtel d'Alsace before Oklahoma-born architect Robin Westbrook set his talented hand to it. L'Hôtel's cellars have been fashioned into intimate drawing rooms where non-residents may dine until 2 A.M., but if two are planning to spend a week rather than a fast few hours, this hotel is as *particulier* and certainly more luxurious than any ordinary *hôtel particulier.* The twenty-five rooms (from 130 to 550F a night) are done in various shades of linen and velvet, and all open on a marbled airshaft that runs the five-story height of the structure, which was enlarged in 1835. They include the chamber where Oscar Wilde died in 1900 (No. 16) and another that contains the fabulous mirrored bed of Mistinguett (3B).

This book cannot avoid the restaurant AU MOUTON DE PANURGE, though in order that some may, the address is omitted. Not that it's difficult to find. Ask among tour-bus operators or conventioneers. The latter are particularly amused by the Rabelaisian murals, the phonebooth fashioned from a confessional, snails in chamberpots, and phallus-shaped rolls. For the *pénis de résistance,* brass testicles sound a loud gong that signals the entrance of a wandering sheep who punctuates the meal by jumping into your lap while his shepherdess runs a garter up your companion's thigh. The food at 130 or more francs for two is a dirty joke.

LOVE FOR SALE

"Where men have nothing but physical desire one finds strumpets, and that is why strumpets in France are charming, and Spanish ones so very inferior. In France strumpets can give many men as much happiness as virtuous women, that is to say, happiness without love; there is always one thing which a Frenchman respects more than his mistress, and that is his vanity."
—STENDHAL, *On Love*

A Bordello

Brothels have been absolutely illegal in Paris as well as the rest of the country since 1946. The most elegant of these is found just off the avenue

Kléber, in the heart (or kidney) of the posh 16th *arrondissement*, near the Étoile. So sumptuous and discreet is this elegant *fin-de-siècle* whitestone mansion, and so select its girls, that many diplomats and important figures of finance, government, politics, and industry—both foreign and domestic—have been regular patrons for years. Indeed, it is known colloquially as "The Diplomats' Brothel."

A plumpish, motherly madam with blue hair greets you warmly—though she has never seen you before this evening, you seem well enough set up in your dark suit and conservative tie—and ushers you inside quickly, past the stand-up mahogany bar and into a large Louis XV salon whose bas-relief ceiling hangs some twenty feet over the Oriental-carpeted floors. Relax with your 10F Scotch or champagne cocktail, admire the tapestries, and after about ten minutes a stunning blonde, twenty-three or so, will arrive for your inspection. She is conservatively dressed in a simple Chanel suit, adorned only by a single strand of pearls, and her manner and bearing are that of an ambassador's daughter. Etiquette requires that you purchase a 10F drink for her (always the champagne cocktail) and that you chat of small things before getting down to business. That will cost you exactly 300F for an hour of her sweet time in one of the lavish upstairs bedrooms, some with ceiling mirrors.

At your inquiry the madam assures you that should you return with a group of friends, additional girls of similar quality will be displayed. But it is difficult to imagine a more magnificent-looking young woman than the Deneuvelike beauty who sits primly before you, awaiting your decision. The interlude is pleasant enough, and one can have a couple of drinks in the parlor, wander about the bar, admire the paintings in the first-floor lobby, and leave without going for the big bed in the sky. *Warning:* temptation is difficult to resist in "The Diplomats'." All the girls are said to be of outstanding quality (if the one you have seen this evening is typical, you are prepared to believe it), and available from 3 P.M. to 2 A.M., every day but Sunday. (No joke here: the place is closed on Sundays.)

You return a few months later for a spot check. This night you are immediately ushered into the bar where a madam produces an album displaying color photographs of ten beauties.

"Make your choice, monsieur. One is four hundred francs, the rest are three hundred francs."

Whichever you choose, you suspect, will be the 400F prize. So, after scrutinizing all the photos, you shrewdly inquire, with apparently real curiosity, which is the expensive one. The madam indicates the photo of a statuesque brunette who resembles Jane Russell in her *Outlaw* days and assures you that the girl speaks perfect English. Her price is dearer, apparently, to pay for the Berlitz lessons.

Whether they are displaying photos or flesh on approval, The Diplomats' management extends to all prospective buyers the same courtesy and restraint as would Tiffany in showing a collection of fine diamonds. And if one chooses not to buy, there are no hard feelings.

A Recent History of Prostitution

When lady legislator Marthe Richard mothered the April 24, 1946, laws (principally No. 46–795) that closed the classic sporting houses of France, the pimps of Paris rejoiced: a panderer's box had been opened. A French house may not have been like home, but at least the brothel system afforded opportunity for strict police supervision and control, as well as medical supervision of the girls.

Cast out of the brothels and into the streets, the girls found the procurers and "protectors" waiting—those criminal parasites who fill the void left when a government attempts to deal with a social problem by the expedient of declaring it partially or wholly illegal. (Just as Prohibition in America helped put "organized crime" in business by handing criminals the exclusive franchise to sell liquor.)

The closing of the houses was deeply mourned by the former clients. Besides being convenient and serving human needs as basic as eating and sleeping, many of these places had a certain elegance and class. The French sat back skeptically. Some even hoped for the miracle of a decline in prostitution. Instead, they were visited by three plagues: an alarming increase in venereal disease; an increase in the number of prostitutes; and a new kind of violence, as large criminal organizations turned prostitution into big business and petty pimps fought among themselves for the leavings.

Thus many people who had supported the 1946 law are now clamoring for the reopening of the houses, Madame Richard being among the strongest advocates. She has called for the strictest governmental supervision of the brothels. proposing that the girls be employed as "social workers."

What to do? It was one thing for the government to pass the law and then reflect that perhaps it was ill advised. But to repeal the law might be construed as governmental approval of prostitution. To initiate a social program of strict supervision of the houses would put the government into the whorehouse business. *La Belle France* would become the world's most prominent madam. And the French government just isn't that French; at least the De Gaulle government wasn't. But a large body of opinion insists the French will once again legalize brothels shortly.

The question is a neat one and offers no easy answers. And because it is representative of the paradox found throughout Europe, this discussion serves as an introduction to prostitution found here and elsewhere on the Continent. As you wander from city to city it is interesting to see how each culture has approached the problem.

But why a problem at all? Why not pass strict laws and attempt to enforce them strictly as the Americans have done? The European answer is that the American "solution" has merely solved small dilemmas while helping to create bigger ones. In spite of tough laws, tough police, and the puritanical attitude of the majority of Americans, there is as high an incidence of prostitution in the United States as in many other Western nations—the so-called American sexual revolution notwithstanding. One sees fewer pretty young girls for sale in the streets and houses of tolerance than in many European cities, but America certainly has its share of hookers.[5] The problem is finding them. And that *is* the problem. Driving prostitution underground with hypocritical attitudes and inflexible laws merely serves to jack up the prices and thus makes it more difficult for those whose needs are great but whose funds are limited.

Take New York City, for example. For the middle- and lower-income groups there is nothing, unless you count those sorry specimens who cruise midtown, East 86th Street, large parts of the West Side, and, of late, Chinatown, offering their diseased, often drug-addicted, and often black bodies— for in America there is at least one profession that has traditionally offered equal opportunity to all races—in order to buy their next fix. Faced with such a limited selection, many New Yorkers would prefer to go out and rape somebody. And more than a few do. Between 1955 and 1965 New York City had 15,133 reported rapes—and countless numbers unreported—and 10,777 arrests for rape, according to figures supplied by the New York Police Department. (In the United States somebody gets raped on the average of every nineteen minutes.)

By comparison, in 1965 Paris and its suburbs, with a combined population of nearly 6 million, showed seventy-eight violations or attempts. In 1966, when the violations or attempts reached seventy-three by late November, people considered it a mass ravage of Sabine proportions. Newspapers and magazines sensationalized the "new crime wave" and Parisiennes became so alarmed they quickly exhausted the city's supply of black and gold perfume flacons that squirt tear gas—and that had gathered dust in the gun shops for years. Yet as Gloria Emerson noted in the Paris *Herald Tribune,* "comparing this city to New York or Chicago . . . Paris is still considered one of the

[5] The term is a tribute to Civil War General "Jumping Joe" Hooker, who spent so much time in New Orleans' red-light district that the area came to be known as "Hooker's Division."

safest cities in the world, where women can walk the streets and not be bothered—unless they want to be."

Of course, New York's high crime rate is attributable to—among other things—its peculiar pressures, tensions, lack of any real human amenities, and lack of federal funding. All the more reasons why the city needs a few legitimate whorehouses.

In 1958 two laws officially recognized that French women may sell themselves, provided they do it with a modicum of discretion and do not engage in blatant solicitation. This merely legalized what was already tolerated. The French view, then, coincides with that of St. Thomas Aquinas: "Prostitution in the towns is like the cesspool in the palace. Do away with the cesspool, and the palace will become an unclean and stinking place"; and with a widely held psychiatric theory that many liaisons with prostitutes are enactments of sex crimes that might otherwise be committed.

And many French just plain enjoy having the prostitutes around. As an American finds some comfort, levity, and release from daily cares in his friendly neighborhood tavern, so many Europeans also like to chat up a prostitute every now and then. Or joke with them, or bargain, or merely stand and stare. And sometimes they even go to bed with them.

Throughout the De Gaulle regime the government made many attempts at suppressing or at least mitigating activities. However, the attitude of the Paris police has remained flexible—"tolerance and control" appear to be their bywords. General De Gaulle, and his wife were well-known for their prudishness, and his media censorship carried over into other areas. But the basic character of the French could not be changed, of course, even by De Gaulle. During his regime one could have said that the French still didn't care what you did, as long as you didn't print it.

There have been several recent crackdowns on prostitution, particularly in the wake of the Markovitch affair, and no doubt the status of prostitution will continue to fluctuate in the next few years. For example, every time a foreign dignitary or head of state arrived to visit De Gaulle, the police were ordered to clear the streets. But it was business as usual, as soon as Kennedy, Nixon, Brezhnev, or whoever had left.

One afternoon, Madame De Gaulle (known affectionately as "Tante Yvonne") chanced to be shopping at FAUCHON, 26 place de la Madeleine (8th), the most elegant and expensive gourmet food shop in Paris. After making her purchases of Asturian salmon, English biscuits and, perhaps, Vermont elderberry jam, the First Lady was shocked to discover, just outside, a number of street tarts who had marketed their wares in the place de la Madeleine for many years.

"Now!" Madame De Gaulle is said to have demanded upon returning to the nearby Élysée Palace. At the President's orders, the Madeleine was cleared by the following afternoon. But shortly thereafter (and ever since), the Madeleine, and especially the adjacent rue Godot-de-Mauroy, have become a speedway for motorized prostitutes, none of whom appear until well after Fauchon closes—from 11 P.M. to 4 A.M.

Similarly, in a recent drive roughly paralleling the sandblasting of public buildings and monuments, the police cracked down on blatant street soliciting, particularly during the August tourist season. (Many prostitutes move to the Riviera at this time anyway.) The effect of this new diligence has been to force the customer to make the first move, or at least to present himself as open to suggestion. Usually this amounts to no more than walking past the girl's beat or pulling up next to her car at a stoplight.

The Markovitch scandal has had its impact on the city's most exclusive madams—the more exclusive, the more impact—but at this writing most of them are still operating, though not quite as openly as before. And at the other end of town, Les Halles is no more a marketplace, and hundreds of 30F teen-aged prostitutes have scurried to . . . no one really knows where they will go.

Recently, when the police closed more than twenty seedy hotels that housed many of "les fleurs" ("The Flowers"—the girls of Les Halles), Lloyd Garrison of The New York Times asked Michel Jean, head of the vice squad, how the closings would affect the future of prostitution in the city. Seated in his "austere office in the Interior Ministry, its only decoration . . . half a dozen pin-up girls taped over the wall opposite his desk," M. Jean had this to say:

"In this country, a woman is free to do with her body what she likes and get money in return. It is a civil right. It is the oldest profession in the world. It has always existed and is likely to continue for a long time.

"We figure there are about twenty thousand prostitutes in France, about half in Paris. It's not a dramatic problem. Our job is to keep it in bounds."

And so, business goes on as usual. On the boulevards, in certain streets, cafés, and bars, in the lobbies of some of the elegant hotels, in parks, and in the doorways of many decrepit hotels. Motorized prostitutes are no longer a novelty in Paris, or most anywhere else in Europe for that matter. And there is an elaborate call-girl system, run with all the efficiency of a Madison Avenue model agency—and the girls are just as winning, and cheaper.

Call Girls and the Markovitch Affair

The French love a scandal as much as the Americans love a parade, and when no scandal exists, they will invent one. For a time it appeared that the "Tout-Paris" gossip surrounding the murder of Stephan Markovitch—small-time hood and bodyguard, valet, and companion to film star Alain Delon—was a mere invention, or at least a distortion of the truth. Even some French newspapers, and almost all the American ones, at first accepted the official police version: Markovitch was a minor drug peddler, undoubtedly murdered by a former associate. Believed it in spite of the fact that immediately upon learning that Markovitch's gunnysacked body had been found in a garbage dump near Versailles, Charles De Gaulle mobilized the entire Paris police establishment and demanded he be kept in constant touch with their investigations.

From late 1968 through the spring of 1969 there was anxiety among some of France's most illustrious statesmen, film stars, writers, and . . . madams, for it had now been clearly established that Markovitch was a remarkably resourceful and ingenious blackmailer who had organized some of the most elaborate *partouze* soireés Paris has ever seen. His guests included many important figures of government and the cinema—not to mention some of Paris's most beautiful call girls—who have since learned that Markovitch photographed them with the aid of a concealed camera and an assistant nicknamed "The Story of O."

For a time the Markovitch thing had Profumo potential; some newspapers even dropped such names as that of Madame Pompidou—this was some time before her husband succeeded De Gaulle—and of Charles De Gaulle's grandson. But there is absolutely no basis in fact for these suggestions. At this writing, Markovitch's murderer (undoubtedly a potential blackmail victim or acting for one) is still at large. The government has hushed up the whole business. It is cited here merely because when the scandal first broke, the public and private *partouze* Establishment and the madams had to make some minor adjustments in their respective personal and professional lives.

"The Soirées of Madame Claude," headed that portion of the newspaper *Minute's* October, 1968, story which stated that one victim of the Markovitch affair "keeps near the Étoile a luxurious *maison de rendezvous* where Stephan Markovitch recruited beautiful young women for his rustic group soirées. The worldly gang 'advised her to close shop and go off for a while in the direction of the Riviera.'

"Now . . . at this time," continues *Minute,* "her idle 'belles' exercise their craft in certain bars of the rue François Ier and some in the Champs-Élysées. . . . As a matter of fact, it must be known that this hospitable house was scarcely clandestine. . . . Madame Claude knew how to receive with discrimination foreign personages in transit. In our capital the heads of government and ministers of the Third World, for example, are fond of Parisian pleasures. At Madame Claude's the motto was 'discretion assured . . . no questions asked.' "

Discretion indeed. One of Madame Claude's former employees assures you that even the French government phoned BAL 20--- on occasion. Operating from a portion of a top floor in the rue de Marignan (8th), right off the

Champs-Élysées, Claude, or one of her associates, could be relied upon to make virtually the same arrangements for particularly important foreign dignitaries as she did for the clients of countless business and industrial firms—"arrangements" that were second to none. The client was presented to a girl so exquisite, companionable, witty, and intelligent that even if he were told she was a professional, he would likely forget it after an hour of her company. After an elegant dinner—at a restaurant like Maxim's, Lasserre, or Le Grand Véfour—he would make his *grande séduction* and wake up the next morning in love with Paris, and perhaps a little more ripe for a deal or negotiation than if he had slept alone. And his companion would phone her "aging grandmother" at BAL 03--- for her next evening's assignment.

Whether Claude took the advice of the "worldly gang" and temporarily retired while the Markovitch *mistral* blew over was immaterial. Although BAL 20--- no longer answered ALM 20--- usually did. And if that failed, a number like 527-60--- might succeed. At this writing, Claude has, after a vacation or two, apparently resumed. Considering the patterns of the past, there is no reason to suspect that she will fall from her place of eminence, nor that associates or imitators will not maintain her high standards. These are very high indeed.

In response to what you had thought would be rather extraordinary demands, even for a madam of Claude's repute—four Scandinavian blondes, two long-legged redheads, and two American brunettes, all to be delivered to your "Cannes-based yacht" within the week—you were assured there would be "No problem, monsieur. But because you are not known personally to us, please present yourself at our offices and I am sure we can satisfy your needs."

You visited the quarters in rue de Marignan (8th)[6] leafed through the photo album of beauties, and feigned disappointment when informed that "you may have to settle for one American girl and one English girl rather than two Americans. But they are each quite superb and, incidentally, witty and extremely intelligent, both being enrolled at the Sorbonne. In addition to the four Swedish girls you may also wish to add two charming Vietnamese to your package."

You promised to discuss the matter with your colleagues, shook hands, and left—wishing you had a yacht.

But, in fact, such services are not exclusively the province of the very rich. Anyone can phone (usually from noon to 8 P.M.) or make arrangements through his concierge or favorite barman. Claude's rates are roughly 300F for the first hour, about 2000F for the weekend. She also has "specials." For

[6]Claude also had offices in avenue Paul-Doumer (16th). The numbers do not belong to her any more and have been suggested purely for historic reasons. To print her current number—easily obtainable from the better bartenders, concierges, and hairdressers—would only mean she'd have to change it again.

example, a Danish girl who is described simply as "the most beautiful girl in the world" (by a well-known American novelist now living in Paris) commands 500F an hour.

No matter whom you choose, the girl arrives as promptly and as coquettishly as would a well-trained mistress, and the rendezvous can be almost anywhere you like. The more elegant your hotel, the better connections Claude—or her successors—seem to have for sending the girl directly to your room. Or she can be met in her own apartment, or yours.

And Claude has had special arrangements with three *hôtels particuliers*—one in Passy, another in the rue Boulainvilliers, and a third near rue La Boëtie. RÉSIDENCE DE LA MUETTE has (as previously noted) severed its connection with Claude and acquired a new management. However it has not changed its phone number: 525-13-08. (Just a hotel now.)

When the operation (not the Muette) is functioning smoothly, there is an active file of from one to three hundred girls, including students, models, housewives, starlets, dancers, American and other embassy secretaries, and even a couple of lawyers and doctors. The selection conforms to current supply and trends. Natural blondes—many are Swedish and German models —always seem to be in great demand, particularly among oil-rich Arabians. A great many of the girls are new to this sort of work. Some are putting husbands through medical school, others are between pictures or waiting for that big break. And some dance nightly in the great striptease *spectacles.* But all are of such high caliber that "a King would be proud to be seen with them at Maxim's." And in the case of some, this is no idle maxim.

The foregoing particulars were gathered from former employees. While the *Minute* account was more concerned with Claude's girls' alleged connections with Stephan Markovitch than specifics regarding her operations— perhaps assuming that "Tout-Paris" knows them anyway—the article did suggest that operations have few problems with the authorities.

"Everyone knows that state secrets spoil easily on the pillow of a bed. Certain guests would willingly serve their country and their interests by repeating them to someone in the right place.

"Contrary to what has been written, S. Markovitch had not corrupted Madame Claude's guests . . . for his soirées outside Paris. On the contrary, he would have been strongly recommended to call upon these very 'sure' creatures by reason of the quality of his invited guests. . . . One would be obliged to agree that faithful to a solid house tradition and anxious about the future, the house 'feeds' unceasingly the files on serving government people.

"Left to themselves, the female informers of Madame Claude's tended to show themselves to be talkative recently.

"Fortunately, order has been restored. Saturday, operation 'recuperation' commenced. Hefty fellows, with efficient means of persuasion at their disposal, undertook taking in hand again all the beauties and directing them to other places of work.

"They are breathing easier now. Victor Hugo said in vain of connoisseurs and politicians that they recover from everything . . . and especially from a couch. It would be insufferable to see the lewd performances of our leaders recounted by the American press."

Whatever her future, Claude has had an exciting past. She is, however, not the only madam in Paris—merely the most distinguished. Unless one considers the elusive Madame Daphné, who travels about Europe with an entourage of ten girls said to be at least the equal of Claude's.

More Madams

Of course, there are dozens of madams in Paris, the majority of them offering girls of amazingly high quality—particularly when Claude is on one of her vacations and her charges are thus at liberty—at fees of no more than 120F for an hour's *"moment,"* or from 200 to 300F for an evening of dinner and bed. Several of these entrepreneurs occupy fairly luxurious premises, with bars, light refreshment, kitchens, and suitable "interview" parlors where you may relish the parade of talent. To comply strictly with the law, it is preferred that one complete the transaction on other premises, though some thoughtful madams do maintain a couple of "emergency" mirrored bedrooms. (Some hairdressers seem to know a lot about these.)

Perhaps the best of the better madams is "S," rue de Rome, in the incredible 17th *arrondissement,* which has more easily accessible, civilized action than all of New York City. Also good are "G" in rue La Rochefoucauld, 9th; "N" and "N" in rue La Fontaine, 16th; and "C" in rue de Gramont, 2nd. Again, to print their phone numbers would only mean they would be changed. However, approximately four of ten Champs-Élysées cab drivers know these, not to mention many of the better bartenders and hotel personnel. Or your company's social secretary.

Street Scenes

Les Occasionnelles

Often as desirable as Madame Claude's girls, frequently much younger, and—for Americans at least—the most difficult prostitutes to identify, are *les étoiles filantes.* Many of these "shooting stars" are so genteel in manner and appearance as to appear completely unapproachable. But in Paris it is often axiomatic that the less likely the girl appears to be, the more likely she is! The best way to find out is to try—something obviously subtle like borrowing some sugar from her café table or requesting a translation of a concert or movie listing in your newspaper. If she likes you, happens to need the money, and is indeed a "professional amateur," she'll usually take it from there.

"Shooting stars" appear from every station in life, frequently from the middle and upper classes. Broadly speaking, they are not true prostitutes. Many are students, secretaries, housewives, poorly paid models—and often daughters of very good families. In greatest heat around the end of the month when the paycheck or the allowance from Papa runs out, they are also called "fins-du mois."[7]

"Amateurs" are found throughout Paris, but the youngest (often in their teens) and most desirable frequent the cafés of the Champs-Élysées, especially those in the area of the Rond-Point. Their prices are usually competitive with the best professionals of the area—about 200F for a "short time." With an étoile filante, a "short time" could last a weekend, if you're compatible. Sometimes teen-age girls travel in pairs, offering themselves as a package for 150 to 200F. These duos are more numerous in cafés nearer l'Étoile than the Rond-Point. On the Left Bank one may find much more professional and frequently unscrupulous "amateurs," who lure suckers from certain bars and cafés.

Do you doubt that the charming nineteen-year-old redhead studying a textbook or the expensively pants-suited blond beauty on the café terrace near the Rond-Point, might spend an hour with you in the bed of any nearby hotel for 100–150F? Such a girl would be mobbed on Amagansett, Long Island's "Bay of Pigs" beach, or at some of the bars on Manhattan's "swinging" East Side. You might see the blonde's American physical counterpart browsing in the Museum of Modern Art and you'd judge her a Vassar graduate, employed as art director or fashion publicist, and daughter of a wealthy executive. Some Champs-Élysées café girls have a similar background, although the wide range of careers open to American girls is still fairly limited in France. In New York a girl with average secretarial skills and good intelligence may earn $125, $150 or more a week. In Paris she is lucky to earn $75. And though the cost of living is not quite as high as New York's, clothing —the major expense for most young girls—is just as costly and the fashions are more tempting.

"Money," says *Time*, "tells much about a nation's character because it is so closely entwined with a nation's history, psychology, and destiny." Their general postwar prosperity notwithstanding, the French are always worried about money. Transitory—though no less serious—crises like the devaluation scare, the gold shortage, and the pressures of the incredibly successful Deutsche mark merely bring to the surface a deep-seated apprehension that is an integral aspect of the national psyche. *Time*'s analysis of De Gaulle's policy of fiscal austerity (November 29, 1968) noted the people's apparent unpatri-

---

[7] Nearly all salaried people are paid once a month in France.

otic distrust of their own currency—which manifests itself in the motto "in gold we trust." This attitude is as relevant to an understanding of France's women, as of her bankers: "It is too easy for self-righteous Americans to condemn this behavior. . . . Frenchmen . . . buying bullion and foreign money and transferring their savings to foreign countries. . . . Anybody who has not seen his own fortunes dissipated by recurrent invasions, inflations and devaluations cannot fully understand the miser mentality of many Frenchmen and other Europeans."[8]

It would be similarly easy for morally self-righteous Americans (historically if not currently far more affluent than the large majority of French) to express smug contempt on learning that one authority[9] has estimated that there are twenty-five thousand amateurs in Paris—more than the combined total of all categories of true professionals. Amateurism is so widespread that it extends even to the stolidly proper middle-class suburbs. According to Dallayrac: "Prostitution with the basket . . . is practiced by certain part-time girls. On market days, in the suburbs, they take their shopping baskets and go marketing. The client approaches, proposes to fill the shopping basket . . . buys cauliflower, oranges, bread and meat . . . and accompanies the housewife."

Even for Paris this sounds rather unbelievable. Just to make sure, you visited two suburban supermarkets. Confirmed: a few pounds of groceries is enough to seduce some of the prettiest young matrons in both Épinay-Villetaneuse and Deuil-la-Barre.

Champs-Élysées and Environs

In America a Caravelle is a French airplane. In France *une caravelle* is a top-grade prostitute, especially indigenous to the Champs-Élysées area. However, depending on the season, she works wherever the money goes—from the slopes of the French Alps to the beaches of Cannes, and on to the Frankfurt Book Fair. Found in "American bars" (bars with stand-up counters), lobbies of grand hotels—the "palaces"—and sometimes strolling along the Champs-Élysées and adjacent streets, these beauties are indistinguishable in appearance from the other elegant women who grace this area. Strictly speaking, you don't find them, they find you. The price—from 200 to 500F, depending on the amount of time involved (one hour minimum) and the season. *Caravelles* and *occasionnelles* are sometimes more expensive during the tourist months, for they are in shorter supply and consequently in greater demand.

[8]However, according to Common Market economists (and *Time,* Dec. 6, 1971) sometime during the mid-1970's France's total G.N.P. will surpass West Germany's, to give France the world's fourth greatest economy.

[9]Dominique Dallayrac, *Dossier Prostitution* (Paris: Robert Laffont, 1966).

According to Dallayrac, 70 percent of the city's prostitutes are natives of the provinces, and virtually all of these are among the 80 percent of Paris prostitutes who work for pimps. Many *caravelles*—a large number of whom are native Parisians—have pimps too. Working for *them*. The *caravelle* is simply too sophisticated for bondage. Her man functions as an extremely subtle press agent, and he must really earn his money by procuring the most affluent clientele with the utmost resourcefulness and discretion. For this he receives a small percentage of the take, and usually nothing more.

Motorized prostitutes, "*les amazones,*" cruise the circle around the Étoile formed by the rues de Tilsitt and de Presbourg. They also drive along the avenue George V. For 100 to 200F, plus 20F for the room, the *amazones* of the 8th *arrondissement*—most of whom are young and quite attractive—offer curb-to-curb service. Several years ago an enterprising businessman invested his life savings in a fleet of twelve expensive white cars, complete insurance coverage, and full-time rental of twelve *hôtel particulier* rooms. Today he is a millionaire, and his girls and cars—both always this year's model—cruise the Champs-Élysées area, bringing him a *taxe* of 40 percent on all earnings. In clement weather many of these girls sentinel themselves at the corner of the rue de Tilsitt and the avenue Friedland, and at the corner of rue de Presbourg and the avenue Kléber.

Bois de Boulogne *amazones* ask fifty to seventy-five francs for a fast trick in the back seats of their Renaults and Simcas. "*Bucoliques,*" girls who work the parks or rural areas, range in price from 20 to 50F in the Bois, where the lawns are their beds.

"Lollipops," teen-age prostitutes who look like daughters of the Jet Set—and some are—gather in certain Franco-Floridian snack palaces and drugstores along the Champs. Often they have subtle arrangements with café waiters.

L'Échassière, the woman on stilts, views life from the top of a bar stool. And since there are so many bars in the vicinity of the Champs-Élysées, she is particularly indigenous to this area. Some bars near the rues Berryer, de Ponthieu, François Ier, and du Colisée are particularly active. Prices range from 200 to 300F, plus 20F for the room and who knows what for the "champagne." One can sometimes avoid paying the price of a room if business is slow and the girl has an arrangement with a particular *hôtel particulier.* And during slack periods, some prostitutes of all classes may absorb the cost of the room themselves. But one must usually bargain for this discount.

Last, and in seeming greatest abundance only because they are so bold, are the used *caravelles,* ages thirty-five to forty-five. As serviceable and workmanlike as a Citroën 2CV, these women are usually found in the cafés and are most active at the apéritif hour. A drink, a meal, or 50F will make them happy. Splendid sources of information and gossip, they know all about *partouzes* and other items of special interest, and speak the best English in town. They should—they learned it from your father.

Those tall buxom blond beauties working the rue de Ponthieu and the rue du Colisée do not mean their sister-in-law's little boy when they offer you a *petit garçon*. The phrase is a transvestite prostitute's euphemism for himself. To look at that statuesque mass of peroxide and paraffin, you'd never suspect it was male. Sometimes one can tell by looking at the hands. But in Paris sometimes one cannot.

Opéra-Madeleine

They're waiting for you on the rue Godot-de-Mauroy (9th). Round and round roll *les amazones* on the long, dimly lit one-way street and the perpendicular rue de Sèze and parallel rue Caumartin. The cars are last year's George V model, and so are the girls. Aged from about twenty-seven to thirty-five, they ask 100F and will often take 75F (especially as the hour grows late), plus 20 to 25F for the nearby hotel room. The procedure and route of this minuscule Le Mans never vary. The girl stops her car next to yours, or blinks her lights at strollers. No sale? She whips around the block and is back to offer a second inspection within three minutes. Sometimes these *amazones,* and others somewhat younger and more attractive, cruise the avenue de l'Opéra, where the price is usually firm at 100F. In warm weather, some cruise the rue Daunou.

In the boulevards de la Madeleine and des Capucines one finds some *"chandelles"* (literally, "candles"), prostitutes who arrive and depart from their specific outdoor beat at times arranged among themselves; and the inevitable *"marcheuses"* or *"trottoirs"*—streetwalkers. These range in age from thirty to fifty and command 100F when they can get it. And 50 to 75F when they can't. And long after the cafés have shut down, the ladies break out the stacked chairs and display themselves on the terraces until 4 or 5 A.M.

Pigalle

These girls really mean business. The hardest, toughest, most professional hookers in town. From 30 to 300F, the wide range of prices speaks for itself —whatever the sucker will bear—and also depends on where one finds the whores. The cheapest work the streets. And the most expensive have close associations with the bars and touts. When a tourist asks a cab driver "Where can I find some girls?" he will inevitably be taken. To Pigalle—clip-joint country. The cabbies get a kickback of up to 40 percent from the bars, and customers may get punched, kicked, rolled, and—sometimes—laid. But all visitors should have a look, if only to watch the wrestlers strut and flex outside their tents along the boulevard de Clichy. And you simply haven't been to

Paris if you haven't been importuned by a Montmartre pimp: "Eh? You want see exhibition, two girls making love? Only fifty francs. . . . No? Well, perhaps you would enjoy to watch two men and the one girl? . . . No? Wait a moment. What would you say to an old lady with one leg and a white dachshund?"

"Excuse me."

"No?! Ahh, look, I have something very special. Two men, a small Jewish boy, an Arab boy, three girls, a donkey . . . and a zebra!"

"Look, man, we're just looking for some Italian food."

"*Ahhh, les Américains . . . toujours bizarres!*" shrugs the "mackerel." (These gentlemen are also known variously as *macs; "harengs,"* herrings; *"saurs,"* kippers; *"barbillons,"* fish-hook barbs; and *"barbeaux,"* barbels—large European fresh-water fish with threadlike growths hanging from their lips. While it can be said that the *macs* are literally always "fishing," the proliferation of nautical references is probably also a reflection of the fact that the Corsicans of Marseilles—France's greatest port—have traditionally been to prostitution what the Rothschilds have been to banking.)

Should you and your party crave a private exhibition in properly atmospheric but safe enough surroundings, the HÔTEL SAINT-GEORGES, 29 rue Fontaine (9th; 874-62-03), does this sort of thing as well as anyone in the neighborhood (and that's saying a lot), except perhaps CHEZ GEORGETTE HÔTEL, 5 rue André-Antoine (18th; MON 82–56). At the Saint-Georges one stands in a specially designed reception parlor hung with some fair Renoir reproductions. Fifteen brassy young Toulouse-Lautrecs surround you, each insisting she is the finest 120F *"suckee-fuckee"* in town. It's 250F for a two- or three-girl "lesbian" exhibition, 100F supplement for you to join the act in one of the twenty-one tatty bedrooms. Exactly the same situation obtains at Georgette's, though the inspection parlors have mirrors rather than Renoirs. By all means attend either of these two houses on your own rather than be led—and bled—to them by the hysterical Algerian and Middle European touts who, when they are not flogging warm watches and jewelry in the places Blanche and Pigalle, insist they must "presenta da gorels, da best you find," but invariably lead you to either of these two standbys. One Budapest '56 refugee, on being asked the time, rolled up his sleeve to reveal eight watches labeled New York, London, Budapest, Bombay, Tokyo, San Francisco, etc., and replied, "Where?" Shades of "E," St. Louis, 1959.

There are a lot of street *"suckee-fuckee"* opportunities in rues Pigalle, Frochot, and Fontaine, 70F including the room. Two *vioques* (old prostitutes), their complexions a livid boiled-chicken yellow, their skins the texture of antique eggrolls, hope to shanghai you from beneath the Pigalle Waterfall sign into HOTEL SHANGHAI, 4 rue Frochot[10]: "She suck me, I suck her, then we two

[10]Management here have no connection with such activities.

suck you." There is said to be another *vioque* who roams this area offering a very special deal: any man who succeeds in making her achieve orgasm gets his money back. The proposition is said to have special appeal to Texans.

A Hungarian guide who has worked the hot rue Frochot since he left the old country in 1956 may direct you to a better fate. Ask for him at LA BOHÈME, YELLOW DOG, GRINZING, SOHO, DIRTY DICK'S, or KIU KIU bars (he's the only Magyar hereabouts from Miskolc). He's about as straight as you have a right to expect of a Hungarian who works Pigalle; speaks excellent English, will find what you are looking for, and will see that no harm comes to you.

Don't visit rue de la Charbonnière without a guide like him. A wild and dangerous street just off the boulevard Rochechouart (18th), an extension of boulevard de Clichy, where apparently everything and everybody is for sale, primarily to North Africans. Emaciated, animalistic, very young girls (not North African) in "fun fur" coats, flash naked, standing six to ten deep in dingy doorways. Lately wire screens have been installed to protect the little girls from the pawing of neighborhood residents, understandably rapacious because *their* women are seen only by day and then heavily veiled.

Attend one of those "2.50F" striptease shows along boulevard de Clichy if you must, but be warned that as soon as you enter you will be required to purchase 20 if not 200F worth of champagne. Some interesting photos of flagellation equipment (martinets and cat-o'-nine tails) may be found in SEXA-SHOP and TRUONG, at 29 and 33 *bis* boulevard de Clichy, respectively, but if you want the real thing, wait for Amsterdam and Copenhagen. For something more permanent in porn, see BRUNO TATTOO, who will, according to the photos in his 6 rue Germain-Pilon studio, tattoo your girlfriend's breasts to your taste.

There is a surprising number of attractive young girls working Pigalle streets, particularly in warmer months. If one is here for that sort of business, he is advised to transact it with street- rather than bargirls, only because it is far less expensive. But for a 5F beer you can have some small talk, laughs, and a fast dance or two if you first make it clear that's all you seek. "We drink, we have fun . . . we lie a little . . . we try to dance," smiles the frank Piaf-lookalike in a rue Blanche bar. (Street girls 70–80F.)

The "girls" in rue Houdon are not quite so straightforward. Some of the boldest, meanest transvestite prostitutes in town. Twenty francs to begin, and thereafter anything that rolls out of your pockets.

Les Halles

Les Halles had been the site of a market for more than eight hundred years. Now, after years of indecision, the city has finally moved the raucous, smelly "belly of Paris" to the antiseptic suburbs: dairy, fish, fruit, and vegetables to Rungis, near Orly; meat and poultry to La Villette, seven miles beyond; and the flowers . . . what will become of *les fleurs*—the whores of les Halles? Some of the famed all-night restaurants, where visiting and Parisian night-crawlers have traditionally mingled with *"les forts"*—the strong men, the porters of les Halles—over pig's feet and a bowl of crusty onion soup, are determined to stay on. But no one can really predict what character change the neighborhood will undergo. Office buildings, new housing, and a large park are planned.

Will *les fleurs* follow *les forts* to suburbia? There are, at this writing, many opinions. Although the girls have always serviced *les forts* and people who had business in the markets, usually at cut rates, they have also carried on a good trade with tourists, students, and others who neither work nor live in the area. And *les fleurs* have been a Les Halles fixture since Louis VI ("The Fat") founded the market in 1135. One rumor suggests that the Corsican underworld has already set up apartments in Rungis and investigated the possibilities of turning house trailers into roving bordellos. But prostitutes, like other human beings, are creatures of habit. Once they call a street home, it takes nothing short of heavy bombing to move them to another location. (A characteristic of many European cities is that prostitutes traditionally work areas adjacent to railway stations. Years after the stations are torn down and the sites used for other purposes, the whores, and succeeding generations of them, still keep to the old beats.)

At this writing Les Halles retains one of the largest concentrations of young low-priced professionals in Paris. If and when they do leave the area, it is likely that many will seek a district (or be directed to one by their pimps) that affords a similar ambiance as exists in Les Halles. The following account may give some indication as to the kinds of neighborhoods under consideration.

If you asked a knowing French comrade to show you the most theatrical whore streets, he would never choose Pigalle. He would bring you here to Les Halles for glimpses of life and for scenes and characters out of Lautrec. Ugly, tawdry, pathetic? Yes, but no less human. A tragi-comedy of humanity. Here is life. It exists, and so one should see it. Such is the Frenchman's view.

It is in Les Halles that one finds some vestige of the more honkytonk prewar bordellos and the flavor of that life sought by the freewheeling society couples of the 1920s and 1930s who frequently slummed in them. Explore these slightly spooky but no less safe streets with your wife or girlfriend. The propositions are bawdy but not without humor, and some of the overtures are intended more for the lady than the gentleman.

Read the street signs and you will know some of Les Halles' history: rue au Lard (bacon street), quai de la Mégisserie (hides), rue de la Lingerie, rue de la Grande-Truanderie (big-time racketeering; and the opposite side translates as small-time racketeering), and rue Vide-Gousset (pickpocket).

Wander into the bistros of the pimps. Sit in a corner—no one bothers you. Watch the girls stream in and out for a snack or a game of pinball with the *macs*. There is laughter and gossip as the pimps play lively dice games for drinks and the devil knows what else.

"*Les maquereaux*" . . . running in the gutters of the streets like pus from a sore. Sneaky, silent little men, caricatures of their calling. They guard the girls like money in a bank, and watch every stranger carefully, without seeming to do so.

"*Les poulets*" (the police) . . . making their periodic rounds. The streets and doorways seem to clear before each patrol, as if everyone had a nightly schedule of the visits. The police never bother the girls as long as they keep to their doorways and don't cause too much commotion when they call to "*les chalands*"—whore jargon for male passersby.

"*Les fleurs*" . . . so young. Many seem fourteen or fifteen, none look more than eighteen. They resemble the teenyboppers on American TV dance parties, except they are prettier as a group. And some are beautiful. Though they have lost their generation, they wear its uniform—sweaters, shrunk two sizes too small and microskirts and boots—and here and there a bright satin dress, low-cut and slashed all the way up one side.

A Humbert Humbert's delight, in fluffy white fun fur, flashes from a doorway, revealing sheer bikini panties and breasts the size of the melons that until recently were unloaded nightly in the next street. Eight, ten, and twelve deep they stand, in doorways and long hallways of cheap rooming houses. *Les chalands* gaze transfixed, peering down corridors and up the staircases tightly packed with gossiping youngsters.

The girls come cheap: 20 to 40F, plus 10F for the "room." Turnover and volume have always been keynotes of Les Halles, whether in produce or human beings. These are the fastest tricks in town. Some girls are said to have turned twenty, or even thirty tricks a night. Many earn more than their sisters on the Champs-Élysées. But very few keep much of the take. They are virtual prisoners of their "protectors," either hopelessly in love with them or in fear of their lives to flee . . . to where? And none would believe that life could be any different than it is. Though young, they are already cynical and hard, and brittle as well, because they *are* so young.

Stroll the narrow, spooky length of the rue Quincampoix (3rd, 4th), one of the bawdiest, most colorful streets in Paris. But be wary—Henri IV was murdered here by Ravaillac in 1610. Activity to midnight in winter, later in warmer months. Very young and lively girls ask 40F, 30F if you are French. Denizens of the rue aux Ours (street of the Bears) and the rue des Lombards —the two streets form the northern and southern boundaries of Quincampoix —are even cheaper, 20 to 30F, plus 15F for the room. Some lively, all-night sex shops hereabouts.

The main street of Les Halles prostitution has traditionally been rue Saint-Denis. Its most active points are at intersections with the rues du Ponceau, Greneta, and Guérin-Boisseau—all busy in their own right. The latter is a street so narrow that a man could urinate across it. And many do. It is lined with doorways leading to cheap hotels and 20-to-30F whores. One girl stands in a corridor holding a stopwatch as another dashes upstairs with a client. The winner is she who gets her customer in and out of that rickety bed and back downstairs in the night's shortest time. The record is said to be under two minutes. While in the neighborhood one might visit the rue des Innocents, which has few, and lies between the rues Saint-Denis and Lingerie. Twenty francs *complet*.

Gare Saint-Lazare

Very young girls and some ancients, in some nearby cafés, 40 to 50F.

But it is inside the station that the real drama occurs. A special kind of man meets the trains, ever-watchful for naïve provincial girls, aged fourteen to eighteen or so, many of whom have left poor but respectable homes out of restlessness or depression. (How can you keep them down on the farm, after they've seen the farm?) The man has his counterpart in dozens of European and British railway stations, from Hamburg to Rome, from Munich to Madrid: greedy eyes, slick groom, sharp suit, smooth tongue. Quarry and hunter play their parts as if from memory. Indeed, the man knows his role by heart. It is his profession.

He offers to carry her bag. Then a coffee. She is impressed, flattered. He is so handsome, and smells so good. And he seems to know such important people. On to a "special" restaurant. He is known there. A hot meal, surrounded by his compatriots. She has never known such attention. He will find her a room, but first a celebration. Dancing—a *bal* in the rue de Lappe. Tonight she may stay in his apartment. He, of course, will sleep on the floor.

By the end of the week she is hopelessly in love with him.

A blissful month goes by. Then one day he returns to their love nest with real tears in his eyes. "They" will kill him unless he returns the money he has borrowed to pay for her new wardrobe and the down payment on their marriage flat. Perhaps she would . . . but no . . . he cannot suggest such a thing. Yet, if she could earn some money. . . .

Sometimes the friendly persuasion convinces her. Otherwise the beatings begin. He threatens to write to her village anonymously and expose her shame if she goes to the police (who, in fact, can do little without real proof). Or . . . he will establish her in business.

At first life seems not so bad. She is earning more money than she has ever seen. He, of course, must "keep all of it safe. Banks are so unreliable."

The story is so pat as to be unbelievable. But the circumstances of the gullibility of provincials, their loneliness in big cities, and the ruthlessness of these men give it credence, especially if the man is the girl's first lover.

Of course, some girls are shrewd and resourceful enough to begin "the life" unencumbered by a pimp and to maintain a certain independence throughout their careers. If they are good enough, they find their way to the more lucrative Right Bank beats. But it is the rare French prostitute who does not have some kind of relationship with a pimp, either for purposes of protection (from police or clients), or because of the strange masochism that drives these women to shower gifts of love and money on one man while withholding everything but their bodies from all others.

Miscellaneous Street Beats

Part-time and full-time *bucoliques* grow in the bushes and lawns of the Bois de Vincennes, from 20 to 50F. Place de la Bastille (12th) has some *mineures* as well as has-beens, 30 to 50F *la passe. Les marcheuses* and *les chandelles* ply the narrow, steep, and ghostly rue de Budapest (9th) and charge 50 to 80F. Though the nearby rue des Dames has none at this writing, this whole area may soon be crawling with whores—many observers consider it a likely spot for *les fleurs* if they choose to emigrate from Les Halles.

The Left Bank has less professional activity than the Right, since so much is traditionally given away. However, as Montparnasse has acquired more clubs and discothèques, more tarts have moved in. Rues Vavin and Bréa (6th) are the most active. Hustlers, attracted by some of the area's transvestite situations, and some used *caravelles* ask from 75 to 100F.

Some statistics

In 1965, when the male population of Paris was approximately 2 million and its prostitutes were said to number about eight thousand, vice squad statistics showed that "users" represented 69 percent of the population; 49 percent were occasional customers and 20 percent were regulars. (Dallayrac, *Dossier Prostitution.*) Paris's prostitutes were estimated to bring in more than $200 million a year. As has been noted, Michel Jean, current head of the vice squad, estimates that there are now more than ten thousand prostitutes in Paris. (The figure seems conservative by at least half.)

Nostalgia

"What the hell do *you* know from fancy whorehouses?!" snort those newspapermen, bartenders, and other sentimental souls who recall the *Maison Closes* of pre-1946 days. Details are remembered wistfully, if not always with strict accuracy.

Apparently the delight of the old times was to make an evening of it, visiting a number of houses, accompanied by your pals or your wife and other couples. One drank a lot of champagne, danced with the prostitutes, and watched them cavort around the great ballrooms and reception salons. There was much gaiety and whoresplay as the girls would bait the wives and perhaps even dance with them.

The atmosphere and decor were elegant, the facilities formidable at the world-famed "Old One Two Two" (122 rue de Provence) and 12 rue Chabanais. Also quite good were 39 rue Pasquier, 6 rue des Moulins, 50 rue Saint-Georges, and the legendary Sphinx, 31 boulevard Edgar-Quinet.[11] These houses were frequented by royalty, society, and the rest of the autogyro set of the 1920s and 1930s. Some of these places were, in fact, among the first discothèques, for in addition to live bands there was dancing to phonograph records. A special guide to the houses, Le Guide Rose, was published every two years and listed addresses and prices. (From a few francs in a workingman's brothel to hundreds in palaces where one could dine well and indulge in fantasies worthy of a Farouk.)

Then there were joints like 29 rue Saint-Lazare, 4 rue Blondel, and 13 rue Rochechouart, saturated with dense smoke, roaring men, and near naked chippies. You'd drink beers at small round tables and dance till a floozy caught your fancy. Then she'd drag you to the cashier. You paid in advance, got a receipt from the register, and soap and towels—and up the stairs you'd go.

The architect who designed the House of All Nations had style. One bedroom, the "Marine Room," was fitted out like a stateroom of the *Leviathan,* complete with portholes and a floor that pitched and rolled and could make a man seasick. A foghorn blew when your time was up. The big favorite of Americans—once a nation of railroad fanatics in case you'd forgotten— was the "Wagon-Lit Room." It was an elaborately fashioned replica of a lower berth, with piped-in sounds of the *clickity-clack (clackity-click?)* of the rails and whistles. The Yanks loved it. (They were quite partial to the exquisite whores too, some of whom married clients and are today reckoned pillars of Grosse Point, Back Bay, San Francisco, etc., society.)

Rumor has it that when the 1946 law closed the houses, the heartbroken gentleman who owned the House of All Nations moved it, berths, mirrors, and trestle, to a suburb of Casablanca. One hears that it still exists, housed in a modest Arab fortress of dried mud that looks like a forlorn set from *Beau Geste.*

Le Palais Oriental, which was in Reims, deserves a mention nonetheless. A former client, who says he spent the eight most satisfying years of his life in the place, describes Le Palais simply: "the Lasserre of brothels."

[11] *All* the addresses noted here in "Nostalagia" have, of course, long since passed into total "respectability."

Apparently it had a lot of class. Take the "Black Room" . . .

"Black walls. Black floor. Black rug. Black ceiling. Black silk sheets. Over the bed a small black shelf with a lighted candle. As madam would open the door to show you into the Black Room she would announce softly: *'Pour la blonde.'* "

AN UNUSUAL MUSEUM

Paris has quite a lot of museums. Competition among them is keen, with the Louvre getting the biggest play and the rest of the houses hoping to catch the overflow. One of the most neglected museums is the MUSEUM OF THE PREFECTURE OF POLICE, at Police Headquarters, 36 quai des Orfèvres (1st), fourth floor. The Police Museum contains a fascinating mass of macabric-a-brac collected from sensational and historic Paris crimes of the last few centuries, including actual weapons used, portraits and souvenirs of master criminals, original dossiers on people like Bluebeard, engravings of medieval executions, and case histories of noted assassins and plotters against the French throne. This portion of the museum is, of course, open to the public.

Down the hall, however, behind a sturdy door is the SECRET MUSEUM OF THE PARIS POLICE, devoted to criminal activities with sexual and/or sadomasochistic overtones. Entrance to the Secret Museum is restricted to criminologists, visiting police officials, politicians, *et al.* However, if you have any political or police connections, they may get you in.

The permanent collection, housed in a large L-shaped room crammed with glass display cases and overstuffed filing cabinets, is administered by the chief of the vice squad office and members of his staff. The detective who serves as guide for today's visit is a composite of Inspector Maigret and Arsène Lupin, with all the characteristics you might hope for in a French sleuth, unless he happened to be chasing you. A relentlessly objective little man, his appearance is almost too pat to be true. The frayed graying brush mustache with sleeveless sweater to match, the jaundiced fingers that bespeak thirty-odd years of Gauloises smoked to the bitter ends. His approach to crime detection is academic, scholarly if you will, almost philosophical. But a worldly man, nonetheless, with a Gallic wit that displays cool shrewdness and a real intellect. He shows the treasures with all the relish and pride of a private collector.

For openers, one is handed an erect penis, which one promptly drops.

One is reminded by the detective-guide that when a man is hanged, he achieves a state of violent erection just prior to death. Twenty-odd years ago a particularly frivolous Levantine hangman cut off the private part of one of his victims and took it to a taxidermist. (Is there a word for a man who prepares, stuffs, and mounts humans as opposed to other animals?) The severed member eventually found its way to France and into the collection of a Paris physician whose home was raided by the police in connection with another matter. The *gendarmes* took the thing along as a souvenir.

Because the museum is not open to the general public, the following highly selective "catalogue" is offered:

The Collection Described in Part

1. *Hand-Colored Lithograph.* Extremely rare,[12] circa 1939. 5 x 8 inches. Nude study of Snow White and the Seven Dwarfs. Orgy scene. (Classic mini-*partouze:* seven midgets and a little girl.)

2. *Daguerreotype Photographs.* About five hundred, circa 1860–95. Some portraits. Some rural scenes. Various studies of men and women, attired in clerical robes and nuns' habit, engaged in sexual intercourse; other photographs picturing children, aged four to eight years, making love while being held in position or supervised by adults. From private collection. Acquired by the museum after owners refused to break up set.

3. *Extremely Cheap Reproductions.* About two hundred, circa 1966. All 3 1/2 by 5 1/2 inches (postcard size). Nudes. Including several Rubenses, Goya's "Naked Maja," and reproductions of several works publicly displayed in the Louvre. Sold to unsuspecting tourists as "feelthy" by streetcorner con-men in Montmartre, and donated to the museum by the dealers upon their arrest for fraud.

4. *Glossy Photographs and Set of Blueprints.* Circa 1946 and 1915, respectively. Depicting one of Paris's most elegant bordellos, at 12 rue Chabanais (2nd).[13] Photos made by sentimental police when the 1946 law was enacted closing all bordellos.

5. *Photographs, Original Drawings—Hand-Colored.* Circa 1920–66. By anonymous police artists, recording various incidents involving possession of illegal materials and assordid sadomasochistic activities. (NOTE: The Paris Police employ talented artists and staff photographers to photograph and sketch every "crime of interest," and many of the works are put on permanent display in the museum

[12]In the past few years similar efforts have become available in poster form at certain select American bookstores or from *The Realist.*

[13]Like all "historic" addresses cited in this book, this one, of course, no longer houses such activity. But some people in the office building there may proudly show you the old elevator.

after being used as evidence. In some cases the police go to considerable trouble to reenact the crime for purposes of "realism.")

6. *Oil Paintings,* circa 1400–1600. Two originals, Flemish School. Both depict love triangle—milkmaid, master, and cow. (Could be "Old Master.") Unsigned.

7. *Items of Wood and Metal. Books. Photographs.* One-of-a-kind, handmade walking stick, circa 1949. Incorporates cleverly concealed camera with special long-range shutter release. Album of photographs with accompanying text by the inventor. From recent case of "Mathew Brady of the Boulevards": an extremely resourceful and inventive photographer concealed a small camera in a block of wood at the base of his walking stick in such a way that lens recorded purview from sidewalk pavement looking straight up. The photographer would stand at stoplights and street crossings and snap the view looking directly up skirts of pedestrians. When the "model" walked off a distance, he would snap a long shot with a second camera and mount both photographs in an album. He assigned a name to each subject and wrote fanciful biographies in painstaking longhand. A second album houses a collection of photos of women's behinds, as recorded by a camera the photographer concealed inside public toilet bowls. (NOTE: While this gentleman went to exceptional extremes in pursuit of his vice, this type of voyeurism is by no means peculiar to Paris. For example, visit the steps of the New York Public Library, especially in springtime. Notice the row of gentlemen, ostensibly reading between the Lions, but actually leering over their newspapers at the girls who sun themselves, often open-legged, on the steps above.)

8. *Horse, Goat, Sheep Heads,* circa 1931. Leather, handmade and hand-colored. From celebrated '30s case. Will fit adult humans, and did. Wealthy Neuilly couple staged private backyard circus composed of performing humans dressed as animals. Show was folded by police for excessive whippings and creating a public nuisance.

9. *"Sailor's Wife."* Of human hair and rubber. Traditionally used by sailors in lieu of women. Can be filled with tepid water. This item from 1930 case of

shipboard riot; merchant seaman locked himself in cabin with it for three days before he was discovered by shipmates who, in a rage, beat him senseless for "rape." Also on display, a "pocket" version "for use on trains and in prisons."

10. *Talmud.* Papyrus and leather, circa 200 B.C. Center cleverly hollowed out to hold "sacred soil" of Palestine. Used by a Grand Rabbi of America to carry soil from Palestine to Brooklyn, U.S.A., via Paris. Soil was so "sacred" a pinch could stone an elephant. The Grand Rabbi was convicted of smuggling narcotics by the FBI just before World War II. Conviction was secured with the assistance of the Paris police, who kept the Talmud and the "sacred soil."

11. *Small Gallows.* Wooden. For use in the home. Constructed by a contemporary German for personal use as an aid in achieving sexual orgasm by hanging himself. Gallows was specifically designed to release him at a point short of death. Malfunctioned on only one occasion. Accompanying official photographs and hand-colored drawings of the accidental suicide by police photographer and artist. (See "London.")

12. *Opium-Smoking Matched Set.* Thermos bottle and camera case, both containing false bottoms concealing opium-smoking equipment: collection of matched hand-carved opium pipes. (Probably early Tung—Mao Tse-—dynasty.) NOTE: Under French law mere possession of *any* articles related to narcotics use is *prima facie* evidence of guilt and usually leads to jail term.

But all Paris is a museum of "special things."

LOVE IS A VERY "SPÉ" THING

"Something special? Well, of course, if it exists in the world, it exists in Paris," muses the tall, angular French industrialist in his late forties, "Pierre," whom you have met through a mutual friend. You are seated in the library of his spacious *fin-de-siècle* apartment on the avenue Hoche near the Parc Monceau, surrounded by an impressive collection of books and paintings and two fetching miniskirts, each in her late teens. The girls have been summoned as "a courtesy," out of respect for your visit.

"Well, of course, Joëlle is 'something special,' is she not?" And he indicates the blonde and directs her to the smallest of the room's three fireplaces.

Putting aside the small violet suede thong that she has been playfully snapping at no one in particular, she moves to the marble shelf, places both hands on it and leans forward. Pierre joins her, idly gives her breasts a tweak or two, and offers you some notes on her background and character.

". . . of a very good family from Lyon, where her father is an important merchant. . . . She is a wonderful girl, and very naughty, and must be punished quite frequently."

At that the man selects a thin cane reed from among several standing in a tall floor vase, eyes it at arm's length like a pool shark measuring the trueness of his cue, flexes it once, lifts the girl's aqua skirt and lets it fall on the small of her back, and gives her little *derrière*—hardly covered by its sheer black micropanty—a smart whack. She cries out with a mixture of pain and delight.

The caning will continue for about ten minutes, one stroke approximately every thirty seconds.

"Nowadays it is so difficult to find someone who will accept to be whipped, someone who relishes it. And someone so young and pretty as our delicious Joëlle."

Whack!

"Of course if one merely wishes to be whipped himself, no problem. Go to London. And even here in Paris there are a number of places. But most of these are of little consequence—here today and closed tomorrow—and have no ambiance and a bourgeois clientele. But you are curious to find a place that has a permanence and a good reputation. A place open to the public, but selective."

Whack!

"Well, there is the house in the avenue off avenue Victor-Hugo. Go to this house ; join the diplomats, politicians, important figures of government, men in high positions of industry and commerce, who have been regular clients for years. Ask for *'spé'*—argot for 'something special'—and you will get it. Here one finds opportunities for scatalogic rites, and rights. Or perhaps you would prefer beautiful prostitutes attired in the latest nuns' fashions, as you make love to them *à la Genet?*"

Whack!

"And, of course, there are always at least two or three darlings who will accept to be whipped or will allow themselves to be taken by the bottom. There are also many other activities that one can witness or join. It is literally up to your own tastes and imagination. As the English say, 'They've got the lot.' But whatever you demand they will respond, 'It is difficult. Perhaps we can accommodate you. But it will be expensive.' And it is, though one receives value for his money."

He commands the redhead to bring writing materials. She places the tablet against the blonde's rear and to "Pierre's" dictation scribbles a vague map showing portions of the 16th *arrondissement,* and references to issues of the magazine *Pan* and *Minute* (Those who always demand specific locations and phone numbers will not be disappointed in Amsterdam among several other cities.)

"We call it *'Le Palais Mignon'*—the 'Cute Palace,' " smiles your host as he sees you to the door.

Whack!

By eleven that same Saturday evening, after a quick perusal of newspaper files, you have staked out the Cute Palace. "Cute" is not exactly the word. There is something spooky—sinister is even better—about the big ghostly white, three-story villa, and this is not merely because its façade is so dark and no cracks of light appear from its tightly shuttered windows or great oak door. You are struck by a feeling that though the big stone townhouse—somehow massive in comparison with other *meublés*—is in immaculate condition, no one has been inside for a decade or more. Or perhaps it is just that once inside, no one has come back out.

In spite of your fear—and it is real—you ring. And ring. And finally resign yourself, ten minutes later, to banging hard on the door. But there is no answer, nor will there be this night. A fraud? Could it be closed at this hour? Impossible. A Paris week, you have come to observe, builds with the intensity of a roller-coaster. Monday is dead—even the Champs-Élysées is practically lifeless. But momentum builds quickly, and by Wednesday—a very good night in Paris—business is booming in the cafés, the discothèques, and, doubtless, the brothels. By Saturday night the music of Paris is so loud that there is enough left over to make even Sunday swing. How could any establishment—especially a brothel—be closed at 11 o'clock on a Saturday night?

Could the information be absolutely false? Hardly likely. This is not London, where the more apparently impeccable the source, the more rich, enthusiastic, and detailed the directions—the more likely it is that the facts are wrong or at best misleading or long out of date. This is Paris, where all rumors seem to come true; where the upper classes are unusually candid and painstakingly helpful to the discreet foreigner who is genuinely interested in discovering the curiosities of the city. Paris—where one can rely on the existence of a thing. But apparently not this time.

Pedophilia at the Pool

Two days later, fifteen miles outside Paris, you approach a villa so intricately and obviously chained and barred as to suggest to any child of no more than grade-school age that the occupant is—or was—the Marquis de Sade. But your host is merely a kindly, distinguished diplomat—now retired. You have come to talk about little girls. Like so many Frenchmen, the diplomat is devoted to them.

The Frenchman will try anything once, but if there is a single so-called aberration that one might call peculiarly French, it is the preoccupation of middle-aged and elderly men with girls at and below the age of puberty. Of course, men of all cultures covet and sometimes pursue preadolescent females. But somehow the French have greater success catching them than anyone else, at least among Western civilizations. In France the pedophile is no more extraordinary than the masochist in England or the sadist in Germany.

Because so many young French girls are objects of desire from an early age, they generally become aware of their sexuality sooner than girls of other Western nations. This constant sensual byplay may account, at least in part, for the Frenchwoman's reputation as being the most purely feminine of all women.

Some existing French laws still reflect a historical tolerance of pedophilia. Dr. Georges Valensin, in his *Sexual Life of the Young French Girl,* cites the case of a young Alsatian girl who was raped with particular violence by a neighbor. Two of his compatriots followed suit while the girl was still in a state of shock. But the court, citing well-established French law, held that the last two men could not be guilty of rape because the girl had offered no resistance.

Nonetheless, the authorities are generally harsh on violators. Because little girls are so often on the minds of Frenchmen, the police tend to be supersensitive.

"Especially since '*Les Ballets Roses*' scandal of 1958," sighs the diplomat as you two relax in deck chairs set on a catwalk halfway below the water level of his château's swimming pool and gaze through the large picture windows set in the pool's walls. Though some of the nude beauties who glide by appear to be no more than fourteen or fifteen, he assures you that they are all over eighteen.

"A pool like this is not so uncommon in France, particularly in the south. Two companies specialize in their construction; the casing may be entirely of glass—very expensive—or, as you see here, cement walls with large windows.

"*Les Ballets Roses,*" he continues. "Well, it's long past and not so important any more, though the phrase is in general use to mean *partouzes* with little girls. As you may know, it was not merely André Le Troquer who, in the course of his duties as President of the National Assembly during the 1950s, felt called upon to dispatch to some of his colleagues and old friends—some were in their early eighties—beribboned packages and rugs containing some fourteen-year-old girls. Many, many other important figures of government and industry were involved in the thing; there were countless soirées and expeditions to the mountains and the seashore. Much of the activity occurred at a charming *pavillon de chasse* near Paris, which was rented from the government by the hosts.

"Nowadays such affairs are very dangerous. Of course, if one is shrewd and well connected. . . . For instance, I have a colleague, quite high in the government, who has devoted a great deal of time to the study of our woman's penal institutions. He visits them frequently, in the course of his work, finds out which inmates have younger sisters, and, in return for a promise to try to commute the sentence, he receives introductions to the unsuspecting little ones.

"But for the average man, the law is so strict as to apply even with a prostitute if she is under eighteen years. And if the hotel employee is suspicious and asks for your papers as well as hers—for the hotel is liable under the law as well—and calls the police . . . well, it can be two years in prison for you. And this is so even if she is a hardened prostitute and has enticed you. Of course, in such a case the law might not be strictly enforced, as in the manner of some of your American antifornication statutes. But there is always the danger that it will be.

"There are at present three madams—well known and respected, for they deal primarily in some of the most beautiful young call girls, but these of legal age—who, for a large fee, provide girls aged ten to thirteen to dance nude at private parties and gatherings. One is permitted to slap a bottom or two, and perhaps make 'French' love, as you Americans call it. But the law is respected and their virginity is protected. No, I cannot tell you the names of the madams, but it is a simple matter to inquire of any madam whether she can provide young girls.

"There is also a discothèque where one may watch films while being fondled by little girls. There is one bordel in Paris where one can usually expect to find prostitutes of teen age. But it has moved five times within the past two years. At present I cannot tell you where it is, but with proper inquiries, perhaps among hairdressers, one could find it. No . . . little girls are hard to come by—although they are available everywhere, from the cafés of the Champs-Élysées to the discothèques and beaches of the Riviera, if one is capable of making his own arrangements. But in a brothel or through a madam . . . it is difficult. Why, not even in the famous *Le Palais Mignon* . . ."

"What!" you exclaim. "I was there Saturday night. It was shut tight."

"No, no . . . never in the evening. It is open only in the afternoon, from two to seven or eight P.M. In the evenings the girls are employed by other madams. Or they dance in the striptease. So go about four o'clock, but be sure to phone ahead. You are apt to find most anything there, except, of course, *des mineures.*"

Indeed, you return to the house in the 16th *arrondissement* the next afternoon, after first telephoning in advance for an appointment. A well-dressed matron answers the door and promptly shows you to a possible Louis XIV drawing room, generously furnished with antiques of the period. The madam withdraws. One by one five girls enter silently, close the door, announce their names, do a slow turn, and leave. They range in age from twenty-two to twenty-eight. Three are extremely pretty, one might be called beautiful. Four of the five are blond, one is brunette. The madam returns, announces the price—250 francs for a half hour—and awaits your choice.

You appear to hesitate, thinking, "So it *is* a fraud. Merely another elegant brothel."

"Does monsieur wish to see Béatrice again? Or perhaps Colette? Or Geneviève?"

"I'd like something *spé,*" you announce defiantly. And without another word, madam leaves and returns one minute later with the brunette, about twenty-seven and not quite so attractive as the others.

"La perle! Her specialty is . . . specialties. You may beat her intermittently for ten minutes at a cost of three hundred and fifty francs," suggests the madam. "Or shall we dress Colette in clerical robes? You can then have your pleasure with her—but not the whipping—for three hundred francs. Or for five hundred francs three girls will . . ."

"Could I just see a room . . . for ten francs?"

This is perhaps the most curious request of the month. But it is answered with no more than a tired shrug.

The second-floor bedrooms are of particular interest, being quite large in comparison to those of most *meublés*— two are at least thirty by fifteen feet —perhaps to accommodate group floggings and exhibitions of one sort or another. While more than adequately comfortable, the rooms are not so luxurious as those of some elegant lovers' *meublés.* But in those houses one must bring his own partner and provide his own accessories. This house— even by Parisian standards—is in a class by itself. What you can do here is pretty much up to your whims. And you can do it with attractive young girls. But no *mineures.*

The reasons for the traditional Parisian kick for the offbeat are not so easily explained. For one thing, although the French have always been some kind of monarchists, they are also a nation of rigid individualists. The two are not necessarily mutually exclusive. The French are truly democratic and exhibit real tolerance in respecting other people's special tastes and appetites, and they demand equal respect for their own. Thus the French, particularly Parisians, are a people open to suggestion; a nation of great innovators and inventors—in the scientific laboratory, the kitchen, and the bedroom.

The Parisian seeks flagellation in the 15th, 16th, or 18th, or *partouzes* in the 17th because it may be amusing. But the German goes for his four-o'clock whipping because something in his soul tells him he *deserves* it! The Englishman will follow along for his own beating because he has gotten accustomed to it in his public school. The American might go, just to see what it's all about. (The Americans, at heart a friendly, open people, have perhaps more potential to become French than any Europeans.) But he'd rather attend *partouzes,* especially if his neighbors go first, and if his wife goes with him. (Many French find this latter fetish extremely "funny.")

Historically the Parisian taste for the bizarre is laced with touches of ironic, sometimes macabre humor. But this pursuit of the unusual is more a reflection of a genuine curiosity and an uninhibited appetite for life and new experiences than of any special national aberration. Aside from the preoccupation with young girls, there is no precise *"vice français."* Basically, the French are a pretty straight heterosexual people who have, at one time or another, been into everything. But there is no particularly high incidence of homosexuality, sadism, masochism, or abnormal addiction to drugs or hard liquor. They do, however, drink a lot of wine.

It is no use, then, to inquire "why" the French do what they do—the answer is the inevitable *"pourquoi pas?"* Better to ask "what, when, and where?"

PARIS FROM A TO Z

The following is a random alphabetical grouping which reflects a variety of Parisian tastes and appetites:

Absolutists: There is a society that calls itself Absolutists whose members believe they will live forever if they find the right companion. Under the direction of their high priest they spend their lives switching from mate to mate with but one goal (so they say): eternal salvation.

cemeteries: Fair game for all manner of fanatics. One group is said to dance regularly at midnight—in the nude—on the graves of the Père-Lachaise Cemetery (20th). Some of the statuary here, covered with centuries of verdant moss, is noteworthy, particularly those male figures whose sex organs have no moss, thanks to the generations of neighborhood women who have visited Père-Lachaise for midnightly masturbations. (Well, of course, this is only a legend, so go and see the *Naked and the Dead* for yourself.)

Daughters of the American Revolution: The local DAR chapter is at 55 avenue Kléber (8th).

dildoes (*gaudmichés*): These are, of course, available in sex shops here as everywhere. But Paris has long been noted for the handmade dildo. Try vendors in the rues Vavin (6th) and Montagne-Sainte-Geneviève (5th). Occasionally one finds a bargain at the Flea Market. Though the managements have no knowledge of the transactions, dildoes may change hands in the ladies' rooms of such bars and clubs as KATMANDOU (rue du Vieux-Colombier, 6th), CHEZ MOUNE (54 rue Pigalle, 9th), and LE MONOCLE (60 boulevard Edgar-Quinet, 15th). LE DRUGSTORE (135 Champs-Élysées, 8th), and the branch at 149 boulevard Saint-Germain (6th), sell battery-operated backscratchers. Knowledgeable lesbians have, for at least a decade, substituted their own attachments; they prefer these to the recent battery "massagers."

The Grand Dada of all dildoes has been selling well in Paris for some eight years and has it all over the trendy competition. Available through two of the city's finest hairdressers, it is handmade by German elves, its casing fashioned of soft pink rubber and hair guaranteed human. The minute battery-operated motor and cams enable the thing to writhe, push, pull, frug, and move from side to side. About 500F, constructed exactly to your specifications.

A woman in the rue Lepic (18th) sells ping-pong balls that she half fills with mercury by means of a hypodermic needle.

A British film dubber recommends "honey and flies."

In 1966 an artist modified an exercycle to accommodate a rubber-encased cylinder designed to enter and exit a woman as she peddles. He periodically attempts to test this apparatus, offering 100F to street prostitutes. No takers thus far.

dog shows: There is a woman who walks Les Halles with a dachshund in a bag. Honest. She offers exhibitions. About 50F. If you decide to attend, resist any impulse to congratulate the woman by touching her (don't shake hands, for example) because the dog will attack you. It is not that the couple are merely having a casual affair. They have been living together for nine years and the animal is extremely jealous.

flagellation: When one thinks of "discipline" on vacation, one surely thinks first of London or The Hague. But rest assured that in this field Paris—the capital that above all others offers something, and that usually the best, for everyone—more than holds its own. Jean-Jacques Rousseau would be tickled blue that some 195,000 *martinets* (a wicked antagonist consisting of about a dozen thin leather tendrils attached to a twelve-inch wooden handle) are sold annually in this country, ostensibly solely for the chastisement of children. Now that Devil's Island is finished, and unless you fancy French jails, France offers no public disciplinary facilities comparable to the fantastic medieval-style torture dungeons found pre-1946 in the "Old One Two Two" and Sphinx bordels. But talk of governesses in Harry's American Bar or that other famed old newsman's hangout the California Hotel, and modern Paris can be justly proud that her own Jaky Duprey plays second ferule to no one —not Lady P of London, nor Frau Karen of Hamburg, nor even the peerless Baroness Monique von Cleef of The Hague, late of Newark, New Jersey, and New York City.

Brunette, thirty, and slightly chunky, but not at all unattractive in her properly severe manner, especially when *en grande tenue* from her vast wardrobe of black leather coats, capes, boots, and corsetry, Madame Jaky is a ten-year veteran fustigator and has acquired such a wide and distinguished following that she is in the process of enlarging her already substantial quarters at 127 rue Marcadet (18th). It's building B, third floor, first door on the left, the one with the peephole. Business hours from noon to 8 P.M., during which time you may phone 252-26-52 for reservations.

Two hundred francs for a basic hour's session, supplements extra—and limited only by your funds and imagination. But, definitely, *"Jamais l'amour!"* This is simply not *that* kind of establishment. Nor is there even much soft-core "domestic" chastisement—diapered spankings or mock cleanups. This is a very "hard" house.

While the cheery, contemporary look of the recently constructed apartment building clashes with the rest of this traditional, hilly corner of Montmartre and might at first put off those avid fetishists who'd prefer something rather more *fin de siècle* if not downright Sadesque, Jaky has turned it all to good advantage. The large, coldly antiseptic five-room apartment has been intelligently done in Nazi Party modern, with colors of the Reich dominating: stark black-and-white-tiled floors throughout give a Goebbels chessboard effect; complementary black swastika on white and red background over the breakfast table and compatible red draperies in the three torture rooms. What's more, an elderly Polish cleaning lady tidies up mornings so that clients feel good and humiliated should they make even the slightest mess.

Jaky has done wonders with the furnishings. Very *Springtime for Hitler* are the several large lock-up boxes, inside of which you can get, but out of which you cannot, what with those ingenious imported German locks. The claustrophobile has a nice sunken U-Boat effect with these though some of the boxes have portholes so one can surface for face thrashings and excrement sniffings. A unique cupboard has an ample anus hatch should the occupant require an enema or higher colonic irrigation while simultaneously enjoying his deprivation-of-oxygen kick. Just beneath the enema-bag rack is the Chinese crib cage with its go-together "chabouk" horsewhips.

Get away from those now, however—it's time for a spin on the iron torture wheel. And later you've a heavy cross to bear and another with leg-irons and hand manacles while lashed to which, according to Jaky's photographs, you may be soundly thrashed or expectorated upon. Further excruciating possibilities are offered by various pillories, iron maidens, a fully adjustable surgical operating table (can't seem to avoid these), a medieval rack and, of course, plenty of accessories.

Jaky's wiggery, whippery, and wardrobe would shame *The Damned*'s property man. Other display cabinets show all the with-it phalluses, dildoes, electric whirrers, and every conceivable bauble, bangle, banger, ring, clip, and fish hook that this bad peri of "Gay Paree" will expertly affix to your ears, nose, penis, scrotum, nipples, or whatever else you have in mind.

Strap on the fine preburred English saddlery and Jaky will canter you round the tiles (again, according to the photos that are available to get you in the proper mood), taking extra care to give you some good ones in the ribs with those vicious spurs, you naughty Camargue pony you! Fierce halters and nasty bit chains too. Or perhaps you'd rather a simple relax on the Procrustean bed or have a satisfying grovel at Jaky's long spiked heels while she sits astride her *grand trône* and scatters feces from a tambourine.

Basically the woman works alone, though she can beckon several ferocious young apprentices who will heighten your distress with some good *sjambok* (South African whip)-cracking and prancing about in high laced boots, sheer black stockings, and nothing more. As long as you remain on your knees you may lick a *"moutardier"* ("mustard-maker," and thus "the behind"), *but don't you dare touch!*

Those people between planes who find Jaky fully booked may be referred to a colleague of perhaps equal talent and, some say, even more extensive facilities: "Madame H" in the rue de Javel (15th), quite convenient to the Eiffel Tower. But if bad is really your bag, Jaky's worth a layover, if not a special trip.

fortunetellers: Paris is very keen on them. Among the best is Frida-Wion, 4 rue Royer-Collard (5th; ODE 38–55). If her ball is busy, authentic 50F séances are held at 38 rue Charlot (4th).

French lessons for Spanish domestics: These are given (at 30F a month) at Mission Catholique Espagnole, 51 *bis* rue de la Pompe (16th; no phone). Even if you are not a Spanish domestic, you may be interested that most of these girls are quite young, adventurous (or they wouldn't have left Spain), and have at least one night off a week. (Of course they are all highly respectable girls.)

guards: If you are giving a party, you can hire a full detachment of France's celebrated Republican Guard—plumed helmets, polished swords, and all.

Rates range from about 12F for an enlisted man to 15F for an officer, and 400F for a full complement. There is a small catch here, for you must know a Cabinet minister to rent the Guard. And he must attend your affair.

guides: Why mess about with scruffy sidewalk touts? Were Sade, Casanova, Lloyd George, Ben Franklin, and Catherine the Great reincarnated for an evening in Paris, Oscar could get it together. A tour in his Rube Goldbergesque cab is unforgettable. No police dog up front for safety (common here), not for optimistic Oscar. His sleek Opel's cushy seats are as buoyant as he is—like riding on a water bed. And flashing psychedelic interior lights, sirens, horns, buzzers, wolf whistles, cassette recorders (wide range of music and sound effects), and various scents (American perfumes, new-mown hay) fed through a blower system. For lovers, Oscar does sonnets in English, German, Russian, Japanese, Italian, and French. Write OSCAR ZUCCA, 154 rue Jules-Guesde, Levallois-Perret 92. Have him meet your plane.

Henri IV: Among the several people of Paris who think they are Henri IV, one man is *sure* he is. Every Wednesday noon he visits a certain young lady in Neuilly who at first resists his advances, pleading her virginity. The performance never varies. Protesting in archaic French—a requisite of the bargain —she begs, weeps, and finally, her strength spent, succumbs to the honor of losing her innocence to the noble monarch. She has thus disposed of her virtue once a week for the past two years, in the process acquiring over 20,000 francs. *New* francs: "A game is a game but business is business."

lighting for lovers: After dinner in a *salon particulier* and before retiring to a *hôtel particulier,* you might want to play God, or at least water commissioner. Fine. For a price the city will floodlight monuments or statues on your behalf or turn on the spigots of your favorite fountain at precisely the moment you select. The idea is to stroll past Notre-Dame with the lady of your desires, stop suddenly, whisper *"pour toi,"* snap your fingers . . . and cause the whole building—and her heart—to be bathed in the light of your ardor. (For 50F, about $10, they throw in the statue of Charlemagne.)

One must reserve two days in advance with the SERVICE DE L'ÉCLAIRAGE, 9 place de l' Hôtel de Ville (4th). M. Gilbert Caulert (227-15-40, ext. 40-95) is the sentimental civil servant on the third floor who will make all arrangements and acquaint you with the wide range of hourly rates and choice properties. For the more expensive and well-known sites like the Arch of Triumph (154F, or about $31) or the Eiffel Tower (341F), one might split the cost with other romantics. There is nothing to prevent five or six couples from thrilling to these spectacles of devotion, as long as they stand far enough apart so the women don't suspect that anyone else is in on the deal. (Take care. This might also lead to *partouzes.*)

Some typical prices: Place de la Concorde, 22F for hydraulics only, 70F for hydraulics and light. Statue de Clemenceau, 7F (remember, all these are hourly rates). Sacré-Coeur, 55F. (In case you're interested in how the cost of living, and lighting and loving, has risen in France, Sacré-Coeur cost a mere 41 francs, eighty centimes to light in 1967.) But there are still many bargains; the miniature Statue of Liberty on the Pont de Grenelle, for example, is a steal at 9.35 francs (not even $2) per hour. And don't pass up the many gems in Le Marais, a charming old quarter which has been restored to its grandeur of the sixteenth and seventeenth centuries when it was the intellectual and social center of the city. The Portail de l'Hôtel de Soubise (rue des Archives in Le Marais) costs about sixty cents (in 1967 you could have lighted it for 99 centimes). The Cloître des Billettes is exactly one franc and ten centimes.

Bear in mind that Paris's choice structures are lit for the masses on summer evenings and on weekends until 11:30 P.M. Afterwards they're yours.

mirrors: The ceilings of room Nos. 6 and 9, among others, in RÉSIDENCE MAUROY (11 *bis* rue Godot-de-Mauroy, 9th; 073-88-33) are *all* mirror.

Napoleon (penis of): See London chapter, p. 516.

poets: One can rent one of either sex at CLUB DES POÈTES, 30 rue Bourgogne (7th). Specify avant-garde, beat, lyric, romantic, or erotic. Very nice.

prostitutes (specials): Males catering to women are, of course, to be found in the *partouze boîtes,* not to mention in many Paris bars. (Admittedly, these are, for the most part, amateurs.) There is said to be a very select bordello for the ladies near place du Trocadéro (16th). Varieties of men—pretty, husky, gentle, or rough, but all of them ready—are said to cater to one kind of woman: rich. A feature of the place is its large wardrobe of period costumes that the gentlemen don for their performances. About 300F.[14]

Pregnant prostitutes are said to be the specialty of a Montmartre madam who procures for them in the tradition of a famous bordello (now closed) in rue de la Huchette which, pre-1946, specialized in crippled and pregnant prostitutes. A one-legged prostitute wanders both the Left and Right Banks along the Seine and has become a living legend. Benjamin and Masters, in *The Prostitute and Society,* report seeing her and note that she has a "steady clientele, mainly composed of Englishmen."

[14]Dallayrac *(Dossier Prostitution)* notes such brothels were not uncommon in Czarist Russia. And see Amsterdam and Hamburg chapters.

sex shops: Since the death of De Gaulle a great deal of censorship has been abolished, if not by actual statute at least in the relaxation of official enforcement. Dozens of sex shops have sprung up throughout the city. While one finds little of the truly hard-core books, magazines, and implements available in Holland, Denmark, or Sweden—and Times Square for that matter—French shops are distinguished for their unparalleled taste and whimsy, and are especially strong on good reproductions of serious erotic art and antiquities. (But no pubic hair allowed in magazines.) Some recommended shops:

4 rue de Sèze (9th), from 9 A.M. to 1 A.M., convenient to rue de la Paix and the rue Godot-de-Mauroy. 4 rue Petit-Pont (5th), knowledgeable Left Bank students and homosexual clientele. Corner of the rue des Lombards and the rue Quincampoix, open to 2 A.M. and handy if you want to put into immediate practice what you have read, for lots of whores (and one grotesque sadist blonde in Hitler Youth regalia) hang about the street. Right on the Champs-Élysées, at number 34. Those requiring something to read on the way up the Eiffel Tower should stop at TRUONG, 70 rue Castagnary (15th), a shop popular with UNESCO personnel. Truong may also send you a free catalogue describing the latest French gadgets, records, films, and books if you write them at the latter address.

sexual club for millionaires: An establishment said to be housed in an elegant co-op building in the avenue Foch. Usually reliable sources report that it has the facilities of a good London club—billiards, library, nightly buffet, bar, etc.—plus much more. Annual dues of about $3000 entitle members to nightly use of all facilities and an ever changing supply of beautiful young women who are always available on the premises. Members receive a weekly program of activities, hand-delivered by messengers. A typical week is said to include: Monday, erotic heterosexual color films; Tuesday, guest lecturer on the effects of amyl nitrate during sexual climax and the use of ground housefly wings as a female aphrodisiac; Wednesday, lesbian show; Thursday, demonstration of technique by Nigerian male and Japanese female. It is also said to be a policy of the club to supply *anything* a member requests, at extra cost of course.

All efforts to verify the existence of this club proved fruitless. But then, perhaps if one really is a millionaire. . . . (But see ''The Hague.'')

sexual massage: Available in some of the smaller massage parlors, usually one- or two-room apartments with small exterior signs reading *''Soins Esthétiques,''* though of course not all parlors with such signs supply such services. At some of the better beauty salons young men oblige.

subways: In Paris some subways run on sensuous rubber wheels. They are clean, heated, and seats are reserved for the elderly and for war veterans. There are pretty paintings to admire in the Louvre station, and nobody bothers you if you have a smoke while waiting for the train. In the city's newest *Métro* station, La Défense (8th), they'll do a quick urine or blood analysis for you between trains. While you're waiting, the lady can have her hair done and you can buy her a bird of paradise in the station's pet shop.

zebra: See The Vincennes Zoo, or that terrible tout in Montmartre (see p. 39).

THE THIRD WORLD

In *The Second Sex* Simone de Beauvoir also spoke of the third. Citing literary authorities from Colette to Casanova, she observed that "the male homosexual, the pederast, arouses hostility in heterosexual males and females, for both these require a man to be a dominating object; both sexes, on the contrary, spontaneously view lesbians with indulgence. 'I avow,' said Count de Tilly, 'that it is a rivalry which in no way disturbs me; on the contrary, it amuses me and I am immoral enough to laugh at it.' "

Whoever the Count was, he speaks for all Western cultures, including this one. Was it coincidental that since De Gaulle's departure *les pédérastes* at last enjoy a semblance of freedom from police harassment? Over the past two decades, at least, female rendezvous have been confidently enough lit from without and usually open to curious, discreet strangers, lesbian or not. And of late, male haunts have become immeasurably less peephole-paranoid, but Parisian lesbian life remains of special interest because there are comparatively so many female homosexuals here—perhaps correlative to the widespread prostitution—and the fact that it is such an open if not salacious book.

Sadly gone is Frede Carroll's wonderful lesbian discothèque in the rue Sainte-Anne, where the clever lone male wolf might ensnare some of the confused little *yé-yé* vixens before the butchy drink hustlers got their *gaudmichés* into them. But somewhat the same situation may prevail at Yvonne's (late of Frede's) LE POUSSE AU CRIME (15 rue Guisarde, 6th), or if one can crash it, the very hot KATMANDOU (21 rue du Vieux-Colombier, 6th).

In Montparnasse the mannequins of LE MONOCLE (60 boulevard Edgar-Quinet, 15th; DAN 41–30) dance to an all-girl orchestra that will not make you forget Phil Spitalny. Meanwhile back in Montmartre testy tomboys in tuxedos or severe business suits menopause at the bar and small stage of CHEZ MOUNE (54 rue Pigalle, 9th; PIG 64–64). Lesbians get the glory, the girl, and the billing at ELLE ET LUI (31 rue Vavin, 6th; MED 29–52; drinks at the bar 20F, 30F at table), but the Hollywood-Rome filmmakers and the ga-ga Middle America tourists are the principal attraction.

Performers reverse roles next door at CARROUSEL (326–66–33), where most of the world's great female impersonators have appeared—Bambi, Fétiche, Coccinelle, Les Lee, Dany Dan—but the composition of the audience remains the same.

Of course, Paris is tops for the devotee of female impersonation in cabaret. Here one finds the most beautiful, talented, and convincing performers. Among them sex-change operations were no novelty even a decade ago. Eschewing common triangles, the puzzling parallelograms, even pentagons, of their complex love lives remain a topic of bar gossip and the basis for much cabaret humor. (Operations forbidden here; Casablanca price, 20,000 F.)

A recent fiasco concerns a male transvestite whose exquisitely feminine face and figure were earning him a handsome living in one of the best nightclubs. He fell in love with his mannish dance partner, but the lesbian wasn't having any. Not even after the comely gentleman increased his already ample bust to forty-one inches with the aid of paraffin injections. Undaunted, the man had a complete sex-change operation, from soup to nuts as it were. This failed to stimulate the sapphist, who chose now to elope with a confirmed male homosexual. As you might guess, the story has a Maupassant ending. The male transvestite (now a transsexualized "woman") was so shaken by this turn of events that "she" married a heterosexual male. This finally got to the lesbian. She came pounding on the newlyweds' door in a jealous rage, shrieking that they were breaking up the act.

The eternal Carrousel aside, LA GRANDE EUGÈNE (12 rue Marignan, 8th; ELY 58–64) offers probably the most glittering female impersonations in the world outside a good English public school, as Eugène himself nightly stuns even "Tout-Paris" with his shrewd impressions of Mistinguett, Yvonne Printemps, et al. In bawdy, lusty bal musette ambiance, L'ALCAZAR (60 rue Mazarine, 6th) offers nonstop revues—camp but not always transvestite—so jolly that reservations (326–53–35) are imperative whether you drink, or dine from 75F. These two rank among Europe's most exciting clubs.

Boys will be boys, but at Montmartre's traditional MADAME ARTHUR (75 bis rue des Martyrs, 18th; 076–48–27) they will not—insulting "method" actors who enjoy their work but spoil your supper. You're only here for the beer? Even that ferments at the entrance of the malevolent Maslowa, a brilliantly cruel master of many strange ceremonies who is Madame Arthur himself. For another quiet night in Clichy join the truckmen and mechanics at BRASSERIE AUX CASCADES (60 boulevard de Rochechouart, 18th) pitching woe and overripe avocados at Armando, an ex-pipefitter who stuffs his hairy torso into a provoquante pink satin, silver-garnished miniskirt, sheer dark hose, baby-blue garter belt, and blond wig that he might better touch you with chansons like "March of the Second Tank Division." Sing along, but do not feed the waiters.

In LA MONTAGNE's nearly half-century history, no tour bus dared disgorge at 46 rue de la Montagne-Sainte-Geneviève where, amid mini-Palladium architecture and ancient cinema-postered walls and ceiling, semiamateur (or maybe semipro) chanteuses defied heckling from the mixed bag of lesbians and cat burglar types—who were more likely plumbers' aides—while a low-slung, very fat old lady, who looked like an old man (or perhaps an old man who looked like an old lady), took her clothes off to cheers, piano, jeers, drums, and accordion. Georgette Anys has transferred the memory of all that to 13 rue des Petits-Champs (1st; 742–45–16), with two important differences: one can dine from 20F and they've taken the band down from the ceiling.

Under French law sexual relations between people of any gender are permitted provided they are both (or all) at least twenty-one years of age and there is no instance of force or duress. Thus, considering that there is no law forbidding adults from offering their bodies for sexual hire, you may be sure that Paris, one of the world's two or three most touristed cities, offers the visitor scores of male whores fit for a king, hundreds suitable for commoners, and several accommodating rich little old ladies, most of whom never leave the 16th or 17th *arrondissements.*

Actually, the life of a homosexual male prostitute is a great deal more arduous—and the span of his career inevitably far shorter—than that of his female counterpart, if only because he must live by the creed "It is as blessed (and profitable) to give as to receive." Considering their tolerance for "normal" prostitution, *partouzes,* etc. (and their museum), the Paris constabulary might afford professional pederasts the same rights and courtesies as female whores. They do not. Insisting that the male homosexual is particularly vulnerable in France (but in fact no more so than in any other socially stigmatized society), the police keep as assiduously their files on pederasts as on "politically dangerous people." In truth this does provide a worthy measure of protection for those who may need it—if one is threatened with blackmail he should immediately report it to the police who will make available, for identification or simple titillation, photos of some of the most beautiful boys in Paris—but sometimes the authorities show a certain confusion in distinguishing between the hustler and the hustled.

In their zeal the cops have recently carried out so many hotel raids that the *Incognito Directory* (published here and available for 15F in many gay bars and clubs; or order by mail, £1, from the Private Swedish Book Service, 283 Camden High Street, London, N.W.1) currently has only one hotel in its Paris listings: HÔTEL LAKANAL, 9 *bis* rue Lakanal (15th; 828–09–13). Homey, warm ambiance, rooms from 25F with breakfast, just a short distance from the bustling markets of rue du Commerce and rue de Javel flagellation house of H. (You may be sure Paris has other sympathetic hotels.)

If there is a homosexual brothel in Paris on the scale of the apocryphal House of the Naughty Boys, it must surely be disguised as something else. In that legendary pre-1946 house, so the story goes, masked sons and daughters of "good families" along with barefaced common whores of both sexes, danced and posed in tableaux while, from a gallery above, wealthy clients made selections and bets. There was a homophile brothel in rue du Dragon (6th), but it closed around 1967. During the reigns of Louis XV and XVI Madame Gourdan directed a similar establishment in the rue des Deux Portes (20th). But perhaps Saint-Germain-des-Prés obviates the need for such places (except when it rains).

Exactly at the intersection of rue de Rennes and rue du Four, near a huge public works department sign, *"Déviations,"* randy gamblers may pull a full house of tough young queens in blue jeans, or tie-dyed flushed *minets. Soldes!* 30 to 50F. The police usually shoo bona-fide transvestites from this beat, but if you are shopping for this sort of merchandise and are well-heeled, don't despair. *"Petits garçons"* await your pleasure in avenue du Général Lemonnier, the Tuileries, or in rue du Colisée and avenue Gabriel, if not in Champ de Mars behind that grandest of Freudian symbols, the Eiffel Tower. Like most Right Bank trinkets, these come dear, 50 to 100F, but some take traveler's checks.

Ask the transsexuals of Pigalle's rue Houdon or Bois de Boulogne's Allée de Longchamp (known colloquially as *"l'Allée de la Longue Queue"*— "Long-Dong Lane") to recommend their surgeon and they may well exhume the memory of "Papa Doc" Duvalier. From 20 to 40F, depending on whether you want a simple *"pipe"* and rapid reconnaissance of their paraffined *"roberts,"* or wish actually to *"se faire foutre."* But avoid carrying identification or the names of any loved ones lest you pay much more to avoid blackmail threats. If you like Arab lads, cultivate the friendship of at least two trustworthy Parisian homosexuals (preferably big ones) before venturing along boulevard de Rochechouart (18th), particularly around rues de la Charbonnière and de Chartres, both of which, incidentally, offer splendid views of Sacré-Coeur. Nor should strangers wander the Bois de Vincennes without a protective guide. If one is a novice to Paris he may find friendly, knowledgeable shepherds who will protect him at some of the following bars and cafés. Then again, he may not.

LE FIACRE (4 rue du Cherche-Midi, 6th). In Iowa a frappe is a kind of fancy dessert. In France *"les frappes"* are fancy young homosexuals. A Cedar Rapids American Legionnaire would not feel much out of place in the gallery restaurant here, but down below he might have his medal blown off. Now that the beloved Louis is dead, the Fiacre is dead—it's CHEZ GUYLAINE now. (Louis' *ami* Charles continues at LE BUREAU, 4 rue Bernard-Palissy.)

Strictly speaking, LE FLORE at 172 boulevard Saint-Germain (6th) is a literary café of great repute. But although Sartre, Camus, Beauvoir, and others worked here during the Nazi occupation, the onslaughts of *les tantes* have proven quite another matter. At nearby LE SPEAKEASY (4 rue des Canettes, 6th) the mix is more homogeneous. And just as pretty.

On the Right Bank the venerable LE FESTIVAL (22 rue du Colisée) is a prudent first stop for newcomers, particularly at apéritif hour when the multilingual barmen and regulars have more time to chat about the neighborhood's *"petits garcons,"* many of whom would fool their own mothers. And did. Near the Opéra in the lavender rue Sainte-Anne (1st) is the cliquish (a word of French derivation, of course) but eclectic CLUB 7. In his glittering bar-discothèque-restaurant the golden Fabrice has gathered a few cheeky lesbians and some of their straight *minette* admirers. And some hetero males and couples. And many beautiful young men who couldn't care less. Best scene of its type in Paris. Nearby (32 rue Sainte-Anne) is the dowdy SIDONIE BAR. Quiet civil servants. Loud valets. Nearby (4 rue Chabanais) CÉSAR has more gentlemens' gentlemen. Spanish ones. All night. Nearby PETIT VENDÔME (3 rue de la Sourdière) has still more Spanish fliers. And flys. And nearby (3 rue Villedo) is NEW BOOTH'S, a flash discothèque.

CLUB LITTÉRAIRE ET SCIENTIFIQUE DES PAYS LATINS—"ARCADIE"—(19 rue Béranger, 3rd; 887–09–63) sounds impressive, and it is. If you are a senator or a celebrated artist or writer your chances of membership improve. However, don't despair. Some Mr. Arcadians are not so remote that they can resist the young attractions of LE NUAGE (5 rue Bernard-Palissy, 6th), which has a glass case in which Farouk used to keep trivia, and L'ABREUVOIR SAINT-HILAIRE (7 rue Geoffroy-Saint-Hilaire, 5th) which hasn't. *Luxe,* gadgety (closed-circuit TV scrutiny, so wear something nice) is L'ANGE BLEU (50 boulevard Pasteur, 15th; 734–53–18), an important Montparnasse night club. Best after 3 A.M., when transvestite performers from other clubs drop by for jam sessions.

In the following saunas and baths homosexuals are not unwelcome. Nor is anyone else. The biggest and most popular is BAINS PONCELET (7 rue Poncelet) in the good old 17th. Everyone goes here at one time or another. Newcomers may have to display their bona fides at BAINS DE MILAN (22 rue de Milan, 9th), for this one is popular with brokers and bankers. To an extent so is BAINS DU LOUVRE (272 rue Saint-Honoré; 1st).

Though women may dance *"Le Slow"* in close embrace in public, such dancing between males is by custom discouraged. Ergo, it was probably French homosexuals who began the modern mania for non-body-contact dances—not so much to turn on the world but to tune out the authorities.

Geographically, homophile Paris cuts a cavalry charge swath directly through the heart of the city, beginning at the top of the map in the 18th and 9th *arrondissements,* which are characterized by some clip-joint bars and the roughhouse street trade of Pigalle and Clichy, those heavily touristed specialty cabarets of Montmartre that offer more acid in the food than in the drag presentations, and an ever-growing number of more intimate *boîtes* where, happily, the reverse is more the rule. Thus, though on CHEZ MICHOU's little stage (80 rue des Martyrs, 18th; 606–16–04) *la plume de ma tante* is likely to turn out to be the pen of your uncle, the audience will be a cross-section of the sextrum, the parodies of Miss Glassex, Scarlatine, and Phosphatine cutting across all fetishes. Inclusive full-course tasty dinners from 50F. Highly recommended.

Several neighboring "sympathetic" restaurant-bars have dancing—LA MANGEOIRE *cave,* for example (17 rue Ganneron, 18th; 387–10–95). Others, among them LE COUP DE FREIN (high up at 88 rue Lepic, 18th; 076–90–06), rely on inexpensive good food served in romantic enough surroundings, perhaps with strolling guitarists (AU PIERROT DE LA BUTTE, 41 rue Caulaincourt, 18th; 606–06–97) and, best of all, candlelit AU BISTROT DU ROY (4 villa Saint-Michel, 18th; 627–67–51). A real find is LE PETIT ROBERT (10 rue Cauchois, 18th; MON 04–46). Nineteen-thirties' ambiance, 1950s' prices. Affable, long-expatriated American owner. Honest food. You might be able to hoist up a suitable dining companion if you are alone at DON CARACOL bar (5 passage Cottin, 18th). In the adjacent 17th is LE WAF *cave* (35 rue Davy). And nearby are several cunning restaurants, among them LA VALLÉE D'AUGE (144 rue de Tocqueville, 17th; 227–12–22; about 40F for dinner), and L'ÉCUREUIL (22 bd des Batignolles, 17th; 522–50–65), open to 4 A.M.

Continuing our tour of the more indigenous nightlife, we come upon Palais-Royale embracing (but discreetly, for this is a very conservative neighborhood) the 1st and 2nd *arrondissements.* The lineages of several of Paris's more important families have abruptly halted in LE VAGABOND (14 rue Thérèse, 1st; RIC 90–97) for it may be the oldest restaurant of its type here. One may also dine late and amiably at LE BRIGNOLET (29 rue Montpensier, 1st; 742–71–42) and still have time for the previously noted distractions in and near rue Sainte-Anne (Club 7, etc.).

In the 4th, along the Right Bank quais and in the Île Saint-Louis opposite, a cluster of versatile restaurant-discothèques has lately emerged, exemplified by LA MENDIGOTTE (80 quai de l'Hôtel-de-Ville, 4th; 272–19–76) and L'AQUARIUS (18 rue Greneta, 4th, Les Halles; 231–56–91). And also LE ROCAMBOLE (9 rue Budé, Île Saint-Louis, 4th; 633–09–01) and L'ENTRE-NOUS (22 rue Petit-Musc, 4th; 272–16–29). You don't have to be gay to enjoy all to their fullest. Well, almost.

On the Left Bank, two of the oldest and most interesting caves are GLI-GLINE SAINT-GERMAIN (66 rue Saint-André-des-Arts, 6th; 633–00–77) and LA BOÎTE AUX CHANSONS (3 rue Grégoire-de-Tours, 6th; 326–83–09). A bit of the old Fiacre ambiance in the latter. Nearly splendid meals (40F) in the charming, lavender LE BISTRO DU PORT (13 quai Montebello, 5th; 033–81–06). Here, ask Gérard to send you on to LES QUATRES SAISONS, an astonishing little inn 20 kilometers north of Paris (exit Porte de la Chapelle) in Nerville-la-Forêt (phone, 469–10–35). Sunday lunch is best. But on entering who'd know? A large, homely zinc bar caters to the villagers as it always has done. And to the left a very basic dining room. But proceed all the way to the rear and . . . *voilà!* as they say. All is purple and lavender. *Cadre* 1900. Another dashing host called Gérard. An old man who looks like Eugene Pallette plays the organ. Young men who look like Valentino serve the food. Here you may find a bit of *Tout-Paris,* and a bit of *Tout-Nerville-la-Forêt* too, for one needn't be gay to appreciate such food (30F for lunch; add the cold Beaujolais) in such surroundings. Fireplace. Large terrace (paved with stones from Notre-Dame that Gérard bought for 1.50F each) affording gentle valley view of the rolling countryside. A few overnight accommodations. Find it before the guidebooks do.

If your hair needs doing on the Right Bank, see GUY SAINT-ROCH (121 rue Legendre, 17th; 627–83–39), on the Left JACQUES SART (20 rue du Cherche-Midi, 6th; 548–09–87). And though LAURENT DESBOIS (33 boulevard Magenta, 10th; 208–17–75) is not a gay florist,[15] he is at least a florist who courts people who may like gay florists.

NUDISTS, AND TWO FRIENDS

Among the nudists of the world the French are certainly no tartuffes. At least their nudist colonies—like the celebrated Île du Levant off the coast of the Riviera and the large camp in Sète near the Spanish frontier—are not characterized by volleyball nets separating the sexes, as in the manner of the traditional American nudist colony. However, they are apparently not quite straightforward enough to suit Kienne de Mongeot, who in 1926 founded the first "serious" French nudist magazine. You have met him this otherwise gloomy December afternoon, in the boulevard Malesherbes (17th) studios of Serges Jacques, the noted photographer of nudes.

"I have lived for forty years among naked women and children and at seventy I am about to abandon nudism. Why?"

Very natty and distinguished in an artfully cut banker's suit set off by a diamond stickpin, M. de Mongeot, who physically resembles Jean Gabin, fingers his lapel—he is a Chevalier de l'Ordre de St. Jean de Jérusalem—runs his hand through a shock of dark hair that shows not a trace of gray, and defiantly gazes out the window, trying to find a good enough reason why the "Pope of Nudism" has suddenly decided to give it up. He discovers several:

[15]Whatever a "gay florist" might be. Nor are the others named, "gay barbers."

"Because, although nudists are by definition people who take their clothes off . . . they clothe themselves in hypocrisy. Human beings are not civilized; they are merely tamed. . . . Nudists pretend nudism is asexual. Nothing is further from reality. Who can control his physical reaction when he is nude among other nudes?"

He coughs.

"Having certain responsibilities as head of the movement, I have learned to control myself through hypnotism. . . . Nudism is pure only when you are with your wife. When her girlfriend arrives and takes off her clothes . . . well, then you have got a *partouze*—or you are a damned fool if you think you haven't. . . . I am a member of the Anti-Alcohol League," he announces as he contemplates his tumbler of Scotch, which M. Jacques has just refilled. "In Europe I am the Pope of Nudism.

"And like Diogenes who used to masturbate in the streets merely to prove he was a free man, I am the freest of men. . . .

"It is impossible for a normal man to give as a gift to the community his wife's nudity. That man is not normal who does it. Some men have begun that way, and ended giving the wife completely. . . . Nudism as we know it began as a movement more than a century ago in Austria. There are today a mere twenty thousand nudists in France. There should be two hundred thousand. But women don't want to be nudists. Their problem is that they are women. If they have a pimple on their ass, they don't want anybody to see it.

"But our nudist camps are more liberal than those of the United States. Here one may wear his clothes if he wishes.

"Once at a lecture I was delivering there came a question from the audience: 'What, sir, must one do to become a nudist?' My answer: 'Take your fucking clothes off.'

"Read my book, the definitive history of nudism—*The Story Is Ours*. And for a list of European nudist camps and information on their facilities and regulations, I recommend that your friends write for the *International Naturist Guide,* published by the Naturist Federation, 16 Lyngvej, Skaering, Hjortshoj, Denmark. Among the best camps near Paris is L'ÉLAN GYMNIQUE, near Soignolles-en-Bire (Seine-et-Marne)."

"And don't forget," adds Serge Jacques, "there are several baths in Paris that have, on certain nights, mixed nude bathing. One does not need to go outdoors to discover nudism."

"Exactly my thesis," adds Kienne de Mongeot.

Further investigations reveal that LA PISCINE DE L' ETOILE (32 rue de Tilsitt, 16th; ETO 50–99) has coed nude swimming on Friday evenings. Tuesday is the big night at the BATHS HAMAN in a Jewish quarter of Paris (4 rue des Rosiers, 4th; 272–71–82) whose feature attraction is a restaurant where one may dine in the nude. One would be well advised to phone in advance, to check on membership formalities, which are nominal.

Serges Jacques, at thirty-eight, has by his own estimation seen and photographed more unclad women than any man in the world. Indeed, his work has appeared in hundreds of magazines—from *Elle* to *Playboy* to *Vogue* to countless nudist publications throughout the world, especially in Southern California; his files contain some 150 thousand photos of nudes.

"Write about me. Anything you will say. I am the man who says *any* woman can be made to take off her clothes and be photographed in the nude . . . in *any* location." He produces two photos—one of a nude on the top platform of the Eiffel Tower, another showing a nude on the Métro. "It merely takes the proper approach. All those chicks who come up here and strip for me. . . .

"This girl, you see, she makes eighty-four dollars a month as a stenographer. I give her eighty-four dollars a day to pose nude. . . . I spend six months of each year traveling the world for my work. It's so easy . . . photography . . . it is nothing. Surely it is not art!

"In the war, I was a boy in the Résistance. High up in the mountains . . . I was afraid of nothing. But now! I am afraid of this man . . . he will ruin me!"

He hurls a copy of the *Reader's Digest* at you. According to the article "War on Smut Peddlers," Ronald Reagan is angry at West Coast distributors and publishers of nudist magazines, including one who happens to be one of Jacques' biggest clients.

"One thousand a week my client used to send me," Jacques fumes. "But now this Reagan. Never has such a small man reached so far."

From beneath a pile of negatives and photos you dig out (at Mongeot's hinting wink) *La Légende de Saint-Germain-des-Prés,* photos par Serges Jacques—a yellowed, musty book, orphaned amid the gleaming glossies of breasts, legs, pubes, and faces that bring Serges Jacques $100,000 and more a year.

"Jacques Prévert listens . . . Juliet Gréco speaks . . . ," read the captions under the haunting, evocative, exquisitely composed glimpses of Parisians of the late 1940s and early 1950s. There are Sartre and Simone de Beauvoir. And Tristan Tzara, the father of Dada. And a particularly dramatic study of Armand Fèvre, the last of the Bonapartists, who tried so hard to live like Napoleon—his flat was filled with busts of the Emperor—but who at least managed to die like him. Alone.

"But come, here are photos of six of the most beautiful women in Paris. Choose three . . . any three! . . . and the six of us will go to Castel" says Serges Jacques.

And he proved to be a man of his word.

DISCOTHÈQUES

The French probably invented the discothèque in the 1920s without fanfare, when some swinging madam put a phonograph in her whorehouse and encouraged the customers to dance with the help before bedtime. They did it again, officially, in the early 1950s. Although the discothèque may be considered passé in America, and even in some European circles, the institution is alive and relatively well in Paris.

The classic Parisian discothèque is small, or at least designed to give the illusion that it is always crowded. Ambiance created by the members is more important than lighting or architectural gimmicks. To say that a particular discothèque has "lots of pretty girls" may not be an exaggeration. Some rooms simply bar or discourage the patronage of unattractive females. (The practice is followed in certain clubs throughout Europe.) Some rooms gain their reputations for exclusivity by the quantity of people who are not allowed in rather than the quality of those who are.

The closed-membership policy applies to only a few clubs in Paris. There are many with comparable ambiance, as many pretty girls and interesting men, and easy admission. Some clubs insist they are "private" out of false snobbery or on nights when the whole town is crowded anyway. But when the place isn't completely stuffed or during summer months when many members are on vacation, entrance is no problem.

Discothèques can provide as cheap and exciting an evening as one can spend in Paris. Admission is rarely more than 10 to 20F, which may include the price of a drink. Even in the most exclusive places, one can dance all night for the price of one drink; the more crowded it is, the more difficulty one has getting served anyway.

The best places are mélanges of people. One sees men of all shapes and ages, some with extremely young women, their own mistresses or someone else's. (In Paris, as in Rome, someone's mistress is often someone else's wife.) These men do not fill the tired American image of the "sugar daddy." The Frenchman, who tends to fanfaronade, brashness, and generally making a spectacle of himself in his youth appears to acquire a certain polish and appeal with age. At least the women insist it is so. Perhaps this explains why Frenchmen seem so well adjusted to life. No matter how old they get, they live as if the best is yet to be.

The discothèque has been called a kind of adult sandbox. And there is no better opportunity to know a people than to join them at play. It is a travel-guide cliché that an invitation to a Parisian household is difficult to obtain. This may be because nobody is home. The discothèque is one mirror of French postwar prosperity; a prosperity created, in part, by De Gaulle's paternalism. A paternalism that has also bred a certain emptiness and lack of purpose among many French people. Two American newsmen who spend their days filing stories that tell how the French despise Americans, and their nights at Castel's or New Jimmy's, put it this way:

"The upper classes have always been decadent, and proud of it. Decadence is part of the national character. It's why the food is so damned good. But this is all filtering down to the middle classes. The young men seem somehow undersexed, for all their physical charm and jazzy clothes. I'm not saying we're headed for a desexed society in France. Not while their fathers are still around. Look at that old guy. The bald fat one. Really enjoying himself with that little beauty. She's no more than 17. And she really adores him. Not simply because he's rich, but because in France—as in Europe—in the kingdom of the young the middle-aged man is king. If he wants to be.

"Listen. The French have an expression, *'M'as-tu vu!'* Did you *see* me! . . . Characterizes everything the Frenchman does. He is saying it when he's driving his car, when he's making love . . . every time he dances in a discothèque. And you can bet your ass, every time Charles De Gaulle spilled some more soup on Uncle Sam, he was saying to all the French people, *'M'avez-vous vu, mes enfants?' "*

"All the people who matter go to Castel's and New Jimmy's. Everybody else goes every place else."

CASTEL, 15 rue Princesse (6th; 326–90–22), 11 P.M. to dawn. Incredible selection of beautiful girls who are treated with studied indifference—or is it contempt?—by the regulars, owner Jean Castel's poker buddies. James Baldwin is here tonight in a watermelon-red sports jacket. Also Belmondo in a droopy tramp's overcoat and lavender velvet tie purchased at the upstairs boutique (opens late afternoon). Other regulars include an ex-emperor's delicious daughter, currently a rue de la Pompe shopgirl. And a man recently returned from a trip to the Himalayas in a Citroën 2CV. His companion is an Afghan hound who smokes little cigars and drinks Scotch at about 20F the shot.

"De Gaulle rules France. Régine rules Paris."

Régine is still around.

RÉGINE (NEW JIMMY'S), 124 boulevard Montparnasse (14th; 326–74–14), 10:30 to dawn. Known by the company she keeps . . . out, this ex-Whiskey-à-Go-Go hatchick and daughter of a Polish-Jewish matzoh-baker has created the world's most circumspect discothèque (it is smaller than Annabel's). Drinks cost the same as at Castel's, but the money that buys them is older. Homaged by her rich or titled or world-famous members, plus the inevitable campy followers, Régine has divided "Tout-Paris" into three parts: the galled "outs," who unwittingly give her further notoriety by gossiping bitterly because she denies them membership; the "outs" who don't give a damn; and the few "ins" who adore the place.

Decor is nothing special—that's part of the snobbery. Atmosphere less colorful than Castel's; everyone is thinking of his money. The women are predictably beautiful, but recall Clemenceau's reaction to "swinging" New York—of the 1920s: "So strange that while the posteriors of the dancers are so gay, their faces seem so sad."

But when Régine senses boredom, she has only to create a new dance. With that easy grace all the more remarkable for less than thin people (Zero Mostel has it; Oliver Hardy had it) she soon has the "innies" applauding this, the true umbilicus of their universe.

As many pretty girls and easier entry at RUBY'S, 31 rue Dauphine (6th); ROMEO-CLUB, 71 boulevard Saint-Germain (6th); and KING CLUB, 17 rue de l'Échaudé (6th). All open to dawn, 15F drinks. And LE BILBOQUET, 13 rue Saint-Benoît (6th), a cellar discothèque where some exquisite females are admired by a Hollywoodish male clientele amid the 2001: A Space Odyssey decor. Dancing to records and occasional English and French groups.

No point listing many nonprivate discothèques. You'll find them indicated in the weekly guide Pariscope without the note "Club privé." At this writing LE PRIVÉ (12 rue de Ponthieu, 8th) is très privé indeed. Central station of les locomotives (a kind of Gallic "swinger". . . who shops at JAP or VOG). More than twice as large as Régine or Castel, Le Privé is equally difficult for strangers to negotiate. Try wearing a funny hat. Or delivering a telegram. Or five hundred francs. FRANÇOIS-PATRICE SAINT-HILAIRE (24 rue Vavin, 6th) is as much fun, slightly easier to crash. CLUB D'O (9 rue Princesse, near Castel) is easier yet; usually only unescorted, unknown men are barred. Ditto the show-biz CLUB PARISCOPE (4 rue Balzac, 8th). And easier yet are LE GREENWICH VILLAGE (10 rue Descartes, 5th) and WHISKY À GOGO (57 rue de Seine, 6th).

B33, 33 rue Saint-Benoît (6th), is another of Maurice Casanova's enterprises. Unlike his Bilboquet, this one is for the masses. Noon to 1 A.M. Boutiques, a beauty salon, translucent fitting rooms, canned goods and music, rooftop restaurant. If all that bores the Saint-Germain-des-Prés yé-yé, she can also dance.

RÉGINSKAYA in rue La Boëtie is New Jimmy's on the Right Bank, with Czarist overtones.

FARWEST SALOON, 11 rue Jules-Chaplin (6th), 10 P.M. to dawn. Jack Kennedy loves this pseudo-Western Left Bank discothèque-bar-hangout. He ought to. Since he gave up plans to teach Indian philosophy, this ex-Californian has been packing them in. Good chili and hamburgers. Difficult for a man to be lonely here.

MILORD MOD'S, 5 rue de Beaujolais (1st), from 9 P.M., and sometimes matinées. Groups and records for younger mods. CLUB DE L'ÉTOILE, 4 avenue

Victor-Hugo (16th), 10 to dawn. Father's car, mother's gas. LE TOQUET, 1 *bis* rue Jean-Mermoz (8th). Mother's car, father's gas.

If your mood isn't mod and you crave a nice uncomplicated shopgirl or non-executive secretary, dancehalls are a good bet (though not nearly the factor they are in Northern European cities). Female travelers, however, had best stick to discothèques and jazz clubs. French men in the "dancings" range from heavily pomaded slickers of the MIMI PINSON on the Champs, to rough 'n' much too ready self-styled *Apaches* in the rue de Lappe (and adjacent streets; 11th) *bals*. LA COUPOLE (102 bd Montparnasse) has dancings too.

JAZZ

Paris is one of the world's jazz capitals because "these French cats may not always dig what you blow, but they let you blow, you know, man? They let you blow." Jazz clubs are among the few places unaccompanied daughters of the middle and upper classes will visit during the wee hours.

Dixieland translates well. Try SLOW CLUB, 130 rue de Rivoli, (1st); Marc Laferrière and his New Orleans Stompers. CAMÉLÉON, 57 rue Saint-André-des-Arts (6th) has students, musicians, poets, and artists seriously listening to French groups.

LA BOHÈME ("*ambiance soul*"), 18 rue d'Odessa (14th): *Ebony Magazine* once called this location the most notorious white G.I. club in town. Then Bud Powell's wife took on management and "Buttercup's Chicken Shack" became a haven for jazz musicians and mavens. And almost fashionable. Now she is gone and so is the atmosphere. Remaining are black men looking for French girls, and French girls looking for black men. And Louis, a sympathetic barman. And no more live jazz.

LE LIVING ROOM, 25 rue du Colisée (8th), is a favorite of Ella, Duke, Miles, etc., when they're in town. At the wonderfully versatile and elegant boîte, LA GRANDE SÉVERINE, 7 rue Saint-Séverin (5th), in the first-floor Blues Bar, Mae Mercer has a divine right to sing the blues.

Student and young people's favorites include LE CHAT QUI PÊCHE, 4 rue de la Huchette (5th); LES TROIS MALLETZ, 56 rue Galande (5th); and LE CAVEAU DE LA HUCHETTE, 5 rue de la Huchette.

RANDOM NOCTURNAL ATTRACTIONS

Paris is one of the great late late shows—it never really closes—but you'll wait a long long time for that drink hustler to "meet you later." At least prostitutes are honest about the deal; you get what you bargained for. How to tell a B-girl from a prostitute? The B-girl is the one girl in town who's always having more than one. Prostitutes are usually no more interested in whiskey than in milk. With them it's strictly money, then bed. With semipros or "occasionals" it's bed, then money. Paris ranks well behind Rome, New York, and Munich in its proportion of clip joints. The quality of Parisian entertainment, the talent and beauty of the performers, make underhanded practices less necessary than in other cities.

But avoid cabbies who have deals with the "cleep joints." Make sure your man takes you to that address you've printed and shown him. If he insists he knows a better place, tell him you know the best of all: 36 quai des Orfèvres (1st), police headquarters. Unlike in London, cabbies are plentiful throughout the night, though rates go up after dark. And unlike New York cabbies, the French hacks won't bore you with small talk, even French small talk. By and large they are a sullen lot, and good luck to them.

The otherwise excellent *Parisian's Guide to Paris* (among the best yet written) won't tell you René Cousinier's exact address since the "police forbid giving too many details about him," but you'll find him at ZANFAN DE LA BOÈME, 4 impasse Marie-Blanche (18th; MON 49–46). 10 P.M. to 4 A.M., closed Monday. It is said that Dr. René was once a surgeon. Perhaps he still is, by day. By night this hairy, ribald professor of love, billed as "René the Shaker," gives nonstop lectures to mostly under-thirty-five audiences who find the advice sophisticated and hilarious, if not always practical. Eternal subject: how a man can make love to a woman. Time-honored methods, and some improvisations. Loaded with puns, anecdotes, visual props, heroic gestures, and blackboard diagrams. Highly visual, and enjoyable for at least a half hour even if you have no French. An interesting place to bring your new French girlfriend. You will treasure her translations.

CRAZY HORSE SALOON, 12 avenue George V (8th). John F. Kennedy visited this house of elegant striptease before he became President. Though he enjoyed it, he fled as soon as the show was over. Claustrophobia. While the Crazy Horse has always put one in the laps of its nude goddesses, that same close relationship with the other patrons dampened one's ardor, not to mention the armpit. Impresario Alain Bernardin, with the aid of a fortuitous fire, has now enlarged the place and continues to pack 'em in.

A literate and debonair man who physically resembles Noel Coward, Bernardin assumes an intellectual approach to striptease. His shows—*all* nude, with the passing of De Gaulle—combine imaginative use of film, slides, and sound with taste and showmanship. And those girls.

"Certainly we succeed. History ordains it. On this spot Josephine de Beauharnais danced naked, behind a veil of course, and seduced the poor unknown officer, Napoleon. . . . I brought striptease to Paris—to all Europe. No, actually it was Mata Hari. . . . Since 1951 the Crazy Horse has had about two hundred girls. For a girl to strip, she must have no illusions. For one thousand years barbarians have assaulted and raped Poland. These people are bitter realists. The only barrier to strip is the father. Significantly, many of my girls have some Polish blood. [Uri Brezhnev was a spring 1972 guest.]

"You could say this is a good place for American tourists to bring their French friends. Everything is a parody but the prices" (58F per person, two drinks all in). The phone number (BAL 69–69) isn't bad either.

LE SEXY, 68 rue Pierre-Charron (8th). Striptease—bare as any, better than most. The manager, Claude, is a gentleman. Drinks 25F, 40F at the table.

CHEZ TANIA, 43 rue de Ponthieu (8th). After the Revolution stranded and impoverished Russian aristocrats became cab drivers in Paris; others went to Nice, where they were awarded the garbage-collecting concession. And others opened Russian bars and nightclubs. This saloon is more haimish than most with an escadrille of presentable and exceptionally friendly dearhearts aged thirty to forty. Dancing in the basement discothèque to rhythms of the Red Army Orchestra. Upstairs Vladivostok-born Tania dances, sings, plays recordings of emotional Russian folksongs, and hangs around the bar. 15F vodka. And caviar.

KIT KAT, 23 rue Bréa (6th), 10 to dawn. 20F drinks. Striptease-bar-discothèque. Good value. Very young and pretty strippers. Routines have polish, run to whips and pseudosadism, striving to arouse the somewhat jaded twenty-five to thirty-five swifty patrons. It can't be done. This night a stripper succumbed to a lit cigarette; another flagellated herself to death with a red gladiolus. A third managed to die by her own hand. Nobody blinked.

L'ABBAYE, 6 bis rue de l'Abbaye (6th), has become fair game for guidebook putdowns. The Julliard guide notes: "No clapping: you have to snap your fingers, apparently so as not to disturb the neighbors. None of this is madly gay." Temple Fielding finds the folksinging "too too exciting to the self-dubbed intellectuals of the long-haired set . . . teen-age fan-club reverence toward these performers now bores us stiff." Young people—many, many of them females—think otherwise. They have been coming here for well over two decades. Yes, there is an atmosphere of almost churchlike reverence. But people come here to listen to the music, not to themselves. And if applause is appropriate in concert halls and shouting in bull rings, why not quiet finger-snapping in small intimate rooms of folksingers? The atmosphere seems to attract shy and lonely females. Drinks 12F, mixed by an indifferent "bartender" who prepares them as if he never touches the stuff himself. Very uncomfortable chairs. A particular favorite of Dutch, Scandinavian, and German girls, in addition to the Americans. Periodic breaks for whispering.

Paris also has a Lido, a Folies Bergère, and an Eiffel Tower. Of the Tower, Oscar Wilde once remarked, "Turn your back to that—you have all Paris before you. Look at it—Paris vanishes."

THE LEFT BANK AND STUDENT LIFE

Those discothèques, clubs, and a few *hôtels particuliers* previously noted to be in the 5th, 6th, and 14th *arrondissements* are all on the Left Bank. In addition, the Left Bank is inhabited by students, and others, aged roughly sixteen to twenty-eight, many of whom live or at least congregate socially in the well-known Latin Quarter.

These people have no sexual problem. The proportion of sadists, homosexuals, and *partouzeurs* among them is relatively low. Many of them have steady bedmates, and a high percentage of the couples live as if they were married. Nothing special about this; it's been going on here for a long time, pretty much as you imagine it. Of course, the students change partners from time to time, as people do everywhere else; but often the girl a boy goes with in his last year at university is the girl he marries.

There are few *hôtels particuliers* in the Latin Quarter because many hotels catering to students permit them to entertain guests in their rooms without additional charge.

One could say the May, 1968, student riots started because of sexual questions, as one could say World War II began because of Poland. Students who lived on the campus at Nanterre and Cités Universitaires demanded the right to receive girls in their rooms. After a number of strikes and demonstrations the university authorities relented. Then the girls made similar demands and the authorities agreed only on condition that females be twenty-one and obtain written permission from their parents. None of this freedom was gained without a good deal of student agitation, and because of it the police "took the habit" of visiting the campuses without invitation. (Previously a university was out of bounds to the police—as was the custom in Latin America—unless a specific request was made by university authorities.) Of course, the intervisitation demands were only a part of the grievances, in France as elsewhere in the world.

Students do not spend a lot of money to find or keep girls. They go "dutch" or else whoever has the money pays. "One cannot say the boy is a mackerel because the girl pays." If a student is looking for a girl, he prefers to do it in the daytime when he can get a better look at her and when she is most apt to be in the streets, the gardens (Jardins du Luxembourg are very appropriate), or walking along the Seine.

An aspect of Left Bank life is its tradition; often students frequent a particular café because their fathers did before them. Provincials tend to gather among people from their own area of France, and often they make a café their favorite because the owner is from their department or region.

"There is complete sexual freedom among us," one girl remarks. "If my lover leaves me, I will not try to hide it. Everyone will know it. He will tell his friends 'She is free.' It is like a divorce. . . . Limited contracts of varying duration. . . . The biggest problem, of course, is children. The girl may become pregnant and need an abortion. There are people who perform them . . . a kind of *sage-femme* [midwife] we call *'faiseuses d'anges'*—makers of angels."

Price of a Left Bank abortion (illegal of course) is 500 to 1000 francs . . . for students. "There are some students who know how to make this, or if the family has money she can go to Switzerland where the price is about 1000F. One must have a certificate from a French doctor about a mental disorder, but this is not difficult to obtain. . . . But very often the students do not find anything. And so they marry."

There is comparatively little narcotics usage among students; if they need it, they can buy it in the rue de la Huchette. They drink almost no alcohol —surprisingly, not even much wine or beer.

There are few "eternal students" in France; certainly the scene does not compare with that of Germany. If they fail the same course twice, they are expelled. And the sobering, mandatory one-year military service makes male students "very, very serious . . . interested to graduate, get money, have the business."

Those students who are from Paris usually live at home with their families. Often the building is an old one and has small rooms once used as servants' quarters, with private entrances. A boy can bring his girl here and his parents will never intrude.

There has been a traditional tacit agreement among prostitutes and the police that there will be no action in the Latin Quarter. It is difficult, of course, to sell what is available gratis. However, "some students who want to improve their financial situation make this, but never in the Latin Quarter. Never here because there is little money for it and, of course, because they are known here." And so one finds such girls on the Right Bank—especially in cafés on or near the Champs—or hired out as babysitters to elderly gentlemen.

Focal points of student cafés and activity are place Saint-Michel and Saint-Germain-des-Prés, and streets in the vicinity of these time-honored gathering places.

Not to be confused with students are the hippies of Paris who congregate in areas like place de la Contrescarpe (5th); at the intersection of the rue Mazarine and the rue Saint-André-des-Arts; and between the Pont-Neuf and the Pont-Saint-Michel, and the Pont-Saint-Michel and the Petit-Pont. A nice collection is to be found in Contrescarpe where, amid the numerous small cafés, one meets many "orphans, runaways, and girls who do not know where to sleep."

Not all the students of the Latin Quarter keep steady company. "Here a girl who is a virgin is said to have a cancer and must be operated upon immediately," says the *dragueur*—the "scavenger" who has no special girl. If you're like the *dragueur*, that is, seeking companionship, you might visit some of the following places after dark.

CHERRY LANE, 8 rue des Ciseaux (6th), from 11 P.M., is among the most popular of young people's Left Bank discothèques. Also CLUB UNIVERSITAIRE, 7 rue de la Huchette. CAVEAU DE LA BOLÉE, 25 rue de l'Hirondelle (6th). LE RIVERBOAT, 67 rue Saint-André-des-Arts (6th). And French folk-singing in CAVEAU DES OUBLIETTES in the 12th-century Church of St. Julien-le-Pauvre, rue St. Julien-le-Pauvre (5th).

Compared to their elders, Parisian students care little about food, though the dinner hour is a very lively time in the Latin Quarter because many student restaurants—like those in the rue de la Harpe and rue des Ciseaux—encourage single people to sit at any table; you choose your dining companion without having to pay for her meal.

> Black as the devil
> Hot as hell
> Pure as an angel
> Sweet as love.
>
> —TALLEYRAND, *recipe for coffee*[16]

Every so often the Paris police go on a hippie-hunt, catching a few students in the net as well. On one visit to CHEZ POPOFF in the rue de la Huchette and LE PETIT BAR, rue du Petit-Pont they caught fifty-one. Lest the kids suffer identity problems, the 5th *arrondissement* police took pictures of each with the word "beatnik" as caption. Interesting events often occur in these two places. The police and their paddy wagons are active throughout the Latin Quarter. Always carry some identification.

Other popular Left Bank cafés include LA COUPOLE; where Alice B. Toklas, Gertrude Stein, James Joyce, and Fernand Léger once sat, *yé-yés* feed pet ocelots. Nearby is the hallowed DÔME, in the 1920s the epitome of the Left Bank café. Though it has seen its day, many young painters and students don't know it. LES DEUX MAGOTS is at 170 boulevard Saint-Germain. LE FLORE, at 172, has young men playing on the sidewalk. Some are homosexuals. Some are poets. And some are not. BEAUX-ARTS, 11 rue Bonaparte, is not a café, but a restaurant where the food is cheap and adequate, and where one finds

---

[16]Paris' first café was opened in 1675 by François Procope, a Sicilian. Ten years later he moved from the rue de Tournon to 13 rue de l'Ancienne-Comédie, hoping to catch the overflow from the Comédie-Française which had just opened at No. 14. He did, and in centuries to follow Café Procope saw Diderot, Rousseau, Voltaire, young Bonaparte, Danton, Robespierre, Balzac, George Sand, Lamartine, and Oscar Wilde. But by the early twentieth century the site had become a vegetarian restaurant of little consequence. After World War II it was refurbished and made a valiant effort to recapture past glories. In vain.

artists and the girls who pose nude for them in the ÉCOLE DES BEAUX-ARTS across the street.

MISCELLANEOUS MEETING PLACES

To find tourist girls as well as natives, try the following random locations. SMITH'S ENGLISH BOOKSTORE, 248 rue de Rivoli. SHAKESPEARE AND CO., 37 rue de la Bûcherie (5th) offers opportunities for browsing, lounging, snoozing. Selected "writers-in-residence" are given free room and board in exchange for minor chores. Easy place to make a liaison or to have a bowl of chicken soup on the house. Good books too.

It would be impractical to discuss every hotel lobby in the city, but the "palace" lobbies are, of course, always lively, as they are in every major European city. And in Paris you can rely on the STOCKHOLM, 24 rue Vernet (8th) to have a steady selection of Swedish girls in spring and summer. And the MONTAIGNE, 6 avenue Montaigne (8th), is a particular favorite of singers and dancers, for whatever that will get you. (Perhaps a song and a dance.)

Paris swarms with *au pairs,* though they are not the factor here that they are in London. If you'd like to find a charming Swedish, Danish, German, or Dutch *au pair,* hang around ACCUEIL FAMILIAL FRANCO-NORDIQUE, 66 rue Saint-Lazare (9th), or ACCUEIL FAMILIAL DES JEUNES ÉTRANGERS, 23 rue du Cherche-Midi (6th), both of which help *au pairs* find work; the latter special-izes in girls who are attending the Sorbonne or Alliance Française.

AMERICAN EXPRESS, 11 rue Scribe (9th), is an obvious, but no less intelligent place to meet fellow travelers. Always a large number of girls waiting for something—a check from home or a "safe" affair. People leave names and addresses in the log book offering rides or "share-expense" proposals to other cities. The Paris office, more prudish than others, tries to obliterate the more blatantly sociable offers, but generally they have more important things to do —like taking hours to sort the mail. (You are now charged 1F per inquiry.) The second-floor cafeteria of the Louvre is usually crowded with tourist girls.

SIR WINSTON CHURCHILL PUB, 5 rue Presbourg (16th). All the English beers, the Irish whiskeys, the American colas. And lots of English and American girls; a favorite of American Embassy secretaries. Among the many Right Bank cafés, those on and near the Champs-Élysées, including COLISÉE, LE PARIS, DES THÉÂTRES, and LA BELLE FERRONNIÈRE, usually have a good selection of single girls, especially the latter two which have a high quota of fashion models.

The guidebooks can tell you all about Paris's bars—most Right Bank bar-tenders speak English and are splendid sources of information. The RITZ HOTEL, 38 rue Cambon (1st), has three very smart bars, each with its particu-lar character and characters. On the Left Bank visit BEDFORD ARMS, 15 rue Princesse (6th), a Castel's adjunct. Elegant carpeted pub, open to 4 A.M., women welcome alone. James Jones and Irwin Shaw have found four more for poker here.

Lastly, one must not forget the laundromats, always handy places to make acquaintances, especially when one is short of funds. A particularly lively laundromat is ECONOMY LAVERIE-PRESSING, 34 rue Delambre (14th), 8 A.M. to midnight. And nearby is LE ROSEBUD bar.

If the café ever disappears from Paris, the French will blame it on the "American-inspired" LE DRUGSTORE, 135 Champs-Élysées. But if the French know a drugstore in the United States where you can buy Christian Dior ties, enjoy the best champagne with your oysters, caviar with banana splits, select gadgets Hammacher would be proud to give Schlemmer, and admire the beautiful *minettes* (playgirls or "pussies") . . . the Americans do not. "Le Pullman" section in the rear is decorated with the only genuine carpetbags in Europe and the most beautiful twelve-year-old blondes in the world. And some gentlemen who prefer them. M. Finkel is the maître d' in the pharmacy. If he runs out of aspirin, try one of the several branches, including the Saint-Germain-des-Prés hangout at 149, boulevard Saint-Germain.

These and other drugstores have dispensed contraceptives quite freely for some time, although it was only in 1967 that the Senate and National Assembly passed the controversial bills that legalized the sale of oral contraceptives. Even before passage of the bills, however, French doctors had freely prescribed the Pill without much fear of prosecution. By 1968 some 250,000 French women were said to be using the Pill.

GOD AND MAN IN PARIS

A 1920 French law—passed by the National Assembly in the hope of increasing France's male population after the decline caused by World War I—banned the sale of all contraceptives and forbade people to advocate birth control publicly. But in its 1968 interpretation of Pope Paul VI's encyclical "On Human Life," the Roman Catholic Church of France showed a delicious French pragmatism as regards matters sexual in deciding that the user of artificial contraception "is not always guilty." The French Church left it to the individual to decide whether such use would be sinful in his or her case.

In its subtle but firm discord with the Vatican, the modern French Church reflects not only the will but the essence of this proud, independent people whose unparalleled genius for pleasure, cannot be any the less "God-given" than a Pope's law. Decades earlier Charles Péguy had written, "It's a nuisance, God said. When those French are gone, no one will be left to understand certain things I do."

Indeed, is it not supernatural how Paris (where all Frenchman, from Dijon to Djibouti still stash their mistresses) remains so rich in harmonious amoral diversity despite all efforts by all governments? Or, more temporally, in this nation of libertines and bureaucrats, does the former perpetuate, or at least make *partouzes* with, the latter? And vice versa? Descartes, a logical fellow and thus a Frenchman if ever there was one, once remarked, "The greatest minds are capable of the greatest vices as well as the greatest virtues." Did he mean the world's few really brilliant voluptuaries, or all Frenchmen?

Although other cities may better her on this count or that, none can touch Paris's encyclopedic versatility. This century several great cities have had their day: Vienna, Berlin, New York, Rome, London; the cycle will doubtless continue, and add others; but Paris nights—through wars, peaces, communes, marshals, and De Gaulle—continue to offer the warmest and most diversified welcome for the sensual traveler. For the French really don't give a sou what you do. As long as you don't care what they do. And *that* is the essence of Paris.

AMSTERDAM/
THE HAGUE

Netherlands

The basic unit of currency is the guilder, also known as the gulden or the florin. Each guilder can be divided into 100 Dutch "cents." At this writing you'll get about 3.18 guilders for each floating dollar. Thus each guilder equals about 30 U.S. cents. You can leave or enter with guilders galore.

INTRODUCTION AND BRIEF HISTORY

The most surprising aspect of "Surprising Amsterdam" is that the Nethe:-lands Tourist Authority, and KLM, continue to assume that visitors will find it so surprising. Undeniably, Holland is home to lots of puritans (though some of the most fanatic emigrated to the Colonies), but the country is even better known as a bastion of freedom for *all* kinds of idiosyncratics, not merely religious or political. All during the 1960s, one popular KLM-sponsored guide saw fit to reassure Americans that Amsterdam bears "not the slightest resemblance to the picture of tulips, cheese . . . wooden shoes . . . plump, red-cheeked people . . . strolling along quaint canals . . . most people expect to find." But why bother to dispel an image that has dubious historic basis, and one that probably precious few people believe nowadays anyway?

People do stroll the canals, not only because they are quaint, but also because whores have been sitting along them for hundreds of years. Amsterdam has always been a good place to have your dirty book published, if the authorities in your own country were less than cooperative. *My Secret Life,* for example, first saw print here. The book's reputed author, Henry Spencer Ashbee, in a bibliography of his own private library *(Index of Forbidden Books)* recalls the remarks of a nineteenth-century traveler: "Don't take an English lady to the Dutch Fairs. The chief dramatic exhibition there is a large-arsed woman who plays a sort of Female Pantaloon. She is whipped on her naked bottom by both Harlequin and Clown, on every occasion and in every attitude. A favorite notion is for Harlequin to take her across one of his shoulders, while the other personages spank her backside. This must be an agreeable and lady-like profession: bless her fat bum!"

In fact, not a few English females, many of them just into their teens and with certificates from Harley Street physicians certifying them as *virgo intacta* tied round their quivering bellies, did visit Dutch fairs, never to return, thanks to the enterprise of Dutchmen like "Klyberg" who "with his wife, was the principal importer, during the whole of the 'seventies' of girls from London to the owners of houses of ill fame in Holland, Belgium, and France," according to Iwan Bloch, the early-twentieth-century sexologist whose *Sexual Life in England* describes some of the Dutch treats: "The most luxurious brothel in the world was that known in Amsterdam as 'The Fountain.' It consisted of a large building with restaurant, dance-hall and private rooms, café, and a billiard-room on the roof of the house, where the most beautiful girls played billiards stark naked. At small tables round sat serious, blinking old gentlemen, comfortably smoking their long pipes, drinking their glass of grog and enjoying the remarkable spectacle."

Though such establishments were declared illegal by a 1911 law, prohibitions did not extend to prostitution per se. Control passed to the smaller independent entrepreneur, if not the girls themselves.

Whoever, then, started the rumor that wooden shoes aren't made for kicks should be put into the pillory at Buiten. Wieringerstraat 3–5, made to watch a reel of their extraordinarily dirty color films, horsewhipped by the young governess, mock castrated in a small custom-made vise (available on short order at nearby specialty shops), bathed, *shtoomed* under water by the breathtaking blond "masseuse," then locked up in the special masochist's jail to think things over. The whole deal comes to around 125 guilders (written f125, for guilders are also called florins; one guilder equals about 30¢; approximately 3.18 guilders equal each floating dollar). But never mind that part of town. For now. (Jordaan and a special area to the west of the Dam Square.) It's somewhat esoteric, even for flying Dutchmen.

THE RED-LIGHT CANALS

Begin with the known but no less interesting red-light district, one of the few that really deserves the term, for it does indeed have red lights, and green ones and blue and purple fluorescent as well, the latter particularly effective in vamping the already flashy charms of some of Europe's most fetching prostitutes. You will only occasionally see a *beautiful* girl here—perhaps one in eleven—but considering the charm of the area, the quaintness of the canalside sixteenth-to-eighteenth-century houses, the youth, forthright sexual appeal, and linguistic abilities of the whores, and the uniformly low prices (from 20 to 40 guilders without "extras"), it's time the Amsterdam Tourist Authority and KLM gave Holland's *snols* the same good press as diamond-cutters, ecdysiasts (many of the strippers are not Dutch anyway), genever-tasting taverns, and Hans Brinker's silver skates. If you're on a three-day group-tour pass, take the very practical Arthur Frommer trot: "From the Krasnapolsky Hotel on the Dam Square, walk down the narrow Warmoesstraat until you come to the bottom of the Zeedijk, near the Centraal Station. Then walk up the entire length of the Zeedijk, until you reach the Nieuwmarkt. From the Nieuwmarkt, walk across the Barndesteeg to the Oude Zijds Achterburgwal, and walk down Oude Zijds Achterburgwal to its end, near the station; then cross over to the parallel Oude Zijds Voorburgwal and walk up that canal until you reach the Damstratt, where you can turn in again to the Dam Square. Did you ever expect to find *this* in Amsterdam?" asks Frommer. Since, through some ten or more editions, he has not a single sentence telling people just what in fact "this" is, it's not surprising that some people never trouble to find out.

If you have some special interest in this area (known as the *Walletjes*) or at least more time to be disorganized, don't plunge right onto the Zeedijk. Get a good map and ease from the opposite (south) end of Oude Zijds Voorburgwal, say 9:30 of a soft summer's eve when the northern sun has finally faded. The simple little streetlamps give barely enough light to scare off spooks (except in Spooksteeg) but never so much to make you feel that you're just emerging from anesthesia, as does the Orwellian fluorescence of cities like Madrid, racing technology to escape their past. Be bold. Poke up every slender alley like a goatish gynecologist. But crisscross the sturdy tippy canal bridges too, for there's more to the area than whores and ship rakes.

A left at St. Pieterspoortsteeg, for example, brings you into an alley so narrow that it's nearly bridged by dimpled legs of sprawling adolescents, swathed in sheer minimumus. Pass gently over bearded boys humming kazoos, strumming Jew's harps into CAFE DE PIETER where among old Provos (thirty or so), new Dolle Minas, and Kabouters you can barter a beer or wine for a guide. One of the first things she may point out is the happy coexistence of the students, hippies, and commune residents who have recently moved in to join the area's longtime residents—artisans, churchmen, at least one enlightened member of the Netherlands Tourist Authority, and . . . the *hoers*.

Left on little St. Annenstraat it really begins. Picture windows with fast-draw curtains frame the tidy parlors of somewhat larger than doll-house-sized furniture. Neatness counts for as much as anything in Holland and whore dens are no exception. It is really quite Dutch to relish the world peering up your parlor; travel throughout the country and, by early-evening lamplight, you'll see the details of as many Dutch living rooms as you'll see battened-up shutters in Latin lands at siesta time. Double back St. Annenstraat to O.Z. Voorburgwal. Now a left into Begijnensteeg, five feet narrow. Six crotch-level (yours) windows here. In the harsh fluorescent front lighting, crocheted white microskirts, theatrically madeup bosoms, and shapely legs glow a weird deep purple. Black pubic hair shines with a wicked iridescence. These girls can't possibly be as exciting to bed as to watch. Still you stare and wonder . . . like considering an affair with an android or a half-dressed mannequin in a chic lingerie shop. Price, f30 ($9) including the room for a short time, but sweet enough if that's what you want. Browsing seems by far the better deal for the amazed, bewildered, bemused, or simply horny visitors who include businessmen, hippies, arm-in-arm lovers, and the inevitable packs of hungry sailors. The majority of the sightseers stick to the well-known main arteries of the area—the picturesque canals; comparatively few venture into the little side alleys where your contact with the whores is very close indeed, whether you're buying or browsing.

Double back out to O.Z. Voorburgwal again, passing a poster for the Free Sex Party: Hans Hofman wants "Free birth control, pills, condoms, pornography, sex shows . . . more sex education in primary schools, more nudist camps . . . sex for the prisoner, the handicapped, the crippled." "And for the Viet Cong too," some considerate soul has added. Don't miss Trompettersteeg, though you may, as it's said to be the city's narrowest street, barely a yard wide. Proceed past more f20-to-30 whores into a T-shaped *cul de sac* where the location of "Dardi Hamburger's" business can only be described as "priming." Surrounded by a dozen or more whore fronts—one or two girls are real beauties, command up to f50—ADAM EN EVA SEX SHOP (Sint Annendwarsstraat 3) is among the most hidden of Amsterdam's many sex shops, which are, in fact, scattered throughout the city, but none is busier. Some days (11 A.M. to 2 A.M.) the gross well exceeds f2000. There is, as you'd expect, an enormous selection of rip-roaring sex magazines, offering nearly everything you could dream of, and lots you couldn't. And there are contact magazines. ("Dardi" also sells the *Reader's Digest,* which, he insists, is avidly read by the neighborhood's business girls.)

Pornography and the Sex Shops

There are sex-contact magazines and there are *Dutch* sex-contact magazines. Not only are the advertisers encouraged to list their phone numbers and home addresses to make meetings happen quickly (you avoid writing to an anonymous box number and enclosing a "mailing fee" to the magazine itself as in the manner of many British and American publications), but very candid photos of the advertisers often appear as well, centering on closeups of proud erect penises or carefully groomed vaginas. The ads are grouped according to special interests—group sex, sadomasochism, homosexuality, etc.—and when the advertisers are in fact "professionals" they so state. According to Hans Baiij, chief editor of *Sextant,* the official publication of the Netherlands League for Sexual Reform, sex-contact magazines have increased their publication by 1000 percent in the past two years and now sell approximately seven hundred thousand copies a month. That's in a country of no more than 13 million people.

Without a tedious description of sex magazines, one can say that Holland appears to offer pornography every bit as strong as may be found anywhere in the world. *One wonders why all the fuss about Copenhagen.* There are apparently some prohibitions regarding the Danish-made animal/human relationships and particularly sadistic German-made films (whose sales are, of course, forbidden in Germany itself), but even such material can be easily found under the counters of several Amsterdam shops. Just ask. Moreover, the authorities, being Dutch themselves, are exceptionally lenient about what may be displayed in the windows. You've never seen such frank outdoor displays *anywhere*. And the variety of articles—sexual apparatus, machines, special condoms, portable phalluses and vaginas, "aphrodisiacs," creams, lotions, candies, drink mixers—is unsurpassed in any Western nation.

Like most Dutch shops, Adam en Eva is bright and cheery. And like most sex shops it is basically heterosexual. Browsers are welcome. The second floor houses an art gallery—erotic and pornographic prints, lithos, oils, and watercolors, and some sculpture, most of it by local artists. Soft rock music keeps things breezy. None of your Soho sleaziness, nor the semiseediness of Copenhagen shops, nor even the inhibiting clinical aspects of the German sex supermarkets. "Dardi Hamburger," thirty, merry, and resembling a pudgy Ringo Starr, tweaks the full mustache reaching round to his heavy mutton-chops as he tosses what resembles half a huge pink Tootsie Roll to a visiting policeman. On closer inspection the thing proves to be made of soft rubber and vinyl plastic, has a puce silk bow, a pink rubber passage whose entrance is fringed by soft black cat fur, and is large enough to accommodate a man's erect penis. The beauty of the thing is that it is completely washable; after you've done jazzing it, just toss it into the washing machine; f95. Now "Dardi" straps on its male counterpart (f49.50, hard rubber but not so hard that fluid cannot be spurted out the tip) and poses for your photo. The policeman laughs.

Adam en Eva is so close to the NH Oude Kerk, one of the oldest Dutch churches, that in late afternoon you can hear the shouts of its sexton and his young son sparring with a soccer ball. Sometimes they accidentally kick it off BABA SEX SHOP's window (evil-looking black leather masks, electric penises) or into the parlor of the red-haired beauty nearby, one of several sex dens that virtually surround the church. "How long have they been around here?" "The girls were here before the church," replies the sexton of the church that has been in Oudekerksplein since before the fourteenth century. The tomb-stone of Rembrandt's wife, Saskia, was found here recently.

Into Enge Kerksteeg, where a plaque dates a building from 1634. Looks in fine condition, but no newer than many others in the area. You get lucky in CAFÉ MAZZEL TOF, and meet a customer who controls a lot of real estate in the neighborhood. He also has a large house in the country where live several of the whores and their children. He says most of the girls are from the provinces and on days of a big soccer match involving teams from their home towns, they take a holiday to avoid meeting someone who might gossip. Most girls leave the canals by age thirty, many marry, settle to comfortable bour-geois lives. None actually lives around here. They pay 50 to 60 guilders daily rent, some paying less and giving the landlord a cut on each actual customer. There are three work shifts, roughly as follows: 10 A.M. to 6 P.M.; 6 P.M. to 2 A.M.; 2 A.M. to midmorning.

"A girl may not sit in the canals if she is under twenty-one years, but she can do it even as young as fifteen, as long as she is married," declares one of Chief Molenkamp's officers in the police station at Warmoesstraat 48. Metal filing cabinets contain records and pictures of nearly every neighborhood working girl, largely for income-tax purposes. Though it's not absolutely required by law—"this would mean the government absolutely sanctions prostitution"—the girls do visit a very busy neighborhood physician for regular medical inspection.

A drunken Greek, bleeding copiously but not seriously from the forehead, is brought in by two smiling cops and quite gently locked away for the night. Too much fandango, or did he slip during the zesty Zorba dances? Both big favorites at the rousing KENNEMER CLUB, Warmoesstraat 63, where you can bring the whole family.

Little Lange Niezel is short but packed with interest. If you like loose amateurs, give your regards to the BROADWAY BAR. Looks very hot. Next door the PLAYGIRL SEX SHOP has for years filled its windows with cards from dominant males calling submissive ones to The Hague. The beauty parlor across the street is much in fashion among ladies of the neighborhood. The lingerie shop nearby displays filmy panties with apertures at the crotch; important to men who like that sort of thing. Even more important to the canal whores, almost none of whom remove all their clothing—such as there is— for the stated "short-time" price unless you've bargained hard *before* they make you ready. Otherwise prepare to add a "tax" of about f10 for complete nudity. It's not that they're bashful or even mean. Snapping off a garter belt or brassiere takes time and only money buys time in the canals.

Feeling frisky on Molensteeg Bridge one 2 A.M., you segue a young American guitarist and his fellow students from "We Shall Overcome" to "House of the Rising Sun." The whores take it good-naturedly enough. Out with your camera for a snapshot. Quick as you can say *pooier* (pimp), strong hands fling you up over the railing to follow a long line of documentary filmmakers and still photographers. It's cold in the canals.

Be careful around here. The police often look the other way when the "protectors" are out protecting. And they are protecting everywhere—from Bloedstraat (literally "Blood Street," with its alley Gordsteeg several little windows, about f25) to Spooksteeg (Street of Ghosts) to Boomsteeg. Pimps are also called *bikken* and when these men aren't "eating" from the girls, they hang around cafés and bars near the Nieuwmarkt.

Between window-shopping along the canals themselves (in addition to O.Z. Voorburgwal and Achterburgwal, don't neglect the foot of Geldersekade) browse SEX-ART GALLERY, O.Z. Achterburgwal 92, from noon to 4 A.M. Try their *Zeemansbruid* ("sailor's bride") on your custom's agent: midportion of a female torso, roughly thighs to waist, with appropriate aperture. Heavily weighted for realism. About f225. "All-in-one" pair of black rubber tights with molded phallus, to be worn inside out and up the vagina "while she goes dancing," explains helpful owner T. Bijlsma. For the man in her life . . . a variety of Disneyland condoms, one shaped like the head and trunk of an elephant, another a reindeer, another a human hand. "Because she like the form." Chiang Kai-shek grins from a packet of "aphrodisiac" candy from Taiwan, f1.50. But here's some "Spanish Love"! Does it really work? Is it Spanish fly? "Spanish fly forbidden," explains mijnheer Bijlsma's manager. However, "Spanish Love" moves in its own mysterious ways—it is made from extract of powdered housefly wings and does some very irritating things to the urinary tract. "Make her crazy . . . she want more." Fifteen guilders for enough powder to make five women crazy, or one woman five times. Deheer Bijlsma has a sandwich snack shop in the basement should you get hungry.

The catalogue of the exhibition at Sexmuseum, O.Z. Achterburgwal 62 gives you a good idea of what's to be found in the many sex shops scattered throughout the city. What's more, it is one of the few printed in English so you might want to send to Postbox 1848 for it. "Item 007: 'Laverta Top Trade 3' condome [sic] with germ-killing innerfilm and a special paste on the innerside that gives a very particular radiant heat at the moment of orgasm; contents three . . . f3. . . . Special extra quality condomes, which can be used many times. . . . Developing Cream: men with a small member are now able to develop the penis within a few months by massage with this hormonal cream. Absolutely harmless. With directions for use. Per tube f19.50. . . . Item 48: Arabian Goat's Eye ('Mata Kambing'): a very stimulating means, which was used already a few hundred years ago, to enlarge the gathering during coition. You have to soak the goat's eye 10 to 20 minutes before using in lukewarm water, then put it behind the acorn. During the erection the ring tightens itself around the member. During the coition the soft little hairs give an exciting stimulation, both to man and woman, but especially to woman! Using this goat's eye, even the most cool woman will have an unknown extatic satisfaction. Wash it after use. Unlimited tenable. Sterile packed in plastic sack. Per piece f15. Item 49: ditto long-haired and even more stimulating, f19.50."

Sex Theater

There are no really raw, live legal sex shows in Amsterdam such as you'll find in Copenhagen and Hamburg. Yet. But while the wife is down the street visiting the famous Our Lord in the Attic Church, give the gang of young performers at Sextheater, O.Z. Voorburgwal 88, a break. Three couples alternate and switch around through continuous performances in the small, off-Broadwayish theater; admission f5. Nearly everything but actual fornication. Nearby live shows include Exclusief (O.Z. Achterburgwal 76). The very hot CLUB NUMBER 1 (Zeedijk 86; 24–67–87) has "topless hostesses, lesbian love, sexual intercourse, and free intimate massage demonstrations." For your added theatrical pleasure an ad also offers "rape." If and only if you are Chinese will you be admitted past the bedsheets of Binnen Bantammerstraat. The Chinese came to Holland from England in the 1920s, scores already stupefied because somehow the economy of nineteenth-century England required that the Indians harvest opium and the Chinese consume it. Most of the old addicts have died off—God Save the Queen!—but for those poor devils who remain, the police tolerate a couple of opium parlors. Once, in Binnen Bantammerstraat, there were a score or more. While you're around here go to BOHEMIA JAZZCLUB, Kromboomssloot 14, one of the best jazz bars in all Europe and a good place to get yourself a nice girl- or boyfriend. The guidebooks haven't found it yet.

The Zeedijk

If you'd rather genever than jazz or opium, get into the Zeedijk (though you may find all three along here), the rowdy but rarely dangerous sailor's midway. There's some *tippelem* (streetwalking) and f25 whores on the steps, corner Stormsteeg, but the most characteristic distractions of joints like JOKE'S PLACE, ZANZI BAR, CAFÉ HAPPINESS, and HOTEL OLOF are "good-time" girls and friendly, forthright amateurs. (Lots of new sex shops and shows lately.)

Some of the Sadie Thompsons in the streets take much longer to take much more from the sailors than common whores. In the fashion of their sisters in Rotterdam's Katendrecht district, some Zeedijk sweethearts (and perhaps even more of them in cafés in the Nieuwendijk) have been known to remove a thousand and more dollars from a sailor just off six months at sea "helping him buy presents for the family." But you can have a good time on the Zeedijk without being had. CASABLANCA, a hard-rock disco-bar, is the hottest house around. Amazing variety of pickups. At 5 P.M. the *borrel uur* (hour of the bubbles), walk into CAFÉ ZEE-EN-RIJNVAART (Zeedijk 4), blow on your cupped hands, and grunt *"Guten Abend."* They'll think you're just another old Rhenish bargemaster. Huge 1820s porcelain beer pump. Billiard table. Marvelous old brass genever pump. Drink the *jonge* genever. The older the yellower, and some genever is over fifty years old. Normally when you ask for old, it means young with a dash of old. Straight *oude* will grow hair on your liver, perhaps require a lambchop transplant. At the far end of the Zeedijk, CHAT QUI PELOTE offers moderately priced French cuisine, and a splendid view of the neighborhood's antics.

The walls and patrons of CAFÉ BET VAN BEEREN, Zeedijk 65, are plastered with memories of forty-five years of banquets, parties, and brawls. Hanging brassieres, jockstraps, an autographed photo of Abbott and Costello (master and slave?), a Chestnut Hill-Philadelphia railroad timetable, and other souvenirs attest to the action. Now mixed, but perhaps the oldest bar of its type in Amsterdam.

H.M.S. *Blackwood* was a very tight ship in OLD NICKEL CAFÉ the night you visited this otherwise rather restrained hotel pub at the bottom of the Zeedijk. So smashed was a *Blackwood* mate that he "married" the barmaid in a wild beer-drenched ceremony officiated by a waiter named Kees who wore full parson's habit and provided six pretty waitresses from nearby KOOPER-MOOLEN (cabaret theater, restaurant) as bridesmaids. If you enjoy the Scottish Navy, English girls, BEA stewardesses, Old Nickel is not to be missed.

Maybe you prefer old leather. Proceed then to nearby Warmoesstraat 20, where in the f13 rooms of the ARGOS HOTEL you can finish what you started in their ARGOS BAR (a short walk away at Heintje Hoekssteeg 15, no more than a slave's scream from the police station). "It's a leather bar, the Argos Bar," had said a homosexual whore cruising down the Singel Canal, "a sadist's heaven. If they ask if you are 'S' or 'M,' better say 'S' or they will hit you." It is indeed a leather bar, the Argos Bar. Cher, the bartender is wearing leather. Many patrons are wearing leather. The walls are wearing leather. But some of the trade, gentle souls mostly, are not at all interested in leather. They are, however, very interested in *people who are wearing leather.* "We had a lot of equipment behind the bar we lend formerly. But these people, they never give it back," says Cher, the bartender of Argos Bar, the leather bar.

They have equipment at TOTAL SEX, 14 Nieuwendijk, a street of even gamier, and far less touristed bars than those of the Zeedijk. In fact, you are now in an area (*left* of the Dam Square facing north) less well known for vended venery, or anything else for that matter, than the Zeedijk and its adjacent red-light canals, but actually light-years more pregnant with special-ized opportunities than any area yet discussed. Total Sex is a sadomasochistic boutique. They sell handcuffs that would hold King Kong (f45), vicious black-snake whips (f20–50), frightening avenger face masks (f125). There are "ball-binders"—a lavender leather testicle pouch with choice of silver or gold padlock; and "-busters"—a penis strap with silvery spikes, to be worn orna-mentally, spikes out, or spikes on skin, in which instance you'll doubtless require the (optional) leather scrotum-restraining sack to insure that your sexual intercourse is all the more trying and therefore more "pleasurable" . . . and a saleswoman who thinks it's all "pop art."

S/M, ETC.

It's not pop art to the husky old whorehorses of Oude Nieuwstraat and Teerketelsteeg. Stolid and solid, they sit like windmill bases in the long narrow ribbon between the lower Singel and Spuistraat. Housefly eyes peripherally ferret your aberrational tapeworm in the convex truck-driver mirrors that extend from weathered window ledges, plot to feed it paces before you pass their frumpy parlors. Twenty guilders puts a tiny, tremulous peter 'tween those Brobdingnagian thighs. Fifteen gets it sucked by gums that last held teeth when Zog kinged Albania. And for f45 they'll beat the living hell out of you. Or lock you up in a dark closet. Or force you to do terrible things with excrement and Edam cheeses. Several of these old red hands (some, as you've guessed, are refugees from the Zeedijk canals) have houses of gear dear to the *stoutertje* ("naughty boy"; also "masochist"). Even the comparatively attractive young girls standing in the street, in doorways, and at the old church, at the corner of Teerketelsteeg and K. Korsjespoortsteeg, can easily rent or borrow, though not necessarily effectively *wield,* a whip at extremely short notice. But maybe you hated your grandmother. Around the corner two fat old frights flank the flatboats floating in the Singel canal. Flail away, f50 the pair. Or watch them "do bad" to each other.

Custom-made Gear

Perhaps you want to contact a different class of subjugator. Hurry past the corner of Teerketelsteeg Church to CALIENTE in Korte Kolksteeg who are to custom-made sadomasochistic gear what A. Sulka is to custom shirtings, and also act as a master-slave marriage bureau.

Shackles, fetters, trammels, manacles, gyves, chains, handcuffs, darbies, stocks, bilboes, and a few dildoes; hobbles, halters, harnesses, yokes, collars, bridles, gags, tethers, masks, pickets, leashes, locks, straitjackets—a remarkable display of restraint in the show window, a veritable thesaurus of human bondage within Caliente's roughly thirty-by-thirty-foot salesroom. Dangling from the ceiling, the tendrils of five hundred whips undulate to the breeze of your entrance, a cruel sea of sadism. Every inch of display and rack space is packed, and the posh, lacquered feel, and *odor,* of a millionaire's racing stable tack room pervades the place. People come with etchings of medieval torture chambers, illustrations from early Sade editions, or their own plans, models, and spec sheets. And Caliente's owner, mijnheer Van Herwerden, a bulky Faustian figure with immaculately close-cropped full black beard, acts as psychiatrist, couturier, and inventor—fashioning things for each according to his needs and physique.

Particularly successful creations appear in near Avedon-quality photos of the quarterly catalogue, posed by beautiful young models. Are they *really* stabbing each other with those silver-handled daggers (with thigh-binding sheath, f85)? Is that true blood spattered over the leather-bound vagina and nearly exploding breasts of the Raquel Welch double who lies lashed to a wooden oxcart wheel (*Discipline tuig, geheel compleet,* f225), pelvis bursting into the wide-angle lens as her handsome young lover snaps her neck back in a vicious body-tauting kiss?

Deheer Van Herwerden will gladly offer you the address cards of various establishments where one pays up to f100 for "all possibilities". But he derives far greater personal satisfaction, and not a single guilder, playing matchmaker to erstwhile strangers of particularly complementary tastes. Though your own impression is that the Dutch are no more perverse than Pennsylvanians or Peruvians, and that the incidence of sadism, masochism, prostitution, or homosexuality only *appears* to be higher in Holland than elsewhere—because so much that is forbidden by law in other countries is quite legal or at least tolerated here and therefore right out in the open— mijnheer Van Herwerden insists that there is more to it. And so do several candid Dutchmen you've spoken to.

"It is in the Dutch character to be this." It's the sincerity of his husky yet high-pitched voice that makes the man seem oddly sympathetic. "It is beneath the surface but it is there. . . . They *want* to have the sadistic love but they cannot get it at home. But here in my shop the husband *and* even together the wife, they feel free to talk about it. Maybe there is two, three hundred thousand masters and slaves in this country. Of course, everywhere, many homosexuals is slaves. . . . I don't have much friends, but many people come to me. Everything I have heard from one I give to the other."

And he "gives" it in Dutch, German, English, or French.

"These days people wants *hard* sadism. If I make a bra with play pins on the outside they say make *real* the pins, *on the inside.* And the same against the penis. At first I think it is for show but they want it real. . . . Many people is trying it that never did it before. Their problem is to be sure if they say to stop, the sadist does not think this means you want more and he hits you more strong and makes you stay locked up for more time."

You are in Van Herwerden's top-floor workroom, watching him add a thoughtful fluid hole to a lavender scrotum sack.

"There are normal men, big as I am, strong as I am [he is a bit over six feet, about two hundred pounds], more money as I am, who want to . . . walk like a dog. They really want to eat from the back of a dog. There is a man coming here, he is about fifty years . . . who want he can razor her. All the hair from her body. If he can see that they are doing it, he pay seven and a half hundred guilders. If he can do it himself, he pay thousand guilders. . . .

"Here, anything is possible. But not the high-heeled boots. I did buy them from Luís 'A' in Guadalajara, but now he have hang himself. It's a problem in Holland to get high boots with spikes. Do you know someone in America who can sell me this?

"Comes here a man with a gold ring through his foreskin like an earring. A ring *so big!* [the size of an American silver dollar]. And through the bag of his penis he does have a smaller ring. And when he is making love or has to be punished by his master, the two rings is joined by a lock. I did seen it.

And a man who has on his chest cigarette burns and on the behind is made with a hot iron an 'E,' the French for slave . . . *esclave*. . . . Fifty kilometers from Paris there is a castle from a strange rich millionaire. I did not see it but I hear of it from Belgian and French homosexuals. There you have all strange things you ever dreamed. Men who want to be slaves are hanging at the top of the room in chains. If you are visiting, you can punish them for a hundred and twenty francs. But you can only give. And if you are a member of this group or a friend of the club, then you can be hanging up too. . . .

"But you cannot play you are a sadist or you are not. Go to 'Maison Cent-Sept' in The Hague. It is . . . *the best house in the Netherlands.* 'S/M Centrum,' where you go now, it is no more than a 'playhouse.'"

You leave a hearty Van Herwerden pretty much as anyone might find him: humming as he fashions a black leather full-head mask with a small brass mouthscrew that will allow the purchaser just enough eating and breathing room to stay alive. (The shop has recently moved to Spuistraat 21.)

S/M Centrum: "Playhouse"

Cross the Haarlemmerstraat bridge at the bottom of the Singel into Jordaan, roughly equivalent to Rome's Trastevere, Stockholm's Södermalm, or pre-1945 Brooklyn. Since the seventeenth century, the area has had about it the smell of leather, though this largely emanated from Jordaan's tanneries, not its veneries. Thus it is largely people from more prosperous neighborhoods who phone 22–04–74 to reserve an hour's pleasure or pain at S/M Centrum —open 11 A.M. to midnight, from 1 P.M. on weekends. The curtains of the two large plate-glass windows at Buiten. Wieringerstraat 3–5 are always drawn, but you're given a warm welcome by Goni, the attractive twenty-three-year-old resident sadist, who, with her man, operates this neat little "house of all possibilities."

A staff of four young girls, a pair on duty at any given time, offer sexual intercourse, massage, and other comforts. In the twenty-five-by-thirty ground-floor-left room (the far end is fully tiled) a twenty-two-year-old blonde —pert, pretty, and pigtailed as Hans Brinker's sister—will get into the big bathtub with you, lather your essentials, dry you on the enormous bed while you watch in the backwall mirror, then receive you between her delicious golden gams for f50. Don't be a cheapskate. Spend the extra f30 and she'll run Super-8 porno films while you two heat up in the tub. All the way for f125 and, rub-a-dub-dub, the other one, her equally slim blond body belied by a pair of Junoesque breasts, joins you with an Archimedean splash. There's a little bar for genever and those good Dutch liqueurs you've heard about, and a nice Delft candy box filled with rubbers for the squeamish. Electric vibro-massagers too.

But douse the main lights and tiny bulbs come alive in the black ceiling.

A pin spot highlights the chrome steel torture rack from which hang manacles and, facing a vertical mirror, *you* by the wrists—if you prefer Goni to blondes. From the wall rack of whips, dog collars, and leashes she selects a snake and prepares for her f100 specialty—"Russian Massage." (Why the Dutch don't call it "English" or "German" is not explained.) Full breasted yet limber (a wonderful characteristic of many young Dutch girls), Goni has the gamin features of an evil-looking Leslie Caron, her dark-brown hair worn quite short —but not "butch"—to reveal pointed pixie ears. She wears an almost transparent micro-skirt, but don't you dare touch her. She is a Taurus and her husband is a weightlifter. Goni "only gives," she "don't get, except from him," actually quite a sunny fellow who's usually off somewhere on the top floor, repairing or building more contraptions.

"We charge them extra for that," giggles Goni as you bump your head descending the elaborate black metal winding staircase. Van Herwerden was right, there's nothing frightening about S/M Centrum. If you want terror, bring your own. Even this "dungeon" feels more like a postwar-America finished basement than a torture chamber. But instead of the home-sized pool table and lacquered pine bar, chains and manacles dangle from a mock-brick wall and there's a pillory, just like the "stocks" you saw as a kid in Williamsburg, Virginia. Say the word—*stoutertje*—and Goni will lock up your wrists and head and thrash your bottom soundly. Perhaps you'd rather go directly to jail. They've got one, eight square feet of cell surrounded by black bars that would look more at home in a Coney Island funhouse. But there are endless possibilities. You could bring your wife or girlfriends and rent whichever room suits your needs. Or have Goni and her mates join you and your business associates in conference.

JORDAAN

But explore Jordaan while you're here. Even many Amsterdammers aren't aware that between the Singel and Herengracht canals, in the vicinity of tiny Kørsjespoortsteeg, there are several gaudy *snol* shops housing some of the youngest, brassiest whores in town. Tiny Bergstraat is also active; number 14 isn't a brothel, although it resembles a dormitory of teen-age nymphomaniacs —not so eager they don't ask f20 to 30. Much street action.

If by now you require some peace and quiet, avoid CAFÉ NOL, Westerstraat 109. No whores, just good solid Jordaanese at their boisterous, practical-joking best. Instead make for CAFÉ TWO SWANS, Prinsengracht 124, where quiet, sober Dutchmen get phlegmatically drunk for bed while an accordion wheezes an ancient jig. And in a back corner, deep in lonely contemplation, the distinguished inventor of the electronic penis puffs on his white clay pipe.

The Electric Preservative

"Did he say something like 'Eureka I've found it' or 'Watson, come here, I want you' when he first discovered the principle?" one wonders out loud.

"No, he is really a very quiet, serious man," replies Nephew Charlie, who has agreed to act as interpreter for the inventor, a shy dimpled chap who, physically, rather resembles a bespectacled Nehemiah Persoff.

"What inspired him to do it, Nephew?"

"A man coming to his sex shop says if the wife buys this thing [describing a phallic-shaped 'face and neck massager' of the type sold in many American drugstores and beauty shops], she don't need him at all."

Faced with this vibrant problem and determined to bring the husband back into The Act, the inventor evolved, from the simple massager, that machine all Holland now knows as "The Electrical Preservative." It is little more than a heavy rubber condom, two wires connecting the tiny motor in the weighted tip extension to a rheostat powered by two 1.5-volt flashlight batteries (not nearly enough voltage to risk shock). The machine virtually electrifies the penis.

After reading the instruction sheet, you suggest he should have called it "The *Eclectic* Preservative":

"Even the most frigid woman has fully appeasement with this preservative. . . . The vibrations stimulate the circulation of the blood and the erection appears; therefore this is THE REMEDY for men who are impotent. With this preservative you can reach fully the appeasement viz. without any bodily exertion. The solution for men who have heart and back affections. By use the extension piece you will be more MAN. For cleaning and powdering (after use) an artificial penis will be delivered. For lonely women many possibilities (further explanation not possible). The duration of pairing can be lengthened by stopping the vibration or to let vibrating the preservative very slowly. . . ."

In the workshop atop the inventor's Haarlemmerdijk sex shop (he was formerly a maker of women's hats) you are privileged to observe his careful, punctual nephews soldering up the latest batch. Not only does he invite inquiries from American dealers—the Electrical Preservative retails here for f75 (about $23), and wholesales for about half that—but *any* traveler who appreciates a first-hand look at real Dutch craftsmanship, wants to see the original working model before it is sent to the Rijksmuseum, and is bored silly with diamond-cutting-plant tours, can arrange a visit by writing Haarlemmerdijk 78, or phoning 23–48–03. As you have undoubtedly already guessed, the inventor's name is Freek Post.

That Mr. Post's invention has encountered some sales resistance in Holland —though it is a big seller among tourists—is not surprising considering the traditional Dutch resistance to "self-improvement." The beauty parlor, for example, is still by no means as normal as the dentist. In many parts of the country, particularly among Calvinists in the north, beauty shops are "closed" houses—no sign out front, unlisted phone number, far more difficult to locate than brothels. Similarly, the Dutch can't stand psychiatrists. If you're seeing one, it's simply not done to tell anyone about it; they might think you're crazy. It's considered far more sensible to indulge your fetish than to pay some stranger to listen to you talk about it.

THE DUTCH: SOME GENERALIZATIONS

As a visitor you are in an enviable position. The Dutch have no xenophobia; instead, they have xenophilia. It has always been an advantage in Holland not to be Dutch. People are as tolerant of foreigners' eccentricities as of their own, which does not necessarily imply approval. Not accidentally, Holland has become a haven for the disgruntled youth of the West, but young visitors shouldn't have been surprised that Amsterdam authorities—and some naval personnel acting completely outside the law—overreacted when the hippies' occupation of the Dam Square appeared to preclude other peoples' use of it. "Show weakness in Holland and you will be protected," mused an elderly actor to his young mistress on the terrace of the Hotel Schiller, "show strength and you will be persecuted. . . . We are a narrow-minded but tolerant people living in a socialistic country run by capitalists who hold some very liberal views in their own conservative way."

These paradoxes are reflected in certain local laws that—however illogical, meddlesome, or ridiculous—cater to the national sins of envy and backbiting. Thus it is decreed that all Amsterdam butchers must close Monday afternoons —a law perhaps lobbied into existence by some powerful but lazy butchers fearful of their more enterprising competitors. Hairdressers Tuesday, green-grocers Wednesday, and so on. And nobody's open evenings—except of course the sex shops, some of which stay on till 4 A.M. And, of course, the whore parlors run round the clock. Any adult can pursue these latter two careers with one-tenth the red tape involved in opening a small cheese shop. You can smoke hash at age sixteen, but must wait until you're eighteen to see the film *Fanny Hill*. For all the freaky condoms sold and manufactured in Holland, abortion has only recently been legalized.

The Pill, in fairly widespread use for the past five years, has been as emancipating here as in England and America. Up to the early 1960s one could generalize that Dutch girls were as shy and reserved as their German contemporaries, warmer but less approachable sexually than Swedish girls. If dress is one criterion of lifestyle, the Dutch girls, especially those of Amsterdam, have blossomed marvelously. In the warmer months they appear to wear the flimsiest, shortest clothing seen in any major European capital. Of course they are easy to meet. Because Amsterdam's nightlife is so inexpensive it has never become terribly snobbish or clannish. And unescorted women are welcome in nearly all establishments.

GENERAL NIGHTLIFE

On weekdays bars close at 2 A.M., discothèques at 3, nightclubs and striptease at 4, and all an hour later on weekends. Taxis are expensive, but drivers honest. (However, ignore those early-morning touts in Rembrandtsplein who offer you excursions to blue-film houses, brothels with bathtubs, etc., at 50 to 100 guilders the trip. If you've seen one—and by now it is presumed you have—you've seen them all.) Don't forget, the meter charge includes your 15-percent tip. There are excellent tram connections; they run swiftly and frequently, but power goes off shortly after midnight. Considering that night life is fairly well centered in two proximate areas (neither terribly far from Jordaan and the red-light canals), the Leidseplein and the Rembrandtsplein, and that Amsterdam is so compact and flat—built to such a tiny scale that people never feel dwarfed or inhibited by their surroundings—by far the best methods of exploring it are by foot or bicycle.

If you've already seen striptease in Hamburg, the Amsterdam version—the clubs are centered around the Rembrandtsplein and adjacent Thorbeckeplein —can be as exciting as watching your sister take her clothes off in your grandmother's living room while your brother-in-law plays the accordion. But when such an atmosphere prevails in cabaret bars like CARROUSEL (no striptease) where the antics of the waiters, bartenders, *and* the patrons are a show and a half, you'll agree it's the perfect ambiance for making new friends. The Carrousel (Thorbeckeplein 20) is really what Amsterdam nightlife is all about. And so is the BIRDS discothèque, and the venerable CORRIDA CLUB.

But then, so is nearby Utrechtsestraat, apparently the only street in the center of town where streetwalkers are openly tolerated by the police. Some comparatively overpriced stalkers—from f40 to 50. But the real attractions are the flaming creatures who favor the corner of Keizersgracht, some so deft with their wigs, tiaras, and waxed legs that it is impossible to tell that they are actually transvestites. Fifty guilders for one is not quite sure what. And the opportunity to visit a real Dutch home.

Amsterdam nightlife is at its most vibrant and sociable around the Leidseplein. "Respectable" females of all ages and backgrounds—perhaps even some *uitgaande vrouwen, i.e.,* "good-time women"—are found in dozens of clubs, discothèques, bars, and pubs. A highly representative few: THE BLUE NOTE CLUB, LUCKY STAR discothèque, BAMBOO BAR (66 Lange Leidsedwarsstraat; maybe the best singles bar in town), and BRITANNIA PUB. And don't miss the terrace and cavernous indoor café of the AMERICAN HOTEL, or the CAFÉ REYNDERS and the CAFÉ EIJLDERS. Because few clubs charge admission (and that only nominal)—drinks are reasonably priced—and unescorted women are made to feel welcome in nearly all establishments, a man's best approach is the most obvious one: wander in and out of several places and see what suits you. If you must pursue the Jet Set, try beating on the very choosy door of GROOTE CLUB. The Amsterdam Hilton's FIETSOTHÈQUE is also considered quite chic, as are some of the private *partouzes* occurring around nearby Beethovenstraat. If you require a guilder-by-guilder guide to the tamer aspects of Amsterdam nightlife, get Arthur Frommer's KLM-sponsored *Surprising Amsterdam* or Thomas Vincent's *Fun Lover's Guide to Surprising Amsterdam,* both available throughout the city in cheap English-language pocket editions.

SUPRISINGLY GAY AMSTERDAM

Nothing is more indicative of Amsterdam's tolerance than the fact that most gay bars and clubs are within one to five minutes' walking distance of the Leidseplein, and not buried in some murky far-off corner of the city. Even if you are not homosexual, you are doubtless aware that Holland, and most specifically Amsterdam, is as a lamp to moths for homosexuals throughout the world. Each year tens of thousands arrive on vacation, many by the charter planeload. It is because of the liberal law that they come, plus the fact it has been in force for a number of years and thus presumably well accepted by Dutch society, and not because the Dutch make more or better homosexuals than anyone else.

In the Netherlands sexual relations between consenting members of the same sex are legal, if accomplished in private and without corrupting minors. (The age of consent has apparently been lowered to 16.) Only the youth are permitted to corrupt one another. To cite the most extreme example: if one party is exactly sixteen and the other is just a day shy of that age, the elder has technically violated the law, even if the younger is the seducer; but if both are fifteen there is no violation. (Apparently.)

One of the most curious things about Dutch homosexuals is that they appear to hold little of the thunder their fellows enjoy in societies where they are in fact social outcasts or subject to legal persecution. Contrary to New York City, here it is neither chic nor especially prudent to court their favor or to be seen in their bars, clubs, or restaurants if one is "straight." Nor do they have inordinate clout in the fashion or theatrical milieu; nor are they celebrities of café or discothèque society as in Paris. Dutch heterosexuals find them quite ordinary. Which is exactly the way the homosexuals like it. Most disappointed are those naïve homophile tourists who think they've journeyed to a kind of gay heaven where the streets are paved with beautiful available young men. There are such streets. There are such young men. But most of them charge from 20 to 100 guilders for their favors, depending on what the traffic can bear and how well hung it is. Unlike most heterosexual female prostitutes, many male hustlers find it difficult to avoid doing the thing for love as well as money.

Of the two main homosexual organizations, the C.O.C. and the D.O.K., the former is definitely more "serious," in the sense Europeans use that word. With substantial headquarters just off the Leidseplein at Korte Leidsedwarsstraat 49 (6–45–11) it is more than a mere cruising ground for lonely queers, though certainly it is that as well. C.O.C.—it was called "Shakespeare Club" before World War II—offers members a library, discussion and TV rooms, lecture and film programs, psychiatric and religious counseling (it has its own minister), and is engaged in a variety of political and social activity on behalf of homophiles. Members come from all walks of life and are thus assessed dues according to their incomes; of the seven thousand actives, some five hundred are lesbians. *Any* foreign adult, on production of a passport and f3,50, can effect temporary membership. Last year over fifteen thousand sought new friendships at the affable, sober bar and discothèque—decor: 1955 Seattle bowling alley. For the straight and simply curious visitor perhaps the most startling sight is the middle-aged men, in quiet conservative business suits, clinched in a slow foxtrot or holding hands in a corner.

On the door this evening is Jan Thijssens, a friendly mine of information and the operator of a hotel-booking service. Bear in mind that certain homophile hotels also function as lovers' hotels. Depending, then, on whether you seek love, discretion, or a combination plate, or if you're merely intent on booking a room, ascertaining prices, and basic amenities (gay hotels are often fully booked far in advance of the summer tourist season), contact Jan's HOTEL-BOOKING, 22 Frederiksplein (22–27–37; or 76–40–89, private). One C.O.C. member maintains that Amsterdam's many sympathetic hotels fall into only two classifications: ". . . those used by members of the C.O.C., the rest for people from D.O.K." To which he added, "If you come here to C.O.C. with your friend, there is no reason to lose him . . . in D.O.K. it's not so sure. . . ."

The D.O.K. club has a flash, bitchy discothèque at Singel 460 (23–75–03) whose members, in large part, are younger and more with-it than those of C.O.C. Many very beautiful boys, but several old queens as well, contribute disproportionately to the eclectic three-ring circus comprising the flesh-market bar, the rows of back booths, and the toilets. Much serious primping and combing at the men's-room mirrors, set *outside* the toilets to insure that you don't miss a trick. Temporary overseas membership f3.50. Just next door at Singel 458 the HOTEL COME BACK (67–519) gets f30 to 35 a night. Perhaps it should be called "Hotel Comeon" for many passersby are tempted to peer through the low picture window to admire the semiprecious antiques—silk-papered walls, cherubed chandelier—among the attractive young guests gathered amid the rococory. The dashing night clerk refused even to dignify with an answer a well-meant—but admittedly loaded—query: that one had heard a possibility of the house was four and more to a room. Draw your own conclusions. And the silk brocade curtains.

Here along the Singel f15 to 20 "business boys" abound, especially near the bridge at Heisteeg. Though homosexuals find several items of interest in most S/M shops, TEDDY BOY sex shop in Torensteeg, farther down the Singel canal, appears from its window display to specialize in homophilia; especially strong on KY-type lubricating jellies and on reading matter including the monthly *Seq,* which is noted for the reliability of its contact advertisements.

It's the law in Holland: males are not permitted to dress as females in public. Apparently no problem, however, with toreador pants suits, much favored by the f20 to 50 "better boys" of Leidsestraat, a main thoroughfare leading into the Leidseplein.

"You're not gay?" muses the affable night manager of HOTEL UNIQUE (Kerkstraat 37; 24–47–85). "It's all right, I had a father who wasn't either." Careful scrutiny through the peephole here, no women, not even lesbians, allowed. The Unique is generally acknowledged to be the best managed of Amsterdam's gay hotels, and not merely for the fact it has been in operation over twenty years. Recognizing that so many travelers come to Holland with basically one thing on their minds and are thus easy prey to unscrupulous hustlers and con artists, the Unique exercises a policy of strong paternalism. Those who prefer a freewheeling atmosphere should seek other houses. Here, "if you bring in a boy off the street, he must present to us his passport; and if we know him and he is a 'good boy,' of course you do as you wish with him in the privacy of your room. But we don't give the guest a key to the front door like some other places, and so he has no chance to be beaten or robbed by a 'bad boy.' Somebody is always here on the desk who knows most of the streetboys and barboys."

The Unique thus functions as a kind of lovers' hotel; all rooms either f42 or f54, whether for single or double occupancy.

By contrast, the WESTEND HOTEL (the peepholed door across the street) is strictly from Sparta—baths in the hall, but some may like that—charges f25 the night, adds f15 for each additional guest even if you've found him in their adjoining COSMO BAR, which is not unlikely. Kerkstraat is certainly the main drag of gay nightlife. At number 49 AERO BAR-HOTEL-RESTAURANT (22–77–28) features early-morning candlelight entrées (f11–15) and appetizers . . . insomniac homosexuals, lesbians, and many straight pairs too.

(You found only two other restaurants where one can enjoy a good meal in pleasant surroundings until 6 A.M.: RESTAURANT 66, Reguliersgracht 26, off the Thorbeckeplein, whose sole attraction is the good French cuisine. It is not at all gay, but of course welcomes all people, just as do *all* establishments cited throughout this book. Ditto CALIFORNIA, Leidsekruisstraat 12.)

Because homosexuals, like other Amsterdammers, have ample opportunity to drink and fraternize in public places into the wee hours, private parties and tight little cliques are not nearly the social factor they are in London, for example, where early closing hours, cumbersome and often bewildering club-membership policies, and the endemic secrecy of the English combine to make you feel the best things in life happen behind other people's closed doors. Amsterdam's not like that at all. Just wander, and see if you don't meet "somebody nice who takes you by the hand and leads you to the C.O.C." If you don't, try THE HUNTSMAN (Kerkstraat 334). If you still have bad luck, perhaps VOGEL the hairdresser (Herenstraat 3; 6–51–05) can change it with a new hair style. At INCOGNITO (Kerkstraat 59) you needn't be gay—except perhaps in the sense the word was used in Victorian England—nor even particularly physically attractive to have a fine time. A younger mélange of mannequins, lesbians, actors, artists, and odd lots of pretty, talky girls who don't know quite what to do with their lives at FIACRE (Lange Leidsedwarsstraat 19). Similar varied mix, but perhaps a little less talk, more music and action, at ELDORADO (Amstel 14, by the Muntplein).

If you are lesbian, TABU is for you (Leidsekruisstraat 19). But leave your husband across the street at number 14, ORFEO-BAR-HOTEL, (23–13–47) because Tabu is taboo for *all* males, except perhaps those in very convincing drag.

Homosexuals under twenty-one have their special society which meets each Sunday evening at Keizersgracht 138 (the club is open only on Sundays from 8 P.M. to midnight).

Some young homosexuals dance at STAR CLUB discothèque (Korte Leidsedwarsstraat) on weekends, though it is basically straight. If you're really on the prowl for the gay young set, you'll love JAMAICA! (Voetboogstraat 4). Old Dutch masters hanging on the softly lit red walls, a few youthful ones on the bar who might gleefully change your money, at extremely high rates of commission. They've become especially greedy since Formosa Tearoom closed (just around the corner on the Spui which has a fair quota of street hustlers after 10 P.M.). Until recently Formosa was *the* place for grass widows who preferred pretty, attentive young men even to their lap dogs. (The tearoom has, somewhat ironically, been transformed into a Madame Tussaud wax museum.) There are also some interesting young men in MACDONALD BAR (Reguliersdwarsstraat 11), REGINA (Amstelstraat 27), and KROKODIL (Amstelstraat 34).

If you enjoy exciting, authentic homosexual cabaret, planes leave Schipol frequently for Paris and Berlin. Don't even open one of the apparently gratis bags of nuts (two guilders if you open one; champagne up to $25 a bottle) at MADAME ARTHUR (Korte Leidsedwarsstraat 45). The ads say "every night a travesty show," and they're accurate.

Though closing hours for bars and clubs are firm, several hotel bars swing in the wee hours by the technicality of remaining open to serve their own houseguests.

Some hotels that are not unfriendly to homosexuals[1] are: NEW YORK (Herengracht 19; quite nice; 24–30–66), PALACE (Raadhuisstraat 33), ALBANY (Pieter de Hoochstraat 86B), TABU (Marnixstraat 386), and the AMSTEL I.T.C. (Frederiksplein 22; 22–27–37 which, as you may recall, is also the phone number of Jan's hotel booking service). And PHOENIX (Prinsengracht 418).

If you are insatiable, don't forget the Zeedijk area. They say the sea air does things to a man. Try the lovely XANTIPPE in the Zeedijk, TOP HIT (Warmoesstraat), the very mixed VRAAGTEKEN (Lange Neizel). And please do not forget our good old friend ARGOS BAR, the leather bar (Heintje Hoekssteeg 15).

On the beach? There's room at ZANDFOORT—reached in less than half an hour from the Central Station—for all kinds of people, but homosexuals prefer a section at the far end of the beach called ZEEZICHT. Also known as "Zee nicht," "nicht" meaning "cousin," a term of affection among homosexuals. In a sauna? The "best" people are said to be found in SAUNA THERMOS II (Raamstraat 33). And in the rather leathery SAUNA ATHLETIC (Nieuwendijk 100) even the most insensitive will discern what Angelo d'Arcangelo in his *The Homosexual Handbook,* described as "that high, unmistakable odor that permeates the atmosphere whenever two hot boys. . . ." And more of the same around the statue of Vondel in the VONDELPARK, and in the following toilets: at Frederiksplein; below the bridge on the right side of the Central Station; at Keizersgracht, corner Spuistraat; and near the D.O.K. on the Singel.

YOUTH AND DRUGS

An unmistakable odor also permeates PARADISIO (Weteringschans 8, near the Leidseplein), but it is the scent of hash, not sex. One of several such youth clubs supported by the city of Amsterdam (others have included KOSMOS and FANTASIO II, among the many *"Provadayas"* throughout the country where soft-tripping is permitted), Paradisio was converted from a church, offers light shows and rock groups. But most of the three hundred or more kids who jam it nightly are too busy smoking their brains out to notice. Membership is f3 and thereafter the entrance fee is f2 for anyone over age sixteen. The worst

[1]But of course all these, like all establishments cited in this book cater to all other well-behaved people as well.

time to come is in summer when the place is virtually taken over by young American tourists (201,000 Americans were among the two million foreigners who came to Amsterdam in 1971).

As is well known, soft drugs are tolerated by the Dutch authorities, but hard stuff and dealing in anything is strictly forbidden. What may not be generally well-known is that *possessing or using any sort of drug from marijuana up is officially illegal* in Holland. However, smoking hash or grass in places like Paradisio is okay. If all that sounds confusing consider: the Dutch are, at this writing, much too conservative, basically, and as hypocritical as any nation to enact a law legalizing drug use; but for some among the Dutch ruling Establishment the only good revolutionary is a stoned revolutionary. (See "Prague" chapter. See the U.S.A.) Perhaps that's what happened to the militant Provos.

Signs in Paradisio forbid pushing (of all the people arrested in Amsterdam for 1971 drug offenses, virtually all were charged with dealing, or possessing large amounts), but upstairs in the "lounges" during one July, 1970, visit it was the Kabul bazaar as several dealers circulated through the pungent funky fog, literally hawking their wares. "Offering a very nice chunk of Turkish Delight"—not your sorry green stuff but the rich brown color of the striking surface on a safety match box—25 guilders. Here's some pitch-black Nepalese, there a new shipment from the Lebanon. Careful with the Afghan, they say it's laced with catnip this month. Average price, about f2 a gram. (A local station broadcasts soft-drug prices regularly and gives crop reports.) Very good grass is hard to come by, but one young man—he swears his name is "Günter"—promises all the Golden Congo one can handle on two days' notice; about f75 the ounce.

The most De Quinceyesque room is a long narrow passage with facing benches that provide exactly forty seats—when you scrunch up—and facilitate the passing of the enormous roaches. Very few pipes in evidence. Soft drinks available, running to very sweet fruit juices. Good cinnamon pancakes, 85 Dutch cents.

Paradisio is a good place to find lodgings, and friends in communes; shouldn't cost you more than a guilder or two a night. And of course you will meet many Dutch activists here; one of them is attempting to launch a call-boy and brothel service for housewives.

ACTIVISTS

The Kabouters, successors to the Provos (who were perhaps more militant), have their headquarters at ATHENEUM bookstore on the Spui and may also be found at the commune at Singel 52, and at St. Pieterspoorsteeg 3. "Kabouter" is Dutch for "dwarf" or "brownie," and the whimsical but pragmatic utopianism of the group has caught on fast. In a recent municipal election they received 37,836 of 344,626 votes cast, won five of the 45 Amsterdam City Council seats. (The Free Sex Party got only 1058 votes.)

Dolle Mina (Herengracht 88) are latecomers by comparison with American women's liberation groups. They have similar objectives, but for the most part, different temperaments and tactics or at least the whimsical approach is more common here than it is in the United States. *"BAAS IN EIGEN BUIK"* ("Boss in our own bellies") is painted on many a tummy, and the girls aren't shy about baring them. In an attack on double standards the Dolle Mina have been whistling at, ogling, even pinching men in the streets, "just to let them know how it feels." Thus far everyone reports it feels just fine.

WOMEN'S LAB: "INTERNATIONAL CALLBOY"

Jan Bik has a callboy service which caters, "on a commercial erotic basis," to females of all sexual persuasions and "perversions" and all ages—from consent to well past the grand climacteric.

In his files Jan Bik has "about fifty male students, executives, athletes, etc. . . . mostly quite young attractive fellows. . . . We charge, but it is a pleasure as well as a hobby and a business. If she is a rich woman or well off she pays perhaps one hundred guilders for an hour. Even a woman of fifty, sixty, seventy is *very* interesting for a young man. Several in my files actually prefer women over fifty; such men are not difficult for me to find. And I myself enjoyed last night the woman of fifty-five you have just seen leave with her husband—he has spent an hour in the room upstairs with films and the seventeen-year-old girl who serves you milk—and the wife said to me she had only ever five orgasms with her husband. And she is having several with me. Some women over fifty, if you treat them properly, are moving and crying all the night. They pretend with their husbands for years and years until they come here and we talk. But you must not only love to fuck them. You must love them to fuck them."

Jan Bik is a very pleasant-looking young man with rosy complexion (and future), a strong, compact (five feet seven) build, and a high, wise forehead. The contrasting precision-cropped jet-black beard and gentle yet shrewd dark eyes cast him as a benevolent Mephistopheles. Born on the Fourth of July, 1938, Bik is a sympathetic, sensitive Cancerian with a passion, a mission, and a very Dutch business head: "First we will try to change people's minds about sex, second about *commercial sex in a commercial society.* Just till that point where we accept the people who do any erotic act for the daily bread, like any other human being doing any other job for a living.

"My people, the males as well as the females, are trying to make you believe that they *love* you, not simply to deliver mere sex. Of course a man cannot fake the orgasm and the erection. Either he has it or the woman knows he doesn't. In this business, as in life, a man can *never* be sure of a woman. But a woman can *always* be sure of a man. . . ."

HOUSEWIFE "WHORES"

Of course International Callboy is still in the laboratory phase. Comparatively few women are paying money for on-the-spot sex/love these days (if only because they don't know where to find it), and so comparatively few men are able to sell it.

But as long as men are buying and women are selling, INTERNATIONAL CALLGIRL is thriving. In the past two hours Jan Bik's three phones have rung sixteen times; about half the calls are from women answering his shrewd ads —placed in daily newspapers as well as sex contact magazines—among them two nurses from Rome who need some extra money to extend their holiday in Surprising Amsterdam.

Jan Bik indicates the large-scale map of Holland dotted with 1022 push-pins, each representing one of his "housewife whores" (the terminology is overly harsh, if accurate). A great many of the women are married—"the husband has to know about it or I don't accept a woman in my system"— some are divorced, not a few are students, secretaries, mothers, air hostesses, models, etc., who, but for Bik, couldn't afford that second car, new washer, or trip to Ibiza (people will do anything to be in Ibiza these days). Ages range from seventeen to forty-five, mostly twenty-five to thirty-five. Surprisingly few have ever traded sex/love for money before (except with their husbands), and all receive lovers "on a commercial erotic basis" in their own homes or apartments (except those few who work atop Jan's office); in many instances while the husband enjoys the brand-new color TV in the next room.

They don't come cheap. (Jan charges 50 to 100 guilders for each *new* introduction; the women charge a further 50 to 150 guilders—$16 to $47.) But they do come, if you cooperate, and that *you* will is nearly guaranteed. You're entitled to at least an hour, probably two, often with dinner. And perhaps breakfast and a lower fee next time. Few of the women have paying clients more than once a week, many no more than once a month. "With many of these girls it is really a hobby."

Jan Bik sends people "only where they will be treated well. And if there are problems, I warn in advance. Every man going should expect *to be loved*. She must make him *believe* it or it is not successful. All the girls all over Holland in our system really get their orgasms, or sometimes, if not possible, they convince their guests by acting. But if it is not a good situation and it does not improve, I cross her from the list. Like a man was telling me today . . . the girl was beautiful but the floor was dirty! And the supper was cold."

Any adult is welcome to drop by Jan Bik's neat four-room flat-cum-office any time from noon to 2 A.M., sip some cider, vermouth, or tea served by a beautiful Javanese handmaiden. ("You can go upstairs with her right now, or the blonde, Petra"—five feet nine, 38–26–36, long natural-blond hair—"for one hundred guilders each, plus ten guilders for films. And when you do it here of course there is never a charge for the contact.") Of the thousand women waiting all over Holland for your call (most in Amsterdam, The Hague, and Rotterdam), more than two hundred are represented by their photos in several large albums. Many nudes. Many in color. Jan Bik knows them the way a rabid Mets fan knows his team yearbook.

"She is brand new to this, costs f125, just divorced, she is twenty-six, likes chess, Saint-Saëns—the Organ Symphony and the piano concertos—and chocolates. This one looks twenty-four, yes? She is actually seventeen, but has been married so is legal majority, like all my people. I am very careful about that. If you want her tomorrow it is 150 because she is together with her sister in a first-class apartment here in Amsterdam, very luxurious. And these two beautiful black girls are models from Surinam. This one only does it when the man is on the sea."

"She only does it with sailors?"

"Yes . . . no, only when he is sailing. Her husband is a sailor."

"What about flagellation, Jan?"

"I have last month a man who pay 10,000 guilders for three hours."

"Ten thousand! Why didn't he go to Monique von Cleef?"

"No . . . he wanted to torture a woman. I found a student because he wants a girl who never do it before. . . . But this photo here, the blonde, she is masochist. You can beat her for hundred guilders. Her husband brings her here last Saturday. He is tired. This one is a doctor's wife. If she likes a client he won't pay after the first time. She needs sex very bad. And they are rich. They don't need money. And here this one, the black hair, is twenty-nine and has wonderful legs. But you see she is cool. A student from psychology. She is hundred fifty guilders. If you want a woman from a distance in a very luxurious environment . . . but she is very cool."

"What about a virgin, Jan? A real virgin? Doctor-tested, hospital-tested, no cavities?"

"I would only start looking for at least 3000 American dollars. The total price might be up to 7000 dollars. . . . Medically certified, of course. If the man is a really tender lover he could have her as a good girlfriend for weeks, months. Perhaps marry her. . . . But this one is only seventeen, a normal housewife so not a virgin; a very simple girl but very kind. She started here when she was sixteen. And of course we are always putting couples together. Like the Englishman and his lady—very Oxford, you see—who were leaving with the Dutch couple as you arrived. . . . Now this red-haired woman has very beautiful breasts; three children and no marks. But she is cruel. She doesn't convince the men I send. I warn them, but they like her photo. The brownhair she makes all her own dresses. She is lame. I get many requests for cripples. Some people like that. . . ."

"Jan . . . with all these girls answering your ads in the daily newspapers and the contact magazines and with all you seem to know about them . . . do you . . . do you try them?"

"For me," says Jan Bik, "it is primarily my responsibility to know how my clients will think of her. . . ." But he grins broadly. "I do it sometimes, if she's my type, and I like her, and she is really brand new. That's only personal pleasure. But only if I am sure I won't lose her with that."

The door opens, and a pert zoology student who lives here in Jordaan and a Welsh rabbit flop on the large damask-covered mattresses in Jan Bik's office. It's the six-o'clock swing shift as the statuesque blonde, Petra, and the Indonesian girl hurry off to their pottery class.

The Welsh girl is twenty-one, has long lovely long, long legs, peach-colored hair, and a sloe-eyed face that Marie Laurencin might have painted. She has slept with three men in her tiny life, two through the facilities of INTERNATIONAL CALLGIRL.

Jan Bik. Haarlemmerdijk 118, in the Jordaan: 22–27–85, or 25–24–97, or 22–89–07. Have the overseas operator add 020 for the Amsterdam area code.

"And don't forget," adds deheer Bik, "every first Saturday of the month we have a group sex party here. Couples only. On a commercial erotic basis. Bring ten dollars and an open mind, and we will do the rest."

GROUP SEX IS GROPING, BUT SWAPPING IS WHOPPING

Swapping is sweeping Holland. Not everybody is doing it, but a lot of people are trying. You won't find such elaborate surroundings as at Southern California's ranches, swings, or treehouses, but the Dutch meeting places are commendable for their easy accessibility (to singles as well as couples), lack of psychological ritual, low cost, and sensible, if not opulent facilities.

Consider, for example, SOCIETEIT MILO (Kruislaan 237; 35–75–05). Any adult—single males, females, couples, small groups—is welcome to drop by from 9 P.M. to 2 A.M. any week night. Like the 1100 other members, you pay a f30 yearly membership fee. At the convivial but low-pressure long bar, have a beer (all drinks f2,50 except Cognac and whiskey, which are f5). As a newcomer you are welcomed less as a sex object than as a fellow human being by the several couples, lone secretary-type young women (some of whom are apparently grossly underpaid in their daytime jobs), and merry off-duty executive specimens. And "all-round masseuses" too. In spite of Milo's proximity to the stadium of the famous Ajax football team, there are no TV games. But on the five square feet of home movie screen a salacious film is unwinding. And so are several snuggling couples in the booths. Try the on-premise group sauna (open 1 P.M. to 11 P.M. to the public with no special connection to Societeit Milo, though all members may use it), or take a sex shower. Two private fur-padded nookie rooms in the rear for couples who wish to be relatively alone. "Anything can happen here . . . suppose a group wants to see a live show and participate in it. We can make that," says Tony J. Klassen, "public relations director" of SWINGERS '70, a club which meets here every Saturday night (couples only).

Striptoe in the Tulips

By contrast, CANDY CLUB leans more to tentative "grope sex." Nothing much, other than a bit of amateur striptease, occurs. At this writing. On premise, that is. But this is to be expected, considering that Candy is located smack in the heart of Amsterdam at Thorbeckeplein 5, just off the Rembrandts-plein. Up to fifty couples squeeze into this discothèque, Friday and Saturday nights only. From 10 P.M. to 5 A.M. Best action at 2 A.M., when everyone is entitled to strip off while a hoedown caller directs the square dancers. Semi-potted house "plants" try to set a good example for the timid but anxious suburban couples.

Wall hooks.

One-time entrance fee f15 per couple, or f50 yearly membership. Drinks from f4 to f7. Singles may acquire partners (but only to accompany one inside, and to dance, chat, etc.) if they inquire of the jovial, rotund doorman. Candy's motto is: "Everything is allowed" (not really, though what you do when you leave and with whom is your own affaire) "but nothing has to be."

The outrageous, lavishly slick contact magazine *Candy* (no known connec-tion with the club) is on sale as you enter at f3,75, not to mention all over the nation. The hopeful couples' and singles' photos accompanying the "body copy" are somewhat more revealing and whimsical than those found in the praiseworthy American publication *Loving Couples:* a chained woman poses nude with a vacuum-cleaner hose suctioning her left nipple; many shaven vaginas; towels hanging from erections. But you get the idea.

Holland's most famous *"kunt u contacten . . . werelds meest unieke en bekendste besloten sexclub"* is 'tSCHOFT, Dr. Baumannplein 4, in the village of Halfweg, a ten-kilometer, ten-to-fifteen-guilder taxi from central Amster-dam. Singles welcome during the week (partners available), and couples. Couples only Saturday nights. Often a live show with audience participation. Jan Bik says 'tSchoft is "the best contact place. A bar, fifty people can be inside. Surroundings and people is very good." But don't take his word, phone Leo at 02907–5008 and find out.

SEX PARLORS

MASSAGE-INSTITUUT YVONNE (Spuistraat 122A; 67–561; from 10 P.M. to 2 A.M.) is, perhaps, the best situation of its kind in town, if only for the opportunity to meet the beautiful blond Yvonne herself. The place has the charm and discreet savoir-faire of an intimate French bordel, and the characteristic civilized informality of so much of Amsterdam's night life. No films, but occasionally a well-planned "lesbian show." Membership is only 10 guilders for the year; all drinks are 5 guilders.

"Have a drink with the girl and then to go with her is f125 for a very nice time. We have four girls. All must be multilingual. But when we need more on the weekend we can call them." Seven massage rooms, sauna, showers, flowers, but no bath. Member of the Diner's Club, according to Yvonne and Johann, and, so they say, the only club in Holland where you can charge sex on your Diner's Club card.

While you're in the neighborhood, don't forget that deheer Van Herwerden has moved CALIENTE-SADOMA shop from Korte Kolksteeg to larger quarters at Spuistraat 21.

If you prefer a nice piece of asp to Caliente's black-snake whips, SOCIETEIT CLEOPATRA CLUB INTERNATIONAL, a posh, modern establishment facing Lijnbaansgracht's picturesque canal, will not disappoint. But don't barge right in; phone 22–01–67 first and discuss your needs. Live shows with audience participation. Massage "sex en relaxen" girls at f100 a time, a strapping fellow for the ladies too. And, most important, a huge double bed in its own huge bedroom just off the ultramodern bar. From 8 P.M. to 5 A.M. F10 entrance-membership fee.

Incidentally, while in this charming area of pricey but fascinating antique shops just off the Leidseplein, have dinner at LA CACEROLA (Weteringstraat 41), an extremely worth-while late-night (to 1 A.M.) Spanish restaurant whose food is as appealing as its flamenco guitar. Call 65–397 and say, "Shalom." Highly recommend for the entire family.

Next day do the Rijksmuseum and afterwards relax at RELAX (Balthazar Floriszstraat 37–39; 76–21–76), a nearby no-nonsense sauna where, from 11 A.M. to midnight on weekdays and noon to 6 P.M. Saturday (closed Sunday), "you can have sex with the girl [four-girl selection] in a bubble bath, a pornographic color movie, love in the French way, and a sauna for altogether one hundred fifty guilders." All drinks at the tiny, dimly lit bar are f7.50. Russian massage too.

Nearly the same situation at SAUNA ATLANTIC, but, considering it is located back across town in Jordaan (Haarlemmerstraat 60; 62–361), the facilities are more mundane—but no less functional—than those of Sauna Relax. You can flounder around the Atlantic with any of three mermaids for 50 to 75 guilders, from 11 A.M. to half past midnight.

The Atlantic has some new competition of sorts—and so does every other house in Europe—for at Haarlemmerdijk 78, Mr. Freek Post, our old friend the distinguished inventor of the electronic penis, has transcended himself with . . . *the electronic woman!* She is f120 without her motor, and f150 with it. Inflates with air. Feelie bosom and fuzzy vaginal aperture. Dealer inquiries welcome.

Facilities at nearby S.M. Centrum still overshadow personnel, at least insofar as S/M is concerned. Consider, for example, the recent "treatment" of one client, bent on masochism.

Good news: On arrival he was immediately locked up in the basement jail by the young lady on duty.

No news: She thereupon went away.

Bad news: She let him out an hour later.

Forthwith he was ordered to pay a fee of f75 and summarily sent home. Mean, yes, but is it S/M?

GOOD NEWS

Fortunately there is always more good news than bad for visitors to Amsterdam. For example, THERMOS I male sauna (Egelantiersstraat 246) has now become an all-nighter, from midnight to 9 A.M. And the new THERMOS II (Raamstraat; noon to 11 P.M.) is already reckoned one of the best of its type on the Continent. If that's what you like.

If you don't, the outdoor bohamish cafés on the Rembrandtsplein are among the best in Europe for young adult heterosexual people who wish to acquaint themselves with the joys of life and each other. Have breakfast here every single day of your stay if you want a nice tan (the sun can be strong enough from late April to early October), for the tables all face the morning and noonday sun. All the better barrel organs pass here too.

(This is entirely off the subject, but how could you possibly have passed up a place with a wonderful name like CAFÉ PRONK—O.Z. Achterburgwal 37 —"in the middle of the red-light-district"?)

Whoever you are in this troubled world, Amsterdam remains a triumph of man's ingenuity, humor, rational compromise, and tolerance. And woman's too. It is suggested you save it for last on your intinerary if you're visiting several countries; or at least make it the mid-point oasis of your journey. If you come here first, other places (Copenhagen, for example) can be a letdown. (And don't be afraid to come in winter; it's milder than you may think.)

For Amsterdam contains more man/woman-made beauty—albeit a peaceful, unspectacular sort of environment—than any city visited by this book. And probably more woman/man-made opportunities for sex, love, and romance than any city its size in the world.

THE NOT-SO-PROVINCIAL PROVINCES

One can't ignore the Dutch provinces for two reasons: the Netherlands is so small and trains run so swiftly and frequently—but the railbed between The Hague and Amsterdam is bumpy; go first class if you can afford it—that virtually the whole country is a suburb of Amsterdam; and, most important, an incredible number of interesting things are happening out there.

Take Utrecht, for example, a mere thirty-five minutes by electric express, most of them along the fascinating Amsterdam-Rhine canal, which at times rises to a higher level than the parallel railbed. At first sight a somber city, more dull than cold perhaps. But it should be as proud of its many domestic tranquilizers as of its splendid fourteenth-century cathedral. Virtually in its shadow at Obrechtstraat 17, MASSAGESALON BARBARRA (71–81–89) has been advertising in the classifieds for at least two years. Barbarra herself is a somewhat blond, roughly forty-seven-year-old person who works "with the hand for fifty . . . and French massage with the condom and penis in the mouth is seventy-five. . . . Nothing more, but I can call another girl who will." If you aren't inhibited by the architecture of this, and the neighboring at-tached single-family stone units—rather like the gloomy working-class areas of London's East End—Barbarra's two scampering monkeys (caged) may persuade you to seek solace with IDA MASSAGE (7 Adriaanstraat; 129–23). Somewhat dingy digs, but at least here you have a sauna and films.

The thin goodbody found at nearby Hofstraat 10 (51–49–43) has her workshop up a ladder of steps for which perpendicular is a better adjective than steep. No, that is not her husband downstairs, "it's the telephone man." In case the two of you want to plug in (f35–50), goodbody can also call a good friend.

Like all these Utrecht ladies, the interestingly constructed blonde who lives (apparently) at Ondiep 24 (44–69–38) advertises and agreed to chat in her parlor (the others agreed to chat in their parlors too). She has somehow just purchased a new color TV and can expertly program your desires for 50 but might take 35. Nearby, in the district called Overvecht, in a large modern housing development, lives a young woman (Naxosdreef 143; 61–56–99) who resembles the typical swinging single girl. But she charges like a pro: "One hundred for what you want."

Should you prefer the great outdoors—and the Dutch countryside is so flat, though by no means tedious to the eye, it has the biggest sky in Europe and lots of water to watch—vice is waiting on the Vecht, a dreamy rural canal located about midway between the Amsterdam-Rhine canal and the great polders which begin where Overvecht ends. Thirty-four houseboats—gaily painted and with names like *Aurora, Mary Ann,* and *Agnes*—contain about seventy young and several pretty girls. All quite cheerful, for "this is a pleasant place to work, if one must do this work." From 15 to 25 guilders, but don't fall overboard.

In the city of Arnhem it's the Spijkerkwartier; in Rotterdam every sailor knows the Katendrecht. And in scores of towns and villages from Breda to the Belgian border the sex mill is becoming as common as the windmill.

THE HAGUE

LOVE AMONG THE DIPLOMATS

But it is in The Hague that things are really happening.

The Hague? That stronghold of Calvinism where by 8:30 P.M. one hardly sees a pedestrian or a moving car, let alone any sign of the sparkling, uninhibited nightlife just now getting under way in Amsterdam, a mere forty minutes away by train? In fact, there is no such *public* high life in this sober, deadly quiet city whose expatriate residents of the diplomatic and corporate communities have for years assured the folks back home that it's the dullest capital in Europe. To be sure, 10-to-20-guilder whores—some very young, others veterans of a dozen peace conferences—beckon from the dingy windows of Helenastraat, Doubletstraat, Nieuwe Molstraat, and Rozemarijnstraat. In the cozy *pieds-à-terres* off the little squares that fan out from the venerable Hotel des Indes, bored secretaries cloy bored executives with Vandermint and sex. And by 9 P.M. some of those well-informed diplomatic sources you're always reading about are perhaps probing the better homosexual bars—the best of them, coincidentally, within two minutes' walk of the American Embassy: MARS BAR, VENICE, and ADONIS.

Occasionally, but then only briefly, The Hague makes headlines. A Red Chinese diplomat attempts to defect. The Second Secretary of the Soviet Embassy is expelled by the Dutch government for spying. (The post is known here as the "Spy Seat.") The Brazilian Second Secretary, age thirty-four, is discovered mysteriously dead in his automobile, parked in a wooded rendezvous. But all such incidents are quickly hushed up by the police and the Dutch Ministry of Foreign Affairs. Nobody enjoys a scandal in The Hague. The Brazilian thing, for example, was immediately declared a "suicide" by the police, though there are, perhaps, more logical ways of accomplishing the job than cutting one's own throat.

All of which is only to say that the game of diplomacy does have its tensions. It should thus come as small surprise that for not a few delegates from your government, mine, and nearly everyone else's, "Congress in The Hague" often as not means sexual congress. For decades they've spent as much of their time and your taxes getting themselves whipped, *shtoomed,* bathed, and fellated in fancy houses as they have getting you fornicated at the peace tables.

MAISON CENT-SEPT

If you doubt such a broad generalization, take a hard look at the current state of the world. And if that contemplation strikes you as rather obscene, stake out MAISON CENT-SEPT, mark carefully the distinguished-looking clientele, trail several back to their official residences, then corroborate your findings with the staff.

Maison Cent-Sept is simply "the best house in the Netherlands," according to several men who should know, among them deheer Van Herwerden. You certainly can't fault the facilities, even if you don't quite understand them.

Behind the purple mosaic façade of Asterstraat 107 are two large floors of equipment and "hurting rooms" designed and constructed with such manifest expertise and insolent permanence that they frighten on sight. Is this a massage room or a Dürrenmatt conception of a mad Swiss millionaire's milk farm? What are all these ointments, salves, and liniments, and why do they keep them in blue bottles? What's in the medicine cabinets? Why do they need so many different kinds of vibromassagers, and what is this contraption that looks as if it's designed to give one an electric shock?

Crank-operated adjustable padded tables, yes. But with straps? The young masseuse assures you nothing more esoteric happens in this room than a genuine therapeutic or "sportif" massage (f25; f35 with a bit of sexual afterplay), but you're happy to get out and move down the corridor past a couple of locked doors to the "waiting room," actually the client's first stop. Here one chooses a masseuse from a rotating staff, at least three of whom are always on call. The young ladies are attractive after the fashion of Pieter Brueghel's people, and they are strong, having been selected and trained as disciplinarians, not lovers. Of course they stand ready to do most anything required. But Rhea, your guide, reckons nine of ten clients to be dedicated masochists who certainly aren't about to *pay* for the dubious privilege of ordering someone else about. And no member of the staff remembers a client requesting both punishment and straightforward intercourse during the whole of Cent-Sept's existence. Before you leave the first floor, you should have a look around the small bedchambers and the private quarters of the proprietors (who are at this time on holiday, it being the slack summer season). But they won't let you.

In the basement the big stuff happens. There's a dungeon with manacles and a large white cross painted on a gray brick wall. One end of a heavy chain is bolted to the wall at the top of the cross. From the other end dangles a thick iron collar that, when clamped round your neck, leaves not even enough slack for you to kneel and pray. Another area houses a large tiled sauna, capable of accommodating fifteen adults, if they are well-greased and squeeze a bit on the tiered, padded shelves. From this vantage point you have a good view of what's going on in the huge bathtub, no more than two feet from the bottom shelf.

The basic charge is f100 for an hour's run of the house (f150 per couple; some clients do bring their wives along), but Rhea reports that the average slave spends up to f300 for a really satisfying session. Reservations: 070–60–18–22 (070 is The Hague's area code. Dial 030 for Utrecht, and 020 for Amsterdam).

WILLY-NILLY

The facilities are less extensive at MAISON WILLY (Delistraat 23A; 070–60–32–48), but it has an enviable reputation among its select few clients who relish the privacy afforded and the f70-f100 extra-long sessions. No group stuff here. Though it's not far from the center of town, the management apparently has a complex about its quiet, semirural situation—there's a spectacular park nearby where deer run wild behind a fenced enclosure of forest and meadow—for the house number, "23A," is repeated no less than three times: on the gate, the window, and the door over which hangs a large gold coat of arms. Two hefty women in their early thirties putter about the garden, respond frankly enough to your serious inquiries, but won't let you go inside.

"Why do you need such big jugs in this business?"

"Hah. Hah. Ha. Good for flagellant. He like everything *strong.*"

"Who comes here?"

"Ohhhhh, many Dutch people. Many English and German. Embassady people. Very good people."

"Direct from the peace conferences, they come here to make war on themselves!"

"Hah."

"What do you do for them?"

"We hang them up. They like this most."

"Why are the Dutch like that?"

"From child, I think."

"But this is a very happy country."

"Only on the outside."

Lately four young ladies have been added for straight "sex intime" at f35. And f60 "with French," and f75 without a condom.

HETEROSEXUAL DUTCH TREATS

Not every house in The Hague caters to fetishists. The management of 44 WESTEINDE (right in the heart of town) believes in good old-fashioned man-on-the-top-woman-on-the-bottom heterosexual sex. And they've got the pretty girls to give it to you. Very comfortable, rather old-fashioned rooms. Some with mirrors, some with sheepskin comforters; f35 for fifteen minutes with a tall, leggy twenty-three-year-old blonde. f50 for half an hour. f75 for two girls, and f25 more for films. If you insist, they'll do a thrashing for around f50, but their hearts aren't really in it. Try to be here around 8:50 P.M. when the incredibly programmed chimes of a nearby cathedral (is this the one where Spinoza is buried?) tintinnabulate like the Moog Synthesizer.

Just next door to 44 Westeinde (which advertises as "MAISON ANGELIQUE"), but having absolutely no connection with it or its activities, is the new SAUNA WESTEINDE at 44a (39–99–51). Thoroughly and exclusively therapeutic. Some nights the sauna is co-ed. Admission f12.50.

The situation is quite different at the very basic parlor of nearby Westeinde 131 for their handout cards say "2 lieve meisjes zoeken Sex ontspanning." And the two limber but stacked blondes say "twenty five with a rubber, fifty without." Reservations, 33–04–08.

The versatile Chez Nana (Hoge Zand 100), which offered both male and female administraters is closed at this writing.

DISCIPLINE

Though scores of houses all over the Netherlands offer punishment services of comparatively high standard, and indeed some form of chastisement, however inept, is available from countless whores throughout Europe—but less so in southern regions—there are precious few governesses who can be accused of virtuosity, even in England and Germany, where the demand for their services is abnormally high. As in any highly specialized field, you can count the really great ones on the fingers of your hand or, if you prefer, the tentacula of a cat-o'-nine tails. And in most instances they are well known to each other, if not personally, at least by reputation. Thus, as a top nuclear physicist in Osaka probably knows of his counterparts in Dnepropetrovsk and Palo Alto, so the leading governesses of those cities, whoever they may be, probably could put you on to such as Frau Karen of Hamburg, Madams E or P of London; and the already-noted Jaky Duprey of Paris. Probably.

Baroness M.M.K. von Cleef

But it's odds on that virtually everyone in the trade has heard of Baroness Monique M.K. von Cleef. She is surely well known to certain film stars, lawmakers, and powerful executives and industrialists among the many rich and prominent Americans who have paid her homage—and fees of a thousand or more dollars. Several even had her on permanent retainer and called regularly at her penthouse on East 75th Street, New York City, during the late 1960s. So influential were some of her clients that when Newark, New Jersey, police raided her house there and confiscated her precious weapons and address books,[2] the contents of the latter were never made public. Though her conviction was later reversed on appeal to the United States Supreme Court (illegal search), the Baroness had already left America—not without much sadness—to return to her native Holland, and this comfortable modern apartment in Rigolettostraat. You're seated on a cool-pink velvet couch that could have come from Bloomingdale's while the Baroness fixes little cakes, soda pop, and genever in the kitchen. It's the slave's day off.

"You know, I was really sorry to leave," she calls from the kitchen, "and not just because you could make millions there. I had a lot of friends in America. But at first I almost didn't know anybody. Then I put an ad in _____, you know, the paper by 'Uncle Schapiro' in Brooklyn, and in three months I got more than eight thousand replies!"

It's a bright end-of-June afternoon in The Hague. You're sure there's not a single cloud over the whole of Holland. It's very quiet, the only sound the boxer dog (she's always had a boxer dog) snoring sputum into the otherwise immaculate high-pile gray wall-to-wall. Sunlight filters through the drawn blinds splaying Mondrian patterns on the nostalgic etchings and photographs. Brooklyn Bridge. Woolworth Building. Barry Gray. (She was interviewed on his radio show.) But there's nothing sentimental about that new Manhattan telephone directory right beside the phone. Many of the old clientele fly over regularly, and not only from New York. The Baroness acquired admirers throughout the American provinces when she had a sort of fuller brush road show.

"I got to see a lot of the country in my work . . . Dallas . . . Chicago, San Francisco. I was very careful always, like when I checked into the Beverly Hills Hotel, I locked the equipment away every night. . . . And to think I got raided in my own home in Newark! . . ."

The face is quite merry today, not at all unattractive. Fleshy, nearly dimpled, but with good cheekbones. There's a passing physical resemblance to Debbie Reynolds. The eyes are dark, deep-set in two caves under perfectly traced half-moon black brows. The shining white-blond hair is worn full, but cut just below the ears. The Baroness has a good figure, a shade stocky but certainly not fat. The hands are freckled, veiny, puffy. Her English is fluent,

---

[2] The Baroness had switched all the area codes. Her discretion, as regards her clients, borders on the fanatic. All clients are, of course, referred to only by a numbered code.

with just a slight accent to lend authority, though she's got that to spare, and an occasional curious syntax—oddly, it is vaguely Yiddish—that brings an unexpected humor to her speech. She is an aristocratic-looking woman, in the sense that she might have come from a solid bourgeois family and been widowed by a Rommel. In fact, she is a baroness by marriage and a native of Holland's oldest city, Maastricht, in Limbourg, that southern, very Catholic province of Holland that hangs, like a fetus suspended from a thin umbilical cord, between Belgium and Germany. (A painter from there once assured you that the Catholic Church has always been the biggest Provo in Holland.)

"Yes, I was married to an old baron." She pronounces the word to rhyme with "drone," accent on the second syllable.

"It was a perfect marriage. He was, of course, a masochist . . . but then he killed himself in a car crash. Very sad because it was a beautiful Ferrari car. . . . I was broken in by Tina, the mistress of the friend of my father, when I was seventeen. And since that time I have always had slaves. . . . No, I don't think there is a sudden interest in these things. I'm forty-five now, and when I was seventeen nothing was new. We just didn't talk so much about it then, we didn't think it was necessary. But nowadays people talk about every-thing!"

She seems incredulous that they do, sounding for an instant like a PTA mother who cannot quite keep up with the carryings-on of her hip teen-age daughters.

"Of course, the law has always been good in Holland. You could always do it here. . . ."

"What exactly do you do, Baroness?"

"Well, I'm just here by myself, and I'm strictly dominant. And if you're masochistic, you're all right. Otherwise you go to a place where maybe you get massage, maybe sex, maybe you get all kinds of things. But I'm strictly sadistic."

"Yes, but what do you *do!*"

"Well, I have slaves here, like I had everywhere else. . . ."

"And you, uh . . . whip them?"

"People always talk about *whipping!* You know there aren't too many real flagellants around. . . . I have a lot of fetishists. They like high heels and boots. And then I get an awful lot of people who like to act like little naughty children . . . who like me to spank them. I do a lot of spanking. And I put 'em in bibs . . . and in diapers . . . and in rubber sheets. . . ."

The last three activities are described in a singsong matter-of-fact lilt.

"There are different kinds of slaves, you know. I mean, I once had a friend with a dwarf from the Belgian Congo, he was deaf and dumb, somebody down there they cut his tongue out. . . . But of course I know a lot of transvestites . . . And I have a lot of bondage people. . . . In Staten Island I had a beautiful pillory. I rented a house there for seven or eight months. In Newark I kept the pillory in the attic. Only three weeks I was there before I got raided. . . ."

"My fee depends on how much time you want to spend. For instance, a man flew in this Sunday from Boston. I put him in a hotel, I pick him up later on, and we have a small session because he's tired from the plane. Then next day a little sightseeing—he wants to see some pictures in a museum. Then we have lunch and then a session. Then some dinner and another session. For four days he gives me thousand dollars. That's maybe six or eight sessions. For a weekend, say from Saturday afternoon to Sunday night, it's maybe four or five hundred dollars. Of course sometimes if I'm free I see people for two hundred guilders an hour. . . ."

"Actually, Baroness, you should have a cable address."

"You know, I *should* have a cable address."

"And you should work up a package deal with some airline or travel agency . . . sessions, sightseeing, meals . . . all-inclusive. . . ."

"Well, they can't stay here—there's only one bedroom. And I don't give them food, except maybe a little bread and water. . . ."

You both laugh at the joke.

"But I'm buying a house. Here's the new address. And I don't think the phone will change."

It rings.

"Excuse me, it's the slave hour."

The Baroness is on and off the phone almost before you have time to copy her richly engraved calling card: Cornelis Houtmanstr. 2A; phone 070–85–63–92.

"You know, I just got back from London. I've got a lot of people there. I'm staying at the _____. It's a wonderful place to go with slaves. They don't bother you as long as you don't mess up the furniture. (And it's only two hundred guilders a night.) And London is the best place to buy leather corsets. I get mine from Madame Medeq in Duke Street, Mayfair. And Johnny Sutcliff is very good for apparel. I can't show you a lot of things because it's all packed up for when I move, but if you really want to look at equipment, when you are in Hamburg go see my friends in the Herbertstrasse. They have a lot of stuff there for when they go out with their slaves. . . ."

"Go *out* with them!"

"Sure! A lot of people like to go out. Imagine you like to go out to dinner in a corset . . . or a chastity belt. . . . I *never go out* with my slaves or send them they don't have *something*. . . . "Either he has a little chain around his testicles or a thing for his cock. . . . Like the one who just called me. . . ."

"The slave hour?"

"Yes, from four to seven," she laughs. "That's when they can call me. He is calling from Ostend. He asks permission to take it off, he's had it on for a week now. . . ."

"You mean he calls for the . . . for the combination? to a lock?"

"*No,* of course he knows *how.* He has the key. He calls me for *permission.* Otherwise he wouldn't do it."

"Who are these people, Baroness? I mean what kind of people, not their names."

"Well, I have an earl in London, he has his nipples pierced. He comes here once in a while . . . and now he has the foreskin of his penis pierced and his wife is divorcing him. Because that's too much for her. The nipples, she could stand it. He's happy, he's been trying to get a divorce for years. He went to a gay doctor in London for the penis. . . . It hurt him a little, it got inflamed, but he liked it.

"Here, you've got some lint on your coat," observes the Baroness, not without a twinkle in her sharp eyes. "I brush it off for you." And as you prepare to take your leave she gives you a sharp, bracing brush-down with a big clothesbrush. During this gratuitous, unsolicited "treatment," one remembers the Ray Bradbury short story about a man who hid behind a dune and watched as Picasso doodled in the sand with a sharp stick: figures of birds, flowers, incredible three-eyed women. As the frustrated onlooker watched from behind the dune, he fantasied frantically that he might keep the tide from coming in. Similarly, one theorized about somehow "bottling" or otherwise preserving this brushing. . . .

After all, one of America's most important politicians once paid a lot of money for not much more than a brisk whisk brooming from the Baroness M. M. K. von Cleef.

What a house Bad has bought. At a spring 1972 visit to Monique's Cornelis Houtmanstr. 2A mansion just off the lovely Haagse Bos park (where romp her two boxers and Madame Blanche, the cat), you enjoy a tasty silver-serviced snack at sunset with the Baroness and her friend Pia, a formidable but pleasant (when she isn't working) Titanness who comes in from the Amsterdam canals Tuesday and Thursday to help out. Business is good.

Only halfway through the meal do you notice that the ivory disk hanging round the neck of the saccharine-faced blond young man in orange crepe dueling shirt who is serving has a number on it. This is not the slave's day off.

Upstairs in Monique's new torture chamber—which can best be described as "the best in Europe"—there is, amid the expected array of strappings and machines, a large board containing some seventeen numbered slave medallions . . . and empty spaces for eleven more. And pejorative signs like "FAGGOT!" and "SCHMUCK FAIRY-QUEEN" printed in reverse so their wearers can read them in the floor-to-ceiling mirror.

"Yes, I designed the room myself," says Monique. "My slaves made it, and I had a wonderful carpenter who, when he came here, wasn't, but I made him a slave too."

Her bedroom isn't bad either. Black satin sheets and pillows, elaborate silken canopy and exquisite tear-drop crystal chandelier after Landesman. Flanking the bed are centuries-old life-size figures of Christ and the Virgin, rescued from demolished churches by "one of my priest friends." In the hall there is an excruciating rendition of the Crucifixion. ("The Original Masochist.")

The Baroness is turned out like a fetishy Florence Nightingale in eight-inch spiked red boots, black mesh stockings, black satin hot pants, starched white middy blouse, black latex floor-length cape, and starched nurse's cap. And Red Cross armband. "I think it's good for people," she observes as she fingers the snout dangling from the suspended red bag. "It cleans you out."

A report in this evening's newspaper suggests that Xaviera Hollander, the Hapless Hooker, is returning to her native Holland. Apparently she, or a press agent, has suggested that Miss Hollander may set up a joint practice with "her friend" Monique.

"I don't even *know* this person!" growls the Baroness, and she slaps the red bag for emphasis. And you nervously *back* your way to the door, preparing to leave. "She couldn't even carry my enema bag."

MILLIONAIRE'S SEX CLUB AT POPULAR PRICES

Back to basics. The best sex club in The Hague is located in a fabulous townhouse at Groot Hertoginnelelaan 108 (65–86–92). The address is absolutely unpronounceable unless you were born in Holland, so just show it to the cabbie. A truly gorgeous blond girl greets you at the door with authority yet humor and says something like: "One-time membership is ten guilders, plus seventy-five for the whole evening, which includes films, live show, all drinks you want, the company of the girls—but not the intercourse, which is extra, but not required."

A few minutes spent in the comfortable grand salon and bar watching the big-screen porn films, observing the contented executives and embassy personnel lounge about the expensive couches, and you agree with the scrolled cards of MASSAGE INSTITUUT SEX-FILMCLUB CONTINENTAL: "In a delightful and refined setting, our idyllic bar included, our nymphs will see to it that you at last enjoy paradise on earth."

Who needs that unfound "Sexual Club for Millionaires" in Paris. Continental has twelve girls, fourteen lavish bedrooms. "You can have upstairs with girl fifty guilders, and seventy-five guilders for also French, and without condom is hundred guilders. Take your time."

It may be worthy of note here that virtually all Parisian and most Spanish and Roman professionals interviewed say they disdain condoms, on esthetic if not religious grounds. German whores insist a man use them, however, and so do most Scandinavians and English. Of course when you get yourself into higher price brackets and semi-pro situations all bets (and rubbers) are usually off. Only in Holland—such a country of choices—and especially The Hague, is the "with or without" option offered so frequently.

Vienna is next. The pros and other girls prefer a *gummi*, but in Vienna a little piece of strudel (in her mouth!) can sometimes work wonders.

VIENNA/ SALZBURG

AUSTRIA

The basic currency unit is the schilling, which can be divided into 100 groschen. At this writing you'll get about 23 schillings for each floating dollar. Thus each schilling equals approximately 4.3 U.S. cents. Austrian law says you can take no more than 15,000 schillings out of the country. Bring in as many as you like.

VIENNA

A "LOVERS' HOTEL"

From the façade it resembles the sort of building Sydney Greenstreet and Peter Lorre might choose for a rendezvous to plot the assassination of Stamboliski. But whether the structure derives its furtive, almost sinister character from the squints of the extremely oblong, heavily curtained double windows —five stories of them in the balconied graystone late-Austro-Hungarian pile —or your own imagination is immaterial. The only architecture on your mind is that of your *Wiener Mädel* as you two skip across the cobblestoned Tiefer Graben—in the heart of Vienna's Inner City—into number 30–32, passing beneath the elaborate cupola of iron filigree, smoked glass, and the glowing, promising legend: HOTEL ORIENT.

Had you the inclination to admire the lobby, you'd note the dark wood paneling all around, the inlaid antique clocks, the huge oil portraits of forgotten Hapsburg cavalry officers and their ladies. (In fact the decor hasn't changed much for over sixty-five years, save for a brief interruption when Russian officers used the Orient as a headquarters and—the oafs—destroyed the grand old *Grossvater* clock.) Pay in advance, get your key, the *Gummi* (condom) and a wink from the deskman, and off you go—the girl her heart aflutter like an aviary of canaries in heat. For this is the most atmospheric *Stunden* hotel in Vienna, and because this city has more short-time rooms rentable for romance than any other save Paris and Barcelona, that is saying a mouthful of *Strudel*.

Take suite No. 4, for example. By all means take it, for it's the most *Küss die Hand* in the house. The sitting room is roughly fifteen by twenty-five by sixteen feet high, dominated by two big paintings—one six feet long of an Arab muse in seraglio motif, the other an oil painting of a lady who might be the Empress Maria-Theresa but is not. There are several rickety chandeliers and a heavy white-marble fireplace on whose mantel sprawls an elaborate gold French Provincial clock mounted with cupids mounting one another. Black Forest-green carpeting, dragoon-maroon-clothed walls—probably colors of the Empire. In the far corner, at a pull of the frayed tassel, the matching maroon brocade drapes fall away to reveal an eight-by-twelve alcove encasing a canopied bed, delicate night table, and phone should you require champagne, apéritifs, or dainty snacks. Whether you need to or not, go to the bathroom, for it is enormous and fully marbled in a shade of faded orange-taupe you have never seen.

If you like to swim, you should have called in advance (63–72–07, or 63–73–07) to reserve suite No. 5. Here is the large sitting room-bedroom which, like No. 4, has a queen-size bed—smaller than king-size so lovers cannot wander far from each other—and those complicated Viennese bed-clothes you had better get used to: top sheet with a two-foot-diameter circle cut out to reveal the pretty pattern of the comforter underneath. Just opposite the bed is a round mirror of nearly twice that diameter. But here is the bathroom—one should really say the Natatorium! All fifteen by twelve of it gray marble—yes, the ceiling as well, with a dome that enhances the spectacular echo. There is no tub. Instead you have a plunge pool, reached by descending four marble steps. Careful now, hold on to both two-inch-diameter silvery tubular handrails. It's four feet deep down there, commodious enough to accommodate nearly three couples, about two if they are Viennese. (It is perhaps a cliché to observe that the Viennese eat too much pastry, but the Viennese do eat too much pastry.)

Four and Five are the Orient's finest suites. Each commands 220 schillings (about $9.50; one schilling equals about 4.3¢) for a period of two, maybe four hours. You liked No. 4 so much that you ran downstairs and begged the clerk to let you stay the night. His look suggested that you were trying to book a Lippizza stallion from the Spanish Riding School to run in the third at Wheeling Downs. Apparently these suites are so popular that only such a luminary as the Emperor Franz Joseph—who, however, is no longer the most popular man in Vienna. He is dead—could luxuriate in them for the whole night. The price would be 440 schillings. Maybe if you hum a little. . . . If you can't, rooms 6, 9, and 11, though smaller, provide an equal sense of saccharine sin, cost no more than 160 schillings *Stunden,* or 240 the night.

A pause to stress that no so-called *"Stunden"* hotel herein described is presumed to be exclusively a short-time, good-time house. One assumes that all establishments welcome the weary as warmly as the wanton. It was only mere chance that the ORIENT, GOLDENE SPINNE, BAUER, MODERN, WIESER, and NORDBAUM were all *besetzt* at your telephoned request for a single for the night. However, when you showed up shortly thereafter at each with a female on your arm and inquired after short-time double rooms—somehow the respective clerks all managed to come up with accommodations. Rack it up to romance in Vienna.

Opulent it may be, but admittedly the Orient is somewhat fusty, if not somewhat musty. Why, then, should a traveler use it when Vienna has some of the world's most glittering ordinary hotels—"ordinary" in the sense that they *only* rent rooms for days, not hours. Time and the money that buys it are the obvious answers. Some of us do not have a lifetime to consummate our affairs in the Grand Palaces of Europe. Moreover, Vienna's best hotels are usually heavily booked far in advance, with a long list of favored clients occupying the choice suites; in the Bristol and Sacher, for example, these can often cost four and more times what you'll pay at the Orient.

SACHER AND BRISTOL—NO STUNDEN *BUT GOOD ATMOSPHERE*

Undeniably, these two, among others, do offer a bit of that old Hapsburg hocus-pocus, this mainly reflected in the strategically placed mirrored screens and headboards of suites like SACHER NO. 11, and BRISTOL No. 265, and in the retinae of the help. It seems general policy to change the sheets two and three times a day, and the maids are a constant threat to swoop in at any hour to smooth a ripple, but this may be only because Austrians are so nosy, not because the guests are so carnal. (No rooms by the hour, of course, in either of these two fine hotels. They are cited here merely for their romantic atmosphere and history.)

Only the decor and a couple of night porters recall the Sacher's romantic past: as when the Archduke Eugen—or was it the Prince Otto?—came marching down the grand staircase, answering a wager, wearing only his sword on his hip and his mistress on his arm, and she no more than her stockings. Actually it may have been the *Prince* Eugen. Like all sentimental people the Viennese have lousy memories. Anyway it was apparently the same fellow who caused another scandal by jumping his horse over a coffin while its inhabitant's funeral was in full procession, and himself later died of syphilis.

Speaking of Prince Eugen (sounds something like "Oy, again?"), if the Orient is fully booked (and this is possible during the height of the Opera and Carnival Ball seasons), you'll obtain almost as much *Schmalz*—surely more than ordinary chicken fat—at PENSION MONOPOL (Prinz Eugenstrasse 68, 4th district) just across from the Belvedere Palace. Superb doubles from about 186 schillings, many overlooking a charming garden. (*Stunden,* 136 schillings.) Phone ahead, 65-85-26, because for years *Europe on $5 a Day* also touted the place to its readers. Moreover, the Monopol is set near the Roumanian and the Bulgarian Embassies. And you know those crazy Roumanians. And how about those hot-blooded Bulgarians? These, along with other Balkan cousins, have over the years given the Viennese much needed transfusions. And don't overlook the strong Hungarian and Bohemian influences—fed anew recently by the tragic, abortive revolutions; it is said that every Viennese has a Czech grandmother or a Hungarian grandfather.

A NATIONAL HERITAGE

But nothing is so purely Viennese as the *Stunden* hotels. Not the cavernous, drowsy *Kaffeehaus*[1]—one hears they are being replaced by fast-service espresso bars, but Vienna still has some 1460 coffeehouses—nor even the waltzes. The *Stunden* hotel is found in various parts of the city, but the most active examples are in or near the first district—the Inner City, which comprises historic landmarks like St. Stephen's Cathedral, smart shops and fine restaurants of the elegant Kärntnerstrasse, most of the general nightlife, and the principal red-light district. What is it about the nature of the Viennese that enables such an anachronism as the *Stunden* hotel to survive, if not thrive? After all, such capitals as London and New York have long since lost their "accommodation houses."

VIENNA WOMAN

Well, in the first, and possibly last, analysis, there is a little bit of operetta in the Viennese woman (not to mention a lot of pastry and champagne). She differs from the German female in that she has a great deal of *Scharm*, which is, apparently, not quite the same thing as "charm." The typical woman here is what is called *mollig*—that is, she is not exactly fat, but certainly never thin. Like Vienna, somewhere on the frontier. (*Mollig* also means, "cozy," "snug," "comfortable," and there is nothing so *mollig* as a good *Stunden* and no state of being these people prefer more.) Never is she the suffragette; rather, she prefers to subordinate herself to the man. (There are some notable exceptions like the Mahler woman, who was very strong-minded and wrote a great deal, but these only confuse the issue.) With all this you would expect the Viennese man to be quite overbearing, domineering. Well, he is not, being quite as passive as his uncomplicated little dumpling. The last thing this man likes is a big *Tumult* and he will go to some lengths to avoid one—usually to a little beach resort on the Adriatic; Viennese and Austrians are not particularly well traveled.

Though Austrians coincidentally share several of these characteristics, none of this has much to do with them. Viennese have as much in common with their countrymen from the Tyrol, for example, as with Hamburgers, with whom they have nothing at all in common. Austrians, according to seven Viennese you spoke to, simply do not exist, apart from the odd ski instructor or racing-car driver. Austria is a nation of peasants or, to put it more kindly, farmers. Why else does that enormous building on the Ring, which once housed the Austro-Hungarian Empire's Ministry of War, now belong to the

[1]The first, near St. Stephen's Cathedral, was opened in 1684.

Ministry of Agriculture? As almost everyone knows, this city remains as an anachronism from a time when it ruled an empire (of which Austria was only a province). But the Viennese don't know that. It is not that they are living in the past; it is simply that they are living in Vienna.

In all fairness to Austrians, it should be noted that even in its *Belle Époque* days, Vienna was a very bourgeois city; not so much because the bourgeois were bourgeois, but because the aristocracy were. And so it remains.

LAZY LOVE

The Germans, among others, insist that the Viennese are the worst lovers in Europe. Whether they fail to reach Teutonic standards because they are too sentimental or too "bourgeois" (if this is a mitigating factor) is uncertain. But the brain of any man who consistently goes to *Heurigen* and drinks two liters of the new wine will be hard put to send enough signals and blood to make the "*Peder*" stand at proper attention. However, there is general agreement among Viennese that it is very important to have "the affair," but mostly for reasons of health . . . like going to a spa.

Considering all that, and the real prudishness of these people—it is not uncommon for a man to spend all afternoon in bed with a woman and never once bring up the subject of sex—why *so many Stunden*? And what about those several restaurants that, though they refuse to admit it to strangers, maintain a few bedrooms behind the kitchen and, for favored customers, present the *Schlüssel* ("The Key!") with the check? And if the Viennese didn't invent the *séparée*, at least it is aboriginal to them.

"Romance" is the Viennese answer to all that. "Of course, sex is not the center of the relationship. Rather, it is more important to go and see the woman. To have coffee with her. And yes, to have champagne in bed with her."

Let's not overdo it. While all Vienna hotels cited as "*Stunden*" are patronized primarily by married lovers or families who may remain all night, a tiny amount of bed and *séparée* space in this town is available to other people. This is not always apparent (apparently). Take the HOTEL GOLDENE SPINNE (Golden Spider) at Linke Bahngasse 1A (3rd district), just outside the Ring and near the lovely canaled Stadtpark. Tradition has it that even when the city of Vienna had walls (the thoroughfare of the Ring encompassing the Inner City traces their line) a bawdy *Gasthaus* occupied this site. The present structure, a more than century-old six-story Hapsburg wedding cake, has been recently renovated inside and had its lobby lifted. Plopped like maraschino cherries in the new coat of white marble icing framing the entrance are the impressive plaques of several of Europe's great auto and touring clubs, assuring NATO and Common Market families this is their kind of accommodation. Moreover, for years *Europe on $5 a Day* touted it to students and little old ladies alike as "a traditional hotel, with much Viennese character. . . ." Character it may have on the upper floors, but characters it surely has on the first and mezzanine levels. In the words of a cabbie who commutes between the Golden Spider and the Ring red-light district, "Our grandfathers already loved here, and not with our grandmothers."

It is hard to imagine what the little old schoolteacher from Dubuque might do with room No. 8, for example, but younger Iowans might adore it. This is the *Bauernstube* (the farmer's room); indeed, his bed takes up half the space. It is an enormous adult crib whose floor-to-ceiling head- and footboards are handpainted after the *Dorftrottel* (village idiot) school in a colorful Alpine riot of tweety birds, giant zinnias, grapevines, and embracing marathon yodeling teams. The thing is fully covered by a mirrored roof and if you tire gazing up at yourselves, there's a tilted six-foot reflector on the side wall. Room No. 9 has a similar namby-pambiance. Napoleon Brandy, Beefeater Gin, Schlumberger Sekt are among the many soporifics on call from the well-stocked cellar any hour of the twenty-four. And they bring the Veuve Clicquot (480 schillings) in silver buckets.

Turnover is keen on the first and mezzanine floors, so no need to call ahead (72-44-86, or 73-17-42 if you must). But if you stood on the *Spiegel* (the mirror) of room 8 or 9 you couldn't touch these two for the whole night. *Stunden* rates vary, 100 to 150 schillings, including taxes, service, and contraceptives. Overnight doubles to 280 schillings.

PROSTITUTION

Prostitution is unequivocally legal in Austria—none of this "toleration" hypocrisy. Vienna has more than a thousand "registered" prostitutes and untold unofficial ones ranging from once-a-month secretaries and shopgirls and very beautiful call girls, to the old *Quetschen* and several of their illegitimate grandchildren who prowl the park behind the Prater ferris wheel (2nd district), ambush you from Rustenschacher Allee. Their *Stunden* is the cold hard ground, their price from 30 to 100 schillings. Colleagues in the 4th and 6th districts (roughly between the Ring and the Westbahnhof) sometimes bring off a 200-schilling killing, more often they settle for 100 to 150, but they do enjoy the comforts of cafés somewhere not far from the Gaudenzdorfer Gürtel, and PAPAGENO off the Naschmarkt, Vienna's mini-Covent Garden. With some few exceptions these women are of interest only to social scientists, though perhaps you might enjoy matching them to some neighborhood *Stunden*. A not very taxing game, as the women are often schnorring close by. Should you grow weary, the hotel ZU DEN DREI KRONEN has modest, tidy doubles at 125 schillings for a couple of hours, 159 for the night (Schleifmühl-gasse 25; 57-32-89). And so does the WIENZEILE (Gaudenzdorfer Gürtel 63; 83-56-82), though room No. 4 commands a premium 200 schillings, apparently because they are still paying off its mirrors and "Naked Maja" reproduction. A desk clerk here thought it quite wasteful that you occupy No. 4 on your own, suggested several alternatives. Someone at HOTEL BAUER (Graumangasse 3-5; 83-11-61 might be equally sympathetic.

WESTEND AND WESTBAHN

There are some peppy, reasonably attractive young girls awaiting you and your 200 schillings in and around the intersection of Kaiserstrasse and Maria-hilferstrasse, the latter a long, wide, winding, middle-class shopping thoroughfare (yes, all of those) that runs from the Ring to the Westbahnhof. (Several connoisseurs insist these, and not the more celebrated streetwalkers of the 1st district, are the choicest in Vienna.) These girls spoke so highly of HOTEL WESTEND you hurried over to nearby Fügerstrasse 3—didn't even bother to phone 57-67-29—and were impressed by its intimate late-night espresso bar, happy to renew there old friendships made four and one-half minutes ago out on Mariahilferstrasse and confused by the room rents: 85 schillings for two hours, 100 for the night.

Actually your confusion began earlier in the evening in a fruitless search for the HOTEL WEST*BAHN*, which, a friend had assured you, was a kind of "*Stunden* Hilton": lots of modern gimmicks and a catalogue from whose photos a couple could select a chamber with just the right combinations of colored lighting effects and angled mirrors to suit their mood or birth sign. Could the Westend and the Westbahn be one and the same? No, says the Westend clerk, there is indeed a Westbahn, just to the right of the Westbahn-hof station, though he can't vouch for the catalogue part.

And so there is, at Pelzgasse 1 (92-14-80), but it doesn't look very promising. It's a big place, recently modernized, lobby done in cold "airport waiting room," some rubber plants and plastic children, and their parents who may have read about the Westbahn in *Europe on $5 a Day*. You're sure you've got it all wrong because of the desk clerk's reaction to your standard opening, in halting Viennese: "*Haben Sie ein Zimmer mit einem Spiegel bei der . . . uhhhhh . . . ceiling?*"

"A *mirror!* in the *ceiling!* In a nice respectable family hotel like this!" No, he's never heard of such a terrible thing, and you'd better get out of here before you frighten the children.

But as you start for the door he calls you aside. Actually he *has* heard rumors, but only *rumors* mind you. Whispering now, he suggests you proceed down Pelzgasse, go in the very next doorway on the left and there you may, perhaps, find someone who knows something about this kind of situation.

You follow the direction scrupulously, marching thirty feet or more down Pelzgasse, taking the first door on the left—which is actually a swinging door —into a small Formica-floored room containing absolutely nothing but a perfect replica of a glassed-in cinema box office, complete with whisper tube. But there's nobody in it.

Suddenly the door behind the booth opens and who should appear? Who? Well, surely not Engelbert Dollfuss. It is none other than . . . the desk man from the Westbahn next door, with a move and a grin right out of a Marx Brothers movie. In fact, the Westbahn is *two* hotels, and this "annex" is one of the fastest, vastest *Stunden* in town. Though Marcel was much too busy running back and forth to show you many of the mirrors or the nice 87-to-150-schilling rooms, the "Spiegels" you saw would make Sam proud[2] and the whole place should get Academy Awards for lighting and special effects.

SCHLAMPEREI *AND THE POLICE*

By curious local law, brothels are forbidden in Vienna, though they flourish in several provincial cities like Innsbruck and Salzburg. The police do their best to insure that lovers' hotels provide only rooms, not "love," but have enough trouble dealing with their own *Schlamperei*. What's *Schlamperei? Schlamperei* is when a big-city police force attempts to form a cadre of sixty policewomen, only to discover suddenly that more than half (thirty-six) of the candidates—all aged nineteen to twenty-five—are . . . pregnant. Pregnant because some official with *Schlamperei* to spare had, in early 1967, housed the female recruits in the same building as the males.

Of course, the Vienna police also spend a great deal of time prowling the streets—mostly in the Inner City 1st district—checking the *Büchl* (license) of each streetwalker to insure that she has recently visited a doctor as required by federal law. Vienna's *Unterwelt* are an eternal problem; many *Galeristen* (small-time criminals who play an illegal card game called *Stoss* in cafés of the 3rd and 4th districts) are attached to the whores for one reason and another. Perhaps the earth-shattering edict of November 17, 1969, was in response to the particularly violent gang wars of the period, culminating in a bad shooting in the PICCADILLY BAR (Annagasse 12; at that time Vienna's leading gay bar, just off the Kärntnerstrasse). Suddenly, after three centuries' occupation of the heart of elegant Vienna the choice girls of the 1st district

[2]Only in the sense that his name happens to mean "mirror" in German. This goofy charade at the Westbahn and its "annex" occurred in the spring of 1970 and then was played out again, exactly as recounted here, in the spring of 1972. In both instances the principals were the same.

were to be moved. Moved to where? To hear the strumpets' wail—not to mention the complaints of several prominent Kärntnerstrasse businessmen who argued that the whores brought valuable tourist trade to this so-called *luxus strich*—and to scan the sensational newspaper headlines, you'd have thought the cops were sending them to the Alps or at least the Vienna Woods. In fact the new law forbade them from hustling within fifteen yards of the Graben and directed them to relinquish their territory in all streets intersecting the Kärntnerstrasse, with the exception of the Krugerstrasse. This was like moving them from the corner of Fifth Avenue and 56th Street to 56th nearer Madison.

"Come and have a nice love," they beckon in Krugerstrasse, not three minutes' walk from the Sacher and the Opera. Thirty-odd young women and old girls, as assorted in shape and size as the contents of a five-pound box of chocolates. "Such a nice love we go make right here in the HOTEL MODERN [Krugerstrasse 11; 52-43-66.] Yesssssss, they got a *Spiegel* in the ceiling in Number Eight room or on the wall in Number One. C'mon . . . three hundred for me, ninety-five for the room, five for the *Gummi*," begs a big nougat-filled naughty opposite No. 10, where Beethoven spent a lot of time with the Countess Erdödy. When it rains, business picks up in the KRÜGERSTUBERL, and even when it doesn't you'll find a few blazing young blondes playing an Austrian version of Kalooki in CAFÉ PICCOLO[3] around the corner in Akademiestrasse. Outside you meet *"Zuper-Katze"* and friend.

BUT NO WHIPS

"C'mon . . . Suck the peder too. That's the penis by the man. Six hundred for we two girls." But that's about as kinky as Krugerstrasse gets. In Vienna even the prostitutes are too sentimental to give you a sound whipping, though no doubt they'd be willing to try, just to help a pal. This is, after all, the city of Freud. In sex or in love, if you must hurt, you hurt the soul, not the body. Besides, whipping is *uncomfortable*!

If you are looking for directions, the policeman standing outside the station-house in Herrengasse is usually one who speaks English. But let's hope you don't draw Inspector Karl Silberbauer, the former SS sergeant who arrested Anne Frank. (*Some Schlamperei?*)

Like all 1st district street girls, those in Seilergasse arrive at their posts at 11 P.M. sharp; no one is served after 4 A.M. Ditto Tuchlauben.

In the smart Kohlmarkt, (Chopin lived at No. 9 and Haydn studied at No. 11), you've a choice of *Portnoy's Beschwerde* by day or some really attractive *Afferl* (monkeys, of course) walking around by night. No one's the wiser

---

[3]No soliciting occurs in either of these two cafés.

if you choose the WIESER, nearby at Neubadgasse 4 (63-83-30). In fact the Kohlmarkt girls seem to prefer it to others. A somewhat spartan but very discreet and well-scrubbed hotel, the Wieser had no single accommodation for you but suggested a 100-schilling double (recommending No. 8 with an overhead mirror) in hopes you'd find someone to share it, for it is quite large. They said. If you had no friends in Vienna, a leggy redhead met outside in the street volunteered to help out if you'd give her 300 schillings to buy nail polish remover. Otherwise there was always the CAFÉ RABE just next door in Wallnerstrasse.

CAFÉ RABE

The Rabe is the classic Vienna café of its type, with the angriest, readiest stock of liver dumplings in town. They really put it to a man in this place, but by law it is the customer who must make the first move in the transaction. In the Rabe that amounts to no more than a quiet cough, though if you kept your nose in your *kleiner Brauner* and just observed the action and the table-hopping from midmorning to midnight—most entertaining in early evening—Rudi, the black-tied waiter with the Chaplin mustache, wouldn't even want to know about it.

OPPORTUNE CLUBS AND BARS

It is difficult to establish precisely how the hostesses in certain *séparée* clubs can afford so many helpings of *Tafelspitz,* the superb boiled beef that the Sacher does better than any place in the world. Many of them are knockouts and most are prepared to go all fifteen rounds, so unless you have a large research grant and an insatiable thirst for knowledge, not to mention "champagne," you are advised not to venture into their *séparées.*

No narcotics in OPIUMHÖHLE (Habsburgergasse 4), just friendly "*Anier-mädchen*" and a cozy *séparée.* CHEZ NOUS (Kärntnerstrasse 10; open to 5:30 A.M.) has a posh back room whose chairs convert to sofas quicker than you can say Bernadette Castro; and BB BAR (Mariahilferstrasse 8; 3 P.M. to 5 A.M.) has a mini-hotel in the back of the house with a whole row of roomy, comfy booths and, according to their advertisements, a harem of "teen-agers, waiting for *You!*" (However despite these gimmicks nothing illegal occurs in any of these three establishments.)

ELEGANT LADIES AND NICE GIRLS

Please don't squeeze the *Scharm* in EDEN-BAR (Liliengasse 2; open to 4 A.M.; 1st district; 52-74-50, booking recommended) for this is café society's favorite rendezvous, the most appropriate *boîte* to toast Viennese womanhood. In exactly the same elegant league is SPLENDID-BAR (Jasomirgottstrasse 3). Here, dressed to the nines, you may dance till 4.

As for Viennese *girls*—they are charming, fragile, very gay, quite approachable if the thing is handled delicately (though they often travel in pairs), and shy. (Which may explain why the bathrooms of so many hotels are larger than the bedrooms; the dears sometimes take hours of coaxing, and it thus wouldn't do for the thing to be a mere watercloset.) Why not begin your search in the bohemian (small "b") CAFE HAWELKA, Dorotheergasse 6, surprisingly the only one of its kind here. Don't miss it!

If you'd prefer her in a dress, albeit a very short one, ATRIUM (Schwarzenbergplatz 10; 4th) and SCOTCH (Parkring 10; 1st) are two discothèques offering some lovely opportunities. (People standing outside the former sometimes know a thing or two about the exotic drug trade with the East.[4]) In summer the VOLKSGARTEN (Burgring; 1st) is perhaps your best bet of all for meeting pretty girls. Less well-known to tourists but a great stopover favorite of airline stewardesses is COCKPIT CLUB (Rechte Wienzeile 23; 56-34-96). An extraordinary little bar is LOOS-BAR (Kärntner Durchgang), designed by Adolf Loos in 1907. High and middle-class society. Pretty girls too.

If you think you can talk your way into the exclusive OPERA BALL, the social event of the Vienna year, try your luck on Mrs. Christl Schönfeldt, the lady who handles invitations. Dr. Mühlbauer of the Austrian Tourist Office (63-96-71) has her number.

"Can't miss" shopgirl, secretary pickup spots include the WIENERWALD in Annagasse. While you're in this lively little street (where Schubert attended school—at No. 3, 3A—while a member of the Vienna Boys' Choir) just off the Kärntnerstrasse, look in on the espresso bar next door and TENNE jazz house. And woo-woo, goody-goody, there are lots of cuties in CHATTANOOGA snack bar-discothèque (appropriately, Graben 29).

FINGERLN *AND FILMS*

If all else fails in the 1st district, RONDELL KINO (Riemergasse 11) runs some of the worst sex films in the solar system, and it's the only cinema where you can smoke and eat. Lot of *Fingerln* going on in here. (This Viennese term is as difficult to spell as it is to translate, but it refers to a kind of "petting.") Rondell also has some striptease (performers hang around the lobby during intermission) and a very funny topless bar in the cellar.

There's much advanced *Fingerln* occurring in the *séparées* and boxes of

[4]As in several European cities drug users tend to gravitate to the sidewalks near selected discothèques, despite protestations of the respective managements.

many striptease houses, and some daring-do on stage as well. Sometimes, when nobody's looking, they take it all off. The ways of all flesh-peelers are pretty much the same, though cabbies (many of whom are very stupid, very corrupt, or simple *Ausländers* like yourself when it comes to finding your way about town) have their favorite clubs, usually obvious 1st district spots like MOULIN ROUGE and MAXIM. But members of Vienna's foreign press corps insist the rowdy CAFÉ RENZ (Zirkusgasse 50; 2nd district near the Prater) offers the worst or best—depending on your point of view—of this ancient art. While the girls are doing their raunchy beauty-contest parade up and down the runway, you have ample opportunity to establish whether in fact they do represent all those far-flung reaches of the old Empire, as the drag narrator claims. Hopefully the recent modernization efforts won't dilute the flavor.

The third is a classic red-light district and it would be discourteous of you to leave without dropping by CAFÉ TOSKA in Praterstrasse to help the old mathematics professor and his girlfriends do his crossword. The Toska sirens sing in a lower key than those at Café Rabe; here you do not feel the eyes of every *Trutschel* boring through to your billfold. Not that a few young Czechs and Hungarians aren't quite anxious to waltz you across the street to the HOTEL NORDBAHN (Praterstrasse 72; 24-54-33)—200 schillings for the Refugee fund, 50 for the room. (Johann Strauss II composed "The Blue Danube" at Praterstrasse 54.)

BATHING & NUDISM

If you can somehow avoid the prowling *Schlumpen* just beyond the Prater ferris wheel you will arrive at the largest and best-equipped sauna—more like a small resort compound—you have yet seen in Europe: PRATER SAUNA (Waldsteingartenstrasse 135; 24-74-73 and 24-53-27). While the Viennese are a bit too conservative to throw it open to all the sexes all the time, they have dipped one big toe in the water (more than can be said for public facilities in New York), having designated Monday evening from 7 P.M. *Familien* night.

Apparently Austria is the birthplace of modern nudism—the practice took hold here sometime in the early nineteenth century. There are some thirty designated areas throughout the country where you can legally go around without your clothes in the open air. Most convenient to Vienna is the LOBAU, a general bathing compound and bird sanctuary just outside the city on the Danube; in certain sections if you have the marks of bathing trunks people look at you as if you were a leper. Homosexual nudists have also staked out a small portion of this area.

HOMOSEXUALS

If you are homosexual, stay away from this country. The best meeting places are the jails, where you may spend two or three years if you are caught violating what is perhaps the most strict and rigidly enforced statute on the Continent. "The only thing we are allowed to do is masturbate in front of each other," laments a dapper businessman, typical of the middle-aged regulars at ALTE LAMPE (bar-discothèque-restaurant, Heumühlgasse 13; 4th district) who are occasionally joined by lesbians and the odd drag queen. If you resemble a Vienna Boys' Choir boy, someone may buy you dinner here, or at KOPERNIKUS STÜBERL (Corneliusgasse 8; 6th). Competition is keener at the rather flash BRÜCKENSTÜBERL, 22 Tiefer Graben (1st) near the Hotel Orient. In the recent good old days, when Larraine and the Baron stood in drag on Opera Ball reception lines to have their hands kissed by unwitting dignitaries, then waltzed over to the PICCADILLY BAR (Annagasse 12, 1st) to collect their wagers, this was one of the funniest nightspots in town. Now, like all homosexual rendezvous you have visited, it is pitch-black from the outside, nearly so inside. Since the bad gangland shooting here, the ambiance—homosexuals, pimps, streetwalkers, etc.—is neatly summed up by Fritz the bartender's response to your "Guten Abend."

"Forget me."

Apparently the law regarding homosexual relations has been recently modified—but nobody is quite sure yet what this means. Vienna gay clubs appear to be as inhibited—little identification as regards signs or marquees, poorly lit within—as they ever were; and surely public attitudes have not changed much. As to men dancing together in public, local ordinances and police attitudes govern. In Vienna, for example, "the law does not forbid it, but it does not permit it to be encouraged," a typically Viennese solution.

A CHICKEN IN THE POT, A KEY WITH THE CHECK

A "Heuriger" is an inn where people consume lots of chicken amid lots of balloons and can get quickly *sinnlos betrunken* while a *Schrammel* band plays selections from Strauss and *South Pacific*. Most tourists know they can find this kind of situation in a place called "Grinzing," which is why many Viennese prefer less crowded and, in fact, more charmingly situated suburbs like Nussdorf and Heiligenstädt. *Heurigen* like H. AND R. RIBITSCH (Heiligenstädterstrasse 215, 19th; 36-24-47) charge about 50 schillings a head for the feast, drink, and fun. Should your lady pass out, 80 schillings more bring the *Schlüssel* to a quiet double room. In case she wakes up it might have a mirror in the ceiling, and if not, surely a magnificent view of the Danube.

SALZBURG

As every Austrian schoolboy knows, Salzburg has a world-famous music festival—founded in 1920 by such as Richard Strauss, Max Reinhardt, and Hugo von Hofmannsthal—Mozart's birthplace, and four whorehouses. Three of these latter are in Herrengasse on the west bank of the swiftly flowing Salzach River, which bisects this magnificently situated town of 120,000. But if you can distract a constable from his chess in the police station near Mirabell-Platz, he will assure you the house at Steingasse 24 on the east bank is by far the best of a mediocre lot.

A PLEASURE HOUSE

Located in a narrow, cobblestoned, tunneled, perfectly preserved medieval street, with a sensational vista across the river to the imposing ramparts of the Hohensalzburg Fortress and the majestic Eastern Alps that surround the city and its countryside, Steingasse 24 has perhaps the most breathtaking situation of any bordel site in Europe. And the most charming. With its bright stucco façade and the kooky cast of the purple lettering announcing MAISON DE PLAISIR, they might be selling gingerbread cookies inside. But the young girls hanging out between the gaily painted shutters assure you they're not—200 schillings. (A couple of farmer's beds, a few ceiling mirrors.) You may spend double and more than that, and wait until 5 A.M. to woo a girl away from OSTERIA, a chalk-white pseudo*cave* nightclub just across from Maison de Plaisir.

DISCOTHÈQUES AND OTHER MEETING-PLACES

Austria is Grand Fenwick with a railroad, and even in summer a good portion of Salzburgers are tucked up tight just after the last light has glinted off the baroque Fischer von Erlach churches that give the town much of its unique architectural character. But at least one striptease house, CASANOVA BAR, rocks Linzergasse (No. 23) all night.

Daughters of some of Salzburg's best families may be met in HEXENTURM discothèque, off St. Julienstrasse; direct entrance via passageway to the ELMO HOTEL, doubles to 130 schillings.

"With mirrors?"

"*Ja,* but only for shaving."

On the west bank of the Salzach only an Alpine mountain goat could easily negotiate the cobblestoned incline of Herrengasse, and perhaps only he would be enthralled with what he found at MAXIM—No. 18; and its neighbors at Nos. 20 and 22A. The latter two are part of an ancient stone fortress-like compound built into the side of a mountain, complete with turrets and musket portals. Sometimes the girls cavort in the courtyard in their skivvies, an appropriate word, for a faded, peeling sign warns "Off-Limits to U.S. Forces." 150 to 250 schillings.

Descend to the cafés GLOCKENSPIEL and TOMASELLI (Residenz Platz and Alter Markt, respectively), among the best meeting places in town. If you prefer a local wildflower ("good" girls only) to the foreign adventuresses, students, and divorcees—for Salzburg's cultural attractions make it a mecca for lone female travelers—it's certainly not hard to attract attention. Because so comparatively little occurs to disturb the equilibrium of this part of the world, the slightest untoward action on your part—a sneeze will do nicely —is greeted by a chorus of geishalike titters and giggles. As the waitress arrives with the pastry tray a dozen or more fluttering eyes zero in on you, as if by your selection you will reveal all sorts of embarrassing little secrets and idiosyncrasies. Salzburg is certainly a very friendly city to the *Ausländer,* if one can somehow overcome the paranoia that he's walking around with his fly open.

It had better not be. Remember the hard line on homosexuals. But the Salzburg police are still too busy with that chess game to take much notice of the TIROLER WEINSTUBEN (Steingasse 51), or what's happening in MIRABELLE PARK after dark, or in the toilets of the railway station. Or on the west bank promenade of the swiftly flowing Salzach, "where everything is forbidden but nothing is discouraged."

Caution: the SALZBURG TOURIST OFFICE (Auerspergstrasse 7) city map reads "Herrengasse" but the street signs read "Herrngasse." Better check on this with them before you climb that hill.

HAMBURG

Frankfurt, Hanover
and 14 City Mini-tour

WEST GERMANY

The basic unit of currency is the coveted Deutsche mark, which can be divided into 100 pfennigs. At this writing you'll get about 3.18 marks for each floating dollar. Thus each mark equals about 30 U.S. cents. You can bring in or take out as many marks as you can carry.

SEX SHOWS

Colibri: Past Its Prime

"The next lady will work with her own body," announces the *Conferencier* of the COLIBRI (Grosse Freiheit 34—"Great Freedom Street"), until recently the most erotic strip club in Hamburg's lickerish St. Pauli quarter, and therefore in all Europe. This will be novel, for in the previous fifty minutes an assortment of cigarette holders, broom handles, and live reptiles have half disappeared between the shapely legs of fifteen naked lovelies, the capacity and dexterity of whose voracious vaginas would be the envy of the most expert circus sword-swallower or contortionist. Strictly speaking, the performers are not completely naked: local law specifies that some article of clothing must always be in contact with some part of the body. With characteristic literalness—this time tempered by Teutonic whimsy—compliance takes the form of a small scarf worn at the neck, or a ribbon tied around a nipple.

Two girls have carried on a brief but exciting simultaneous affair with the wriggling ends of a three-foot bull snake; two others, housed in an enormous champagne glass have, between breaststrokes, joined their pudenda in what was surely more than a mere charade of lesbian love; and there were several vignette and tableaux stagings of rapes, seductions, and sadomasochistic orgies so explicit and realistic—though the parts of males were taken by females with appropriate costumes and appliances—that you could describe them as stag films come to life. And as a sort of running gag, a six-foot-tall blonde with a startlingly angelic face has punctuated the little dramas by executing full splits at the apron of the small stage and emerging having suctioned up a *pfennig* coin (100 pfennigs equal one *Deutsche Mark,* one DM equals about 30¢) with her remarkably adroit orifice.

You are seated—your eyes crotch-level to the performers—among several dozen well-dressed district-manager and sales-executive types (if there is a sailor among them, he is wearing his conservative Sunday best) who applaud with polite enthusiasm each time she executes her little trick. Germans have a nice appreciation for specialized talents and clever gadgets—the more esoteric and gimmicky the better.

Salambo: Team Sex

There is nothing especially esoteric about an attractive young couple copulating, nor even, in this permissive age, about the fact that there is another pair also doing it next to them on the same sheepskin-covered bed. But when the thing is lit by a battery of kleig lights, strobes, and multicolored gels worthy of a fairly lavish Off-Broadway musical; accompanied by stereophonically reproduced orgasm sounds and suitable background music; narrated by an ridiculously buxom drag queen play-by-play announcer who also does her own color commentary; and when all this is happening on the apron of a twenty-foot-wide stage in full view of an audience of more than one hundred people, including several well-to-do young couples on the edge of their front-row seats—well, even in Hamburg, even on the Grosse Freiheit, when SALAMBO first presented live sexual intercourse between members of the opposite sex it was considered a major breakthrough. Up to then, Colibri had been considered the hottest house in town. In fact, the authorities were not quite sure *what* to do when producer-director René Durand brought his showmanship to Salambo, but he convinced them that his spectacles were more in the nature of "theatrical performances" than mere sex shows. Apparently this was the rationale that for years enabled Colibri to get by with much stronger stuff than anyone else.

Unquestionably Durand does the best show in town, and not merely the most erotic. The "team sex" (as Dave, the sound-and-light man who came to Hamburg from Liverpool when the Beatles did, calls it) was preceded by a series of topically satirical sketches juxtaposing color slides and live nudes with a few touches worthy of Dali or Jacques Tati. One satire on the Arab-Israeli question began with a rear-screen projection of the late President Nasser minus his mustache. This was added by a long-legged lovely, wearing only a helmet, who positioned her jet-black pubes just beneath Gamal's ample nostrils. The political spoofs were followed by the most intricate and exhaustive demonstration of lesbian lovemaking you can imagine.

At your meeting with René Durand he was in the process of renovating the nearby Star Club, first a cinema and more recently a cavernous hard-rock discothèque where the Beatles once did $45-a-week gigs. (Let's hope he somehow preserves the wonderful photo murals of Paul, John, Ringo, George, Pete, and Stu, looking so prehistoric that Mathew Brady might have shot them.) In this new Salambo, Durand dreams of doing for erotic theater what Paris's Alain Bernardin did for striptease. Europe's "first Theater Erotikon" promises vast Felliniesque orgies, naked girls flying in from high in the wings, sadomasochistic ballets staged à la Busby Berkeley, choreographed after Gene Kelly.

There is a great deal of jealousy among St. Pauli's entrepreneurs. Some weeks after you left town you heard that Salambo's show had been temporarily suspended by the police (to reopen *sans* stage copulation) on the grounds that "one of the couples wasn't married." But there is no reason to suspect that one can't see similar exhibitions either here or in whichever house can convince the authorities of their "theatricality." Surely Durand, who has been in Hamburg for many years, will more than survive. (A dashing black-bearded Frenchman, he defiantly carries numbers tatooed on his left wrist, memento of three years in Buchenwald.)

Backstage you chatted with several of Salambo's cast, being particularly interested to learn that the two swarthy Algerian male members of the sex team did "five or six shows a night, six nights a week." You returned the following night, sat through five shows just to see if they could do it and were amazed to report that they did. All five shows. As in Copenhagen, however, there is some difficulty getting native males to perform consistently. (No problem at all finding capable and willing German females.) The brunette German girl and her partner are true Stanislavskians: they're married. So is the second fellow—the one who's wearing the high laced boots throughout his performance—but not to his blond Glasgow-born partner. He claims his wife has no idea what he does for a living. According to the blonde, neither does he. As she prances into her dressing room after the last show, she's complaining with all the fervor, and in exactly the tone, of a West End veteran who's had her lines stepped on by some ingenue just up from the provinces.

"That bloomin' bastard couldn't get it up all night. My gums are killin' me!" But then that is, after all—at least in Hamburg—show business.

THE BAWD AND THE BEAUTIFUL

This is the most beautiful of the large German cities. Of its 285 square miles, 139 are made up of rivers, lakes, canals, woodland, or meadows. In the free and Hanseatic city of Hamburg a stripper has for years been at liberty to display her pubes, but she cannot chop down a tree in her own backyard, once its diameter has reached ten inches, without obtaining permission from the authorities. And so for every dollar spent per week among St. Pauli's more than 500 bars, strip houses, jazz cellars, sailor dives, discothèques, dirty-movie houses, and brothels (over $25 million a year) Hamburg has a tree. Over five hundred thousand trees, 94,000 of them lining the streets. Among St. Pauli's 11,000 residents only 3000 are registered prostitutes, slightly less than one for each of Hamburg's 3800 horticultural firms. But in all Hamburg there are an estimated 10 to 15,000 prostitutes, not to mention uncounted numbers of part-timers, amateurs, strippers, and bar hostesses. And, until recently, you could throw in a few lady wrestlers. In the mud.

Hamburg: the bawd and the beautiful. A city of five symphony orchestras, eleven theaters, and a justly renowned State Opera—yet many of its 1.8 million yearly visitors (almost one for each Hamburger or each ten square meters of flowerbed or lawn) never get out of a whore's bed.

Connoisseurs and statisticians agree (the average tourist dallies no more than two nights) that if one wants to sin efficiently and economically, and cares little for elegance, St. Pauli's anything but square quarter mile offers more opportunities than Billy Graham's vision of Sodom. Hamburg has been a free port since the Emperor Barbarossa's 1189 declaration, and St. Pauli rose to ill fame as a sailor's quarter during the late eighteenth century. Today, as West Germany's premier port and Europe's third, Hamburg has more consulates (sixty-six) than any city but New York and hosts ships from eleven hundred ports around the world. In a given month a whore may entertain representatives of the entire "free" world, not to mention goodly portions of the rest of it. But Hamburg cannot live on seamen alone. Seventeen hundred ocean-going ships a month may promise plenty of customers, but they've not much time: the port and its seventeen hundred dockworkers are second to none for speed and efficiency. Eighty thousand banana bunches will be unloaded in fifteen hours; thirty-one thousand tons of mineral oil in ten hours; eight hundred automobiles in seven and a half hours. Which is why the whores of Herbertstrasse must be prepared to handle up to ten men an hour.

And so St. Pauli is first and foremost a playground for the middle classes of Germany and neighboring Northern Europe whose time is not quite so limited—a kind of Deutsche Disneyland whose most typical merrymakers are whole families of German and Scandinavian rubberneckers, the latter just stopping by for a beer on their way to Spain. "It is the juxtaposition of obscenities with round German shop-keeping faces and solid German shop-keeping virtues that makes St. Pauli's commercial sex obscene," wrote George Feifer for *Holiday*. But it would seem that the quality of obscenity loses little, whether the eye of the beholder belongs to the dirndled Frisian schoolgirl, the ubiquitous Japanese businessman, or the Cuban merchant seaman (who hasn't seen anything quite like Hamburg since Castro ran Superman and the Bongo Club out of Cuba)—all of whom may feel equally at home in St. Pauli.

PITFALLS, AND HINTS FOR REVELERS

The best of the Hamburg establishments cannot, in comparison with public entertainments in other cities, be termed mere striptease. These are *sex shows*. That of the Colibri or Salambo, for example, ranks with any Parisian private "exhibition" you may find, but all it costs you is the rather high-priced drink (Colibri, 11,75DM; Salambo, 18,30DM) and you're in and out in twenty-five to fifty minutes, well worth it if that's what you want to see. The performers are well paid—about 150DM a night in Colibri, perhaps nearly double that for Salambo's professional fornicators—and profit is made from turnover, every fifty minutes a new show and a new packed house. Beware of clubs with long intervals between shows; they may need the time to sell you lots of drinks to compensate for their mediocre attractions. As a general rule, the less exciting the show, the more on-premise opportunities for mingling with the hostesses or even the performers. The following suggestions can be applied not only to visitors to St. Pauli but throughout the Federal Republic.

Never take a commissionaire's word for it. Well-run establishments have no need for these touts dressed as doorkeepers. By law these parasites—some euphemistically attired in nautical uniforms—are not permitted to lay hands on you, even in a friendly manner. They and the waiters and the bargirls all have a keen fiduciary interest in what you spend. They will try all tricks to increase your bill and will take ingenious pains to distract you from the drink card. Promises of *ultimate* on-premise sexual rewards accompanied by demands for more drinks usually won't be kept. However there is often ample opportunity for intimate hanky-panky short of coitus.

Be a good literal German and *point* to the drink you want on the list. Quantity and quality are of crucial importance. One can order, for example, cola-Rum with 2, 4 or 8 centiliters of rum. A vague order of "whiskey" will inevitably lead to the most expensive disaster. If you are not adamant, your hostess will always be served a double. Always settle with the waiter after each order. The law requires that there be reasonably priced drinks in all establishments; take the trouble to examine the drink card closely to find them, often on the back. In those equitable places that offer nonstop shows, no one expects you to buy more than one drink at from 7,50 to 19DM. All establishments with a show should offer reduced prices for orders after your first drink.

After the war and through the late 1950s, St. Pauli was largely controlled by racketeers and gangsters. Beatings and even murder were a constant threat to revelers. The dangers are largely past, thanks to an erstwhile civil servant, Kurt Falck, who brought law and order to St. Pauli with threats and the revocation of many licenses. However, it is suggested that one take only as much money as he is prepared to spend, and only in bills of small denomination. The character of the touts, bouncers, and enforcers has not necessarily changed—in fact a few of them are ex-convicts or minor concentration camp straw bosses—but the Hamburg police do a creditable enough job enforcing the rules and regulations that Herr Falck instituted. If one does have problems he should avoid discussions with employees, and should never accept an invitation to step into the back room. *This could be dangerous.* Instead call the DAVIDSWACHE POLICE STATION, conveniently located on the Reeperbahn and appropriately neoned (blue). Dial 41-11-1, ext. 6251, and ask for the chief, whose name at this writing is Kretschmar. If he's no longer in office, all the better. Say you're an old friend of Chief Kretschmar and they should send a man around posthaste. All-purpose police or emergency number is 110. (Thanks to Dr. Walter Stahl of the "7 to 7" guides.)

GREAT FREEDOM STREET: FLEA MARKET OF FLESH

The Grosse Freiheit has the length of an American football field and the flavor of a carnival—more appropriately "carnal ville"—midway. A flea market of flesh is Great Freedom Street, but not a free market. Yet there is a certain economy to St. Pauli's hottest strip, for within its swift length one can, in a short time, see enough live sex shows to last him a lifetime—or at least until he returns to Hamburg.

Were the *Guide Michelin* to rate sex shows with symbols as appropriate as those used for restaurants, Salambo might receive some ultimate accolade —that is, four Volkswagen stickshifts, two Ipunkt Space Needles, and the Eiffel Tower for upright dealings and efficiency. On the same scale you might award two stickshifts and the Leaning Tower of Pisa to TABU (Grosse Freiheit 16). A nearby club compensates for its comparatively tame shows by stocking the house with friendly companions some of whom, usually for no more than the price of a drink (5cl. Scotch, 18DM), will hold the spectator's hand, or whatever else may be in need of holding. Customers enjoy reciprocal privileges. Meanwhile, on stage, this night the headliner is a miniature redhead having a go with the nine-inch wooden whacker of a ventriloquist's dummy, followed by a very dirty blonde who decides the audience has more need of her pubic hairs than she does. ("Pubic Enemy Number One, that one," mutters an English shopkeeper.) The hard blue-white glare emitted from the translucent glass stage floor—not unlike the effect of raising the windowshade at sunrise after an all-night poker game—makes it difficult to distinguish the female hostesses from the few but active transvestites.

Some may call it pubescent hairsplitting, but there are certain advantages (none of them financial, however) to having an on-premise rendezvous with a striptease performer, as opposed to the ordinary bar hostesses. Aside from the undeniable pleasure some men take in seeing the lady perform for the mob, all the while fantasying about having her later, there is the practical advantage of seeing on approval *all* of what one may be buying. Certain clubs in St. Pauli are very popular with stage-door Johns. In these the price of a bottle of wine (35DM) doubles if the girl closes the *séparée* curtain, and perhaps doubles again if you choose a performer rather than a hostess.

Relaxing, low, low pressure, nearly charming, is CAFÉ MEHRER (Grosse Freiheit 5–7) with its late-1930s dance band and mirrored decor. No strippers, *séparées,* or sex shows, just 61 telephones and large, number placards at every table. This is *"Dial-a-whore,"* but their motto is, "If you don't call us, we'll call you." However, you're made to feel as welcome taking a reflective two-hour *Kännchen Bohnenkaffe*-break (3DM) as the exhilarated party of foxtrotting Osaka businessmen who need expend no more than the one DM entrance fee and a 5,40 Cola mit Rum for the pleasure of their partners' company (usually a blonde or redhead). Preliminaries can be delightful here, but you don't even have to buy that 3DM French tickler from the men's-room attendant. Just promise a Mehrer girl 100DM and she will immediately accompany you next door to one of the LUXOR HOTEL's 25DM *Stunden* rooms. As the Luxor also offers a small selection of bedmates at its own little second-floor bar, its rooms are sometimes fully booked, but HOTEL HACKER across the street usually has several durable doubles available at 20DM. The nearby HOTEL PARDON appears to be "modified American plan": you'll have some difficulty obtaining accommodations without also taking one of their 30-to-50DM barflies to bed.

Back down on Great Freedom Street they're running big sales on *Gruppensex* (but programs are subject to change without notice). A brute in a yachtsman's cap tries to haul you into "Fuckshow Fuckshow Naturell, blackman whitewoman, whiteman blackwoman, one beer and one brandy ninefifty, take a look for nothing." EROTICA is showing films twice as blue and half as cheap as anything you'll see in London's Soho or in New York City for that matter. Torture show at REGINA and MONTPARNASSE—whips, chains, a naked girl with a black widow spider crawling down her breast. MOONLIGHT's commissionaire assures you there's "real hot stuff inside," but he'd do better quoting Temple Fielding's rave review: "One of the dirtiest, rottenest, most tasteless shows we've ever seen anywhere, anytime. Ugh!"

Caution: those beckoning beauties in ROXA BAR's front window—enticingly attired in strategically apertured lingerie, some sporting color-coordinated pubic hair—are Loreleis to all but homosexuals. Similarly surgical are many of the proffered breasts in several bars hereabouts. Beware the BARCELONA (Grosse Freiheit 35). In this rough-and-tumble temple of transvestites, strong sweaty hands wait to tear at the testicles of unsuspecting male visitors. They grab with the glee of men hoping to see a girl get her skirts blown over her head in a fun house, but if they succeed, you'll feel more than chagrin . . . sometimes for a week or longer. The 25DM drinks don't numb the pain. Ha! Ha! Ha! Barcelona is a big St. Pauli joke because everyone hopes you'll mistake it for *BAR'CELONA* (Wohlwillstrasse 21), an eminently civilized transvestite cabaret where the *chansons* and comedy can be outstanding, and the stripteasers unbelievable—even when naked these boys look like girls. (Same ownership as Berlin's excellent Chez Nous.)

If you like animals, you'll hate the HIPPODROM (Grosse Freiheit 12). A drunk donkey named Knorke challenges you to ride him once around the circus ring. Avoid being thrown into the sawdust and you win a bottle of dubious champagne. Three anonymous horses and their near-nude equestriennes also offer rides, the latter varicose and bellicose, in the *séparée*. Pray for these unfortunates at St. Joseph's Church, right in the heart of Grosse Freiheit.

After mass (adults 7:15, children 9:15) the BLAUER PETER (Grosse Freiheit 10) is de rigueur for that last supper. As much a cliché as a tradition for its clever soups, Dixie dance band, and dinner-jacketed doyens representing some of Hamburg's oldest money—some of it very old indeed, considering the city was founded by Charlemagne in 811—the Blauer Peter is open from 3 A.M. to 10 A.M. to coincide with the 4-to-5-A.M. closing of most St. Pauli cabarets. (However, many bars and cafés remain open to 7 or 8 A.M., and some around the clock.) Perfect timing for off-duty strippers and haute-coutured business girls; the former may also be found, at this time, in SKANDINAVIAN EXPRESS (Hein Hoyerstrasse 12) and the latter, in the early evening, on the public terrace of the Alster. Sunday morning St. Pauli revelers head for the very theatrical FISCHMARKT in nearby Grosse Elbstrasse. Other days you may want to dry out in the mixed sauna of the SAUNABAD HOTEL (open 10 A.M. to 4 A.M., closed Sundays) just around the corner from Grosse Freiheit in Kleine Freiheit, next to the bakery whose window display this week features birthday cakes decorated with candy black spiders.

DRUGS AND YOUTH

There's more to Great Freedom Street than pros and peelers. There are peddlers, several of them sprawled on the sidewalk outside the GRÜNSPAN[1] discothèque, dealing hash at 5DM a gram. Nearby PAST TEN (Detlev-Bremmer Str.) sells an extraordinary amount of sweet fruit juices. This one has no dancing, just dreaming. Decor and ambiance of a teen-age opium den: seating on stacked-up little painted barrels, sheets of aluminum hanging from the ceiling reverberating to the eerie sounds blasted at a constantly Wagnerian level. No one under sixteen admitted after 10 P.M., which accounts for the very youthful dealers to be found outside around midnight and the unhappy pile of stoned little girls on the pavement.

That Hamburg has become a Northern European center of drug dealings is as much related to the fact it hosts so many vessels from places like Mexico, Morocco, the Middle and Far East, and the United States, as that, pop musically, it was Liverpool's sister city during the early 1960s. Hamburg has substantial numbers of middle- and upper-middle-class youth, yet compared with their alienated and rebellious counterparts in America, there are com-

[1]As in several European cities drug users tend to gravitate to the sidewalks near selected discothèques despite protestations of the respective managements.

paratively few young sexual revolutionaries or drug dropouts here. One could cite the traditional reserve and restraint of the archetype citizen: Hamburg has been called a city-state between England and Germany, and the temperament of the classic (upper-middle- or upper-class) Hamburger lies closer to the Englishman's than, for example, his Bavarian cousin's. There is also the traditional threat of the back of a strong paternal hand, characteristically stronger in this country than elsewhere. Speaking specifically of the drug question, one could note that the habits of two thousand years are hard to break—and that young Germans still prefer drinking the fruits of hops to smoking leaves of grass. As to morals, it appears that Germans may be mollified in their youth by the fact that their laws are more strict where the morals of minors are concerned and less so when dealing with the morals—or, rather, vices—of adults, at least in comparison with most other Western nations.

Thus it is *verboten* for children under the age of six to attend the cinema. (Granted this may also be intended for the comfort of adults.) From ages six to twelve they must leave by 8 P.M.; from twelve to sixteen by 10 P.M., and to eighteen by 11 P.M.—all enter on condition that the film has been cleared by the censors for their particular age group. (Similar regulations apply to attendance at dance halls and restaurants.)

COMPUTER-AGE CATHOUSE

And after age eighteen they may attend the EROS CENTER. This is the ultimate cathouse of the computer age. If the Federal Republic should last a thousand years, it will produce no monument more exemplary of the celebrated German genius for efficiency than the Eros Center. Of course, the Americans could have brought it off almost as well. One can imagine that if prostitution is ever legalized in the United States and Howard Johnson's adds favors to its flavors, American brothels will have all the Orwellian charm of this Space Age bawdyhouse. But they'll have to choose another name: the far-sighted Germans have registered "Eros Center" with the federal patent office.

In this four-story erection of frosted glass and white brick there are accommodations for a hundred and thirty tenant whores. Each bedroom is done in mid-twentieth-century motel, with identical modern furniture, wallpaper, carpeting, and curtains; and all the rooms have wall safes as well as alarm buttons wired directly to the Davidswache Police Station. There is an underground garage discreetly accommodating sixty-eight customers' cars; and, for the girls, a twenty-four-hour beauty salon and rumpus rooms. Several entrance arcades front Grosse Freiheit and lead to an infrared-heated courtyard. (With its proximity to the North Sea, Hamburg has a brisk winter climate but, overall, a far better one than you might think: its annual rainfall is two thirds that of Munich, and over the past fifteen years it has had three percent more sunshine.)

In the courtyard stand dozens of girls, aged twenty-five or so, weary but ready under the intense but rather asexual scrutiny of the men, the majority of whom seem middle-aged and "respectable" middle class. For many, this is a leading Hamburg spectator sport, which may account for the fact that the girls are sometimes in a bad humor. "I am bored," observed one apparently innocent male bystander. (English is spoken here far more widely than in Bavaria.) "But I am not bored *stiff,* you may be sure of that." Some of the girls are smartly dressed and relatively attractive. But plain or pretty, lean or plump, each charges exactly 30DM for a dose of her very experienced services. Like all of St. Pauli's card-carrying prostitutes (the cards identify them as "working single women"), all Eros Center girls receive frequent medical attention.

Like Dante's Inferno, the building complex is divided into nine parts; the houses are built around the open courtyard and each contains twelve to fifteen rooms. Each house has its resident male custodian, responsible for keeping things neat, clean, and, above all, ORDERLY! No photographs are permitted—two husky bouncers discourage drunks, journalists, photographers, and other undesirables—but at the entrance to the courtyard a series of Automat-style vending machines dispense nudie photos and films, as well as stockings, racy panties, maps of the city, picture postcards, canned strawberries . . . and sweetheart roses (six for 2DM).

Herr Direktor of the whole aseptic affair is called "The Kaiser of St. Pauli" in deference to his considerable real-estate holdings in the area. Though the city of Hamburg has no official connection with the enterprise, the Kaiser received generous civic cooperation in the planning and construction. "Of course we are Germany's most tolerant city," assured the innocent bystander. "After all, there are only thirty thousand Jews in all of Germany, but one of them is Mayor of Hamburg!" His Honor, Dr. Herbert Weichmann, is himself a man of no mean tolerance. "It cannot be supressed, but we are controlling it," he replied to an inquiry on prostitution. The Mayor's views are apparently shared by a large portion of the electorate, which gave him 61 percent of the vote in the last election.

Since the October, 1967, opening, at a reputed cost of more than $1 million, the Kaiser has been lionized as a civic hero for moving at least a hundred and thirty girls off the streets into clean and comfortable quarters. As will be discussed more fully in the Munich chapter, there is a federal law against living off the "immoral earnings" of another, but the hairsplitting German interpretation does not consider the collection of rent a violation. Just to make sure, the owner leases each of the nine houses to a group of independent investors, including a jeweler, a retired government official, an insurance salesman, an old salt sea captain, and other pillars of the community. For a 10–12,000DM down payment (plus 2000DM for "furnishings") each lessee secured a five-year lease. The lessees pay the Kaiser 450DM a month, collect 50 to 60DM a day rent from each girl, and project a minimum 15-percent net annual return on their investment. Apparently the Eros Center is working out very well for all parties, including the tax collector, who is a regular caller here as well as at similar establishments in several other German cities. But the Hamburg tenants complain that it now takes them twice the time it took to earn a given amount of money on the streets. And they, like many of their customers, deplore the clinical surroundings.

"Why stay here if you are unhappy with your working environment?" an Alsatian was asked.

"I stay because it is warm," she barked coldly. "When these clever Germans discover how to heat the streets, I will return to them."

PALAIS d'AMOUR: TEENYBOPPERS A MARK A MINUTE

Imagine you are visiting the playground of an all-girl high school at recess, surrounded by dozens of vivacious teenyboppers, all offering you thirty minutes of sexual instruction at a mark a minute in their upstairs dorm rooms (50DM for *Ficken mit French* . . . and to take off *alles, even the love beads!"*). That approximates the atmosphere in the courtyard of PALAIS D'AMOUR, which opened in the wake of Eros Center's success and whose accent is on youth. At 3:30 A.M., with the sun already up this mid-June morning, you counted exactly forty-five girls—none *looks* more than eighteen—on display under the red lights of the central Oriental-style pagoda and several awnings extending from the mod mosaic walls. Most of the admiring clientele are young men, many, apparently, students. Both Eros Center and Palais d'Amour can be entered from the Reeperbahn, the latter at number 140A. But do not mistake Palais' neon sign for that of just another strip joint, as so many people do, presuming the better-known Eros Center is the only game of this type in Hamburg.

THE REEPERBAHN

Infamously known as a shopping center of sex, the Reeperbahn is, strictly speaking, the name of St. Pauli's main stem and very much a promenade of middle- and working-class tourists, though many people refer to the entire St. Pauli area as "The Reeperbahn." As sportive, exuberant, and luminant as it is, and for all the lusty attractions offered within its six-hundred-yard length, the Reeperbahn is surprisingly clean. "Well-scrubbed" is more apt, for the street always seems to have the aspect of a subway toilet recently disinfected or a whore just douched. This although the innumerable restaurants, bars, cafés, strip joints, dance halls, dirty-book stores, quickie hotels, street whores, and the wax museum stagger their hours to insure that diversions are available at all hours.

The blazing neons, the gaudy façades, and the vivid advice of the touts create a frank, uninhibited—but not wanton—atmosphere, aptly reflecting the pragmatic liberalism of the city fathers. Hamburg's seaport traditions are a great source of pride (at a point in the Elbe approaching the harbor all ships are greeted by loudspeakers blaring their country's national anthem), but because today's average St. Pauli sinner is somewhat more discriminating than a horny seaman, fleshwares must be displayed effectively and advertised with candor. This is simple business acumen and sound psychology.

That the Reeperbahn feels tamer than you'd imagined is partly because everything appears to be so methodical and matter-of-fact and partly because St. Pauli's showcase street is in fact not quite as wicked as it would like to have you think. The striptease cannot hold a candle, nor a dildo for that matter, to Grosse Freiheit's. KARRUSEL BAR, for example ("champagne" 55DM and up), opens by noon to accommodate visiting rurals who, after all, have Holsteins to milk by next light. Here, as in MOULIN ROUGE and GOLDEN NUGGET, the greatest evil appears to be in the fly of the beholder, for all three are strictly family striptease. Not that the area lacks excitement. One of Temple Fielding's field men reports that he was "shouldered into a doorway and ringed by several thugs," then "raked open from nostrils to lip" from a "roundhouse slug" courtesy PIRATEN CABARET's bouncer. A more characteristic Reeperbahn excitement is possible on the terrace of ONKEL HUGO's restaurant, where the percentage of Scandinavian tourist girls is particularly high in warmer months, and they cost no more than a coffee.

Willing young amateurs frequent TOP TEN (Reeperbahn 136, hallowed by the Beatles even earlier than the Star Club) or GROUPIE. Their older sisters and fathers prefer the rules of the gamey CAFÉ KEESE (Reeperbahn 19/21), where custom insists that the lady ask the gentleman to dance. One finds another sort of young lady, one who has completely lost her amateur standing, at cafés MENKE (Nos. 31–35) and LAUSEN (No. 59). More later about these two important cafés, among the Reeperbahn's most worthwhile attractions. But first, to savor that salad of brutality, and bestial sexuality, seasoned with the smell of salt, sweat, seamen, and tar, and a dash of Hamburg humbug—all that you'd always imagined to be the epitome of the Reeperbahn—you will now please to get off the Reeperbahn.

HERBERTSTRASSE: WOMEN IN THE WINDOWS

"It is known you have had sexual relations with many partners. In view of your habits, it is presumed you have been infected. You are therefore suspected of having a venereal disease and of being a carrier," begins the official document duly issued by the Hamburg Central Advisory Board of Health to all registered prostitutes and requiring that they report for weekly medical inspections given without charge, Monday through Friday from 8 A.M. to noon. With all due respect to the tenants of the nearby Eros Center and Palais d'Amour, no one has more need than the very busy harlots of the Herbertstrasse. (Unless you consider the countless unregistered street prostitutes who prefer to risk infecting you than be included in the files of the police and hence the tax collector.)

Through the green gates of Herbertstrasse daily pass hundreds of men, some blatantly concupiscent—at last! here there be sailors—others simply curious, and these sometimes with *Frau* in tow. (But signs forbid entry to anyone under eighteen.) At first sight it is an amazing spectacle, this quick, compact little alley barriered at the far end and lined on either side with adjoining houses three dwarf stories high whose first-floor picture windows are so large and set so low that even a myopic troll won't miss a trick. The windows of these tawdry, yet somehow tidy structures are front- or back-lighted with red, the preferred color. How like zoo cages—the comparison is odious and thus all the more appropriate—for the rooms have been designed to deny the inmates any privacy whatsoever during their long shifts, save when they close the curtain for coitus. (It's simply bad business to keep the curtain closed otherwise.) The total architectural effect of the street is that of a movie set created by a misogynistic sex maniac who learned scenic design as a "trade" in a penitentiary workshop. And the odor! It simply cannot be described, but its components include beer, cheap perfume from Seville, certain other cosmetics unknown, urine, dead rats, offal, disinfectant, sausages frying, seminal discharge, and spew.

And the women in the windows . . . skimpily dressed in cheap copies of the latest fashions, some of their microskirts no more than belts. Though most wear boots, their attitudes vary. Some crochet demurely or fix foods on the hotplate, tiny TV at hand, all the while ignoring the taunts and cruel jokes of passersby. Others good-naturedly join the banter, crowing coarse chanteys back at passing jackeys, lascars, and galiongees. In the Herbertstrasse few men make antes at girls who wear panties. Though nudism is technically forbidden, someone always seems to have something in her eye and nothing handier to haul it out with than the edge of her sheer microskirt. From time to time there are some really frightening arguments as overly enthusiastic or antagonistic window-shoppers hit a particularly delicate nerve. Surely there is no language more appropriate for a whore's rebuttal than the guttural, brutish, very low German of the ladies of the Herbertstrasse. But their oath is worse than their bite, perhaps because the Davidswache Police Station is only two minutes away by patrol wagon. *"Liebchen"* sounds lovely cooed softly, but when bellowed out by a burly Brunhilde at four o'clock of a rainy, windswept Hamburg morn—the Elbe is but three short blocks away—it sounds more like somebody selling a fungus.

Each year thousands of girls leave the provinces of West Germany for the big cities—until the Wall, many arrived from the East as well. It is estimated that some three thousand go to Berlin, sixteen thousand to Munich, and twenty thousand to Hamburg annually. Of these not a few wind up as St. Pauli prostitutes. At any given time there are from two to three hundred girls working the Herbertstrasse, occupying the apartments at a daily rental of 20 to 25DM in shifts from 7 P.M. to 4 A.M., or from 7 A.M. to 7 P.M. (The thing is closed for scrubbing in the early morning.) The girls range in age from twenty-five to about thirty-five and in appearance from surprisingly attractive to better left unsaid. They will obey most any request short of murder or suicide, and a few of the second and third stories of the little houses harbor facilities for all manner of exhibitions and special devices—whatever the problem, the Germans seem always to have a machine for it—designed to satisfy the most sophisticated, masochistic, or sadistic proclivities.

THE BEST S/M HOUSE IN TOWN

The very word "masochism" was contrived by Krafft-Ebing in commemoration of the strange bent of Leopold von Sacher-Masoch. Though born in Austria, Sacher-Masoch had a police chief father and a German libido and mother. From age ten little Leopold was mightily attracted to whips and chains, and he thrilled to exhibitions of cruelty with sexual overtones. As he matured he became obsessed with whips and furs, employing them in the coat of arms on his stationery, upon which he wrote several novels with masochistic themes. The most celebrated is *Venus in Furs.* In private life Sacher-Masoch married twice. The first wife could tolerate the fact that he required daily whippings to inspire his literary output, but when he advertised her in the press as sexually available to any "energetic man," that straw broke *her* back.

In spite of history and your own very strong preconceptions, there are few genuine sadomaso houses in Germany, at least according to no less an authority than Baroness Monique von Cleef of The Hague who theorizes that most Germans with such needs seem to be affluent enough to travel to London or Holland to satisfy them. However, she did suggest that of all Germany's governesses none is so skilled as Karen who, with her assistants

Christine and Madeline, operates an S/M house in the Herbertstrasse which has no peer in the entire Federal Republic.

Unfortunately, at your visit to the four-story house of brass-lined windows and tiled façade, Karen was on vacation and Christine was thus unable to show you her mistress's locked chambers. However, you are assured they are quite elaborate, containing, among other fixtures, a "big jail and a cross [iron of course] for crucifixions." Christine, a not-unpleasant-looking mini-skirted woman in her late twenties, chats with you amid her own quite respectably equipped quarters. Her torture room contains all the latest in pulleys, trolleys, whips, chains, rack, and a pillory, but none of it has the faintest false sheen of newness. The whole house, even the front parlors, has the acrid smell of leather. One of Schleswig-Holstein's leading wholesalers does periodic rounds, attending to any needed repairs or replacements. In her sitting room—containing a studio bed against a mirrored wall, a washbasin, some nasty-looking prints of women in black stockings and garters, and a stuffed vulture—Christine assures you that "There is a lotta kinky woman in this street, but none like Karen. None in Germany like Karen.

"For a good session costs maybe one hundred, maybe two hundred marks. Most coming is over thirty, but comes some young ones too. A few woman comes alone . . . and married couples . . . we whip them, hang them up on the cross [said as offhandedly as 'We serve them coffee and cakes']. . . . Maybe comes with the couple another guy. We order some slaves maybe, and he gets some whips, maybe she fucks some other guy. You know, it's always different."

Apparently one cannot go far in this profession without a second, if not a third language. You can't get by simply screaming *"Raus! Raus! Raus!"* all the time, no matter how skilled you may be with the appliances. Even the Americans would get bored with that. Evidently the tone, the inflection of the command, are as important as the words themselves.

"You know, with Madeline, unless they is German, they don't know what she want them to do. Most who comes, after the Germans, is English. And we get lots of Swedes and Dutch. Not many French. You come back when Karen is here. She make you do it in five languages!"

Karen, Christine, and Madeline. Herbertstrasse 14. Advance bookings: 31-22-96 for Germans; 31-49-09 for other nationalities.

BAWDY BARS, STREET WHORES, AND THE TOUGHEST BAR IN TOWN

For years Germans have relished strolling their "trade streets"—Herbertstrasse is the last of them—for reasons not all that different from those of the people who paid $25 to sit in the first eight rows of *Oh! Calcutta!* and brought opera glasses to make sure. The public still seems to prefer the "charm" of the Herbertstrasse to the more impersonal courtyard courtships of the much heralded Eros Center. It was hoped that Eros Center and Palais d'Amour would supplant what many officials consider an eyesore, particularly since a great deal of new construction is planned for the area. But certain sentimental civil servants consider the Herbertstrasse as valuable a tourist attraction as the charming inner-city lakes. Perhaps this last of the trade streets will be preserved in the manner of a New York City landmark, P. J. Clarke's saloon, which, rather than succumb to the wrecker's ball, stood its ground to have an office building constructed around it.

Further questions about the Herbertstrasse girls should be addressed to the man who may own one, in one of the neighborhood pimps' bars. Or inquire of some of the more regular customers in ISTANBUL, open round the clock at the corner of Davidstrasse and Herbertstrasse. Considered among the most atmospheric and authentic of all St. Pauli dives, Istanbul enjoys its finest hours from 4 to 7 A.M.

While you're in the neighborhood, pay your compliments to the lineup of 15-to-20DM Kastanienallee street whores, few registered nor many older than eighteen. Proceed into nearby Hans Albers Platz and adjacent Friedrichstrasse and Gerhardstrasse, which area contains the greatest concentration of streetgirls in Hamburg. At 6 A.M. of a June Sunday morning such *trommelfellerschütternd!* A cacophony the like of which you've never heard, at least not in concert. Birds cheeping, foghorns groaning, martial band music blaring from CHIKAGO discothèque, rock and pop from a dozen wideopen bars like HAWAII and BARCAROLE (dirty color movies here), and the siren songs of half a hundred harlots (you counted thirty-nine in the Platz alone) dancing in the doorways; 30DM for a short haul, 40DM to take all clothes off plus selected short subjects, for many girls carry reels of film. Move on to Silbersackstrasse and you are approaching the most dangerous and authentic area of St. Pauli, that portion lying south of the Reeperbahn and ending (forever, if you're not careful) down at the docks of the Elbe.

Here is ZUM SILBERSACK, a very tough sailor bar. And nearby, among several, there is one of the grimmest, toughest, and potentially most violent bars in this galaxy. From dawn to dawn you have opportunities for on-premise frolics and dancing with the barmaid while you are accompanied by a gasping hand organ and carefully watched by an enormous Hun of a bouncer who might be mistaken for the result of a full-moon union between the Wolfman and one of the Amazons who wrestled in the mud of Hamburg's now defunct Bikini Club. Well, he *might* be if he were not so big and ugly. Drinks are cheap here—50-pfennig beers served by a bartender with a face like a clenched scrotum—and so is human life. Go with four big friends and a small wallet.

There are many bars and pubs in the immediate vicinity. Of particular interest are those near St. Pauli Fischmarkt and Hafenstrasse which serve as homes away from home for foreign sailors. Among them are KINGLING (Chinese—corner Lincoln and the appropriately named Trommelstrasse) and CASABLANCA (African—Bernhard-Nochtstrasse 89); both open to 6 A.M.

You never know what you'll find in this dark, somewhat spooky neighborhood. One midnight you stand in the little park of Bernhard-Nochtstrasse admiring the wonderful view of ships passing along the Elbe and the enormous dockside loading cranes. Breathe deeply. The brisk North Sea air smells of fish and chippies. Climb down the two flights of stone steps into Hafenstrasse where not one of the nine hitchhiking teen-agers will have a thing to do with the likes of you, a simple pedestrian. They are strictly for passing motorists who might require a quick 20DM snort in the back seat or a fast 15DM fellatio in motion.

You hail a passing cab, direct the driver (a blond woman of about thirty) to park overlooking the Elbe and to let the meter run.

"Just want to chat a minute. . . . What's the *best* club right now in Hamburg?"

"I don't know, but I hear a new club, TRIANGEL."

"It's good? What's happening there?"

"I don't know, I never been there. But I take lots of diplomat people there. It's private. . . . I *hear* it's the best. . . . Just near here in the Hafenstrasse. But you must have a card. . . ."

You thank her, give 2DM over the meter price and walk back along Hafenstrasse.

THE TRIANGEL CLUB

No. 126 is a small nondescript building whose glass front window is completely blackened. The little red neon barely whispers "Triangel Club." There's a Diner's Club decal and a small card warning *"Strengstens verboten . . ."* to persons under twenty-one. You knock and the tiny peephole winks.

"Haben sie eine Klubkarte?" growls the huge black cigar that opens the door a sliver.

"No, but I'd very much like to get one." The door opens and a second cigar appears. A mystic Arabian melody beckons from somewhere in the rear.

"Who are you! Who is send you here?" demands second cigar.

"Uhhh, uh, the Ambassador," dropping, in fact, the name of a local consul. Apparently it's a very good name to drop in this town, or maybe it's simply the fact that you're wearing your dark-blue suit with the quiet maroon tie, for you are immediately whisked along a narrow, dim corridor. The chorus of Arabian drums, pipes, lute, and flute grows louder and a muezzin cries out.

Hookah Heroics

You never did get the room decor down pat. It's dark, intimate, seating no more than forty, and *very* posh—lots of velvet and good crystal. A battery of lights spot only the tiny stage on which a nude, rather plump Middle Eastern girl of about twenty-five with marvelous golden skin is sitting cross-legged, smoking a huge hookah with her vagina. You make for the tiny eight-stool bar, no more than fifteen feet from the stage, and are at first appalled to learn that a drink costs 35DM ($10). But the bargirl promises that you won't have to order a second one (and you don't), and none of the ultrarefined capitalists at the small tables looks to be anybody's fool. Moreover, the girl with the golden skin has now given up smoking and plugged in a two-inch-diameter candle. She shoves it halfway up the Suez Canal and lights it. You buy the drink.

Through five minutes and thirty-two seconds of gyrations, handstands, situps, plus all the usual contortions ordinary belly dancers do, this one kept that candle up and lit. There are all kinds of applause. What you hear at a rousing team sporting event surely differs in mood, tone, and intensity from that which acclaims the concert pianist. Each time the Arab girl paused to pull out a bit of melting candle the audience responded with a kind of applause most nearly approximated by what you'd hear at the end of a game *(not set)* at a tennis match.

Sex for Two . . .

The girl takes a brief curtain call and, during the short break, the tape-recorded voice of a comedian tells five jokes about salamis, knockwursts, and various other types of German meats and produce, all somehow involved with vaginas and Fallopian tubes. Now a tall young man and a leggy blonde come on stage in street clothes. To the strains of "Clair de Lune" he slowly, carefully undresses her, takes his own clothes off, and sits her on the bed. After some friendly persuasion she takes his flaccid member in her mouth, sucks it ardently, and soon has it standing out like a flagpole.

"Hello, I'm Tonia. Do you like my body?"

"I'm delighted to meet you under these circumstances, and your body is sensational!" And it certainly is, as is the face of this luscious little brunette who has nuzzled up to you. Remember Dorothy Lamour? In her prime? Tonia looks quite like that, but instead of a sarong she's clad in sheer pantaloons, nipple tassels, and a tiny puce *cache-sexe.*

Meanwhile back on stage the girl is polishing the boy's penis with her palms, he is fiddling with her breasts, and Florian Zabach is doing "Hot Canary" over the stereo system. (Even for a German rig the fidelity is unbelievably high.)

"Won't you *please* buy me a drink," begs Tonia. "It's only thirty-five marks."

From the loudspeakers a basso voice begs the question, "How must it be?"

"It must be wet. It must be wet," answers the recitative chorus of sopranos.

"No, Tonia, I can't . . . stop putting your body on my hands. . . . I can't afford to buy you any drinks. . . ."

"Ohhhh. . . ."

"Das ist schön?" inquires the male audio as the man begins to investigate his partner's venter, alternating his fingers and his tongue. Segue into upbeat bongo-bongo rhythm.

"You've a lovely snatch, Tonia, and it's very accommodating of you to throw it into my knee . . ."

"Schön, schön," coos the female audio.

". . . but I can't afford to buy you a drink."

"You must speak slowly," begs Tonia. "I am just now learning English in the school." The foreplay at Triangel is certainly more good-natured than at any club you've attended. She really doesn't care a damn whether you buy her a drink or not.

"Fick mich! Fick mich!" screams the girl on stage and, accompanied by the "William Tell Overture," her partner begins to do just that.

"He's really fucking her, isn't he, Tonia!"

"Yesss . . . of course."

"Makes you . . . almost want to do it yourself."

"Ja?" smiles Tonia hopefully.

"JA!" shrieks the man on stage triumphantly.

The couple are really going at it now. Back to the beat of the bongos, building wildly as the man bangs away amid gasps, groans, growls, and moans. Can't really tell what's coming from the sound system and what's from the performers, but the action's certainly authentic enough.

"Would you like to fuck me right now?" pleads Tonia who is really even more attractive than the pretty enough blonde on stage.

"Look . . . I'd really like to . . . watch this. . . ."

"Listen, you fuck me for a whole hour downstairs after the lesbian show. Two hundred fifty marks, ja?"

"Ja . . . ja . . . Fick . . . Mich. . . . JAAAAAAAAAAAA!" says the blonde.

"Will the lesbians please now get ready for their next performance," intones the PA announcer and Tonia kisses you *Wiedersehen* on the cheek.

"Hast ihn? Hast ihn?" inquires the man under a crescendo of Liszt's "Les Préludes."

"Ja! Ich hab ihn," replies his partner, perhaps referring to the *Höhepunkt* (the German word for "climax," which, of course, is a *masculine* noun). At this the audience breaks into vigorous but polite applause . . . oh, say, not

unlike that offered a chess master who has used his rook and two knights wisely at the endgame to score a neat checkmate. And the music segues to a Hawaiian medley to sail away into the sunset with Jon Hall by.

. . . And Three

"That, ladies and gentlemen, was an act of two. A man and a woman fucking," declares the narrator. You are reminded of a room you once occupied in a Munich hotel. Above the lightswitch was a small printed sign reading *"Lightswitch."* "And now, for an act of three, Triangel Club proudly presents . . . Lesbian Show!"

To make a long story as short as possible, your old flame Tonia is cowering on the bed nude, as a big blonde (whom you later learn is Scottish) prowls round it, swinging an enormous dildo as if it were an Andean bolo. Now the blonde pounces on Tonia, gets her tongue stuck in Tonia's vagina, can't seem to get it out, and Tonia eventually capitulates, and more than reciprocates. The dissonance of shrieks, screams, and yowls, apparently coming from the audio system (surely the girls can't eat and talk at the same time), sounds like an alleycat fight.

"Saug, saug," wails Tonia.

"Trink, trink," demands the blonde, she herself quite thirsty.

"Beiss, beiss"—bite, bite— suggests a wonderful-looking redhead who makes her entrance from stage left with a big black dildo strapped on, ready for action. She jumps on the pile.

"Through your applause you can stimulate the performance," orders the PA announcer. But they are going at it with such gusto and relish—and lots of mustard too—as to be completely oblivious to the audience. Tonia and the redhead are having a sixty-nine and the blonde is doing a number into Tonia's rear end with a dildo. The background music is from *The Man with the Golden Arm.*

At this point you momentarily lost your place, for Isabel, a smashing blond Marseillaise in slave slacks, slinks up to you, extends her hand. But as you move to take it she undercuts you and shakes your *Schwanz.*

"You have there a nice paynis," says Isabel, making it rhyme with "anus." "What is your name?"

"If you'll give it back to me, I'll tell you."

Other than your penis, Isabel wants no more from you than a cigarette, though she does offer to go immediately to the downstairs "bedrooms" and make a half-hour's love for 200DM. After some chitchat she disappears with a tall distinguished-looking gray-haired gentleman who looks like a bank president.

On stage the girls have made a choo-choo. Tonia is up front being jazzed from the rear by the dildo of the redhead who is being similarly tended by the big blond Scot. As the latter is the caboose she can do no more than reach around with another dildo to rectify her own backside. The thing ends with a fantastic strobe-light effect, giving the illusion of watching an old silent movie; it is then slowed down for a "stop-motion" trip. Sometime later the bank president returns, looking very pleased with himself, Isabel tagging along, holding his hand.

Still later you are taken for a tour of the three downstairs dressing rooms, so large they'd make a Broadway star drool; each contains an enormous couch and mirrored walls. An affable employee of the Private Club Triangel assures you one should pay no more than 185DM to make love here with any of the "slave girls. . . . All the best people come here, *only* the best. Many from the consulates," assures Affable. And considering that after the mandatory 35DM first drink a second can be had for as little as 8DM and the fifty-minute shows are so good there is no need to hustle the customers, Triangel is probably as equable a club as you'll find anywhere in Germany. ("Members' " phone: 31-27-84.)

It remains only for you to meet the star performers, but the French girl is indisposed, having done five shows from 9 P.M. to 5 A.M. Her twenty-four-year-old Parisian partner, Michel, however, still looks very fit.

"Marvelous performance."

"Thank you indeed."

"When you make love here, monsieur, do you . . . really mean it?"

"Well, yes, yes, of course."

"How many times a week?"

"Two, three, four times a night . . . depending. Six nights a week. I rest on Sunday.

"You like the work?"

"Oh yes, it is very agreeable."

"How much are you paid?"

"I am paid *very well,* as is mademoiselle."

"And I would like to add," notes a German assistant manager, "that when it is standing up, he has more than eleven inches." (Some changes in the locales of "fuck-shows" are noted near the end of this chapter.)

OTHER EROGENOUS ZONES

Considering that the amount and variety of bawdy amusement in this vicinity is greater than one finds in most *countries,* it is not surprising that many travelers assume that St. Pauli contains all that is salty in Hamburg. But the city has other erogenous zones as well. Proceed east from the Reeperbahn along Holsten-Wall and Gorch-Fock-Wall. Best take a taxi or the underground, for Hamburg is considered to be among the most confusing of

Europe's cities to drive in, even by its natives. Continue along Lombards Bridge, which, with its immediately parallel Kennedy Bridge, separates the Inner from the Outer Alster. To your right the smaller of the two lakes and the shoreline of the City Center, which contains large mercantile establishments, banks, and elegant shops. The view has been compared with Geneva's.

St. Georg

Proceed east to the huge Main Station and you have reached St. Georg, a throughly respectable and solid quarter of good restaurants, sidewalk cafés, theaters, office buildings, important hotels, and museums. Scattered among these innocent establishments are the elements of what may someday become a sort of gentleman's St. Pauli.

Chérie Tanz Café: Coffeehouse Whores and Prosthetics in the Men's Room

Even if you don't have to go, go to the men's room of the CHÉRIE TANZ CAFÉ (Steindamm 7) in the heart of St. Georg. Nothing particularly unusual about the design of the urinals, nor the tiled decor. It might be any well-appointed men's room in any respectable club or hotel in the Western world. (There is an odd *déjà vu* of the lavatory of New York's late Astor Hotel.) But as you pass the black-tied white-coated attendant in the anteroom, do not expect obsequious attentions to the invisible lint on your lapel. Nor does Herr Fritz ply you with the usual bonbons of his trade—phony cologne, lilac water, or tacky combs. This cat is far too busy looking after his brisk trade in complicated prosthetic devices, multicolored French ticklers, mysterious ointments and salves to prolong orgasm and aphrodisiacs to induce it, illustrated booklets and instructive pamphlets—all devoted to insuring a gentleman's success and a lady's pleasure in bed whatever the handicap, real or imagined. One old fellow has just purchased a ten-inch phallus, complete with body strap, for 25DM. The second toilet cabinet has been converted into an archive of dirty films like *Surprise Attack* and *Teen-Age Erotics*.

Back upstairs now, you resume your table in the rear of Chérie Tanz Café's two adjoining rooms, observing that the fixtures and appointments, though so gleaming and well-polished, appear to have been manufactured in another era. It's as if the whole place had been carefully wrapped in excelsior and cellophane for forty-odd years and just now unpacked. Tacky nude oils and 1920s-modern mirrors offset the blushing red walls. Hovering on a platform above the tiny dance floor a geriatric band of organ, cello, drum, and violin (an old lady who looks like Wanda Landowska and plays with the verve of Liberace doubles on organ and fiddle) delivers the melodies of waltzes and ancient foxtrots to the cadence of military marches. "It is important the beat be most conspicuous," confides a waiter, "otherwise many of our patrons could not hear it."

Five P.M., the height of the tea-dance hour of a somnolent November afternoon: a prominent local butcher, his arms frozen in a pose more suited to shooting a bow and arrow, woodenly waltzes his lovely young partner about the front room; a retired feed dealer and his guests, a delegation of high-living Schleswig-Holstein dairy farmers, doze, dream, and dawdle with their *Strudel*. Like a goose about to peck his tailfeathers, one man cranes around from his elegantly silver-serviced coffee to apprise some newly arrived females, his wizened, gnarled neck scratching audibly at its high detachable collar.

Here come the girls, fresh from the ladies' room. Some are twenty-one, some are thirty-two, but most are in-between. Handsome creatures, leggy, and "very high in the breasts," their daytime attire tends to the conservative: high-necked wool suits and dark-toned smartly tailored skirts and sweaters, set off by cameos, single strands of pearls, or other simple antique jewelry. The purposefully naïve and schoolgirlish look is also well represented by sheer or dotted-organdy chiffon blouses with ruffles and puffed sleeves, perhaps in memory of long-lost loves of the gentleman patrons or recent fantasies of their granddaughters. If you want company, all you have to do is whistle or wheeze, though a simple nod, proper movement of your eyebrow, or dropped monocle is in better taste and quite sufficient. (The St. Georg area police are *very* strict. Even the occasional 50DM streetwalkers found outside near the little pensions along the Steindamm have to be careful. St. Georg is not St. Pauli.) As far as the law is concerned, Chérie girls are well within their rights as long as they do not make active solicitations: technically a gentleman must make the first move. If a girl does accompany a man to a nearby hotel (*Stunden* rooms 18DM; 30DM for the whole night) in the vicinity at 100DM for up to an hour, all that is required is that she be registered with the health authorities like any other law-abiding prostitute.

By 8 P.M. the hemlines are much shorter, the cleavages lower, and the new band somewhat more with-it, in deference to the middle-aged business executives who dominate the Chérie during the evening. Some of the night-shift girls hold daytime jobs as bank clerks, secretaries, or models, and not a few are employed in Hamburg's considerable communications enterprises. A convivial formality reminiscent of a Geisha house prevails, exemplified by four dark-suited, pompously mannered technocrats who have invited Heidi, a statuesque five-foot-ten redhead with excellent cheekbones, to join them. As she approaches they rise, click their testicles, shake hands with her in turn, and introduce themselves. Seated now, 5DM Scotches all around, they chat gently and weigh her whispered appraisals (Heidi wouldn't lie) of other girls in the room. After much consultation three of Heidi's co-workers are invited to join. More formalities and presently all eight retire to a nearby hotel for a "party."

It should be stressed that Chérie has no fiduciary connection with the girls even though, the delicious pastry and coffee notwithstanding, business might fall off somewhat without their attendance. Even the manager avoids speaking to them lest, perhaps, he be considered a "procurer." Just to test, you invite a handsome blonde in a low-cut orange dress for a piece of chocolate cake and some coffee. Noting that you are a foreigner and under sixty, she is somewhat disappointed. With studied civility she declines food and drink and quickly gets to cases. "Come on, 'Mouchie,' one hundred marks for me and eighteen for the room." When you insist on some preliminary conversation and order a second piece of cake from a real nice waiter who has been here twelve years, thereby setting yourself up as a perfect creampuff for any B-girl, she establishes her true vocation and independence by dashing off in an orange-crepe silver-lined huff.

Founded in 1945, Chérie is by no means the only game of this type in town, merely one of the most tolerant, if its business hours are any criterion—open from 10 A.M. to 6 A.M. Just around the corner at Steintorweg 4, CHARMAINE is a kind of Chérie with jugglers, refined (for Hamburg) striptease, and on-stage audience participation (with the jugglers). Between 10DM Scotches you are invited to hold the female acrobat during the course of her performance. However, should you attempt to tumble her into a nearby *Stunden* hotel, well, the managers will undoubtedly intervene. However Charmaine has a number of good-looking girls seated throughout the large house. Some just dance with you and others will go right to bed for 100DM. Just ask who's who. Charmaine has a well-deserved reputation for upright dealings, and it's one of the few places in town you'll find an honest crap game. There's also baccarat, roulette, and a couple of nice Swedish and Yugoslav girls too.

The CAFÉ MENKE (Reeperbahn 31–35) is the oldest coffee house of its type in Hamburg, having been established in 1912, destroyed during the July 24–August 3, 1942, incendiary bombings—the eleven-day *Katastrophe* saw 48,000 people die—and completely rebuilt since. Open from 10 A.M. to 7 A.M., it's still a pretty hot place. Considering the Reeperbahn location, one finds girls of many backgrounds here, though ladies with tariffs and needs similar to those of Chérie's beauties seem to prevail. However, they are less expensive in the morning and daytime hours.

A similar situation prevails at CAFÉ LAUSEN (Reeperbahn 59). In fact, here you recognize some Chérie regulars. But because the band is so versatile— the music responds to the composition of the clientele, ranging from the "Tennessee Waltz" to the latest pop and rock tunes—and the pastry, coffee, and drinks are so reasonable one finds all sorts of people here. However, there is no mistaking that many of the girls mean business. So does Herr

Ludwig, the gents' room Lord of the Flys—you can't miss him for his surprising Hitler mustache—whose line of prosthesia is similar to that of Fritz at Chérie. Herr Ludwig's specialties are French ticklers that pay homage to the memory of Walt Disney. "Yes, it's very funny, to have a Mickey Mouse *Gummi* so your girlfriend has an adventure. Almost as funny as putting him on your wrist to help you tell the time."

Club Hotel: The Most Elegant "Lovers' Hotel" in Town

At Reeperbahn 54, conveniently located a couple of doors from Café Lausen and near enough to the Menke, is CLUB HOTEL. It has been passionately recommended to you by a discriminating womanizer from the French military mission in _____. You press a call button, wait two minutes (you later learn the pause is so that someone upstairs can carefully scrutinize you on closed-circuit TV), and the door is electronically buzzed open. Up a long flight into . . . what? The inside of Hermann Göring's cufflink box? Here is surely the most luxuriously *recherché* (in the sense that the word means "farfetched") bar in town. Extravagant silken wallpaper with subtle metallic threads. Twinkling crystal chandeliers. Soft lush glows from somewhere illuminating the lavish, but tastefully equipped bar. *This* is the Club *Hotel?*

"This is the Club Hotel," nods the barman, suave, bronze, silver, and smiling. He looks exactly like Curt Jurgens—and knows it—but is actually a native of Tarragona.

"But where's the check-in desk? . . . And the . . . the rooms?"

"Here you may register," indicating the bar with a soft but no less expressive shrug. "I am the room clerk, and these," bowing with his shoulders to the four Marlene Dietrich types grooming the stools, "these are the charwomen."

"Okay. I'd like to see a room."

"Single or double?"

"Double."

"But you are alone," shrewdly observes an ice-cool blonde.

"I move around a lot in bed."

"Fine," says the barman, "because we *have* only doubles."

In fact, the Club Hotel has only two rooms. But such rooms! You've never seen prettier ones, even in Paris—each with velvet-canopied bed, perfumed pastel satin sheets, and lots of abracadabra crystal candelabra. Everything tinkles, rustles, and glitters. Rates are 22DM for one hour, 35 for two, but if you prefer a partner from the bar to your sweetheart, the room is free. "Write it correct in your book," says a dour blue angel. Two hundred marks costs a girl in 'Kloophotel.' " The other charladies nod solemnly.

Some of Hamburg's most exclusive call girls occasionally bring clients to the Club Hotel. These are under the direction of a man, not a madam, who operates out of the exclusive Epindorf district, near the university. Many of his girls are, in fact, students and some come of very fine old families. The girls are on call only occasionally, perhaps no more than once a month. Often a visiting businessman is "introduced" to one of these girls by his host and never knows the evening has been arranged and paid for in advance (up to 1000DM) by the local corporation courting his trade. The phone number of Epindorf's male madam changes frequently. The German branch of your company might have it; or the Gold Key men—members of the European association of hall porters—at two of the city's best hotels may confide it to a guest with proper connections . . . or with 50DM.

BEATE UHSE'S PROSTHESIA EMPIRE

"I need soldiers, not lovers," growled Hitler as he ordered that contraceptives be fitted with surreptitious holes, thereby insuring future fame and fortune to Beate Uhse, a pert young Luftwaffe captain who was at that time ferrying Focke-Wulfs, Stukas, and ME-109s from their factories to the Russian front. Later, in 1945, as Der Führer and Eva Braun prepared to exchange wedding vows in the bunker and the advance guard of the Red Army hurtled through the outskirts of Berlin hoping not to miss the ceremony, Captain Uhse, her baby and wetnurse in tow, commandeered a rickety Siebel-104 from Gatow Airport, artfully hedgehopped across northern Germany, and narrowly evaded her Soviet pursuers to land safely in Schleswig-Holstein.

Good thing she made it, for if modern German couples are happy in their beds—and tonight more of them are happier than ever before—no contemporary individual is more responsible than Beate Uhse. Today every fourteen and a half seconds someone buys one of her products, each of which is designed to prevent birth, enhance sexual pleasure, or accomplish both jobs simultaneously. "She has led us along the difficult road to Seventh Heaven," lauded the highly respected *Frankfurter Allgemeine Zeitung.* Difficult indeed, if you know a little about Germans. But Fräulein Uhse obviously knows more than a little.

Noting the general ignorance of birth control in early postwar Germany (the tale of Hitler's punctured condoms is apocryphal but it is well documented that the Nazis suppressed dissemination of all birth-control information), Fräulein Uhse began peddling a pamphlet on the subject. On Washington's Birthday, 1951, she opened the Beate Uhse Mail Order House and, with a staff of four, cranked out a little book, *Is Our Marriage the Way It Should Be?* It is still available to customers, though now at no cost.

By 1953 the little Flensburg company had sold enough books and rubbers to purchase the Honemann Pharmaceutical and Cosmetic Company; in 1959 the lingerie holdings of Madame Cotelli; in 1960 the C. Stephenson Publishing

Company; and sometime later a General Electric Bull Gamma computer. Today the firm employs some three hundred people (over two-thirds women), grosses more than $6 million annually, lists more than 2 million steady mail-order customers and over 20 million occasionals, and includes a chain of twenty-one sex supermarkets in Hamburg, Berlin, Frankfurt, Stuttgart, and other German cities.

Forget Fritz in Chérie's men's room, though one must award him points for location. Dismiss those latecoming Southern California imitators whose sniggering ads pepper the "underground" papers. No American entrepreneur can match the solid technical excellence, nor all of them together the variety and ingenuity, of the Beate Uhse line.

Of total sales the major portion (30.9 percent) is still derived from birth-control products—condoms and other mechnical devices, creams, jellies, etc. Interestingly, the company does not market birth-control pills, perhaps because of its stated policy that the Pill should be taken only under the direction of a personal physician in view of the possibility of side effects, or perhaps because of government prohibition. A library of over two hundred books—some dealing with problems like frigidity, impotence, or nymphomania, others providing instruction in technique, and still others frankly salacious—accounts for another 24 percent. A specialty of the house is cosmetic and pharmaceutical preparations (20.3 percent of sales) like Amatella, described in the catalogue as an "Aphrodisiac drink which hastens away worries and complexes. Being freed he and she can together enjoy the 'cruise of pleasure.' They are ready to enjoy intimacy. Amatella is *the* love drink [32 percent alcohol] . . . price: 14,80DM. Pleasant coffee flavor." Included in this category are various other cocktails, liqueurs, chocolates, hard candies, tonics, and pills designed to up the ardor. For those with Amatella in their veins, as it were, there are *Antipraecox* or *Longtime,* creams that delay ejaculation and prolong the duration of a gentleman's erection by reducing his excitability —7,20 or 9,90DM.

Mechanical devices that increase the size of the penis or give other general aid and comfort to the female during the lovemaking process—vibrators, splints, penile extensions, strap-on dildoes, and so forth—account for a brisk 9.2 percent of sales. In America the achievement of simultaneous orgasm is largely a matter of luck, favorable astrology, or even love, and if not achieved within reasonable time, do consult *Cosmopolitan;* in Britain one might turn on BBC 2. In Germany, Happiness for Two Is . . . number 51–019–39 in the Beate Uhse Catalogue: a rubber cushion equipped with "scientifically designed" soft buttons that operate gently and naturally on the clitoris to achieve more efficient orgasm, while an attached rubber ring fitted about the base of the penis is simultaneously agitated by the couple's activity to stimulate the gentleman to ecstasy as well. Considering the equitable 16,80DM price for

Happy End, not even the lowliest peasant couple should miss out on the coveted double orgasm. Or try 51–050–39, *Apollo 2000,* whose soft air-filled nipples "stimulate the clitoris" while the base "counteracts premature ejaculation" in the best traditions of the Space Age: 14,80DM.

Yes indeed, the Beate Uhse Company is a veritable Alice's Restaurant of sex: you can get most anything you want at Beate's, except Beate herself. However, some of her acquaintances appear in some of Beate's photographic studies of male nudes, and these, along with other spicy photos, color slides, and films, account for 7.6 percent of business. Sexy underwear (4.7 percent), including a line of what might be called "breakaway lingerie"—flimsy corsets, brassieres, panties, bathing suits, housecoats, and pajamas that all fly off the female form at the touch of a hot hand—and "miscellaneous" (3.3 percent) round out the catalogue, which is not so dull on its own merits: many of the items are pictured in action photos employing live nude models.

Seventy-five percent of sales are by mail order, the rest through the twenty-one retail stores of which Hamburg's (Grosse Allee 10, corner Kreuzweg, near Chérie) is typical. The goods are displayed on racks and in bins amid dignified, trade-fair-modern carpeted surroundings. Beside all items are numbered tags that the customer has only to take to the cashier, who notes the appropriately coded number and brings forth the article, already sealed in a plain wrapper. Each store has a consulting physician to provide free counseling and, not incidentally, to lend an aura of respectability and scientific authority. Even more popular—perhaps for the anonymity afforded—is the firm's counseling service, available free of charge to anyone who drops a line to 12 Gutenbergstrasse, D239 Flensburg. No subject is too delicate for these Rose Franzblaus of Flensburg who, with the aid of that computer, have got the answering of thousands of troubled letters a month down to a science. Literally. Female secretaries classify each letter according to the writer's basic problem. Dry vagina? Push number 3150 and out of the Bull Gamma's mouth pops the appropriate answer. This, along with a description of an appropriate remedy, found, of course, in the catalogue, is forwarded to the troubled correspondent with a reassuring *personal* signature. Diameter and length of penis in relation to virility? 3146. Premature ejaculation? 3141. Or what have you?

SEXWELLE

Not by coincidence, the growth of Beate Uhse Company has paralleled the development of the *Sexwelle* (sex wave), latest in the postwar series that began with the *Fresswelle* (eating wave) and the *Vespawelle* (motor scooters), and progressed in logical yoke with the country's economic miracle through the *Autowelle, Wohnungswelle* (homes), and *Reisewelle* (travel).

Many observers trace the beginnings of the *Sexwelle* to 1961, when an inferior court in Flensburg ducked a ruling on a government case against Beate Uhse and dumped the matter into the lap of the Karlsruhe Constitutional Court, where it has remained pigeonholed ever since, much to the delight and profit of filmmakers, ad men, publishers, and certain members of the medical community. And opportunists and panderers among all these.

The *Sexwelle* does not describe a wave of promiscuity. It has only a vague resemblance to what has been going on in the States and England, and is not a revolution of the young against established mores. Rather, the phenomenon is characterized by adult Germans who, with unprecedented enthusiasm for the subject, now discuss sex freely—*dissect* is more precise—and happily gorge themselves on every morsel of information the mass media and pseudoscience can provide. To what ends? Not primarily for a mass orgy of *Gruppensex* (though the practice has its new adherents here as elsewhere; see the classified columns of *St. Pauli Nachrichten* or *St. Pauli Zeitung*), but more in keeping with the German tradition of knowledge for its own sake, and for the sake of efficiency . . . around the house! "If we cannot master the world, we shall at least master sex."

It should surprise no one that Germany reported the first successful artificial insemination using frozen sperm, according to a June, 1969, UPI dispatch. Dr. Georg Sill-Seidl of Frankfurt (admittedly Hungarian-born) said his discovery "offers itself not only for cases in which the husband is prevented from being present at the ovulation time but also gives the possiblity of concentrating semen or collecting it." However the husband in this particular case, age thirty-three, had donated his sperm for freezing primarily because "his job kept him away most of the time," according to Dr. Sill-Seidl. At birth the baby was normal, weighing six pounds three ounces—if not an immaculate conception, certainly a tidy one.

Contrary to apocrypha, Nazi Germany never achieved such a *Schlag.* Not for lack of effort. Authorities like Professor Wolfgang Hochheimer, director of the Institute of Educational Psychology, West Berlin Teachers College, consider the *Sexwelle* a healthy reaction to those repressive years, and a much-needed filling of the psychological cavity that exists because for the first time since anyone can remember, Germany has no immediate future as a military power of consequence. (Cross your legs.) Whatever the causes of the *Sexwelle,* Germany appears to have gone quickly from the supine to the ridiculous.

Whether the ads are pushing machine tools or motor oils, they haven't a chance without a naked girl slinking around—or in front of—the product; nor has the periodical itself—be it a newsweekly or a pharmaceutical trade paper —without one on the cover. Needless to say, the market in bare magazines is goatish. Werner Jungeblodt, head of the Federal Censorship Office (under the Ministry of Family Affairs, and concerned primarily with material considered objectionable to youth), recently resigned the position, citing "personal reasons." Boredom could not have been among them. In a recent year 345 magazines were blacklisted; 342 another. Of these latter, for example, only 3 were domestic publications. Because the Scandinavians export so much of their "pornographic" output to West Germany, the Federal Republic is at this writing considering legalization of all pornography, just to protect their own industry (and not, as Germans piously suggest, because they feel their society is now mature enough to require no protection).

Writing in *Der neue Vertrieb,* Herr Jungeblodt gives some insight into the German character and, incidentally, provides an interesting comparison with the American: "There has never been much demand for publications lacking sexual ingredients and devoted entirely to violence and crime, but there has always apparently been a wide market for crude orgasmic propaganda and perverse nonsense. Some periodicals treat the subject in ways that are nothing short of animalistic."

Of course, Germans exhibited a strong stomach for "special" diversions long before any *Sexwelle.* The Bundestag recognized this facet of the national character, and revealed a good deal of its own, by enacting without debate a 1969 law that provides for "voluntary" castration of habitual sex offenders. The *Stuttgarter Zeitung* called it "long awaited." A proposal for forced castration was rejected, although, according to the *Zeitung,* the practice has a great deal of support throughout the country.

Germany's new-wave films are little more than modern medicine shows —*Doktor*-narrated documentaries (enlightenment movies). *Du,* an exceptionally heavy-handed chronicle of masturbation, had a big triumph, and *Helga,* the mother of them all, which cost $150,000 to produce and starred a baby making its entrance from a womb, made $25 million and is still grossing. Even the Bonn government, which originally sponsored *Helga* as sex education for the public schools, was amazed.

Perhaps in hopes of sparing the children a future *Sexwelle,* the Fatherland has been in the forefront of nations offering sex education for the young. As the first nation to introduce sex education as a separate subject, it has recently issued a forty-eight-page *Sex Atlas* throughout the school system; it contains twenty-three pages of four-color illustrations depicting sexual relations. Among the program's basic tenets: intensive sex education should begin for everyone by age fourteen, and all first-year pupils should know the facts of birth and the differences between the sexes. A 1969 Health Ministry poll showed a whopping 83 percent of respondents considered sex education in the schools essential. (Compare American attitudes.)

From admittedly subjective observations, teen-agers and young adults appear as bemused bystanders to the *Sexwelle.* They are no more sex-happy than other Western youths, but by comparison their elders seem quite sex-mad. At the height of the *Sexwelle,* the late Professor Hans Giese of Hamburg University's Institute for Sexual Research (and regarded as the German Dr. Kinsey) conducted a youth poll that received wide publicity. Replies from thirty-six hundred students in twelve universities were rather a shock to churchmen and sociologists who had voiced the conviction that the young were being corrupted by the *Sexwelle.* But no one doubted the veracity of the replies or results. The respondents were mostly middle- and upper-class Germans—frank and open about sex—who would characteristically take any such study quite seriously. Some findings:

Promiscuity among the young is rare: 90 percent believe that "sex without love is immoral." Two-thirds of the young men and over three-fourths of the girls remained faithful to one partner during the previous year. Only 5 percent of the men and 2 percent of the girls admitted sex relations with more than six partners in the previous year. Only two hundred of the students were married: of these only 4 percent admitted to adultery. Not that young Germans aren't realistic about sex. By the time they are twenty, at least 40 percent of men and one-third the women are no longer virgins. Petting is common, but most respondents considered any activity that does not result in coitus as childish and timewasting. (Of course, as in any such study, there is some gap between beliefs and practices, but probably less so in Germany than in most countries.) Ninety percent approved of sex before marriage, and 40 percent saw no harm in extramarital sex. Eighty percent did not disapprove of homosexuality, though only 3 percent of men and 1 percent of women admitted practicing it. Of those who did, half reported heterosexual activities as well.

Compare that sober picture of German youth with the fact that, by her own figures, 69.9 percent of Beate Uhse's 2 million regular customers are over thirty-one years of age; and a substantial 31 percent are over forty-one. Or ponder the rather free translations by German distributors of these American film titles (as compiled by *Variety*): *With Six You Get Egg Roll* became *The Man in Mama's Bed; The Girl with the Motorcycle—Naked Under Leather; Under the Yum-Yum Tree—Marriage Bed for Probation; What's So Bad About Feeling Good?—Wedding Night in Front of Witnesses; Come Blow Your Horn—If My Sleeping Room Could Talk;* and *Good Neighbor Sam—Lend Me Your Husband.*

TOO MANY WOMEN

As a legacy of World War II, of West Germany's approximately 60 million people there are nearly 3 million more females than males, 2 million of these over forty. Draw your own conclusions as to what role this situation may have played in instigating the *Sexwelle*. But it is axiomatic that any society that habitually commits large portions of its male population to military slaughter will be left with a good many anxious, lonely, unusually approachable, if not downright promiscuous females. In fact, Germany has been a good hunting ground since the days following the Kaiser's follies. Four observable manifestations of the female surplus are: prostitution, which, paradoxically, flourishes when there are too many women or not enough of them; the matchmaking agencies; the peculiarly Germanic dancehall, which encourages instant communication among strangers by setting phones on the tables or by establishing *rules* that permit the lady to make the first approach; and lesbianism.

MATCHMAKERS

Two hundred forty matchmaking agencies have been founded in the past twenty-five years, mostly in Germany's Protestant north; before that only ten existed. While the primary goal of the matchmakers and many of their female clients is matrimony, they are fair game for suitors of every conceivable intention. But *Achtung!:* each year about 14 percent of the Federal Republic's marriages result from classified ads in the press, many of these inserted by marriage brokers. Altmann of Hamburg, for example—which was founded in 1928 and now boasts that it's the world's largest—employs an IBM 36/50 computer and claimed 2188 marriages, 2520 engagements, and 8216 "continuing relationships" during a recent year. Fees from 400 to 2500DM guarantee up to 99 new introductions a year for up to three years. Ten thousand people a month shop at Altmann's, most of them female.

TURNABOUT DANCEHALLS

The archetype of the "girl-asks-boy" dancehall *(bal paradox)* is CAFÉ KEESE (Reeperbahn 19–21, and also in Berlin). The combination of *alt* Prussian light-green-silk-walled decor, big loud bands changed religiously each month, inexpensive snacks, meals and drinks, and *strict* policy that a gentleman never refuses a lady, has produced nearly thirty thousand marriages in the past couple of decades, according to Wilhelm Bernhard Keese. The men are passively lecherous, ages twenty-five and all the way up, but mostly between thirty-five and forty-five; the girls eighteen to forty or so, but mostly twenty-five to thirty-five. Yes, they will walk right up to you and ask you to dance: no, that does not necessarily mean they will ask you to do anything else. A shrewd management, under the direction of Charley Orth, passes out cards to the prettiest girls, inviting them back next time for free drinks. By and large a convivial middle-class crowd, but in summer these are joined by legions of tourist girls, particularly Scandinavian and British, who enjoy the novelty.

DREYER'S AHOI *Bal Carré* is a good bet if you're between trains, for it's right next to the Main Station in St. Georg. A younger crowd (eighteen to twenty-five) than at Keese and, judging by all those Sunday-best suits on Wednesday nights, mostly working class. Any girl, even if apparently escorted, is waiting to be snatched . . . as long as the yellow ball is lit. Red ball, she chooses. Of other dancehalls whose opportunities are similar to Dreyer's and Keese, BOCCACCIO, directly opposite the station at Kirchenallee 50, is surely among the best. No telephones or rules, but the dark-green velvet chairs, good linen, coffee in silver service, black-tied waiters, and danceable Italian bands draw many, many single women, principally of the career girl, divorcee, or bored housewife variety—from about twenty-eight to forty-five. Open from 4 P.M. to 4 A.M., but 4:30 to 7:30 P.M. is the optimum pickup hour. Lead the band at ZILLERTAL (Spielbudenplatz 27) in case you missed Munich's Oktoberfest. EDELWEISS (Reeperbahn 110); LIDO (Grosse Freiheit 36); and BALLHAUS BARBERINA (Reeperbahn 2), are also in St. Pauli. And if you simply cannot wait for Berlin and the Resi, ARNO'S BALLHAUS (Neuer Pferdemarkt 15) and BALLHAUS CENTRUM (Alter Steinweg 42) both have telephones at every table, and stay open to 2 A.M. on Saturdays, in case you make a bad connection or two.

Hamburg's women outnumber the men by more than two hundred thousand. This fact, coupled with the unusually large number of predominantly or exclusively lesbian bars and pubs, and the city's legions of prostitutes (who traditionally include a much higher proportion of lesbians than women of other occupations), leads one to the superficial assumption that Hamburg may just have a higher proportion (if not actual number) of lesbians than any city of Europe.

MOSTLY GIRLS

Lesbians are particularly indigenous to that area north of the Reeperbahn[2] comprising Paulinenstrasse and immediately adjacent portions of the perpendicular Budapesterstrasse and Wohlwillstrasse. A most exciting part of town for those who crave the company of their own sex. A focal point of the neighborhood is IKA-STUBEN (Budapesterstrasse 38; 31–09–98). This is Hamburg's most traditional lesbian club, so don't miss it. Wednesdays through

[2]The police station in this area is at Budapesterstrasse 20; or phone them at 31–13–55.

Fridays are exclusively for women and the door*man* is tough about it. But a gentleman might gain entrance if he is accompanied by a female, especially if she is known to the management. In spite of the rather homespun decor —jukebox, two small bars, walls papered with fading fan-magazine cutouts —you meet a very good class of lesbian at Ika-Stuben.[3]

And your chances increase with a short three-block walk north on Budapesterstrasse. At 84A of the left-fork Schulterblatt, the strict SUNSET 77 (43–32–66) is closed to all males the first and third Fridays of the month (even the Herr owner can't get in) and is predominantly female other nights (to 4 A.M.). *Yé-yé* dancing in a refined enough atmosphere. Or take the right fork to DORIAN GRAY (Schanzenstrasse 6; 439–56–23), a juke-box dance bar near the appropriately named Kampstrasse. Saturday till dawn it's ladies only in the main room; here one may do her things in discreet alcoves. Other nights Dorian Gray is about 80 percent female.

Last, and surely best, is the recently opened CAMELOT discothèque in St. Pauli's Hamburger Berg which can also be Camelot for accompanied male voyeurs (lot of see-through blouses) if they sit back quietly watching the action and behave themselves. This is *"Dial-a-Dike":* telephones at every numbered table, and the prettiest *young* lesbians in town dancing, drinking (Coke 1DM, whiskey or big stein of beer 2DM; no admission charge) and feeling each other up up in the back-bench bleachers. In the same building is HOTEL CAMELOT, doubles at 25DM.

MOSTLY MEN

Until September 1, 1969, West German law was as Prussian as most of America's, considering homosexual acts and sodomy, with or without consent, to be criminal offenses; prison terms varied with the tempers of the times and the respective communities. Under the first major revision of the penal code since 1871, only forcible acts, those committed with a person under twenty-one or by a person taking advantage of a position of authority, are actionable; but penalties remain strict: up to ten years' imprisonment.

In spite of past Prussian mentality, or perhaps because of it, Germany, and particularly Berlin, has always been a homosexual haven, if not heaven. (No need to pursue the legendary Nazi faggotry.) Since the war, Munich and Hamburg have taken the play away from Berlin. It should be stressed that no suggestion is made that any of the following establishments is frequented

[3]As in the case of all establishments cited in this book, none of the establishments in this or the "Mostly Men" section following are patronized exclusively by members of only one sex, except where—as here—*explicitly* stated in the text.

exclusively by homosexuals. As is the case with all public establishments cited in this book, you might find anyone on the premises . . . bankers, lesbians —even your brother-in-law.

Tramp steamers and rough-trade cruisers are found, appropriately in the parallel Kastanienallee and Hopfenstrasse, just in from the docks and a short block south of the Reeperbahn.

Among others, choose from the leathery FLAMINGO, and LAUBFROSCH, after which you might have need of a hotel like the ballsy BALTIC back in St. Georg in the Spadenteich. After which you might also require a good proctologist.

Continuing up St. Pauli's gay ladder (for, if you will note a map of the area's confusing pattern, you will observe that Hopfenstrasse, Kastanienallee, the Reeperbahn, Seilerstrasse, and Simon von Utrechtstrasse are consecutively parallel rungs with the equally hot Detlev Bremerstrasse and Hein Hoyer-strasse forming their sidepieces), at Seilerstrasse 45 you may enjoy observing the LA BOHEME'S make-believe-ballroom belles. Pause with MAX UND MORITZ at Simon von Utrechtstrasse 19. Some of these old gentlemen may teach you a thing or two. And in ROXI (Schmuckstrasse; near a tattoo parlor) there's a rousing transvestite show.

If you're cruising, be sure you know what you're getting into if you happen to pick up a beauty in hot pants or miniskirt in this appropriately named (for New Yorkers) street—they're transvestites, and for 30DM will prove it. Don't forget our old friend the BARCELONA in Grosse Freiheit. Back on the ladder sidepieces, Detlev Bremerstrasse has PETIT and LORELEY; and parallel Hein Hoyerstrasse features DANDY BAR, a rather refined situation—the decor and the clientele. A few steps east on Wohlwillstrasse the aforenoted BAR'CELONA CABARET (11 P.M. to 4 A.M.; first drink 12.50 DM, excellent transvestite cabaret, wholesome atmosphere; bring the wife) and the SIT-IN BAR at No. 48.

Stroll east on Paulinenstrasse if you seek street boys. But if you are merely curious and/or accompanied by your wife, sweetheart, or daughter, you'll find a welcome of sorts at SPUNDLOCH (Paulinenstrasse 19), a popular disco-thèque–cum–pub whose young gentlemen are quite well off without you, thank you, but not unfriendly to curious strangers. Amateur cabaret Sunday nights.

The action along the main drag strips Budapesterstrasse and Schulterblatt coexists peacefully enough with the good burghers of neighboring Eimsbuttel and Altona districts, but the mothers of these archetype-middle-class areas take care that their little boys avoid the Alsenplatz public toilets.

If your appetite is voracious, or if you merely believe that if one has a good eye and is resourceful, quantity can produce quality in any enterprise. STADT-CASINO, in the city center on the lovely Grossneumarkt Square, is by all odds the most fruitful game in town. (If you'd rather watch the dancing and have no interest in making a friendship here, you may still enjoy a visit.) Old hands have lately been moved out by younger ones to the nearby NEUE STADT-CASINO. Also in city center, HANSEAT BAR (Kaiser-Wilhelmstrasse 55) and ABC-STUBEN (ABCstrasse), one of the oldest male bars in Hamburg.

From the gay purview there is far less quantity east of the Alster than west, but perhaps more quality. Those with an intellectual bent may satiate it at NA DENN (Hofweg 58), a painters' and writers' pub. Gay travelers between trains may establish a relationship at TUSCULUM (Kreuzweg 6; no women) and consummate it at HOTEL MÜNCHNER HOF (Pulverteich 25; reservations, 24–28–50). Beate Uhse (lubricants, etc.) is but three minutes' walk at Grosse-allee 10. Also nearby are KOPPEL-KLAUSE (Koppel 34) and ROBBI BAR (Lange Reihe 113).

A truly elegant sauna–discothèque–"boys club" has recently opened in the lovely Uhlenhorst section, just off the Outer Alster. CLUB UHLENHORST (Adolf-strasse 25; 22–59–54) is one of the best of its kind in Europe. Some very old families. End of the line?

GENTLE BLOOD

"Quality homosexuals" . . . "better-class lesbians" . . . 100DM prostitutes —surely there must be other aspects of high life in Hamburg. Indeed, this is a city whose considerable mercantile aristocracy dates back centuries. Its gentle blood—if not blue, it is certainly a very distinguished money-green— is rarely warmed by St. Pauli prowlings, though there are escorted slummings to the Fischmarkt, Blauer Peter, and Triangel. Custom and parental authority are perhaps more comparable to that of Madrid than Berlin or Munich. Still, the times they are a-changin', here as everywhere, and it is no longer considered improper for a young lady of good family to have an evening out on her own. Serious jazz houses provide a cover of respectability in many cities, and JAZZ-SALOON NO. 1 (Paul-Roosenstrasse 33) affords a favorable environment to make some worthwhile friends. To a lesser extent so does STREIT's BAR and CAVE (Jungfernstieg 38) in the City Center—especially from 5 to 7 P.M.—and the bars of the ATLANTIC and VIER JAHRESZEITEN Hotels, and the terrace of the ALSTER PAVILLON during warm weather and any Sunday afternoon.

JEUNESSE DORÉE

Alone, or in company of a female friend, the *jeunesse dorée* are most likely to be found in several elegant rooms west of the Alster. Among the best: AMBASSADOR discothèque (Heinickenstrasse 6), ROYAL CLUB (Fruchtallee 106), GIGI (Grindelberg 81), and DIE INSEL (Alsterufer 35). The last-named, in a striking white townhouse overlooking the lake, is Hamburg's most traditional supper club and provides warm and elegant surroundings for cultivating a particularly eclectic group, among them members of Hamburg's very international consular community. For reservations, call 45–10–55.

"A well-educated rather than an intellectual city," observed a bookseller, perhaps an indication of why Hamburg's student and/or intellectual gathering places lack the musty veneer or hippie frenetics of the Left Bank or Greenwich Village. There is, too, less intellectual pretension, but this does not connote a lack of charm or pace. On the contrary, Hamburg's mini-Saint-Germain-des-Prés, newborn in the Pöseldorf area between the university (twenty-five thousand-plus students) and the lake, is a tasteful blend of antique shops, boutiques, chic little art galleries, and cafés housed in what were graceful coach- and townhouses. Milchstrasse is the center of this stimulating activity. Here you find ALT-PÖSELDORFER BIERSTUBEN; there is no better place to be in Hamburg on a summer's eve than under the trees of its lively terrace. In fact, all year round Alt-Pöseldorfer is second home to *Ewige Studenten* ("eternal students"), artists, rich people who live nearby, and pretty girls of all three categories. Also a brace of discothèques in and about Grindelallee.

Reflecting the somewhat conservative student temper (compared to Berlin's, for example) and the city's traditional view of art as a byproduct of commerce, the intellectuals' cafés and pubs—always among the freest and easiest places to encounter young women in any city—are as likely to be thronged with recent graduates now employed in broadcasting, publishing, and the cinema, as with students, poets, and artists. No matter whom you encounter in the following pubs and cafés, you may be sure that a high percentage of them are among the 80 percent of Germans whom the Bielefeld Emnid Institute learned approve of the Pill.

Political discussions, an art gallery, chess games, many varieties of tea, and many, many pretty girls are staples of WITTHÜS-TEESTUBEN (Brandsende 4) in the city center. AM KAMIN (Curschmannstrasse 24) features nurses, whether it knows it or not, and young doctors too, in case one has a problem. In COSINUS (Bundesstrasse 15) it is difficult for any young man or woman to be lonely.

Last noted, but perhaps your best first stop in Hamburg, is RATSHERRN PILSTUBEN (Mundsburgerdamm 21). Host Armine Ewald, a former journalist who spent time in the States and has fluent English, can tell you much about the town, if you can keep your eyes from the attractive patrons, one of whom might be willing to guide you about. Some are students from the nearby fashion school, others straying housewives and career girls. According to one, now that Hamburg has replaced Berlin as the communications capital of Germany, and with the advent of the new penal code under which adultery is no longer a criminal offense, Hamburg is well on its way to becoming Germany's swingingest city. And this has not a bit to do with St. Pauli.

NUDISM AND SYLT

But if during the summer months you happen to find many of the worth-while natives away on vacation (the slack is somewhat taken up by Swedish girls), a situation which anyone who visits Europe's major cities during July or August may encounter, do not despair. Head north for the Frisian island of Sylt, Hamburg's favorite summer playground (aside from the Elbe with its colorful bars and opportunities for sailing). In 1971, 60 percent of Sylt's visitors bathed in the nude, a 10-percent increase over the previous year. Inquire in the Main Station about the "discothèque–train" to Sylt.

GERMANS—TAKE THEM AS YOU FIND THEM

Take the Germans you meet as *individuals*—try to forget whatever collective prejudices you may have—and you may enjoy them. *In no European country are the young more different than their parents.* (It remains to be seen what happens in the next twenty years.)

Of course, certain aspects of the German national character have not changed for two thousand years. Many of P. Cornelius Tacitus'[4] (A.D. 55–117) insights could have been gathered yesterday, though this Roman senator, knight, and historian wrote his *Germania* in A.D. 98. Not a few scholars consider it the first, if not the last word on Germans:

"They have only one form of public show, which is the same wherever they foregather. Naked youths, trained to the sport, dance among swords and spears." The old rascal certainly got around (though he was quite disgusted with what was going on back in Rome). "However adventurous the play," continues Tacitus, "their only reward is the pleasure they give spectators." The play is certainly as adventurous as ever, the swords and spears having simply been joined by a few more inventive phallic tools, although the rewards are considerably more tangible. The Hun girls of Tacitus' experience wore "undergarments of linen, embroidered with purple" with "forearms and upper arms bare. Even the breast, where it comes nearest the shoulder" was "exposed too."

"Marriage in Germany is austere," Tacitus found, "and there is no feature in their morality that deserves higher praise. They are almost unique among barbarians in being satisfied with one wife each. . . . Clandestine love letters are unknown to men and women alike. Adultery in that populous nation is rare in the extreme. . . . Wives must not love the husband so much as the married state."

The divorce rate has gone up, but remains considerably lower than in other

[4]Tacitus, *Germania*, Translated by H. Mattingly (London, Penguin Books).

Western countries. (The itchy year is the fourth, not the seventh, incidentally, according to the *Stuttgarter Zeitung*.) Appearances—very important to Germans—suggest that those who stay married fool around a lot less than the French or Italians, not to mention Bob, Ted, Carol, and Alice across the sea. By and large, modern German couples banquet together, often attend sex shows together, and stay together. That women remain chaste to all but their spouses seems largely true. This is not a promiscuous country. A wife turns to Beate Uhse rather than her best friend's husband. Certainly Tacitus' love-letter reference remains appropriate. These are basically unsentimental people, and the man, if he does seek an affair, is rather unimaginative and unemotional about it. (Unless she's French! Germans have always been suckers for French girls. Bismarck had a fantasy that he'd create the greatest nation on earth if he could marry all the German boys to all the French girls. And so, every twenty or thirty years for the past century Germany raped its lovely neighbor.) Generally, married men prefer quick, unentangling alliances—very often with prostitutes—to long clandestine Gallic love affairs or whirlwind Italianate courtships.

The local governments have legalized and controlled prostitution to varying degrees throughout the country. In Bavaria, where the weather is balmy and also the mentality, people are more often out in the streets and traditionally more gregarious and, Catholicism notwithstanding, they mingle freely with the opposite sex. But in the north adultery is as discreet as it is among the English, and so the need for and availability of prostitutes is greater. German businessmen do quite a lot of traveling within their own country, and much organized public pleasure is geared to their needs and tastes. Surely "vice" is so ruthlessly well packed and well marketed that there is no small loss in flavor. "Above all the gods they worship Mercury," said Tacitus, and in modern Germany the brothels are as rapid and efficient as the trains. In this country, unlike England, for example, everything and everybody works.

"They inspire or feel terror according to which army roars the louder," continues Tacitus. "What they aim at most is a harsh and hoarse murmur, and so they put their shields before their mouths, in order to make the voice swell fuller and deeper as it echoes back."

Speaking to today's Germans remains a matter of self-defense. Above all, take the initiative: be precise, demanding, harsh if necessary, with hall porters, waiters, lovers, and prostitutes, for Germans respect, nay worship, authority whether they wield the whip or bend to it. Everyone has said it, but Churchill said it best: ". . . They're either at your throat or at your feet." The quality of the language has improved little since Charles V's oft-quoted "I speak Spanish to God, Italian to women, French to men, and German to my horse," but it sounds better up north.

"Their horses are not distinguished either for beauty or speed, nor are they trained in Roman fashion to execute various turns. They ride them straight ahead or with a single swing to the right, keeping the wheeling line so perfect that no one drops behind the rest," wrote Tacitus. The average German drives his car much as he performs in bed, according to several non-German girls who've been there and lived to tell about it; and he operates a motor vehicle much the same as his forebears rode their horses. Orderly in all things—not even a toe off the curb until the Hamburg light changes—Germans drive strictly by the book, and still manage to be among the Continent's most ill-mannered and dangerous drivers. Though they may be as unimaginative behind the wheel as in bed, this does not imply any lack of skill in either situation. In both cases technology is heavily relied upon to compensate for human error.

In traffic and in bed Germans press their advantages and like to sound their horns, particularly when the other fellow is technically in the wrong. Romans and other Latins "executing various turns" remain a national nemesis. They have improved the beauty and speed of the beast and treat their cars like beloved mistresses in the fashion of Americans (though they don't cast them off as often) lavishing great care on them, covering them with gifts—foxtails, fancy reflectors, wobbling dolls and trolls, etc.

Of course Germans have certain preconceived notions about *you*. They've always had strong opinions about foreigners and foreign relations—even as far back as Tacitus:

The Germans' neighbors were "the stuff of fables—Helusii and Oxiones with the faces and features of men, but the bodies and limbs of animals." Germans still have misgivings about their neighbors to the east: they've always despised the Poles, hated, and feared the Russians. They also consider the Italians competent in nothing but lovemaking; they think the French decadent, frivolous, and sneaky; they fear and admire the English, who have beaten them badly in two wars, and with whom they share some common ancestors; they are remarkably bigoted toward blacks for a country that has so few. Until some Jews moved here some time before the year 1000, Germans didn't care much about them one way or another. Now that Israel is again formidable and lots of Jews have gone to live there, Germans by and large have a healthy respect and admiration for them. German feelings toward Americans change with the times; Germans are, above all, a pragmatic people.

As to Germans themselves, Tacitus found that ". . . the physical type, if one may generalize . . . is everywhere the same—wild blue eyes, reddish hair, and huge frames that excel only in violent effort." One still finds such specimens in the town *Brauhaus*. But you'll meet lots of ash blondes in Hamburg and the north, quite sleek and trim. And Tacitus would hardly know Bavaria: it's all mixed up with a lot of wandering Greeks and some of his own descendants.

Statistics provide valuable insights into the national character, not only because they are so abundant, but also because they are unusually accurate. The Germans, in their passion for self-analysis, are pathological polltakers . . . and responders. To a German a poll is a lie-detector test and, in the interest of science, he will answer truthfully (or not at all) the most personal questions.

For the record, the average married German male is fortyish; he is named "Hans," is 5 feet 9 inches tall, weighs 172 pounds, has blue eyes and a blue collar, and a wife named "Elisabeth." She is 36 years old, 5 feet 6 inches tall, weighs 145 pounds, and lives with her husband and a dozen potted plants in a small town where they annually consume 230 pounds of potatoes. They prefer an ocean cruise (34 percent) to a vacation amid a big city's fleshpots (10 percent), and the women apparently have a good deal more dignity than their American counterparts: 87 percent of women interviewed considered shopping in hair curlers in poor taste. All this according to a recent *Public Opinion Yearbook* published by the Allensbach Research Institute.

In your personal relationships beware the inconsistencies, literal and thus predictable though these people may be. "They are so strangely inconsistent. They love indolence, but they hate peace." You can say that again, Tacitus, and so he does: "The Germans have no taste for peace."

Modern Germans love the comforts of home, and they have thrown themselves into work, war, and whorehouses with equal zest. This is only one of the paradoxes. Germany is decidedly schizophrenic, and the diagnosis is not limited to the classic national and personal delusions of omnipotence and persecution. The various political parts united later than those of any major European power, and today there remain marked differences between the personalities of southern and northern Germans (not to mention those of the east). Germans of every region, so well controlled on the surface, are said to hide within their souls some great monster, ever threatening to surface and destroy the host as well as innocent bystanders. No wonder many foreigners regard these people as afflicted with a kind of national epilepsy.

The difference between the personalities of men and women is also marked, but this is pleasant for the visitor and seems to cause no conflict among the natives themselves. A Hamburg journalist expressed this vividly: "You like our German women . . . so intelligent, yet so attentive to your jokes and whims; so frank and willing, so obedient, yet not servile; so long-legged and slim, yet with the big tits. You like our German women? Well, it is we fat, cold, cruel, dominating, demanding German men who have created and trained this lovely animal. *Never forget this!*"

Okay, okay, it won't be forgotten, but you don't have to holler.

The men are, variously, somewhat pretentious, given to exaggeration when drunk, irony when sober. Witty, precise, and blunt, rarely does a middle- or upper-class German refuse to discuss any question regarding morality, prostitution, vice, crime, etc., as long as the queries are not personal. He is proud of his country's pleasures and women, and more than unusually eager to initiate the foreigner. German men have a nice zest for life—food, wine, women, and music—and are unusually literate and well informed.

The women can be an absolute joy. They are as intelligent, but warmer, more lighthearted than the men. Their physical beauty is well known, the Brunhilde image gone, perhaps forever, in the wake of food shortages following the war. It is no longer fashionable to be fat in Germany, though the middle- and lower-class elderly strain to keep the tradition alive. However if there is a national neurosis, the young women seem unafflicted. But then, nobody here ever overate from *nervousness*. (For the record, the typical West German female has hips slimmer by two and a half centimeters and a bosom fuller by half to one centimeter than she did ten years ago according to the Hohenstein Research Institute, which measured ten thousand females aged fourteen to sixty-six.)

The most significant characteristic of women: *they know how to please men.* They are brought up that way. Obedience is still the first law of German homes of all classes. Daughter watches mother who wouldn't dare cross father in this, the most patriarchal of large European nations. (Until the 1969 penal reforms there were penalties against adults who knowingly permitted their children to have premarital sexual relations.)

Though they are as frank and uninhibited as their Scandinavian sisters, German girls are not as promiscuous. And unlike many Swedish girls, the German girl makes love not merely to gratify herself: she is genuinely interested in her partner. But *caveat;* though Germans, unlike the French, don't care how you pronounce it . . . you had better do it properly.

BROTHEL FOR LADIES—"WHORHOUSE"

This is especially timely advice for gentlemen, considering the advent of Hamburg's new bordello catering to women, staffed by men. (What should they be called? "Whors"? And what does one call such a situation: "bordella"? "House of the Rising Sons"?) German Women's Lib groups have already lauded the project as a "meaningful step toward sexual equality." On the other hand, Hamburg's city *fathers*—who've never been bothered about houses wherein the boys do the girls—have shown grudging approval at best (they've no choice; it's perfectly legal), promising no difficulties "unless the thing gets out of hand." Whatever that means.

Surely director Dieter Glocke is a serious businessman. (He's also thirty-three and happily married.) Nearly 1600 anxious gentlemen of every intention rushed to respond to the first help wanted advertisement, whereupon Glocke began a great separation process—the men from the toys, as it were. A three-page questionnaire ranged from probes of general physical capacity —"we expect no man to satisfy more than four or five customers per eight-hour shift"—to whether the applicant "could satisfy a seventy-year-old woman." (The majority of the clientele is expected to be aged forty and over; many women's social and professional organizations regularly come en masse to Hamburg for a night on the town, "often wishing they had some place like the men have to finish off the evening," according to Herr Glocke.) The chosen studs then "appear before an all-female panel to be tested [this was not explained] for intelligence, tact, good manners, and general suitabil-ity," before at last they are permitted to staff the brothel for ladies ("Tom Cathouse"?).

"YELLOW HOUSE," as Glocke chooses to call it, will have a connecting beauty parlor affording discreet entrance for timid Janes. "Rubbernecks, tour-ists, and people who come to stare are expected for the first few months of business" before things settle down to accommodate the anticipated flow of regulars—the backbone of any successful bawdy house. Many of the rooms have baths and kitchenettes, and the whors are encouraged to decorate them for the occasion—flowers, paintings, erotic sculpture and art, etc. (Perhaps some *Cosmopolitan* magazine foldouts.) Clients will be charged 100DM (about $30) a time—rather high, considering that men pay only 30 to 40DM in comparable environments, the Eros Center, for example.

As with all so-called "bordels, whorehouses, brothels, etc." cited in this book, such terms are used only in the strict dictionary sense, as for example *Random House's* " . . . a house or apartment where *women* [italics mine] work as prostitutes." However, as with all these situations, whatever the Germans or Random House choose to call them, the whors of Yellow House share none of their fees with the operators; the only monies accruing to management will be derived from room rent—in this case 50DM per day—and food and beverage concessions. With an initial staff of seventy sexy, sensitive stallions, Glocke expects to be operating profitably within several months. Just to make sure, "the only stipulation we make is that our staff shall not fall in love at once with the customers."

Because Yellow House was just preparing to open as this book went to press, it is suggested that you secure its exact address in Simon von Utrecht-strasse and further particulars from the extremely efficient and amiable HAM-BURG CITY TOURIST OFFICE (Bieberhaus, next to the Main Station; an under-standing, discreet young woman will answer if you ring 24-12-34). Or ask a policeman. Actually, virtually the whole town knows, for the enterprise has caused a mild sensation, even in bawdy, beautiful Hamburg.

LIBIDINOUS LIBRARY

You've come a long way, baby. But you've still got a long way to go before they build you a doll house to play in like CLUB RONDEEL (Sierichstr. 74; 279-33-60), located in portions of a mansion set among the weeping-willowed canals and columned, balconied mini-estates of Hamburg's Winterhude quarter, just in from the sailboat-dotted *Aussen* (outer) Alster. Rondeel's facilities approximate those of a good Englishman's (or naughty one's) club, which suits some Anglophiles among the *haute* Hanseatics in this neighborhood and nearby Eppendorf. To the right of the large entrance foyer there is a splendid little library of more than a thousand volumes, ranging from *Life of Bismarck* to *Death in Venice*. Rich Harleian bindings. Hefner (not Hugh; F. von Hefner-Alteneck, nineteenth-century electrical engineer) reading lamps. Brahms (born Hamburg, 1833) on the excellent stereo. And, speaking of smoky Johannes, good cigars in the humidor.

You will not find the seven or more gorgeous librarians in the library, although some were recently first editions (aged twenty-one to twenty-four) and all are best sellers. They are in the large candlelit drawing room, sipping sherry (from 5DM) and whispering at the small, unadorned check-out desk which doubles as a bar, or playing card games like "pisher paasher" at little doily-covered tables.

Browsers are treated as cordially as buyers. However, for 200DM (somewhat more than $60) one of the girls will take you into one of the smaller reading rooms (which have beds) and read to you. For about an hour. The walls have mirrors in case you like back numbers or house organs in reverso.

Like many libraries, Club Rondeel is closed Sunday, but, unlike some others, it is open the other six nights from 8 P.M. to 2 A.M. Considering that the Rondeel stacks offer some of the finest hornbooks in the country—and perhaps the best in this town—Sierichstr. 74 might be worth a stopover before or after the Frankfurt Book Fair.

SAIL TO A MIXED SAUNA

While you're in Winterhude take a short stroll from Rondeel to Andreasstr. 18. Better yet, come back the next day because the SIERICH SAUNA is open from 9 A.M. to anything from 11 P.M. Tuesday and Thursday to 6 P.M. and 1 P.M. Saturday and Sunday respectively.

Here's what you should do, especially if you have your wife, husband, or whatever kind of sweetheart with you. Catch a 3, 16, or 33 Toonerville-type trolley in front of the Main Station and, after about five minutes, jump off at Lohmühlenstrasse. Walk a block to the Alster and, after coffee on the terrace, rent a little motor boat or sailboat. Note the lovely whitestone hotels in the area facing directly on the lake, probably no more expensive than the one you may be occupying near the Main Station or in the center of the city. Anyway, sail up the Alster and take your second right (the first is okay too if you have a map) into Langer Zug. Pass under Sierichstrasse bridge, then make a left up the narrow Mühlenkamp Kanal and keep going for two bridges (two city blocks) until you intersect the next canal (Goldbek). Make a left into Goldbek, pass quickly under the three little bridges, stop at the third one (Sierichstrasse) and pull your boat up on the mossy bank under the weeping willows.

Stop necking with your wife and climb the bank. Ask the man who wants to know why you're putting your boat in his back yard where the Sierich Sauna is. It's only a block south and, considering that people who live in this lovely upper-middle-class area are very happy with their lifestyles and not adverse to showing them off, he'll probably walk you to it.

Be sure it is either Saturday or Sunday, because on these two days Sierich is a mixed sauna (but only a therapeutic one; it never "swings") with all facilities, except dressing rooms, coeducational—lounge, saunas, showers, outdoor room, sleeping rooms. It's mixed Tuesday and Friday nights from 9:01 P.M. to 11 P.M. too. Phone 27-21-35 for further details, and ask them to have a fresh fruit salad waiting for you. You may also find this kind of situation and equally civilized people across the Alster in Pöseldorf at OLYMPIA-SAUNA (Magdalenenstr. 25; 44-33-80).

SEX SHOWS REVISITED

Speaking of Frankfurt, as we were a few moments ago (we'll arrive there for a short visit in about fifteen minutes, ten minutes for speed readers), West Germany's center of publishing and traditional capital of finance offers its bankers and bookmen no live sex shows on a par with those of St. Pauli's, for all Frankfurt's raunchy reputation. However, before a recent trip to Hamburg one heard that all its clubs have now been forbidden to stage live team-sex, not to mention two-party heterosexual intercourse ("except private clubs," whatever that may mean).

Sure enough, a spring 1972 phone call to TRIANGEL (31-27-84) elicits a gruff male voice which suggests the premises (126 Hafenstr., facing the Elbe as you remember) are no longer occupied. "But go down there anyway. You will find a guide who takes you to a new Triangel."

Indeed, you are met in front of the heavily boarded-up 126 Hafenstrasse (Triangel's old sign is still visible) by several guides (some of whom might be equally at home at racetracks), the smallest of whom you choose for the three minute Volkswagen bus ride to Nobistor 14, an extension of the Reeperbahn and just around the corner from the ever-grossing Grosse Freiheit.

This is a "private club," says the hostess—whom you have never met in your life—as she shows you to a comfortable couch, "so of course you will see a real fuck show tonight. No problems here." You are required to order two drinks (total 55DM; about $17) which arrive simultaneously. On demand you are given a menu that says, "SEX CLUB TRIANGEL" but has no address . . . perhaps in case the management decides to move again. The room is nondescript, well carpeted, and too big. This is Saturday night and there are perhaps nine customers among the one hundred or so empty places. And several relatively attractive waitresses or hostesses in scanties.

You recognize the old Arabian vaginal candle act, and the narrator's voice on the tape-recorded soundtrack sounds very familiar. In between live "lesbian" performances a very stylish porn cartoon called *Sleeping Beauty and the Seven Dwarfs* proves to be the hottest thing you will see this night at Triangel. That there was no "fuck show" is perhaps your own fault. (Though when you left and angrily complained, the management stiffly replied, "There were not enough people here tonight for that.") Two hostesses offered you the chance to go right up on stage and perform with the professionals if you'd only buy a mere 60DM worth of champagne. And when this suggestion was declined a girl suggested a private audition for 250DM.

Daunted, you return to 126 Hafenstrasse to complain that Triangel wasn't on the square this night and there you find the "guide." He's sorry, he says, he took you to the "wrong place. A fuck show for sure if you go to CLUB AMPHORE," he says as you chase him a few yards along Hafenstrasse to number 140 (31-52-09).

This is more like it. (Familiar narrator and Arabian music?) Tiny but poshly enough upholstered *bôite*-like L-shaped chamber with small stage and production values nearly equal to those experienced during Triangel's 1970 "May of life" (see Schiller). Fair visibility from the bar but better from the cushy couches. That is if the almost naked (wearing socks) waitress will only get off your lap. After bringing you the mandatory two drinks (at 55DM) she suggests you massage random portions of herself while she consumes 60DM worth of champagne. She persists gently and sweetly at your decline (but not fall, although she is very very pretty), but then gives up and leaves because she must get ready for the "lesbian" show.

Another nearly naked (wearing socks) hostess joins you, invites you to come on stage and "make a fuck show" with her, but you decline again, pointing out the professional couple who, at this moment, seem to be carrying on well enough. "How about we do it in the *séparée* for hundred eighty marks?"

"Sorry, I forgot to pick up my Amatella at Beate Uhse."

And though audience participation seems to be the latest thing at certain Hamburg live shows, there were no takers this night among the audience of well-dressed consular types, several with their wives, apparently. However, a male employee here at Club Amphore says they are planning to install a Turkish bath in the basement. Perhaps that will stimulate the patrons.

In contrast to the so-called "private clubs," the authorities have forbidden René Durand to stage live sexual intercourse in his lavish new SALAMBO SEX THEATER (Grosse Freiheit 39; 31-56-22; 319-34-73). He couldn't care less. This same Saturday night Durand's place is packed out, a tribute to his stunning sex showmanship, which, it is submitted, may now surpass that of Paris' Alain Bernardin; people also appreciate Salambo's sensible 15DM entrance fee and one-5DM-drink minimum. Salambo has emerged as a somewhat larger and more exciting version of Bernardin's Crazy Horse Saloon (and Durand also runs a Hamburg "Crazy Horse," just a few paces down the Grosse Freiheit).

In case you are tempted to get up on stage and join the ravishing chorus of eleven Siamese beauties ("just flown in from Bangkok") or if your companion relishes ravishing the equally splendid malemen (none gay), don't. Don't bother, that is. At the rear of the top-floor SALAMBO-BOUDOIR (smaller of the two sex-theaters), Durand is just putting the finishing touches to "Europe's finest *partouzes* room." A lavish four-hundred-square-foot chamber of scarlet ceiling and wall-to-wall beautyrest mattress, the *"Gruppenzimmer"* also has clothing racks, douches, mirrors, and showers. Couples welcome, but partners may be provided for singles. Everyone will be given a gold bracelet for identification purposes, or in case one gets lost.

DEUTSCHLAND, DEUTSCHLAND ÜBER
PHALLUS—IN 16 CITIES

Own a Share of the Oldest Profession

If Merrill Lynch is bullish on America, Kurt Kohls, founder and managing partner of KOHLS LIEGENSCHAFTEN KG is positively goatish on Germany. For the first time in history, according to an item in *The Wall Street Journal,* you and public investors all over the world have the opportunity to invest in its oldest profession. "It is also the solidest," states the prospectus, "because *Irma La Douce* never has a recession. . . ." A minimum annual return of 9% is guaranteed on your investment.

This is more than enough inducement for a train ride (always a pleasure in modern Germany) from Hamburg to Ulm-on-Danube, a cathedral city which gave the world Albert Einstein (not terribly proud of it until recently). At Neuestrasse 115 in a modern office building opposite the fifteenth-century Three Kings Cathedral you find the corporate headquarters of Kohls' activities (principal activities: housing and office-building construction, real-estate development and investment) and the hearty forty-three-year old executive talking on his telephones 0731-23009, 23008, 23208, and 28095; telex 07-12533).

Kohls Liegenschaften is seeking equity capital of $2.5 million, about $400,000 less than the market value of its two existing enterprises, where quarters are rented to young ladies who in turn rent their bodies: 1. ARABELLA HOUSE I, shrewdly set just across the border from Switzerland, a country which has no legal prostitution, in the city of Konstanz (Bahnhofsplatz 4, with other entrances at Nos. 2 and 4 Rauheneckgasse, comprising two houses totaling 57 rooms and a "V.I.P. Club,") and LA PETITE MAISON, "A special house for connoisseurs." 2. ARABELLA HOUSE II, set just outside Kaiserslautern, a Rhineland-Palatinate city of some 89,000, less than three hours by train to the northwest of the Ulm corporate headquarters.

This latter operation is perhaps even better located than the one in Konstanz, for in Kaiserslautern and vicinity (otherwise whorehouseless) is the largest complex of NATO bases in Europe. The Kohls operation here includes seventy-six modern single-room apartments (all with private shower and douche), canteen, and relaxing lounge for the girls, public beer bar, night bar, two automatic bowling alleys, lockup garages, discothèque-dance hall, tennis courts, access to adjacent horseback-riding facilities, infirmary with staff physician, large community sauna with solarium, and torture room. A separate compound of apartments for children of the prostitutes and a swimming pool are planned. In Kohls' prospectus the appraising architect notes that the property could be converted to "a hotel, motel, or privately run old-age home." And from the photos in the prospectus Arabella House II resembles a large modern secondary school of the type that might be erected by an affluent suburban American community.

By early 1974 Herr Kohls will have eight such houses in Germany and Austria—that is if he can raise the necessary $12.4 million. To accomplish this he is selling partnerships through investment consultants, newspaper advertisements, and an enthusiastic sales force, which includes some former mutual-funds drummers, not to mention his own considerable acumen and effusive drive. Five feet nine of bearish (but half Teddy) jut-jawed, well-fed Baden-Württemberg muscle, Kohls laughs all the time, is a good family man, is not a Scorpio, and likes white ties and wide-striped shirts.

Kohls isn't kidding. At this writing he has sold nearly $2 million worth of limited partnerships to some 145 investors. Each share is sold as a 50,000DM ($15,500) unit. But to accommodate the small investor and to afford everyone anonymity, ten people may get together and each put up $1,550 to achieve the minimum for one unit.

Inquiries have come in from all over the world, not a few from the United States, including several from investment counselors for some of America's largest universities.

And "First National Bank of Santa Barbara, California," says Kohls as he merrily sifts through the pile of perhaps one thousand letterheads.

"Manufacturers Hanover Trust!"

"Hey, that's my bank," you exclaim.

"Hornblower Weeks . . . Shearson Hammill!"

"Hey, that's my broker!"

" . . . And here England's greatest broker. And here, Hayden Stone. And Fidelity Fund."

"And my mutual fund!"

"Don't forget, our operations are a sound financial investment, and not only for the theoretical reason that prostitution has survived every recession and depression for over 2000 years. But we also have something no one else has . . . *Sex mit Herz!*" exults Kurt Kohls as he points to the heart-shaped sticker with his corporate slogan affixed to your two-suiter and waves good-bye to you and the 7:30 P.M. Intercity pulling out of Ulm station. His roar of laughter nearly drowns out the p.a. announcer.

People on the train are laughing at your baggage sticker too. "Sex with a heart, is it?" says the conducter as you glide through the hills that surround Stuttgart. He graciously points out the principal attractions. Chartered in the thirteenth century, Stuttgart now includes a pretty good house (30DM) just off Königstrasse between the railway station and the town hall. There is also considerable street activity near Leonardsplatz and Wagnerstrasse, and there are bar bargains in the vicinity of Katharinenstrasse.

At 9:30 change trains in Heidelberg, whose university was founded in 1386. A current student favorite is the "Eros-Center" in Güteramtsstrasse, tuition from 30 to 40DM. Students who have cars patrol Speyerer Strasse, and those who don't take tutorials with the 20DM streetwalkers of Messplatz.

This is not some two-bit express linking tank towns like New York City and Boston, it is, rather, the ordinary Intercity connection between those great metropolises Ulm and Kaiserslautern. Therefore it pulls in right on time at 11:14 P.M. Arabella housemaster Joe is at the station to meet you, Kohls having wired ahead. Joe instantly recognizes you by the *"Sex mit Herz"* sticker, which, by now, has been affixed to your sleeve by a pretty secretary. (Secretaries are available in the first-class sections of most Intercity trains . . . but only for secretarial services. However this one took dinner with you and, liberated and well-paid by the German Federal Railways system, paid for her own.)

Housemaster Joe is a formidable barrel of a man, feared by potential troublemakers (he's a Scorpio and keeps a "wolf" for a dog), admired by Kohls and the peacekeepers and maintenance personnel who make up Ara-bella-Kaiserslautern's staff, and well liked by the prostitutes for his compassion and sense of humor. He is also a man of decision and action. After an hour tour of the small city discloses that all the moderately priced hotels are full . . . Joe looks at you . . . and you look at him. He throws the big Mercedes into gear.

"Do many people stay overnight in your whorehouse?" you ask Mitzi the floormaid as she flips the switch which turns on the red light atop the entrance to your room (number three), signifying to anyone wandering the halls that this one is "occupied." The whores posing in mini-chiffons outside rooms 2 and 4 are giggling and two G.I.'s feign jealousy.

"No," says Mitzi as she turns down your fresh sheets.

"Am I the first?"

"Looks like it."

It's 2 A.M., you keep falling out of the round bed, and the big mirror seems ready to fall off the wall. Next door a soldier doesn't know whether he's coming or going. A wolf barks down the hall. The . . . douche leaks. You fumble for the bedlamp switch and eleven seconds later the door crashes open to reveal a laughing Joe and a snarling Alsatian called Max. Joes shakes with laughter (the dog continues to snarl), for you have accidentally switched on the alarm. All seventy-six rooms have them, each wired directly to a master board in the first-floor-left office where someone (and Max) is on duty twenty-four hours.

Arabella House is open for business from 11 A.M. to 5 A.M., and Joe had scheduled your inspection tour for noon of the following day, but you have decided to take it now.

At present the house is a bit over 50 percent occupied by some forty-one tenant prostitutes ranging in age from twenty-one to thirty, most of them in their mid-twenties. Every morning beginning at 2 there occurs the check-off ritual in the canteen-restaurant, which serves as an oasis for the girls and is strictly off limits to clients. Joe sits at a desk with adding machine and a stack of ledger books, one for each tenant-whore. Relying on a complex chit system, he records the amounts spent by each girl for snacks, meals, and innumerable cups of coffee. This can be considerable, but monies for rent (50DM per day) and food are the only sums the girls pay to Kohls KG. The girls may also, at this time, deposit their daily or even hourly take in the safe and, of course, make withdrawals on demand.

By terms of their rental contracts the tenants are advised to charge at least 30DM a time. When business is poor—and it always is in the days immediately preceding the Army's monthly payday—fees may drop that low, but the standard price is 50DM ($15.50) or $20. Thus G.I.'s, who apparently haven't the opportunity regularly to convert their money to marks, are charged more than Germans or anyone else with German currency.

Working conditions and morale appear to be as good as could be expected in this business. The girls are free to come and go as they please, of course, and while many do live in their Arabella rooms (and are under no obligation by Kohls KG to entertain so much as one annual customer), some maintain apartments in town. Many have their own cars. Not a few have been here for more than three years.

A tour of the four floors reveals that the rooms (all about fifteen feet square) are done in any of four basic color ensembles—red, blue, aqua, and something Joe keeps referring to as *"Bauernhaus"* ("farmhouse"; see Vienna chapter)—with coordinated drapes, spreads, and modernistic lamps. The girls are encouraged to decorate to taste, and most rooms resemble young teenagers' bedrooms with lots of pinups (and some *Playboy* magazine-type nudies), enormous stuffed animals, incense receptacles, and huge colorful candles. Several rooms have film projectors and the dirty films to go with them, some have TV receivers, and Nos. 29, 48, and 3 have round beds. The tenants are required by their rental contracts to keep their rooms clean and orderly; the halls, where they pose on stools or rocking chairs, are scrubbed daily by Arabella's maintenance staff.

A portion of the second floor is "off limits to colored boys," according to one lithesome blonde found there. *This is not a house policy,* it is simply that certain girls refuse to entertain black men and therefore a section of the house has been reserved to honor this prejudice. But it's not so simple. The blond girl tried to explain with an analogy that " . . . it's the same like some girls don't like fat men."

"Undoubtedly. But is there a section of the house that's off limits to fat guys?"

"No . . . but we could refuse them. We have the right to refuse anybody."

"Have you ever refused a fat man? Even a very fat man?"

"No." She laughs. "In Germany these are usually the ones with most money."

"But you refuse black men—fat ones, thin ones, rich ones. . . . "

"These people are a little bit rough . . . can't work with them. . . . A lot of houses in Germany have a floor like this one."

(But Joe and the other peacekeepers—including an ex-GI and former M.P. from a large southern state—agree: When trouble, fighting, or excessive drunkenness occurs, Germans are the worst offenders followed by white GI's, followed lastly by black GI's. And worst of all was the furious French soldier who, in 1970, launched a one-man, three-grenade attack on Arabella House, causing $155,280 damage—which the French Army paid—to fifty rooms.)

"Well what about Jews? Does anyone refuse to go with Jews?"

"What! Hell, no . . . nowadays in Germany who can tell who is Jew and who is not?" says the girl.

"Yes, that's probably so, although there was a time when Germans *could* tell who was who."

"? . . . *Ja,* the noses!"

"*Nein* . . . the Yellow Stars."

In Germany, though practical application may be quite another matter, even the whores are capable of engaging in pseudo-Hegelian dialectic.

Continuing your tour, you find that room No. 15 contains a well-equipped infirmary where the girls are examined each Tuesday by a physician. The stirrups are attached to a kind of adjustable dentist's chair surrounded by sterilizers and all the latest miracle drugs.

Another sort of stirrups—these for clients—dangle from the fine English saddlery in the basement torture room or *Folterkammer.* Also crops, whips, syringes for enemas and colonics, handcuffs, shackles, etc. Though many girls are willing to administer to S/M clients (at rates from 100DM) it is doubtful they get much opportunity to do so and hence acquire no real proficiency. Surely there is no call for torture from American soldiers who face the possiblity of the real thing in Vietnam, if they haven't experienced it already. Only one girl suggested that she would submit to torture—but not for less than 1,000 per hour.

For 100DM an hour clients may join the girls in the large sauna and solarium next door (best times; 5 A.M. or 11 A.M.), the latter equipped with expensive sun lamps, paneled in sandalwood, and carpeted with a sort of AstroTurf. There is also a large plunge pool.

With all the fairy tales one hears about whores who save their earnings to retire at thirty and live happily ever after running boutiques or small hotels, it is submitted that few prostitutes anywhere have a better opportunity to do so than Arabella girls. (An added factor, of course, is the characteristic German thrift.) A stunning slim brunette insists she has already made a substantial down payment on a shop. Three years ago she gave up her interesting but grossly underpaid job as translator with a wire-service and embarked on her current career with equal parts of terror and determination.

"With my first man here I was so frightened I couldn't even look at him. (I had slept with only three men previously, each of whom I loved.) And of course he was aware of my fear. He loved it. He 'raped' me but paid double the price. He fancied me so much he kept returning each night for a week. It was horrible. But later we became friends." She speaks the Queen's English, having learned it in London, as so many German girls do.

"I had great difficulty my first few months. I was too softhearted . . . gave too much away . . . stayed too long with the men and listened to their problems afterwards. But after six months the girls put me straight." (There is a good *esprit* and camaraderie among the girls, considering the similarity of their day-to-day experiences, whatever their backgrounds. This is exemplified by the periodic group sings in the canteen when, after Joe puts way his ledger books, he plays the Hamond organ, his "first love" aside from wife and children. And that big dog.)

"Even now," continues the soft-hearted brunette, "if I get to know a man on a level other than sex-business I cannot have relations with him for money."

Psychologists (or whorehouse architects) might be interested to learn that virtually all the clients turn to the right when they come into the halls from the stairwell landings. These choice right-hand chambers—on whichever floor—are assigned according to a girl's seniority, says Miss Softheart, who further states, "Most men seem to go into the room of the first girl they see, whatever she looks like. I don't think the men who come here even look at our faces!"

Their boyfriends may visit the prostitutes, but if "boyfriends" come it is a direct violation of Arabella House's regulations. Considering that Kohls' policies and innovations leave the girls as free from the menaces of pimps, the pressures of corrupt police, and the taunts of society as it is possible to be in this line of work, it comes as a disappointment that some girls do share portions of their hard-earned incomes.

Perhaps the psychiatrists can explain it, but as Joe's Mercedes roars you toward the Kaiserslautern railway station and NATO jets zoom over Arabella House (did a wing waggle?) a quick glance at the scrolled lettering on the stone entrance gate affords reason enough: SEX MIT HERZ.

FRANKFURT

The Kaiserslautern-Frankfurt run involves a change of trains at Mannheim where, "Whatever is not forbidden is permitted" (see Schiller, whose career effectively began at the Mannheim theater in 1782), among the 20-30DM street girls of Luisenstrasse, Hafenstrasse, and Lupinenstrasse. Arrive Frankfurt 7:07 P.M.

Within one hour you've ascertained that the simplest way for this book to cover Frankfurt would be to enumerate those areas immediately east of the monstrous main railway station—at the heart of the city—wherein there is *no* action. In downtown Frankfurt there are virtually no such areas.[5]

For all its bright neon, the wide main stem Kaiserstrasse remains a grim thoroughfare of strip joints, whore bars, quick-eats joints, touts, striptease houses, and porn sellers. And streetwalkers (to 50DM) and auto-borne whores (from 75DM) available from about 10 P.M. to about 4 A.M. The CAFÉ EXPRESS (Kaiserstrasse 42) is, however, a pleasant contrast to the riffraffishness of the neighborhood (the parallel Taunusstrasse and the intersecting Elbestrasse have even more concentrated action than does Kaiserstrasse). In glittering, somewhat old-world surroundings you may enjoy delicious deli snacks, excellent coffee and pastry to 4 A.M. while, from about midnight on, tables of truly beautiful sugar puppies hope you'll invite them to join you, perhaps even to dance in the cabaret. The black-tie waiters and management know nothing of these hot-stuff arrangements, nor do they profit from them in any way, for, aside from its name, Café Express is a pretty laconic situation.

The greatest concentration of very young, pretty pros (99 of them!) is in the nearby GRAZY SEXY (Elbestrasse 53), a classic house of its type. This one is even more theatrical than Hamburg's Eros Center—which it closely resem-

[5]The all-purpose police number is 110.

bles in architecture as well as theory—so accessible for bargaining ("fifty marks for fifteen minutes; *mit* French and all clothes off . . . seventy marks") and even dancing (pop Muzak on the speakers) are the scantily clad Grazies. The stone street-level contract cavern is brightly lit in red, the girls are amazingly good-humored considering that the scene resembles a concentration camp roll-call, the crude erotic murals after Diego Rivera (well after) are more Rough Rider than *Blaue Reiter,* and the bedrooms are upstairs. In the midst of it all is a porn boutique. Connecting compounds house a flashy pub and posh, expensive striptease nightclub.

Get out of there and walk two blocks north across Mainzer-Landstrasse, where begins a lovely area of little parks and attractive villa-style residences, characterized by the great townhouses built by Frankfurt's mercantile aristocracy—for the city has traditionally been more a center of commerce than industry—many of which have now been converted to consulates and small office buildings. From 10 P.M. to about 2 A.M. 50DM streetwalkers—who have apartments in the neighborhood and, as do so many Frankfurt prostitutes, thus obviate the need for clients to pay for hotel rooms—patrol Westendplatz, Westendstrasse, Erlenstrasse, and Rheinstrasse. The cute little brothel in Savignystrasse, however, has recently ceased operations. Never mind. Five blocks south of the Palmengarten and even closer to the university compound, the sidewalk in front of the imposing townhouse at Westendstrasse 104 is packed with well-spoken and attractive pussycats who suggest you spend fifteen minutes and fifty marks.

From here it's mostly downhill. For example, one doesn't have to enter the ugly gray stone piles at Gutleutstrasse 97 (midway between the Hauptbahnhof's south side and the River Main) to imagine what grade of whore is prancing its hallways and, amazingly, charging 50DM.

Moving east into the area that comprises what was the old city (the path of the original twelfth-century walls and moats is marked by street names ending in *"graben"*), in the vicinity of the ancient Hirschgraben (where Goethe was born in 1749), one sees a great deal of 100DM *Sturm und Drang,* particularly among the auto-borne whores of Kirchnerstrasse. Passing by the 500-year-old Römer town hall, anachronistically set amid the glut of steel and glass that is central Frankfurt, you encounter even more storm and stress (and some very complicated traffic patterns on the way) among the brassy whores of Allerheiligenstrasse. Two houses, "fifty marks to take the clothes off and put the *Gummi* on." A short walk down Klingerstrasse across the Zeil leads one to yet another house; 50–60DM zealots in the courtyard, some on the sidewalk.

The world's first high-tension alternating current power-transmission installation was accomplished at Frankfurt's 1891 Electrical Exhibition by its director, Oskar von Miller, the celebrated (in Frankfurt) electrical engineer. Perhaps that is why the whores of Oskar-von-Miller-Strasse 8 are so very highly strung, and overcharging at 30DM. They are conducting themselves badly with men who get up the courage to take a peek into the open-air courtyard behind Sexy Pirat Bar and the little house there. Too bad, for the complex affords a nice river view, it being set directly on the right bank of the Main.

Should you become involved with one of the better street or auto girls of Kaiserstrasse and environs, she'll likely consummate the transaction in her flat in one of four houses across the Main in the Sachsenhausen quarter. (There are no less than ten bridges which connect the central city to the left bank.) Cabbies know them well. The girl who charges a client 100DM after bringing him to one of these might take 50–60DM if he first encountered her outside one of these apartment buildings. But don't prowl the halls banging on the peepholed doors. These are *residences,* not brothels. Similarly the high-class dwellings in Grosser Hasenpfad and Oppenheimer Landstrasse can only be negotiated if you arrive with one of the beauteous tenants in her new Mercedes or Porsche. Her fuel bill is high, so the session will cost from 100 to 200DM.

HANOVER

Hanover is hot. The capital of Lower Saxony, located south of Hamburg and west of Berlin in northwest Germany, has some 580,000 people and at least five thriving public whorehouses—and if you want to be technical, there are actually over twenty!

Hallerstrasse 33 and 35 are the best. Although they are modern structures with all the latest security devices—buzzers, switchboards, glass partitions behind which sharp-eyed custodians scrutinize prospective clients—the Haller twins offer a decidedly un-Teutonic, almost Geisha-like ambiance, what with the comfortable exhibition parlors where up to ten young and uniformly attractive girls parade on approval among the conservatively dressed clients, so comfy in their soft leather lounge chairs. From 30 to 50DM. A favorite of touring Japanese businessmen, so you know it has to be good. There is a second house in the neighborhood, in Friesenstrasse (just behind the Main Station, but so much construction is occurring in Hanover, and will for some years to come, one is advised to take a taxi). With the 30DM tricks hanging out the windows, one can't miss it. But one would be wise if one did.

Ludwigstrasse is preposterous. The whole street—well, one whole side of it—is one big whorehouse, or rather some fifteen individual adjacent buildings, some of them interconnected. The houses are of recent construction and seem specifically designed as machines for vending women. The architect apparently devoted a great deal of effort to insure maximum exposure. (And the eye-level, large windows afford maximum vulnerability to the taunts and vicious humor of the steady stream of jeering men and boys who would rather march Ludwigstrasse than attend a boxing match. Or a pigsticking.) Highly recommended to those males who believe female prostitution to be a lazy, easygoing occupation. It would be interesting to see how some of the beer-slobbering bullies for whom Ludwigstrasse is a Circus Maximus night out would fare if they were placed on the *inside* of the windows (those at ground level around the far corner are grilled). Up to one hundred courageous, good-natured prostitutes, from twenty-one to forty or so, all of whom, you may be sure, earn every pfennig of that 30DM.

Don't wander Hanover after midnight. It's safe but you'll be lonesome. Your likeliest encounters will be with construction and demolition workmen, their acetylene torches slicing the crisp Saxon air as they dig and fill an enormous (at least five square blocks wide) hole in the heart of town on the Opernplatz. Using the height of the five-story structures which surround it as a guide, you reckon it to be as deep as the combined height of two of those buildings. By midnight the lovely OPERA KONDITOREI (opposite the magnificent Opera House) has closed, as has the smart PASSPORT PUB (journalists and some very worth-while *jeunesse dorée*) in Luisenstrasse which emanates from Ernst-August Platz in front of the main railway station. But long after 3 A.M. in JENSEITS, a new cellar club and attractive discothèque (just off Ernst-August at the corner of Rosenstrasse and Schillerstrasse) you may encounter attractive and well-spoken ladies and gentlemen who can explain Leibniz' Law (he was entombed in Hanover in 1716) or point out some of Sir William Herschel's (born here, 1738) astronomical discoveries—Uranus and the snow caps of Mars, among others.

It's 4 A.M. How about . . . delicious steaks or other grills served on wooden slabs at butcher-block tables . . . with hot fruit salad; endless varieties of the good German cheeses, beers or white wines (the best white wines come from this country, of course); engaging, theatrical fellow diners; black-tie waiters with the sauce of Paris' Brasserie Lipp but none of the lip of New York City's Ratner's. There is apparently only one restaurant of character in central Hanover that is open until dawn, but it has all that: HERRENHÄUSSER—a veritable Lindy's-on-the-Leine, Hanover's little river—corner Gëorgstrasse and Karmarschstrasse, right at the edge of the big excavation.

MINI-TOUR OF THE PROVINCES

In modern Germany it seems virtually impossible to find a city of any size without a house of prostitution and/or midtown streets where such commerce does not flourish. But let's try.

We've already failed in Kaiserslautern, Heidelberg, Stuttgart, and Mannheim, not to mention Hamburg, Frankfurt, and Hanover. No luck in Ulm either. A short distance from the splendid Gothic cathedral (begun in 1377), virtually in its shadow (no metaphor, it's 528-foot tower is the world's tallest ecclesiastical erection), stands a "nunnery"—again no idle metaphor as such houses were thusly described in sixteenth- to nineteenth-century England. This is Schülinstrasse 12. Five windows wide by five stories high. Forty marks for fifteen minutes. Awful place. Smells of chicken fat and liver and onions frying in the halls.

The HOTEL HERZOG-ALBRECHT, corner Zinglerstrasse and Schillerstrasse, near the Bahnhof, is infinitely more appealing. Which is saying little. Like Schülinstrasse 12 (which was constructed in 1898 for more mundane purposes) Herzog-Albrecht is a nineteenth-century structure, but here you find a certain working class *Belle Époque* ambiance in the dark coffee room where some attractive, though unilingual, girls are available from the late afternoon to the early morning at 50DM or less. Phone 67-535 if you'd like a room for the night (for the H.A. is also an ordinary hotel)—singles 17DM, doubles 30DM. No mirrors, but no chicken fat either.

You finally lose the odor in Cologne (founded by Romans in A.D. 50), which has a cathedral even more celebrated than Ulm's (begun in 1248, it contains relics of the Wise Men of the East), and more "nunneries." Ordinary ones in the Im Stavenhof and Kleine Brinkegasse and a rather class operation in the Parkgürtel. Cabbies know all these. Street girls disrupt Cologne traffic in Hohenzollernring, auto girls in Kaiser-Wilhelm-Ring, and coffee-house girls stir things up in Friesenstrasse.

Düsseldorf is a fashion-conscious supermodern city—but pleasantly so—having been virtually destroyed during World War II. A center of the textile industry, it is overloaded with models and would-be models. A very *haute* class pleasure house in Gustav-Poensgenstrasse. And more mundane establishments in Rethelstrasse and Hinter dem Bahndamm. And several more throughout the city.

Duisburg was, through World War II, an armaments center and sure enough, Vulkanstrasse contains no less than four fireworks fornifications. Some roaming candles in Juliusstrasse. In Flensburg the Beate Uhse factory continues to make Germany safe for sexocracy, but the 20DM houses in Neuestrasse owe their existence solely to the street's proximity to the town's harbor. Bochum has a house in Im Winkel, street girls in Ferdinandstrasse and Mauritiusstrasse. Bonn, which begat Beethoven (born 1770 at 515 Bonngasse), has an "Eros Center" in Immenburgstrasse but otherwise the capital of the Federal Republic is a pretty dull place. Bremen, on the other hand, is quite another story, particularly along the Helenenstrasse. Ditto Dortmund's Steinplatz and Linienstrasse. Thomas Mann, a Lübeck boy, describes his city in *Buddenbrooks,* among whose lines are "Beauty can pierce one like a pain." Good chance of this happening the morning after a night on this Baltic seaport's uproarious Clemenstrasse, where 20DM opens many portholes.

Considering the estimable efficiency and comfort of the trains and the proximity of most of the foregoing situations to the railway stations of the respective cities, the German Federal Railway System would be wise to institute some sort of bawdy beltline tour of the country. But if you don't stop using your Eurailpass (unlimited first-class travel throughout continental Western Europe, three weeks for $125, etc., passes available from any travel agent) and get off the trains, you'll never see Munich.

MUNICH

WEST GERMANY

The basic unit of currency is the beloved Deutsche mark, which can be divided into 100 pfennigs. At this writing you'll get about 3.18 marks for each floating dollar. Thus each mark equals about 30 U.S. cents. You can bring in or take out as many marks as you can carry.

"In Germany people do not walk about in public naked."

"Oh, but my uncle did," rejoined co-producer Bernard Castelli, whose local production of *Hair* was threatened with the padlock by police sent from the Ministry of Culture if the very brief, dimly lit nude scene and the profanity were not omitted. "Right here in Dachau too . . . on the way to the gas chambers."

Few guide books can resist describing Munich without using the word *Gemütlichkeit* or belaboring the *Kameradschaftlichkeit* of its beerhalls. And for Thomas Wolfe, Munich was no less than "some kind of German heaven." But for Gerome Ragni and James Rado, *Hair*'s authors, the City Tourist Office brochure's description of Munich as a "small town of one million inhabitants" is far more pointed than was perhaps intended.

"Haare" was eventually presented here, and with no cuts, but only after much fuss, not a little from the authors' intended hotel, whose militant management denied Messrs. Ragni and Rado admission simply because their hair was too long. Further, when a taxi driver refused to transport Mr. Ragni on similar grounds, an altercation resulted and both authors were hauled off by the police. The morality of the authorities, the taxi man, and the hotel—a perfunctory, small, second-class house opposite the Main Station—is as reflective of the Bavarian mentality as all the wild rumors you've heard (many of which happen to be true) of sexy, sensual, madcap Munich.

SEX AND THE SINGLE ROOM

Paragraph 180 of the West German penal code provides a jail sentence of not less than one month for anyone who registers unmarried couples in the same hotel room. As long as lovers register as man and wife there is no danger of prosecution, but if they fail to observe this formality, the chance of embarrassments is somewhat greater than you might suppose. Especially in Munich, where innkeepers are particularly strict. Of course, you'd never take such a law seriously, unless you happened to arrive late at your hotel one night (near *Hair*'s, by coincidence).

"You are late, sir," snaps the cadaverously thin, renitent room clerk.

"Yes, I know I'm late. And *you* knew I would be. I wired from Prague about my difficulties. It couldn't be helped."

"Yes, sir. We got your message. But you *are* late!" (How can a man be arrogant and polite at once? Must be ex-SS.)

"Well, do I get the room?" You are begging now.

"You can have the room for two nights only. After that it is reserved for another party." You have the feeling you are being punished.

At this moment a large, squarishly built Oriental in mourning clothes and a tiny black bowler comes charging down the stairs, rushes the desk, slams his key down, and stops short to glare red-eyed hatred at the clerk.

This has to be Goldfinger's Oddjob! Nobody else looks like this. But what would he be doing in Munich? Visiting Gert Froebe perhaps. Incredibly, the clerk proceeds to stare the big Chinese down. Not a word passes between them and at last "Oddjob," or whoever he is, stalks downstairs to the garage, displaying a most un-Oriental angry frustration.

"Oh, yes, that was Mister Oddjob of the films," offers the clerk, suddenly rather friendly and enjoying your astonishment. "Real name, Charles Sakata, South Korean national. The man is a 'catcher' on tour, appearing this week in the competitions. His home is Aachen." The delivery is flat, objective, as if read from a police dossier.

Bizarre confrontation. A three-hundred-pound Korean wrestler and karate expert and this arrogant, brittle little desk clerk. But "SS" never flinched.

Next morning you get the background from the hall porter. Mr. Sakata, though he can kill you eighty-three ways to Tet with a flick of his hand or his hat, must play by the same rules as the rest of us. Apparently he was to be interviewed by a local female journalist. A very private man, Mr. Sakata understandably chose to chat in his own hotel room (which happened to be a single), the hotel lobby being small and affording little privacy. No one questioned his motive, which makes the incident all the more pointed, and Teutonic.

Although the circumstances were entirely innocent, Mr. Sakata's several requests were denied. He in turn refused to acquiesce to the hypocrisy of taking a double room and registering the reporter as his "wife." Under hotel regulations this would have technically absolved management and clerk of all "responsibility." (Western passports are rarely examined in West Germany.) Obviously the rule has little to do with sin. Germans are more concerned with rules than morals. Whatever the equities, it is the *rule* that must be enforced to the letter. For if Mr. Sakata had proposed a compromise—that is, that he register the lady as his "wife" while retaining the single room— the answer would still have been an unqualified *"nein!"* After all, no rational man takes his wife, nor surely his "wife," to a single room.

Under current West German law a multitude of sins is covered by the word *Kuppelei*—procuring. For example, a hotelkeeper can be technically charged under the concept for renting a room to an unmarried couple merely because he gave them the *opportunity* to be "immoral." For years Berlin and Hamburg hotels have taken the law about as seriously as Newark prostitutes regard New Jersey's ancient antifornication statute. At this writing a new law has been drafted which will replace the concept of "immorality" with far more liberal and ambiguous legal language—"sexual acts of some gravity"—which simply means that all hell may break loose in Berlin and Hamburg, and what was once "immoral" in Munich will now become "grave."

Mr. Sakata, obviously a highly principled and very cultivated gentleman, checked out the following morning. Fortunately you first had a chance to meet him and found him to be a man of many parts, not the least interesting of which was the hood ornament on his black Mercedes—an eighteen-carat-gold bowler hat. The room clerk, too, lived up to all your expectations, if one can believe the Yugoslavian chambermaid. According to her, the man is indeed a former SS man. Balkan rather than German, however.

MAVERICK AND PARADOX

For Germans, Munich is a maverick. For foreigners, rather a paradox. The puritanical attitudes of the police and other civic authorities seem at variance with Munich's otherwise justly deserved reputation as the most uninhibited and eccentric of the large German cities. Perhaps there is a very real cause-and-effect relationship here. As a police officer observed, "Bavarians require more discipline than other Germans. If left to themselves, they would quickly eat, drink, or fornicate themselves to death." Without getting into a comparison of the respective passions and capacities of southern vs. northern Germans—in passing, however, it should be noted that Münchners are veritable human garbage pails at the table, consuming up to eight meals a day, many on the run—it is sufficient to observe that no German city has created, or been blessed with, more excuses for bohemian behavior than has Munich.

A balmy climate and magnificent geographic situation certainly contribute to Münchners being a great deal pottier than any other kind of German. But it is the *Föhn,* the strange warm wind that originates in Africa and sweeps down from the Alps, that is said to make Bavarians really crazy. Münchners seize the slightest change in wind direction as an excuse for anything from nymphomania to Hitler. But the *Föhn* is no mere myth. Scientists at Munich University's department of climatology have recently constructed a special atmospheric chamber in order to conduct detailed experiments on the relationship between the *Föhn* and psychic disorders. And some Bavarian courts have considered the wind a mitigating circumstance in crimes of passion.

OKTOBERFEST

Similarly, a state's attorney might have a difficult time prosecuting a case of rape allegedly committed during the *Oktoberfest* (which actually begins in mid-September). This is the beer party to end all beer parties, but they've been doing it annually for the past hundred and sixty years (taking time out for a few wars), with no letup in sight. The focal point is the huge Theresienwiese fairgrounds, where the major breweries erect large tents and stock them with food, drink, funny bands, freaky sideshows, yodelers, and serving girls noted for their good humor and accessible bosoms. Imagine the *Tom Jones* eating sequence as directed by Pieter Brueghel the Elder, catered by the combined resources of Anheuser-Busch and Armour & Company, staged over a period of sixteen days and nights with a cast of millions.

If you prefer purer statistics, digest these: during a recent *Oktoberfest* 400,000 grilled chickens, more than a million sausages, and 4 million quarts of beer were consumed. Even when bad weather curtailed another recent *Fest,* police still managed to arrest 187 drunks and break up 538 fights, and the Red Cross administered to 5025 visitors, of whom 159 required hospitalization. Of these, 26 were felled by flying beer steins and one, a matador, was gored during a specially staged bullfight.

FASCHING

Though no figures are available, a graph representing the incidence of fornication between erstwhile strangers would doubtless show a significant rise during the time of *Oktoberfest.* The line would fairly leap off the graph paper during the climax of the *Fasching* carnival, if only because the celebrants wear masks, which not incidentally inhibit their activities at the trough and stein and, most importantly, conceal their identities. A time-honored custom of carnival in Munich encourages married and otherwise bonded couples to separate from time to time; to pursue sexual adventures with anonymous partners during carnival is considered as exciting as it is pragmatically discreet. Lawyers, in attempting to minimize alimony in cases that arise out of peccadillos committed during *Fasching,* rarely fail to plead the holiday spirit as an extenuating circumstance. The bench is generally sympathetic.

Raise New Orleans' Mardi Gras to the tenth power, add the Carnival in Rio, put blinders on the police, and one has some concept of the licentious gaiety of *Fasching* time in Munich. A traditionally sexy holiday, it has fairly ancient origins. For Tacitus' Bavarians, the end of the harsh winter and the coming of spring—a time when women were thought to be in greatest heat and most fertile—seemed most appropriate for celebrations. Thus, though *Fasching* begins officially at 11:11 on the eleventh day of the eleventh month, the real celebrations and merrymaking occur during the four weeks immediately preceding Ash Wednesday.

It is only slightly excessive to claim that nearly all Munich goes slightly mad in a balmy, good-humored, hedonistic way during *Fasching:* official estimates claim that over 90 percent of the population take part in the festivities in one way or another.[1] There are balls for all, and strangers are welcome to choose from hundreds—the entrance fees are comparatively nominal—including those sponsored by firemen, journalists, actresses, models, hall porters, maids, doctors, homosexuals, and many others. If you are especially fond of little boys and girls, there are even balls for children over the age of two.

Among the most elegant events are those held at the HOTEL BAYERISCHER HOF, the official residence of the *Fasching* prince and princess; for sheer spectacle, gimmickry, grandeur, and a colorful cross-section of society, don't miss the Deutsches Theater balls. The REGINA PALAST HOTEL and P-1 in the HAUS DER KUNST are particular favorites of young people, though the *Fasching* mood prevails in every discothèque, beerhall, and club in town. For a complete list of activities consult the *Fasching* calendar, published daily in the newspapers. Costumes, though not mandatory at all events, are easily obtainable through your hall porter or at several rental shops. Semi- or near-nudity is the latest *Fasching* fashion, but you're a damned fool if you don't wear at least a mask.

SCHWABING

Comparatively few Americans visit Europe during the winter. Actually it's a fine time to be there and, with the airlines' increasing cooperation less expensive too.

For those who can't make *Fasching,* however, some of the mood and freedom of Munich's carnival prevails the year round in Schwabing. "In Schwabing," your hotel porter had promised with a kind of elbow-in-the-ribs fit of laughter. "Ahh, in Schwabing!" As if the very word itself were pregnant with all manner of delicious secret sins and carnal delights.

Superficially Schwabing—it sounds more like something one does than a

[1]However, the 1972 *Fasching* was unaccountably dull, according to a *Time* magazine report. Not only were the revelry and ribaldry visibly restrained by comparison with previous years, but restaurants and hotels reported their business down by as much as one third. Among the many theories propounded for the decline (but not fall, it is hoped) of *Fasching,* the most plausible seems to be that of Dr. Emil Vierlinger, a leading *Fasching* m.c.: That young people, with their mod lifestyle, now "celebrate *Fasching* all year long."

But perhaps Bavarians were simply girding their gullets and their gonads for the Summer Olympics, for *Time* also notes that "this year's festive gloom clings only to . . . Bavarian cities. In the Rhineland, the freewheeling *Karneval* was going strong last week, as noisy and popular as ever."

place to do it—is commonly described as Munich's Greenwich Village. The comparison is facile but surely apt, for Schwabing is both the intellectual heart of the city—15000 people engaged in the graphic arts, 5000 of them painters—and a highly commercialized center of discothèques, convivial taverns, cafés, and restaurants. Here one finds the young girls, easier met and cultivated than anywhere else in Germany; some roving part-time pros and semipros; an active drug culture; and, among all the aforementioned, thousands of students, some serious, some in their early forties.

Most important, in Schwabing you are not likely to encounter those spontaneous outbursts of violence—not mere impoliteness but explosions of vicious temper—on the part of utter strangers which are commonplace in the central city, particularly near the Hofbräuhaus.

For a European center of intellect and amusement, Schwabing is physically surprising, being quite modern and rather gaudy, though not tawdry, with ample bright neon and chrome and only a few narrow streets branching off the far end of the main artery, Leopoldstrasse. In warm weather this wide thoroughfare's outdoor cafés offer unlimited opportunities for inspecting and wooing young women: simply walk down Leopoldstrasse and stare. Someone is bound to stare back.

Citizens of Berlin, Hamburg, and Munich brag of nothing more proudly than that their own particular city is Germany's "most tolerant." Ignoring your cynicism, each place can make a good case. In Munich "Schwabing" is synonymous with tolerance, particularly of experimental artists and lovers. Its past includes such innovators as Kandinsky and Klee; and Isadora Duncan, who danced naked on tabletops in the early part of the century when Schwabing gave Montmartre some nice competition. But above all Schwabing was and remains a haven for students, of whom the university contains more than 38,000. If Munich has any reputation for antics or raucous sexual abandon, its students have for years claimed most of the credit.

At Leopoldstrasse 29, THE PICNIC restaurant is one of Munich's most tolerant establishments (P-N DISCOTHÈQUE is another). Outside The Picnic some students and druggists loll on guitar cases (they opened one for you to reveal a very small man who lives in there) and occasionally mooch likely strangers for the price of the self-service, ample, several-course meals. You offer meal money to anyone who will talk to you for fifteen minutes. One farts, the others look bored. But finally a youth emerges from the pack and you are presently installed across the street in SCHWABINGER CAFÉ. (Lively, unpretentious pastry café; some interesting and very attractive young students; you pick your favorite stranger and sit at her table, as is Munich's custom. Poetry and dancing in the basement.)

The young man, twenty-eight or so, is a student, though presently "on sabbatical." You speak first of dried cabbage leaves, which he smokes, and kings, of whom Bavaria had some dandies. (Including old Ludwig I, who lost heart, libido, and almost his entire domain, thanks to the voracious appetites of his notorious mistress, Lola Montez. And Ludwig II, the "Mad," who took the country to the brink of bankruptcy with his wild construction projects and outraged the good burghers with his confused sex life.)

"Something special in Munich? I know a policeman who will tell you something about the prostitutes, but they are not so extraordinary here. Something *very* special in Schwabing? Of course, such things exist, as they do in your own country, I am sure. But they are mostly private and unknown to me. No, I cannot help you."

One thing about Germans: they will rarely fake it. It is unusual to be led down false trails here, as happens so often in Rome and London, for example, where everyone professes wide knowledge and experience, but comparatively few are willing to share it with strangers.

"Move about Schwabing. Visit the little pubs and cafés. People are friendly here and you are bound to find someone who can help. Some of our cab drivers are excellent guides. Try and get one with a beard; he is therefore likely a student and will speak English well."

A leisurely stroll about the "typical" areas of Schwabing (in and around Occam, Feilitsch, Ursula, and Haimhauser Strasses) begins at NACHTEULE (Occamstrasse 7). Many lone girls, but approach them with tenderness for they've mostly come to hear the songs of owner Walter Novak. More good luck, but no information, at SCHWABINGER SPRITZEN and SCHWABINCHEN. Across Occamstrasse to the famed GISELA's, whose chanteuse-owner, a kind of Bavarian Piaf, is a great favorite among Münchners of all ages. Really extraordinary pickup opportunities in pizza restaurant BOLOGNA, Leopoldstrasse 23, where you are encouraged to sit next to anyone you like. Two nights wandering northern Schwabing and you've made several warm friends but learned nothing special.

Nearly last on your list is a small café whose peculiar hours (5 A.M. to 8 A.M.; 6 P.M. to 1 A.M.) attract actors, artists, writers, and lonely girls who seek them. Owner "X" and his manager "R" served, as teen-agers, in the *Wehrmacht*. The two have made a standing offer to help any shut-out traveler find accommodation; they feed indigent actors, which makes them the most charitable of men; and they are among the most quietly ardent pacifists imaginable. (Sadly, the café has closed.)

R belongs among the *Reader's Digest* unforgettables, though his politics and lifestyle might preclude the coverage. In speech and mien he could be a youngish Walter Slezak, but he lacks a left eye and right arm, lost in the war. Undaunted, he is a tennis and riding instructor, a horse-breaker, a marrier (four times), and an actor. "I was in *The Vikings* with Kirk Douglas. Portions were shot here in Munich, you know. But that was a long time ago. I enjoy acting, but with half the requisite number of arms and eyes, I find the roles available limited."

With his black satin eyepatch, neatly cropped full black beard, 1970 blue jeans, and 1967 Porsche, R is a familiar figure to the girls of Schwabing. And he is an expert on them.

"The incidence of clap, syphilis, and crabs is so much higher among the 'nice girls' of Munich than among the prostitutes," he observes after a careful analysis of German law and prostitution. "Well, of course, I should know the law well. My father is one of Munich's leading prosecutors. He was put in a concentration camp. For aiding Jews. A great man, my father. I am his black sheep." He says this last with some pride.

"Something *really* special in Munich, in Schwabing? I, even I, cannot really help you. But perhaps *'Der Ewige Student'* can. . . ."[2]

AN ORGY AMONG FRIENDS

One evening the following week you meet *Der Ewige Student.* He is about forty, with short black hair silvering at the sides and a *Schmiss* (dueling scar) on his left cheek. And that's all you care to know. About him. You never ask his name, nor does he offer it.

Two nights later, at 8:45 P.M., you and your newfound guide proceed across Leopoldstrasse to the corner of Franz-Josefstrasse and turn into this street of handsome well-kept townhouses. Entering one by a rear door, you climb two flights to a small hallway containing four substantial doors.

You enter one that leads to a large rectangular parlor. At the far end of the room is a large wooden table, about two feet high, supported by heavy, intricately carved legs. On the table is what appears to be a human form, hidden by a sheet of the same black velvet material that also covers the tabletop.

An inner door opens and thirteen men, aged approximately twenty-five to thirty-five, file into the room. Though flushed, glassy-eyed, and gulping beer from huge tankards, they are strangely silent. None acknowledges your presence as you and your guide make yourselves as inconspicuous as possible in a corner. Each man bears a *Schmiss,* a couple of which look freshly earned. All are naked from the waist down.

Two men move to the table and whisk away the velvet coverlet to reveal

---

[2]"The Eternal Student" is actually a generic term, it being a principle of West German higher education that the student decide how long he will labor for his degree. According to recent statistics, the average student is over thirty before he receives his degree and enters his profession, and thirty-five is not uncommon. Several years ago a Hamburg court expelled a student of forty-five who had maintained his seventeen-year academic standing by never failing a single examination. And never taking one.

the naked girl. There are sighs and whispered exchanges among the men, indicating perhaps that few if any have seen the girl before, at least not in these circumstances. She is apparently no more than eighteen, slim and nearly flatchested, her breasts being nearly all nipple. But these are large and rosy-pink, standing stiff and pointed directly at the ceiling, which bears an interesting pastoral fresco depicting a boar hunt.

The girl is shaking from cold and appears frightened, but you are assured she is here of her own free will. Further, your guide whispers that she is an artists' model and has posed often for two of the assembled men. Indeed, her face is lovely, though now contorted by fear—or is it expectation?—and the long hair spread about her head in an arc is pure blond, almost white.

One of the two unveilers whispers something in her ear and she immediately responds by spreading her legs nearly ninety degrees. The two men, known as "policemen," each take an ankle and carefully widen the gap.

A third man comes forward. He is the "fireman" and proves it by striking a wooden match on his teeth and expertly lighting her pubes. The downy blond fuzz, sparse to begin with, singes fast and "fireman" pats the little conflagration out quickly. Throughout, the girl utters no sound.

Now the policemen each kiss the spot. Fireman pays similar respects, followed by each of the ten others in turn.

The ten line up single file, facing the spreadeagled girl, each policeman at attention and flanking her ankles. Fireman stands to one side, facing the lineup and holding a tray. From his pocket he extracts a pair of dice and hands these to the young man at the head of the line in exchange for his beer stein, which is placed on the tray.

This first fellow (truly he can be called a "plunger" in at least two senses of the word) shakes the ivory bones with much enthusiasm and, calling upon some forgotten Hun gods, lets fly the cubes hard against those tender inner thighs. One die caroms off the girl's vulva and she gives a startled shriek of pain, for she lies stretched out flat and cannot see that portion of herself. And the things have struck without warning.

"*Drei!*" call out the policemen in unison as the dice settle on "three." The crowd boos lustily as the roller feigns shame and disappointment. There are shouts of mock encouragement, and the room is suddenly alive with clamor as the man mounts the girl.

"*Drei*" he rolled and *drei* he gets: three strokes in and out. No more. No less. The rules of the game. The crowd counts in unison, and the policemen pull him off, gently but firmly. Somewhat embarrassed but apparently determined to do better next time, he marches to the end of the line, and the next suitor exchanges his beer mug for the dice and rolls "nine." Hoarse cheers, shouts of glory, and a stanza of rousing song greet this roll, for a man can do quite a lot with nine strokes, if well placed and expert. The young lady is also warming and at "six" she gasps something that suggests things are going well for her. But at the stroke of "nine" the man is pulled off, with an *Achtung!* for good measure, for he has taken his sweet time between counts.

The next man craps out quickly with "snake eyes." You're rooting for "boxcars," but it takes eight more rolls before this point is achieved. By now things are quite heady, what with the counting, singing, drinking, toasting, bragging, and so forth; but the line remains orderly and everyone waits his turn in place. As each man achieves satisfaction he drops out of line, the first three changing places with the policemen and fireman. The man who happens, by circumstance or through his own skill, to be in place when the girl achieves climax, is accorded some special honor. You never learn what this reward might be (perhaps some sort of betting pool has been prearranged), for the girl, though pleased, never achieves *Himmel* this night.

On your way to P-1 CLUB you recall Tacitus' Huns who "for auspices and the casting of lots" had "the highest possible regard. . . . They go in for dicing in all seriousness and in their sober hours, and are so recklessly keen about winning or losing that, when everything else is gone, they stake their personal liberty on the last decisive throw." To add local color, your guide notes that Münchners are reputed to be Germany's most avid gamblers: the city has no fewer than eleven public card and gaming parlors.

Who was the girl? Her patrician good looks and white-blond hair suggested a north German, perhaps upper-class background; but she could as well be the daughter of a Hamburg merchant as a refugee Danzig whore.

And the men? Were they members of one of Germany's infamous *Korporationen* "dueling" societies? Though they had the hideous scars, one cannot say for sure: the guide refused to discuss it. And there were none of the bloody trappings—bandages, dueling jackets, sabers—hanging on the walls of that room. But there were other walls, other rooms in that flat. . . .

BLOODY BROTHERHOODS

What had occurred, however baroque, seems no more peculiar than the more widely publicized practices of some *Korporationen*—the student societies that are literally "blood brotherhoods" for life. What little you gathered on the subject is well documented and expanded in Amos Elon's *Journey Through a Haunted Land,* a major thesis of which is: the physical rebuilding of Germany was so hasty—and so successful—that there has been no time or inclination for a spiritual rejuvenation. And Elon's account of brotherhoods certainly reinforces the theory:

"Today, about 40 percent of all male students belong to various *Korporationen* and *Burschenschaften.* A quarter of these practice the so-called *Mensur,* that is, dueling.

"Two duelists *(Pauker)* stand facing each other, the upper part of the body, neck, arms, and nose protected or wrapped in bandages. Skull, forehead, and cheeks remain exposed. The opponents wish each other *Waffenschwein* (luck with their weapons) and then begins an unwieldy flailing about with sabers above their heads until an exposed spot is struck and the opponent has his dueling scar. In the *Mensur,* the duelist does not fight his antagonist, he fights himself. His enemy is his 'worse self,' his 'inner pig.' Neither of the duelists comes out victorious—the ideology of the blood does, proof of which are the nauseating, blood-encrusted dueling jackets, sacred relics kept along flag-draped walls."

Dueling is banned in East Germany, but the new legal code adopted by West Germany in 1969 provides no penalties against the practice, which always happens in secret anyway. The past few years have shown a marked liberalization among West German students, characterized by a proposal to ban dueling submitted at a conference of the *Deutsche Burschenschaft,* the nation's oldest dueling fraternity, founded in 1815. However, the measure lacked the required three-quarters majority to change the dueling statutes. At this writing the matches—consisting of twenty-four to thirty "rounds" of about eight slashes each, with a doctor at the ready to stitch cuts—and the *Kommerses* (all-night drinking orgies) continue.

THE BEAUTIFUL BAVARIANS

Had you seen a brotherhood at play this night? The P-1 discothèque (housed in the Haus der Kunst) makes you soon forget to wonder. This is the Bavarian Castel's and New Jimmy's, *the* place to find the beautiful Bavarians. Regulars refer to it simply as "Alecos' " after its host, a gentle, rolypoly, gregarious Greek teddy bear—5 feet 6 inches, 240 pounds with Sebastian Cabot beard—who, now 35, arrived penniless from Athens in 1955. Even when he operated small clubs—which were often harassed to close earlier than other clubs for reasons which remain unclear—Alecos was the darling of the Bavarian Jet Set. Today his following is as wide as his belly. "It will always be a Club Alecos in Munich," he growls smilingly.

Before Alecos took it over, P-1 was undistinguished. He's transformed it to a stylishly sober olive-drab cross between a swinging Smithsonian Institution and the Prado. Back-lighted glass cases house stuffed birds and very-deep-sea fish. Several good Goya and El Greco reproductions, and a portrait of your host in white lace collar after Velázquez. Clientele include Soroya, who lives around here, Prince Philip, and Teddy Kennedy, according to Alecos.

You spot Prince X, recall that you met him at Alecos' old Club 13, though he's never met you. The Prince—you have been warned *again,* he is Bavaria's "*top* prince"—is a unique-looking man. Very tall and erect, as if he wears an iron corset or has a saber stuck up his pants. He has certainly had one stuck in his face, which seems dominated by the inevitable *Schmiss*. Rather bald, the large head has lacquered black hair splayed forward. The combination gives the Prince a frightening, almost cruel countenance. (This, of course, is entirely subjective. Everyone else apparently finds him enormously attractive.) Perhaps it's those algid ball-bearing eyes that seem to look nowhere, but apparently register everything. More likely the Prince—an apparently practiced intimidator—vexes you because he does no more than nod to acknowledge your presence on this Earth, of which he is said to own considerable ("half of Munich and suburbs, breweries, farms, estates, factories, etc.").

THE "JUNKER'S DAUGHTER"

Between two lesser princes is a particularly haughty and aristocratic-looking female of about twenty-five who could be no one but the daughter of some Prussian Junker. You strike up a fair conversation, and though she seems even more bored by your inquiries than the princes, she agrees to lunch the following afternoon.

Lunch next day at tiny A. BOETTNER (Theatinerstrasse 8; 29–08–81, reservations imperative). Here one finds more Bavarian princes, Krupps, and Soroya again for this is one of Munich's choicest restaurants, though not well-known to tourists.

The Junker's daughter has you at an immediate disadvantage. Her bearing and dignity are well nigh overwhelming. She wears a simple but rich-looking high-necked suit of pearl gray with a single strand necklace of amethyst and silver. The steep, sharp cheekbones give her a severe, almost Oriental look, and the narrow triangular face is framed by glistening black hair. This is tied back and fastened with a good cameo. She's more handsome than pretty and her heavy-lidded gray eyes heighten the severity. You proceed slowly, swapping travel notes and losing badly, hoping eventually to gain some insight into Munich and Bavarian society.

"Would you like to have it in the bed with me?" She asks this without looking up from her Helgoland lobster, a house specialty.

In the worst tradition of Ian Fleming you drop your goblet of Urziger Würzgarten 1953 in your pheasant and try to let out a deep sigh. But it comes out sounding more like a belch. Before you can stutter a reply in the astonished affirmative she clarifies everything. Or nothing.

"The price will be one hundred dollars . . . until the sun sets."

To say no one would have imagined Magda to be a whore is superfluous, though many Europeans would have hardly been surprised. Men are being similarly duped every night in hundreds of European resorts where so many students and working girls—many are well-to-do daughters whose allowances are small or spent—can always use a bit of extra cash to extend their vacations. If you ever doubted it, you never should again: prostitutes are as much landmarks of the European scene as sidewalk cafés, discothèques, churches, and museums.

Magda began at the top, but remained there only briefly. Born in Berlin, 1942. Father a high *Luftwaffe* official, both parents killed during the devastating Allied incendiary raids on Hamburg. Raised humbly but decently by an uncle in Hanover. Graduated from high school and trained as a cartographer, but the work bored her.

She has been "doing this" for three years, and enjoys the life. "At least it is honest." Never does she see more than one man an evening—mostly these are middle-aged and elderly businessmen, industrialists, and politicians—and her dates usually consist of dinner and the theater or opera or a concert. (Munich has four symphony orchestras.) She fancies herself more an escort or consort than harlot. Her usual tariff begins at $50, and this is paid "whether or not there is bed." She lives in a comfortable modern apartment in Schwabing with a young man her own age.

Magda has propositioned you as a "little joke" in view of your researches; for one thing she *never* acquires clients at Alecos', but goes there "only to relax with friends." Oh, yes, if you really want to "make the bed," she will oblige. Right after dessert if you wish. (*Note:* the pastry here at Boettner, as everywhere in Munich, is superb and freshly baked. Munich is a town where you'll never get yesterday's tart.) And the price would be special, perhaps $25, "because you are a friend." No, she does not need the money, but she must ask something. "It is a matter of principle."

"Much as I'd like to make the bed with you, it's somewhat a matter of principle with me too, and mostly a matter of twenty-five dollars. . . . Have you ever worked the streets?"

"Never! But I know them well, and tonight I will show them to you."

PROSTITUTION

Prostitution in Germany is a local affair. Each municipality exercises such authority and control as it deems appropriate and practical, within the wide latitudes afforded by West German law, which provides that prostitutes cannot "offer themselves for immoral purposes in an obvious way, or in a way liable to annoy individuals or the public." (The girls must also register with the local health authorities, and submit to periodic medical examinations.) The statute is a refreshingly worded one, admitting, or designating, an activity to be "immoral" yet sanctioning it.

And the Law

Munich is less permissive as regards prostitution than other major German cities. Though women of Magda's appeal are discreetly available in the lobbies of some of the best hotels and nightclubs, the situation is transitory. Such women are not as characteristic of the scene here as are the chic young beauties who grace the cafés of Berlin's Kurfürstendamm. Nor does one experience the rowdy, bawdy atmosphere of Hamburg's St. Pauli. Brothels per se are forbidden, but there is a nice hairsplitting way out of this, later discussed. (Similar to the tenant-whore scheme found all over Germany.)

Each year for the past eight or more Munich civil authorities, perhaps considering that Schwabing offers enough gratuitous sex, have exercised ever greater controls and restrictions over streetwalkers. Once all Munich was their open-air marketplace. They gave Schillerstrasse and Goethestrasse bad names, made Nymphenburgerstrasse an apt one, and ran rampant round the Town Hall square. But now streetgirls are primarily restricted to one small designated area along Landsbergerstrasse, an arterial dual road heading west out of town.

And the Syndicates

Such rigid control breeds opportunities for corruption and the inevitable need for "protection": the city crawls with pimps. Such men are apt to be heavy gamblers, and as Munich has so many gaming parlors, the girls are pushed to earn to the hilt to support their protectors' habits. Some of these fellows are independent entrepreneurs, but others are organization men.

If Munich is a kind of German heaven, it also has the attributes of a tart tycoon's paradise. There are at least eight good reasons. (1) Heavily restricted but legal prostitution; the girls are free to operate, yet they still require protection from overzealous policemen. (2) No municipally operated brothels, in which even a Mafioso might have difficulty gaining a foot in the door. (It is significant that organized prostitution is less a factor in German cities which have such establishments.) (3) The fastest-growing population of any large German city. (4) A great deal of loose "play" money, and a permissive "live and let's live" attitude among the citizens. (5) Thousands of foreign blue-collar workers who arrive, almost to a man, womanless. (6) Tourists by the millions. (7) Munich's two big festivals, *Oktoberfest* and *Fasching*. (8) Proximity to United States Army bases.

According to Magda, a Munich policeman, and Judge Clemens Amelunxen of Düsseldorf, several of the syndicates pay the girls on a weekly, regular salary basis, with fixed working hours, days off, paid holidays, and hospitalization.

One syndicate, with men in the field throughout the country, is said to have in its headquarters a large map of Germany, with colored pushpins designating the various trade fairs that are so much a part of the German businessman's and whore's life. The syndicate also keeps abreast—as well as do the Russians!—of American and West German Army troop movements. (These are constantly shifting, particularly along the East-West border in response to East German activities.) For example, a Philadelphia supply sergeant, stationed in Mainz, receives $200 each month in return for such scraps of information as when a new base quadruples its supply of toilet paper in anticipation of new arrivals. Needless to say, the syndicates made big plans for the 1972 Summer Olympics.

And the Tax-Collector

The German authorities are, understandably, disturbed by the sex syndicates. After all, the country is losing money. *Tax* money. A 1964 court ruling declared that income from prostitution is legally taxable as "miscellaneous income." ("Indiscretionary income," an American CPA might say.) But whatever you call it, more than a billion marks are spent on prostitutes annually in the Federal Republic, according to Reuters.

A Drive-in Whorehouse

Some portion of this amount is spent out on Landsbergerstrasse. Just beyond the intersection of Elsenheimerstrasse the city has shrewdly constructed a short parallel road that extends for about an eighth of a mile as far as Fürstenriederstrasse. A "service" road if ever the word were appropriate. Rain or shine, through all seasons, its sidewalk is packed with up to seventy-five ladies in various shapes, sizes, and even colors. (Some are illegitimate daughters of black American troops, sad souvenirs of the last war.) Most of the girls are under thirty and range from surprisingly attractive to absolutely out of the question. But each costs 50DM for a tumble in her apartment or 30DM for a rumble on the seat of a car. Landsbergerstrasse is probably the most active drive-in whoreway in the world.

With Magda at the wheel, you join the line of cars that prowl along at less than five m.p.h. Some men make a whole night of this cruising—like "bowling night" in the United States—but too many times around the track and the girls may throw stones or, worse, signal their pimps, who watch menacingly from cars parked along the curb. If the girls suspect you are U.S. Army, they may reject you on sight for many soldiers consider it great sport to taunt the whores from the safety of their cars.

The truck in front of you stops, its window rolls down, but no girl moves until the man signals his choice. (It's the law.) She is among the most attractive of the group, a very pretty young blonde, about twenty-one, in black leather miniskirt with matching leather jacket, peach sweater, and lime-green accessories—umbrella and boots.

Pimps

"The *Kupplers*," notes Magda, indicating the pimps. "The police do not like these 'big ones,' but tolerate them because they keep order." Though it is the city of Munich that has constructed this area, a new girl cannot simply apply at the Town Hall for space. She must have one of these "big ones" to fight for her right to do business here. And when there are violent disputes for choice spots at the entrance to the road, the *Kupplers* settle them. One can understand why the police would not wish to be involved in arbitrating such discussions.

In addition to Landsbergerstrasse the police also tolerate curb-service prostitution (15 to 20DM) in Ingolstädterstrasse, Floriansmülstrasse, and Freisinger Landstrasse, all in the northern suburbs. The truck stop in the suburb of Grosslappen is particularly primitive and busy.

On the drive back to the center of town, a short course in whore argot. A man who goes with whores is a *Freier*—literally a "suitor," and pronounced "friar." This word is derived from the "old times" when a suitor went meekly to a girl's father and begged for her hand, just as a man who seeks prostitutes is said to go on *Freier*'s feet. The *Kuppler*—literally a "coupler" or matchmaker—calls his little workhorse a *Traber*, that is, a sulky horse or trotter. The girls travel the *"rue de la Trab,"* and so forth.

Until about six years ago Goethestrasse and Schillerstrasse—near the Main Station in the center of town—had more trotters than a season of Yonkers Raceway Daily Doubles. For many Americans seeking "action" this was the first, and sometimes the last, they saw of Munich. The area crawled with diseased, non-card-carrying pros ("wild cards" the GIs called them), tough, unscrupulous con men, pimps, thieves, and muggers; and there were dozens of villainous clip joints. In short, a German Times Square. But the police are proud to have "cleaned up" the area. That is to say, the streetwalkers and gangrenous dives are gone; instead you have B-girls standing in the doorways of gaudily refurbished clip joints that charge 18,50DM for a beer! (Recall what Hamburg delivered for 18DM.)

RACKETS, DIVES, AND CENTRAL MUNICH NIGHTLIFE

One infamous bar near the Town Hall was said to have had one girl behind the counter and fourteen out in the streets enticing hopeful *Freier* to sip a small drink before a promised—but rarely delivered—bedtime. Though beer and wine were priced reasonably enough, the sucker's drink was *Sekt,* a kind of peasant's champagne, at 400DM the bottle. A slightly tipsy tourist might "order" a few of these, for the menu was printed in red and almost impossible to read, the room being lit by one red bulb of extremely low wattage. Upon being presented a bill large enough to rent the place for a month, the customer could holler for the police (dial 21-41). Even if they came, he would be required to pay up in full. German bars and clubs can charge whatever the traffic will bear. Best way around this is always to demand a drink card. Then demand a flashlight.

Achtung: Munich remains a sucker's town!

In Am Platzl, a center of nightlife, you're likely to be approached by an apparently innocent young girl (known here as a *"Schlepper"*) who has fallen in love with you on sight. She insists on immediately going to bed with you —no, of course she wouldn't think of taking a *pfennig*. But first, because she is "nervous," a "small drink." Whereupon she chooses, apparently at random, from among the many Platzl bars and "strip" clubs. Here she receives 35DM for each bottle of *Sekt* sold to you at 108DM. (A bottle is considered "sold" if she accidentally smashes it on the floor.) The owner gets the stuff wholesale at 3,10DM the bottle and you, you Schlep, have been schlepped.

If you must see what's happening in those Platzl bars which employ schleppers (by now the word should be part of your Munich vocabulary) by all means have a look. But go in alone and leave alone. And be sure to visit the riproaring HOFBRÄUHAUS, built in 1589, according to the concession man who, without your even asking, assures you *"This is not the place from Hitler. He was never here. That was the Bürgerbräukeller at Rosenheimerstrasse 29, across the Isar."* But remember, this area is no Disneyland: in one hour you witnessed four savage fist fights, then helped the victim of a stabbing into a waiting police ambulance.

At Am Platzl 4 is TILBURY-CLUB, surely the best discothèque in town, thanks to millionaire-playboy James Graser, its owner-impresario. Tilbury attracts Munich's prettiest girls, of all backgrounds. If the air you breathe makes you crave something sweet, large orange juices are served.

THE BIG TEASE

If you are in Munich and want to see striptease, go to Hamburg. Here it is no more than a big tease. Typical is LOLA MONTEZ (Am Platzl 1), whose takeoffs are more tasteless than total, thanks to the strict authorities and the jealousies of the various clubowners who inform on one another. Best of a mediocre lot is EVE (Karolinenplatz 2A), whose production values take a fig leaf from Paris' Crazy Horse Saloon and whose prices are perhaps even higher. Situated in a lovely mansion that Ludwig II built for Lola Montez and around the corner from a big platz Hitler created to give Thousand-Year-Reich speeches in. Fifteen delicious hostesses.

A typical, pseudoposh strip club in the Maximilianstrasse area, had no female shills on the streets. They're all inside where it's so dark you can't see a breast in front of your face. It was "suggested" that you order champagne. Demands for a wine card were ignored. One must assume they're ashamed of their prices (15DM at the bar), 2.50DM door charge, coat-check fee, noxious band, and surly bartender.

Back to your tour of central Munich's other cheek. Around the corner from LUIFILLIP'S SEX STORE (Damenstiftstrasse 4; brightly lighted window display of flowers to use as nipple pasties), at Josephspitalstrasse 5 (trouble here of late; see p. 236), 50DM prostitutes stand in the doorway, hoping to lure *Freieren*. Nothing illegal here—as long as the enticements are reasonably subtle—for the girls *live* at this address (and so do people in less colorful professions) and no law forbids a girl to stand in her own doorway. Nearby are numerous bars, for GIs and teeny camp followers. You try one at random. Jukebox dancing, garish red lighting, cheap, vulgar, and colorless. Not a clip joint, however, according to its soldier patrons. But why is Abraham X, a Jew from Lodz, Poland, spending his last precious years running such a place? And in Germany of all countries!

Magda, as usual, has an explanation: "Many Jews, not the German ones but mostly Galicians, Poles, Ukrainians, own these places, and also the cheap gambling halls, and some of the houses where live prostitutes. This is so throughout Germany, but especially in Munich, which has so many foreigners."

Indeed, Germany has a mere thirty thousand Jews (once there were more than half a million) and by the time you leave the country, you must concur: a disproportionate number of Jews are in the "entertainment" business.

"It is simple," says Magda, as if it were. "The government gives them money if they have been in concentration camps. It is part of the *Wiedergutmachung* ['reparations']. Most of these people were old, ignorant ones; some cannot read. And so they invest in places like these; they are not capable of much else. It is just as well. Somebody has to do this."

You look at Abe X's weary face, his blank eyes. You're glad yours have not seen what his have seen. He has a story, perhaps among the best in Munich. But it is too late for him to tell it.

ROSEMARY'S BABY

"Don't turn left," laughs Magda as you whip around Stiglmaierplatz, "or we go to Dachau," pointing to the casual roadsign. And so you swing right, go a block on Schleissheimerstrasse, and park in front of No. 14, right behind a gaudy sports car. "This is Y's car. He visits the prostitutes here."

Y is well known throughout Germany. He was a friend of Rosemary Nitribitt, the Frankfurt call girl who attempted to blackmail her wealthy industrialist clients and was subsequently murdered. Rosemary's career has been dramatized in a number of films, the most successful starring Nadja Tiller. Y's has not.

In 1968 there appeared a red commemorative stamp whose inscription read: "Deutsche Bundespost, 1958–1968, Ten Years of Mourning for R. Nitribitt." The quality of the forgery duly impressed the Federal Ministry of Posts and Telecommunications, but only increased their zeal to apprehend the counterfeiters who, still at large, are liable to prosecution under Paragraph 13, Section 1, of the postal regulations which prohibits the mailing of "immoral material." "Is nakedness in itself sufficient cause for the Bundespost to intervene?" *Welt am Sonntag*'s reporter asked Herr Frick of the Federal Ministry. "No," he replied, "but just look at the stamp. It requires little imagination to work out what she is lying down for."

A HOUSE THAT IS A HOME——and some that are not

Schleissheimerstrasse 14 looks like an ordinary modern apartment house until one turns the corner. The entrance is on Rottmannstrasse, where a dozen women wait next to the condom machine in the dimly lit doorway, ready to take on all comers at 40 to 50DM. But this is not a whorehouse: *it is a house where whores live.* In Germany the distinction is important. No law forbids the girls to occupy dwellings, nor forbids large groups of girls to occupy the *same* dwelling. And as long as the landlord collects a fixed rent, and not a percentage of the take, he is not considered to be living off the earnings of prostitutes, any more than would a Houston hairdresser who happened to number a few call girls among his clients.

Some of these girls spend some of their *off-duty* hours in Philoma Café, which has dancing and a convenient back exit leading to No. 14. Sometimes, whorelike, the ladies go to the cinema next to the Peugeot garage on Rottmannstrasse where they mingle with potential clients among the steerage of immigrant foreign workers who first charge their batteries watching the spicy Turkish, Greek, and Italian films. The children of these workers are meanwhile kicking tin cans around the courtyard of Schleissheimerstrasse 56. Upstairs their mothers are frying beans and onions behind doors labeled *"Familia"* just so you won't confuse them with certain other tenants behind the peep-holed doors. These will if you will, for 50DM.

Some girls in the ill–famed Schwanthalerstrasse house work out at the drive-in on Landsbergerstrasse, and some do not. Though several of the girls are listed by first name on the call box, a Rosemary by any other name is still a Rosemary, sometimes even after you've seen her.

The best house in Munich is undoubtedly the modern structure at Baldurstrasse 79, in a lovely northern neighborhood conveniently located near the

Olympic Games compound. No amateurs these, but some splendid specimens at 100DM.

THE REAL THING

If you want to see a *real* Bavarian whorehouse go to " MEX"-HAUS, Hohen-
zollernstrasse 112. This is not a house of Mexican whores—it's simply that
a company called IMEX, INC. demanded the joint change its name.[3] At last
look, Phi Kappa Epsilon had left its "Zorro" mark on the front door. In any
case, if you have a nostalgia for the ambiance of those quonset-hut things in
the hills behind Tijuana where five hundred roaring sailors jammed bleachers
to cheer putas having it off with roosters and donkeys, this is your kind of
cathouse. (No avisodomy here, however. Just Wham! Bam! . . . Not even a
Thank You, Sir.)

Owned by B, who is said to charge the tenants 400 to 500DM a month
for *work space* (no one could *live* here), "Mex"-Haus is a sizable yellow
stucco building, six well-spaced windows wide by five stories high. Unlike so
many houses where the girls pose quietly in the halls or await your knock
demurely behind closed doors, the "Mex" is wide, wide open, and it has
NOISE! (It's not terribly clean either.) As you move through the iron front
doors, past the battery of condom machines (six for 1DM) you're certain that
the hollow, monstrous melody echoing and re-echoing off the stone walls and
floors will ring metallically in your ears long after you leave: police dogs and
dachshunds howl and urinate in the hallways through which their mistresses
also wander—about ten to a landing—in a cat's chorus of gossip and song
among themselves, or cajoling, and cursing the mobs of delighted American
soldiers; Schwabing students; Turkish, Greek, and Italian workers tramping in
review up, down, down, up: five whole floors of whores! All this to the
auditory assault of rock tunes and *Regimentsmusik* blaring from every other
open door. "She won't take nothin' awf!" bawls a red-necked Tennessee
corporal. "Got a hole down there in her panties you gotta stick it clear on
through. . . ." Two whores interrupt their Monopoly game to explain that the
basic rate is 40DM, and 20 more to take all clothes off. Considering that most
of the girls—aged roughly earlier to late twenties—wear little more than
mininighties with plunging neckline blouses, whoever owns "Mex"-Haus is
crazy not to charge admission. It's the best striptease show in town.

BOCCACCIO: LESBIANS AND EPICENES

In contrast to the sound, smell, and fury of Munich's whorelife are the
decadent elegance and high antics of BOCCACCIO. Though you won't find it

[3]According to Temple Fielding.

in *Fielding, Fodor,* or *Europe on $5 a Day,* this can be one of Germany's
—one of *Europe's*—most colorfully wicked night places, if you hit it on a
good night. (Best take a taxi to Klenzestrasse 47.)

Boccaccio's infamy derives from its elegant homosexual patrons, particularly the lesbians. However, the guests may include any Bavarian who has
made a success of being rich, famous, talented, beautiful, or debauched.
Chances are good that some women met here are lesbians, but they could
also be better-class prostitutes (off-duty) or absolutely heterosexual fashion
models, film starlets—or a combination of all these. There are comparatively
few obviously homosexual males, except for the prettily painted bartenders.
Some obvious lesbians growl about in black *Le Smoking* suits and string ties
for comic relief. But on the whole most of the women are quite feminine-
looking and some are stunningly beautiful. That's the way owner-host Rudi
Gaugg likes it. Herr Gaugg is a European water-skiing champion.

The freedom and spontaneity of the place are reflected in the lighting
that, even before the 1969 criminal code eased homophile inhibitions,
was always exceptionally bright in contrast to the guilty twilight one
gropes with in most homosexual clubs. This has for years been one of the
few clubs in Munich where members of the same sex danced together in
public. That in itself has always been a major attraction for the dancers,
as well as the spectators. Though there is no scheduled floor show, the
guests themselves more than compensate. As everyone here appears to
have led a full life, the lesbians, transvestites, showgirls, and occasional
visiting actors and singers have a tendency to try hard to top one another, whether trying out a new act or bawdy song, belly-dancing on tabletops, or stripteasing. If good stuff happens, it's likeliest after 1 A.M.,
when they lock the doors. Reopens at 5 A.M.

The decor is gilt, though not gaudy, favoring white, gold, and satin. Framed
in shadowboxes and covering the walls are five-foot-high blowups of original
illustrations from an early edition of Boccaccio's *Decameron.* One depicts
a nude lad and maiden tied back to back at a stake and burning quickly, while
a frenzied mob cheers the youngsters on their way. Another features a
husband surprising his wife in her bedchamber as she is about to be cunnilin-
guated by a half-cow, half-eagle. The other reproductions run the gamut of
woman-beast relationships, sadomasochism, and flagellation.

Boccaccio's prices are not high considering what you may get. But this is
common in places that rely on a following of regulars, no matter how affluent,
and discourage the patronage of tourists who act like tourists. Champagne
cocktail, 5DM; double Johnny Walker Red, 7DM; fair meals from 14DM.

Voops! *Halt* press! recently Boccaccio has gone completely straight. Stet all
the stuff about the freedom and spontaneity, and keep the bit about the erotic
decor . . . but throw the lesbians out. And the gay boys too. (Sorry bartender,
you too.) Somehow or other—perhaps the Olympic Games had some influ-

ence—the most beautiful *demi-mondaines* east of the Maginot line have painted this formerly purple palace a bright shade of red. Many look and speak as if they've just graduated finishing school and none starts at less than 200DM. Don't worry about a taxi. Some dwell in the neighborhood, and the others have the Mercedes outside and a good apartment near Maximilian-strasse.

GAY LIFE AND HIGH LIFE

As a traditional center of the arts and as the new capital of Germany's film and high-fashion industries, Munich attracts some of the country's most talented homosexuals. But their public rendezvous usually close by 1 A.M., sometimes at 3 on weekends, though many reopen at 5 A.M. Virtually all gay bars and clubs are confined to the immediate vicinity of Gärtnerplatz and nearby Sendlinger Tor Platz. Though local homosexuals consider this municipal circumscription quite undemocratic—some say downright fascistic—they admit that it is a boon to weary strangers. Surprisingly, the gay ghetto is some distance from Schwabing, where, one was told, anything goes. Homosexuals, talented and otherwise, are not unwelcome in the following establishments, most of which are found within areas H-6, G-6, and H-7, G-7 on the Loden-Frey map of the city distributed by the Munich Tourist Authority.

In Klenzestrasse, dominated by Boccaccio, one also finds two highly re-garded *gemischte* (mixed) establishments. CASANOVA discothèque (No. 43) has separate bars for lesbians and male homosexuals; BEI COSY (No. 8) is a bit looser, segregation being confined to the dance floor. Most other gay places in this neighborhood are primarily for males. In nearby Reichenbach-strasse the welcome is warm at DEUTSCHE EICHE bar and hotel. The aforenoted are all near Gärtnerplatz, as are IM MOSQUITO and ESTAMINET, Nos. 2 and 9 Corneliusstrasse, respectively; TEDDY BAR, Hans Sachsstrasse 2, is a comfort. Playful is LE TROU bar and restaurant, and if you like games, KATZ UND MAUS, both in Baaderstrasse. If you are gay, you will consider MANDY'S one of the best discothèques in Europe. Difficult to find: at Baader Platz and "Buttermilk Street." (Tiny sign outside.)

Just a few blocks west, in and around Sendlinger Tor Platz, pass up the dangerous rough trade (20 to 30DM) lurking under the ugly stone arch by the public urinals, and make for ALI-BABA, an all-male bar and nightclub at Augsburgerstrasse 21. Or try *"Die Bar mit der exklusiven Note,"* FRED'S PUB, Sendlingerstrasse 30. One of the current rages in discothèques is run by a gentleman called MRS. HENDERSON (Rumfordstrasse 2, tricky peephole screening; entrance in Müllerstrasse). Huge double-horseshoe bar so the varied clientele—fashionably turned out hot young bloods; dour dark-suited executive types—can get a good look at one another before dancing cheek to cheek on the tiny dance floor.

Hungry? It's the GRÜNE GANS ("The Green Goose") around the corner at Am Einlass 5; you might find some nice green thing to pluck here between courses. Tired? PENSION LINDTNER (Dultstrasse 1; 24–25–57) is waiting.

This area of Munich is *extremely* complex geographically. Get your map out and find Pestalozzistrasse, running off Müllerstrasse from Sendlinger Tor Platz. Homosexual or not, you'll agree that a moonlight walk along Pestalozzi's amazingly pea-soup-green canal is quite romantic. Pass under the weeping willows and gnarled oaks, back and forth across little wooden footbridges, until you come to the swiftly flowing Isar River, no more than seventy-five feet across. On the far side at Sternstrasse 6 is MYLORD, mostly female. Nearby, in Innere Wienerstrasse 2, males meet in KING CLUB's basement.

The most romantic homosexual outdoor meeting place is the bridge by the waterfall behind the Haus der Kunst in the English Gardens, near Schwabing. Other rendezvous include the toilets at Karlsplatz, Peterplatz, and Feilitzschplatz, and the parks at Maximilian–Brücke and the Max II monument in Maximilianstrasse.

"A KIND OF YOUNG GERMAN HEAVEN"

One afternoon you go to CAFÉ LUITPOLD (Briennerstrasse 11) with Franz Spelman, author and *Time*'s Munich bureau. Every city in the world should have a Café Luitpold; fortunately, many in Europe do. A tradition since the late nineteenth century, it was wrecked during the last war but has been completely rebuilt. Though now quite modern, it has lost none of its vitality and is still the place to debate and cultivate fired-up intellectuals. But the main attraction is the beautiful women. Around the corner is an interpreter's school that trains daughters of Munich's upper middle class for careers in industry and business. At lunch and apéritif hour they like to practice their English here. And, of course, Munich's custom of sitting at any table you please prevails. An especially great place on rainy afternoons.

Like most everyone you've met in Munich, Franz Spelman is not a native. He is expatriate Viennese. Once these two words would have been mutually exclusive. But Franz Spelman says, "Vienna is as dead as Munich is now alive. It is ironic—no it is *symbolic* of the new Germany that Munich, where Hitler rose to power, has become Germany's greatest melting pot. And this, of course, only further enriches the city's vitality. Russians, Yugoslavs, Poles, Czechs, Jews, Hungarians, Spaniards, and Italians . . . well, of course, the Italians have been coming since the artists and architects of the Middle Ages. Today, one-tenth of the population was born outside this country. Two-thirds were not born in Munich!

"Of course, the population of Bavaria has always been changing. And, like China, Munich has had the capacity to absorb and capitalize on foreign influences. It is Germany's most tolerant city.

"Munich has seven seasons (the four, plus *Oktoberfest, Fasching,* and Strong Beer time), seven breweries and twenty-five hundred bars and clubs. There is, here, a nice Catholic immorality. German yes, but also Italianate without changing the basic efficiency of the population. This is important. Go to the discothèques: Munich has Germany's best. The sexual life has been most advanced here for quite some time. What happens in Munich happens five years later in the rest of Germany, if ever.

"For a long time, perhaps from 1890 to right before the Second War, the old screwed the young. [The "old" being mostly men over thirty; the "young" under twenty and mostly female.] Then, after the war, until perhaps ten years ago, the old screwed the old. *Now* it has finally become exciting: the young have at last got around to screwing with each other. First here in Europe, and now at last in the United States. Yes?"

Yes.

"In Munich, and various other parts of Europe, London for example, one sees the differences between former times, when one had to buy many things to get love. Now the boy has only to buy the high-collared shirt. There is actually such a surplus of beautiful, young girls."

And some willing highborn widows and divorcees as well, relaxing tensely amid the Chippendales and Rosenthals of CARLTON TEAROOM, directly across Briennerstrasse. A fortune-hunter's paradise—but approach with grace and manners.

Meanwhile, out on the pavement, some of Munich's higher-priced whores (150DM) prowl around the nearby elegant Maximilianplatz, at the moment favoring the flattering lighting given off by the showrooms of Galerie Handwerk (Ming vases, Persian tapestries, pre-Columbian art). Best hours, 10 P.M. to midnight. It's only a three-minute walk to Arcisstrasse, near the Alte Pinakothek art museum, where some 30-to-50DM pieces have staked out the area near the cemetery.

NIGHTLIFE IN BRIEF

Of course, if you succeed in Schwabing's GASLIGHT (Ainmillerstrasse 10), Arcisstrasse becomes no more than a ghoulish stroll. Ages eighteen to twenty-three or so; to 1 A.M. (to 4 A.M. during *Fasching;* most clubs extend hours during festivals). Also under Josef Samel's direction is BLOW-UP (Elisabeth-platz in Schwabing), the biggest noise in town and Germany's largest discothèque. Big-name pop groups, blinding light shows, admission 2 to 6DM (depending on the group) entitles you to a drink and your pick of up to two thousand pickups, most aged nineteen to twenty-six. For slightly older young adults, Mr. Samel provides BA-BA-LU, across from Gaslight. A similar clientele is found at nearby SUBWAY (ages twenty to sixty-five), no admission charged; thus *many* girls come on their own.

If you're between trains, CAFÉ STADT WIEN, directly across from the Main Station, is a time-killer. Modified pop groups, ballroom dancing with lots of single shopgirls, secretaries. CITTA 2000 is a Bavarian Le Drugstore.

ST. JAMES BAR (Briennerstrasse 10). James Graser bought a whole village to acquire one five hundred-year-old farmhouse with which he created what *was* Munich's nobbiest, most elegant bar. Now that he's sold it and Fritz, a bartender with a clever, loose tongue, is gone, who knows?

The nightclub of the HOTEL BAYERISCHER HOF is considered Munich's best. Excellent opportunities to meet sons and daughters of the better and best families at weekend 4 P.M. tea-dances in the big ballroom, from October to February. Same big chance during the summer at garden fashion-show teas. Always check the sixth-floor swimming pool to see who's lying about. Otto von Bismarck slept here, and so did the Beatles. And so can you, even on a modest budget. Avoid the elegant suites and request one of the rooms reserved for chauffeurs—only about 20DM if available.

This is a stay-up town, and after they close the twenty-five hundred night places, all those strippers, hookers, musicians, waitresses, night-crawlers, and insomniac students get hungry. Some go to DONISL's near the Town Hall, which is traditional. Less known and perhaps more interesting is BEI PETRE (Blumenstrasse). Opens 5 A.M. Black walls and ceilings with all light supplied by one violet bulb. Soothing. Specialties: champagne splits and onion soup. At SPEZI's (Max-Planckstrasse 7, on the far side of the Isar) owner-chef Max Anselm should get the Iron Cross for the hours he keeps: 6 P.M. to 3 A.M. Pause for a catnap. Then, 5 to 7 A.M. resumes serving moules, lobster thermidor, escargots to a fascinating assortment of dawn people.

Before St. James, BEI HEINZ (Herzog-Wilhelmstrasse 7) was "the" Munich bar. It's gone down in chic, but up in opportunities. Current owner "Puppi" (Hildegarde Auer), a former fashion model, has employed a few of her old colleagues. Best-looking collection of twenty-eight-to-forty-year-old women in town. Jacqueline, the barmaid, sings risqué French songs. There's a little dancing. Nice plate chicken soup, 2,50DM. Good cheap steaks. What could you lose at 4 A.M.?

DR. SCHÜTZE'S Rx

In 1970 ladies passing through the Black Forest could lose what ails them —not to mention their virginity, if they had it—by visiting the Bad Boll clinic of Dr. Werner Schütze. After careful diagnosis he might have prescribed and administered a good dose of sexual intercourse. But *one could not enjoy herself* lest she jeopardize the good doctor's good name. He was, after all, recently tried for performing such operations on three epileptic patients. All of them, however, admitted the treatments were beneficial. Speaking for the Freiburg District Court, Judge Paul Mueller ruled that because (1) one of the patients was sixteen years old and (2) she admitted that Dr. Schütze's treatments were enjoyable as well as therapeutic, some sort of violation had occurred . . . if only of medical ethics. To put things *korrekt,* Judge Mueller ruled that Dr. Schütz (fifty-six) could continue administering his sexual therapy as long as a third person was present to insure that neither patient nor doctor got any enjoyment whatsoever from the treatments. Meanwhile Dr. Schütze (rhymes with "Cutesa," but should not be confused with the noun *"Schütze,"* which means variously, "marksman" "sharpshooter," "archer," or "Sagittarius") sued the state of Baden Württemberg for briefly shutting his clinic during the trial. (February, 1971.)

In early 1972 Dr. Schütze wrote to a prospective patient that he keeps an "open house for guests . . . one day with all special food, all lodgings, treatment with massages, water, hot and cold, exercises and my special psychologic care . . . generally 60DM." Take the train from Munich to Löffingen; from there phone Dr. Schütze at 07703-210. He'll come to you, then drive you to his clinic. Of course you must write to him first: 7823 Bonndorf in Bad Boll.

SKI BUFFS IN THE BUFF

And for the bare ski bum too. The FAMILY SPORT SOCIETY (F.K.K.) invites you to ski in the nude with them. Non-members are welcome to use their ski area in the Allgäu Alps in Southwestern Bavaria. Six marks a day includes your transportation (by jeep or snowmobile); half price for the kiddies. Write F.K.K., 896 Kempten, Munich, for further details.

AN INTEGRATED SAUNA

Warm up for Berlin at SAUNA-SOLLN (Weltistrasse 65; 79-65-19), at this writing apparently Munich's only full-time public sauna that does not segregate patrons as to sex (though they're planning a branch near the football stadium). Buried in the sticks by bluenoses, so best take a fifteen-minute, 7DM taxi, or No. 8 trolley, then bus No. 63 to the suburb of Solln. The 10DM entrance fee gives you free run of the tiny rock garden, indoor pool, and some forty chaise longues, and the bar and TV room. But keep your hands off anybody you meet (ages mostly thirty to sixty), especially any pretty young girls, for they usually are accompanied by husbands or boyfriends who're liable to give you a good *Klopfe.* This is a deadly serious place. There is a certain camaraderie if you join the crowd (capacity ten) in either of the two

Schwitzen rooms, but no chance of anything phony happening with your baloney, even during the massage (15DM extra), as in the special "massage" houses of London, Amsterdam, Copenhagen, Rome, Stockholm, or New York.

While Sauna-Solln's twenty-eight-year-old and handsome, but formidable, blond masseuse Helga hews a huge slab of gnarly old *Bürgertugend* into filet mignon, and fortyish Otto Hyman makes *Nudel* of a lithe brunette *Mädel* stretched out on the *adjoining* table, fifty or more other naked Bavarians insure all is *korrekt,* for the massage tables are set right at poolside. Often several people stand quite close around the tables, apparently awaiting their respective turns but, to an *Ausländer,* looking more like medical students watching a delicate operation being performed in a hospital amphitheater.

Debauch—Bavarian style.

MASSAGE AND HOSTESS SERVICES

On a given day one finds over fifty massage parlors advertised in the classifieds of the lively newspaper *AZ.* None has more attractive young girls and few give more varied services than SALON GUDRUN (Leopoldstrasse 71, second floor; 34–86–92), in the heart of Schwabing, where so many of the better parlors are located. Thirty marks for a basic rub, 70DM for several other good things.

SALON MARLIE (Orleanstrasse 43; 45–21–09) must be doing something. Right? They advertise *"Massage mit Herz."*

The better hostess services—and there must be twenty or more—include HAPPY DAY (Mainzerstrasse 15; 34–77–75) and HOSTESSEN–SERVICE (Barerstrasse 50A; 28–68–43).

DRUG TOPICS

For years Munich has been a major terminus and way station for narcotics traffic (mostly soft) from the Middle East to points west. The police, those here as well as officials along the trade routes, seemed to care little about it. But recently with the increased pressure on Marseilles and the French by American agents Munich has become perhaps the leading European point of entry for hard drugs. Frequent truck caravans (their otherwise innocuous cargo sealed and undisturbed by customs agents through international agreements) pass through Adana, Ankara, and Istanbul, Turkey, and on through Sofia, Belgrade, and Vienna, bringing thousands of pounds of hashish and significant quantities of heroin to Bavaria, much of it destined for export to the U.S. Now that Munich authorities admit there are enough hard-drug users here to "make a market," the police have begun to take significant action against dealers and importers. In 1969 only 170 pounds of hashish were seized. In 1971 the police confiscated 6000 pounds. In one single 1972 deal over 65 pounds of high-grade heroin were impounded, with the aid of American and French agents.

The penalty for the sale of hard drugs has recently been raised in West Germany from three to ten years in prison. The Cabinet has authorized wiretapping and unannounced searches of suspects' residences. Foreigners are not immune. As many young Americans already know, because of the collusion with dealers of so many police and customs officials in so many countries, the innocent bystander with one small joint may be prosecuted as harshly as the dealer (who somehow can usually afford and arrange "bail"). By mid-1972 nearly 1000 Americans, mostly young ones, were languishing in foreign jails for violating drug laws. Of these German jails held 78, Spain's 41, Holland's (yes Holland's, most of these in Surprising Amsterdam) 35, France's 27, and Italy's 24.

MIXED-UP MORALITY—WHOREHOUSE RAID

The police are busy on other fronts. Had you strolled Zweigstrasse on the night of April 10, 1972, seeking Munich's new "Eros Center," strategically located a block from the main railway station, you would have witnessed a hilarious but no less perplexing example of the new Munich morality, which by now should be old hat to you. Here, in this raffish quarter of B-girl bars and all-night cafés favored by Yugoslav, Turkish, and Italian laborers, stands the city's latest whorehouse—the late (for the moment, at least) LEIER-KASTEN.

This means, literally, "barrel organ," but this night it was no one's turn in the barrel. Men were jumping out of windows, half-naked young whores (from 30 to 40DM) were angrily clawing at squads of leather-coated cops, and the most persistent (and publicity-conscious) among the girls and their clients were handcuffed to their captors, hauled off in paddy wagons. Many press photographers just happened by—they had been given advance notice, apparently—and within an hour a large crowd of excited workingmen and boys had gathered to enjoy the spectacle of this, one of the biggest and funniest vice raids in Bavarian history.

The morning papers, filled with some extraordinary photographs, announced solemnly that the police had closed Leier-Kasten, and the poor little house at Josephspitalstrasse 5 too, for the sole reason that "both are in the center of the city."

"City center, hell!" shrieked a well-stuffed shrew as she feigned squirting a burly sergeant in the eye with her right udder, "What about the Schleissheimerstrasse houses, and Imex House. They're in the center too! And why don't they go bother the big shots in Baldurstrasse!" In the nights to follow wisecracking, catcalling crowds gathered outside *Leier-Kasten* to give support to the whores who, by now, had barricaded themselves inside, appearing in shifts on the window ledges to hurl abuse and women's liberation slogans through electric bullhorns at the cops, who, in turn, good-humoredly strolled their beat behind hastily installed steel crowd-control barriers.

The general consensus seemed to be that, considering the lively bargaining scenes encouraged by *Leier-Kasten*'s sidewalk courtyard, Munich's Town Hall comstocks had simply decided to clean up the town a bit in preparation for the Olympic Games. Let the American newspapermen and television commentators keep their minds on the *Gemütlichkeit* in the beer halls and the stadium, never mind the *Kameradschaftlichkeit* in the whorehouses. When the amateurs had left town the pros would go back to work.

WEST BERLIN

WEST GERMANY

The basic unit of currency is the Deutsche mark, which can be divided into 100 pfennigs. At this writing you'll get about 3.18 marks for each floating dollar. Thus each mark equals about 30 U.S. cents. You can bring in or take out as many marks as you can carry.

THE GERMANS HAVE COMBED THE EARTH

Pubic hair has fascinated laymen (apparently far more than women) and scholars since other body hair began to disappear. Galen, the early Greek physician (A.D. 130–200) whose authority in these matters was virtually undisputed until the sixteenth century, considered the function of pubic hair to be purely ornamental. Caspar Bartholin, pioneering Danish anatomist, regarded it as nature's screen of modesty. And Gerdy, a French authority, saw it as nature's tease, noting with a certain Gallic irony that the growth appears almost coincidentally with the ripening of the genitals. But it remained for a German, Burkhard Eble, to tell us what our pubic hair is really about:

1. It is absorbing perspiration in the genital area and that trickling down from the abdominal area.
2. It is preventing excess friction during coitus.
3. It is acting as a symbol of sexual maturity.
4. It is facilitating "the accumulation and mutual interchange of electricity between the two individual opposite poles in copulation."

Apparently the Germans got into gynecology generally, and hair specifically, earlier and heavier than anyone else. Before the end of the nineteenth century they had pretty well combed the earth.

Wernich, for example, reported on the comparatively sparse pubic harvest of Japanese women in contrast to their luxuriant heads. Doenitz discovered total pubic baldness in an "amazingly large number of cases" (which rather begs the question of just how many Japanese ladies he managed to examine). Baelz found several Manchurian candidates with flat, smooth-skinned mons veneris and scarce, coarse hairs around the labia majora. Schliephake reported the situation to be similarly arid among the Eskimo women of Cumberland Sound. Stratz managed to get into nearly everybody's hair in a region of Java; after examining over twenty-three hundred native females, he concluded, "a hirsute mons veneris is rare," and as a filigree added that "in cases where the genital hair has not been . . . artificially plucked out . . . it is apt to curl slightly and be lighter in tint than the hair of the head." Von Meyer examined only one Tierra del Fuegan, and she a rather elderly one, but he made the most of it. Noting that her mons veneris was oddly flat with a slight fatty mound he went on to observe that her pubic hairs were soft and downy. For the main course he measured each hair, and for dessert calculated their average length to be precisely five-hundredths of a centimeter.

Conradt was confused. Returning from Africa he reported that the crop among Togoland's females was always black but varied from "rather profuse" to "sparse" to "patchy." Finsch was flabbergasted to find fair hair in New Britain but suspected that the girls used an acid bleach. And Bässler arrived breathlessly from the Bismarck Archipelago to report to the Anthropological Society of Berlin that the South Pacific beauties dyed their pubes red and wiped their hands there in lieu of towels.

The first authoritative tabulation of such researches comes to us from the Berlin gynecologist Eggel, who, just before he died (of exhaustion?), directed that his work be continued by his colleague Max Bartels. One thousand German women were examined and found to have the following characteristics in various combinations:

```
Dark eyes  ........................................239
Dark hair on head  ..............................333
Dark hair on mons veneris and genitals  ..............329
Light eyes  ......................................761
Light hair on head  .............................667
Light hair on mons veneris and genitals  .............671
```

The great truth to come out of these researches is that while there is some tendency for color of pubic hair to correspond with color of head hair, this is by no means an absolute rule. Not a few brunettes with blond bases were found, for example. Further, there is absolutely no relation between color of eyes and color of pubic hair. (At least not among the *women* of north Germany; none of these fellows seems to have displayed much scientific curiosity about men.) As to length, density, texture, and arrangement, you may be assured these were tabulated exhaustively and checked against all other characteristics (and this in the early twentieth century, before the advent of modern computers), but no significant patterns emerged.

Determined to confirm what he had not found, Bartels somehow persuaded his friend Rothe the gynecologist to carry out a further study on another group of 1000 women. Rothe found that of the 977 north German women, most had fair hair, and 52 had hairs on the labia majora a good deal paler than on the mons veneris. Further, the redheads invariably had either red or light pubes, never dark. Two-thirds of the brunettes had brown or black forests down below, nearly one-third red ones, and two cases dark blond. Nearly all the Jewish women ran to brown pubic hair. In a further study on yet another group of women—477 north Germans, 11 Jews, and 2 Poles—Rothe found "two main types on the mons veneris . . . the hairs grew mainly in a longitudinal strip" or were clustered in a roughly triangular patch. "In both main groups, there were several subtypes." In 420 North German cases curly pubic hair occurred most often and straight hair least. As to numbers and length of hair, he found moderation the rule.

Apparently hooked on research, Rothe went on to study the breasts of 1000 North German women, 75 percent of whom were Brandenburg Prussians. Of these, 16.2 percent had cup-shaped breasts, 51.2 percent hemispherical, 8.3 percent bowl-shaped, 21.4 percent conical, and only 2.9 percent had what he described as the "goat's udder" type. Of these latter, 82.76 percent were found on women with light hair and eyes, 13.9 percent on light-haired dark-eyed women, and only 3.45 percent of "goat's udders" hung from dark-eyed dark-haired women. You may be sure Rothe didn't stop here. Further researches included an apparently definitive nipple probe ("knob-shaped," "cone-shaped," "low cylindrical," etc.; red 30 percent, dusky-brown 27 percent, reddish brown 20 percent, rose-pink 15 percent, etc.). Several of these studies, along with much of the foregoing statistics can be found in *Femina Libido Sexualis* (New York: The Medical Press, 1965). However, should you yourself wish to do some of your own field work, Berlin still offers the finest facilities and opportunities in the world.

TURNABOUT

Begin your observations at Heerstrasse 39, a handsome complex of low white stucco buildings surrounded by a white wall and set in a small park in the British Sector on the edge of Grunewald. The 8DM ($2.40) entrance fee covers use of a locker and all laboratory facilities in Dr. F. Runge's THERMES HEERSTRASSE (3–04–98–70). Like so many Berlin saunas, this one is thoroughly democratic, welcoming all people regardless of race, creed, and sex. Other than toilets and dressing rooms, there are no separate facilities for men and women. However, Thursday is reserved for females until 3 P.M., but gentlemen who arrive at 3:01 P.M. will find this an especially fortuitous day because many women remain well into the evening.

But the Heerstrasse Sauna is popular any time (9 A.M. to 11 P.M., every day), partly because the facilities and accommodations are so extensive and lavish, and very much because an unusually stimulating and accomplished group of people are thus attracted to come here.

If it's your first visit, you might want to run around a bit and get the feel of things. Inside there's a restaurant, a large swimming pool, community and smaller saunas, and a sleeping room with rows of padded bunks. The staff of masseurs and masseuses (one is free to request either) is courteous and professional and fully clothed, for there is no hankypanky with the help, in contrast to some of the smaller Berlin massage institutes. The decor, a sensible combination of chalk-white stucco, lacquered and stained wood, and flagstone walkways, lends a healthy, robust atmosphere, but not an antiseptic or pristine one. The effect conveys the feeling that you're supposed to enjoy yourself and, incidentally, get a little healthy in the process. Outside sweet-smelling pine trees surround a Japanese rock garden, and an artificial brook runs under a wooden bridge and empties into the open-air swimming pool.

It is mid-November, and though the sun shines brightly and the air is dry, invigorating (Berliners compare the intoxicating briskness of their *Berliner Luft* to brut champagne), it is still a brisk 35°. You're no physical-culture maniac, and nothing could make you jump into this pool unless it were warmed by dozens of beautiful naked women. You record only eleven naked women in the pool (and six men), three about twenty-five, the others from thirty to forty. Only five of the women could really be called pretty, and only two really beautiful. So you just stand around the edge for about an hour, making notes on arrivals and departures.

This is a very intelligent way to work up a good sweat, and certainly worth the 8DM admission. But there are some worthwhile extras, all of them quite reasonable in price. The "sport massage" (7,50DM) is supposed to aid the circulation of the blood and, as executed by a lively blond girl of twenty-three, it does. The sunlamp (1DM) is superfluous today, but who can resist a vigorous 50-pfennig shampoo? Follow this with a facial (9DM) and a free hour on a padded bunk in the sleeping room, and you'll work up a good appetite.

The restaurant is a hot, very dry room, so to dress is optional; few do, except the waitresses. Heat emanates from a copper-funneled fireplace, and you sit on little Scandinavian reindeerhide hassocks. The philosophy of the place is exemplified by this room, which has the look and ambiance of a small chic ski lodge. The health faddist or body-building fanatic would not feel at home at the Heerstrasse Sauna (nor, perhaps, would the confirmed homosexual). No tiger's milk, monkey droppings, or wheat germ, not even a bottle of Diet Pepsi. But if you enjoy a tasty small steak (5DM), excellent goulash or noodle soup (2,50DM), fruit salad (2DM), and a glass of wine or beer (1 to 2DM), and the opportunity to dine, swim, and sweat with friendly strangers who incidentally happen to be naked . . . this is your kind of bathhouse.

You're lunching with a smart-looking brassiere model (Berlin is Germany's garment center), an especially pretty red-haired (all the way) airline reservations clerk, and an amusing old man who claims to be not only a member of the West Berlin House of Representatives but also the redhead's uncle. You're smoking a big black cigar and nobody cares. The steak was fine and the wine more than adequate. There is a poker game at another table to which you are invited. The redhead wants you to take her walking in the rock garden and then join her for a nap in the sleeping room. Her "uncle" is about to begin a chess game with Bra Model and your noodle soup was nearly all noodles. If you have ever been better off in your life, you don't remember it.

MORE SAUNA AND MASSAGE

Solf Sauna: Plentiful Young Women

A subsequent visit to Berlin (meaning *West* Berlin unless otherwise noted) and the chic new SOLF SAUNA (atop the modern white apartment building at Bundesallee 186; 213–21–14) may qualify that statement, for this is reputed to attract the largest proportion and number of unattached *young* women of any of the city's several mixed saunas. Sure enough, at 3 P.M. on a hot cloudless sunny June Sunday afternoon, of the ninety-eight people enjoying the large roof-garden sunbathing area and sauna, the spacious indoor pool, sauna, and snack bar, you recorded 40 percent women, of whom perhaps 30 percent were under thirty and attractive. Of these the true blondes tended to blond pubic hair, the bleached to black, the brunettes to brown or black, and one redhead had red fire down below. Three girls never took off their bathrobes. Perhaps 60 percent of the nude men were in their twenties or thirties, 30 percent in their forties or fifties. All, including the baldheaded and over fifties, had pubic hair.

Why has Berlin, for years since World War II, offered more mixed public sauna and bathing facilities than any European city? Proprietor Clemens Solf is sure he doesn't know. As to why Berlin girls are so uninhibited about mixed bathing and sunning on their own, rather than arriving with a male escort as is the custom in Munich or Vienna, for example, the pretty blond receptionist —who does not savor the practice at all—could offer no explanation except to suggest that the girls who come here do so not so much to look as that they enjoy being *looked at*.

Filanda Sauna: Plentiful Women

SOLF'S FILANDA SAUNA (Filandastrasse 5; 792–45–42; a good stop to or from nearby Tempelhof Airport) is reported to attract the highest proportion and number of females of all ages. And indeed, one weekday afternoon (the best time for men, especially for the overflow Tuesdays, which, until 1 P.M. are reserved for females) you record 75 percent of the sixty-two guests as female, a few in their twenties, but most beyond thirty. Many well beyond. Adequate but with crowded, nearly tacky facilities, especially the jammed roof garden and tiny open-air wading pool, the Filanda is probably Berlin's oldest mixed sauna.

Haus Paulsborn and Finnia: Mr. Berlin for the Ladies

More up to date is the sauna at HAUS PAULSBORN (just off the Kurfürsten-damm in the heart of Berlin at Eisenzahnstrasse 14; 880–22–22) set within a handsome modern apartment complex, many of whose well-off tenants are regular clientele. Like most mixed saunas, Herr F. J. Schnock's is open every day, and the 8DM entrance fee covers use of all facilities except massage, food, and beverages. Excellent borscht. Large card room. FINNIA SAUNA (also just off the Kudamm at Johann-Georgstrasse 7; 881–77–82) features a large well-equipped gym; reserves Mondays and mornings to women when they may be expertly manhandled by the masseur, a former Mr. Berlin; and is mixed all other times, except Saturday mornings, which are strictly for males. The sauna by the Olympic Stadium (3–04–44–72) is mixed noon to midnight every day; females only from noon to 7 P.M. Thursdays.

Though most of the foregoing offer massage, think of them also as meeting places. For more intimate and specialized massage there are several smaller establishments that feature private rooms, Muzak, and scantily clad mas-seuses. It should be stressed that all the establishments cited here are highly respectable places whose raison d'être is therapeutic. However, depending on the girl, *not* the management, various exotic and erotic massages may sometimes be had in the smaller places, rather like the maraschino cherry on a tart. ("I will massage any part of your body with any part of my body," suggested one girl.)

It should be noted that Berlin is a municipality with the legal status of an independent state; West German federal laws become operative here only after being ratified by the West Berlin House of Representatives. And if the old Representative met in the Heerstrasse sauna is any criterion, Berliners are stubborn and tolerant and wary of making laws that govern adult morality. Hence there appears to be no law in Berlin which prohibits one having any part of his or her anatomy massaged by a member of the opposite sex. By comparison, the laws of most of the United States seem oddly obsessed with preventing *heterosexual* contacts in public baths. Consequently, American baths have traditionally been as much places of homosexual assignation as anything else. No such hypocrisy exists in Berlin.

Schwarz Gymna: For the Men

The SCHWARZ GYMNA is a homey place, owner-managed by a motherly matron. It is housed in a comfortable fifty-year-old townhouse located in quiet tree-lined Württembergischestrasse (at No. 31; 8–81–85–96), just off the bustling Kudamm. It offers a lot of complicated medical apparatus, various rubbing machines, showcases of trusses and liniments. Everything looks and is highly professional. Advertised services include "medical," "*sportif,*" and "cosmetic" massages, as well as pedicures. Average massage is 14DM for thirty minutes. (Compare New York City or Los Angeles prices.) Private rooms have very high ceilings, soundproof walls, strong oak doors, hand-colored engravings and French prints, and some good antique furniture. Hours 9 A.M. to 8 P.M., to 4 P.M. on Saturdays. After the strong but lithe and attractive twenty-nine-year-old blonde finishes kneading, scrubbing, and polishing you to a limp noodle, you may feel like nothing more than having a good snooze, or at best lying back quietly and savoring a bit of penile massage, if you like that. And if she does. (Consider that in Copenhagen they'd charge $20 to do that in some smelly, dirty little room, or before a sex-show audience.)

Depending on the relationship you establish with a masseuse (of which the management has no knowledge), you might make *her* day by offering a bit of reciprocal massage. She might consider it a fair bargain,[1] though it would still be impolite not to leave a small tip. However, for a young lady to climb out of her sheer white miniuniform and shed her white lace panties (no bra) and hop on a rub table with you, well a 30DM gratuity *might* do it.

Massage-Praxis

There is some nice intrigue associated with locating the MASSAGE-PRAXIS. At Kurfürstendamm 30 enter the bookstore of Marga Schoeller. This has a wonderful selection of English-language books, and a relaxing upstairs reading room with overstuffed easy chairs and very good lighting. Never mind that now. Go to the back of the bookstore on the ground floor and walk out the back door into a small courtyard. You'll see a small sign indicating "Massage" and pointing to a doorway. Enter, walk up two flights, and you are greeted by a pretty young woman who appears to have nothing on under her rather sheer uniform. Though the place is rather homely, the masseuses are not. You did not take the cure here and cannot state with certainty the kinds of massage offered, but the girl rattled off a great gush of German that sounded quite promising. When you smiled, she blushed. Any treatment costs 10DM. Although the Kudamm house is at this time on extended holiday, there's another Massage-praxis at Kudamm 130. No connection between the two: "*Praxis*" simply means "practice."

For Ladies Only

Most massage houses cater exclusively or primarily to men. But right on the Kudamm, at 26A, in the same building housing NBC News and the AP, the thoroughly businesslike MASSAGEINSTITUT (833–54–93) handles women

[1]And she might not.

exclusively, particularly those with rheumatism or arthritis. Karlheinz Schumann is a virtuoso in his field—and, only incidentally, quite an attractive chap—particularly expert at helping you recover from accidents. He also treats *Stoffwechselerkrankungen.*[2] But he'll do it only if you can pronounce it.

MORE MASSAGE?

More massage.

The following have no connection with each other, nor with any establishments thus far cited—in fact, unlike in any previously noted situations a massage in any of the following can run as high as 70, 80DM. Needless to say, you get what you pay for. All offer the highest standards of cleanliness and attractive masseuses.

MODERN-MASSAGEN (Lietzenburgerstrasse 54; 883-72-63) is modern. And so are its charming, extremely friendly masseuses. It is also "*diskrete.*" From 10 A.M. to 10 P.M.; from 65 to 80DM.

The 80DM treatments at ROYAL MASSAGE (Uhlandstrasse 77; 87-92-29) are, as the clever, incisive traveler may have deduced, royal. And cost 80DM. Fine classical record collection. Try for the blonde.

At Fasanenstrasse 60 you may be massaged by Jasmin for this is JASMIN MASSAGESALON (883-67-44). Enormous bedrooms. Enormous beds. Look for the sign "De Sade" on the outer door. Don't forget the torture room.

Or you may be massaged by SUJI WONG (Wilmersdorferstrasse 94, third floor; 881-72-35).

Or for nearly three years, if your body can handle a rub—and other delights—of that duration, at MASSAGE SALON OF A THOUSAND AND ONE NIGHTS, Bleibtreustrasse 29/30; 60-80DM.

Which brings us to the versatile MASSAGE-PRAXIS JET (Kurfürstendamm 130; 886-22-52). Some may never want to leave. A beautiful young man who is equally at home with the ladies or his fellows for 50DM. A nice young lady (80DM) for the other fellows.

And don't overlook SALON MADY (Lietzenburgerstrasse 76; 883-65-63). A lovely *Mädel* or two. And films. From 60 to 100DM.

Note that all these situations are just off or near the Kudamm and, considering that they are located in buildings whose other tenants all are engaged in far less exotic or vigoroso occupations, it is imperative you telephone first for an appointment or, barring that, make sure the massage salon in question is clearly identified on the outside door buzzer or building directory.

---

[2]As you have surely guessed, this means "diet problems."

SPIES AND THE WALL

Even without all that friction, Berlin would rank high among the more stimulating cities of the world. The drama of Berlin's fact of life is unique in modern history. Surrounded on all sides by hostile territory (the zone border separating West Berlin from East Germany totals 185 miles of barriers) and cut off from its historic heart in East Berlin by a wall as much symbolic as physical (the sector border dividing the city is seventy-four miles of barbed wire, concrete, and recently added escape barriers that include trip flares, police-dog alleys, trenches thirty-five feet wide and nine feet deep, and antitank traps), the city can be compared to those ancient and medieval walled cities that managed to live relatively normal lives while under siege. But Berlin's situation is really unprecedented. For it is the immediate *outside* world that fears "invasion" and has thus created the barrier.

Spies lurk everywhere. CIA and West German Interior Ministry sources estimate the number of Communist agents (mostly East Germans) operating throughout West Germany as anywhere from fifteen to twenty thousand. (Accurate figures on the number of Western agents are much more difficult to come by.) At some time or other any spy worthy of his code name must come and do some business in Berlin. The possibility that the most innocuous-looking character at the bar could be in the espionage trade gives the town a nice sharp edge. But, admittedly, it does not compare with the convention atmospheres of World War II Istanbul or Lisbon.

There is, however, no ignoring the Wall, the most revolting yet compelling tourist attraction in Europe. Visitors gape at it with that same mixture of horror and fascination usually reserved for three-alarm fires and bloody highway accidents. And even the most blasé Berliner will tell you that the longer the Wall stays, the more dangerous it becomes. Dangerous not only because over twenty-five thousand East Germans have risked death to crawl under, over, or through it (more than a hundred and fifty have died in the attempt), but dangerous because of the political and military realities the Wall represents.

Berlin lives dangerously, but is proud that it also lives normally. If cities had psychiatrists, Berlin's might be amazed that the patient did not suffer feelings of paranoia, schizophrenia, and long periods of manic depression. People tend to ignore the danger, or mock it. The cliché description of Berliners is that they have an uncommonly strong sense of reality. In truth, the city has experienced such a wide variety of realities during the past century that the more absolute the situation appears to be, the more cynical the Berliners' response to it. (It remains to be seen whether the mid-1972 East-West détente pacts really mean what they say.)

CYNICISM: SUICIDE AND SEX

Forty-one of every hundred thousand Berliners respond with the highest cynicism—suicide, the highest recorded incidence in the world. (The U.S. rate is about eleven per one hundred thousand.) The tensions accompanying the city's perilous isolation, and the fact that 21 percent of the population is over sixty-five, offer only partial explanations; at least three prewar periods had even higher ratios. Dr. Klaus Thomas, who founded a center to aid potential suicides in West Berlin, is convinced that sex education is among the most important suicide deterrents. Among Dr. Thomas' findings was that the suicidal urge was greater among females under rather than over twenty, with broken love affairs the most common cause. Of the people who call his center for help, 75 percent are women.

Among foreigners and even other Germans, Berliners have the reputation of being aloof, even unfriendly. However, on initial contact with strangers, they are generally pleasant, courteous, witty people. The acidity has been much exaggerated. But as New Yorkers respond to their environmental difficulties with rudeness, indifference, or despair, the Berliner has evolved a special way of talking back to life. Pointed, ironic, and colorfully descriptive figures of speech, the Berlin *Klappe* is usually good-humored and directed more at man's works than his morals. Not surprisingly in a city 78-percent destroyed and now almost totally rebuilt (often in the style of a Prussian Los Angeles), much of the *Klappe* is directed at architecture. What's left over is aimed at the East Germans. Thus the Congress Hall is either "The Pregnant Oyster" or "The Baby Scale," Philharmonic Hall is "Circus Karajani," the recent reinforcements of the Wall "Ulbricht's Beautification Project." East Germany is known simply as "paradise."

But a city can go only so far on wit. On a more practical level, the exigencies of life are considerably eased by a civic leniency—Berliners quite seriously call it "tolerance"—that the city cherishes as chauvinistically as Green Bay adores its Packers. Though this permissiveness strikes one as analogous to the kind of indulgence one grants a deprived child, it works.

FUN CITY

Among the first proclamations of Berlin's Lord Mayor Klaus Schütz (he is technically a Prime Minister) was that "Berlin must be fun." What he meant was that restrictions on nightlife must be kept to a minimum. In addition to its soothing saunas and massage parlors, Berlin has over four thousand bars and nightclubs.

And at least fourteen brothels (all of these, however, regarded as "unofficial"). Prostitutes are harassed less along the Kurfürstendamm than chestnut peddlers are on Manhattan's Fifth Avenue. There are dozens of homosexual bars and nightclubs. Miniskirts are the shortest in Germany. Since March 10, 1970, the city government has paid for the birth-control pills of all women on relief. And the law requires that pubs close only between 5 and 6 A.M..

But Berlin is not Sodom. The popularly held notion that this city, constantly threatened with no tomorrow, lives accordingly, is erroneous. Berlin's "high life" is neither as homey nor as uninhibited as Copenhagen's or Amsterdam's, nor nearly as extensive as Paris's. (However, there's more happening here than in London.) This is partly because Berliners are not a frivolous people, and mainly because the nightlife is designed for tourists and businessmen. Berlin enjoys itself, but strictly on its own terms. Tolerance here means "you do as you wish as long as you do not disrupt the natural order of things." If you want a pretty, topless girl to massage your privates . . . fine. But go to a private place, request a private room, and a private girl. Do not expect such attentions in a community sauna. Almost every imaginable taste is catered to, but the pleasures of Berlin are . . . measured.

Most of all, Berlin is an extremely friendly city, particularly to Americans, who may be fast running out of towns where they don't risk being stoned in the streets. For one thing, Berliners make themselves very accessible, spending a great deal of time outside their homes. Here you find the best café life in Germany. Parks comprise one-fifth the city's area and there are sixty-two lakes, most of them in the Western sector. This is Europe's greenest city.

AN ADULT CITY, A CITY OF WOMEN

Unlike London and Munich, two cities that pander to youth, Berlin is a city of and for adults. The visitor is struck by the comparative absence of young people, and this is no illusion. A recent census reports that of West Berlin's 2.2 million inhabitants, only about 400,000 are under the age of twenty. About 700,000 are between the ages of twenty and forty-five. And more than a million are over forty-five. Berlin is also a city of women. The same census reported 1.25 million females, and only 940,000 males. Similarly, the Soviet sector has some 600,000 females and only 460,000 males. Berlin has more widows than Richmond, Virginia, has people. And 5000 taxis.

YOUTH, DRUGS, AND COMMUNES

The young women of Berlin are as emancipated as any in Western Europe. Berlin has full employment and most young women work, though not always in jobs worthy of their intellects and capabilities. Because Berlin must be self-sufficient (East and West, it is Europe's largest industrial city), one-third of the people are employed in factories. But to see the uniformly well-dressed strollers on the Kurfürstendamm, it is hard to believe it. Berlin probably has more charming, brainy factory workers, maids, waitresses, shopgirls, and prostitutes than any city of comparable size in America. These people find outlets besides careers for their creative and emotional energies.

The Free University of Berlin (fifteen thousand students) is the Berkeley of Germany. Though her youth are comparatively few in number, the city's students are the most politically and socially conscious in the nation. When not in the streets challenging the Axel Springer press empire or other Establishments, they're planning new provocations and demonstrations in their communes. *Kommune-I,* which Ranier Langhans founded in 1966 in a onetime Stuttgarter Platz whorehouse, is still sharing ideas, toothbrushes, and bodies alike, though it has moved. Sixteen of the twenty dormitory residences in the student village in Schlachtensee, off Potsdamer Chaussee, are coed, right down to the showers and toilets. And there are many other sexually integrated communes throughout the city, ranging from those formed for purely hedonistic reasons (which perhaps have inspired latecoming Americans, though Bard College was doing it unofficially in the 1940s and 1950s, and the Russians, for that matter, in 1925) to others where sharing is more an aspect of sound economics.

If one were seeking information as to the current price of drugs in Berlin, he'd of course inquire among the youth sprawling over the steps of the Kaiser Wilhelm Memorial Church at the top of the Kudamm. Some of the gathering near the bottom of the Kudamm, around Johann–Sigismundstrasse may also be up on such matters.

THE KURFÜRSTENDAMM

The Kurfürstendamm is Berlin's liveliest and busiest street, and has more neon than all of East Berlin. It has always been a center of nightlife—85 percent of today's is on it or just off it—but now, as the hub of commerce as well, the prewar elegance has been replaced by a crisp, businesslike snap. Yet the mélange of modern glass-and-steel structures intermixed with those great townhouses that managed to survive the war is not unappealing. The Kudamm has a nice optimistic feel to it, and many of the local street-level establishments deal in pleasures and leisure. (Even the nightclub touts are dressed in conservative dark suits and make their overtures in an extremely low-pressure fashion.) There are sidewalk cafés, chic shops, indoor cafés, bars and restaurants, cafés in rebuilt hotels with famous old names, and more cafés. (But beware the street numbers which seem to run with no logic at all.)

Café Tarts

Not the least of the commerce is in prostitution; in fact, far more people are engaged in the oldest profession than in any of the newer ones. "If Berlin is to be fun," says a city official, "the Kudamm coffee must have its spice." And so the girls are permitted to operate right in the center of town and are not relegated to remote areas as in Munich. Some of the better cafés may tolerate the girls, as long as they are discreet *and* decorative. But of course no café has any connection whatsoever with prostitutes. The situation is so ephemeral that to single out any one café would be misleading. However, whether one is peddling mechanical rabbits, newspapers, or sex, it is prudent to set the stand up where the action is. And the more elegant the girl, the more elegant and fashionable will be the café she chooses.

To the unsuspecting male, the demimonde who garnish the Kudamm cafés appear to be no more for sexual hire than any of the other charming young women who find café-sitting among the most pleasant Berlin pastimes. Here, as in Munich, blatant solicitation is an offense (and is assiduously discouraged by all cafés), but the Berlin police tolerate café prostitutes as long as contacts are made with discretion. In practice that simply means the gentleman must make the first approach. (Paradoxically, it can be assumed that any girl who makes an overt proposal to a man is probably *not* a prostitute.) The custom of payment in advance prevails here as anywhere else, but should a girl then, for some unaccountable reason, refuse to deliver, West Berlin courts will entertain your charge of fraud!

Once a man makes the first move, the café management is apparently technically absolved from responsibility for operating immoral premises, for what European café could be expected to discourage its male patrons from flirting? The prostitutes are so chicly turned out that it requires great skill and subtlety on their part to indicate, without blatantly advertising the fact, that they are for sale. Usually it is enough merely to raise an eyebrow or a drink, but in cases of naïve foreign prospects the girls resort to such extremes as "reading" *Schmutzliteratur* held upside down.

A Kudamm café girl charges from 75 to 100DM for her favors, prices having remained amazingly stable over the past few years. Some of the girls are merely part-timers—moonlighting secretaries, models, or masseuses— and they may prefer an evening of dancing or theater before bed. Pro or semipro, the café girl's workbed is usually in her own apartment, or in one of the small hotels in the tree-lined streets intersecting the Kudamm. It has been noted that German hotels are particularly sensitive to male guests attempting to fashion single rooms into doubles. For this reason many experienced travelers prefer the excellent first-class pensions within a block of the Kudamm to hotels. Most important, one has his own key to the front door and may go and come as he pleases, with whom he pleases. (It's rather bad form to bring a prostitute into a nice respectable pension, but a girlfriend is quite another story, as long as she is out by morning—otherwise you will be charged for a double.)

In addition to the Kudamm café and street action, one finds considerable *Mieze* (pussy), and a few *Tanten* too (old aunts), in nearby streets like Joachimstalerstrasse, Rankestrasse, Augsburgerstrasse, and Fuggerstrasse. And perhaps a couple of accommodating pensions as well. From 50 to 60 DM.

Café Sweets

But of course you'll encounter many non-professional girls in the Kudamm cafés. "The ZUNTZ? *Ja!* The best place in Berlin for a *Schnack*," says a swell-looking blond schoolteacher. Indeed, the Café Zuntz has a marvelous location at one of the Kudamm's busiest intersections, and the upstairs portion is a particular favorite of writers and artists. The ground-floor terrace is crowded winter and summer, and the sandwich menu is endless. Günter Grass has just ordered No. 286, *Schweizer gebacken mit Preiselbeeren*— grilled Swiss cheese with cranberry sauce. Upstairs, where people are younger and less interested in food, a prostitute couldn't give herself away, for one finds many enthusiastic amateurs who might. Here, among the intimate booths, rocking chairs, and large lounges offering the gossip and newspapers of the world, a stranger has among the best opportunities in all Berlin to meet students and other young people.

The CAFÉ SCHILLING is another matter. Like Munich's Carlton Tearoom, the Schilling is popular with widows, not so merry perhaps, but they're willing in the Schilling. CAFÉ KRANZLER is said to have the most chic and the best ice cream on the street, and this night an airline stewardess who looks as good to eat as Lilli Marlene in her prime. CAFÉ CARROUSEL is Berlin's most cosmopolitan and is especially popular with people over thirty-five, if only because it and the adjoining Hotel Kempinski are heir, at least in name, to the traditions of *Alt* Berlin. Also on the Kudamm, the ROXY BAR appears to be a favorite of models and girls who are not models but look as if they could be.

The Streetgirls

Streetgirls are strung out all along the Kudamm like Prussian sentinels, becoming thicker and cheaper as one moves in the direction away from Kaiser Wilhelm Church and the Europa Center. Their day begins at 9 P.M. and ends at dawn. On cold nights the girls light bonfires on streetcorners.

The Kudamm streetgirls are somewhat younger and less sophisticated than their sisters in the cafés, but not necessarily less attractive. Because they must catch the eye of the passing motorist, they favor garish outfits of mini- or microskirts, tight bright sweaters, and boots. And some carry flashlights and hand mirrors. In keeping with Berlin's antisolicitation prohibitions the girls must keep their come-ons to a minimum. Flat rates from 40 to 60DM usually include the cheap room nearby. Most activity after 11 P.M.

All Kudamm girls are regularly inspected by the health authorities, carry cards to prove it, and are subject to strict police supervision. Though about 75 percent have pimps and protectors, these men are not visible on the Kudamm. There is a federal law in this country, strictly enforced in West Berlin, that "no person shall make a profit from sexual acts of any kind." This has nothing to do with prostitutes, of course, being aimed squarely at brothelkeepers and pimps, though, as elsewhere, it is somehow difficult for the police to completely abolish the activities of the latter.

Beware the "Baroque Blonde"

At the intersection of Clausewitzstrasse and the Kudamm and points east, beware the "Baroque Blonde." These statuesque, white-booted, microskirted, bewigged (*usually* blond) beauties jump right into the car if a driver so much as doubles his clutch. They suggest parking in a secluded spot, then plead menstruation and offer manual or oral sex in lieu of intercourse. Most Berliners know them for what they are (including the police, who have registered, at this writing, over a hundred of them)—male transvestites. But many visitors do not, and never find out, even after they have paid the 30DM and been serviced. Or slugged and robbed.

Because time means nothing but money to a prostitute, the Kudamm girls charge 10DM less than their usual price if the customer is willing to have his business done in the car. And, of course, there is an additional saving on the hotel bill. Some of the homelier and older women offer a 20DM "special" on fellatio and throw in a good feel under their skirts or a long look for an extra couple of marks. Or, for a paltry 10DM, these poor devils will manually service the customer, while he is driving if he wishes. (This only adds to the already high Kudamm accident rate and perhaps contributes to the fact that your chances of dying in an auto accident are about twice as high here as in New York City; 14.6 deaths per hundred thousand population vs. 7.5 in New York City.) These unfortunates are the bottom of the Kudamm barrel and at best lead a meager hand-to-mouth existence. (Sorry.)

THE UGLY GAME

The Kudamm is certainly not the only game in town, merely the cleanest and safest. Potsdamerstrasse is an uncommonly ugly area of prostitutes, pimps, and criminals, especially near the corner of Bülowstrasse. The girls are priced for quick sale (15 to 20DM) and look it. Hot-eyed and scruffy, they strut in front of selected bars. Lurking in the shadows—Potsdamerstrasse is virtually all shadows—are the protectors, diabolic Teutonic versions of the "Murphy Game" in their dark hearts, and knives in their pockets. If every union in some of the hotels in the neighborhood resulted in a birth during the past few years, Berlin could cease its importunings to other West Germans, offering $4000 interest-free loans to any who marry here, with no requirement to pay it back should they remain and bear children—a desperate effort to beef up the dwindling, aging population.

If Potsdamerstrasse is dangerous in the evening, Stuttgarterstrasse is suicide at any time. The area is often put off-limits to military personnel. Even the police are afraid to come here, and though they may mount raids on some neighborhood dives, these are usually carried out by large groups accompanied by big dogs. Some of the whores standing in front of certain bars look no more than thirteen or fourteen. Surprisingly, many are as pretty as the best of the Kudamm girls. But it is an axiom of European prostitution that the younger the streetgirls, the more ruthless their pimps. The price is 10 to 20DM and you get what you pay for. And often a bonus: many of these girls are too young to dare apply for registration (minimum age sixteen) and medical inspection. Or, rather, their pimps prevent them from doing so. One hotel in the area has about six rooms, no name, and averages one hundred guests a night. Even for Germans an all-time efficiency record.

THE COLDEST GAME

At midnight . . . in 40°, on the first of July in the Street of the 17th of June, hard by the Soviet War Memorial (guarded warily by its own soldiers) and in the shadow of the Brandenburg Gate stands a small army of whores—some of the oldest (to fifty-five) and youngest (from fourteen) in West Berlin. From 15 to 20DM in your car, or a certain pension in Niebuhrstrasse. This is one of the toughest beats in town, particularly in winter when the cruel winds from the east sweep down this long, lonely fourteen-lane-wide "street"—fit perhaps only for marching armies down, which is exactly why Hitler built it. It begins in East Germany, passes for miles as Heerstrasse, Kaiserdamm, etc., through the western sector and under the Brandenburg Gate to become Unter den Linden and terminate at East Berlin's vast Marx-Engels Platz.

There is a well-organized call-girl ring in Berlin, and call boys too; very skilled, one hears. For 200DM and up, and that is a lot of money here, exceptional partners are available through contacts with concierges in some of the better hotels. Some say that Berlin has the best collection of whores in Europe, aside from Paris. Economic conditions are not all that good here, despite the glossy architectural façade. To entice visitors, settlers, and new enterprises, prices of most goods and services are kept lower than elsewhere in Germany and the whores do their part. Their tariffs haven't increased for years.

DANGEROUS GAME, CHICAGO-STYLE

One early evening as you turn off the crowded Kudamm into Bleibtreu-strasse, you happen upon three young chaps machine-gunning some of their fellow men. Diving headfirst into the nearest cab, you direct the driver to proceed with haste to Vienna, or at least the Grünewald. On the way you learn that Berlin's prostitution and drug trade are controlled by several gangs, much in the fashion that Chicago was carved up in the 1920s. At the moment two of the leading bands, one Persian, the other German, are fighting a savage war over the fact that while the German boss was away on vacation in Mexico City the Persians moved in on his territory. The cabbie is sure the gunplay is somehow related. For further information he recommends you eavesdrop on certain patrons of the twenty-four-hour BUKAREST RESTAURANT (Bleibtreustrasse 45).

"Okay. Never mind Vienna," you tell the driver, "let's go to Bukarest." Nothing like a quiet bowl of goulash soup to the soothe the nerves.

Next morning's headlines report the gangland shooting. One Persian is dead, four are very ill. The police round up several gang members and offer a 5000DM reward for information leading to the arrest of three particular members of the German gang, one the "big boss," who the newspapers are sure has fled to Amsterdam. Berliners carefully scrutinize their fellow passengers on the U-Bahn and buses and the police (call 66–00–17 if you have news) commence turning the whole city upside down.

"The fools!" snorts the man at the next urinal, also having a *Schlitz* (literally, a "slash," or the "fly" of your trousers, therefore as good a word as any for a pee, whether one is English or American). "Why don't those dumb cops look in the brothels?"

FAIR GAME

Privately operated brothels are "illegal" in Berlin. According to Walter Henry Nelson's *Berlin*—for which he claims to have interviewed one thousand people—there are a dozen or so clandestine little places whose addresses Berliners guard as assiduously as Parisians do their favorite off-the-beaten-track bistros. He says.

Café Chérie and Hotel Nobel

The pink-neon script of CAFÉ CHÉRIE blazes from the six-story, gleaming white stone-and-glass structure also housing the connecting HOTEL NOBEL

(881–01–86) at Xantenerstrasse 4, parallel to and a block off the mid-Kurfürstendamm. If Chérie isn't a brothel, it offers comforts and companions equal to those found in Europe's finest brothels, and an ambiance absolutely superior to any you have experienced. And roulette too. This enterprise is surely worthy of the Nobel Piece Prize.

Begin slowly over simple soups and plain meals served all hours in the homey publike back dining room behind the hotel's supramodern brisk lobby (liveliest time 4 to 6 A.M.). You're having a good chess game with a lovely blonde from Hanover. Five of her pals kibbitz. With their legs and faces, and but for their bosoms, they could be Dior models. Suddenly the room breaks into wild pandemonium, as if Rudolph Hess had just parachuted into the goulash soup.

"What's happened?" you ask the blonde.

"Oh . . . nothing," she stutters. "One of the girls . . . uhhh, her father has just arrived."

Some time after the commotion has died down, you are led down a long corridor whose walls and ceiling are papered with blowups from early engravings of the *Decameron* (same ones as in Munich's Boccaccio Club). Tape-recorded sounds of lovemaking and *Höhepunkte* herald your entrance into the seraglio that is the Café Chérie. The general decor is high-class tarty Prussian. Dark green and maroon banquettes and sofas, lots of crystal chandelier work, more *Decameron* blowups framed in shadowboxes hung with silken tassels.

The girls are a veritable Miss Universe Contest, with representatives from Brazil, Israel, Austria, Sweden, Algeria, Yugoslavia, and a couple of Turkish delights, not to mention many Germans. But best of all, the atmosphere is that of a pub you've been attending for some ten years. The gear is informal too. Some thirty girls wander between the glittering bar, the parlor, and the roulette room in anything from pants suits to cocktail dresses to hot pants. About half the clientele are young men in their late twenties or thirties. One could come by every night for weeks, chat with the girls, and drink no more than his own Calvados (3DM—90¢) or 2 cl. twelve-year-old Chivas (6DM—$1.80), and Doris, the bargirl, would not be offended, though she might be somewhat surprised, for the talent rivals that of Madame Claude's in Paris. And if ever the word *Gemütlichkeit* applied, it does here.

"In a *Puff* like this Germans are free. The mentality of Germans makes the brothel a *necessity* of life. A German must always have *control* of himself. . . . He is constantly afraid he will lose it in front of others. But here, as you see, we have a special, warm atmosphere," observes a luscious, tiny, natural redhead. Huge Wedgwood-blue eyes and a complexion recalling Du Chaillu's description of the loveliest Swedish girls: "like apple blossoms floating in milk."

"Give up this life? Why?" She is twenty-two, daughter of a Düsseldorf surgeon. This night she wears a purple suede jumpsuit with matching cap. "I have here a Mercedes, a fine terrace apartment, much money, and all freedom to come and go and to go with whom I please. I am like the Hetaera."

"The what?"

"You know, the courtesans of ancient Greece. . . ."

Her price is 150DM, plus 30DM for a mirrored-wall room in the connecting Hotel Nobel which can be charged on your Diner's Club card. But the majority of the fifty-odd girls who work here can be had for 100DM for a couple of hours, perhaps longer if you order champagne (Mumm's Cordon Rouge, brut, 60DM; Cuvée Dom Pérignon, 110DM; Pommery and Greno, 33DM).

Good King *Puff*

"Of course, none of this is possible without Hans. We all love him like a father," says the daughter of the Düsseldorf surgeon.

The photo of Hans Helmcke, framed by a daisy chain of copulating couples, glares at you from the first page of the heart-shaped, souvenir program sold at 2DM. It also contains photos of several of the girls in the nude, one lying on a mirrored bed of the Nobel, another barebreasted at the bar, and cartoons of nudes doing handstands on their partners' erections. Helmcke is at this moment in his office off the *Decameron*ed corridor, in conference. Not with the "father of one of the girls," but (he later tells you) with another man. Apparently while the man was briefly out of town, some Persians also sought Hans's confidence. Perhaps to sell him some rugs.

Some days later, according to the newspapers, the police arrest a prominent expatriate Persian. Also arrested are three Germans.

That evening you have a quiet chat with Helmcke. "Oh, these are very nice boys," he says of no one in particular. He's an absolute Damon Runyon character. Big cigar, crushed homburg, bushy eyebrows, jolly-shrewd face, rapid-fire broken English. Always chuckling. "I got five different businesses. I got here the Chérie and the Park Ascona too, and a fruit store in Hamburg, and a publicity agency here, and in New York too." Indeed, he is his own best press agent.

Mounted on the Hotel Nobel's lobby wall is a three-by-six-foot blowup of the front and back pages of a March 29, 1969, Berlin paper whose headlines proclaim *SITTEN-RAZZIA IN KUDAMM-HOTEL*. (A small filler at the bottom notes the coincident passing of Dwight Eisenhower.) The big story, with several action photos, described how vice-squad police collected fourteen girls, aged seventeen to thirty-three, from the Hotel Nobel. An outraged lawyer was interviewed: "This is going too far. If a guest pays for a hotel room he is entitled to strict privacy. What will this do to Berlin's image for tourists!"

The story goes on to note that police cannot raid unless they have specific reasons. Herr Helmcke is not the Nobel's chief—she is described by the newspaper as a certain Ms. "G"; Hans, apparently, merely has the concession here and at the Park Ascona. The police responded weakly that certain girls did not have the required health permits, but the paper noted that the hotel maintains the highest hygienic standards. Indeed it does. But what the newspaper forgot to mention was that until March, 1965, Helmcke operated one of the finest brothels in the world. The police hadn't forgotten. Nor had the United States Army.

Whores, Espionage, and the USA

The HOTEL CLAUSEWITZ at Clausewitzstrasse 4, just off the Kudamm, "was like a big family," according to an Israeli girl you spoke to at Chérie. The large comfortable parlor had the atmosphere of a good St. James's club. The decor roughly approximated Chérie's but was somewhat more *alt* and authentic prewar Berlin—hand-embroidered linens in the old bedrooms, etc. A terribly fashionable place, its patrons included top company directors, diplomats and . . . a number of high-ranking members of the military. When the police finally raided and closed it (permanently), they simply announced that it was a brothel and therefore illegal. But perhaps they never would have bothered if pressure had not been brought to bear by the American government. Apparently Army officers were doing more pillow-talking than fornicating at the Clausewitz (appropriately named for von Clausewitz, the great Prussian strategist. Pre-Helmcke, Goebbels had the place wired for sound).

Hans winks. When the police arrested him and threw him into Moabit Prison following the closing of the Clausewitz, "it had nothing to do with the Clausewitz. It was espionage. . . . Well, that's what *they* said."

"Espionage?"

"Hah. Hah, I was spying. . . . I was talking one day with somebody over there in the East, *just talking,* you know. And they gave me a business card and asked me to be their representative in the West . . . at trade fairs, you know. But listen, coming to me at the Clausewitz was around-the-world *big shots.* Still they come here. And I got some of my girls from there still with me, and we try to keep the same atmosphere. We have a lotta fun here . . . but if you want some peace and quiet, go over to my place in the Park Hotel Ascona. Tell 'em I sent you."

Park Hotel Ascona: "Mae West" at 50DM a Breast

Indeed, the bar and lounge of the PARK HOTEL ASCONA (886-70-95 or 96; Telex: 01-183-482 npa-d), four blocks from Chérie at Münsterschestrasse 11, is comparatively subdued but by no means cheerless. It's a very discreet operation; you are buzzed through the formidable white iron gate that guards the large multistoried building. Candlelight, fresh roses in tiny vases, bright-red-papered walls and white organdy curtains give the assignation parlor a foolish and romantic feel. Five or six cunning *Kätzchen* pose at the bar, several more chatting among themselves or with clients at the small tables. A matched set of twenty-four-year-olds who look like Mae West as painted by Rubens give you the glad eye and a sip of giggly (25DM the bottle), their *Zitze* (50DM each, 185DM the four in one of the connecting Park Hotel Ascona's 30DM rooms) flouncing in undersized gauze Mädchenforms.

The Hotel Badener Hof: "For the Man Who Is Hiding"

The man who wants real discretion—the man who is *hiding*—should proceed immediately out the Heerstrasse corridor and turn off into Badenallee to number 4, the HOTEL BADENER HOF. Helmcke says he operated here for a time when he emerged from prison, but he no longer has a thing to do with it. (He must have had a thing for the number "four." Among Berlin's radio-controlled cabbies, the Clausewitz at Clausewitzstrasse 4 was known by the code "C-4," the Badener Hof is "B-4," and the Chérie is now "C" or "X-4.") You phoned ahead per instructions (304–85–45), rang the bell at the huge iron gates and nine-foot-high walls guarding this dour three-story villa, once a Prussian nobleman's residence. "Tuxedo," the tall, rugged, handsome barman and custodian rushes out to welcome you. It helps if you are carrying an attaché case, or if you resemble a Japanese or Milanese industrialist, for the mahogany-paneled anteroom is filled with them, chatting softly by candlelight at little tables with several of the two dozen young women on call. On the whole, Badener Hof has some quite attractive girls (100DM) but their dress and attitude are far more conservative than that found at Chérie. However, the huge, ornate, late-Bismarck bedrooms are surely worth 25DM. Moreover, if you're a regular and you show Tuxedo a photo of your mother-in-law, or wife's attorney, he'll be sure not to buzz them in while you're on the premises.

Carola: A Typical Small House

Of the dozen or so smaller houses operating throughout West Berlin, CAROLA (Niebuhrstrasse 76, three blocks off and parallel to the Kudamm; 883–83–65) is perhaps typical. Enormous bedrooms, so large the unextraordinary girls (80 to 90DM includes room price) met at the bar (Coke 2DM) could probably flagellate the whole Polish cavalry in them. Nice calling cards printed on wood shavings. Madame speaks excellent English. The Carola also doubles as a *Stunden* hotel.

A Lost Brothel

From the standpoint of facilities and architecture, the finest brothel in Berlin is said to be housed in a mansion in Lynarstrasse, in the exclusive Grunewald section. However, after hours of house-to-house snooping about the large mansions of this lovely district (whose landscaping and architecture recall areas of Los Angeles built by 1920s movie moguls), you've learned nothing more than that hereabouts lived many high Nazi officials during the 1930s. Wandering Johannaplatz and Herbertstrasse (a far cry from Hamburg's Herbertstrasse) certainly gives one a feeling of prewar Berlin. Then at Lynarstrasse, corner Wangenheimstrasse, you come upon a large stone mansion, brightly lighted but with all shades drawn. A peek through a basement window shows an enormous kitchen and a pretty maid bustling about with trays of beer. Moreover, there are at least twenty-five cars parked along the street, but all other streets in the neighborhood are empty of parked cars, for all these huge houses have their own garages. Smells good. *Burschenschaft . . .* you read on the heavy bronze plaque at the stone gate. Sounds good.

You ring the bell set between two large brass carriage lamps. It is answered promptly by a popeyed man of about thirty wearing a dark business suit, beer stein, skullcap, and a black, red, white, and yellow silk rep sash across his shirt; and a nasty cut on his cheek. At your indiscreet inquiries he bursts into laughter, summons more beer steins, sashes, and skullcaps, several of whom are also wearing *Schmisse.* More laughter. Of course! *"Burschenschaft!"* A chapter of one of the dueling societies. You'd forgotten Munich.

You are informed that there are twelve or thirteen such societies in Berlin, this particular one founded in 1862 by Bismarck, who lived just round the corner. All right, it isn't a brothel, but it's a whole lot spookier. However, they had no naked girl under a black velvet sheet upstairs, and nobody even offered you a beer.

THE GOLDEN '20s: A PROFESSOR RECALLS HIS YOUTH

Those who were there, and even those who weren't, mourn the Berlin of the 1920s which produced a genre of baroque café society that will never be duplicated. The intoxications of that Berlin sharpened rather than sapped the senses, and though Germany was poor, Berlin was witty, wicked, and wonderful. At the Picasso Café in London's King's Road you met a German-born art professor, now at an American university, on his way back to Berlin for the first time since fleeing in 1933. In return for updating him on the latest saunas he searched his memory for the Berlin of his youth:

"The most celebrated and interesting homosexual place was the Eldorado. It was near the Scala Vaudeville Theater. You'd see always famous people there, like Max Pallenberg. Not much of a show, but the most fascinating thing was . . . you had lesbians looking like lesbians with short hair, lesbians looking like beautiful women, lesbians dressed exactly like men and looking like men. Then you had men dressed like women so you couldn't possibly recognize they were men, it was so realistic. Then you would see couples dancing and you wouldn't know any more what it was. . . .

"The first nude shows after the First War were in the Friedrichstrasse, near where it crosses Unter den Linden, in East Berlin now. George Grosz would come to these sex shows, cabarets they were, to make his drawings. And they showed these crazy homosexual films. Better . . . well worse! than Warhol makes now, with that actor that later made a career playing all those homosexual sadists in Hollywood, what was his name? . . .

"There was a place with a glass dance floor with colored lights underneath, and the first in Europe with telephones on the tables. And records, yes, it was really the first discothèque. And the most beautiful whores in the cafés on the Kurfürstendamm . . . the Café Schiller. And they had these *fantastic* whores in the Kakadu, that was a bar that also had the glass floor and colored lights. . . . And another discothèque in Nürnberger Platz, very small. Famous actors would come here with girls they didn't want to be seen with in bigger places. The Jockey Club! You are sitting so close together you can't move. A chanteuse is standing on the piano singing erotic songs. There were several bars like this you couldn't get into them unless you were well known. What was that café on the Kurfürstendamm, Victor Hollander's place, the man who wrote the music for *The Blue Angel* . . . you could see Marlene Dietrich sing there before she was known.

"The Romanisches Café maybe between Tauentzienstrasse and Kurfürstendamm where was gathered all the intelligentsia, the good writers, the essayists, painters, sculptors, they all had their own tables. Many got their mail delivered to them there. . . . There was so many characters. One guy, what was his name? He had long black hair, he was a great chess player. He lived from playing chess . . . like Paul Newman from *The Hustler*. Schmeling, you'd see him with his manager. And the director of the Flechtheim Gallery, who was crazy about boxers. [Albert? 1878–1937.]

"There was a show with a very clever MC but a brutal man. And it consisted of old people, all over sixty, some of them seventy, even eighty. Some had been famous performers. They would perform with their varicose veins and arthritis. What was this place, the Kuka? The Keka? Pragerplatz maybe, or somewhere off Kaiserallee. The MC was coming out announcing these great acts and all these sophisticated sadists in the audience would make these actors and dancers think they were seriously admired. You could go all night there.

"It was the most interesting city in the world in 1925, Berlin. Why? Why Berlin? Because it was *decadent!* [He pronounces the word as if it had all capital letters and two Ks.] It was a defeated city where morals and everything had broken down. It was for sophisticated people who wanted to have all sensations. . . ."

SODOM ON THE EXPENSE ACCOUNT

Since World War II Berlin has experienced the same kind of leveling affluence that has afflicted winners and losers alike. And so, much of today's nightlife is the same here as everywhere: somewhat inhibited, well packaged, and baldly laid on for the new middle-class masses—tourists in groups, company men on expense accounts, and soldiers. Yet Berlin offers far more illicit activity than Munich and more possibilities for friendship than Hamburg, for a night or a month of nights.

A large number of the more than four thousand bars and clubs remain open till dawn or later; one need never be lonely in Berlin at any hour. When the strippers, dancers, acrobats, musicians, and whores finish work at 4 or 5 A.M., they must go somewhere for a drink, "dinner," and relaxation. Where they go is often the best place to be in Germany at 6 A.M. The philosophy of Berlin dancehalls and clubs is that the customers should mingle freely and get to know one another. There are a number of places where it is the rule for girls to ask the boys to dance (a carryover from the days immediately following the war when there were hardly any young men left in the city). For some people this almost forced mixing is a bore, for others it is one of Berlin's great attractions.

One could begin a fruitful nocturnal tour by acquiring a new friend at the skating rink of the futuristic EUROPA CENTER—and then avoiding most everything else in the building. A cold front of gleaming steel and glass dominating the head of the Kudamm, the Europa Center is a gigantic Dagwood sandwich of so-called "authentic" bars, clubs, and restaurants, each with a different international motif. (There is even a pathetic attempt at duplicating the Romanisches Café.) It is as if the entire 1964 New York World's Fair had been neatly stacked up in a German Rockefeller Center. Unhappily, few American tourists can resist it, so they are about to be warned.

The epitome of Europa Center is the RED ROSE NIGHTCLUB. It is claimed that this club is "Germany's most expensive." And they work hard to prove it. Over "1.5 million DM" was spent to create a large, red, coldly plush amphitheater, perhaps more suited to insurance company board meetings than performances by tricky dogs, jugglers, and stripteasers. The dogs are clever, the girls beautiful alabaster, and in few clubs is the audience made to feel more remote from the entertainers. "We spend sixty thousand Deutsche Marks a month on the show alone," and the patrons contribute their fair share of it: hot dogs 4DM; German wine 59DM; a bit of caviar 30DM. And if you don't begin by paying the 6,50DM door charge, they won't let you in in the first place.

So instead of striptease, go for SPITZE (Lietzenburgerstrasse 82, a block off the Kudamm), a clever complex of boutiques, pubs, and sidewalk terrace with some marvelously atmospheric little cafés in the rear. Great example of what someone with patience, taste, and comparatively limited funds can do with the ordinary ground floor of an apartment building.

STRIPTEASE

RIFIFI (Fuggerstrasse 34) has about the best striptease in Berlin. A typical main event features a girl who manipulates a formally attired life-size male dummy so that it apparently seduces her. This is a classic of Continental striptease, but only rarely does one see it performed with such a combination of artistry and eroticism. Very nice *separée*. The owner, a Warsaw refugee, runs a good straight place, and there is no hustling. Ballantine's Scotch, 2 cl. 5,50DM; wine 45DM the bottle; 3DM cover.

DE PARIS is quaint. Every night till 6 A.M. one can drink 2,50DM beers in this fusty, musty old saloon that resembles the parlor of a 1925 dentist's office, relax in doily-covered stuffed chairs, and watch dirty movies. You won't see *Mexican Dog* here, but the films are ancient and funny enough as period pieces. Superfluous telephones at the tables, for there is no one to call but Gerda the bargirl or her boss, both of whom resemble John Carradine. While you're in the neighborhood say hello to the 50DM girls in Berlin's new "Eros Center," GRAZY SEXY (Fuggerstrasse 20). A very lively street.

PICKUPS

Rolf Eden, who was once a Teddy Boy but now looks more like Pierre Trudeau, is Berlin's most successful nightclub entrepreneur. Once you reach puberty Eden has you for life, for each of his four clubs caters to a fairly specific age group. Though all are tourist-infested (bear in mind that "tourists" in West Berlin refers as much to other West Germans as to all other kinds of tourists put together), Berliners consider them among the best pickup spots in town.

The OLD EDEN SALOON—ages eighteen to twenty-five—has seven rooms, cheap drinks, campy movies, nude slides, Rube Goldberg gimmicks galore and many, many unattached young girls. Also pinball machines, jazz groups, a Russian pianist, and an upstairs "make-out room" fitted with school desks and a blackboard for the rebellious. The EDEN PLAYBOY CLUB—ages twenty-one to thirty-five—attracts the counterparts of the "swinging singles" who have made such a thing of Manhattan's Upper East Side dating bars. Highlight of the evening occurs at 11 when a dozen or more bikinied girls—and you too if you wish—take a dip and dance in the large water tank. Mr. Eden, who might be called the "Playboy of the Western Sector" and has a legendary Hugh Hefner apartment, sports cars, boats, girls and some nice neckties, always declines to swim. "Unless you fill up the tank with champagne, sir." A Texan once called him on it, spent 12,000DM on six hundred bottles of champagne, and Rolf Eden jumped right in. The NEW EDEN—ages thirty and up—has a Borscht Belt ambiance. Eden himself MCs the vaudeville and amateur striptease. BIG EDEN, an enormous discothèque on the Kudamm, is the latest addition to the empire.

COUPÉ 77 (Kudamm 177) is perhaps Berlin's most elegant bar-discothèque, decorated with handsome fittings from posh old German railway cars, purchased from the Hanover Museum, and the city's *jeunesse dorée*. Same management and crowd at CIRO'S BEACH CLUB (Rankestrasse 31), fashioned from the remains of North German Lloyd's late flagship *Hanseatic*. BLACK BOTTOM (Uhlandstrasse 20) is nearly as nifty; girls on their own sometimes have to pass a rigid pulchritude test at the door. (Visiting a country that has comparatively negligible humanistic and democratic traditions has, at times, certain advantages.)

The BIG APPLE (Bundesallee 13) is a mammoth discothèque for people sixteen to twenty-five. Not beat; many boys in ties and jackets, girls in the latest pop fashions. RIVERBOAT (Hohenzollerndamm 174, a former Nazi Party headquarters) is a bit rockier, attracts a slightly younger or same age group. In accordance with West German law, it should be noted, one must be sixteen to drink beer or wine, and eighteen for all other alcoholic beverages. Other places where young people gather include GO-IN (Bleibtreustrasse 17) activist nightclub, many single, open-minded girls. Not to be missed is LEIER-KASTEN (Zossenerstrasse 1) whose many attractions—jazz, old movies—draw droves of hippies, students, many lone girls among them. Similar crowd at DANNY'S PAN (Fasanenstrasse 78). Perhaps the best jazz house for meeting unattached females is JAZZ GALERIE (Bundesallee 194B).

Berlin has no touristy Schwabing or Greenwich Village artists' quarter, but many serious artists sleep and work in the cellars of Kreuzberg, a modest working-class district. Their hub is DIE KLEINE WELTLATERNE (Kohlfurterstrasse 37), a small, homely café open to 7 A.M. Artist-owner Helmut Diekmann and *Kunst-Mutter* Hertha Fiedler also run a small gallery in the rear. If you'll buy them a beer or *Schnaps* (50pf) or Pernod (2DM), the artist patrons will splash a masterpiece on your beer coaster. All jukebox tunes are over thirty years old; waiters use *"Du"* form. Outdoor paintings market held from 10 A.M. Saturdays on Kreuzberg Hill. Bring a flower child from PINTE, corner Gneise-naustrasse and Solmsstrasse.

THE RESI, "THAT TELEPHONE PLACE," AND "BAL PARADOX"

The RESI (Hasenheide 32–38) is sheer nonsense, and no trip to Berlin is complete without a visit. Unescorted ladies are not only welcome, they drag them in off the streets. This is "that telephone place." Every table has one and the house welcomes up to twenty-five hundred callers a night. One gets a floorplan, wanders about, picks a girl, notes her table number, and either telephones or, if he's bashful, sends her a note through a system of pneumatic tubes. Most tables seat five so the note must be addressed to "Little Brunette in brown dress with white organdy dots, holding gray fur muff." A central censor passes on all communications and if yours is not obviously the work of a psychopath, it will be dispatched swiftly. There is a fourteen-piece band, gigantic dancing-waters shows three times a night, art-nouveau murals, and a beer cellar seating eight hundred. Except for tourists, Resi is mostly for lower-middle-class Berliners. A somewhat more prosperous middle-class Berliner enjoys the attraction of the KEESE (Bismarckstrasse 108), which is *"bal paradox."* As you'll recall from a visit to the sister establishment in Hamburg, women ask the men to dance, but here, once every hour, the procedure is reversed; and the rules are much more rigidly enforced. If a man is asked to dance and refuses, he is "warned" twice by the management. The third time he declines he is ejected from the playing field. The bar is neutral ground. The system seems to work well enough. According to manager Willy Aster, "More marriages are made here than in Heaven and Hell together." This may be so, but the large Sherry-Netherland-type ballroom, which holds eight hundred, looks just as suitable for Bar-Mitzvahs.

Bal paradox is also the specialty of PALAIS MADAME (Nürnbergerstrasse 49). This one is more intimate than Keese, really a small night club with five-piece foxtrot and waltz band, slowly turning mirrored ball, and a friendly stand-up bar. Decor in the style of Berlin's Golden Twenties, and so are the male patrons; the eager females are somewhat younger. If you decline a dance, the management pitches you right out.

WIDOWS AND ELIGIBLE CHAMBERMAIDS

The WALTERCHENS BALLHAUS (Bülowstrasse 37) is a ridiculous old place where *alte* widows are very glad to meet you and may sleep with you for a glass of apple juice. The Berlin Tourist Office describes it as a "dance hall for mature youths." Even higher *Kampf* is the RHEINISCHE WINZERSTUBEN (Hardenbergstrasse 29A), "historical place of entertainment since 1899," which has an elderly dance band, a rousing storm scene of the Rhine depicted on a huge mural, and Berlin's most eligible chambermaids. (No professionals in either of these venerable ball rooms, of course.)

Afternoon tea-dances are held at many discothèques and dance halls, but the very best of this Berlin tradition is found, ironically, in the roof garden of the BERLIN HILTON. An admission of 4 to 7DM includes coffee, tea, or pastry. The good international band plays everything from waltzes to quiet pop tunes, depending on the mood of the house. Many, many lovely single girls in their twenties and thirties (at least they arrive alone). Particularly active Wednesday afternoons. That day the city's lawyers and doctors close their offices and go tea-dancing. The German custom of cutting in is honored to the hilt here; to make a fuss is bad form. The Hilton's roof affords a dramatic view, particularly by night, of the contrasts between West and East Berlin. A Gold Key man here could write you a thick book on the pleasures of Berlin. The barman is nobody's fool either.

GAY BERLIN AND HIGH LIFE

Though transvestism achieved its greatest notoriety here during the 1920s, Berlin's unusual tolerance for homosexuals was apparent even during Victorian times. Krafft-Ebing quotes an 1884 newspaper article that describes a "Woman-Hater's Ball. . . . Almost every social element of Berlin has its social reunions—the fat, the bald-headed, the bachelors, the widowers—and why not the woman-haters?" WHY NOT (Fasanenstrasse) indeed?

The tolerance remains, but transvestism is no longer the international cabaret attraction it was during the 1920s. CHEZ NOUS (Marburgerstrasse 14) is the best TV cabaret Berlin has to offer, and very good it is, presenting striptease and variety acts in mock Louis XIV surroundings; elegant silver service, crystal chandeliers, pleated satin curtains and couches, and paraffin breasts. Michel claims his Boucher and his Marie Antoinette miniatures are originals and together worth 1,040,000DM. Be careful: the performers who grace the bar between shows (best at 2 A.M.) appear equally authentic. Chez Nous isn't Berlin 1928, but impresario Michel is. He had to leave town in 1938, but returned in 1956 to open this club and TROIKA (Wittenbergplatz 6), a Russian nightclub—smashing place for *heterosexuals* in love who like to sing along with a cymbalom.

What Berlin's gay scene may lack in quality (and youth) by comparison with its halcyon days, it attempts to overcome with a quantity of bars, clubs, and cafés. KLEIST-CASINO (Kleiststrasse 34) is the traditional male homosexual rendezvous, but even though recently redecorated with tinny mobiles that look like struts from the Red Baron's Blue Max, the place gets more depressing as the years pass. A very mixed-bag clientele—some pretty young knaves, some old queens, and this night a U.S. Army private in *From Here to Eternity* Hawaiian short-sleeved shirt, weeping his guts out to three very attentive listeners. He's on his way to Vietnam.

Nearby, NEUF TROCADERO (Courbièrestrasse 13) is roaring at ninety-five miles an hour, even though it's 6 A.M. of a Tuesday morning. Nearly a hundred lesbians, *off-duty* midnight cowboys, and a seventy-five-year-old cleaning woman in rags twisting with an elegant blond boy wearing a leopard-skin and gold ballet slippers.

Outside in and around Courbièrestrasse there's a panzy division of rough-trade transvestite Hessians (20 to 50DM).

The components of Jean-Claude's PIMM'S CLUB (Knesebeckstrasse 70; 883-35-31) however, are much more finely tuned. One of Berlin's most interesting clubs. Discothèque, lively bar from 8 P.M. to 8 A.M. Fascinating cross sexion of people. Regal African queens at LE PUNCH (Passauerstrasse 8), often a German "freak-in." Until 4 A.M. rather homosexual—some stunning young lesbians and pretty males—but later they may be joined by an eclectic bag of jazz musicians, actors, Jet-Setters, pretty girls (straight but curious), and perhaps some underworld celebrities. "Hildegarde" says his club is "exclusive but democratic. We don't exclude straight people, but they must be ornamental, or at least 'interesting.' But soldiers and sightseers are not welcome." Apparently Le Punch has become TAM TAM. FIFTY-FIFTY (Nürnberger-strasse 46) is just that. And a friendly discothèque for young people too. MOBY DICK (Grolmanstrasse 39) is a restaurant and coffee bar for people of all sexes.

GIRLS AND BITCHY BOYS

The two most interesting lesbian clubs are L'INCONNUE (Goethestrasse 61) and SAPPHO (Uhlandstrasse, corner Pariserstrasse). The latter is particularly warm and rococo with large, comfy chintz sofas. Other female *Treffpunkte* (rendezvous) include CLUB 10 (Vorbergstrasse 10) and FESTIVAL (Holstein-ischestrasse 29). A typical *Schwulen—Lokal* (queer pub) is BEI ELLIE (Skalitzer-strasse 102), one of Kreuzberg's most venerable *Kneipen* (affectionate term for a pub or "joint"), of which this borough has dozens. Front room for men; middle room with dance floor, lesbians; rear, epicenes.

After 10 P.M. in Savigny Platz bitchy boys in tight hot pants and tough guys in trenchcoats will take you on in the filthy toilets for 20DM. Favorite S–Bahn station toilets are at Wilmersdorf, Witzlebenstrasse, and Tempelhof stops.

Strichjungen (little boy blew) 20 to 30DM at Bahnhof am Zoo. Other favorite outdoor rendezvous include Tiergarten Park at the monkey cages of the Zoo, Böcklerpark in Kreuzberg, and the following public toilets: Boppstrasse, Ernst–Reuter–Platz, Hermannplatz, Weddingplatz, Winterfeldtplatz, and Wittenbergplatz. Sleep that off in HOTEL-PENSION CENTRAL (Kudamm 185). Doubles from 46DM with breakfast.

Heterosexuals may be pleased to visit the apartment house at Klopstockstrasse 2 which has for years rented primarily if exclusively to single people (secretaries, executives, etc.) and has perhaps provided a model for this recent real-estate innovation in America. The building's GIRAFFE BAR, as you would expect, is a good place to make friends, and perhaps secure a night's accommodation.

LATE-NIGHT HAUNTS

Should you find none, let Tacitus' remarks on the ancient Huns console you: "They count, not like us, by days, but by nights. It is by nights they fix dates or make appointments. Night is regarded as ushering in the day." Berlin thus has dozens of late-night, early-morning pubs and restaurants. BEI HEINZ HOLL (Herr Holl is a movie character-actor who resembles a fireplug) at Damaschkestrasse 26 serves open-face sandwiches on wood slabs: "a place where a man comes with a woman other than his wife and nobody talks." LEIBNIZ KLAUSE (Mommsenstrasse 57) serves actors, politicians, opera singers, momzers (see The Bible, Deuteronomy 23:3), businessmen and some off-duty business girls (too tired by 5 A.M., however, to do business). KORALLEE (Bleibtreustrasse 45) serves ox tongue in Madeira sauce (6DM) to strippers, cabbies, intellectual insomniacs, sleeping beauties, and sleeping bags too. Next door is the BUKAREST RESTAURANT, open twenty-four hours to "crazy peoples, policemen, entertainers, and flying-carpet salesmen," according to one of its many regulars. EL FLAMENCO (Leibnizstrasse 62), run by Spaniards, has authentic flamenco guitar and paella, and is as romantic a place as you can find at 5 A.M.

LE MAÎTRE (Meinekestrasse 10) is a magnificent French restaurant, even by Parisian standards (its French chef-owner has about every diploma the Swiss and French cooking schools award); no prices on the lady's menu.

LOVE ISLAND

In summer on the beaches at Lake Havel one has a wide choice of girls, as well as young men. From here you row out to Lindwerder Island, nicknamed "Love Island," the most favored trysting place. While you're outside don't forget the renowned Berlin Zoo, which is Europe's largest and contains the world's biggest lionsteppe in captivity. In fact, the Berlin Zoo pioneered in the recreation of the animals' natural habitat. The Zoo, incidentally, is a fine place to select sleeping companions, particularly during secretaries' lunch hours.

After the Zoo, visit the nearby BEATE UHSE sex supermarket, Hardenberg-strasse 28.

UP AGAINST THE WALL WITH A PRETTY GUIDE

If one is unable to get home after a night on the town, a call to 32–47–14 will bring a student who will manage the job for 9DM. Berlin has many other kinds of guide and escort services. Among the best is SEVERIN AND KÜHN'S Hostess Service (Kudamm 216; 881–39–36). Choose from a selection of fifteen charming girls who speak a total of ten languages—including Chinese and Arabic—and act as guides or escorts for the zoo, museums, nightlife, etc.[3] Hostess Service claims its girls are available for any legal job short of those that the Kudamm pros perform so expertly. For an extra 5 to 10DM above the basic 15DM-per-hour rate, a girl will take dictation in your hotel room and make breakfast in the bargain. Severin and Kühn also offers a unique method for exploring East Berlin. At competitive rates they supply a young West German female or a nice young man who arranges for you two to be met on the other side by an East German guide. If you insist that your two new friends keep their discussions in English, and if you can keep them from physically harming each other (the DDR guide is sure to be a militant Communist), your short trip to "Paradise" will be unforgettable.

---

[3] In the same vein, something called "RENT A DAILY GIRL" supplies photogenic models, escorts, translators by the hour or by the day (887–44–54).

EAST BERLIN

GERMAN DEMOCRATIC REPUBLIC (EAST GERMANY)

The basic unit of currency is the mark (or *Ost* mark), which can be divided into 100 pfennigs. At this writing you'll get about 3.18 East marks for each floating dollar, according to official East German rates. Thus each mark equals about 30 U.S. cents. The East Germans peg their mark at whatever the West German mark happens to be worth. On the black market and in many Western banks, however, you can get up to five times the official rate for your Western currency. Don't. East German law says you can neither bring in nor take out *Ost* marks. If you're caught they may not let *you* out. Entry Requirements: Valid passport. Visa is obtainable at the border or East German Consulate in countries which recognize the German Democratic Republic (remember, the U.S. does not): $1.25 fee for stay up to 3 days, $3.75 for longer. Prepaid hotel voucher and confirmed reservations required for overnight visits.

NOBODY WALKS A DOG

East Germany ranks ninth among the industrial nations of the world, but the faces in the streets of its capital rarely smile. Economically the system is working well enough, but socially it is a crashing bore. Apathy hangs over the land like a big gray tent. There is full employment, a labor shortage in fact. Per-capita TV-set ownership is higher here than in West Germany; 55 percent of families own washing machines, and well they do, for more than 75 percent of women work in industry, agriculture, or the professions. Clothing, though plain and somewhat behind Western styles, is not at all shoddy. But nobody walks a dog.

East Berlin by night is dark. Much of the city's candlepower is trained on the Wall. Each year these lights grow brighter and and the Wall grows higher and more sophisticated. (And the West Germans keep pace by building higher viewing platforms.) Mesh fences with sharp-edged rims have replaced much of the barbed wire, and the crumbling houses that once formed portions of the barrier have been torn down or reinforced. At each attempted escape the Wall goes off like the Houston Astrodome scoreboard after a home run—rockets, flares, and three pitches of sirens. In 1961, its first year, the Wall was a sieve as eighty-five hundred got through. Only a handful a year attempt it now; few make it.

The most animate sign is a large Times Square kind of news bulletin atop Friedrichstrasse Station which flashes the latest riot tolls from American cities. During the Johnson Administration his name appeared so frequently in connection with the Vietnam atrocity that the city might well have renamed the area Unter den Lyndon.

Americans enter East Berlin on foot or by car at Checkpoint Charlie, or by underground (U-Bahn) or elevated (S-Bahn) trains that arrive at Friedrichstrasse Station. Visas are easily obtained at the East German control point. It is recommended you cross at Charlie *and* that you tell the very efficient GIs there precisely the hour you expect to return: if you are so much as fifteen minutes late they're on the phone to G-2 as to your whereabouts. The possibilities of "misunderstandings" are greater for American travelers here than in any other European communist nation, with the possible exception of Albania. But one should not miss the opportunity to cultivate some East Berliners. Though initially more guarded than citizens of other Warsaw Pact nations, many are as eager for dialogue with Westerners as their government is for diplomatic recognition from *anybody*.

SEX AND YOUTH

"A sexless nation! Do not let appearances and preconceptions deceive you," says a twenty-two-year-old engineering student in the cafeteria of Humboldt University on Unter den Linden. (Another good place to meet students is the STUDENT CLUB (Linienstrasse 127). "Here is a study, recently published by Professor Rolf Borrmann of Leipzig University. As you can read it, 78 percent of the girls interviewed and 84 percent of the boys have admitted having premarital relations by age twenty." Your question of whether the 78 percent carried on exclusively with the 84 percent, and vice versa, is ignored. "Also you may be interested that 83 percent of males do not expect their wives to be virgins." (The study, *Youth and Love,* was apparently the first such inquiry conducted on a scientific basis in East Germany.) "But confidentially," winks the student, "the results are not so extraordinary. What else is there to do in this country but masturbate and fornicate?"

PROSTITUTION IN "PARADISE"

"Prostitution is against the law in the German Democratic Republic," says the pretty brunette prostitute near the brand-new TANZ CAFÉ just off the Alexanderplatz, which is being developed into what is hoped will be an East German Kurfürstendamm. (But the massive buildings and incredibly wide thoroughfare merely add digits to the citizen ciphers who move self-consciously through the strange quietude at the heart of their capital.) "But I will do anything you ask if you will pay me fifteen dollars or fifty marks. West German please. The police do not interfere as long as we approach only foreigners. The government is, of course, happy to have the Western currency. . . . You are surprised to see our skirts as short as those of girls in the West? Be sure that what we have underneath is quite as nice as well."

Walking down Unter den Linden is like strolling on an airport runway. At the intersection of Friedrichstrasse, where George Grosz could wander from one roaring sex show to the next in the 1920s, there is nothing now. Nothing save the stone-cold-sober socialist-modern HOTEL UNTER DEN LINDEN. A few tense $20 whores in the bar.

Though the Party interpretation of "socialist morality" remains characteristically prudish, the Ulbricht government defecated such a sewer of comstockery at the "orgies," "depravity," and "dissipations" of the West

German "facists" (Example: "The Sex Wave has been invented by vindictive imperialists to distract the people from discussing serious problems like struggle against nuclear destruction") that it had little wind left to convince the people the only good socialist is a sober socialist.[1]

SEX RIPPLE

In fact, East Germans are quietly experiencing a sex ripple, if not a sex wave. This is due in large part to the emancipation of women of whom the professions (and not merely the oldest) contain 47 percent, compared to 36 percent in West Germany. Little grumbling greeted recent legislation that eliminated alimony, on the grounds that all able-bodied women should be able to provide for themselves. Certainly not from the new and growing elite class of women—doctors, government and party workers, teachers, technicians, and fashion models, designers, and artists, many of whom average $800 and more a month. Often more than their men. (Average earnings in the GDR are about $300 a month.)

The fashion industry, centered here and in Magdeburg, is symbolic of the new affluence and resulting independence of women, not to mention the nation's emergence as a style-setter—though not yet a swinger—among socialist-bloc nations. Paradoxically this once somber satellite is exerting its greatest influence on the Soviet Union, which, for example, publishes only two fashion magazines, but eagerly devours any of the two dozen imported from East Germany. Similarly, with only one sex clinic in all the USSR (under the able but harassed Professor Viktor N. Kolbanovsky of Moscow's Institute of Philosophy), an East German primer on sexual problems quickly sold out its standard Soviet edition of a hundred thousand copies. The Russians never reprinted it, but in East Germany the guide is in its eighteenth edition, as thirty-one houses specializing in youth fashions hike (ten inches above the knee in 1969) or lower (four inches in 1970) their skirts in response to public demand, not government command.

There are several sauna baths in East Berlin, but since none, at this writing, is mixed . . . the hell with them. On the other hand, who knows, perhaps next year at MARIENBAD (Chausseestrasse 42; 42–33–79). Or give the RUSSISCH-RÖMISCHES BAD (also in central East Berlin, in Gartenstrasse) a ring at 42–59–81.

---

[1]But the new regime may be thawing, at least according to what *Time* calls "the rule of skin: the extent to which a regime [in Eastern Europe] tolerates the exposure of female flesh often indicates the future direction of its cultural and sometimes even political policies." *Time*'s Feelers, usually highly reliable in these matters, sense an impending cultural liberalization in East Germany because the official Party newspaper, *Neues Deutschland,* in early 1972, displayed a bare-bosomed East German beauty in its pages for the first time in its twenty-six-year history.

THE NOT-SO BITTER PILL

In the GDR over one hundred thousand women are on the Pill, many in response to the critical housing shortage. Some young couples share tiny flats and may switch through several accommodations and partners before they contemplate marriage. So say two actors in full makeup and costume, kibitzing a chess game in the PRESSE CAFÉ across from Fiedrichstrasse Station, as they wait to perform (7:30 P.M.) in the adjacent DIE DISTEL theater of political satire. The acting is excellent and the humor comes through, even if one has no German. Most of the "Thistle's" barbs are aimed west, but mild attacks on the regime get saucier each year and are usually enthusiastically received. The Presse was the most amiable of East Berlin's cafés, and not only because it was packed with pretty young hustlers. From $5 to $10 or equivalent in West German currency (they won't take Ost marks).

CAFÉ GIRLS

Besides these and the actor and theatergoer patrons, there were many attractive young East Berlin fraüleins—students, shop girls, etc.—who came here specifically to talk with Westerners. Because of all this action the police have closed the Presse at this writing, temporarily it is to be hoped, for surely it was the most interesting café in East Berlin.[2] The girls have dispersed, some of them to CAFÉ BUDAPEST (Karl-Marx-Allee 90), others to the bars of hotels which attract Westerners. In this town, there is a fine line between professionals and amateurs because of the fact that hard currency from the West is so very precious here.

In the MITROPA CAFÉ of Friedrichstrasse Station, a coffeehouse where a sign says "No Smoking," hash may occasionally be purchased from disgruntled young patrons at the equivalent of five Ostmarks a gram.

HOMOSEXUALS AND THE BIRTHRATE

The Presse was a mélange of people, and so it attracted many homosexuals. Some gay East Berliners now gather at ECKSTEIN in Schönhauser Allee near the S-Bahn station. (Or perhaps at CITY-KLAUSE or G-BIER CAFÈ, both in Friedrichstrasse). Here a taxi driver notes that in East Germany homosexual acts between consenting adults (at least twenty-one) are not illegal. "However, in this country it is not merely indiscreet to be homosexual, it is unpatriotic." Indeed, the East German birthrate is among the world's lowest. No wonder

---

[2]Of course all establishments cited in Warsaw Pact nations are under the exclusive control of the state (or presumed to be), and no individual or group of individuals is suggested to be responsible for the morals therein.

abortions cost citizens between $300 and $500 here. And the Swedish girls who fly in on weekends pay up to $700.

The GDR has always had a lower birthrate than the Federal Republic (the overall population actually decreased here by some three thousand from 1967 to 1968) and the Wall was constructed primarily because an estimated 3 million of the country's most valued citizens—many scientists, technicians, workers, and intellectuals—had fled West. (Recent figures show both Germanies total 77,549,000—of whom 41 million are women—17,087,000 in the East.) But there were economic reasons for the Wall as well, though the government usually denies it.

MONEY, PICKUPS, JEUNESSE DORÉE, "BLOODY BUSINESS"

In MÖWE CAFÉ (Luisenstrasse 18)—artists, intellectuals, writers, and girls who like them—a painter recalls better days:

"One could live cheaply here before the Wall, and spend his money each night in West Berlin. Our government was losing millions each year. For example, you could buy a beer here for eighty pfennigs and take the empty bottle for refund to West Berlin, where it would bring thirty pfennigs in their currency. Back here, that thirty pfennigs would get you up to one and a half Ostmarks on the black market. Theoretically this exchange is still possible. The *official* rate is one to one. But this is unrealistic nonsense. On the black market you'll get as much as five Eastmarks for one west."

You may also get caught.

The OPERNCAFÉ (Unter den Linden 5) is considered quite chic by Party members, successful bureaucrats, visiting North Korean and Cuban trade delegations, and open field for high-priced (up to $40 a night) easy marks. People drink things like "*Kaffee Baltimore*" (with powdered eggwhite) at prices like 1,46 OM (everything in this pfenurious, most toilet-trained of bureaucracies is figured to the last dismal decimal) and dutifully enjoy the palsied rhythms of an ancient, formally attired unstrung quartet. Don't sit too close to the stage—the violinist and cellist have whopping consumption. There is a nightclub of sorts, and some loose ladies, in the Opern Cellar, where a Party member lets you hear it for religion: "Everybody has a hobby so why not go to church?"

If one has some leftover nostalgia for even more swing music played in waltz time, there are also "possibilities for dancing" at TANZ CAFÉ in Straus-Platz, Karl-Marx-Allee, SCHUSTER'S CASINO (Ackerstrasse 144), and BEHRENS CASINO (Chausseestrasse 102).

If there is such a thing as a *jeunesse dorée* here, you'll find them in the MILCH BAR, Karl-Marx-Allee 35. Ladies note: some of the most attractive

Russian officers in the world are stationed in East Berlin. The uniforms are of an exceptionally brilliant cut. Looking like something out of a modern *War and Peace,* the Russians gather, almost too plausibly, at the cavernous Moscow Restaurant (across from the Milch Bar). The room seems specifically designed for discreet conversation (though there is some dancing), almost as long as a football field and nearly half as wide. Tables are set very far apart and none of the diners speaks above a whisper. None but an Italian journalist who insists the place is irresistible to all Russians who pass through East Berlin. "Even members of the Thirteenth Department!" Could be. The Moscow menu offers a variety of authentic Russian specialties at reasonable prices. (For about 50 cents you get a bowl of borscht so good you could cry. The Caspian caviar is a bargain at 25 OM a large portion.)

The Thirteenth Department of Russia's First Directorate for Foreign Intelligence is engaged in the more colorful aspects of intelligence work—murder, sabotage, abduction, and sexual blackmail. In Russian slang this kind of business is known as *"mokriye dela"*—"bloody business." The chief of all this bloody business is a man called "Rodin" who uses the name of Nikolai B. Korovin when he travels. The Italian journalist insists that Mr. Korovin dines at the Moscow when he visits East Berlin, and further states that he has seen him here frequently. This in spite of the fact that no one outside the Kremlin knows what Mr. Korovin looks like.

SEX AND THE SINGLE SPY

It was under the Thirteenth Department's direction that swarthy, debonair Heinz Sütterlin was given some highly specialized training, then sent out to Bonn in 1959 (age thirty-five) as some kind of phallic phantom. Assignment: seduce someone with access to most secret documents in the Bonn Foreign Office. Heinz did better: he married the hawk-nosed, pudgy private secretary of the ministry's administrative Zb Section Director. Lunchtimes his Lenore came home to serve Heinz all 57 varieties of *Spezialitäten,* including the complete Allied contingency plans for the defense of Berlin and the West German diplomatic code, then quickly returned them to the ministry. For five years the Thirteenth Department received Heinz Sütterlin's cigarette-case-camera photographs of these and more than fifteen hundred other snacks. They trained Heinz well. Lenore spied for love. Only after Lt. Col. Evgeny Evgenievich Runge of the KGB defected west with wife and son to a CIA "safe house" in West Berlin and blew Sütterlin's cover in October, 1967—not to mention that of several other Soviet agents under his immediate command —did Lenore learn the true and only reason Heinz had married her. Whereupon she hanged herself with her pajamas in a Cologne prison.

MORE BLOODY BUSINESS

Most bars, cafés, and restaurants close by midnight, though the Moscow Restaurant is privileged to remain open later, by which time East Berlin begins to swing as much as the Vatican during Lent. But the lights burn through the night at the East German Secret Police Headquarters in Alexanderplatz (one wonders if they send out to the Moscow for sandwiches). Here an infamous man, known to his former prisoners as "Great Dog" for his specialty— knocking out teeth with his fist—and his colleagues aid in the interrogations of some of the twelve thousand people who have been arrested on political grounds since the 1961 erection of the Wall, over six thousand in connection with attempts to go west or breach frontier regulations. Nor is the work ever done in the basement interrogation rooms of the Supreme Court building in Scharnhorststrasse, where "Schräger Fürst" ("Twisted Prince") and "Schweinebacke" ("Pig Face") twist the testicles and minds of not a few of those more than five thousand who have been caught with forged passports and other documents hard by the wrong side of the Berlin Wall.

MADRID

SPAIN

The basic unit of currency is the peseta, which can be divided into 100 centimos. At this writing you'll get about 66 pesetas for each floating dollar. Thus each peseta is worth about one and a half U.S. cents. Spanish law says you can bring no more than 50,000 pesetas in, and take no more than 2000 out.

THE MAGIC IS LOST

The good thing about Madrid is that it's less than an hour's flying time to Barcelona. Politicians, policemen, and priests rule Madrid, the anarchists have kept things more human in Barcelona. Here they toast *"Salud, pesetas y amor"*—"Health, money, and love." In Barcelona they add "Death to your mother-in-law and strength to the stick!"

Still, this is very much the night city, for Spaniards are the original night people. Though Franco has had notable success suppressing freedom of speech, press, and profligacy, he has never been able to make the people go to bed on time. Pope knows he's tried. Some years ago, laws were passed aimed at putting Spanish shops and offices in time with the rest of Europe. But these were largely ignored, even in the capital. Businessmen still arrive at the office at midmorning, lunch at two, retire for siesta or otherwise until five, return to work until eight. The real life of Madrid does not begin until the Caudillo's 10 P.M. bedtime; dinner at 11 is commonplace, and the subways are jammed at midnight. Some nightclubs remain open until 4:30 A.M., but there is apparently something immoral about an all-night restaurant.

There is a maniacal hustle to daytime Madrid, an extension of the Madrileño's "more-cosmopolitan-than-thou" attitude. The faster he moves, the more important and businesslike he feels. At first the city wore its new shroud of smog with smug pride, smothering the visitor with tangible proof of Spain's recent industrial boom. But urbanization has now overpowered the city.

Once there was a real magic to midnight in Madrid. As you wandered the dark alleys of Old Madrid, or explored the eerie oasis of El Retiro park, you had the unmistakable feeling that *something*, be it macabre or romantic, was about to happen. For generations this hint of the unknown has exemplified the charm of the city. But the Stygian promise of Madrid has been broken by the glare of thousands of recently installed streetlamps that cast a mundane brightness over virtually the entire central city. Gone are the spooky shadows of Calle Cava de San Miguel behind the Plaza Mayor. Though many of Old Madrid's *mesones* remain excellent places to encounter females, these will be tourists from Duluth and Dulwich, not the *chulapas* who gathered round Luís Candelas, the swashbuckling, unbuckling bandit-hero of nineteenth-century Madrid; nor even the *chulapas* of the late 1950s and early 1960s. Gone, too, is Candelas' ghost from Calle de Calvario, street of his birth, and the *mesones* of Calle Imperial.

And yet, the blazing futuristic illuminations also remind you that Madrid is the all-powerful capital of a new, booming Spain. This is where the big-time generals live, and the big politicians. And their mistresses. This is the home office of newly prosperous corporations; the residence of Spain's largest foreign colony and, thanks to the inordinate amount of publicity laid on by the federal tourist organization—by comparison Barcelona's allocation is preposterously small—an irrational "must" for tourists; and the goal of so many young men and women escaping the provinces for a better way of life, or at least a few more pesetas—the population has tripled in the past fifteen years.

RISCAL: PAELLA AND THE DEMIMONDE

Something must be going on around here.

Avoid the obvious, the garish clip joints in and around Avenida Jose Antonio. Begin your search at RESTAURANTE RISCAL (11 Calle Marqués de Riscal). Many discriminating Madrileños never look anywhere else.

It is often reported in the gossip columns of the newspaper *Madrid* that so-and-so High Official or Army officer and his entire family enjoyed the *paella* (specialty of the house) at lunch here. But it is not reported what further delicacies the gentleman savored upon returning alone later in the evening. For by day Riscal is a thoroughly proper restaurant, very popular with the upper classes (reservations, 223-62-06), and by night (224-00-00) a dashing rascal of a room where one may meet some of the most beautiful demimondaines in town, and therefore in all Spain. For if the capital has traditionally the "toughest police chief in the country," it also attracts the prettiest girls.

No one questions that Riscal wears two such diverse sombreros. No good wife, however proper, thinks twice over lunch that a few hours hence a party girl may occupy her place. (Whether she enjoys some secret tremolos at the prospect is open to question.) For Spaniards this situation offers no paradox. It is simply the way things are, and no one save God and Franco can change the natural order of life. Besides, Riscal is a Madrid institution. To bring one's wife or *novia* here after 11 P.M., however, would be an unthinkable breach of taste.

The armada of regulars begins to arrive around 10:30 P.M. Eagerly they crowd the elevator of the small office building and emerge at the top (seventh) floor to be greeted in all their pomaded glory by the maître d', Señor Palomero, a handsome palomino of seventy or more who is a ringer for Maurice Chevalier and knows it. He ushers the guests into a large, airy, rectangular room, pleasantly scented with ferns and freshly cut flowers. On warm nights the ceiling rolls back to add a healthy, outdoor touch. A small orchestra stands by. Waiters in white tie make last-minute adjustments, fussing with the champagne buckets at each of the fifty-odd tables.

By midnight Riscal is the most amusing show in Madrid.

Statuesque blue-eyed blondes from Galicia and volatile black-eyed beauties from Andalusia move with confidence and class among bureaucrats, bullfighters, businessmen and their clients and cronies. The men are obviously comfortable, very much at home. The jokes are witty, if off-color only in pastels. The dancing enthusiastic, but comparatively sedate. There is good small talk, big cigars, and great *paella*, wonderful Asturian smoked salmon. It might be any smart *boîte* in any city. But all the women are young and many stunning, and few men are under forty. Americans are welcome if they behave, but few appear to know the place. (It is helpful if one is accompanied by a Spaniard.) And, of course, the management does not employ photographers to snap souvenir shots at the tables.

A girl will never approach a man unless he suggests it; generally he does this with a small gesture. If she remains alone, she pays her own bill. There is no question of the girls hustling drinks. They have absolutely no connection with the management, nor any employees, though Riscal's evening trade might fall off somewhat without their attendance.

The place has a definite rhythm and a certain dignity. The men are *courting* the girls, and everyone seems to enjoy the situation enormously. Money alone is not enough. These beauties must be wooed.

FOR LOVE AND MONEY

Eventually final arrangements will be made, but often with no more than a shy smile and a nod. By this time the girl may be even more eager than her partner. She is, after all, a woman, and though she makes love for money, she'd rather have it both ways. It goes without saying that a Riscal girl entertains but one man an evening.

Lines of cabs wait patiently in the street below. Like a mass honeymoon procession, they peel off one by one into the night, joined by Mercedes and Alfas.

The girl will have her own apartment, of course. The *meublé* is not tolerated here, though it flourishes in Barcelona. She will probably live in one of the hundreds of huge modern apartment houses, often quite lavishly if she has an arrangement with a wealthy lover. Five rooms, terrace, air-conditioning, and parents from the provinces in their own little room is not uncommon. A small child is almost inevitable.

The sleepy maid is roused to open the door. (Is she the mother?) She must be tipped, about 25 pesetas. (One peseta equals about 1.5¢; about 66 pesetas equal one floating dollar.)

In the bedroom the game really begins. She is shy at first, shows her collection of stuffed animals, or perhaps grabs a book she has been reading and seeks your opinion of it. It could as easily be Hemingway as a pulp novel. Presently lights are dimmed and she giggles like a schoolgirl as she undresses. There will be a crucifix and a representation of the Virgin over her bed, and she does not want them to see.

As true to her glands as her God she won't hear of a contraceptive. Such things are "immoral," and besides they spoil the fun. And, of course, she is clean. After all, this is her profession.

The price is often an afterthought. Maybe 3000 pesetas. Maybe 4000. Maybe a new pair shoes.

It is very important to her that the man satisfies her. Generally there is no problem with the Spaniard. He considers it a matter of honor. But American men have a rather bad reputation among Madrid's demimonde. Many Yankees won't even stay for breakfast!

These women are spoiled, of course. They have had the best of Spanish men in their prime of manhood. Spanish prostitutes thoroughly enjoy sex for its own sake and are certainly far less inhibited about it than the average Spanish housewife. Because the prostitute accepts her role in life, she has few complexes or guilt feelings. Her religion does not interfere, for it has told her to accept things as they are, not to attempt to change them. And so she makes love and money with Christ's blessing. And she does so with humor and abandon (but with the lights low or off for the sake of propriety). And that is why the men of Spain find her so irresistible.

HYPOCRISY AND CORNEAL COITUS

Sexually, Spain is a working hypocrisy. Bullfights are popular but the national pastime is staring. Any Latin male can ravish a lady with a leer, but Spanish women stare as provocatively as the men. And with good reason. In a nation where Church and State have traditionally forbidden sexual intercourse to all but whores and their clients, tourists, and married couples, lovers must resort to corneal coitus.

One thing the Spaniard prizes above all is love—or the *illusion* of love. (It is difficult for a foreigner to discuss illusion and reality in Spain; many Spaniards—perhaps it is the Moorish influence—cannot distinguish between the two. And don't want to.) While the letter of the moral law of the land is fanatically puritanical, the spirit of the people is not. The Church promises hot times in Hell for those who ignore its warnings against sin (*i.e., sex*). And the State, which equates purity of the soul with the return to greatness of the Spanish nation and its destiny to cleanse the world, sees to matters in this life. Spain is not quite as sexually austere as it was five or ten years ago, but the following remain the rule rather than the exception in many parts of the country:

•Young ladies of "good family" are unapproachable to strangers and, for the most part, have little social contact with anyone but their own families and immediate circle of friends. They are never seen alone on the streets after dark, except during the evening *paseo*. Even during this ritual charm parade, a girl must be accompanied by another female, a *dueña*, or her fiancé (*novio*). Or perhaps all three at once.

•Civil Guard authorities (nicknamed *El Moral* by youth) patrol the beaches, often on horseback, and make arrests if bathing attire is considered too revealing.

•In some towns a man may be arrested for kissing or lightly bussing a woman in public, even if she is his wife.

•Unmarried tourists and other potential fornicators are liable to a night in jail if they attempt to consummate their affairs in a hotel or pension. The traditional nasty cahoots of Spanish police and snoopy innkeepers harks back to the days of the Inquisition (which didn't end officially until the nineteenth century) when fornicators were burned at the stake.

Yet with all their fanatic repression, and perhaps because of it, the Spanish are among the most sensual and erotic people in Europe. Because the pleasures of the flesh are so proscribed by Church, State, and family custom, and because the Spanish are such a physical people, sex has an almost mystical aura and attraction for them. Sex and the Single Spaniard may not be synonymous, but he's always thinking about it. A Madrid prostitute who should know observed that "There is more happening in the head of one of our men than in all the bedrooms of Stockholm."

This average Spaniard is likely to suffer (or enjoy) the celebrated "Don Juan Complex." And it is not merely that he thinks he is Don Juan. He *knows* it! Like Juan, the Spaniard has a reputation as an active lover. Part of his charm is that he can be daring, witty, gallant, childish, brave, passionate, tender, and given to flowery, outrageous compliments (*piropos*)—all in the course of a single evening. He is also a peacock—boastful, self-indulgent, spoiled, and preening. There is no question that he is a "woman's man," but there are many who whisper that Don Juan and his heirs are merely bent on an endless series of conquests to prove a masculinity they themselves doubt. Why else do so many Spanish men have the habit of constantly searching their pockets to make sure everything is still there? (Or is that the Italians?)

Traditionally the sexes are segregated from early childhood on—in church, school, and even in the home when it is economically possible. Until recently few Spanish women worked outside their homes, except peasants, servants, and prostitutes. And so there has been no tradition of office sociability, without which the American birthrate might be considerably lower. Thus to the average Spanish male any new female acquaintance may represent a strange and wondrous adventure, and he is apt to become infatuated and immediately fall in love as he glimpses a woman passing by in a train. (And a fast train at that. The Spaniard has a very quick eye.)

Part of the Don Juan thing is to tell about it, and so Spanish men have a preposterous compulsion to confess—to their pals as well as their priests. This is a very Spanish thing to do. Being able to brag of the affair is an important fringe benefit to having a mistress, and many Spaniards will dismiss the woman if she protests. Of course, the only women who can abide such wide notoriety are prostitutes or foreigners; since many kept women do a bit of whoring on the side, the system works well enough.

Habits form early, and in most instances the young Spaniard will have his first sexual experiences with prostitutes. This is not a generalization to be debated. Social customs make the conclusion obvious. There are simply no other girls available for the majority of young men. Often it is the boy's father who arranges the first lesson, in somewhat the same spirit of American fathers who—until recently—sent their adolescent sons to the family doctor for that first, all-important lecture on the facts of life. In Scandinavia, where social customs are traditionally somewhat different and schoolboys bring school-girls home to bed, a great proportion of men do not think of marrying until their early thirties. ("Why buy the book when you can get it from the library?") But in Spain a young man who has the financial means may marry quite young, often long before he has really matured. The occasion marks his first opportunity to make love to someone other than a prostitute or foreigner and, if nothing else, he is passionately curious at the prospect. Of course he loves his *novia* deeply, but much of his fire is fanned by a worshipful satyriasis for the fact of her virginity.

Pity the poor Spaniard (and there are millions of poor Spaniards, notwith-standing the recent prosperity) who cannot afford to marry early and must hoard his pesetas during an agonizing courtship that may last ten years or more. What with the frustrating nightly *paseos*, occasional stolen kisses, and titillating lovers' conversations fraught with sexual innuendo (at which all Spaniards excel), the couple is apt to be climbing walls. (Don Juan again.) For the lady there is no relief until her wedding night, by which time she may be approaching menopause. But for the man there are always the prostitutes. And many Spaniards sadly admit that their nightly courtships are preceded or followed by visits to whores, "just to protect my *novia.*"

Far less is generally known about the women of Spain than the men. Social customs make research difficult. Like the American virgin Jewish Princess, one can do the Spanish girl justice only by marrying her. Because of her previously cloistered existence, she may be a poor match for her husband. She has probably seen little of the world outside the strict confines of her parents' home, her school, and the Church, and her knowledge of sex is next to nil or at best confused. The chances are not remote that her husband may become quickly dissatisfied, and after a year or two the marriage finds its level: the *señora* is someone to bear children, mind the home, and stay there. And the man returns to the more exciting women of his youth. Even in the best of families, by Spanish law a wife needs her husband's written consent to work, open a checking account, get a driver's license or passport. Unless they marry or become nuns, women remain under the legal control of their families until age twenty-five; men achieve majority at age twenty-one.

The Spanish national character has changed little if at all for hundreds of years. Nor has the Church changed. Nor the family structure. And the reign in Spain remains pure totalitarian. Yet mass hunger is gone because the country has finally opened up to foreign investment and tourism, and these two facts of life promise to change the face, if not the soul, of Spain for the first time in five hundred years.

A mere million and a half tourists passed through the country, virtually unnoticed, in 1952. The regime was not hard-pressed to keep alien thoughts and customs from "polluting" the people. But even the austerity of a Franco cannot cope with the current 20 or more million annual visitors. Moreover, the natives are friendly and the travelers bring two things desperately needed —cash and the seeds of sexual freedom. Spain, nothing if not hospitable, responds with sunshine and passion. A fair bargain.

There is no question that tourism has brought modest but welcome prosperity to millions of Spaniards, and it has fostered the growth of a rapidly emerging middle class. Yet no one can say tourism has spoiled or soured the people, as is the case with many French. Perhaps it is the inherent nobility of the Spanish spirit, or the fact that the bonanza has been spread rather thinly. Probably a combination of both, for if Diogenes could search Spain for an honest man, he'd find a nationful, but you'll still be hard-pressed to find many fat ones.

No one can predict how substantial and lasting will be the social effects of tourism. Spaniards are stubborn by nature, independent by instinct, and non-joiners unless forced. But they are amused, excited, and sometimes awed by the parade of English mods and minis, forthright Scandinavian beauties, and the flotsam and jetstream of American hippies, yippies, hillbillies, millionaires, schoolteachers, students, and itinerant bullfighters. (They've never really recovered from the fact that a Jewish boy from Brooklyn—Sidney Franklin—could learn to fight a bull.) To a deeply religious Spaniard, a Protestant or a Jew has always been as alien as an Eskimo. Nowadays he may be sleeping with the first one he meets.

If Spain is experiencing a minirevolution, it remains confined to individuals and small groups—most of these among the young men of the upper classes. Yet that is exactly where many revolutions have begun, whether political or social. This time the battleground is the beach, the bed, and the discothèque.

But the choreography is a steal from Lenin: two shakes forward and one shake backward.

Some examples:

•Ten years ago on Majorcan beaches even the men wore tops. Today the authorities consider themselves fortunate that the girls do. Most of these are tourists, but Spanish girls are tired of losing their young men—if only for the summer—to foreign bikinis.

•In the late 1960s a young Londoner, sent to Spain by the British Travel Association to demonstrate the latest mod gear, was arrested in downtown Madrid for being indecently dressed, and charged with wearing "obscene clothing." The modster spent eight hours in jail, a light sentence by Madrid police standards considering his offense: striped Regency jacket, purple satin shirt, blue bell-bottom trousers, knee-high boots, and shoulder-length hair.

•Foreign investment, and the hundreds of American and British concerns that now maintain offices in Spain, have produced a new social phenomenon —the Spanish working girl. Freer, more independent, and more sexually available than any other women in the country, with the exception of prostitutes and tourists.

•Young couples, girls in pairs, and sometimes even single girls frequent discothèques, coffee bars, and chic saloons. Their curfew hour gets later each year. They may chat, flirt, and even dance with strangers, unheard of five years ago. However, it remains the exception for a stranger to escort an unchaperoned Spanish girl of the "better families." Still, thanks to the new atmosphere and the "new music" (relatively new to Spain), if the stranger is exceptional, it sometimes happens.

•The discothèque scene here is a culture unto itself. It began with American jazz caves in the early 1960s, exploded when the British and French opened their discothèques. The basic pattern remains: Spanish or foreign boy meets and sleeps with foreign girl. But Spanish girls are beginning to feel more left out than shocked.

•There is a substantial expatriate scene in Madrid; and resort areas like Majorca and Ibiza, and the Costas Brava and del Sol are deluged with thousands of very willing female tourists. The foreign girls enjoy the anonymous, exotic attractions of making love with a Spaniard, whatever his class and their own background. The passionate Majorcan fisherboy whose *piropos* include such endearers as "I cry twice when you cry once" is a perfect vacation love match for the English, German, and Scandinavian beauties who are accustomed to slightly less demonstrative males back home.

•The Spaniard still holds his own women sacred, and presumes that any newly met girl who sleeps with him is a "bad girl," but that only seems to make him more exciting to female tourists.

•There is, of course, no such thing as "divorce Spanish-style." But then again maybe there is, for lately the Church has, in rare instances, granted legal separations.

•Though all birth-control devices are forbidden by law, many pharmacies quietly dispense contraceptives. Unless the proprietor is particularly devout, your request for a *goma* is no longer answered with a look of horror and a phonecall to the police station. And in Barcelona there is an area of the Barrio Chino where *gomas* shops abound—shops that sell *nothing* but contraceptive devices and dispense on-the-spot cures for the milder social diseases. A recent congress of the World Medical Association held in Madrid was informed that some 1.25 million packs of the Pill had been dispensed throughout Spain that year, a 78.6-percent increase over the previous year.

•Franco ordered all brothels closed in March, 1956, ostensibly to make Spain more attractive to tourists. The tourists were attracted all right, but by all those low-priced *putas* set loose to hustle the streets. The authorities have clamped down on streetwalkers, and now the official word is that all prostitution is illegal. Which means it flourishes as before, though somewhat less openly, confined to designated bars and clubs. There are some bordellos, particularly in Barcelona, a city with a mind of its own if ever there was one.

MADRID HIGH LIFE

It is a paradox of prostitution that it flourishes during periods of economic crisis as well as prosperity. Surely Spain is no longer the "one vast brothel" Richard Wright described in *Pagan Spain* (1954). With the rise in standards of living the actual number of working girls has decreased, prices have climbed, and, particularly in Madrid, the new laws have created a situation very confusing to strangers.

B-girls: *Promises, Promises*

In certain nightclubs and bars, especially several in and around *La Gran Vía* —Avenida José Antonio—B-girls and hostesses will promise you *everything,* but at best you must invest in more than one 2000-peseta bottle of "champagne" on the very slim chance you may escort her to her apartment after the 4 or 4:30 A.M. closing. It is axiomatic of Madrid clubs that the more anxious management is to have you drink, the higher the prices, and the less likely the girls are permitted to deliver, particularly during business hours. Moreover, in hothouses like YORK CLUB, MICHELETA, and HAPPY CLUB the management is absolutely incredulous should you imply that their many dancing partners are anything but vestibule virgins. In some of the less frenetic houses, the staff may offer delightfully candid opinions as to why the girls are there and what may be done with them.

ALAZÁN (corner Paseo de La Castellana and Calle José Ortega y Gasset, a block from Riscal) is no more than a case of *Promises, Promises* but is surely worth a visit. Though the thirty or more girls have strong affections for the management and must remain to the 4 A.M. closing, they are perhaps the most attractive and international assortment to be found in any Madrid club (a few Swedes, English, French, and the odd American art-history student). Four mysterious dressing rooms in the rear are in constant chaos as the girls change from midi to mini to maxi to hot pants. Very confusing. "If you have real *machismo* . . ." winks a customer. Alazán is a real challenge. Maybe, if you say "SHAZAM!" someone might meet you for coffee the following afternoon.

Straightforward but Wholesome

CASABLANCA (7 Plaza del Rey) is more straightforward, but wholesome (and closed Holy Week to prove it). This suits the middle-class families who may come at any hour (closes 4 A.M.) for the vaudeville shows and dancing, and the shopgirls and chambermaids who come to dance in the afternoon. In the evening some other girls arrive to peddle their 2000-peseta pelts amid bus-loads of bewildered American tourists. These girls are somewhat younger than those at Riscal, less sophisticated, and on the whole far less attractive. They do not push drinks, are not required to remain until closing, and might leave with any apparent gentleman at a moment's notice, only to return less than an hour later. According to Raúl Abril, the late manager, "Our girls pay the entrance fee [150P, which includes the first drink] and do *not* work for 10 percent as in some other clubs. They are guests like everyone else. We have a very good name with the Air Force base, and not just with the enlisted men. The girls speak enough English to know to go to bed. We have had about ten marry American soldiers. I have postcards here: 'Have two children . . . happy with my Sidney in Jersey City' . . . 'I have joined the Spokane PTA. . . .' "

Calle de la Ballesta and Street Scenes

Though the ordinance against streetwalking is strictly enforced in Madrid, when the José Antonio clubs let out at 4 to 4:30 A.M., the wide avenue is literally mobbed with B-girls. Some make straight for the greasy embraces of their *chulos* (the word sometimes connotes a pimp, but more often refers to the Madrid equivalent of the classic 1940s Brooklyn wiseguy or the Soho cockney). Many hop into a cab alone, however, and cruise up and down José Antonio, pulling up to every likely looking prospect to offer the remainder of the evening plus breakfast at 1000-1500Ps. Similarly, the price of Casablanca girls drops from 2000 to 1500 or less if you catch them emerging from the club and coming into the Plaza del Rey at around 4:15 A.M.

Much 3-to-4 A.M. street commotion in Calle de la Ballesta when the tease bars regurgitate their regulars. This Castilian "Grosse Freiheit" was a disreputable whoreway for many years but it has calmed down in recent years. It is just off José Antonio but quite well hidden and so narrow you might spit across it if Madrid's smog and altitude hadn't got all your wind. You may be sure Calle de la Ballesta is quite well known, however, to the busy gentlemen around the corner in the police station.[1] Also close by is SCARLAT CLUB. Go and see if you can figure out this odd bowl of salty characters and . . . and what? A billboard photo seems to imply they may have had a transvestite perform here recently. If so, muses the manager of the nearby KING CLUB discothèque, it's the first time in Madrid's memory since Franco.

If you've done the Ballesta dives, don't bother with those joints along the road to the airport that constantly change their names, but not their girls or linens. Some of these are off-limits to military personnel.

A National Monument

CHICOTE (Avenida José Antonio 12) is literally a national monument, however, having been so designated by the government. Ostensibly this may be in tribute to the fascinating basement booze museum, which features an 1852 Chartreuse and an 1811 Napoleon brandy, together said to be worth nearly $3000. Neither is for sale, but upstairs some lovely, much younger concoctions can be savored for 2 to 3000 pesetas each.

Chicote is truly a classic. Hemingway loved to come here and watch the action. There is no particular decor, the lines and fixtures being fairly spartan. It is a cool, wise, shrewd room with the look and aroma of the inside of a cigar box. Though tourists are welcome it is the regulars who give the place its flavor. Musty but prosperous-looking gents—sporting men of means, landowners and bullbreeders who affect heavy knobbed ivory canes, carefully cultivated paunches, and expensive black-and-white wing-tip shoes. Every man in Chicote seems to say, "I have a great deal of money, and now I am too old to spend it." They stare like sleepy old lions . . . at the whores. And the whores stare right back at them. At apéritif hour things may liven up somewhat. A few Riscal cuties cruise by. Now and again a dapper midget drops in to give the place an extra touch of class. For some reason, Spanish kings and courtesans have always found comfort in the company of dwarfs.

El Abra

Directly across José Antonio from Chicote is EL ABRA. It too is an afternoon and early-evening scene, albeit a rather brash place by comparison, notwithstanding the richly paneled wood decor, heavy white silk curtains, and for-

---

[1] The all-purpose police number is 221-65-16. An ambulance will arrive if you call 227-20-21.

mally attired barmen. Fat, talky ladies crowd the bar, but in the rear, where an elderly professorial type arrives at the grand piano promptly at 8, the girls are slimmer, and dearer. (To 1500P up front, 2000 in the rear.) There is a discreet little back exit, leading to the narrow Calle Caballero de Gracia.

"American Bars" and "Brothels"

A colorful aspect of Madrid's nightlife is the numerous "American bars" scattered throughout the city—"American" merely connoting that one may stand at the bar. These correspond to English pubs. There are bars for workmen, bars for bullfight *aficionados,* bars for the Jet Set and for American expatriates. And along Calle de Serrano there are bars favored by the growing numbers of working girls, many from the so-called "best families," who go to see and be seen, and occasionally to be picked up by *hijos de papá*— spoiled young men who have no work. Many American bars are manned by young women. But do not be misled by those six unwed mothers behind the counter. They'll tell you all about it for the price of a beer, but none can leave before the 3 A.M. closing. If one then accepts your company, it's a tribute to your *machismo,* not your money.

Scattered throughout the city are several "floating" brothels. One must always have an introduction, as police keep proprietors constantly on the run. If you do secure a phone number from a Spanish *amigo,* keep it to yourself, though chances are you'll find nothing more exciting than a former madam, who cannot acquire today's jobs with yesterday's skills, letting her flat evenings to three office girls.

Spaniards are not particularly disposed to orgies. Meals and available women are not taken for granted in this land; a man is generally more than satisfied with one of each at a time. Alexandre Dumas (père), who recorded his observations of life in nineteenth-century Spain in *Adventures in Spain,* described a Granada bordello:

"Never can the evening degenerate into an orgy, for there is no question of eating or drinking, and at 10 o'clock the princess [prostitute] prepares to depart. . . . She rises, graciously allows you to kiss her forehead, sweeps you a curtsy, and withdraws. . . . During all the time we were in Spain we saw only one drunken man, and then the whole population was following him to observe the phenomenon."

There are, of course, excesses among the expatriate and artist colonies, but Madrid is much too gossipy and the authorities too strict for any kind of wild, illegal scene to exist in one place for any length of time. Of course, anyone who can afford it may hire two or three prostitutes at once, but the whores of Madrid are essentially a jealous and modest lot and prefer to work alone.

Hollywood-on-the-Manzanares

By the late 1960s, if there was something "special" happening in Madrid, chances weren't bad that some residents of a certain large, newly constructed apartment house in the Calle Dr. Fleming area might put you on to it. Known affectionately as "The Clinic," because of "all those sick cats living in there," this *edificio* remains a favorite residence of members of the film industry, other expatriates, and assorted international wanderers who can afford the comparatively high rents. Inhabitants of "The Clinic" spend a good deal of time in the smart little bars and sidewalk terraces along Calle Dr. Fleming, a kind of mini-Sunset Boulevard with high hopes of maturing into a Castilian Via Veneto. Typical of these bars is ALADIN, which, when it first opened, provided low tables and high-priced Scotch to the film-cutters, second-unit cameramen, and would-be starlets doing their damndest to make Madrid Hollywood-on-the-Manzanares.

But lately dozens of ultramodern high-rise apartments have sprung up around here, and the neighborhood appears to have been almost completely overrun with newly affluent Spaniards (however, in all Spain no more than eight thousand people admit to earning over $14,000 annually). Architecturally the area may resemble those residential portions of Miami that front Biscayne Bay, but certain quaint Spanish customs are retained. Each block has its *sereno*—the old night watchman with the big stick and ring of keys whom you summon with a *clap-clap-clapping* to open the outer door. And a "Bar Americano" with *amistosa* barmaid[2] is as *de rigueur* for each new high-rise as ostentatious lobbies are in America. Similarly, several Calle Dr. Fleming bars have gone rather native. In Aladin they've stopped pushing the Scotch. In fact nobody cares just how long you dawdle over your 20P espresso, least of all the posse of very pretty young pussycats who are anxious to have you inspect the model apartments in "The Clinic" (its street number has been mysteriously changed; the girls still know where it is, however), or those of another nearby apartment building. Intimate tours range from 2000 to 3000 pesetas. Nor are they hustling *drinks* in elegantly California casual Dr. Fleming bars like KOKETT, etc. Your opportunity to examine closely the new Spanish interiors may run as high as 4000 pesetas ($60). Unquestionably, then, the most exquisite and costly examples of modern Spanish architecture (not to mention a representative collection from the schools of Nice and Marseilles) are no longer to be found back down in the center of town on Avenida José Antonio, but rather here in the suburbs, along the "Costa Fleming." (Interestingly, the Calle Dr. Fleming honors the memory of Sir Alexander Fleming, Scottish discoverer of penicillin.)

[2] *Not* a prostitute.

Discothèques and the Mini Social Revolution

Until recently it was American and British management and foreign clientele that made a Madrid scene "in"; wealthy young Spaniards might come by six months after an opening just to see what the fuss was all about. These were jazz clubs, where people came to *listen* to the music. Most of them have evolved into discothèques—places where people come to dance with and meet strangers, and where women may arrive unescorted—concepts alien to the Spanish. Even the sheltered daughters of Madrid's most upright, uptight families can't sit still in a discothèque, and while the girls usually dance with the Spaniards who brought them, sometimes they don't. And sometimes they even dance with a foreigner. In Spain these are not small gains. In discothèques like STONES, BOURBON STREET, CARNABY STREET, and ROYAL BUS it is now actually possible for a foreigner to introduce himself to one of the young señoritas who come in pairs or groups, and in rare instances to make a date to see her again. Often the introduction may be arranged by her brother or by the young man who brings his own *novia* and her girlfriend or sister. (An only child is comparatively rare in Spain.) A few years ago your overture might have involved you in a nasty duel. Until recently it was rare to see a single girl—other than a prostitute or foreigner—out after 10:30 P.M. The curfew grows later each year, and some stay out till early morning. By far the best pickup possibilities are to be found at LA BOMBILLA, an alfresco dance emporium in PARQUE DE ATRACCIONES, The "Tivoli" of Madrid. *Dueñas* are becoming as rare as streetwalkers, and the absence of the former may soon make the latter obsolete.

Young Spaniards are also creating their own smart nightlife. One example that they've arrived in their own capital is LA BOÎTE, an elegant discothèque in Plaza de las Comendadoras, which strives for all the chic and smartass of clubs wealthy Spaniards enjoy when they travel. Another is DON JAIME'S (Avenida de America 31), founded as Nicca's discothèque by Nick Ray, the gifted but luckless director of *Rebel Without a Cause,* and now impresarioed by Don Jaime de Mora y Aragón, gray sheep brother of Belgium's Queen Fabiola. At this writing Don Jaime's is perhaps the smartest *jaleo* in town.

Jaleo is argot for "noise," "action"; a *lío* is a "mess," "confusion," a kind of Spanish *tsimmes.* If you want a little *lío* and a lot of *jaleo*, go to CAFÉ GIJÓN, Calvo Sotelo 21, the Brasserie Lipp of Madrid. Here one finds an animated and varied collage of actors, painters, journalists, Swedish girls, and students foreign and domestic. The latter are also easily met in the *mesones*—the caves and inns of Old Madrid like SÉSAMO (Principe 7), and MESÓN DEL SEGOVIANO.

Kif (as marijuana is known in North Africa) may be purchased in or around certain *mesones* (*not* these two), as well as along the Costa Fleming. Alexandre Dumas' observations about the dearth of inebriated Spaniards notwithstanding, the pace and tumult of modern Madrid are such that even some young Madrileños have turned to turning on.

If you get sufficiently stoned to enjoy a bullfight, buy your tickets in one of the special outlets in Calle Victoria. That way you'll avoid the scalper's rakeoff and accompanying package tours of a night of pseudoflamenco which the hotels and travel agencies push with fervor. Or fight your own bull. Some Spaniards do it as casually as their American counterparts play tennis or golf. On certain mornings bull ranches in the suburbs and surrounding countryside offer laymen a cape, a bottle of wine (for courage), and the opportunity to jump into the ring with a baby bull. (Up to two hundred pounds of baby, but don't worry, his horns are padded.) About 1000P. Sr. Luís Fernández Fuster of the Government Tourist Information Service (Avenida Generalísimo 39; 254-22-00 or 253-83-08) should be up on which ranches are having specials on tame bulls. Perhaps Señora Amalia Gabor's EL PLANTIO; Don Juan Ruiz Ramirez' ESCUELA TAURINA TORREMOLINOS EN MADRID; or Don Antonio Moreda's LA GUAPISIMA.

If bullfighting makes you hungry head for the *tapas* stands and bars. Spaniards have been making their early evening *tapas* rounds since Roman times. A little stuffed mushroom here, some fried shrimp two doors down, and those succulent mussels across the plaza. Each little stand specializes in a certain delicacy, rarely more than 15 pesetas for a handful. Good *tapas* streets include Manuel Fernández y González, Calle Barbieri, Nuñez de Arce, and the general area around Calle Victoria. The local breakfast of champions is bulls' testicles, revered by Spanish men for its potency potential. (Spaniards have ambivalent feelings about bulls, however. A memorable sight at the conclusion of provincial bullfights is the surging crowd of men and boys who descend on the dead bull's carcass and stomp, kick, and mutilate his testicles with sickening ferocity.) The finest selection of bulls' testicles can be found at LOS MOTIVOS in Calle Ventura de la Vega. Here you may see fathers feeding this delicacy to their young sons . . . hopefully.[3]

Not so Gay Madrid

Some Spanish boys, however, are not partial to "bulls' testicles." These unfortunates are jeeringly called *maricones*—the Spanish equivalent of "fag" or "queer"—and are regarded as the ultimate disgrace to their family. And

[3]Should you require a bull's penis write Major Noel Corry, Steeple Bumpstead, Suffolk, England. He imports these from Madrid where they are first stretched with weights and then fashioned into 40-inch whips.

even to the State. The Madrid police periodically harass, and frequently beat, homosexuals because, in the words of one official, "It is necessary to purge this impurity from our society. They are an insult to the glory of Spanish manhood. They are the shame of Spain." Nevertheless, social customs, which have had the effect of depriving young men and women from having all but meager contact during their formative years, have for centuries made Spain a breeding ground for homosexuality. Coincidentally, the Spanish lisp, particularly that of Andalusians, makes Spaniards somewhat suspect to the unaccustomed foreign ear, especially to Latin Americans. According to legend and Nina Epton *(Love and the Spanish)*, Andalusia, and particularly Cádiz, is famous for its crop of homosexuals. People speak of rampant lesbianism in the Church, but thus far no one has made any definitive report.

Barcelona may be mecca for Spanish homosexuals, but Madrid has a fair-sized community as well, though they enjoy somewhat less mobility here than in other European cities, or resorts like Málaga, Marbella, and especially Torremolinos along the Costa de Sol. (In the latter town you will find a fair number of gay bars and clubs.) Through the mid-1960s a few artists, writers, and actors might gather in quiet corners of the Café Gijón; homosexuals serving in the armed forces of the United States could meet their Spanish counterparts in certain bars near Barajas Airport; a few local sophisticates seeking wealthy foreigners might cautiously cruise the RENDEZVOUS ROOM of the HILTON hotel. And one could always slink about EL RETIRO park, sniff round the toilets at SINDICAL park, or case some of the better baths, if not the worst ones.

More recently the authorities have shown a grudging tolerance to the smart little bars clustered in two areas just off Calle de Serrano, Madrid's King's Road. BOURBON STREET (Calle de Diego de Léon 7) is surely not completely gay—in fact it was one of Madrid's pioneer discothèques. But after 2:30 A.M. it bends more than a little as the neighborhood bars close. Lesbians arrive from LE CARROUSEL, just around the corner at Lagasca 118; St. Laurented (he has a shop in Calle Serrano) homosexuals from TONI'S (Lagasca 103); and a slightly less elegant mixed bag from several other clubs. Back down Serrano in the direction of the Prado, shy lone males seeking their fellows may enjoy the two tiny bars (especially the basement one) at the rather posh DON RODRIGO (Calle del Cid 8); if not, check modish BAGLIONI (del Cid 1). Nearby in Calle de Recoletos the very mixed PINBALL is long on quantity, but *guárdese* what you do with your machine in the streets. Any sexual couplings between homosexuals are implicitly illegal by statute in Spain, whatever the ages of the participants. Considering the law and customs of this country, *all* situations cited are, of course, mixed. That is to say, lots of heterosexuals come to all these too. (Note: The Madrid and Torremolinos police have been especially active recently.)

A NECROPHILE'S DELIGHT

Don't leave town without visiting one of the least-known museums—but in fact even more typically Spanish than the Prado—the ANTHROPOLOGICAL MUSEUM (corner Calle de Alfonso XII and Paseo de la Infanta Isabel, near the Atocha Railway Station) founded by Dr. Pedro González de Velasco, pioneer Spanish anatomist, who was so passionately devoted to his science that he cut up more than eighty-five hundred corpses during his long and distinguished career. Among the many curiosities collected by Dr. Velasco, endeavor to see the skeleton and plaster cast of the giant, Agustín Luengo y Capilla. So fascinated with Luengo's case of acromegaly was Velasco that he agreed to support the huge peasant for the rest of his life if Luengo would will his body to the museum. The giant readily accepted, but died shortly thereafter, the fleshpots of nineteenth-century Madrid being too much for a nouveau-riche Asturian peasant, albeit a seven-foot-four-and-one-half-inch one.

Dr. Velasco, a singularly dedicated and humane physician and scientist, had but one great love—his daughter Concha. So griefstricken was he at her untimely death at age fifteen that he performed the embalming himself. And such was his skill that when, eleven years later in 1875, he exhumed the body for reburial in his home, even he was startled to discover the corpse was perfectly preserved. So amazingly lifelike was the little body that when the good doctor lifted it from the coffin he found he could even flex the elbow and knee joints. Overcome with joy and emotion the doctor had the naked corpse installed in a chair before a window near his study, in spite of his wife's vigorous protests. After the body had mummified, Velasco had a wedding dress fashioned for it, draped it with costly jewels, and summoned the best hairdresser, manicurist, and beautician of the day. The neighbors began to rumble. (They had always been somewhat anxious about his midnight deliveries and the bone-boiling vats out back.) Soon all Madrid was gossiping. It was reported that periodically Dr. Velasco removed Concha from her specially constructed glass case to dine with the family. There were wild stories of midnight rides in black carriages, the radiant, bejeweled little corpse propped up between Velasco and one Dr. Múñoz (to whom Concha had been bethrothed). And there were wilder stories. . . .

But don't you believe a *word* of them. After taking in the museum—originally Dr. Velasco's home, incidentally—pay your respects at San Isidro cemetery, where repose the good doctor, his wife, and, at last, little Concha.

Now make for EL CRIOLLO in Calle Barbieri where you can get what may be the cheapest good meal in Western Europe: about 35 cents for a wholesome three courses of white-bean soup, fish, meat, potatoes, and a vegetable.

AUTO-DA-FÉ

Someday they'll make a movie, *To Drive in Madrid*. It will be a tragedy. Rush hour is as jammed as New York's, as chaotic as Rome's, with a dash of the Spanish death wish added for color. The Spaniard is as passionate about proving his manhood behind the wheel of a car as he is in a strange girl's bed. What he may lack in experience with automobiles he attempts to overcome with hair-raising courage and élan. If the light suddenly changes to red, you must not stop short or the madman behind will charge right into your trunk and emerge from his vehicle screaming that it was your fault. And the policeman will undoubtedly agree that the accident would never have occurred if you hadn't displayed the reflexes of a cow and the courage of a tapir.

When the Spaniard finds himself on the open road, he considers the event a *corrida*. If he is operating a truck or bus and you happen to be coming the other way in a small car, he fancies himself a raging bull and swerves to the center, charging you right off the road. He is less fond of the matador role, but will play it out to the end, advancing toward your larger oncoming vehicle with frightening abandon. Notice how gracefully he moves to the center, then pulls slightly away as your cars meet and pass with no room to spare. A perfect *verónica!*—if he's young and well coordinated. Another coat of paint and you're one more death in the afternoon.

The drive to Barcelona is 620 hard kilometers, and pathetic accidents are far too commonplace considering the comparatively sparse traffic. The road is mostly flat, but given to mirages and freakish optical illusions when the sun is high; the land, harsh red desert—mountains, plains, and bizarre, often spectacular shapes on the horizon that make you feel you're motoring across Mars.

Far fewer *"Viva Franco"* signs are scrawled on peasants' huts than ten years ago.

The Spanish have discovered a new advertising medium: endless irrigation aqueducts strung with long messages that add to the traffic hazards, especially if one is a slow reader.

In summer the heat is suffocating, absolutely moistureless. Only fools and vultures dare the awesome sun from two to five. But fifty miles from Barcelona you begin to smell the sea, and the road is suddenly cooler as it winds pleasantly through tall waving marsh grasses. Sea gulls flap a welcome, young girls wave frankly from green fields growing more lush with every mile. Happy fat dikes flash out of sideroads on motorbikes.

Highway police stop every vehicle coming down out of the Pyrenees with Andorran license plates. The Andorrans are a very industrious people and their chief industry appears to be smuggling. Cars are emptied, seat cushions and occupants searched, but smiles all around say, "We've been doing this for a long, long time, and what's a bit of smuggling among neighbors . . . as long as one is willing to share his good fortune."

You begin to get the feeling that if Madrid is the rule of Spain, Barcelona is the exception.

Meanwhile, back in the capital, Parliament is at last removing from the civil code that portion of Article 57 which denies women under twenty-five the same rights granted men twenty-one and over. María Belén Landaburu, one of eight women in the 561-member unicameral body, led the reform movement, but you can be sure it was no fiesta. During committee debates some of her male opponents suggested that there was only one way to handle all this women's equality business in Spain . . . "raise the age requirement for men to twenty-five."

BARCELONA

SPAIN

The basic unit of currency is the peseta, which can be divided into 100 centimos. At this writing you'll get about 66 pesetas for each floating dollar. Thus each peseta is worth about one and a half U.S. cents. Spanish law says you can bring no more than 50,000 pesetas in, and take no more than 2000 out.

"LOVERS' HOTELS"

The Pedralbes Is the "Plaza"

The *meublé,* or hotel, PEDRALBES stands high on a hill overlooking the city of Barcelona. From its tiny windows there are magnificent vistas of the Catalonian coastal range, whose hills form the western rim of the natural amphitheater half surrounding the city. Mt. Tibidabo rises to the north and, looking east, there is a breathtaking view of Barcelona's bustling harbor, dominated by spectacularly lit Montjuich. But none of the Pedralbes' guests is much interested in scenery, and there are no complaints that the windows are always tightly shuttered. The management spares no effort to insure maximum privacy for its guests, and with good reason. Set well back from the main road and surrounded by a high wall, this forbidding little fortress is the original Hernando's Hideaway.

And Juan's, and Carlos', and Miguel's too. It is said, only half apocryphally, that during siesta hours one need look no further than here or in certain of Barcelona's many other *meublés* to find a healthy quorum of the more prominent members of the commercial, industrial, and political community, along with their favorite mistresses or prostitutes. The Pedralbes, and houses like it, is not—it should be stressed—a whorehouse. (*"Meublé"* means, literally, "furnished," as in "furnished room." See the "Paris" chapter.) You cannot rent a woman here; you bring your own. The Pedralbes is simply a discreet, ingeniously designed hotel for lovemaking. As one regular put it, "We do our sleeping at home."

Spain needs such institutions as badly as India needs the Pill, yet they are rare outside Barcelona's province of Catalonia. By law, single females are not allowed to visit a gentleman's hotel room (suite is okay, apparently) after nightfall. And in many parts of Spain an unmarried couple traveling together may find it impossible to share a room. At the least the hopeful pair will be politely refused a double. Should they resign themselves to separate singles with plans for late-night rendezvous, the male must be sure to return to his own room before dawn. Maids and other hotel personnel are extremely suspicious and will summon the police at the drop of a second pair of shoes. Spain's jails are crowded with lovers and Communists.

And so the Pedralbes operated twenty-four hours a day, every day for years. It is hoped that recent police actions have not disturbed the following ritual: A car containing a man (whose age is of no importance) and a young woman (who must be at least twenty-three) moves swiftly south along Carretera de Esplugas seeking number 90, high above the city in the exclusive Pedralbes section. Just beyond the Pedralbes Gasoline Station it makes a sharp turn east into a short dead-end street, then a quick right through an arched gate into a large courtyard flanked by some thirty garage doors. An attendant in white jacket and black tie rushes to the auto, whistles, and directs the car to one of the garages whose door has swung open at his signal. Inside the garage a canvas rolls down to conceal the car's license plate as another attendant meets the couple even before the overhead door swings shut. He leads them through an inner door that opens onto a long corridor, down which they tiptoe past several rooms until they reach their own. No time wasted checking in at a front desk. Apparently, no passport formalities, except perhaps during the evening. (A rare omission in Spain.) And, most important, no chance of meeting a friend, relative, or enemy in the halls. Only one couple is checked in at a time, a house rule. If others arrive during this time, their license plates are quickly covered and they wait in their garage.

The bedroom is good-sized, perhaps fifteen by twenty-five feet. Directly above the ample double bed hangs a massive contraption of mirrors and fluorescent lighting. The side walls and headboards are mirrored as well. Left night table has four switches that control various lighting effects. An attendant reports that the management plans to install a sound system that will provide taped sounds of the sea, sounds of rain on the roof, and soothing flamenco guitar music. The Pedralbes is so discreet and secretive, and is operated with such flair and earnest, that you may even see your own wife in an entirely new carnal light (red, green, blue, fluorescent overhead white, or any combination of the four). Exemplary of all the loco hocus-pocus is your concierge, who moves through the heavily carpeted hallways in soft slippers or stockinged feet in order not to disturb the guests.

There are some fifty rooms, all doubles surely, ranging in price from 200P ($3.00) to 500P, whether one remains one hour or five. (It's about 50P extra to have the car washed.) Children and dogs are forbidden, luggage is discouraged, and, of course, female guests must have reached their legal age of majority. Spanish champagne can be ordered at 140P the bottle, and contraceptives are available gratis. The Pedralbes' importance to the community is scored by the fact that in telephone-poor Spain it rates no fewer than three lines: 239-30-06, 239-30-07, and 239-85-44. One does not "check out" of a place like this. Simply press the buzzer next to your bed and one of the attendants arrives, takes payment, checks the halls to insure they do not contain your father-in-law (in case he's been following you since Paris), and then leads you back down the long corridor to your garaged car.

And the De La Fransa Is the "Hilton"

If the Pedralbes is the "Plaza" of *meublés,* the MEUBLÉ DE LA FRANSA (Calle de la Fransa 40; 223-84-73) is more comparable to the Hilton. Some regulars consider it to be the most modern in the city. A really sumptuous room with every convenience can be rented for 300P and 650P commands an extravaganza: a Louis XIV suite with black marble floors, a sitting room whose couch is walled and ceilinged with mirrors for an "infinity" effect, and a bathroom the size of most hotel bedrooms. Bedside switches control the ingenious lighting system—which includes dimmers and indirect colored lighting—hi-fi music, and air-conditioning by Chrysler. Full meals are served at any hour and the wine list is more than adequate.

Though it is large—about a hundred rooms—always active, and convenient to the Plaza de España, the Bull Ring, and the Palace of Sports, the Fransa is quite difficult to locate. First-time visitors are advised to arrive by taxi; the concierge is glad to phone another when you're ready to leave. Like any of the better *meublés,* the Fransa is scrupulously discreet and has no sign. The innocuous exterior reveals no more than a nondescript long low building with two auto portals. The only apparent entry is via the underground garage inside which huge hanging canvases conceal each of the thirty car shelters. These latter lead to a passageway and thence to the rooms via one of the three enormous elevators whose walls and ceilings are mirrored, just to get you in the mood.

Space-Age Service: The Casita Blanca

Only slightly less opulent than the Fransa but just as highly respected in the community for its Space Age professionalism is the CASITA BLANCA, which serves—or rather *helps* serve, for there are several *meublés* nearby—the upper-middle-class Balmes quarter. A vast, rather grim-looking modern sandstone structure fronting on no fewer than three streets (auto entrance at Avenida Hospital Militar 43; exit at Calle Ballester 87; pedestrian portal at Calle de Bolívar 2–4), the Casita Blanca is particularly eclectic, offering three huge floors of nearly a hundred rooms to suit every budget and taste at 150, 200, 300, 400, and 600 pesetas. Probably no need to phone 227–9085 for reservations; cars rocket in and out around the clock, and the large ground-floor parking emporium with its hanging canvases is operated with the cold efficiency of a New York City Kinney System garage. Payment is made in advance to the parking attendant, who provides room keys and gratis contraceptives, and directs couples to elevators that lead directly to the upstairs hallways and rooms. Though everything's up-to-date in this Catalan "Love City," the Casita Blanca has never compromised on discretion. Their business cards contain neither phone number nor address, nor even the name of the house, offering merely a map showing its exact location on one face and, rather incongruously, a color photo of a 1900 Renault on the other.

Rosaleda and Nido d'Oro: Neither the Best Nor the Worst

If you'd prefer a slightly less with-it house, though one that also offers underground parking facilities, try ROSALEDA just up the Calle Ballester at 77–79 (21-20-262). "Not the best, not the worst," suggests a regular patron. But a 1972 renovations program has seen Rosaleda emerge as a real comer. Gimmicky rooms from 300P. Particularly active when the neighboring Casita Blanca is closed for re-styling.

Of course no self-respecting *meublé* will admit a single guest. Should you find yourself alone, but curious to see the inside of one of these places, always check nearby bars in the immediate neighborhood. PISCIS, for example, across the Avenida Hospital Militar from Casita Blanca.

Moving east now, back down the mountainside toward the waterfront, the little streets east of Ronda San Antonio (a main thoroughfare in the heart of the city which leads into Plaza Universidad) yield several cheap, workmanlike *meublés*. At Calle San Erasmo 19, corner Calle Nueva de Dulce, is what appears to be the entrance to a coalmine. But drive down into it and you are ensconced in the underground garage of NIDO D'ORO, "The Golden Nest," whose golden nests rent from 200 pesetas. Of course there are a lot of houses in the nearby Barrio Chino waterfront quarter, but they are so numerous and many so leprous as to be hardly worth identifying.

An inquiry at the Ministry of Tourism failed to disclose how many *meublés* there are in town; in fact a gentleman in charge suggested that he had never heard of such institutions. But a very uneducated guess would place the number at at least fifty. Multiply this by a conservative average of, say, twenty rooms each—at least one thousand rooms, many of them occupied by from five to twenty couples per twenty-four hours—and you get some idea of the amount of sexual hankypanky going on every day in Spain's second city, population about 2 million. Many *meublés,* especially those in the deluxe category, were designed and built specifically as lovers' hotels and represent a considerable economic investment. It goes without saying that they are inextricably bound to the economic and social life of the community.

CATALANS: MORE FRENCH THAN SPANISH

It is difficult to believe one is in Spain, but then Barcelona is the capital of Catalonia, and the Catalans are a fiercely independent people, traditionally a thorn in the crown of whoever happens to be ruling the nation from Madrid. For brief periods, and as recently as the 1930s, Catalonia achieved political independence. Among Spaniards, the Basques and Catalans have shown the central government the most resistance, and none but these two peoples has ever shown any "consistent attachment to liberal causes and democracy," as V. S. Pritchett has observed.

Catalans have always felt themselves to be superior to Spaniards and have worked hard to prove it, particularly in industry and commerce. They are intensely proud that their culture and history antedate Madrid's by more than a millennium and a half. Picasso spent his early formative years here and is surely more Catalan than Spanish. And so are Dali and Casals. And Tápies. And, if you believe historian Salvador de Madariaga, Christopher Columbus was a Catalan Jew. But before one gets carried away, Xavier Cugat comes from around here, too.

It may be specious to generalize about the morality of peoples, but one can be assured that the Barcelonan makes a great deal more mischief than the Madrileño, and he needs no tourists to show him how. For background one can point to the proximity of the "immoral" French and the fact that Barcelona's great port has afforded centuries of contact with the rest of Europe and the Near East, and more recently the United States Sixth Fleet. And, for observable proof, one can note that Madrid has no "hotels for love," unless one counts those few scruffy pensions maintained by retired madams. Hotels for love cannot prosper in a society that forbids non-professional females extra- or premarital relations. Which leads one to conclude that the Catalans are more French than Spanish, and none of the three would argue the point.

Liberality notwithstanding, the attitude of the Barcelona police is arresting. They will arrest anybody—often on the smallest provocation—being especially keen on protesting young priests (who champion workers and peasants and are therefore suspected Communists), students, tourists (particularly tourists from small countries), Swedish and German girls who have committed the offense of paying a young man's café bill (thereby letting him open to a charge of procuring), Communists, homosexuals, gypsies, more homosexuals, and occasionally a prostitute. (Usually expatriate.)

¡Mira! ¡Mira! In December, 1971, and again in spring, 1972, the local authorities persuaded several hotels and bars to close for vacations of varying duration. Several reasons were offered in the press, none of which seems plausible. Because these closings seemed quite arbitrary to at least one lay traveler (and many Barcelonans as well)—many establishments were undisturbed—and because a large body of local gossip suggests, or at least hopes, that "all will be again normal soon," this book will not speculate how long each of the situations in question will remain shut. Several of these houses have been serving the community for nearly a decade or more—they are surely no Spanish fly-by-night operations. Rather than omit them from the text they are described at the height of their success (the summers of '70 and '71 were very good indeed) in hopes that "all will be again normal soon."

BROTHELS

Though the Barcelonan joins his Italian friends in considering it his birthright to sleep with the family cook and his secretary, the city offers him a wide variety of prostitutes—a thousand or more are said to be in police files. (Phone the police at 222–65–20 for the latest count; or dial 091 for more immediate emergencies.)[1] Franco's cleanup obviously ended somewhere west of Catalonia. Sex for sale ranges from the bargain-basement bimbos of the Barrio Chino to some really outstanding beauties found in bars and clubs. The city also has a few flourishing brothels. And some women advertise their services in the massage columns of the newspapers, like the whores of Rome. One lady even offers "Chinese Massage."

Barcelona is somewhat of an anachronism. So much of its architecture is nineteenth-century and is so well preserved that a visitor from America feels he has stepped back in time. Not 1850, but more nearly 1907. The bordellos of Barcelona add to this illusion. They are among the few in Europe which retain at least some of the flavor of the *Belle Époque.*

Typical is VILLA MONTSE (Plaza Fernando de Lesseps 7, *torre*, in the Balmes area; 227–59–17) housed in a narrow early-twentieth-century townhouse with imposing iron gates and light green shutters. The madam inspects new clients (dark suits are preferred) through a bejeweled lorgnette and escorts them from the entrance hall into a small parlor. Here, on brocade maroon sofas stacked with chintz throw-pillows, gentlemen may relax over brandy and demitasse. Presently ten young women file in, clad in discreet cocktail dresses or long gowns, looking more like members of a local junior league than the working staff of a whorehouse. There may be a bit of pseudoflamenco dancing before the girls settle in for some serious posing, eye jousting, and *piropos.* When a client makes his selection, he does not indicate it to the young lady. She would perhaps be embarrassed and the others might feel slighted. (At least everyone seems to play it this way.) Instead, he whispers her gown color to the madam and proceeds upstairs to a designated bedroom to await his choice. Two thousand pesetas do the trick.

If for whatever reasons a gentleman likes no one on display (or if, as is now the situation, Villa Montse is closed for "vacation"), fret not. Visitors are presented with a card for I. MONREAL, another establishment operating one marbled flight up at Calle Diputación 208 (old hands should note that the phone number has been changed to 254–55–48 or 254–32–28) behind a massive lacquered-mahogany door whose handsome gold grillwork and peephole rather belie the mundane but no less practical interior. There appear to be only a couple of bedrooms, the one you inspected containing no more

---

[1] For dental or medical problems call 213–20–12, THE FOREIGN COLONIES HOSPITAL, Alegre de Dalt 87.

than a large double, backed by a green felt headboard, facing a six-foot-wide gilt-framed mirror. Open primarily during siesta and early-evening hours like other similar operations—in order not to conflict with Barcelona's many late-night *puta* bars and clubs—I. Monreal might be described as a "euphemistic whorehouse," for it tries hard to pretend it is not one.

On entering, one is immediately hustled into one of four curtained booths. The madam whispers, "No girls here . . . only rooms. *I go phone girl!* Wait few minutes, have three beautiful girls, all very good." Whether girls are maintained on or off the premises (they have recently added several more cozy little waiting chambers) is academic, for within less time than it takes to skim through all the cartoons of an ancient *Playboy,* a girl does arrive. She may be no knockout, but she is very expensive—3000 pesetas. "Well, perhaps for you two thousand, and six hundred more for the room." After some bargaining you, and surely a Catalan, might bring it down to 2000, and there is said to be a special rate for students. (I. Monreal is located in the heart of the city, quite near the university.)

A third establishment, whose management is rather nervous and exceptionally choosy about its clientele, is located behind green iron gates and a black door in a narrow street off the Calle de Muntaner. Any policeman in the neighborhood can locate it for the curious. There are several large bedrooms featuring four-by-six-foot mirrors, and nude lithographs that have a certain John Petty quality. Madam will summon a small selection of girls by phone, none of whom should command more than 2000 pesetas. Nothing really so special here, except perhaps the good crystal chandelier in the parlor. But sometimes lurking about the neighborhood, seeking to intercept prospective customers of the house with the green gates (with which he has absolutely no connection), is a freelance gentleman whose headquarters float like a Vatican City crap game. And with good reason. The man offers something "really Spanish," "really typical"—"authentic," as the guidebooks might say.

A Matter of Love and Death

You are led to a top-floor apartment in a nearby townhouse, one of whose rectangular rooms contains a black velvet "tent" supported by several bamboo poles. Inside the tent the sole illumination is provided by a tall thin candle set on a pedestal at the head of an enormous draped coffin. And inside the coffin lies an exquisite young woman, her face heavily rouged in the manner of Spanish corpses. She wears no more than a white lace gown (similar, perhaps, to that worn by Concha Velasco during her first burial) and in her shining black hair—wait for it—a red rose. For 4000 pesetas you may climb into the coffin with her. If the girl makes any movement on her own account, or even moans a trifle, management guarantees a refund. Of course, you fool!

of course she's alive! It is merely her business to *play* at being dead. And, being Spanish, she does it very well.

Throughout their lives Spaniards carry on a love affair with death. This obsession is well reflected in their art and literature, their fascination with funerals, fanaticism at bullfights, and in the trappings of the Church. Though the necrophiliac whorehouse is endemic to Spain, it is not, broadly speaking, unique. For example, Benjamin and Masters *(The Prostitute and Society)* record similar activities in the United States, including the case of the owner of a well-known funeral parlor in a "large Eastern city."

Interesting as they are as anachronisms, the bordellos of Barcelona are few in number compared to the many bars and clubs where women may be hired. The discrepancy appears to arise from practical rather than moral considerations. Vice in bars and clubs is more tolerable to the local police than in secretive brothels because it is easier to observe and control. Streetwalking is rather risky here, unless one counts the *putas* who cajole passersby from the Barrio Chino bars. However, at the corner of Rambla Cataluña and Calle Diputación, during the early-morning hours, streetwalkers, some of them North Africans, are asking 700 pesetas and getting 500. A bartender, paraphrasing the cynical definition of democracy put it this way: "All prostitution is illegal in Spain. But some forms are less illegal than others."

GOOD-TIME BARS AND CLUBS

As in other Spanish cities, those bars and clubs that offer the most attractive surroundings and beautiful girls—in Barcelona these are invariably superior to the women found in brothels—do not cater to foreigners and are located some distance from the usual tourist haunts, that is, the Ramblas, the Barrio Chino, and Plaza de Cataluña. Most of these establishments, as you may surely have guessed by now, are found in the Balmes quarter.

Acapulco: "The Best"

In the opinion of local *peritos,* no place compares with svelte, flashy ACAPULCO (in Calle Manuel Angelón, a short narrow street parallel to the east-west throughfare Calle Balmes and near its 340s block). Acapulco is a fast-paced place with a certain Hollywood hip to it and a large following of slickly groomed, well-heeled regulars, almost none of whom seems much over forty-five. None of your Madrid *hauteur* here, none of El Chicote's somnolent dignity, nor Riscal's brittle, aristocratic gaiety.

There are two frenetic bands, two bars and, between 1 and 4 A.M., when the atmosphere is at its shrill, festive best, about sixty girls. All are young, several are real beauties. One presumes they are strictly on their own for they do not push drinks (*the* drink here is Scotch) though their presence certainly doesn't harm business. They come for fun—for good company, gossip, laughs, and dancing—and, of course, to make a sale, hopefully at least two or three a night. (Usually 2000P, 3000 for something really extraordinary.) The atmosphere is a good deal more boisterous and the bargaining less subtle than in comparable Madrid clubs. Catalans are, after all, a very practical people. (150P entrance fee includes the first drink.)

The right to refuse service is inalienable, however, and to be fair and accurate some of these girls are something more—or less, depending on one's point of view—than prostitutes. Some are secretaries, nurses, or the equivalent by day, and come here no more than once or twice a week, thus maintaining a certain self-respect and income, and ensuring a variety of attractions for those men who spend almost every night of their lives here. It should be noted that Spain is the best of countries for the moonlightress: many offices don't open until 10:30 A.M. or thereabouts.

And Others

Acapulco has had such success that it has brought a certain dubious prosperity to this solidly upper-middle-class corner of the Balmes area. Some latecomers have opened shop in vicinity, including several directly across the street. The best of these is LA PARISIENNE, which is graced by some lovely 2000P imports from the south of France, not to mention a few Andalusians, North Africans, one Israeli, and one Anglo. Similar tariffs, though the quality appears to fall off slightly, in CERVANTES BAR. Fifteen hundred does nicely in EVA BAR. Farther down Calle Manuel Angelón, an arbored courtyard behind a light green door leads to an anonymous *meublé* whose 200-to-300P rooms, you may be certain, get a good workout in a neighborhood as lively as this one. (The particular shade of light green apparently has some significance in Barcelona—recall the shutters of the house in Plaza de Lesseps, and the gates of the one near Calle de Muntaner, both, incidentally, five minutes' drive from this neighborhood.) A short block away in Calle Ríos Rosas the 2000P talent in JB BAR is anxious to "*tracka track*" with you to the little *meublé* opposite. Similar business (1500 to 2000P) in other nearby bars. That all these little "Malibu-modern" bars close by 3 to 3:30 A.M. keeps the business flowing to Acapulco right up to its 4:30 A.M. closing.

"MODELS"

"Where have all the young girls gone?" you might wonder if you happened into BAR MARFIL, Rambla de Cataluña 104, or the BAR CLUB, around the corner in Calle Rosellón 230, at about 7 of a Sunday evening. In the richly paneled back room of the latter you find nothing but several of the sharpest male minds in town, intently engrossed in the video adventures of Sr. Bugs Bunny. One hears (from Temple Fielding) that these are two of the city's most "in" spots for that early-evening drink and "model." A barman advises that indeed the Marfil is, but only between 8 and 10 P.M. during the week. By ten minutes after the hour the gentlemen have gone home to their families to dress for dinner and the girls (an amenity, just like the dishes of potato chips and peanuts) have gone to wherever models go in Barcelona between 8 and 10 in the evening. Of course, as in so many "class" establishments cited in this book, the girls who come here are attracted by the high caliber of the male patrons and have no arrangements whatsoever with management or personnel.

CAFÉ SANDOR

Timing is so important here, as it is throughout Europe. At 3:30 Sunday afternoon, for example, the sophisticated terrace of the CAFÉ SANDOR, which faces on elegant Plaza Calvo Sotelo, is deserted. But by 4 it is smartly packed with some of the city's most prominent families (the *entire* families) having brunch. And between 6 and 9 P.M. of a weeknight the Sandor is graced by many attractive young ladies who stop by for an *aperitivo* after work or school, or even a mild flirtation with an interesting stranger. Even the most discreet semi-pros do not attempt to work the Sandor, for the management refuses their patronage, perhaps in deference to those dashing male terrace sippers who may see quite enough of such girls in the mirrors of a nearby *meublé*.

NEIGHBORHOOD PLAYGROUNDS

A short block away from lovely Calvo Sotelo is Calle Buenos Aires, a street of pizzerias and bars, some of the latter containing 1000- to 1500-peseta slices of life. There are, among other bars, LONDON SCOTCH and FUJI YAMA, whose authentic Japanese decor and blond female playmates make it very popular among the neighborhood's residents. These are, after all, *neighborhood* bars. All are open to 3 A.M., but the action appears hottest between 7 and 9 P.M. Nearby, incidentally, is SEARS, considered a quite "with-it" store by the young set: all the latest King's Road and 7th Avenue gear.

Hard by the waterfront and at another end of town, literally at another end of the world from Plaza Calvo Sotelo, is the infamous Barrio Chino, where one finds many strange things, but no Chinese. The most appealing aspect of the Barrio Chino is that one must stroll Las Ramblas to get to it.

THE WORLD'S MOST EXCITING BOULEVARD?

If global war should come and the so-called great nations of the Earth blow most of it to eternity, those survivors who have traveled it and known its great cities may mourn most the memory of boulevards like the Ramblas. Even now cynics and nostalgics will tell you the Ramblas pale by comparison with their 1920s heydays when the vibrant café life rivaled that of Paris. All those authentic bohemians—writers, artists, poets, anarchists, and separatists who gathered nightly at the Café de la Rambla and others like it to plan and plot what was to be no more than their own extinction—all are in fact now dead, or in prison, or at best in mourning for a Spain that never happened.

Many of the cafés along here, and in nearby Calle del Marqués del Duero, have been converted into more profitable automobile showrooms and cinemas. But for all it has lost the Ramblas remain a delight to the senses, a showcase of life where Barcelonans of all classes come to see the world and be seen by it.

For Sale: Books and Women . . .

It has been said that one can buy anything along the Ramblas and in the immediate vicinity, and this is still true, with some qualifications. Books and women have always been particular specialties of the area, the variety available and price depending on the temper of the times. Today one can browse dozens of fascinating *librerías* offering all manner of rare antique volumes, old maps, and religious parchments. The racy pornography of the 1920s is now as proscribed as the Marxist books and pamphlets of the 1930s; but recently mild sex manuals and girlie magazines have begun to appear. You'll find no such thing in Madrid. One can still rent a girl or young man, especially in the innumerable bars toward the lower end of the Ramblas near the waterfront. (Some fair 500-to-700P treaties can be made in VERSAILLES, near a shop that must be fifty yards deep and sells nothing but guitars and swords.) And there is the odd streetwalker at late hours. But the boulevard beauties of the nineteenth century are gone, and so of course are the small booths, cribs, and lean-tos that have housed prostitutes hereabouts since the Middle Ages and before.

. . . And Little Girls, Dirty Birds, "Toys," and Love Potions . . .

Today, wandering Catalonian con men—ordinary pimps, gypsies, and so-called *gomoso* (literally "gummy," "sticky" fellows)—offer strangers everything from a ten-year-old boy and his little sister to a wide selection of narcotics. Drugs, brought in largely from North Africa and the Middle East by way of Tangier or Marseilles, are available in Spain "as a matter of convenience to the American sailor and foreign beatnik element." At least that is how the Spanish authorities explain it. (*But caution:* recently in Madrid the police have sentenced several British tourists *and at least one American girl* to six years and a day for mere possession of hash.)

At the stalls of the wide tree-lined center mall, recently repaved with undulating mauve and gray tiles, one can purchase a monkey for 2000P or a parakeet for 200; 500 buy a foul-mouthed myna bird, 750 his bilingual son. There are live jumping frogs and exotic Mediterranean fish in bowls. Also stamps and coins and an assortment of "sick" toys. Typically Spanish is a soft, cuddly teddy bear. You wind him up and he writhes and dies.

The once ubiquitous herb shops that specialized in aphrodisiacs are not so numerous now. But Barcelona is still one of the few big towns in Europe where one can get a well-put-together compound of monkey droppings, red peppers, and *ginseng* on short notice. "Guaranteed to melt the heart and loose the passion of the coldest *novia*. Does a nice job on her *dueña* as well," winks the herb-seller. As in most poor countries one can buy a lottery ticket or an excellent shoeshine. And there are flower-sellers everywhere.

. . . And Good Clean Fun

Las Ramblas may just be the most animated boulevard in the world, with Marseilles' Canebière a close second. At 2:30 Sunday morning it is hard to find a place *not* open. And there is lots of good, clean but colorful fun. The terrace of the HOTEL ORIENT is jammed with English schoolteachers and there are some funny old opera singers anxious to have an intellectual chat with you in the CAFETERIA DE LA ÓPERA. And at the top of the mall in Barcelona's "Speaker's Corner" some fifteen hundred men engage in heated discussions beneath the blue and red banners of a Falange rally.

. . . And Love Letters

Near the San José market a few *memorialistas* survive. These are professional letter writers who once did a formidable trade composing love letters, but most of their business is more mundane now, being principally composed of executing contracts and writing business letters. However rusty the flowery pen of the *memorialista,* he is always delighted to oblige illiterate or lazy lovers at around 30P the page. And it's 10P extra "with passion."

EL BARRIO CHINO

Directly to the right of the Ramblas (walking east), beginning at a point roughly midway between Plaza de Cataluña and the waterfront, is the Barrio Chino. The narrow twisting streets still retain their sinister look, but the roaring cribs and brothels where women were held in virtual bondage up through the early part of this century are gone now. To oldtimers, this traditional sailors' recreation area appears comparatively tame, at its best more seedy than bawdy. It is, in fact, heavily patrolled by the police and a good deal safer than it looks. Which is not to say that nothing is happening in the old neighborhood.

Not a few *meublés* (where the whores are as thick as fleas . . . and so are the fleas) are as frankly disreputable on the inside as they appear to be from the street. These still rent space to prostitutes and their customers who first rendezvous in the bars and cafés. In the late evening and early morning— when the Barrio Chino is at its most active—the alleys are wall to wall with crowds of shouting, laughing, jostling men, but there are few female strollers, except for tourists and occasional slummers clutching tightly to their student boyfriends' arms. In Calle Robador and Calle San Ramón, perhaps the two most emotional streets in the quarter, hundreds of 100-peseta *putas* garnish the bars with their scabrous wares, and every second story harbors what appears to be the fastest *meublé* in town. Pharmacies (like the one that has thrived at the corner of Calle Espalter and San Pablo since 1802) proclaim *"¡Mira! ¡Mira! Penicilina"* from their heavily stickered windows as proudly as Rexall advertising a one-cent sale. And one cannot avoid the *gomas* shops.

Condomsellers

A curious institution, these *gomas* shops—all the more so in a country that claims to be more Catholic than the Pope. These shops specialize in the sale of contraceptives and have been a Barcelona tradition for decades. And business has never been better. Typical is LA MASCOTA, Calle San Ramón 1. From the outside it looks like a small, rather rundown American drugstore, the type that puts trusses in the show window. A bell tinkles as you enter, and the proprietor, managing to look tacky, distinguished, and knowledgeable all at the same time, emerges from the back room to greet you with all the solemn enthusiasm of Ted Mack about to sell Geritol. He wears a long white gown and a pince-nez.

Between you two is a large glass showcase containing perhaps fifty varieties of condoms, or at least fifty varieties of condom *labels,* none of which you recognize, unless you are familiar with such brands as "Conquistador," "El Cid," "Flower Drum Song," "Moment of Truth," and "Brave Bull." The condoms can be purchased individually (from 5 to 20P each), and American manufacturers could learn a thing or two from Spanish package design. One brand, "Two Flowers," is wrapped in little boxes adorned by scantily clad models. Another, "Kiss Pack," comes in a packet shaped like a miniature book, entitled *"Manual de Higiene."*

After appropriate deliberation you make your selection and the proprietor removes the condom from its handsome four-color envelope and carefully stretches it to fit over a polished-wood phallus-shaped apparatus fixed upright behind the showcase. The contraption's two-inch dimension and that of your prospective purchase increase threefold as the man cranks a small handle and the wood separates in the manner of a carpenter's vise, stretching your condom with it. Now he pumps his foot on a floor pedal, which action feeds a bellows contraption to pump air into the rubber, blowing it up as large as a child's full-blown balloon. If it doesn't burst in your face, you shake hands with the gentleman and the transaction is done. Spaniards, though a gracious and courtly people, are a suspicious lot as well.

If all this sounds like something from the cartoons of the late Rube Goldberg, the framed caricatures on the walls of the shop complete the impression. Drawn in a style roughly reminiscent of "Krazy Kat," with a similar feeling for the zany, these portray in comic-strip panels various stretchings, testings, and embarrassing situations imaginatively associated with the use of condoms. There are also vignettes of man's adventures with pro kits, wire brushes, and other time-honored remedies for the social diseases—all of which goods and services are available at your friendly neighborhood *gomas* shop.

Quick Cures

Besides La Mascota (which is also the brand name of a popular condom), the better *gomas* emporia include LA CRUZ DE MALTA, Calle Robador 29, and LA BOLA DE ORO, Robador 47.

Forty-five pesetas covers the full post-coital treatment at "The Ball of Gold," whose superb laboratory is far more up-to-date and extensively outfitted than Ernest Hemingway's World War I ambulance. The cure here begins with a session in the stirrups, during which the learned host carefully diagnoses your particular species of clap or crab, then a soothing "sweeeeem" in the sitz bath and one, two, perhaps even three different kinds of soothing ointments. Barcelona is also rich in clinics that specialize in the treatment of venereal diseases and other genital disorders. One that appears to have a consultation arrangement with several *gomas* shops is CONSULTORIO MÉDICO SALUS, Calle San Pablo 18 (221-08-20), hours 1 to 2 and 4:30 to 9 P.M. *"Enfermedades genito . . . análisis . . . urinarias . . . piel y sangre"* says their card; apparently they know their business.

The Fastest Street in Town

The concentration of *gomas* shops in and around Calle de Robador is no coincidence. You haven't really tasted the Barrio Chino till you've joined the 2-o'clock Sunday-morning horny river of manhood which surges along this barely ten-foot-wide canyon of roaring bars and scrofulous *habitaciones*. *Always* keep to the perimeter of the mob, along the curbs; periodically the crowd breaks into an apparently spontaneous stampede—often at the mere scent of a police patrol—and the unalert stroller can easily be trampled to death. Sure enough, suddenly the men charge forward like a herd of frightened bulls (what else?), all tuned to a sound or signal beyond the range of your senses. You're rescued from a certain stomping by a strong young arm extended from TAKATA BAR and passed hand to greasy hand halfway down the raucous lineup of twenty fire-drinking, garlic-breathing gorgons before you plead sufficient poverty and impotence to crawl back out into Calle Robador.

Proceed now with even more caution from ZARGOSA BAR to BAR LOS ARCOS (gay?) to BIMBO BAR (there *had* to be a Bimbo bar). Fandangos tarantellas Presley pop Beatles boleros rock Welk? jazz *malagueñaaaaaaaaaaa.* . . . Music blares from the wide-mouthed entrance of every bar, segueing as fast as you can walk. ANDALUCÍA BAR. A bar with no name, corner of Calle San José Oriol whose very pretty young hustlers nearly tempt you at 400P. Can there really be more than forty bars in a stretch no more than one New York City crosstown block long? FANDOS BAR. Whatever they're selling, the good doctor P. Pla across the street should be able to diagnose it. BAR 31 CLUB. BAR ALGERIA. More bars. Geriatricks. More *meublés.* A woman offers a package deal, 200P for herself or her daughter, 300 the pair. The child is at least eleven years old. Another woman, perched like a huge fat parrot on a jukebox, is breast-feeding a baby. It probably comes out whiskey.

For Sailors Ashore

Far better known to tourists than Calle Robador, and particularly to American sailors, is Calle Escudellers, on the opposite side of the Ramblas. Some Escudellers whores take on up to twenty men a night, but the saloons here lack that certain Robador flavor, and many are as Spanish as Times Square or Soho clip joints. A German girl who has worked as barmaid in some of the neighborhood dives reported that each had two different price lists—one for Spanish-speaking patrons and another for foreigners: "The Spanish-speaking man will always pay less," she warned. "For whiskey if it is eighty pesetas for him, it is a hundred and twenty for the foreigner. If you buy a drink for a girl, it is maybe a hundred pesetas if you speak Spanish, a hundred and fifty if not. A marijuana cigarette is only twenty-five pesetas for the Spaniard, but two hundred, maybe three hundred pesetas for the American sailor." Similarly, a Spaniard pays as little as a couple of drinks to 250P for a girl here, but the same hustlers may extract from 300 to 1000P from the foreigner for a "short time" . . . a very short time. The girls range from the homely and prematurely mature to some who are in their early twenties, surprisingly attractive, and always brash, compensating for what they may lack in the social graces with a wide assortment of the social diseases and plenty of experience. Not everyone in the neighborhood works in bars, however. Some are in vaudeville.

Music Halls

At the foot of the Ramblas, facing the waterfront, a right turn brings you into Avenida del Marqués del Duero, known to all Barcelonans, and especially poor ones, as *"El Paralelo."* Once a Roman road and today a promenade of the working classes, El Paralelo is a wide thoroughfare of cinemas, cafés, and newly constructed auto showrooms and office buildings. Barcelona has had a wonderful tradition of music-hall entertainment and though the cinemas have virtually wiped it out here, as they have obliterated it nearly everywhere else, one can still enjoy real music hall along El Paralelo. The place to go is EL MOLINO, Vila y Vila 97.

The most important thing about El Molino is that it appears not to have changed for some eighty years, only to have aged. And you see it and smell it no sooner you pay the entrance fee, take your hard wooden pew, and set your drink on the shelf of the seat-back in front of you. Scattered throughout the two hundred-odd-seat house are sundry hard-eyed gentlemen, some half dozing but all obvious connoisseurs of the school of music hall. No dilettantes or tourists in this house. A far cry from the so-called "last surviving London music hall," the Player's Club.

El Molino is a bawdy, rickety old place, once perhaps a dashing rake of a room, now more a musty old reprobate—worldly-wise, very tired, and almost ready to die. *But not yet!* The lights go down as if someone pulled out the plug and up goes the tatty green velvet curtain. Three musicians emerge from manholes in the stage. Next you expect Junius Brutus Booth. Or perhaps W. C. Fields in his early wanderings.

The jugglers are first, greeted by snores. Then some audience suggestion, followed by constructive criticism, followed by a Valencia orange. This is juggled for a bit, then thrown back at its owner. Next come two of the dirtiest comedians you have ever seen or heard, even though you cannot understand a word of Catalan (it is a *language,* not a dialect), followed by dancing girls and perhaps a singer. And then more of the previous. The surroundings are pathetic, the talent is meager. But it tries hard. During and following the 10:30 P.M. and 1:30 A.M. performances bar girls are free—that is to say they are at liberty—to mingle with members of the audience, sometimes behind the tattered curtains of the boxes; naturally some extra gratuity is expected for these command performances. (100P entrance includes a drink.)

If you crave still more music hall, join the jeering throng at BODEGA BOHEMIA (Calle Lancaster 2, just in from the Ramblas) hurling abuse and produce at the varicose vaudevillians, several of whom are younger than eighty springtimes.

GAY BARCELONA

Though statistics are not available, Barcelona may have more resident homosexuals than any city in the country. A great many of these are not natives, according to a winsome young flamenco dancer who supplements his income at 1000 and more pesetas per private performance. He himself claims descent from "a very fine old family of *maricones* originally from Cádiz. . . . In Spain, when young people leave home, they go first to Madrid, as I did. But if one is homosexual, the authorities say we are a disgrace to our country and should not be permitted to live in the capital. And so the police chase us, send us to Barcelona, sometimes even give the bus ticket. It is a big joke with them, for they do not like Catalans. It is as the American sailors tell us, that in your country the police in Los Angeles and Chicago send all the tramps to New York by bus."

The Barcelona police are not pleased with this situation and spend much time beating, jailing, and shaking down homosexuals. Exile is not part of the local rehabilitation program, however. Strong civic elements are most interested that the many gay bars and clubs operate profitably. The port area is, of course, a focal point of activity; two parallel *calles,* Serra and Codols, just in from the waterfront right off the lower Ramblas, are well stocked with gratis naval stores, street boys (300 to 700P), and bars. If your ship hasn't come in at ANCLA or ARLEQUÍN, chances are it won't at BAMBU or NAGASAKI; nor in any of the several Calle Escudellers sailor bars. Perhaps you'd prefer the intellectual stimulation of CAFÉ DE LA LUNA (Rambla Cataluña; very mixed); or the relatively sophisticated clientele at SCOTCH CLUB (San Eusebio 42), or MITO'S (Calle Descartes 1; downstairs). In these last two (all mixed and in the Balmes area), the majority of patrons tend to arrive after midnight.

FOR STUDENTS AND SCANDINAVIANS

Few homosexuals find their way to EL ESTUDIANTIL, a rousing, vigorous café in the shadow of the university (Plaza Universidad), for many years a city landmark and hangout of students, old grads, journalists, bivouacking soldiers, pickpockets, and prostitutes. The latter—running to badly bleached blondes in their mid-thirties—are *not* a feature of the place.[2] Rather, they blend into the general decor and surroundings, which are faintly seamy but practical. Occasionally the whores (700 to 1000P) repair to a nearby *meublé.*

But far more popular are the amateur German and Scandinavian girls who congregate here in summer, and around the corner at another student favorite, ALT HEIDELBERG. Another important café is NAVARRA, which faces the huge

[2]And have no connection whatsoever with the establishment. They are patrons here like everyone else.

Plaza de Cataluña, and is one of the few cafés in the city where women (shoppers, students, and office girls) generally outnumber men.

NEGLECTED BARCELONA

There's somewhat more to Barcelona than whores, homosexuals, and cafés. One can hear really good jazz at JAMBOREE (Plaza Real 17, an interesting square just off the lower Ramblas with a certain pre-Castro-Cuban flavor), an excellent place to meet Spanish and foreign students. Also on Plaza Real, LOS TORANTOS offers the best "tourist" flamenco in town. But if you want something less trite, take a ten-minute hansom ride from Plaza Real to tiny but explosive BODEGA DEL TORO (Conde del Asalto 103; 241-30-60 or 242-07-77). Extraordinary flamenco dancers and "real thing" atmosphere, but the most electrifying performer there is . . . a Japanese! And for an equally unforgettable evening of Spanish folk and classical music and poetry, follow Temple Fielding's good advice and go with reverence to SALÓN GARCÍA RAMOS (Calle San Elias 42 in the Balmes area, just off Calle Balmes). You'll emerge with reverence, too. Don García is that good.

Largely due to the power of Madrid, Barcelona is among the most undeservedly neglected tourist centers in Europe. Yet besides being the best read and most intellectual of Spain's large cities, and the publishing center (and film, too, until the generals forced foreign producers to move to the capital), Barcelona is the nation's classical music metropolis. The Palacio de la Música is an architectural delight and wonder (1900); don't miss it, whatever's on. The opera season program at the Liceo is as eclectic, the audiences as knowledgeable and elegant as any in the world.

The city has a splendid geographical situation; convenient beaches; a compact and thus visually exciting waterfront area; several gorgeously illuminated colored fountains, including what may be Europe's largest; a fascinating twelfth-to-fifteenth-century Gothic quarter commemorating a rich, colorful history—a history that antedates the arrival of the Phoenicians; and a recent Picasso Museum featuring works of his Cubist period, forty-four oils after Velázquez's "Las Meninas," and a large number of erotic works. Here one learns that the artist's well-known "Les Demoiselles d'Avignon," which hangs in New York's Museum of Modern Art, has nothing whatever to do with Avignon, France, but rather immortalizes a famous Barcelona whorehouse of the same name (there are still a lot of whores from the south of France in Calle Balmes and environs).

Among the city's many unique architectural curiosities, not to be missed, are the bizzare, sculptured works of the genius, Antonio Gaudí. Less well known than his Church of the Sacred Family is Gaudí's PARK GÜELL, whose serpentine walls—mosaically constructed from countless smithereens of crockery, shells, broken tiles—command a striking, romantic vista of the city, and, not incidentally, the nearby Balmes area. Best time to go is Sunday afternoon, when the working people bring box lunches and big jugs of wine, and are more than delighted to share them with you.

But most of all Barcelona is *night town,* perhaps the insomniac capital of Europe. By midnight it just begins to roll and at 3 A.M. it puts New York in the class of Cleveland. Barcelona . . . chic, stylish (fashion and design seem about three years ahead of New York), a bit snobbish. But do not confuse this with Parisian snobbery, for although upper-class Barcelonans are very French in their tastes and lifestyles, they are more than casually interested in foreigners. What a shame most visitors rarely stray from the Ramblas and Barrio Chino to the more elegant sections of the city.

BOCACCIO (Calle de Muntaner 505, in the Balmes area) is, for example, among the most smashing, dashing discothèques on the Continent. At 3:30 A.M. you'll find four hundred or more of the most eligible and beautiful young men and women of the "best" families sprawled all over the plush maroon velvet couches with some of the worst intentions. The Tiffany lamps, beaded wooden-ball curtains, and serpentine Gaudíesque wood paneling combine to give a rich, warm, yet exotic feeling of 1910 extravagance. The sound system is superb, the lighting properly soft; and the men's room has urinals in brown, black, and green marble and gold fish-head fixtures on the sinks. Entrance is surprisingly easy for foreigners, considering that Bocaccio is every bit as exciting as the most exclusive discothèques in Paris or London. Across the street is LE CLOCHARD (or have they changed the name to DISCO?), not quite as fashionable as Bocaccio but the people are just as pretty—perhaps somewhat younger—and the sound and synchronized light show even better.

KING'S ROAD, CATALAN-STYLE

A short distance away is Calle Tuset, a Catalonian paella of London's King's Road, Paris's Saint-Germain-des-Prés, and New York's "swinging" Upper East Side. Singles, aged thirty and up, meet around 8 P.M. at ANAHUAC; a surprisingly large number of lone girls here—solidly middle and upper middle class. Nearby is EL DRUG STORE (closed only from 6 to 7 A.M.), whose opening was presided over by Salvador Dali, and ISCHIA, both very important to the local teenyboppers and young men on the prowl. For an apéritif it's the SNOB, a romantic café-bar whose clever, soft lighting, comfortable red-velvet couches, and curving Beardsleyesque wood exemplify the taste and style of this city. Downstairs, at Calle Tuset 3, is COUPE 77, a romantic discothèque.

SNACK BARS AND YOUNG LOVERS

Throughout the area are many tiny chic bars—like BAR RAFAEL in the appropriately named Calle Casanova at number 202—which appear to be specially designed to afford maximum privacy. Even the snack bars have clandestine little upstairs rooms, designed to the specifications of the hot young patrons. For while dating mores are far less restrictive than Madrid's, Barcelona is as gossipy as any Spanish city. At ground level the LUGANO, for example, appears to be nothing more than a modern, extremely well-stocked quick-meal bar. But the seven or eight young couples sprawled all over each other in the semiprivate upstairs "make-out" chamber are surely savoring more than simple snacks, although not complete dinners. (Ironically, the Lugano is located on Rambla Cataluña, midway between Bar Club and Bar Marfil, where their daddies may this instant be selecting the full-course meal.) Another cozy situation in the comfy couches off an elevated landing at CRISTAL CITY (Balmes 294). People here may be a bit better read than those at Lugano, for Cristal City is a unique combination of library, bookshop, bar, cafeteria, and cozy fireside lounge.

As has been noted, Barcelona is very popular with Scandinavian and German girls. But among the most likely places to find a Nordic beauty in summer—even more likely than in Scandinavia—are Majorca or Ibiza. Barcelona's airport is the main gateway for both, unless one prefers the ferry.

FELLATIO ALFRESCO

On your way to the airport, in the southwest portion of the city, you'll observe dozens of high-rise apartments, just completed or still in the process of construction. In the midst of these, "virgin" prostitutes wait at sundown near the intersection of Calle del Capitán Martín Busutil and the Gran Avenida de la Victoria, and in adjacent streets like Calle de los Caballeros. Gentlemen on their way out of the Barcelona Tennis Club and anyone else in the area may be offered a fast fellatio alfresco at 150 pesetas—in the car or the bushes.

If you prefer dancing, in the same neighborhood is CABAÑA TÍO TOM where gather barmaids, after they have finished work, from clubs all over the city. Rousing native pop groups. Best action after 3:30 A.M.

A ROOM KEY WITH THE CHECK

Continuing toward the airport, and beyond it on the road to Sitges several kilometers south of the city, are two clubs known to many Barcelona blades. For the man who cannot persuade his *girlfriend* to accompany him to a *meublé,* these are said to offer a unique service. Once the dancing and drinking establish the proper mood, a signal to the waiter brings the check —and a key to a bedroom. "Of course, one may make love with his *girl-friend,"* says a man who frequently does. "But *never* his *novia!* That is to say, in Spain, even in Catalonia, one would never think to seduce his *novia.* In Spain is different . . . yes?"

Yes.

PRAGUE

CZECHOSLOVAKIA

The basic unit of currency is the crown, which can be divided into 100 hellers. At this writing the government offers tourists an exchange rate of 14–16.20 crowns for each floating dollar. Thus each crown equals about 6 U.S. cents. Of course you may get up to 30 crowns for your dollar in West European banks, up to 40 or even 50 crowns per dollar on the Czech black market (as will be discussed in the text). But . . . the Czech government forbids you to import or export the currency, or to buy it from any but official sources. You may stay longer than you planned if you get caught. Entry Requirements: Valid passport, visa, 2 photographs, $6 fee. Getting a visa is usually an easy formality at any Czech embassy.

Recent Czechoslovakian history is unique by comparison with that of all other countries traveled in this book. Since 1966 this nation has experienced four distinct sociopolitical periods: (1) Neo-Stalinism. (2) Heady, but brief liberalization—"liberation" if you like. (3) Brief invasion and occupation, but with apparently lasting effects. (4) A resultant revision to the socialist "normality" of the mid- and early 1960s.

By mere chance this book was researched on the spot during portions of all four periods. Although Prague's "lusty life" was observed to have maintained a certain stability since 1966—perhaps simply reflecting human nature, that of the natives as well as the comparatively few Western visitors—the extraordinary foreground events dictate that the structure, if not the contents, of this chapter differ significantly from the others.

FALL 1966

Prague is a hundred spires, a thousand years, a million tears. See them mirrored in the somber still-life beauty of its river whose very name haunts —the Moldau.

For the capital of a modern Communist state the moods of Prague's architecture are misbegotten: Renaissance, Gothic, Baroque, Romanesque, nineteenth-century neo-Renaissance, and contemporary scaffolding and chewing gum to keep it all from crumbling down. The Russians may be the Zeckendorfs of the East, but this geographic center of Europe has largely escaped her very heavy neighbor's monstrous wedding-cake modern. Indeed, in no other Western capital—for east is east but Prague has always looked west—does one have such a *total* sense of the past. The city has miraculously escaped structural damage, as if centuries of occupiers found quite enough plunder in his purse and mind, but stopped short of physically harming the classically florid, if timeworn, Old Professor who is Prague.

A stranger's Prague is, more than anything, the city of one of its most illustrious and bedeviled sons, Franz Kafka, of course. Yet within its forbidding façades—the hundred fabled Jack-and-the-Beanstalk turrets, towering and several-steepled; the jaded copper cupolas—are people more anxious to touch Americans than any Europeans yet met. People who make good food —the 1958 Brussels World's Fair Grand Prize for cuisine; good music—the melodic, schmaltzy symphonics of Smetana and Dvořák, jazz since the 1920s; good drink—try the original Pilsner Beer, "the Czech penicillin"; and good love—after Americans and Japanese, Czechoslovaks (75 percent of whom are Roman Catholic-born) make more birth-control pills than anybody.

PROSTITUTION IN THE OLD TOWN, AND TUZEX GIRLS

Alone, you enter the nightgloom of the city of Wenceslas and Jan Hus, your auto tentative and friendless on the cobbled, virtually lightless streets.

A tough Malinovsky-type, his epaulettes belying that he's a simple city cop, smartly salutes your Western plates, parked outside No. 13 Melantrichova,

"*U modrého šífu*" (House of the Blue Ship), then chases across the street to question three pretty teen-age whores. Until 1770 Prague houses had no numbers, and many dwellings and taverns here in the mazy, gaslit *Staré Město* (Old Town) and *Malá Strana* (Lesser Town) across the Charles Bridge are still identified by signs or reliefs: a black man, three hearts, a gold star, a green crab, and the Tavern of the Green Frog, pub of the infamous medieval hangman Vaclav Mydlar. Prostitution is technically against the law, which condemns "social parasites" in the CSSR, but is not really discouraged, particularly when it attracts precious hard currency from the West. Street-walking here in spooky Melantrichova and at the bottom of Wenceslas Square is tolerated as well. Arrests are made by municipal police—and there are good ones and bad ones here as everywhere—either when the girls get a bit too aggressive or, in rare cases, when the *secret* police require new blood—"prison or help us"—to help gather information or to compromise particularly interesting foreigners. The prettiest and shrewdest become "Tuzex-girls" (so-called because they are among the few Czechs who have the hard currency or equivalent Tuzex coupons to shop for scarce Western goods in the State-run Tuzex shops), easily recognized by the extravagant lengths of their Marlboro cigarette butts.

In the hotel nightclubs, in the streets, even at 3 A.M. among the Main Station's sordid hash of snoring peasants, addled alcoholics, and nightmare homosexuals, *there are no old whores,* nor even many over thirty. What happens to them?

There are no apparent pimps. The State is pimp.[1]

But one cannot say that the majority of girls from all stations of life who eagerly cultivate visitors are prostitutes. They simply enjoy the novelty of foreigners, surely more lively and carefree than their own proud but under-standably ego-bruised men. A hard penis remains more important to Czech girls than hard currency, but who can blame them for bedding down for the weekend in nearby rural lovers' retreats like René Hotel and Hotel Hubertus with Western businessmen or Party officials? The promise of a precious Beatles record is irresistible.

THE SECRET POLICE STATION

The police, suddenly intrigued by your inquiries about the René, have decided to include you in their night's catch and requested you to accompany them to the dreadful Bartolomějská Street secret police station. You are

---

[1] And thus any illegal or "immoral" activities which may take place in any given establishment are at the direction or the sufferance of the Government and not any employees or managers therein.

properly frightened. (The Czechs have only recently renamed Mt. Stalin, their highest Tatra peak, and lagged behind even the Russians in removing their Stalin monuments—the Prague statue, the world's largest, came down only three years ago, its massive site so commanding that Coca-Cola requested it for a billboard. However, one big monument remains: Antonin Novotny, the neo-Stalinist boss of Party and State, apparently as powerful as ever despite recent protest ripples among filmmakers, writers, and students.) But secret policemen Josef and Jaroslav are too busy with Jan Beneš a wiry, intense young writer, and his wife, Šárka, a painter, to trifle much with tourists. That police have confiscated her nudes as "pornographic" is amusing, but their interrogations of Šárka are not. "So she's five months' pregnant," they taunt Beneš. "All the other prostitutes[2] here are pregnant too." Jan Beneš is accused of smuggling Central Committee documents to Paris émigrés having allegedly gotten them from his pretty "lover," Zdena (about twenty-two), who, in a passionate moment, is said to have stolen them from the desk of her father, Jiří Hendrych, second-in-command to Novotny. Lieutenant Colonel Počepický, feared by many Czech liberals as he is head of the Prague police investigative division, first assures himself that you know none of this, then sends you on your way. Outside in Bartolomějská Street you meet a good cop Schweik who knows the sexy underbelly of Prague "like the inner thighs of my mistress."

NIGHTLIFE IN WENCESLAS SQUARE

Western-style nightlife is centered in the New Town (Nové Město, founded by Charles IV in 1348), principally in and around the two hundred-foot-wide half-mile-long trolleyed boulevard of Wenceslas Square (Václavské náměstí), which is dominated near its top by the equestrian statue of St. Wenceslas, and beyond: the massive soot-blackened National Museum. There are many ancient, vaulted wine taverns and some working people's dance restaurants in the adjacent Old Town just across the moat (now paved as the perpendicular thoroughfare Na Příkopě); and more ancient beer cellars and taverns across the Moldau and the twin-towered fourteenth-century Charles Bridge (thirty statues representing the greatest Baroque artists) in the Lesser Town beneath the staggering Hradčany Castle, symbol of the Czech nation, founded perhaps as early as the sixth century A.D.

In the bewildering arcades of Wenceslas Square one finds ingenuous, willing young girls, particularly in the dance restaurants on the even-num-

---

[2]Needless to say not only is this a vicious hyperbole as regards the incarcerated females, but an outright lie as regards Šárka Beneš.

bered west side. At No. 4 there's a cross-section of high blue collars—teens to twenty-five in the upstairs ASTRA, to thirty-five amid the fusty red plush basement CARIOCA, which also has a few semipros for prowling native husbands. Children of the intelligentsia prefer the sparkling modernity and pop music of ALFA (No. 28). TATRAN (No. 22) mixes drinks, drunks, and whores for undiscriminating foreigners and cooperative-farm bosses. A slightly crummy, boisterous situation.

LUCERNA: WELL-ORGANIZED PROSTITUTION

But the real action is around the corner at LUCERNA (Vodičkova 36), where one finds the nearest thing to strippers (bras stay on in 1966, however); and pretty young $15-to-20 pros and semis- trying to learn how it's done while a lusty chanteuse, built like a streetsweeper, belts out a stirring "John Brown's Body."

Defenestration has been a peculiarly Czech sport since the early seventeenth century, but when they're not throwing themselves or their enemies from their hundred spires, Praguers can certainly forget their troubles dancing and drinking as well as any people. "This is Mincova," smiles a narrow-gauge tactile titian with the best pair of vicissitudes in Bohemia. "She has been singing this American song for years. She has no barriers. She just serves it."

At a ringside table a Munich photographer and a Florentine art historian race drinks (about $1, or 16 crowns at the tourist exchange rate) for the loves of a blonde. It'll either be a photo finish or an oil painting.

"Things are well organized here in Lucerna," says T (his initial is not at all "T"), one of the country's first Party members (193?), his body as worked out as the Jáchymov uranium mine (the world's oldest; its ore yielded the Curies' first radium), where he was for eight years imprisoned by Klement Gottwald, Novotny's predecessor.[3] A Ph.D. equivalent, T is grateful for his recent release, moonlights from his position as lavatory-cleaner to perform occasional unofficial guide services. "See, there is the 'head girl,' " groans T in the characteristic monotones Czech males use to pronounce English. "She directs twenty others. She says, 'Yes, go with him, he has money . . . no, not with him, he is too young.' No one in our country can really believe, you see, that a young man can have extra money. . . . Prostitution, well, of course, everywhere you have it, but I know of no other form of government which uses them in quite this way. I know . . . my granddaughter is working in Jalta."

[3]Virtually all of Czechoslovakia's rich uranium harvest goes to the Soviet Union. No atomic research is permitted the Czechs.

HOTEL PROSTITUTION

Of course, the really serious business is transacted in the nightclubs and lounges of the best hotels, among them JALTA, ALCRON, and ESPLANADE. In the large socialist-modern cellar cabaret of Hotel Jalta (Wenceslas Square 45) mid-twenties hustlers, *módní* in minis or pants suits, command up to $25 for anything from a couple of hours to the night if you establish some rapport over a late dinner. Attractions in the top-floor dancing bar include three Hungarian fashion-model types, all agog about a recent scandal back home at a Lake Balaton Communist Party hotshots' gambling casino, where the prizes included a chocolate-dipped Malev Airline hostess. In addition to the Hungarian girls, this carnal carnival includes two natural white-blond Poles, two Roumanians, and a nice Jewish Bulgarian girl. The regular circuits for these Warsaw Pact sex maneuvers include GELLERT HOTEL in Budapest; ATHENAE PALACE in Bucharest where the girls are beloved of Italian trade delegations; METROPOLE, Belgrade; and Bratislava's DEVIN HOTEL. Competition is especially keen in the latter city, however, for the Slovak capital's fiery beauties are as amateurish, openhearted, and inexpensive (as little as $10 the night) as any pros in Europe. In fact, for hundreds of years neighboring Viennese have traditionally crossed the Danube to select their brides from among Bratislava's volatile beauties. Current 1966 price, if she has a university education, about $4000 refunded to the State for the cost of it.

There is much action in HOTEL ALCRON's (Štěpánská 40, just off Wenceslas Square) coffee lounge, dubbed the "Yellow Submarine" by foreign correspondents (*Time, New York Times,* various wire services) headquartered in this thirty-three year-old hotel, perhaps the best in town and always under the close scrutiny of Czech security.

HOTEL ESPLANADE (in gloomy Washingtonova, at No. 19, which bisects the top of Wenceslas Square) has a basement nightclub where you may enjoy the pretty mercenaries as much as members of the diplomatic corps.

From his suite here last August 16, Charles Jordan, head of the American Joint Distribution Committee (resettlement of Jewish refugees), disappeared. Shortly thereafter, sometime between eleven and midnight, he drowned in the Moldau off the First of May bridge. The "Prague Bush" (as the grapevine is known) credits the Czech Secret Police (STB) or even the Soviet KGB. Unofficially, the Czech government implies that it was the Egyptians.

In the Soviet Union, guests must leave their hotel rooms by 11 P.M., and government hotel directives require chambermaids to find some ruse for entering rooms if visitors remain longer than two hours. But a $1 tip to a Jalta or Alcron night clerk may turn your single into a temporary double, though many a syzygy is cemented in the girl's own apartment—somehow, in spite of Prague's critical housing shortage, they manage to find apartments, at least for the duration of their careers. Otherwise, they use one of several B-category hotels that double as quickie joints.

No fancy house for Eva. She pulls clients, usually elderly and always foreign, at any of the aforenamed spas, rushes them by taxi to RIEGROVY SADY park, takes advance payment like any respectable whore, then skips off with their trousers. She has, at this writing, fifty-eight pairs—mostly West German, some British, a few American and Third World, but no Russian. Whatever their status in behind-the-scenes power games, no Soviets move as freely through Prague as Westerners.

Czechs like Russians well enough, though they find them somewhat boorish, traveling in pajamaed groups as they do, and, like Germans, always wanting to know the dimensions of everything. This according to "Miss L," a sparkling schoolteacher met at SLOVANSKÝ DŮM (Na Příkopě), formerly the palace of Vernier de Rougemont, rebuilt after the classicist style in 1798, and now a complex housing several dance emporia ranging from pop music with a Guy Lombardo beat to cello and tuba quartets; a large outdoor bar apparently caters to winos and alcoholics in the arcade. (Of her romances with foreigners, Miss L recalled that her Frenchman said something like, "Did you enjoy yourself?" Her German: "What did you think of my performance?" And her Russian: "Are you still alive?")

Though Russian is a required language in secondary schools, English is the most popular elective and many young Czechs speak it quite well; their elders lean to German.

SOME WORDS: NAUGHTY AND NICE

Some useful Czech and Slovak phrases: *Milovat se sněkým* (melovaht s' nyiekeehm) or *Pomilovat se sněkým* (pomelovaht) are common "polite" Czech ways of saying "to make love to someone"; *"sněkým"* is the someone. You'd better know that someone pretty well before you start tossing around *mrdat* (mrdaht) or *sněkým šoustat* (showstaht). This is extremely vulgar language, especially *"mrdat."* *Jebati* is the bawdy Slovak equivalent. (All Czech words are stressed on the first syllable, by the way.)

Similarly, if the American "prisoner of sex" suggests he put his *čurák* (choorahk) into a Czech girl's *píča* (peecha) or her *kunda* (koondah), which is the same thing, or his *kokot* into a Slovak's (whatever they call it in Slovakia or northern Moravia) . . . well, he'd better have been there before. All these are "very hard words."

Kurva (koorvah) is the raw term for a Czech whore; *prostitutka* or *pouliční holka* (powhlichneeh holka) are somewhat more refined. The latter word means, literally, "street girl."

More Czech phrases: *Prosím* (pros-eem)—please. *Ano* (uh-no)—a confusing word that means yes. *Ne* (neh) is no. *Děkuji* (dyekooyi)—thank you. *Dobrý den* (dobri den)—good day *or* hello. *Mluvite anglisky?* (mlooveeteh anglitzkee)—Do you speak English? *Kolik?* (kohlik)—How much? *Muži* (moozhee)—men. *Ženy* (zhenee)—ladies. *Pivo* (peevoh)—beer. *Víno* (veeno)—wine. *Lůžka* (loozhka)—beds.

THE MONEYCHANGER'S TEMPLE

"Bizness, bizness, come make bizness, time is money," hisses the moneychanger in any of four languages from his shadowy arcade temple next to Hotel Jalta. His brogues are expensive—always a way to spot a corrupt Communist—his mood is expansive. A huge graying man of about fifty-five, perhaps 6 feet 4 inches, too well dressed for comfort in his well-cut gabardine, fur-collared trenchcoat, and homburg, he flashes a huge billfold of new 100-crown notes. At your reticence he shows a passport lavish with Western visas indicating he has recently traveled throughout Europe, as if they somehow should assure you that dealing with him will not be dangerous. Quite the contrary. The "official" rate of exchange is 7 Czech crowns to $1 (100 hellers to the crown), 16 for tourists; Vienna banks give up to 25, but this man offers 30 even though the penalties for private currency exchange are severe for Czechs and foreigners alike. How does the tall man operate so openly? Moreover, why?

Ten years ago Czechoslovak life was synthetic, and this was not restricted to chocolate, cream, and butter. But now in 1966, people no longer trade heirlooms for oranges. Today Prague's lifestyles, mores, and intellectual currents are more vibrant than those of any Warsaw Pact capital. Minis, divorce rates, and infidelity are up; intensive sex education in primary schools is being seriously considered; and when you shout *"Mánička"* ("beatnik," but this is, literally, the Czech equivalent of "Mary") lots of long-haired Levi-clad youth turn and grin. As of April, 1966, *Time* reported that there are five hundred beat groups in Czechoslovakia, all with English names.

Czech females rather relish their reputation as the "Swedish girls" of the Warsaw Pact nations. Their age of consent is sixteen. Among the country's most treasured archaeological finds—so vast that many have not yet been catalogued—is the Moravian "Venus of Věstonice," fertility goddess of the Gravettians, who lived it up around here twenty-five thousand years ago. More recently Casanova chose the Bohemian town of Duchcov to write his memoirs, and the swingers at Čedok (the extremely helpful and unbureaucratic—"only to foreigners," say the Czechs—government tourist organization; Na Příkopě 18) have scheduled a big festival on the 170th anniversary of his death next year, inviting all his namesakes from around the world. Do say some nice words at his grave in St. Barbara's Church, Duchcov. And visit the castle library where he worked as a librarian.

CZECHS AND SLOVAKS

Though the average female industrial worker is 5 feet 3½ inches tall, weighs 139 pounds, and thrusts a 35-inch bust, you'll encounter many blond spareribs (usually Czech or German descent). But a predominant type is raven brunette, suprisingly dark, with broad flat face, large wide-set eyes, and pug nose. Czechs number 10 of the nation's 14 million (all of them generally, though not strictly accurately, referred to as "Czechs"), and have admittedly looked down their snub noses at the more colorful, emotional Slovaks. But if the easterners are the "poor white trash" of the country, no small compensation is that their women are said to be more passionate than the cerebral Czechs, who sometimes would rather think about it than do it.

BIRTHRATES, "THE PILL," AND ABORTIONS

The men of Central Europe, traditionally as proud as a pride of lions, once ruled their households with a firm hand. Their workday generally begins at 7 A.M., and—since more than half the country's women are employed—often ends with them bashfully pushing a baby carriage along the highway home from the State nursery. Thus it is hardly surprising that the men may have less passion left for bed than the playboys of the Western world. This is perhaps a contributing factor to one of the world's lowest birthrates (15.1 per thousand in 1967, the lowest rate since the republic was founded in 1918). However, the Czechs are not alone.[4]

Somewhat ironically, then, the "anti-baby pill" is readily available at low cost for the prescription in pharmacies, and abortion has been legal since 1956 (140,000 successful vacuum-method operations—"technology sucks," as Norman Mailer has described this two-minute process—without a death in 1964; and that year Hungary had only two deaths in 358,000. By 1972 it was estimated that 60 percent of all pregnancies are aborted in Hungary, and 36 percent in Czechoslovakia). Though couples must appeal to a special board, permission is rarely withheld. One of the best grounds is lack of living space. Abortions on medical grounds are free, otherwise cost from 300 to

[4]In December, 1971, the French National Institute of Demographic Studies reported that births are not keeping up with deaths in Czechoslovakia, Hungary, West Germany, Sweden, Denmark, Finland, and Poland. Approaching zero growth are Austria, Switzerland, and East Germany.

1000 crowns; the abortion rate currently equals the number of births. (There is one doctor for every 538 citizens, in the United States one for every 910, according to Czech statistics.)

At ALHAMBRA (Wenceslas Square 5), a regular attraction is the Black Theater, an ingenious combination of mime, rear-screen projections, and seemingly free-floating objects and portions of human anatomies given an antic, bizarre life of their own through the clever use of light and wire. Two male shirts fight for a dancing dress. One wins. "Next morning" several tiny shirts dance. Gorgeous, leggy, singing "nuns" in huge white coifs and translucent gray tights do a Zorba dance around a "Buster Keaton" Indian diagnostician who, with grotesque flashlight, seeks the pregant one. To the accompaniment of cymbalom and wild Hungarian czardas, two midwives proceed to operate in the best tradition of Marx (Harpo, not Karl), extracting everything the lissome blonde has got: galoshes, Gauloises, old washing, dirty socks, a monkey wrench, and a smoking cigar.

LOVERS' PRAGUE

"Hello, my name is Z, I shall be your guide," she greets you, all pupils, eyelashes, dimples, and legs. She has been sent to meet you in your hotel lobby by Čedok. Or Heaven. Later, in the OPERA RESTAURANT (Divadelní 24, a tiny street off the Moldau; reservations imperative: 237–588), Ladislav, the pianist, who closely resembles Erich von Stroheim, shrewdly plays "Natasha," the French saga of the Moscow visitor who falls in love with his guide. If the Opera isn't the best restaurant in town, it is surely the most difficult to get into: only eight tables set at cozy couches, candelabra-lit, heirloom china and crystal in a six-hundred-year-old cavern. Rudolph runs it like his own home—takes your order, cooks the delicious "Chicken Opera" or succulent filets of beef with garlic, takes cash. Opera is a particular favorite of Party profligates, for a man can show up ten straight nights with ten different women and Rudolph will always greet him like a welcome stranger.

Surely Prague is a city for honeymooners and other lovers. Rent a small boat at the foot of Pařížská (in the Old Town) and make love on one of the most sublime city rivers in the world. Then paddle over to the Czech Pavilion of the Brussels World's Fair which has been reassembled to house the elegant RESTAURANT PRAHA (Letná Park; 374–546) overlooking the Moldau. The peal of the huge eighteen-inch native-crystal brandy snifters—filled with Gruzin Russian brandy from Georgia—will make her squeal. In summer BARRANDOV's dining and dancing terraces offer another aphrodisiac setting in Prague-Hlubočepy, on the west bank of the river below the Prague Castle.

LANDMARKS

The Hradčany Castle is simultaneously Czechoslovakia's Tower of London, St. Peter's, White House, and Kremlin. Within its confines soar the great serrated Gothic needles of St. Vitus' Cathedral, the nation's most important church. Much of the vast eastern wing was built from fines and taxes levied on fourteenth- and fifteenth-century prostitutes and their wealthy lovers. A short dance from St. Vitus in the Golden Lane (Zlatá ulička), Z counts sixteen fifteenth-century Grimmlike pastel houses, now quaint shops, where Rudolph II (1552–1612; call him "the Ribald" for the profligacy of his reign) kept his alchemists locked up brewing gold. The steep winding cobbles of the Lesser Town lead to Nový Svět (New World Street), from the sixteenth to the early twentieth century Prague's most squalid and nefarious quarter, heart of the red-light district and site of the infamous medieval Three Spiky Dogs tavern whose specialties were whores and thieves. In the area one finds memories of the gold-freak Rudolph's passion in the names of the old wine taverns— The Golden Stork, Golden Star, Golden Bush, Golden Sun, Golden Griffin, Golden Ball—everything but golden fleece and fillings. But pause for the ballsy "17 grade" dark beer brewed in nearby St. Thomas' brewery and a very nice white wine, Ludmila (after the celebrated Middle Ages queen) from Mělník for Z. For the proper historical mood these should be consumed at U ZLATÉ HRUŠKY (The Golden Pear; Nový Svět 3) whose sixteenth-to-eighteenth-century harlots would have stolen your teeth if the roughnecks in Three Spiky Dogs hadn't got them first. Today, certain Latin visitors in company of a nearby hotel's high-priced bedwarmers keep Nový Svět's traditions alive.

STUDENTS

Beneath the Good-Soldier-Schweik cool (you may find the much touristed Schweik tavern U KALICHA on your own) of Czech students burns the passion of Jan Hus, if not Giovanni Casanova. They are best met at VIOLA (back in the New Town by First of May Bridge at Národní 7, perilously close to the Bartolomějská Street secret police station), which features lively, argumentative girls, poetry, jazz, and warm welcomes for Westerners. Many students recall Allen Ginsberg's 1964 visit with fondness. He was allegedly thrown out of the country for "having a bad influence on Czech youth," having invited them to sleep with him under the Charles Bridge. It is said that he was asked to leave Cuba on similar grounds, though allegedly on that occasion Raúl Castro, rather than the general population, was the object of his affections. More students, and patrons and actors of the adjacent National Theater at nearby (Národní 8) KLÁŠTERNI VINÁRNA. LUXOR (Wenceslas Square 41) has jazz, poetry, and pretty teen-agers. Back on Národní, at No. 20, REDUTA offers the best Eastern European and, occasionally, American jazz groups; and in proper darkness, to enable you to be alone with the music, your girl, or your dreams.

Drugs are scarce but scores can be made through African and Middle Eastern exchange students though some Czechs settle for sniffing cleaning fluid, wearing conspicuous crosses and digging (this is, after all, 1966; but soon they'll groove on) the magnificent organ and chorus of ST. JAKOB's CATHEDRAL in the Old Town. "Some come here to find God, some to find themselves, some to find grass, some to find a girlfriend."

HOMOSEXUALS (also called "teply," which literally means "warm.")

Ginsberg might have done better to cruise the bar of the FILM-KLUB, Národní 40. And better yet, GLOBUS (Ulice 28 října No. 11, a continuation of Národní Třída which intersects the bottom of Wenceslas Square and commemorates the 1918 birth of the republic), apparently the town's only exclusively gay wine restaurant and club; for lesbians and male homosexuals. Homosexual carnality between consenting adults eighteen and over is permitted in this country, and nearly committed in the first-floor balcony of HOTEL EUROPA's (Wenceslas Square 29) very Viennese fin-de-siècle coffeehouse. Also chess games as fierce as those found on New York's West 72nd Street, some infuriating elderly hummers (mostly Smetana), and occasional roving brides who'll barter. Lots of Africans too.

Other gay rendezvous include the sauna and shower rooms of PODOLÍ swimming-pool complex, the KARLOVY LÁZNĚ SAUNA and public baths, SAUNA NA SLUPI (Na Slupi 8), though all also offer fortuitous meetings with heterosexual young girls, for many Prague dwellings have inadequate bathing facilities, if any at all. Rough rent and some well-hung Jiřís cruise, at speed and some peril, VRCHLICKÉHO SADY park in front of the main railway station, and some arcades near the top of Wenceslas Square. Very sour cream in the toilets opposite SMETANA THEATER (Vinohrady; Vítězného února 8) and some leathery love in the back rows of CINEMA ČAS (Wenceslas Square 41).

How plausible, then, is the firm assurance of the sharply dressed young hustler (no "screamers" tolerated, however, nor do the authorities permit public contact-dancing) who contends that Prague, a city of about a million, has a mere six hundred homosexuals, all of them registered with the police? (Surely he cannot mean six hundred are on call to entrap foreigners?) Here in Hotel Jalta's top-floor dance bar, a favorite 3 A.M. nightcap for the gay smart set, Q, a pretty, trim brunette whore of about twenty-five, nods in solemn agreement, then continues her tirade against black Africans with whom, she says, few of her colleagues will sleep at any price. "I don't like this Negroes. You know they have bitten with teeth a girlfriend of mine who would not lick them."

Indeed, the Third World blacks sit silent and bitter amid Jalta's brittle gaiety. Up till now they'd believed that only in America could such foolishness exist.

PRAGUE NIGHTS AND NOSE JOBS AT $300

Most dance restaurants close at midnight or 2 A.M., hotel nightclubs by 3 A.M. But when Prague sleeps, BARBARA's Tuzex girls schnorr; and T-CLUB's gay boys too (when Globus is periodically closed by police), warmed by the "champion" violinist, fogyish felt booths, and dumpling soup. After 3:15 some peephole scrutiny in both clubs (located at 14 and 17, respectively, in the bosky shadows of Jungmannovo náměstí, just behind and east of the bottom of Wenceslas Square but difficult to find), but a Western passport works wonders, particularly at Barbara whose amiable headwaiter looks like Norman Rockwell. One finds some quite interesting girls, at 4 A.M., in this relatively contemporary sunken white-stucco cellar. Though the building is over three hundred years old the chamber has a 1930s-modern "dropped"-living-room effect, overstuffed with comfy sofas, diplomats, journalists, intriguers, moneychangers, and police informers—no one knows who these are though one is rumored to be a porter—but everyone is sure they are here.

Considering the Czechs' skill at plastic surgery, ofttimes a spy's own mother might not recognize him on the job. For example, plastic surgeons from all over the world have accorded accolades to the PRAGUE INSTITUTE OF COSMETICS. The institute, however, is a regular division of the state national health scheme and thus offers full services to all Czech citizens at nominal rates. Foreign patients (most of whom are women) are charged double what Czechs pay but not a few are discovering that the quality of the treatments is very high and prices (1972) are about one-fifth to one-tenth those of New York, Paris or Zurich. According to Osgood Caruthers' *Los Angeles Times* report, even the woman who has a simple facial massage or shampoo is first given thorough medical tests by dermatologists to determine precisely which creams and cleansers should be used. "Those who come in for a face lift or a nose bob or the removal of unsightly hair and other blemishes, including tattoos, must undergo a more thorough checkup. . ." that may include comprehensive examinations by gynecologists and other specialists. With all that attention a complete face lift costs a Czech only about 2500 crowns, a foreigner double that—about $300. Nose jobs about the same price. Your local Čedok office (write them at 10 East 40th Street, New York City) can supply further details about the Prague Cosmetics Institute (and the superb clinics and spas of Marienbad and Carlsbad). Closed Monday.

SPRING 1968:
All the Women Are in Love with All the Men

The Prague spring swings. And swings all night.

Streetwalkers have disappeared.

Lucerna has real striptease, more married couples, fewer whores.

All the women are in love with all the men.

The most observable manifestation of the liberals' revolution is the assertive masculinity of Czech males, their turtleneck sweaters (de rigueur these heady days) taut with pride.

"Serious military pressure . . . is believed to be the least likely" Soviet response, according to a *New York Times* man here. *Time* agrees.

Tuzex girls are not so sure. Among the few Czechs with appreciable hoards of hard currency, some whores are fleeing, confident that their savings and the currency of their bodies will enable them to survive in the West.

A SCANDAL

Maj. Gen. Jan Šejna age forty, one of Novotny's top army henchmen has fled the country with some money too: 300,000 crowns, loot from a Billie Sol Estes-type alfalfa operation. Not surprising, then, that such a man has been warmly welcomed by the Johnson Administration, along with his eighteen-year-old son and a young lady of twenty-two, described by some of President Johnson's aides as the son's "fiancée," but by Czechs as the general's mistress. (Somehow he forgot to bring his wife out of the country.) The Czech people are shocked and humiliated; their newspapers burn with accounts of Šejna's scandalous love affairs, riotous drunken orgies, some said to be in company with President Novotny's namesake son. The Dubček government has demanded Šejna's extradition on fraud charges, but Washington refuses, noting the 1925 extradition treaty is inoperative for charges arising out of "political crimes or offenses." Šejna was co-leader, with Miroslav Mamula, of a military plot last December (1967) that sought to preserve the neo-Stalinist Novotny regime and crush Dubček and his followers: that, the Americans insist, is why the Czechs really want Šejna.

The United States (a country where on October 26, 1918, in Philadelphia, Thomáš Masaryk signed the Declaration of Czech Independence at the same desk used by George Washington on July 4, 1776) becomes, even before the Soviet Union, the first large nation to show its contempt for Dubček and his reform government. "Saňo" Dubček may be the incarnation of *Casablanca*'s Victor Laszlo—tall, blond, self-effacing, and glowing with idealism, he even *looks* a bit like Paul Henreid—but America is on more familiar ground doing deals with the likes of Šejna, the Greek Junta, and that South Vietnamese Dragon Lady in drag.

SUMMER 1968: Smalltalk

Soviet Ambassador Anatoly Dobrynin has hastily requested an 8 P.M. appointment with President Johnson. Dobrynin arrives at the White House promptly, kids Walt Rostow about his new Virgin Islands tan, banters wryly that, in spite of the humidity, "Moscow does not regard Washington as a hardship post." Lyndon Johnson, seeking his place in history, joins them in the Cabinet Room. A Scotch and soda for the Russian. A Fresca for the American President. Some minutes of playful smalltalk. At last Dobrynin extracts two pages of longhand notes and reads them perfunctorily: at her own invitation, because of threats to her security, internal and external, Czechoslovakia is at this moment being visited by military units of the Warsaw Pact nations.

The Washington press corps, according to *Time,* has guessed that the President's reaction was ambivalent: while the invasion might set the SALT disarmament talks back somewhat, there is ample compensation. It would, at least, "discomfit the Democrats who most loudly condemn his war policy."

FALL 1968

BREZHNEV THE TRANSPLANT SURGEON

Leonid Brezhnev is being hailed in the Pařížská Street writers' club as an even greater surgeon than Christiaan Barnard, "for having transplanted the heart of Europe into the behind of Russia."

The 10 P.M. curfew imposed during the early weeks of Soviet occupation has been lifted and most all the old familiar places have reopened, but minus a lot of the old familiar faces. Of the estimated ninety thousand people who have fled, or chosen to extend, indefinitely, their summer vacations in the West, many were valued members of the professions, including a good number who followed the oldest profession. The secret police are finding it as difficult recruiting their replacements as the Russians are in scrounging quislings with even a modicum of ability and stature to form a new government. But time favors the strong and the corrupt, though the Czechs are being as uncooperative as possible. The country's leading pop singer, Karel Gott, for example, has refused to do a concert for Soviet troops, even at ten times his usual fee.

"BIZNESS" IS BETTER THAN EVER

"Bizness, bizness" is better than ever for the tall, husky moneychanger in his shadowy arcade next to Hotel Jalta. He's currently offering 35 crowns to the dollar, more than twice the official tourist rate, and 5 crowns more than the current black-market rate. Hard currency has become more precious than ever, for it buys more than mere goods from the West—the chance to live there; without it no one can hope to leave the country. Czechs who are still permitted to travel abroad must give the government 36 crowns for each dollar, and obviously the amount they are permitted to exchange is extremely limited. One beautiful young coed who offers "forty . . . fifty crowns for dollar . . . or thirty dollars for a night of me" must leave, "not because I know something will happen—what more can they do?—but because I know *nothing* will happen. We are lost unless something drastic occurs inside the Soviet Union itself. Something like what happened here last spring. Otherwise they will never let us go, if only because without our light industry it is not possible for the Russians to go into space. . . . And so, I shall sleep with a hundred men and then I shall have enough money to go to England. Only four months it will take me, but perhaps a bit longer for I have never done this. . . ."

BOURGEOIS WESTERN DECADENCE: THE ALCRON HOTEL

Prague is by no means a dead city. There is a perceptible residue of charged atmosphere, compounded of Schweikian defiance and the fresh memory of the terrifying but no less exciting August events that have bound together virtually the entire population. At the Alcron Hotel, which Fidel Castro cited in a recent speech as an opprobrious example of bourgeois Western decadence imperiling Czech socialism and thus justifying the invasion, snappish young whores and moneychangers have virtually bivouacked in the self-contained outside coffee bar from 4 P.M. to its 9 P.M. closing; $20 to 25 for a short haul, $50 the night.

Upstairs in the grim second-floor double room that serves as *The New York Times* Prague bureau, chief correspondent Tad Szulc—soon to be expelled from the country—inexplicably allows you to babble on about what you think you've found in Prague, having scoffed when you first queried about hidden microphones. But when you announce you have a cryptic message from a Czech friend, he and his assistant, indicate with a "mum's the word" gesture and James Bond nod at the chandelier that the room may indeed be bugged. Nasty pool, Tad.

The door bursts open. It's roving correspondent Clyde Farnsworth, Hemingwayesque in jodhpurs and fleecy bush jacket, rosy and exhilarated from tailgating Soviet troop movements in the hinterland.

"LOVERS' HOTELS"

Prague's hotels have no mirrors in the ceilings, but from time to time they may install even more exciting two-way jobs. Take care, then, you don't experience *coitus interruptus* at HOTEL UNION (Jaromírova 1; 43-82-61 or 43-82-25; tram lines 4, 14, 24, and 27), a serviceable B-category house in the 2nd district whose four floors of sufferable doubles rent from 46 to 60 crowns but jump to 100 if you're in a hurry, arriving at, say, midnight and vacating by 3 A.M.; your passport may or may not be collected for the duration of your stay: however, its number will always be recorded, as will that of your partner's identity card. West Germans, at least three of whom have appeared unknowingly in short stag documentaries shot here, would do well to hang bedsheets over the mirrors; but the Egyptians and other Arabs for whom the Union is a Czech Mecca probably needn't bother. The Union has a splendid location in the heart of the Nusle valley with a vista of the ramparts of the ancient Vyšehrad Castle, regarded as the nidus of Czech history. On the fifteen-minute taxi ride from Wenceslas Square you'll pass FAUST House (Vyšehradská ulice 402, southern side of Karlovo náměstí park) where, legend has it, Dr. Faust exchanged his soul to the Devil—at something more than 30 crowns to the dollar—inspiring Goethe's poem. Some truth is lent the story from accounts of the fantastic chemical experiments of the medieval alchemist E. Kelley who occupied this superb Renaissance house during the sixteenth century.

Pass through the massive portal of the grotesque Powder Tower (constructed in 1475 as part of the original fortifications of Old Prague), and you enter a mysterious quarter of the Old Town rarely visited by Western tourists at night. There is hardly enough light to admire anything but the ghostly shapes of the curious medieval Baroque palaces and Prague's first Cubist house (circa 1912) in Celetná ulice. A right on Rybná ulice brings you to the haunty HOTEL CENTRAL (No. 8) from which occasionally dash underage pretties and lesbians back to the remarkable, extremely beat PLAY CLUB cellar discothèque. Numbers of Play Club's scrunched dancers and manic stair-sitters wear huge crosses: some appear to be smoking navel lint. Next door is CASCADE, which offers twenty five-to-forty-year-old maidens—"red hands" but warm hearts, made warmer yet by the 12 percent beer and traditional Czech folk dancing. Cascade and adjacent Hotel Central seem to have certain reciprocal arrangements. Across the street at Rybná 5, in rousing SEKT-PAVI-LON every night to 3 A.M., is a kind of firemen's ball. Although the accordion has asthma some of the community-property girls may have crabs. If the drawstring-curtained booths don't offer sufficient privacy to feel up the working class in peace, there's always ESPRIT HOTEL at the corner of Jakubská and Rybná (64-137, but don't let them know you're coming; just bang on the door and tip the night porter 5 or 10 crowns). Though this modest establishment is traditionally reserved for lower-echelon Soviet bureaucrats, quickie rooms may sometimes be available at 41 crowns. This night from the top-floor windows lean several tipsy tykes, punctuating choruses of "These Are the Days" by dropping vodka bottles to the pavement. This is curious because supposedly all Czechs have sworn off vodka for the duration.

A conveniently short distance from Esprit, perhaps only coincidentally hidden on Čedok street maps by a rendering of the massive Powder Tower, is Králodvorská Street. The large modern façaded structure at No. 4—prewar Praguers might remember it as the Hotel Steiner—has been facelifted to accommodate visiting "political people." No marquee or sign identifies it as PRAHA HOTEL. No need to phone 663-02. If you're a member of the Communist Party, the Praha always knows you're coming, sometimes even before you do. No chance to snuggle up with the purposeful female bureaucrats lounging in the spacious lobby; this is just not that kind of hotel. Whatever you do, don't confuse Praha Hotel with PRAGA HOTEL, a quite different type of operation on the other side of the river near a sizable gypsy encampment in the Smíchov district. The Praga (Pleňská 29; 54-87-41) is among the more active of the city's B-category hotels. Your unannounced presence here will be immediately reported to the city police, who may or may not communicate it to those "other" police.

WHERE TO FIND RUSSIANS

If you really want to ferret out Russians, go to Haštalské Street in the Old Town, a short distance from the nighttime hot stuff in Rybná. Though the Western press has reported that the military has retired to the suburbs for the sake of appearances, the Russians seem to have permanently requisitioned the HOTEL U HAŠTALA (Haštalské nám 16; 639-62). Several Soviet personnel carriers, two tanks, and a large truck fashioned into living quarters crowd the opposite churchyard whose large gold crucifix glitters in the morning sunlight. Huge Czech and Russian flags hang side by side, dwarfing the tiny hotel's entrance. Elderly shawled residents of the neighborhood hurry by, saying their beads, counting the cobblestones to avoid the steely glare of the two Russian sentinels with fixed bayonets.

A tubby, acned schoolgirl approaches the Russians. Suddenly, quick as a mouse, she pivots, drops her drawers, shows the soldiers a flash of her behind, then defiantly turns to see their reaction. For a frightening instant one young guard, who looks no more than seventeen, teases the nipple of her heaving breast with his bayonet. Then he lowers it, grins, says something dirty in Russian, and the girl runs off in the direction of the macabre death-mask likeness of Franz Kafka which marks his nearby former residence. She nearly collides with the homburged moneychanger, last seen next to Hotel Jalta, who hurries into Hotel u Haštala.

That night in the Old Town Square a gypsy violinist dressed in mourning leaves a trail of haunting Czech melodies from the famous 1410 astronomical clock to the statue of Jan Hus, just as he has periodically done since the Russians arrived.

In nearby Melantrichova, great busty lummox ladies and their fellow lathe operators come brawling out of NARCIS and into BARBARINA across the street.

At PALACE HOTEL (Panská 12; 23-71-51), though patronized in the main by Westerners and with a relatively active semipro afternoon coffee bar and cellar apéritif bar scene, thirty anonymous blue circles in the front-desk registry book indicate that a party of Russian tourists has arrived. (It is said such groups always include at least five KGB fellows.) Each night at 4 A.M. an avicular Georgian, his striped herringbone sports jacket and wide-brimmed gray fedora each a sinister size too large, shrewdly scans the register with the darting black eyes of a famished crow. While Novotny was in the stirrups the Palace manager gave him his undivided support. He then welcomed the Prague Spring. Now, with winter coming on, he is again welcoming the Russians. But who can cast stones at Czechs like him? One must, after all, survive. Palace Hotel was among the very few Prague buildings that willingly flew the Russian flag this past November 7, the fifty-first anniversary of the Bolshevik Revolution. That night police water-cannoned twenty-five-hundred demonstrators in Wenceslas Square. At least eleven Soviet flags burned throughout the city. In Na Příkopě, homosexuals poured out of Globus and one urinated on a Soviet vehicle. An officer leaped out and fired several warning shots. Prague police, after ashamedly beating back crowds of students, acquiesced to the furious demands of their countrymen for badge numbers.

Bivouacking troops have finally left Riegrovy Sady, and Eva the trouser thief has resumed her nocturnal dry-cleaning operations. A block from this park, set behind the main railway station, the most intense battles of the August invasion were fought as Czech students barricaded Vinohradská Boulevard with buses and trucks and Soviet tanks blasted the area in an attempt to take over the crucial radio station building at No. 12. This gray November morning the bullet pox drip with tears of freezing rain. A young girl sells photos (3 crowns each) of burning Soviet vehicles, a dying Czech youth. "Six hundred tanks they had in Prague," she recalls. "It was very crowded, you know, I don't think we have six hundred streets!"

WHORE CARAVAN

An estimated nine thousand of the seventy to one hundred thousand Soviet occupation forces are permanently encamped at Mladá, a timeworn military base where Nazi and Austro-Hungarian oppressors have preceded them. Less than an hour from Prague by fast tank, Mladá is on an historic route along highway E-14, passing through Stará Boleslav where Prince Wenceslas I, later to be proclaimed saint, was murdered in 935. This is no temporary cookout; the Russians have even brought several trailers of Ukrainian whores along. And well they have, for many of Mladá's fifty thousand residents recall the mid-1940s when several Russian soldiers shot Czech youths here and in Prague for refusing to give up their girlfriends. With the presence of the ubiquitous foreign press and the eyes of the world on Czechoslovakia—for the moment at least—such conduct would today result in a swift Soviet court-martial and probable summary execution. However, Mladá women have been pawed and taunted, their men interrogated and beaten. Shopgirls have not only disdained any fraternization but have even refused to sell the bewildered young Soviet troops water. (Some heads were shaved recently in Ostrava, however, hard by the Polish border.)

A tavernkeeper recalls that this time (in 1968) the first waves of Warsaw-Pact troops included "the monkeys." Berliners have similar tales from 1945, claiming that before the Red Army first entered their city, a casting call had apparently been sent out to Central Asia for the most primitive, fierce-looking warriors, the intent being to further intimidate an already demoralized civilian population. The tavernkeeper refused to serve a group of Russian soldiers until they would recite: "Brezhnev is a pig."

When one soldier quickly complied, the Czech asked, "Do you know what is a pig?"

"Yes," replied the Mongol, still not convinced he wasn't liberating West Germany, "but what is a Brezhnev?"

He might well inquire at the forbidding, well-guarded SOVIET EMBASSY, a massive sentinel situated on a strategic hill overlooking the Moldau and the city beyond in the exclusive Bubeneč (6th) district (Pod Kaštany 1; 742-24, but if you must phone, wait until after midnight when the lines aren't so tied up and everyone's asleep). Here, Soviet First Deputy Foreign Minister Vasily Kuznetsov and Ambassador S. V. Cervonenko, the man who originally urged the invasion, supervise the "normalization," prowling around town in their heavily armored, curtained Chaika limousines, frequently strolling two blocks over to the Ministry of Interior housing KGB agents and their Czech counterparts. It is somewhat ironic that the Soviet Embassy building and the nearby EMBASSY OF THE PEOPLE'S REPUBLIC OF CHINA (Majakovského 22; 32-61-41)—not to mention the AMERICAN EMBASSY (Tržiště 15 in the Lesser Town; 53-14-56) and the Ministry of Foreign Trade, which was formerly Gestapo headquarters—were among the several elegant mansions housing the fabulous Petschek family, from the turn of the century to 1938 the country's most successful capitalists.

JEUNESSE DORÉE

More irony near the Soviet Embassy. At Václavkova 12 (trams 11, 18, 23, or 30) is ARI COLA, once—from 1890—a wine club, but since its coincidental opening the day the Russians came, Prague's first "high-style" discothèque. Though the Roy Lichtenstein and other day-glow pop posters lend a decidedly juvenile dorm-style effect, Ari Cola has the same snob appeal for the smartly mod-suited and minied children of Prague's artistic intelligentsia and high-up Party members who live in the Smichov district (the city's most desirable residential area) as Castel's does among Paris's *jeunesse dorée*. "Ivan Go Home, The Girls Don't Love You Here, Don't Ever Come Back Again . . ." has been censored out of the Top Ten, but on Friday nights there's still the members-only striptease performance. "She takes it all off, except a little bell." Surely Ari Cola has the prettiest, most "with-it" girls in town, but "no workers from coal."

"A BED FOR LOVE BUT NO BED FOR SLEEP"

In the nearby villa of a soon-to-be-deposed member of the Central Committee, his son pours the *krambambuli*—a delicious concoction of wine, rum, and all kinds of fruit, far more powerful than it tastes. (Yugoslavian?)

"When the Russians came, there was strong opinion we should fight. A fast war, win or lose it like Israel. Not only the simple people wished this but also many of our top military men. Assuming the Russians would not dare to use atomic weapons, their troops in the field would have had a major supply problem—you have seen how we made their radio-detecting train go around in a fifty-hour circle—and perhaps a morale problem as well. America is not the only country which has deserters in Sweden, you know. Our army is larger and better equipped than you may think [175,000 men, 853 planes] and very well motivated. But at last it was decided not to risk total destruction of the country, and you may also be assured that we do not want to be the cause of a Third World War. Although many Czechs believe the Russians would not have come if there was not some secret agreement with the American leadership, all Americans are very welcome here as you see. We understand the facts of life . . . and power.

"Indra, watch this man, he is very ambitious, though you might not think so if you had lived here when he was Minister of Transport. Not only did the trains not run on time, often they did not run at all. Bilak is also dangerous, but Štrougal most of all. He was Novotny's Minister of Interior, and so when we see the old Stalin faces reappearing among the police, we know Štrougal's star is rising. But perhaps there will be new names. No one really knows but the Soviets. They will find them because they will pay in all the currencies of the world, just as your country pays. . . . Now the excitement is over and the world will again forget us. We have small gifts, in the Old Town Square our first Christmas tree in twenty years. But although we have renamed our Moscow Restaurant 'Moravia,' soon again it will be 'Moscow.' But whatever will now happen here do not believe it is because the Czech people want it. We are good Communists, we do not want capitalism; but we do not want the Soviets either."

Now the man's son speaks. "Perhaps more interesting than that thousands have left is that millions of our people could have gone but have not. Some of us will remain active in our quiet way. For rebels there is a bed for love but no bed for sleep. Perhaps now that your Nixon is elected . . . he has always been strong against the Russians, has he not?"

That's how much hope there is today on this planet of the absurd for the place Neville Chamberlain once called "a faraway country of which we know nothing." A rather effete, snobbish Czech hippie who marched with fellow students from Strahov, on Hallowe'en Night, 1967—one of the singular events that is acknowledged to have led directly to the Dubček reforms the American military and governmental Establishment have so hollowly hailed —tosses his shoulder-length hair, sniffs from his vial of cleaning fluid, kisses the cross in the valley of his girlfriend's breasts, and prays to Richard Nixon.

SUMMER 1970 . . . AND 1971

"NORMALIZATION"

Czechoslovakia has been "normalized." Even more so than during Novotny's last two years. The borders are again so secure that for the first time since 1968 the East German government is permitting its citizens to travel here. Westerners are as welcome as ever and have no difficulty getting entry visas. The government desperately needs the hard currency, and the people, even more desperately, need to be visited. A touching Sunday-afternoon scene at Ruzyně Airport is the crowds of ordinary citizens watching the planes take off, some, their nostrils vaporing the glass wall that sets them a world apart from the departing-passengers' lounge. *If you visit one European country in the coming year, let it be this one.*

DUBČEK DISCREDITED

Now that Alexander Dubček has been throughly discredited politically, a campaign is on to dishonor him personally. Slanderous composite photos, created with head shots made at a public reception where Dubček chastely embraced Marta Kubišová (the country's leading female pop singer and one of his staunchest admirers) purport to show the two in a nude bedroom embrace. The faked photos have been distributed in Central Committee meetings, and several of the members have been spreading the news among the people that they are in fact genuine.

Nightlife is brisk, if not gay. Ari Cola discothèque lingers but has been harassed and may be closed at this reading; news of "floating" discothèques and pop cellars is posted on handbills around Wenceslas Square. Though Globus homosexual club has again been shuttered, the new Wenceslas Square pedestrian underpass and the second level of Hotel Europa's café take up the slack.

LUCERNA, THE SECRET POLICE, AND TUZEX GIRLS

Lucerna—drinks now up to $3.60 equivalent—has renovated and reopened with a whole new crop of pros and semipros, many of them timid on the surface, precocious at the core, high-school students or dropouts, tentatively trying out "the life," sleeping with no more than one man an evening. At first. From $25 to $50 for a short time, up to $100 the night or weekend. These are only *asking* prices, however. The economic situation is so desperate that many girls will take much less.

Though the secret police are as active as the FBI at an SDS convention, some of their dirty work is done by the *Mravnost* or "morality" squad—six overworked policemen and a captain who operate out of a fifth-floor room at Politických vězňu 14 (Street of the Political Prisoners). Not only foreigners but also Czech men patronize whores as well. There may be a vicious circle going here. Such is the rapid deterioration of the economy, and the people's ennui, that many housewives and student girls are hungry for pocket money, if not a night on the town. Rolling Stones albums and other scarce Western luxuries can sometimes work wonders, but since 1967 West German Deutsche marks have been the preferred currency here.

Though business is brisk in the nightclubs and bars of Jalta, Alcron, and Esplanade Hotels, Tuzex girls anxiously await the opening of the INTERCONTINENTAL HOTEL, which has been twice postponed since 1969. The Intercontinental's site at the foot of Pařížská and directly on the river may bring this whole area of the Old Town alive by night, though by daylight its antiquities and charm have always been a great attraction. In the next street, for example, is the most extensive repository of Judaism in Europe, including the largest Jewish museum in the world and the heartrending fifteenth-century Jewish cemetery—layer upon layer of sorrowful stone markers frozen in a chaotic scatter pattern. Here, among many, lies Rabbi Löw, creator of the Golem legend. In the wine tavern of the same name in Pařížská, a pretty journalist notes that Kafka is only one of several noted Jews born on what is now CSSR soil; there also were Mahler, Freud, and Egon Kisch, among others.

BEER SHORTAGE AND SCANT PANTIES

The economic outlook is as gloomy as Mahler's Fifth. In a city that claims a world's record fifty gallons of beer consumed for every inhabitant, there is a serious beer shortage. The outlook for panties is similarly scanty. Panty-planners report only 12.9 million pairs will be manufactured this year, a mere 2.8 for each panty-aged female. Compounding the woes of returning to cumbersome central planning, the Russians have blackmailed the Czechs by withholding credits and raw materials until "normalization" is complete; trade with the West has fallen off; and most of all, there are apathetic slowdowns if not complete stoppages among the general population. Only the whores and the police are as industrious as ever.

"BIZNESS"

Our old friend the husky moneychanger is still at it, now giving up to 50 crowns to the dollar and still commuting to Hotel u Haštala. (The Russian flag no longer flies in Haštalské Street, but the little hotel remains under requisition by police for a procession of mysterious visitors.) "Three people have been doing this money business for the government for fifteen years," says an old man strolling among the dozen or so medallion traders who pitch their shabby little velvet stands in front of Hotel Europa every dry Sunday morning. Bring your old Kennedy buttons, or even a Nixon, Yorty, Harold Teen, or that lot. Most any Western button is prized and may secure up to three Maos, two Castros, or even a Treaty of Brest-Litovsk commemorative. But rarest of all are the once ubiquitous black-bordered Dubček pins. "One of these money changers, a man of very big size, is 'W'," continues the old man. "He is formerly porter at __. He reports to police *all* people who make business with him. If they need something against you they put their finger down for illegal currency dealings. I know three people who have lately fallen down that way, two West Germans and one American."

SEX AND THE SECRET POLICEMAN

The British government has prepared a special pamphlet, "Security Advice About Visits to Communist Countries." The admonitions are not the ravings of paranoid McCarthyites, but based on actual cases of blackmail and intimidation:

"Communist intelligence services also make use of sophisticated technical devices . . . visual or photographic surveillance . . . infrared cameras . . . restaurant tables . . . fitted with microphones. . . . The visitor may . . . be compromised sexually. A liaison [with] a local girl will not long remain unknown to the local intelligence service. The girl may be acting for that service from the outset; if not, she is likely to be brought under its control at an early stage. . . . A homosexual affair carries all the same risks as a normal one, but to an enhanced degree. Local homosexuals are often deliberately [set as bait] before visitors who are thought to be homosexuals. . . . Attempts may be made to induce the victim to sign a confession or agree to 'cooperate' [or] 'evidence' may be stored away for use . . . later . . . for example, after the visitor has married."

That Tuzex shops—until recently not open to the general public but always available to whores as well as foreigners—gather twice the amount of hard currency earned by all other aspects of tourism, far outperforming their State-owned counterparts in Poland and Hungary, suggests that the British Board of Trade pamphlet should be read more assiduously by visitors to

Czechoslovakia than to any other Communist nation, even Albania, China, or the Soviet Union, where opportunities to cultivate the natives intimately are far more limited and thus obviate the need for undue precautions. No matter whom you bring to traditional rural lovers' retreats like HOTEL RENÉ and HOTEL HUBERTUS, check the wiring even before you inspect the plumbing. Better yet, camp out!

RURAL LOVENESTS:
RENÉ, HUBERTUS, AND LOVE IN A BARREL

However, one could not do justice to Prague without some account of this pair of idyllic assignation nests, as indispensable to Western businessmen who frequent the city as to local Party philanderers. The mention of their very names, especially René (pronounced "Rena"), draws snickers and winks from cabbies and night porters, and blushes but acquiescence from pretty girls anxious to escape Prague's more than occasional coal-dust smog for the rarefied ozone and crystal-clear nightglow views of the city the nearby forested Brdy Hills afford.

Of the two, René is smaller, less comfortable, but offers a far more illicit ambiance, if only for the ridiculous cupids lurking impishly about the spacious grounds. Drive, or better yet taxi (about $4 equivalent, one way), twenty-three kilometers south on route 3 in the direction of Benesov. Make a right just beyond Horní Jirčany at the sign indicating Sulice and, after a short distance through dense forest, you are passing through the red entrance gates. Be sure to reserve (Jílové 50), or better yet have a hall porter or friend do it; *but not Čedok!* The irrepressible woman who rules René like a grenadier, runs her own show her own way. Serviceable double rooms 70 crowns; "take a bath," 90; "suites," 135. The René was doing a brisk "honeymoon" trade even before the Communists took it away from __ (but don't feel too sorry for him; they made him headwaiter at __ Hotel), and is particularly cherished for its romantic, huntsy dining room and splendid kitchen. Entrees from 20 crowns. Try the Veal Alexander; and Ham Roll à la Marquise as a starter. This latter is topped with whipped cream, strawberries, and peaches and, most important, is filled with a very strong horseradish. "Highly aphrodisiac," according to one guest.

Because René has only eleven rooms, sometimes the hotel runs in two or more shifts; first-time visitors may stand a better chance of accommodation if they book a room for the afternoon, enjoy an exhilarating walk in the woods and a romantic candlelight dinner before motoring back to Prague for the evening.

In the vicinity of the nearby village of Jíloviště, close to recent archaeological digs that have yielded early Celtic settlements, stands HOTEL HUBERTUS (phone 54-48-81, or have Čedok do it, for this is one of their hotels), a proud stone beagle marking the portal of this large Italianate villa built during the time of Empress Maria Theresa for a very bohemian Bohemian nobleman. If any house in the vicinity of Prague offers opportunities for what the Americans have lately dubbed "swinging," this may be it. Vast ornate rooms feature clever "soliloquy" stone balconies that, though they offer inspiring views of the surrounding hillocks, cleverly hide couples from the voyeurs lurking about the grounds. Choicest suites (260 crowns with breakfast for two) are No. 48, beloved for its perspective of the sunrise, massive bed, and Franz Josef furnishings; and across the thickly carpeted corridor, No. 46 from where, caution, you risk being routed from your passions. Not by the police— conveniently, both 46 and 48 are on the first floor and you have a survivable drop to the plush green lawns should the occasion arise—but by film crews. Because Suite 46 has the largest private bathroom in the nation, with ample space for plenty of lights, camera, and action, the Czech film industry periodically requisitions it for its bigger bath scenes. Don't be fooled by the ornate headboards and size of Hubertus' beds, however. They give in all the wrong places at the worst times and, according to a frequent visitor from Amsterdam, "there's not a good bed in the whole country."

"Whose turn in the barrel tonight?"

"Why, both if you wish," smiles a nice woman at Čedok who can arrange for you and your gal to roll the night away in 140-gallon-capacity beer barrels from the *original* Budweiser Brewery in Cēské Budějovice fitted with beds by VLACHOVKA MOTEL on the outskirts of Prague. Barrels are fun to make love in and offer minimal opportunities to hide microphones or infrared cameras. But enough of this spy nonsense; nowadays, all things considered, an American is held safer from harm in the streets or from having his phone tapped in this country than in his own home town.

STUDENT LIFE: PASSIVE SELF-DESTRUCTION

If you feel you've got something to hide, or are for some reason more vulnerable than the next traveler, chose your weekend partner from among university students, most of whom, even the ruling establishment would admit, have no love for the current regime. The twelve buildings of Charles University are spread throughout the city, and students—they may range from eighteen to thirty—can entertain members of the opposite sex in their dorm rooms until 10 P.M. But as Prague students are as resourceful and libidinous as students everywhere, the curfew is often honored in the breach.

By night Viola is as much a rendezvous of older students and postgrads as it was in 1966 or 1968, though the atmosphere is considerably more subdued. Late afternoons go to CLUB VLTAVA (Revoluční 25), ages roughly eighteen to twenty-five. A flashy, Italianate Bulgarian exchange student, admiring the pretty but listless coeds in the riverside restaurant commons, complains that in his experience "Prague girls have no temperament." Indeed, appearances suggest that the students are hopelessly disillusioned at the "loss of our dream." Many are simply frightened of a government that employs prison guards and ex-convicts equipped with two-and-a-half-inch-long rubber-covered steel truncheons to quash demonstrations like the one marking the first anniversary of the "Day of Shame." There was only a murmur of anguish on the second floor of the department of philosophy's building when the death mask of Jan Palach, the student who immolated himself in Wenceslas Square as a protest against the invasion, was ordered removed from its alcove. Students still lay flowers there, however, and hope visitors will as well.

THE FUTURE IS IN THE PAST

Perhaps it is the land itself which makes Czechs so introspective; there are no inspiring, limitless horizons, no great mountains or oceans. The children of this gentle, brooding landscape, wearied and worn to exquisite but finite vistas, the fiery volcanoes long ago burnt out, have turned inward and reflective as the thousand becalmed little lakes. For now the future is in the past. The best of the young salve their wounds with sex, private parties, drugs, and studies.

Following a pattern characteristic of other Eastern European youth—notably Polish and Hungarian and, one hears, Russian as well—passive self-destruction has become the only form of rebellion left to Czech youth. The authorities, moreover, do not always discourage them. Play Club cellar discothèque in the Old Town remains a surprisingly anarchic temple of teen-age iniquity.

Several young men recently stole some cactus plants from the botanical gardens for their mescaline. LSD is somehow available to anyone who really wants it. But it is apparently against the phlegmatic and purposeful Czech nature for large numbers really to let loose as the Hungarian young seem to be doing. According to the Communist Party newspaper *Magyar Hirlip,* teen-age sex clubs and gang rapes are becoming as Hungarian as Tokay wine. That the VD rate has doubled in the past thirteen years is largely attributed, by Budapest venereologists, to the sudden cult of group sex among fifteen-to-nineteen-year-olds.

Now it is 4 A.M. in Barbara Club in Jungmannovo, still the after-hours Elaine's of Prague, and the professional insomniacs huddle over their petty middle-aged vices. A violin moans the moody Moldau national anthem.

People pretend not to hear. Soon Emil Zátopek—four-time Olympic Gold Medal winner for the long-distance run, more recently an army colonel under Dubček in the Ministry of Defense—will arise to make the rounds of his new position. Garbage collector.

On Slavín Hill in Bratislava, by his modest two-bedroom house a mere five minutes' march from the watchful Soviet Consulate, Alexander Dubček pauses in the vegetable garden before catching the tram to his new post with the Ministry of Forestry. Groundskeeper.

SPRING, 1972

The forestry people have promoted Dubček, but he is by no means out of the woods. If recent trends continue, it is not unlikely he will be arrested and tried soon. Contrary to repeated guarantees of Soviet-controlled Czech leaders like Party Boss Gustav Husák that "there will be no trials and no arrests for political activities in 1968 and 1969," more than two hundred citizens, mostly intellectuals, have been arrested in the first two months of this year.

Brezhnev is sending Nixon a hydrofoil boat as a gift. Nixon has given Brezhnev a Cadillac car.

PARTOUZES *IN PRAGUE?*

Partouzes in Prague? Spy scandal? An adjutant of the French military attaché's office confessed under interrogation "that he was not the only one mixed up with women," according to a secret report sent by Prague's U.S. military attaché to the Pentagon (and, apparently, also to Jack Anderson). The French government is investigating its diplomats in Prague (and the Americans are investigating Anderson), and making bedchecks "in other iron curtain countries as well, with the intention of tightening security."

Meanwhile, in a hotel just outside Prague, two Dutch businessmen are having a hot scene with a pair of Tuzex semipros, one of whom—the blonde —has a degree in philosophy but cannot obtain a teaching position because she and her father, a journalist, too militantly supported the Prague Spring. Beyond the hotel's rococo stone balconies in the Brdy forest a tiny tree—like this land a sapling in a valley of giants—yields to the soughing wind from the East.

Brave, cunning, frightened little tree. It bends and bends in order not to break.

ROME

ITALY

The basic unit of currency is the lira but because, at this writing, you'll get about 588 lire for each floating dollar, the hell with dividing a lire into anything smaller. The Italians couldn't care less how many lire you bring in, but don't leave with more than 50,000 lire or you and your lire may be floating in the Tiber.

A TYPICAL ROMAN "ORGY"

You are invited by Carlo Mariotti to attend a "typical Roman orgy" at his home, converted from an old mill, in the ancient village of Bagni di Tivoli, on the edge of a quarry that his family has worked for a century. Caesar got marble here, and left enough for Carlo to do New York's Lincoln Center.

The food and ambiance are spread informally, much like that of a Texas barbecue, though all the men, most with their wives, wear dark suits. There are some marvelous pheasants that Carlo has shot, a huge suckling pig, and great quantities of the local wine. Several film stars are here, including one whose husband does not discourage you from visually admiring her wonderful architecture. And the village priest, and an American-born doctor of Italian descent who has lived in Rome for many years. At 2 A.M. comes the highlight of the "orgy." Carlo and his wife steal into the nursery, awaken their seven-year-old son, and bring him to the patio where guests form a circle around him. Rubbing slumber grit from his eyes with the edge of his sleeping gown, Carlo Mariotti's firstborn son mugs a grin and drinks the admiration like an alcoholic let loose in a distillery. Now some of the guests kiss the little boy on the forehead. The village priest pinches his cheek. Then the little boy goes back to sleep, Carlo goes to bed with his wife, and everybody else goes home.

HYMEN-REBUILDING, AND OTHER ROMAN REMEDIES

"Take me to an orgy! It's silly. These things just happen, often after a party of friends go to a restaurant, get a bit drunk, then go to someone's house. . . . It always starts with some unknown girl taking her clothes off," observes the expatriate doctor on the forty-five-minute drive back into Rome. Of course, if anybody should know about orgies, he should. In the Roman spring the good doctor is busier than a Tel Aviv mohel. As an avocation to his practice he restores up to ten deflowered aristocratic hymens a fortnight, usually a month prior to the marriage ceremony. If there is enough membrane left (in Rome, because of the climate, "there is always *something* left"), he uses sutures of fine catgut, waits twenty days to remove them. Sometimes he resorts to alum, occasionally leeches, and other time-honored methods that Italian priests and physicians have employed since the Middle Ages. (See Albertus Magnus' sixteenth-century *Albertus Parvus* for a definitive, exhaustive list of *Signa vel probae virginitatus.*) The doctor smiles that you are surprised that such tactics survive in modern Italy, especially among the educated upper classes. In Sicily and in many villages near Rome he has seen many a bloody bedsheet hung out by the bride's proud mother after the successful wedding night. A broken hymen, whatever the cause, may still be grounds for annulment in this country: "that's why they're so big on buggery and blow-jobs." These latter are but two examples of the very Italian way of evolving the simplest solutions to the most complicated problems. "Of course, the bloody bedsheet doesn't *mean* she was a virgin. The night before the morning after, the old lady is sure to stick a chicken bladder up there. They don't even ask her. Even if the kid cries and screams she's never even fingered herself they shove it up there anyway, just to make sure."

ANOTHER KIND OF ORGY

The doctor is determined that *you* should not leave Rome a virgin. At CAFÉ CANOVA in the Piazza del Popolo, opposite the better-known ROSATI, in the secluded rear patio nestled at the foot of the Pincio gardens, you are introduced to the Marchese Camillo Casata Stampa di Soncino—"Camilliono" to his *amici.* He has been brought up with popes and kings, his family is among Italy's oldest and noblest, he has a fabulous fortune, owns a castle, forty-one racehorses, and the Mediterranean island of Zaonne, and he takes out his wallet and shows you six color photos of his wife in the nude—three solo, three fornicating with young men. She looks about twenty-eight (actually is thirty-five), a bit more extravagant in the chest and narrower at the hips than Sophia Loren, with a face somewhat prettier than Claudia Cardinale's. The Marchese, forty-five but with the vigor of forty-four, made her the Marchesa in 1958 after each had obtained divorces from previous partners. Whatever you have heard about the revolution in divorce law here, it was always possible to get a divorce if one knew the right people . . . the pope, for example. Actually Anna was a poor peasant girl who had come to Rome to "break into films" when she met the Marchese.

She's doing all right now, from the look of her husband's fabulous penthouse overlooking the Villa Borghese. You have been invited for nine and arrived precisely—no mean feat in the Rome traffic[1]—for which promptness your hostess considers you to have the *savoir-vivre* of a Visigoth. She finally emerges at ten, a statuesque five-eight clad only in white wet pants cut just so high—or is it low?—that one can glimpse the tiny fringe glistening above

[1]Best way to see Rome: hire a motor scooter from NOLO SCOOTERS, Via Marche 5, just behind Via Veneto; between $6 and $8 per day. (Motor scooters, in case you haven't tried one, are far gentler than motorcycles.)

the small gold padlock and key hanging by a chain round her hips. Actually you had to let yourself into the fantastically furnished foyer and drawing room —priceless antiques, tapestries, and paintings; an exquisite sixteenth-century tea table whose sale could keep one in Rome, in Roman style, for a year. Adriano, the butler, and the other faithful retainers have been given the night off. Good thing, too.

Games Noble Romans Play

In the huge marble bathtub, fizzing with champagne and cognac, bathe three daughters of the aristocracy; a Finnish blonde; a would-be film extra from Turku whom the Marchese found in the lobby of the REGINA HOTEL on Via Veneto; and a *sciamannata* brunette whore in Mickey Mouse T-shirt anyone can find after dark in front of ORBIS, POLISH TRAVEL AGENCY on the lower level Veneto. A man called Nono and another man called FoFo fish for them.

The Marchese is still dressing, slicking down slivers of black hair to cover the semibald moon-faced head, composing all his features—eyebrows, eyelids, mouth—to turn down at the same angle. Above his bed hangs a life-size photo of his wife posed nude on his bed. (Even in Rome this is rather overdoing it.)

Presently eight middle-aged men arrive, seven with beautiful young women —two are well-known film stars—and Guido with a toothless old hag (late of the Baths of Caracalla), who is swinging a cat (late of the Colosseum) round her head by its tail. The women gasp (not at the cat), the men laugh. They know this crazy Guido and his crazy jokes. Sure enough, waiting outside in a Hispano-Suiza, Guido has a gorgeous blonde in silver minidress and matching ballet slippers . . . her Friday-night workclothes when she hustles the corner of Via Veneto and Via Liguria (20,000 lire or roughly $34; 100 lire equal about 17¢; 1000L equal about $1.70).

The Marchese arrives, embraces his wife, caresses her bare breasts, and announces that everyone will play "auction." Everyone, that is, but himself and his wife. Though the money will go to charity, this will be exciting for three of the men have brought their *own* wives, a comparatively rare occurrence: though Rome is a bit bored with itself these days, it remains a "small town," very gossipy and, of necessity, quite discreet—that is, usually a man will attend one orgy and his wife another. The bidding begins at 1000L.

When this *scherzo* is played at the Marchese's castle or on his Mediterranean island, it often ends with a great hunt, the men pursuing the naked "foxes" through the wood. There are other games too, like "Pussycat-Tomcat," "Brothel," and "Roulette." Though she strides regally among the copulating couples, the Marchesa participates in none of it, nor does the Marchese, too busy snapping away with his camera. Off to one side, nervously fiddling a caprice with the feather on his beret, is Carlo, a young soldier the Marchese met on the beach one night last week and paid 10,000L then and there to tickle the Marchesa's *capezzoli* with his plume. This night the Marchese has laid out 52,500L for which the soldier will be expected to perform the whole concerto on the Marchesa while the nobleman makes memorable photos. Perhaps one or two guests will be invited to stay on.

How to Find Them

How might a plumber from Philadelphia or a salesman from Chicago, who knows "it's Tuesday 'cause it's Rome," get himself into such a situation? The same way the soldier did. In Rome there are few specific answers, but there are always opportunities. For openers he'd need to be young and attractive (though the Italians have a saying: "The man must be interesting, the woman must be beautiful"), and hang around the beaches and discothèques of the moment, the more obvious the places the better, where the Marchese and men like him cast their operas.

It's all over with this Marchese, however. A short time after this writing he shotgunned himself to death after murdering his wife, a twenty-five-year-old student, Massimo Minorenti, and the 470-year-old tea table behind which they were cowering. *"Amor regge senza legge"*—"Love rules without rules" —goes another Italian maxim, and the Marchese surely adored his wife and didn't much mind Massimo (whose name, incidentally, means "very large"). But Anna had broken the rules of the game for *she fell in love* with the beautiful student. ("In southern villages, many a wife peddles her pelt," notes the hymen surgeon. "Okay with her old man as long as she gets paid, but let her find a guy she likes and give it away free . . . ahhh, then it's *adultery* and her husband beats the life out of her.")

Police found a diary the Marchese di Soncino kept, recounting the affairs he had arranged for his wife, and some fifteen hundred action photos depicting some of the best people in Rome in some of the worst situations. Though among the noblest modern Romans of them all—the family's intimate ties to the Church date nearly a thousand years—the Marchese had a simple funeral, attended by only a few close friends and relatives. The Vatican sent its regrets. Above the family tomb at Soncino you read their ancient motto: "Always above reproach."

If anyone in this town knows when an orgy's going to happen, it's a man like X. A jazz pianist and singer with the mien and style of Sam, late of *Casablanca*'s "Rick's Place," X once accompanied Louis Armstrong, but has spent the past ten years in Europe, some of them playing Rome's expatriate hangouts. He and his several counterparts are always in demand for villa parties, usually receive at least an hour's notice. Through all the striptease and copulating in whipped cream, Old X just goes on playing songs like "As Time

Goes By" and "Laura." If he's invited to jump in at the finale when everyone else is nearly exhausted, he says he feels like he's being sent to the kitchen for scraps of leftovers after a big banquet.

ORGIES: HISTORY AND A RISORGIMENTO

Rome has been afflicted, or blessed, with an orgy mentality for some two thousand years, perhaps beginning with the endings at the Circus Maximus. Spectators were raised to such *isterismo* after watching the gladiators and animals do each other, a chaser somewhat more stimulating than an *aperitivo* was required. Unquestionably, Rome's emergence as a film-production center has brought a *risorgimento* in the *orgia.* The town is loaded with gorgeous young girls from all over Europe and America hoping to make it as walk-ons or take-offs. For most of them Rome is heartbreak city, one big casting couch —make that pool. By comparison, the cinema is serious business in New York or London. Here, no matter how big or how many the pictures, filmmaking is a game, an excuse to audition sixty naked girls, jump into the pool with them, and call it a day's work. Rome *still* hasn't gotten over *La Dolce Vita.* Though the film merely reflected what was already happening, it has made Via Veneto what it is today. Fellini apparently got the idea from a late 50s party at Restaurant Rugantino (now closed) where a half-Turk, half-Calabrian did an impromptu strip.

THE WORLD'S WORST HUSBAND?

Then you have the weather, an orgy climate if such a forecast exists; and the mentality of the Italian male, who will freely admit that he makes one of the world's worst husbands. There seems to lie just beneath his surface of wit and charm a pathological, animalistic desire to degrade women. Even if he's the funniest-looking bum on the Boot, he's brought up to believe he's cock of the roost, surrounded by doting females who will do everything but sleep with him in this, Europe's most matriarchal society. When he marries, there is constant warfare between Mama and daughter-in-law, the latter often no more than a semiwelcome guest in her husband's house. So when *she* has a son, she gets even by giving him all her attention. And the cycle begins again. As to making a sixty-nine with his wife, the Italian is appalled at the thought. That's the kind of thing you do with *somebody else's wife!* And there's always somebody else's wife who wants it, including his own.

Though Rome appears to be a town with more participants than spectators, if you can't find this sort of action *pronto,* blame it on the very proximate Vatican. The Romans don't care what you do, nor even how you pronounce it, as long as you don't do it in the same place twice. And you're safest of all if you do it in the streets. You won't find any regularly scheduled, organized-group-sex houses as in Paris, for example. Italy is a very Catholic country (though it's not terribly religious).

POPE, "PILL," AND PAPAL SCULPTURE

The 1929 Concordat between Pope Pius XI and Mussolini is still very much in force; by its terms Rome is a holy city and its authorities are required to maintain a certain dignity. The whorehouses were closed throughout the country in 1958, and Rome's have less chance of operating illegally than do those in Milan and Turin, among other cities. Next to Madrid, which has none, Rome's striptease clubs are the dullest of Europe's major capitals.

Not that the Church always gets its way. Two years before the 1971 Constitutional Court ruling that the Mussolini-wrought anti-birth-control law was unconstitutional, an estimated one in ten women were already on the Pill, and contraceptive devices had been freely, though illegally, available in pharmacies for years. Moreover the Church has controlled for some time, among its several commercial endeavors, a Danish firm that manufactures contraceptives. This fiscal note was omitted from Paul VI's encyclical *On Human Life.*

The Church has always shown a practical bent: Pope Clement II issued a Bull requiring prostitutes departing for Britain to leave half their property to the Church. And it hasn't always been so priggish. You don't have to journey to Pompeii to see erotic sculpture: while you're in the Vatican have a snigger at Bernini's baldachin over the Papal Altar, apparently ordered by Pope Urban VIII ("The Urbane" or "The Busy") in celebration of the birth of one of his children. His coat of arms, three bees, is set below a girl's head to depict breasts and pubes. Each of the panels shows a stage of her steadily progressing pregnancy, and the last has the face of a pleased baby. Underneath is a rendition of genitals.

PROSTITUTION

Italy has been described as a kindergarten of 55 million which stopped growing two thousand years ago and remains immature in any civilized activity—marriage, business, war, or love—that requires the participation of more than one individual. Observe the anarchy that is prostitution in Rome, for example. There are discothèques with bedrooms in Turin, Teutonically efficient brothels in Milan, and horrible ones in Naples, a colorful waterfront of whores in Genoa, and gondolas of them in Venice; but in no Western European capital are there *more* whores, more *ugly* whores, more *over-*

priced *ugly whores* (and *more beautiful ones* too!), and more *confusione* than in Italy's capital—ironic, considering that when Italians have established themselves as procurers in countries other than their own they have shown a certain talent for organization. But then, it is rare to find a Roman emigrant. Nobody ever leaves this town.

The Merlin Law and the Origin of "Syphilis"

When, in 1958, Senator Lina Merlin's law closing the brothels was finally enacted after ten years' lobbying, she insisted that she wasn't against prostitution per se, merely against the State's acting as Big Madam. (She didn't bother to mention that the Church owned much bordello property.) But what a *messa* Lina made! There were then perhaps three hundred thousand prostitutes in Italy; today a local newspaper estimates more than 1 million, a hundred thousand in Rome alone (this can't be true, but several other sources concur). Italian men experienced a great psychological trauma at the closing of the houses, especially the proud young laboring class, "forced now to make love like dogs in the streets." Moreover, the VD rate has since risen some 200 percent; the girls are no longer subject to State-controlled medical inspection. (It was an Italian, Girolamo Fracastoro, who originated the word "syphilis" in a 1530 poem, *"Syphilis, sive Morbus Gallicus,"* whose hero, a Greek shepherd, Syphilus, is cursed with the disease for doing the god Apollo dirty.)

The Good Old Brothels

There were some twenty-five large houses in Rome up to 1958, with about thirty girls each, and many smaller establishments; 5000L did nicely in the better places behind Via del Tritone and Via del Corso, 1000 to 1500L in the laborers' and soldiers' brothels. Many of these houses still exist, a couple in and around Via Capo le Case, for example, used by Via Veneto whores and their clients. They remain, to all purposes—though not attentions—brothels, but to say they lack their former amenities is a most un-Italian understatement. In some the waiting rooms were like smart doctors' offices; in others you'd have encountered veils, spangles, mirrors, champagne, lots of bright-red velvet and taffeta, and marble bidets. Today you're lucky if there is a toilet, much less one that flushes.

An estimated 80 percent of Italian men can recall that their first sexual experiences were with prostitutes of one sex or another. Some sentimentalists still carry the little plastic or ivory markers *("marchette")* that the brothel cashiers gave to the girls as proof of a turned trick. The expression "to make a *marchette"* is still used to connote any girl gone on the game. With much *sentimentalismo* does the middle-aged Roman recall the atmosphere and smell of the old houses, a compound of perfume, cigar smoke, and perspiration that Romans have called "the sweat of love" since Seneca (3 B.C.–A.D. 65) observed it emanating from emerging brothel patrons of the day and Juvenal sniffed it clinging to the Empress Messalina.

Bologna Girls

The attitude of some of the 1950s madams was itself worth the price of admission. There would be uproarious and dramatic descriptions of each girl before she passed through the parlor for inspection. Various girls specialized in this, that, and some other thing, many known for the regional *specialità* of their birthplaces. Bologna girls have always enjoyed a splendid reputation: their mouths are said to be the biggest and most sensuous in Italy. Even today, no Italian plane will fly directly over Bologna—they steer pretty clear of the whole Emilia region if they can help it—for fear of being forced down by the incredible suction. (Ironically, many Emiliana women are married to ship captains, pursers, and/or pilots.)

Massages and Manicures

"If there is anyone who thinks that young men should be forbidden to make love, even to prostitutes, he is certainly a man of stern righteousness, that cannot be denied, but he is out of touch not only with the free life of today, but even with the code and concessions which our fathers accepted. For when was that not customary? When was it blamed? When was it not allowed? When was it not lawful to do what is a lawful privilege?" observed the otherwise rather stoic Cicero some two thousand years ago. Following the enactment of the Merlin law, then, Italy, and particularly Rome, has acquired as many manicurists and masseuses as it has always had priests and whores. So ardent were these girls, and many boys, in wishing to attract top clientele by being at the *top* of the classified columns, that many changed their names to begin with "A." The newspapers countered by assigning letters of the alphabet to the advertiser—the higher up the alphabet, the more expensive the ad (and the more the manicurist will charge her clients—from 8000 to 30,000L). Thus in a recent Thursday issue of *Il Messaggero* you noted some 138 offerings[2] under *"Massaggi Cure Est"* ranging from:

A.A.A.A.A.A.A.A.A.   A.A.A.A.A.A.A.A.A.   A.A.A.A.A.A.A.A.A.A.A.A.A.A.A.A.   A.A.A.A.A. BRAVISSIME manicures ambiente tranquillo. Piazza Barberini ore 10–21. . . .

and:

---

[2] How many of these were "legitimate" could not be determined, but of six contacted, all offered sexual as well as therapeutic services.

A.A.A.A.A.A.A.A.A. A.A.A.A.A.A.A.A.A. A.A.A.A.A.A.A.A.A.
A.A.A.A.A.A.A.A. A.A.A.A. ESPERTISSIME MASSAGGIATRICI anche domicilio
[also makes house calls]. . . .

to:

Z. BRAVISSIME manicure ambiente elegante zona Casilina. . . .

The text of the ads was, until recent police pressure, somewhat livelier, many girls forthrightly stating their Bolognese origins and other easy virtues. Now, overzealous copywriters are limited to reassuring you on such fine points as that your manicure will be performed *"senza portiere"* or *"independente!"* Romans having been dodgy of porters and doormen since Napoleon III organized the concierges as spies. (By law concierges are still charged to report all untoward events immediately and to tell the cops the *whole* truth when it is demanded.) If an ad includes *"nuova,"* it's less consequent that the girl is very young or even "new" in town than that she is a virgin who will receive you only with her mouth or bottom. Some of the notices have been running for several years, and even in the unlikely event that addresses may change, phone numbers usually remain the same and the move is duly announced: *"AAAAAAAAAAAAAAAAAAAAAAAAAA* [etc.]*GIOVANISSIME Manicures, telefono 86–32–12 da via della Isole ——trasferitesi adjacente via Malta 6A indipendente 10–23 (Corso Trieste)."*

Sure enough, some three years after the above change of address notice ran, you phoned 86–32–12 and thereupon visited the ground floor of the lovely villa at Via Malta 6A to be greeted by a maid who bade you cool your heels on the Oriental rugs of the handsome, neo-Mediterranean parlor. Presently a rather tubby young blonde emerged to offer the 10,000L lasagne manicure. Answering *"AAAAA[etc.] MANICURE, abilissima 11–21 Corso Trieste, 84–11–14, ambiente signorile,"* brings you to nearby Via Gradisca 5, ground floor, and a similarly sumptuous villa where a honey blonde with Slavic face meets you in minislip and microbra, spreads her properties on the tiled mosaic floor next to a Monopoly set, and requests 30,000L ($51) for an hour's *amore—costoso,* but someone's got to pay for the huge pink chaise and matching vases, easy chairs, and giant stuffed poodles, not to mention the sulphurous maid. No phone listed for *"MANICURE, viale Parioli"* etc. (one of several along here), just come ahead to be greeted at the gate by a slim brunette tiger in silk loincloth. No prices quoted through the iron grillwork barring the chalk-walled patio, but worth a trip to Parioli just to dine at one of the excellent nearby terrace restaurants (complete dinners for two from 3500L, plenty of embassy secretaries living in the neighborhood to enjoy them with).

Call Girls and Whores on Wheels

With such action advertised in the classifieds of papers like *Il Messaggero,* *Il Tempo,* and, occasionally, the *Rome Daily American,* it's surprising that Roman society gets so scandalized when the police break up a call-girl ring like that of "Madame Fury" or, recently, an organization (perhaps *that's* the dirty word) comprising a hundred and sixty students and wealthy housewives which allegedly operated under the direction of Madam Anna from six apartments scattered throughout the better quarters of the city, with fees ranging from 50,000 to 200,000L. Perhaps it was simply that the latter followed so closely on the heels of newspaper and courtroom allegations that a young film actress, daughter of a prominent Vigna Clara quarter resident, and described as the "new Sophia Loren"—was "top filly in the stable" of several well-to-do Saudi Arabian oil sheiks and a Libyan prince who were said to have flown regularly to Rome with 300,000Lire offers she could not refuse.

At lunch in some of the city's finest restaurants, some of the city's finest *ragazze squillo* (call girls) may find you in the toilet, pass their phone number, and Maserati you to sumptuous apartments where dwell moderately wealthy elderly ladies, kept that way by letting a bedroom or two for 4000L the hour; and that'll be 50,000 to 100,000L for the tootsie. Some of these *ragazze* are among Rome's almost three thousand motorized prostitutes, most of whom are financed by wealthy *protettori.*

Brothels and B-girls

The easiest way to make a Roman brothel is to accent the "i" in "*casino*"; hit the "o" and you have a gambling house. The distinction may be academic, for though Rome has several of each—the latter considered highly fashionable—the police would close any whose addresses appeared in print. (It is even illegal to play the old Neapolitan game of *morra*—"choosing"—because so many deaths have resulted from arguments about who held up how many fingers.) Of the former there are at least four, combining sadism and voyeurism, which cater to old men who, for 5000 to 20,000L, may watch secret beatings of dogs and women through one-way mirrors.

Avoid the strip clubs and nightclubs, especially those that maintain "porters" dressed in dark suits who feign that they themselves are foreigners, then literally "carry" you inside for a drink and pocket up to 50 percent of the pickings. Because the *entraîneuse* work permit is the easiest to get (followed by that of pension girl, airline clerk, and model) and because so many attractive young girls are drawn to Rome by film "opportunities" and/or the "Sunshine Syndrome," you'll find a virtual United Nations of B-girls working the clip clubs at salaries of 5000 to 8000L a night—not much in this eternally tempting and extravagant city. Some hang on . . . too long, some jump out of windows. Most are sick of maulings. Many are part-time students or really serious about the cinema, but no matter how much you can produce, none may leave the premises until the 4 or 5 A.M. closing. So make a tea date for next afternoon. (*Never* choose an Italian B-girl: she's more likely wired to a *protettore* than her English or Swedish counterpart.) Bed with one of the Czech, Finnish or four English hostesses you met while on the prowl with an Italian-American film cowboy will cost you anything from 50,000L to a dawn walk in the Forum. You can bet it wouldn't cost the cowboy more than spaghetti for his horse.

Street Scenes

By 10 P.M. thousands of the most aggressive streetwalkers in Europe prowl Rome. The most active markets are in the gloomy hard-bitten arteries just west of the main railway station, particularly where Via Cavour begins at Via Giovanni Giolitti and intersects Via Principe Amadeo. The bleached redheads and blondes range from twenty-five to thirty-five years, from *grassoccia* to *grassa,* from 7000 to 12,000L (the *squallida pensione* included) and have lots of hair on their legs. And plenty *mezzani* in the shadows. Same productions in and around Piazza della Repubblica. In the lesser-known Piazza dell' Esquilino, facing Santa Maria Maggiore Cathedral, they're miraculously younger, slimmer, prettier, and cheaper (6000 to 8000L). And cheaper yet behind the church (5000 to 7000L), site of the "Constantine Miracle." Snow fell in August. As one proceeds north toward Via Veneto, prices rise (10 to 15,000L) and so do penises, for some of the talent along the Via del Tritone and Via Sistina is smashing. (And is smashing your windshield if you haggle too long.)

Grab a seat at CAFÉ DE PARIS or, if its full, DONEY'S, or one of the other Via Veneto cafés. Eugenia Sheppard has observed, "The French invent a fashion, the Americans buy it, but it takes the Italians to wear it well." Don't miss *any* of Rome's clichés: they're what you've come for. Imperative is the *aperitivo* or the 11 P.M. *sfoggio* of gorgeously eccentric humanity along Via Veneto whose *scintillare* and *sovraeccitazione* are packed into such a comparatively small area that the promenade is even more exhilarating than the Champs-Élysées. (But for all its cosmopolitanism, as Barzini has noted, the Veneto is also merely the "enlargement of the *corso* of any Italian small town.") Note the *bambola* in chinchilla coat, pool-table-green eyepatch and lavender kid microskirt. How can you ignore her! Roman terrace chairs show a lotta leg; they're schemed so that a woman's *parti posteriore* sits up to 30 degrees below her knees, just one more triumph of Italian design in the marriage of function and esthetics.

No one's saying that the Sicilian whores own the Veneto area, but even big tortonis like Gianfresco Ciacerci and his brother, proprietors of the classic EDEN HOTEL, have problems getting the Roman police to move the tarts away from the street. The hustlers ask 20 to 15,000L (asking 20, taking 15 when business is off, including the room, but *not* in the Eden). Friday night is formal night at the corner of Via Liguria or Via Ludovisi and the Veneto. Three of the best-looking blondes south of Milan are ready for ball games in ballgowns; 20,000L dropping to 16,000 if you *mercanteggiare,* or after 2 A.M., or whenever it gets below 45°. (And it does so often: in winter Rome's climate can be unexpectedly unpleasant.) Fifteen taking 11 *(più la camera)* in front of HOTEL MAJESTIC, and swinging in the swings outside ANGELO DI ROMA's nightclub.[3] Nearby "special" hotels in and near Via Capo le Case charge 3 to 4000L for the short-haul room, including the condom, which Rome's whores seem to have reluctantly accepted now that anti-birth-control statutes are withering away. These hotels will demand your passport, though perhaps not the girl's (who must be twenty-one).

There are many other street scenes, including that of Piazza Augusto Imperatore whose primarily blond teen-agers shout *"dieci mille"* at tourists too exhausted for love: they've just watched ALFREDO's son Armando "achieve," rather than simply make or create, fettuccine. Less well known to visitors (except those who drive by on their way to the far-flung Hilton), some of the youngest and prettiest hitch-hookers (8 to 10,000L) work the Tiber's west bank along Lungotevere della Vittoria at Piazza del Fante. Very nice at sundown, but avoid 7:30 P.M. when the sandwich boy brings the girls' snacks.

"Grandmothers" and Girls

The police are said to have run the whores out of beautiful Villa Borghese gardens (actually it was the homosexuals), but Rome certainly has no dearth of bucolic and historic locations. By night the ancient Baths of Caracalla is the largest *bordello al fresco* in the world. It's whores also have a long history, some are among the oldest in Italy, and conveniently toothless: 1 to 2000L. (Such a matriarchy is Italy, geritophilia is rather an endemic, if not epidemic, vice. Benjamin and Masters, in *The Prostitute and Society,* recall a "ring" of "grandmother prostitutes" which catered almost exclusively to "young men" before police called a halt some years ago.) Though stray homosexuals and cats have appropriated the Colosseum's interior by night, 4-to-6000L handmaidens and some who will even copulate (8 to 10,000L) grace its perimeters. More of the same on the Appian Way, *siesta* to sundown. And if you crave a quick *spuntino* on the way to Milan or Florence,

---

[3]The whores have no connection with any establishment mentioned. They simply roam wherever they please and congregate at the busiest locations.

just before the Autostrada tollgate wait rail-sitters—tough or tender depending on the quarry—fresh-faced, sweet-limbed country girls, their pubes not yet grown or plucked clean by the gnarly fingernails of truckmen. (Nearly every long-distance Italian truck has a bed in it—and hair under the fenders —fair warning, or promise, to hitchhiking Michigan schoolmarms.[4]) Recalling the *lupae* or "she-wolves" of Ancient Rome, for 2 to 4000L, including "God's room," she'll take you hard and fast, high on the worn flats of little hills with nothing between her thirteen-to-eighteen-year-old body and the hoary, fast-eroding earth but a flimsy patch of cardboard framed by fifty filthy *gomme*.

GAY ROME?

If you must know all about The Italians, reread Barzini's bestseller of the same name. But in its exhaustive 783-item index, between "Abruzzi" and "Zurich," you'll find no entries for "prostitution" or "homosexuality" and precious few references to those subjects in the text. These may be omissions of the obvious, for apparently Italy (along with Holland) has the lowest minimum age of consent (sixteen) for homosexual sexual relations of any Western European country with the exception of Luxembourg (fourteen). This is far more a recognition of *che sarà sarà* than any government program to encourage the mating of little boys and old men.

The Romans owe a great deal to the culture of ancient Greece, but any historic predilection for what the French call *le vice italien* (and the Italians call "the French vice") is as much rooted in an indiscriminate adoration of the anus *per se* as any predisposition toward the members of one's own sex.[5] In February, 1963, for example, *L'Osservatore Romano* warned that "Women's clothes that are too revealing from behind might rekindle a desire for marriage in some homosexual sodomites." Be that as it may, travelers have always remarked on the extraordinary incidence of frank pederasty in Italy, as in this seventeenth-century account of the Venetian scene by D. M. Le Sieur *(Nouveau Voyage du Levant,* The Hague, 1694; as quoted by Henriques, *Prostitution in Europe and the Americas):*

". . . however easy may be the commerce with women and however beautiful they may be, would you believe it but the Venetians mistrust them, and attach themselves rather to a boy, even if he be as ugly as a monkey, rather than the most pleasant girl. It is the dominant vice of the nation.

---

[4]In 1970 Miss Corinne Orr, the Montreal television personality, had all she could do to fend off the passionate attentions of a man dressed in a Santa Claus outfit. The incident occurred in the heart of Rome, in broad twilight. On Christmas Eve, no less!

[5]The family of Pope Sixtus IV formally requested permission to indulge in sodomy, and His Holiness is said to have granted it. (See W.W. Sanger, *History of Prostitution,* New York, 1919.)

. . . There are even those who go to the infamous excess of paying porters and gondoliers to bestialize themselves. All their activities are directed towards this end [*sic*], and where in France conversation between young men may revolve round the love of women, here it revolves round that between men. The Turks are also active in this direction, but I do not think more so than the Italians. The Monks also have a terrible reputation as regards this, as well as regards women.''

Indeed, in March, 1971, Magistrate Luciano Infelisi, with the aid of one thousand five hundred policemen and one general, investigated some three thousand ONMI state-supported nurseries and orphan homes in Rome and environs. In many of those institutions directed by Roman Catholic priests boys gave vivid details of their hyperactive homosexual relations. In one instance a priest was accused of sexual violence against his charges, he being the tutor charged with their "sexual education." (Italians consider pupil participation far more edifying than the puny lectures of the pedantic Swedes.) Corporal punishment is widespread, one priest forcing his confessees to kneel at his knees, place their heads between them and have their sins squeezed out until they faint.

ROMANS ROAM EVERYWHERE

Understanding full well the appetites of their fellow citizens, Rome police not surprisingly, discourage any designated, exclusively homosexual bars, cafés, or clubs. Like all Romans, homosexuals roam literally everywhere, though certain favored rendezvous swing in and out of fashion. All situations cited are mixed. Thus, late at night, you may encounter some lesbians (not nearly the factor here they are in Paris) and gay boys at several *otherwise straight* discothèques and cafés. A very smart, swift crowd—many of the *figli di papà* ("spoiled rich kids") are indistinguishable from the elegantly clad peasants making good their escape from the provinces—gather among the Hollywood international smoothies at Via Veneto's St. James Bar or those of nearby Flora Hotel Bar.

In Rome recall Stendhal *On Love,* specifically on Italy: ''. . . fortunate in being left to the inspiration of the moment . . . where a true sense of honor opens the road to a false sense of honor.'' Thus one season (or even one night) a certain café terrace becomes *"di moda"* and its neighbor the next. The homosexual enjoys a *tartuffo* in Piazza Navona as much as the next man, and for the price of one (about 450L on the terrace, 300 inside) will offer a discreet fricatreat with one hand while he consumes the delicious concoction of ice cream, bittersweet chocolate, and cherries with the other. And in this case the right hand couldn't give less of a damn what the left one is doing.

Among Rome's many floating scenes, check out: Tony's (Via Avignonesi

10A), MADISON BAR (Via Niccolò da Tolentino 76), and BARETTO (Via del Babuino 122). And the TURKISH BATHS at Via Poli 11.

Certain other saunas keep alive certain ancient Roman traditions and don't turn your backside to anyone you don't fancy at LA MARINELLA BEACH.

TRANSVESTITES AND TRANSSEXUALS

Though any Roman is too Roman to show up regularly at the same place for any dependable length of time, this is not true of the homosexual, the transvestite, the homosexual-transvestite, and the transsexual *prostitute*. Thus, at this writing, you need a program to identify the various species of whore (3 to 8000L) who pitch camp and woo in Villa Borghese gardens by night, all looking as uniformly innocent as Italian-American trattoria waiters. By day, when they doff their bright-red shirts and black vests, they make excellent guides (1 to 2000L) to the city.

Why not take in GALLERIA BORGHESE, for example and catch Bernini's "Rape of Persephone" and Canova's erotic carving of Paolina Borghese.

Motoring toward Trastevere along Lungotevere Vaticano, in the shadow of Castel Sant' Angelo, many foreign brakes screech in the night (after 11 P.M.) at the sight of the gorgeous-looking blonde in flaming red cocktail dress, posing in Piazza della Rovere. On closer inspection, this sultry Siren of the Tiber—who has worked these shores, virtually at the same spot in the same red dress, for four years—has the face of a Madonna, the hands of a *stivatore*, a blond wig over a black crewcut, and the genitals of the Pope knows what. *"Dieci mille,"* coos the *dolce voce,* as softly aromatic as Rome's silken summer air. Much sniffing of tailpipes among little Fiats and riverside hustlers hereabouts and on the opposite side of the Tiber. There is some difference of opinion as to whether it is strictly legal for a man to appear publicly dressed as a woman in Rome. The discussion is academic, for the police do on occasion arrest transvestite prostitutes for notorious acts of solicitation, only to release them the following morning after a night of rigorous examinations —whereupon the scandal sheets publish a juicy photo of the just-released culprit with captions like "GEORGETTE! She's available again!"

The Colosseum: Wolves and Cats

For dwellers in a city founded by wolves, Romans have a pathologic antipathy toward animals. A priest explained this: "Perhaps this is because Our Lord had so much to say about human beings he had little breath to pass along many words on animals. Now you take the Germans and the English," sighed the good father with a gesture that implied he couldn't, "they have very strong feelings for animals, but as for people. . . ." Anyway, by sundown the interior of the Colosseum is a *manicomio* of screeching, yowling, tailless cats and bloody human behinds; 2 to 5000L. If you've become sufficiently Romanized to despise cats (they're free), climb the Spanish Steps by moonlight (2 to 6000L) or explore the CIRCO MASSIMO or COLLE OPPIO, ENGELS-BURG, and PINCIO parks. For that matter something may always find you if you give improper vibrations along the Veneto (8 to 15,000L), especially in the public toilets there or those at Via Venti Settembre; or perhaps in the rears of various cinemas.

Of course, many homosexuals advertise their services in the massage and manicure classifieds. If you can't tell whether the distinctions between *"Massaggiatore," "Massaggiatori,"* and *"Massaggiatrice"* are personal or grammatical, neither can some Roman compositors (Italians are fine on plurals but have some trouble with gender). Play safe and phone the operation that advertises in English: "Masseur, young, via Quattro Fontane, also client's home." The boy who answers speaks only Italian but an interpreter comes on the line: "Be assured, *signore,* he is a young and beautiful boy and can make love in all the languages. Whatever you like, five thousand lire."

ROME AND THE SINGLE GIRL

Some of the homosexuals must be doubling in brass, for the woman traveling alone in Rome has no difficulty attracting a man. Getting rid of him may pose somewhat of a problem, however. One recommended *tattica* is quickly to get yourself eight months pregnant and run into a jewelry store. Few except the most ardent of the very young and very old will follow you under these conditions.

Though women's civil rights have drastically improved recently in the eyes of the law, less has changed in the hearts of men. A late-1969 ruling finally abolished two penal code provisions that had allowed women to be jailed up to two years for adultery but provided no penalties against men unless they kept "a concubine in the conjugal home or notoriously elsewhere." (Fat chance of conviction, even among the exhibitionists of Rome.) *Civil Cattolica,* Italy's leading Jesuit publication, attacked the ruling, suggesting it would lead to "murders of honor." But such crimes have been commonplace for centuries anyway. In a March, 1971, case, for example, a Catania, Sicily, court gave a mere five years to a schoolteacher who shot to death a university professor for making love to the teacher's daughter. Though the verdict was widely criticized in the north (as usual), Sicilian judges and lawyers, equally true to form, praised it as preserving a "precious and ancient" custom which combats moral corruption.

La mano morta, "the dead hand," remains very much alive, and you're as likely to be pinched in the cinema (or the *capezzolo*) as at a fancy Via Margutta gallery opening. (The *capezzoli* are your nipples, *cara.*) A well-traveled Italian filmmaker explains everything: "You stare at a woman, as I am doing it to her now, in America she will think she has a new mole or her hem is off. Here it is an art to convey to her, and to her husband, that it is but a gesture of admiration." Recently a party of British schoolgirls and their teacher were so badly mauled by Italian gestures that they ran home and raised hell about it on the BBC. The cordial reply from the Italian Embassy assured that this affection was only a "well-deserved tribute to British womanhood." Which recalls Dean Acheson's recollection that "Even as a boy looking at pictures of Boadicea, Britain's warrior queen (circa A.D. 60), one could see that she wore a brass bra as protection against the Romans— where it may still be needed from what I hear. . . ."[6]

Of course, some women come to Rome with no bra. Others proceed more cautiously, availing themselves of the services of a charming escort who at least avoids clinches until first names are exchanged. Many women have learned that some of the most respectable travel agencies provide some of the most unrespectable and charming guides. About 6500L for four hours. Other women avail themselves of the advice of handsome, sensitive, multilingual Via Condotti area hairdressers.

THE ITALIAN WOMAN

In the Reggio Calabrian night a young Romeo (that's his first name) has allegedly kidnapped his girlfriend, aided by his father. The boy and girl are each fourteen. A twenty-year-old breaks a thousand years of Sicilian tradition by marrying the man whom she loves rather than the rejected rich man's son who kidnapped and raped her in the time-honored courtship-where-all-else-fails Sicilian-style. (Lots of dashes in Rome, and everyone seems to speak in italics.) The community is furious, not with the boy for violating the girl but with the girl for violating the code. Such happenings remain common in the south, and they thus compound the tribute to Italian women who remain among the most justifiably poised, proud, and uninhibited females on earth.

Prudish about sex like Spanish women, hypocritical like some Americans, vulgar or priggish like some English, blasé like the French? *Giammai!* Earthy and ready are Italian women. The blushing bride may be scandalized by the dirty joke, but she frankly enjoys it. Likely she is even more passionate than her husband, hence the *imposed* restraint. No fashion does the Italian male wear so gracelessly as horns. *Never* make a fist with your pinky and forefinger

[6]The Via Veneto "precinct" police station is at Via Toscana 5; tel. 46–42–30. The police have recently launched a drive against the Roman wolves. But in spring, 1972, a 21-year-old Yugoslav *died* as she fought to escape the advances of a young man and was accidentally run over by an auto.

extended at an Italian male—the classic cuckold accusation—even at 95 mph, going in the opposite direction.

Where to Find Her

Though you won't seduce as many as in Milan, you'll meet far more natives in Rome than in Madrid. Again the most obvious places, *and times,* are the best: ROSATI in Piazza del Popolo, 7 to 9 or 11 P.M.; Piazza Navona at midnight; Trastevere when the PASQUINO cinema lets out. Perhaps in this year's discothèque: DOM (Via Savoia 6). Or last year's: NUMERO UNO (Via Lucullo 2). Or the year before's: SCARABOCCHIO; or even the raucous, monstrous PIPER CLUB (as much a curiosity as the Catacombs; Via Tagliamento 9). Or in old, old favorites like the *boîte* ROUGE ET NOIR (Via del Vantaggio 47), where diamonds and dungarees are always in fashion. Owner-pianist Greco Americo looks like Ralph Branca, sings "I Like New York in June" in a voice half Dean Martin, half the late Joe E. Lewis, without a trace of Italian accent —and speaks no English. Nor do some of the *jeunesse dorée,* nor the Arab beauty belting out "Ha-va-na-gila. . . ," but here you talk with your hands anyway.

LOVERS' ROME

"In its lifestyle Rome is the most baroque of capitals; even our clouds are baroque," muses the Countess Maria Gottilega over an apéritif at CAFFÈ GRECO, a trite, but no less suitable place to bring, or find, a countess or model, for Via Condotti 86 is in the heart of Rome's very-high-fashion area. Ask for Peppino, a waiter who has been here since the drawing room (now available for private parties of ten or more) was a billiard parlor forty years ago. Greco may be pat, but if it was good enough for romantics like Liszt, Bizet, Keats, Buffalo Bill, and Orson Welles, it's good enough for you. For the first-time visitor the romance of Rome is that it is a city of clichés come true. Even your arrival by airport bus takes a remarkably scenic and historic route, capped by a thrilling zip around the Colosseum and the Forum. If you're with someone you love, do all the obvious things. Take the horsedrawn hansom (*carrozzella* —and they are metered) through the Villa Borghese by night. Throw three coins into that fountain. No matter how many guidebooks tell you not to miss HOSTARIA DELL'ORSO (Via di Monte Brianzo 93; 56–42–21), don't miss it. Dante didn't, when this was a fourteenth-century inn, nor have Richard Nixon, Peter Lorre, the late Aga Khan, Taylor, Burton, and Cardinal Spellman (now *there's* an orgy!) since its conversion into Italy's most elegant *boîte.* (Note: Hostaria dell'Orso was sold in 1971. Hope the new owners maintain founder Antonio Prantera's high standards.) The "Cabala" room is appropriate for intrigues and dancing; and if you are alone, get the lay of the city over a chess game with Frank—Bogart did during the filming of *The Barefoot Contessa*—bartender of the luxurious "Blue Room," whose forest-green walls and ancient beamed ceiling suggest the inside of a handsomely tooled Florentine jewelry box. Even more romantic is L'Arciliuto (Piazza Monte Vecchio 5); your host was a former guitarist at Hostaria dell'Orso. Reservations imperative: 65–94–19.

"LOVERS' MOTELS"

A man alone in Rome, and a woman too, should be apprised that one has no problems having a newfound friend spend the night in the hotel room *if* it is a suite or has a sitting room. Although your guest's passport may be requested even in the several motels on the outskirts of the city, it is the rare clerk, especially if he's greased 1000L, who compares passport signatures with the illegible scrawls in the register book. Though comparatively remote, many of these motels are sumptuously furnished, and what's twenty-five miles to a man in love, especially in a Ferrari? Among the best, especially for young couples, according to the beauteous Letizia Paolozzi (and in her book *Roma-Sette*) of that glamorous family, is Bela Motel, on the Via Cassia route (*not* the Autostrada) to Florence. Reservations: 699–02–32.

EXPATRIATES

On the prowl for an orgy, high-class *case di appuntimenti,* or pizza, a stranger could do worse than consult among the knowledgeable American expatriate colony.

Considering Rome's tremendous economic, industrial, and political importance in the modern world, not to mention the climate, the United States maintains a massive embassy and staff—about fifteen hundred employees, perhaps seven hundred young and female—right on the Veneto, of course.

You'll find many loose tongues (no one listens, everyone talks) among Rome's bittersweet deadbeats: the fading actresses, career girls, divorcees; the *Catch-22* old soldiers, some of whom haven't seen the States since the early 1940s and still use the "lingo" of that long-lost time; and the inevitable "filmmakers"—all of them living variously, in the soporific limbo of languid Rome, on dreams, alimony, small inheritances, or whoredom, gone not so much to pot as to alcohol. But though Rome is such a marvelous place to live and therefore such a difficult place to work, one must be good at something. At least be a good drunk if you decide to stay on or some of your more energetic fellow expatriates will pass the hat, buy your plane ticket, and ship you right back to Dallas, Denver or wherever—it's happened.

No one will ever starve in this town, it is said, at least not on Thanksgiving when expatriate Jerry Chierchio—who once managed King Saud's kitchen—throws a massive free turkey dinner at his LUAU Oriental bar-restaurant as a gesture of thanks to the city. Rome has been good to Jerry and Jerry has been good to Rome. Whoever is playing piano, Via Sardegna 34, with its meld of Rome's very lively foreign press corps, talky girls, movie stars, and press agents has the aspect of another of those Bogart cafés. Some of the newsmen know Rome like a dirty book, and there's a "Six Hours to Jilly's" sign. Lots has happened in the basement of the Savoia Hotel (Via Ludovisi 15) in DAVE'S DIVE, though former boxer and actor Davey Crowley, whose fund of information comes at you in rapid-fire shifts from low Cockney to high Etonian to Irish brogue, is currently resting from it all back in Manchester. Davey remembers the night those two Arabs plotted here to hijack that Israeli down to Egypt in a steamer trunk; and, as in several other bars in town, Burton and Taylor spent some time here too. Prices kept low, for this is a place of regulars; nice, even male–female ratio. More of the same plus dancing at OLD VIENNA (Via degli Artisti 25), tending to Germans and Scandinavians. And some Africans too: "Black is beautiful in Rome," noted one delightful and delighted black girl met here. "If you're black, brother, Rome always says, 'Come back, come back!' "

Vernon Jarret of the estimable GEORGE'S (Via Marche 7) runs a morning cooking school for some of the handsomest matrons in town when he's not impresarioing this, one of Rome's finest restaurants. Lots of good stuff about diplomats and countesses to be learned in the bar.

Paul and Ben in the HILTON SAUNA will make you feel like a million lire, and charge near that for the course, but it's well worth it if you can pump them on the movie scene. Stewardesses from TWA, Olympic, and Canadian Pacific, among other airlines, bunk at the Hilton, which has a magnificently romantic situation, high on Monte Mario overlooking the city, and in case you couldn't care less, a bellman who assures you that as long as she shows her passport at the desk, a manicurist or masseuse has no problem visiting your room here.

A poor man's Hassler is PENSIONE SCALINATA DI SPAGNA (673–006), directly across Piazza Trinità dei Monti from that classic hostelry at the top of the Spanish Steps. Several rooms with a view of the steps, only about 3000L per person, tax, service, and breakfast included. Or strike up an acquaintance with one of the several charming French students who run the place. Later have morning coffee at CAFFÈ JARDINS in the nearby Pincio gardens, or at BABINGTON TEA ROOM (Piazza di Spagna 23). Founded in 1896 by Anna Babington, descended from Anthony, whose property was awarded to Sir Walter Raleigh after the former was drawn and quartered for a plot against Elizabeth I. This is the place King Farouk lost some of that youthful svelte. Plum pudding.

"DO YOUR OWN THING":
DRUGS AND ELIXIR VITAE

In fine weather the Spanish Steps are one vast jewelry bazaar whose motto, like so many of Europe's great plazas, has become *"Facere Rem Suam"*—rather free Latin for "doing your own thing." Standing at the foot of the steps, boldly eyeing the often pantyless artisans doing it, are many grateful natives. Mood music supplied by a wandering black saxophonist, who plays nothing composed after 1936. The steps are also the best and most obvious place to purchase hash. But be careful—Italian police and courts draw little distinction between users and peddlers. If accused, your pretrial incarceration may last a year or more, and Rome's jails, as someone has observed of prisons the world over, cure but one thing: heterosexuality. For years Italy was simply a way-station for distribution of drugs from the Mid- and Far East and Africa to America. The authorities seem to have displayed little concern until Italian youths suddenly became users. Thus, for years the black "ivory" carved elephants of hash and the heroin-injected tomatoes and oranges passed through in easy transit; in all 1967 less than 9 pounds of hash were confiscated by the Rome police. But during 1970, 450 pounds were found, 132 of them on a discothèque barge in the Tiber which youths had converted into *The Drug Boat.* In 1972 a huge drug scandal swept the city, allegedly involving some of the most prominent members of the international set.

Meanwhile, adults have also become hooked on sex elixirs like the Roumanian-made "Gerovital." Though there are at least four identical Italian-made potions, only the illicitly smuggled Roumanian stuff will do. Because it is illegal, for Italians it must somehow be better. Incidentally, Italy is the only Western European country that does not honor pharmaceutical patents. Any of the country's thirteen hundred pharmaceutical companies is at liberty to steal and sell anybody else's formula.

SKELETONS, SPOOKS, AND SÉANCES

Noise, of course, is the true opiate of Romans. Or is it life? And, like their Spanish cousins, they are very interested in death. If you've tired of the Catacombs, visit the merry monks of COEMETERIUM CAPUCCINORUM at the foot of the Via Veneto near the lively discothèques and terraces of Piazza Barberini. In the church's bone basement the good friars have tucked away some hilarious caricatures and collages constructed from parts of the skeletons and skulls of their dead brothers. Or attend a séance at NAVONA 2000, a pseudo-spooky cave in Via Sora off the Piazza Navona. Most every evening, from 10 P.M. to 3 A.M., Marissa tells fortunes in a stalactited antechamber next to a candlelit coffin that contains the "corpse" of a baby doll. Meanwhile, by the light of a single red bulb in the *sanctum sanctorum,* husband Fulvio conducts very scary séances, choosing volunteers from among the audiences of forty or more who pay 3000L per session. Though a confirmed skeptic, you watched horrified, during one four-hour session, as the large round table did indeed move all round the room, carrying with it six entranced participants. Three young ladies and one old man fainted.

THE HAPPY MEDIUM

Back in Piazza Navona you met one of Rome's several private mediums, a handsome brunette of about thirty-five who specializes in recalling dead wives, husbands, and lovers. (None had any connection with Navona 2000.) She requires up to a week's notice, around 200,000L, and a vivid description of the departed in order to muster her full dark powers so that the succubi will hear the call. You are then at liberty to communicate, verbally or sexually, with your departed loved one who, on close inspection, bears a striking resemblance to the medium herself, or a prostitute found otherwise on the Via Veneto for 15,000L.

COPENHAGEN

DENMARK

The basic unit of currency is the krone, which can be divided into 100 ore. At this writing you'll get about 6.90 kroner for each floating dollar. Thus each krone equals about 14 U.S. cents. You can bring in or take out as many kroner as you like.

AVISODOMY FOR FUN AND PROFIT

Bodil Joensen has a stud farm in the north of Zeeland. On this farm she has some cattle, twelve pigs, four cats, two horses, two dogs, some geese, and a hamster. She makes love to some of the animals and some of the animals make love to her.

Perhaps you'd enjoy seeing Bodil or some of her counterparts perform in one of "Wonderful Copenhagen's" live sex shows. Otherwise in the many porno shops you can purchase color films or color magazines in which Bodil appears with the different animals. For 20 to 30 Danish kroner (one Danish krone equals about 14¢) you can buy magazines like *Animal # 1, Animal # 2, Animal # 3, Animal # 4, Animal # 5,* and so on. And on.

In the booklet of thirty color photos called *Animal Orgy # 1,* Bodil has her mouth open frequently, and other things too. In the opening sequence she is holding the nose of her black horse, Dreamlight, against her vulva. And so on.

Then there's the one about Bodil and the pig.

Her paramour in *Animal # 2* is a three-hundred-pound swine, just about the length of Bodil or the couch in her living room where this sequence was shot, as well as portions of the horse opera. Actually a porker's poker is more cochleate than its proverbial curly tail, with a sharp barb at the tip and so, as Bodil told Lizzie Bundgaard in an interview for *Ekstra Bladet* (Denmark's largest circulation daily, *family* newspaper), if you're going to sleep around with pigs you must "take care they do not make holes in you." There were other problems. The pig, obviously a novice at this sort of business, showed little adaptability for adjusting to the rigors of modeling for modern still photography and kept falling asleep under the hot lights of Rodox Trading (one of Scandinavia's leading porno producers; mail orders: Rodosvej 13, 2300 Copenhagen S; studio: Adelgade 5; 58-36-58). Though Bodil tried very hard with this pig and finally succeeded in bringing him to orgasm—as the camera graphically records—the animal seemed as indifferent to copulation with humans as most human beings would be disturbed at the prospect of making love with a pig. Unless he just didn't fancy Bodil.

In yet another booklet a lesbian touch is added when Smut (that's right, the dog is called "Smut," and no smartass whizzbangs), Bodil's German shepherd bitch, is smitten by a slim, very attractive redheaded girl and adds her large snout to form a tribad trio. Lassie, the collie, gets into the act too.

Lest you get the impression that Bodil Joensen is promiscuous, she assured Lizzie Bundgaard and *Ekstra Bladet* readers that she does her animal act only for money. Bodil has a strict moral code about sex, much preferring, with woman's logic, relations with a dog or bull she knows than with some strange man. "When we made the last porno magazine," Bodil told Lizzie, "they gave me a new partner, a man I didn't know, and it was awful!" Sexually, if not spiritually, she does prefer men to animals, but she is too independent to marry, what with the heavy responsibilities of running her stud farm and moonlighting with Dreamlight, Lassie, Smut, and the rest of the barnyard. To the psychiatrists, psychologists, sociologists, journalists, and, yea, even the mythologists who speculate about why Bodil Joensen does this, her answer is as good as any to the question: "What about sexual freedom in Denmark today?" In a good month of animal smooching she nets about 12,000 kroner.

PORNO CENTER OF THE UNIVERSE

"I'm sick of it . . . sick, sick, sick of sex!" screams Lizzie Bundgaard as she swings her shapely, well-tanned legs from the desk in her *Ekstra Bladet* office, just off Copenhagen's Town Hall Square, and stamps the floor for emphasis. "I can't bear writing about it, can't bear talking about it, hearing about it . . . can't bear all these people who come here looking for it!" Lizzie is laughing, of course, but it's a mocking, derisive outburst. A tough, sexy blonde in her early thirties who, as one of Denmark's leading journalists, has roamed Europe at the whim of her editor covering sex angles from algolagnia to zoophilia,[1] she is also typical of most Danes who are appalled that the world suddenly recognizes what has been a fact for many years: Denmark is the pornography export center of the universe.

Some years before July 1, 1969, when Denmark became the first modern Western nation to remove all restrictions on the creation, sale, and consumption of pornography (with exceptions forbidding sales to minors and tough restrictions on window displays), if one had visited the Danish National Travel Association (next to the Central Station), they would have been happy to discuss any aspect of sex, prostitution, pornography, perhaps even offer names of some of the better shops. During that period of the mid-1960s Denmark was exporting millions of dollars' worth of pornography (the word is used here as descriptive rather than pejorative) and Copenhagen's porno windows were a gynecological kaleidoscope, *far more blatant than they are today*. (Much of what was sold then was "illegal," but police couldn't have cared less about what was produced for export.) But today, as waves of

[1] But a versatile writer as well, Lizzie Bundgaard is equally skilled at covering Girl Scout jamborees, Brownie cookouts, and church socials.

foreigners visit the country in response not only to news of the lifting of the bans but to publicity and advertising created by Danish pornographers and sex trade fair promoters, the travel officials' lips are sealed on the subject of sex—sealed by orders of their government.

Permissive or Promiscuous?

"This is all we can say about it nowadays," one man frowns as he hands over the pamphlet, *Permissive—or Promiscuous,* by Geoffrey Dodd, an Australian freelance based here, and reprinted from the prestigious *Danish Journal* for distribution to the world press by no less than the Danish Ministry of Foreign Affairs. The pamphlet has been much paraphrased, quoted, and parroted, *though rarely credited as a source* by Western reporters, and it is illustrative of the formidable public-relations campaign waged by Denmark in the face of the apparently unexpected foreign reaction to the legalization of pornography.

Why *did* the Danes legalize pornography? According to Knud Thestrup, Conservative Minister of Justice who was instrumental in the decision, "Public authorities should not censor what the adult individual wants to see and read." Fine. But the other reason the learned judge doesn't offer—the authorities simply couldn't handle the situation. In early 1967, for example, after the police had raided porno producers all over the country—mostly in response to local complaints about the outrageous window displays—police actually begged big magazine distributors like Bent Jorgensen of BETEX TRADING (marvelous wholesale selection: address later on) to take the stuff back and store it in their own warehouses until the officials could decide what to do with it; pending court action the authorities couldn't simply destroy it.

The announcement that they were making technically legal what had already been tacitly permissible acted as a gigantic, incredibly effective worldwide advertising headline. But the Danes miscalculated. A nude Frankenstein had been created, or rather had been permanently freed of its coffin. Dilemma: of course they want to continue marketing the monster, but they also shudder to think that tourists and other foreigners might discover an archetype Dane other than the one these public-relations geniuses have labored so many years to create—the whimsical, democratically permissive but certainly not promiscuous, delightful Dane with that marvelously honest, self-deprecating wit. (A key to which is that Danes, like the English, often say exactly what they do not mean.)[2] They hope foreigners continue to regard Danes as synonymous with fine furniture, beer, cigars, bacon (but not fornicating pigs), and butter, and to keep on buying the lot. They want you to continue buying the pornography too, but they don't want to be synonymous

[2]Is that why the weather is such a hot topic in both countries?

with *that!* Some people are aware that the Danes have been mass-producing and exporting dirty books since the 1950s. And a few people knew the Danes were making the stuff even before the Second World War. But in this the age of overfuck, not to mention overcommunication and overtravel, you can't legalize the whole business and expect to keep it a secret. Not even from the little old Dubuque heiress who stays at the Angleterre and commutes from Georg Jensen to Tivoli to the Little Mermaid statue. You can be sure that when charter flight loads from Jacksonville to Morocco began arriving at Copenhagen's sex fairs, the Danish government ran off a lot of copies of that pamphlet.

Sex and History

How insidiously well it has worked is perhaps demonstrated by an article, "Foreign Affairs: Sex and Sense," by no less than C. L. Sulzberger, which appeared on the December 5, 1969, editorial page of *The New York Times.* By coincidence the short piece contains several direct quotes or paraphrases which also appear in the Danish pamphlet. Did Sulzberger get his quotes directly from the learned Danish windbags whose pontifications form the substance of the pamphlet . . . or from the pamphlet itself? One cannot know, for never does he so much as acknowledge the existence of the pamphlet. Never mind; from *Permissive—or Promiscuous* or from Sulzberger, you can get a pretty good idea of what Danes want you to think of them and, more important perhaps, what they think of you:

•The Danes, because of their background, history, and culture, are more liberal and thus more mature. Sulzberger, quoting Dr. Henrik Hoffmeyer, Copenhagen University psychiatrist, exactly as does the pamphlet: "As far back as historic records show, a liberal attitude towards relations between the sexes has existed in Denmark." In the pamphlet Hoffmeyer further theorizes, quite plausibly, that this attitude probably stemmed from an early emancipation of women who, with their Viking husbands roaming, raping, and looting their way around the world, had an inordinate amount of responsibility thrust upon them (not to mention, perhaps, some very large Viking horns) and thus became independent far earlier than women of other cultures. Sulzberger, paraphrasing Erik Manniche (or the pamphlet?), lecturer at the university's sociological institute: ". . . From 1650 to 1880 church registers show almost half of Denmark's women were pregnant at the time of marriage. The drop to about 30 per cent since then is linked to availability of contraceptives." And Manniche concludes, "Sexual mores in Denmark have remained amazingly constant for at least 300 years, and probably longer."

•Danish parents are far more enlightened in the raising of their offspring. Sulzberger quoting, exactly as did the pamphlet, Sten Hegeler, of the celebrated husband-and-wife psychologist team Inge and Sten (whose column began in Lizzie Bundgaard's paper), as Sten slips in a plug for their best-selling *The ABZ of Love:* "When it was published in 1961 a complaint was lodged with the police. Today parents often give it to their children as a present at confirmation."

•The Danish men are kinder, more considerate of women than perhaps you are. "The contempt many men in more puritan societies feel after they have had 'their way' with a woman is very rare in Denmark," says Dr. Hoffmeyer, who further assures us that although Danes have always been liberal in sexual matters, compared to many other cultures . . . this does not mean more promiscuous."

•The Danes are bored by pornography. "As far as Denmark is concerned, pornography is on the way out—the interest has waned since prohibitions have been removed," declares Dr. Hoffmeyer. But maybe *you* are an uptight sex-mad pornomaniac: "Many male tourists come to Denmark expecting to find women available everywhere, but they are usually disappointed. In this country the payment of money for sex, or—the classical background for seduction—false promises, pressure or abuse of a form of dependence, are considered to be much more immoral," gasconades sociologist Manniche, who apparently has never attended an animal-human porno-photographing at Rodox Trading's Adelgade studio, a flagellation set at S/M Centrum's Vesterbrogade "studio," nor visited the WONDERBAR, KAKADU, or the old DIXI BAR or the street corner of Istedgade and Gasvaerksvej, Vesterbrogade and Oehlenschlaegersgade, nor Teglgaardstraede. Nor Colbjørnsensgade.

But let us accept all the foregoing statements as largely true, if somewhat sanctimonious. If there remains anything more boring than the glut of Danish pornography, it is the flatulent, galling glut of assurances of how above it all they are as consumers. They've certainly convinced Mr. Sulzberger, and inferentially many of his loyal readers, who begins his *Times* piece, "There is nothing in the least bit either unwholesome or immoral about the Danes who simply share with Benjamin Franklin . . . a belief that honesty is the best policy."[3] Surely Sulzberger is referring to lack of hypocrisy in matters sexual. But can a people be so honest and moral in one field and dishonest in closely related enterprises?

[3]It behooves Mr. Sulzberger and the learned windbreakers of Copenhagen University who have fed him all those Danish baked beans and blue cheeses to get their hands on an obscure but witty Franklin essay on "farting" for fun and profit and the amusement of one's friends. In speculating how one might perfume his rear winds by imbibing perfumes or fragrant foods to make their emission as fashionable as snuff-taking, Franklin was in fact hoping to let the air out of certain learned members of the Belgian Royal Academy. See *Franklin's Wit and Folly*, by Richard D. Amacher, Rutgers University Press, 1953.

Exports and Smuggling

Unless you do considerable business with them, never mind that "in Scandinavia there is widespread opinion that the Danes, while a delightful people, are insincere and not always to be trusted." (See Donald Connery's *The Scandinavians*.) Who really cares that a recent Danish State Radio poll showed that Danes earn 6 billion kroner (over $800 million) more than they declare in income-tax returns (some of that assuredly in unreported sales of porno); it's warming to know that they're as human as the rest of the world. But consider that for years they've ruthlessly exploited their privileged position to produce pornography and export it to countries where it is forbidden. Not content with the handsome profits, the Danes proceed then to rub the noses of their best customers in the stuff. For it is these very countries that the Danes are criticizing when they refer to less liberal, unenlightened, puritan societies.

West Germany is Denmark's easiest mark, followed pantingly by the United States and Britain. The Danes have several porno shops set right smack on the German border. They've smuggled so much material into the Fatherland—by mail, parachute drop, launch boat, model airplanes—it is submitted that by the time this is read, Bonn may have been forced to legalize all pornography just to protect the interests of Germany's own very lively industry. Lizzie Bundgaard related a hilarious account of one resourceful countryman she interviewed. Thwarted by German border patrols, he loaded a large horse-trailer with hot books and films, and then enticed therein—possibly with a sexy blowup of Bodil—the wildest, buckingest, most ferocious stallion he could rent. If there is anything Germans respect more than a big bad dog it's a big bad horse. The goods got through customs and the happy Dane went on German TV to crow.

One of the great unsubstantiated myths, gobbled up and regurgitated by the Western press, is that sales of porno are steadily declining since all restrictions have been removed here. This is actually impossible to prove; you can be sure that Danish producers do not always tell the tax man exactly how many books and films they've sold. What's happening, of course, is that reporters are talking to certain porno plutocrats who keep crying that legalization is killing the business. What they really mean is that their profits are down somewhat—since legalization volume is up as lots of little guys, who formerly lacked proper rapport with the police, are flooding the market.

In 1966 an official of the Danish National Travel Association estimated that the pornography business amounted to no more than $40 million a year. *The New York Times* of October 22, 1969, in describing the huge success of the Copenhagen Sex Trade Fair, spoke of the estimated $50–$75-million annual volume. The March, 1970, *Holiday*—noting that the fair drew fifty thousand people, "the majority . . . Danish"—estimated annual sales to be $90 million. By now they're probably up over $100 million. Of course, any Dane will tell you that a great deal of the increase is accounted for by foreign sales. This is surely true, but do locals consume as little of it as they claim? Apparently American reporters are talking to the same eleven porno shop clerks you did, all of whom solemnly insisted that almost none of their customers are Danes. (Odd that Amsterdam shop *owners*—Danish entrepreneurs are rather above working their own counters, much like their Times Square and Soho counterparts—freely admit that much of their trade is local. Are the Dutch more prone, or simply more honest?)

Of course the Danes are bored by pornography but not, as they insist, because they have such a sophisticated heritage. We all get bored with free access to the stuff. Maybe the Danes are bored because their pornography is so boring. With all their legendary sexual maturity, the big breakthrough after the bans came down, the hot, number-one bestseller among Danes as well as tourists was Bodil and her barnyard. Up to 1972 most of the better heterosexual porno sold here—truly beautiful young girls, elegantly photographed, slickly produced—came from Sweden. The most arresting films are shot in Germany. The most arousing homosexual epics (lots of ten-year-old Arab boys) are made in Germany, stapled together in Denmark, then smuggled right back to the Fatherland. Ditto much of the slickest sadomasochistic stuff. For years the big cheeses of the classier Danish girlie magazines have relied on French, English, and Swedish models, and foreign photographers.

Crafty, but Is It Arty?

Forget pornography. What about art? If the Danes haven't abused their liberal heritage, at least they've ignored it; otherwise why have they produced so little erotic art or film to compare with that of far more repressed and/or censored societies? Yes, it's a small country (4.8 million), but nobody maintains that Danes can't or even won't come through in the near future. If they're such great beer, ballet, butter, and egg men—if they've given us Hans Christian Andersen (though they ignored him to tears during much of his lifetime), Niels Bohr, and Victor Borge, why give pornography a bad name?

Where to Buy It

A guide to Copenhagen's porno shops is as necessary as a guide to mailboxes. A blind man could find them—though at this writing Danes have not yet committed porno to Braille—even without *Sexionary,* an advertiser's paperback directory of sex shops, available at most kiosks. Many sex shops are open to 3 A.M. and, unlike in their Times Square counterparts, browsers are as welcome as buyers. Quantity varies with the size of the shop, but "quality" is fairly constant—films, photos, and magazines depicting women being done by dogs, dildoes, fish, eels, and every now and again a man. Also in and around the Istedgade several kitchens and parlors have been converted to 10-to-30K "membership" film clubs. Some serve coffee, some tea, all offer the strongest sex films you can imagine. Most are in Super-8 color; some, usually German, have sound.

Anyone who orders pornography by mail runs the risk, of course, that the goodies will never get out of the finished basements of his local postal authorities. Many Danish mail-order houses are no more than kitchen-table operations; they're liable to take your money, never mail the goods, then explain by form letter that the "mailing" was undoubtedly seized by your country's uptight customs agents.

A highly reliable mail-order company is ALLIANCE–X: Marielundvej 37–A, 2730 Herlev. If they manage to get even a free catalogue through—usually with color reproductions of their stock—it's worth the price of your postage. WEEKEND SEX (several shops in the Istedgade) and CONCERNO (G. L. Mont. 17) are among the best retail porn shops. And don't forget, Alliance has a contact club too.

LIVE SHOWS

While the pornographers' trade could do with less guilt and more professionalism, Copenhagen's live sex shows, just because of their amateurish quality and the youth of entrepreneurs and performers alike, are all the more erotic and appealing—and not without a certain charm and humor—than the comparatively De Millean Hamburg productions. Some live shows advertise daily in *Ekstra Bladet,* often in very blunt English, so by all means don't give the cabbie or hotel clerk any 100K for "recommendations." If you insist on being touted, pay no more than 5 or 10K.

Love-Inn

Among the most representative clubs was LOVE-INN (closed recently but several new clubs—later discussed—give performances similar to those offered here). A pleasant-faced fair-haired chino-clad young man of twenty-two, assisted by two merry blond teen-agers, each girl no more than nineteen, makes change from a tin lunchbox for your 25K eight-month membership and 100K admission charge. At around $17.50 it had better be good. You take your comfortable red swivel chair in the rectangular parlor of makeshift plasterboard—a bit scruffy by Danish standards but quite neat and clean—relax with a 3K beer (or soft drink) served by the pretty topless waitress from the long, roadhouse-type service bar. Shortly after 11 P.M. a home movie screen is set up and the Super-8 projector whirs into action with a fish story.

On the screen a pretty redhead is struggling with what appears to be some sort of sea snake, trying to angle it into her vagina.

"What's a nice plaice like you doing in a girl like this," comments an English company director, quickly shushed by his wife.

"That's no plaice," explains a Danish accountant. (The summer eve audience appears evenly divided between Danes and foreigners.) "That's a Danish eel. We've got some very good ones here in Denmark. They know their way around."

Eventually the lights come up, three men cough and an Austrian girl goes to the toilet to throw up as the waitress hands you a précis of *The Girl and the Ealing* should you wish to purchase it at your friendly neighborhood porno shop: "The girl witnesses an orgy and, inspired by it— however without a male—she gets an ealing to function as 'man.' This has never been shown on film before, and the realism in the filmed scenes is beyound description. You woun't believe your own eyes . . . the girl is electric and so becomes the ealing, and the camera lenses register the whole action in closeups."

A rather mannish mistress of ceremonies now emerges and announces that she will sing four love songs, one each in Danish, German, English, and French. To the amazement of every one of the thirty-five guests she does. Next the live striptease. A pretty eighteen-year-old (minimum age for performing in live shows) circulates her delectable bottom among various laps. The fortunate spectators are called upon to help her remove her garments. Finally, with an erotic display of charming fright (it has been announced that this is her maiden performance) that has the whole house licking its lips and creasing its trousers, she permits a German art historian to unsnap her garter belt, a French cook to roll down her black stockings, a Danish electrician to unsnap the black bra. The Frenchman returns to remove her panties and buss her rear. She curtsies to the polite applause like a grade-schooler delivering a valedictorian address.

Now the Murphy bed swings down from the wall, a brunette gamine wanders in carrying a book, peels off her pants suit and undies, lies down on the bed, and begins to masturbate. Having reached the moaning stage she is joined by a sweet-faced blond girl, but even after ten minutes of violent tribadism both remain unfulfilled. To the rescue and the tape-recorded strains of "Green, Green Grass of Home," the box-office boy emerges from counting the receipts, removes his chinos and buries his nose in the gamine's pubes while the elfin blonde takes his temperature by placing his thermometer in her mouth. For a time they behave like three youngsters playing doctor but he finally gets to it, satisfying both girls, then himself, nearly getting a sailor from the U.S.S. *Wasp* right in the eye with it. Do they really mean it? Well, it certainly *sounds* like it (none of the moans and screams are coming from any tape recorder), looks like it, of course, and *smells* like it! In the fifteen-by-thirty-five-foot room, with the bed placed in the middle no more than eighteen feet from any of the swivel chairs, you and seven others have front-row places not more than eighteen inches from the action.

"Well, one thing you can say for that guy," comments the sailor, "every night he comes to work he knows he's going to get laid."

Chino and Gamine depart, leaving the blonde to her own devices, which include a meat-grinder handle and a Danish sausage (which the State Agricultural Board impishly defines as an "edible container with spicy meats"). Not for long.

"Ladies and gentlemennnnnn, we will now have the demonstration of intimate massage," announces the mannish mistress of ceremonies. "If somebody want to try, you are welcome here on the bed."

"First thing I ever volunteered for in my life," explains the pride of the *Wasp.*

"Nonsense," notes a waitress, "he's already landed there twice this week."

The blonde unbuttons the sailor's flap, takes out his throbbing member and proceeds to tie it into a square knot. Up to this point fly buttons had been popping all over the house in appreciation of the freshness and spontaneity of the performers, but as the tape recorder booms out "Anchors Aweigh," the acrid smell of semen permeates the room, and the blonde briskly wipes the Navy dry with a crisp linen towel, the atmosphere has rather degenerated into that of a 1947 college fraternity "circle jerk."

"Anybody else want to try?" invites the MC. "It don't hurt."

Nobody else wants to try.

The lights come up for dancing, you with the brunette gamine who has spent herself three times a week the past eight of her 276 months as a member of the five-girl, three-boy repertory company.

"You all really seem to be enjoying yourselves—not as if you're giving a public performance."

"Yes, of course, we do it for the pleasure. Otherwise we couldn't ever do it."

"But what if a member of the audience attempted to join in, went for you while you were masturbating with the book. Surely that's the next step here after people get bored with the massage."

"Oh! I would run away."

"Even if the man were attractive to you?"

"Yes."

"But you feel free to perform before all these strangers?"

"That's only because I know the boy I do it with."

At this writing the live shows have not got much beyond the stage of Soho's little cellar stripteases, *architecturally,* that is. At the height of the shows' popularity (1970) knowledgeable Copenhageners felt that the thirty-odd clubs would narrow down to perhaps five or ten, and these would become more professional in their presentations and surroundings. And, sadly, less erotic as the "parlor" atmosphere and the ingenuousness were lost. But no one really expected the kind of mass closings which occurred in early 1972. (See end of this chapter.)

Club 69

CLUB 69 YOUNG LOVE (12–33–54), is in Højbro Plads 19 just off the Strøget "walking street" near the Illums Bolighus department store and facing the statue of Bishop Absalon whose stern likeness indicates that this may not have been quite what he had in mind when he founded the city in 1160. You visited the comparatively posh premises, set atop a fancy fish store, just prior to Club 69's 1970 opening, and were informed by the bearded twenty-three-year-old manager that "we're going to have a girl whipped to blood and the blood runs down the back. Anybody in the audience can whip her too,[4] or be massaged by her, but you can't make love with her even after the show. That's of course illegal." While no dearth of Danish girls auditioned for Club 69 (a casting director's dream—or perhaps nightmare), apparently Danish men, like Hamburgers, are "no good at all at it." Though the manager himself said he planned to perform from time to time, he readily admitted he's no match for the eager Yugoslav and Algerian seamen, always in good supply off the Ny Havn docks.

Some clubs have offered live intercourse between humans and animals, but one can't really count on such happenings, thanks to the interference of the Danish counterpart of the ASPCA, perhaps at the initiative of the Danish Agricultural Marketing Board (in whose *Denmark from A to Z* a "goose" is rather narrowly defined as "a distinguished cousin of the duck. An integral part of the Danish Christmas dinner").

Homosexual Shows and Sex Afloat

In 1970 PARTY CLUB (Nansensgade 45; 12–40–26) specialized in live homosexual shows (and by 1972 hetero ones as well) and is currently featuring first-run screenings of films like *Lick My Ass!*

CLUB TABU has apparently had certain differences with the coast guard (Danish, not U.S.), but when her S.S. *Atlantis* is sailing, your six-hour sex cruise along the beautiful Danish coast includes "movies, topless go-go girls, live intercourse (also lesbian and homosexual), Danish gourmet buffet, pirate

---

[4]There is no evidence that such S/M activities or performances ever took place here. The "manager" did appear to be a bit of a Barnum.

girl model hostesses [*the ship sails in international waters*], discothèque and live band dancing, roulette, blackjack, and slot machines.'' Bookings at Saxogade 9; phone 31–74–26.

Rent-an-Orgy

Publisher Tony Winholt has come up with a new Danish *smørrebrod*— ''Rent-an-Orgy.'' Noting Copenhagen Police Chief Kloster Christensen's 1970 dictum that ''we have certain rules for public entertainment but no rules for what happens at home,'' Winholt planned to stage orgies in private homes ''on the sitting-room floor'' or perhaps in your hotel room if the management will permit it. Customers will be restricted to watching, must not touch the girls—he has some thirty on tap, including housewives, nurses, secretaries— speak or take part . . . ''unless invited.'' Free coffee and cakes. Bookings: Club Holiday, Nordre Toldbod 21, 1259 Copenhagen K.

THE THIN BLUE LINE

That the authorities draw a blue line between ''intimate massage'' and actual intercourse is as silly as it is academic. Despite scholarly protestations to the contrary (see Dr. Hoffmeyer in the Foreign Affairs Ministry pamphlet), and despite the foreign authorities swallowing such bilge (Temple Fielding, for example, observes that ''. . . there are very few professional prostitutes, as a result of a healthy, sensible, natural attitude toward sex. . . .''), Copenhagen's whores, while admittedly catering to the recent heavy tourist influx, surely do a bit of local business. And have done it since long before the first recorded case of syphilis in the fifteenth century. Free treatment of venereal disease was available by 1790 (and still is to anyone; in fact, it is a legal offense not to report your infection), and by 1895 the city was a brothel center of Northern Europe. In 1906 the brothels were closed, police supervision and State medical inspections of prostitutes were suspended (the State, as so many others have done, hypocritically not wishing to associate itself with the business of prostitution, whatever the consequences for society), and a law was passed which regarded any woman selling her bun—or man his bum—as being engaged in ''illegal occupation.'' Granted, the number of prostitutes here is far smaller than in most European capitals—but there are more than you might expect—and if they are caught in the act, the police are only likely to force them to accept ''legal work.'' If one already has a job, no problem. Thus apparently all a girl needs as a legal cover is a card showing that she is ''legitimately employed,'' usually as a secretary. A good deal for some executives, for they put girls on their books at ''salaries'' that they declare as tax deductions but in fact do not pay.

Privates Massage?

As to which of those many massage ads in *Ekstra Bladet* will yield some- thing more advanced than "Swedish, Russian, German, or French," just check the classifieds under *"Blandede"* or the photo model listings under *"Stillinger"* (both classifications are usually placed between the sports sec- tion and the sex shows' display ads), and then phone a few. (No need to list specific ones, they're apt to change frequently.) One young woman, for example, quotes Swedish ("with my hand") at 50K, French ("with my mouth, of course") 125K, Danish ("with my pussy") 200K. When not rubbing, munching, or venting she can be found vending at an Istedgade porn shop. "Never on Sunday, but we are here every day from 10 A.M. to 4 A.M., both pretty girls with nice tans," invites another ad. A pretty blonde who lives in a Vesterbrogade apartment house occupied by several other advertisers off- ers Swedish manipulations accompanied by German films projected on the ceiling, 100K inclusive. Book early in the day if possible. Especially in answer- ing ads with long provocative copy, or ads in English (these are often the busiest numbers). It took a half hour to get through to the two beauties living at a Frederikssundsvej address. "We two girls," one said, "both do it. You can have one between the breasts. You can have two with mouth and hand. Depending what you need, massage is one hundred fifty. All the way? Why not? That would be four hundred kroner . . . then it's very good, you know?"

Street Scenes and Bars and Nightclubs

The large apartment building at the corner of Vesterbrogade (Oehlenschla- egersgade 1, named for Adam, a father of Danish theater) has some female actresses (among its many ordinary middle-class tenants) and nearly as many sidewalk Johnnies admiring those who pose in the upper-floor windows. Nearby, the dodgy intersection of Gasvaerksvej and Istedgade is a traditional whoreway. Rough, tough juveniles, some four or five months' pregnant, several under fifteen—from 75 to 150K. Several stand near the appropriately dubbed SEX CLUB ACTION, others in nearby dim doorways.

If you want to see a very Danish working-class nightspot—few tourists brighten its dark door—visit CAFÉ TUNESIA, No. 84 lower Istedgade.

The amazingly high prices and comparatively low quality of Copenhagen whores have been a characteristic of the city for years. Surely this is in no small way due to the gratis competition, though it has never occurred to the pros to lower prices to stimulate trade. Thus the good-time girls of WONDER BAR (Studiestraede 69, if you please) have increased prices from 300–400K to 400–500K. Some of the girls have been around almost as long as has this traditional businessman's (especially Swedes and Americans) favorite. You inquired of one such oldtimer if she had a special rate for children. "This is not an airplane," she smiled, "but I can give you a very fine ride." The venerable barmen may discuss the thoroughbred-horsehobby of the founder; but you'll have no trouble on your own getting acquainted with the human fillies as the early 1940s opulence of Wonder Bar makes it among the friendliest rendezvous in town.

If you can't find your husband when you return from blowing his bonus at Georg Jensen, try KAKADU (Colbjørnsensgade 6). If he's not here, you might pick up an oil sheik, for this is a traditional favorite of traveling horny toads. The girls are very attractive, young, and ask 400–500K, but you might compete if you stuff yourself with Kakadu's succulent Limfjord oysters. Kakadu closes at 5 A.M., but as Copenhagen is one of the world's great round-the-clock rocks, maybe he's breakfasting with the high-priced trollops across the street at MAXIM'S. Still no luck? Check the musty Old World ambiance of ORIENTEN BAR (in Viktoriagade, off Vesterbrogade), where basic charge for dicktation from the late 1920s part-time secretaries is 300K. Convenient entrance directly into HOTEL METROPOLITAN, doubles from 75K (you must show your passport). VALENCIA nightclub (Vesterbrogade 32) has the self-conscious atmosphere of an Eastern European hotel nightclub. What's more, it's expensive (1,75K coat check, 5,75K admission) and the strippers don't remove their G-strings. Some hostesses (but not all of them) might, however, and everything else in the privacy of their flats—no need waiting till the 5 A.M. closing. The lone female traveler who made the rounds of the aforementioned proximate clubs—if she's gamy and perhaps accompanied by a good-sport girlfriend—might find herself positively rolling in, if not with, some of the best men in town, for all these rooms are quite respectable and rank with the best after-hours corporate headquarters the country has to offer. (None of these establishments has any financial connection with professional ladies of the evening who may visit their clubs.)

For years CASANOVA (Farvergade 10, in the heart of the city, near the Town Hall) has been consistent: Swedish girls off the ferry from Malmö, some Danish and Norwegian girls too, irresistibly drawn by the large number of blacks—both visitors and residents—for whom Casanova has been a haven for more than decade.

SADOMASOCHISM IN WONDERFUL COPENHAGEN

Tread tiptoe on Teglgaardstraede—the apex of an isosceles triangle with Town Hall Square and Oscar Davidsen's famous sandwich restaurant at the other angles—for it has been known for its tough whores for half a century, not so much to tourists as to locals. Lately enlivened by a spate of porno clubs and sex shops in vicinity. Trade may not be what it was, but you see several frightening old cheeses beckoning from windows, and the odd 100K street whippersnapper. Apparently some of the professionals hereabouts specialize in sadomasochistic treatments, and some of the formidably built young men lunching on tire irons and bicycle chains round the corner in Sct. Peders Straede may know a thing or two about that sort of business as well. Though at times this street resembles a sadists' camp meeting (and gay city is not far away), PELIKANUN CAFÉ offers nothing more daring than flowsy old floozies flipping the suspenders of ancient mariners and farmers as a wandering concertina-player keeps getting his belt caught in his instrument. Virtuoso saw and spoon players too. Community sing–songs. Don't miss it.

S/M Centrum

In the ground-floor showroom of S/M CENTRUM (Sct. Peders Straede 20), however, a large photo shows a girl lashed to a cross and being whipped to blood by a man many years her senior. To judge from the frightful condition of the lass, she won't outlive him. Upstairs, the acrid smell of leather is nearly overwhelming, for this is Copenhagen's largest purveyor of *"flagellantismus."* They have mouthpieces, arm- and crotch-binders, penis picklers, and vagina vises, not to mention a whole second-floor boutique of leather and rubber—whips, capes, brassieres, body suits, corsets, chains, and other whatnot. "Yes, some of our customers come from America, but most is German," answers the clerk. "And also many English, some Italians, Swiss, French, Belgians, and many Swedes."

Anybody else? Say, uhh, maybe some . . . Danes?"

"Danes!" as if you had said Jovians or Carmelite nuns. "Oh, no. We don't get so many Danes." He fondles the rubberized replica of the lower female torso, heavily weighted with rabbit fur around the vaginal orifice leading to the washable pink latex sex throat (225K). "Yes, I suppose we could install a vibrator in that one but it would be an easier job to put the motor in our 'whole woman' model" (and probably Fallopian tubes as well; 920K or about $129).

A Torture Dungeon

Because S/M Centrum sells articles as well as books and films, it cannot remain open to 3 A.M. like other porno shops but must close by 5:30 P.M. With all the incredible apparatus (much of it available custom-made), perhaps the most arcane items are the line of jailhouse books and films, some of which Centrum apparently produces itself in the large medieval torture pokey that has been fitted out in Vesterbrogade. A Centrum clerk may give you the exact address. Direct your tour-bus driver there and demand that the lot of you be given a tour. If you've no luck, even with a complaint to the Danish State

Travel Association office next to the railroad station, the photo book *Spanking Ritual* gives you a good idea what goes on these days in Danish dungeons. It (and the film of the same name) stars two young men in the latest Centrum mod gear—black rubber gloves, capes, boots, tights with huge matching black snouts designed to accommodate their angry penises, and masks that fit over their noses like dog muzzles. The female lead, a handsome high-cheekboned young woman of twenty-four, signs an ancient parchment, is disrobed, then led nude into the sawdust-floored torture room by a rope attached to the dog collar at her neck.

Following a stern lecture from the two capemen, the terrified lass kneels and receives several introductory lashes from the cat-o'-nine tails which draw "blood." The shots are as realistic as possible, her agony doesn't look at all feigned. One suspects, at the least, "method" actors, but why actors at all? There seems certainly no shortage of sadists or of masochists to oblige them these troubled days. And why not in Denmark, where such performances are as legal as marriage? Meanwhile our gal is hanging by her wrists as the lashing tendrils slash her soft breasts and rip little clumps of pubic hair from their oddly accentuated mooring (retouching elves at work?). At last the boys strike her from the rack like a sack of Esrom ("A soft and supple cheese," explains the Agricultural Marketing Board, "whose mild flavor is the delight of connoisseurs"), but that's only the end of the beginning, for they've found a very clever horizontal rack that tilts the spreadeagled girl to every angle like an artist's easel. By hair-raising torchlight—or romantic candlelight, however you see it—her tormentors, jackals' eyes ablaze through the masks, prod various long, hard dowels up the damsel. (Excellent, properly Gothic lighting by photographer Erik Rasmussen, incidentally; good pacing by editor Ewald Hansen.) There are more pages of lashing, choking, and blood, climaxing with the poor girl doubled up on the sawdust floor as one dreadnought viciously shoves the hard rubber phallus attached to his rubber pants into her anus while his compatriot squats on her pilloried head and beats it about. Now the pair insert a syringe into her mouth, bloating her with air and water, and the finale has the girl hanging by the wrists again, this time apparently to dry. Like *Love Story,* the film of *Spanking Ritual* inspired the book, and the sales of one apparently continue to stimulate the other. Get yours wherever better dirty books are sold for *Spanking Ritual* seems on its way to becoming a classic.

Down the street at number 18 is HIGH CLASS PORNOGRAPHY, a pleasant, well-lighted shop that, for all its bright ambiance, attracts numbers of young female patrons. Not only do they stock all the latest bestsellers—*Fucking!*, *Spritz,* and *New Cunts of 1972*—they'll cheerfully screen the films for you before you buy. Thus did you catch *The Last Door* with a giggling member of the Royal Ballet—but let the producer describe his own work:

"This is the strongest movie ever shown, showing the most brutal rape scenes feasible. The terrified girl is raped normally and in her behind. Obviously the brutal rape does not satisfy her sexually. The scene where she is sucking his penis while satisfying herself by means of her heal, is magnefiscent. . . . [*sic*]."

SEXY JEWELRY

Two streets away at Vestergade 4, KJELD LARSEN custom-makes and purveys sexual jewelry. (H. C. Andersen lived at number 18 when he first came to town, later moved to Ny Havn.) Instructive as well as decorative, the gold bracelets depict various sexual positions as executed by handsome Peruvians; there are copulating Hindu key rings; a his-and-hers gold organ set to hang below your navel on a gold chain. Send for the brochure depicting "over 100 sexy trinkets for every possible taste. Also one for you." (Sales managers please note: this could solve your salesman-premium problem for life.)

GAY LIFE: BARS, CLUBS, AND THE LAW

Is it a coincidence that Centrum and the sadistic sallies of Teglgaardstraede are on the perimeter of Copenhagen's gay ghetto? Homophile sexual acts, committed by consent and in privacy, are legal in Denmark provided the participants are at least eighteen (the minimum age may be lowered soon). Indeed Denmark is nearly as tolerant of her homosexual citizens as of her heterosexuals, which cannot be said of most nations. COSY BAR (Studiestraede 24) is traditional: refined middle-aged queens pursued (a refreshing switch) by intense young men. Apparently no women allowed (except lesbians) unless accompanied by a known homosexual. Nearby MASKEN is a bit younger, more with-it. COPENHAGEN GAY CLUB (Studiestraede 31) is new. Three bars, good discothèque, attractive young people of all sexes. Around the corner, CAN CAN's patrons may do a double-take if your bottom is exceptional; hours 1 A.M. to 5 A.M. This old favorite is at Larsbjørnsstraede 12. (The celebrated thief who pilfered Denmark's greatest national treasure, the golden horns, lived at number 18. Melted them and sold the gold.)

When it was predominantly gay, EL TORO NEGRO (Boldhusgade 2) was one of the most exciting discothèques in town—a fascinating mélange of homo-sexuals, lesbians, beautiful straight girls, dashing black musicians, and a flam-boyant straight Spanish painter-hatchecker called "Plátero." As the club has become straighter it's lost some of the glitter, but not the girls. A traveling homophile's best friend is PAN CLUB (Nybrogade 28) bar and discothèque from 9 P.M. Lunch every day. This one has replaced PINK CLUB (Aabenraa 33) as the meeting place for FORBUNDET AF 1948 CLUB. Other homosexual clubs include VENNEN ("The Friend"), P.O. Box 999, Copenhagen NV; and EOS,

Box 949, 2400 Copenhagen NV, which publishes the estimable EOS directory of homophile bars and clubs around the world ($11). IHWO, DK 4633, in the town of Ostervang, offers "intimate guest house" accommodation for homosexuals in the lovely Danish countryside. A prudent Copenhagen first stop is the gay porno shop at Istedgade 36; homosexual sex films and magazines like *Homo Action, Bottle Games,* and *Triple Lesbian* (sounds a sort of Chinese soup). They also sell *Coq,* a Danish homophile contact magazine. Friendly, knowledgeable proprietor. Intimate massage information.

If you are a traveling transvestite, the transvestite fraternity, PHI PI EPSILON, P.O. Box 48, 4100, town of Ringstead, will advise you on something more, perhaps, than merely what to wear on your journey.

NY HAVN: SEAMEN'S BARS

Istedgade, with its whores and porno shops, is known as the "university of the day," and Ny Havn, the waterfront area, the "university of the night." Though it does have its quota of drunken Swedes and Finns and rough Danish ladies who know how to handle them, Ny Havn pales by comparison with Amsterdam's Zeedijk or Barcelona's Barrio Chino. Still, you may enjoy joints like SAFARI, CAP HORN (great Dixieland), 17 and 41 NY HAVN, TEXAS, and BROOKLYN. And there's a TATTOO JACK—"Mother" with roses and your ship's name from 50K. TATTOO BOB, TATTOO JOHN too.

"MEET THE DAMES": CLUB INTIME

Perhaps you're simply interested in meeting some ordinary Danes. The Danish Tourist Board sadly informs us that the laudable "Meet the Danes" program has been canceled—at least in Copenhagen. People here got bored, if not fed up with it. Don't despair. There is a private club offering somewhat more intimate meetings with Danes of all classes—but apparently one mind. Why not join CLUB INTIME before your next trip to Denmark; a Danish-Swedish contact club with nearly forty thousand "contact-seeking, broad-minded members." It may be the largest club in Europe, if not the world, that consistently promises high-quality no-nonsense sexual contacts.

There are several clubs within the Club Intime, but for the basic $21 entrance fee, males or couples (females are wisely admitted free) receive a membership bulletin that provides addresses of sex clubs and smaller groups of two to four couples "who seek other persons for mutual sexual gatherings." Members are sent contact lists of members of the opposite sex. Males, for example, receive lists of eight hundred (the number grows each month) "unprejudiced and broad-minded women members" whose attributes, desires, and code numbers are listed in the sheets, as are those of male members in sheets sent to females. For the sake of anonymity initial correspondence is sent through the club, which forwards your letters to the proper box number.

If you're really in a hurry, for an additional 8oK you will be swiftly computer-matched with a series of sex partners and sent their names, addresses, and (if available) phone numbers. On your questionnaire be as blunt as possible in describing your desires and what you consider your best features, from jet-black head hair to silky pubes. List *all* your hobbies. Some members, for instance, in addition to "stamp-collecting," etc., may check the box that indicates that they enjoy receiving erotic phone calls or smutty correspondence.

As a member of Club Intime's Privat (six months, 8oK) you are privileged to attend sex parties held at members' homes—"group sex fests, pajama parties, nude bathing, surprise parties," baptizing, camping trips, slave markets, and that lot.

Club Intime also offers a deluxe "Sex Weekend in Copenhagen," which is run with all the efficiency of a Prussian day camp, costs about $300, includes virtually everything but your air fare and contraceptives: room in a first-class hotel, three meals a day (excluding drinks), an attractive female—or male— escort cum guide cum? . . . ; transportation to and from your hotel. A typical weekend goes something like this:

•Friday at 7 P.M. your guide picks you up at the hotel, accompanies you to a selected live show similar to the one described at "Love-Inn." Your guide should be young, attractive, and not a prostitute; likely she's a secretary or shopgirl, perhaps a member of the contact club. What you do after the live show, then, is strictly up to you and her.

•Saturday at 10 A.M. it's off to the porno shops. She knows exactly where to find exactly what you want (be candid), perhaps at a discount. At 2 P.M. you're sweating out last night in the *schwitz* boxes of the "exclusive" International Massage and Sauna Club, where "it is of course possible to get the famous Swedish sex massage treatment, compliments of the house." At 4 P.M. nude models are waiting for your camera in a private porno studio, or be a Russ Meyer and make some hot home movies. A meal is served to you and your companion at 6 P.M., but you are cautioned not to make it a Naked Dinner, for the best is yet to be.

•At 9 P.M., according to the agenda, "a sex party has been arranged for in a large villa in the most exclusive suburban areas of Copenhagen where you may participate in one of the many legendary sex parties arranged for . . . broadminded people. . . . There will be dancing, and drinks will be served by topless waitresses while having group sex [dextrous, these Danes], sauna bathing, etc." A letter from the nice managing director of Club Intime confirms that "it is correct that we will invite a female member as companion, but as there usually participates about twenty-five members of each sex, you are of course free to mix with the other participants. The parties usually end up in common group-sex. Because we are very careful to invite people of equal ages, interests, from the same milieu, etc., this is the main reason for the parties' success."

Similar sex dos are arranged in Stockholm by Club Intime and the same arrangements can be made for female travelers with, of course, a handsome male companion. For further information on all the activities, write Club Intime, Postboks 2081, 1013 Copenhagen K; or wire them at "Clubmail"; or phone them at OR–95–85. The $300 sex weekend is surely a value if: you're in a hurry, don't know Copenhagen, and can spare the money. But assiduous use of this book and membership in Intime's $12 Privat Club, whose members are, perhaps, among your partners at the 9 P.M. sex party, should bring virtually the same results at perhaps a fifth the cost. Of course, you'll then have to provide your own meals, hotel, and guide.

DANISH GIRLS (TICKLISH) AND TIVOLI

Denmark is historically a lonely country that loves to be visited, but the traditional melancholy may return if many Danes continue to regard every male traveler as some kind of sex maniac. Thanks to porno paranoia, it may now take the average man (and the one who does not join Club Intime) a week or more to accomplish with a Danish girl what he could have done in a night five or ten years ago. Generally, however, Danish girls remain friendly, rationally hedonistic, and ticklish. Though available in a variety of shapes and sizes, yours will likely be rather diminutive, perky, and not necessarily blond —the classic, leggy, fair-haired beauties are more indigenous to Sweden, though Swedish males, for whom Copenhagen has long been a favorite drinking and mating port, prefer the temperaments of the warming Danish girls to those of their own frosty *frikadelle*.

Surely TIVOLI is the world's most amusing amusement park, the classic place to find the nice Danish girl, perhaps among the several who are waiting from 9 A.M., May Day, to midnight, September's second Sunday, for you to pay their way in. (But mind she doesn't run off with her boyfriend once you're inside.) If you can't distract someone from the water shows, acrobats, band concerts, ballet, pantomime, 150,000 flowers, and 90,000 colored lights, make for DANSETTEN (teens) or better yet TAVERNA (twenty-one to thirty-five). This Walpurgis Night Taverna is all you've conjured Tivoli to be. Amid the fireworks, light show, and witches with exploding broomsticks riding high wires across the first summer eve sky, 500 sailors from the good ship *Wasp* toss 500 Danish girls to Valhalla at the pregnant pauses of "Get Me to the Church on Time" in a scene straight from a 1940s Gene Kelly-Sonny Tufts musical. Not a Danish male in sight. They're out at BAKKEN (S-Train to Klamp-enbourg), said to be the world's oldest (and most advanced) amusement park. Things have become so heavy there of late that the city has planted "antiso-cial plants" to protect the flora and shrubs from the flower fauna and the rolling stoneds. Striptease and spicy songs too.

MISCELLANEOUS MEETING PLACES

With comparatively little class distinction in Denmark, Copenhagen's night-life, like Amsterdam's, is unusually democratic and relatively inexpensive. However, the QUEENS PUB & GRILL in the KONG FREDERIK HOTEL is considered rather fashionable by communications and advertising people. Some of the prettiest girls in Scandinavia, many of them models, pause here from shop-ping in the nearby Strøget . . . the "walking street." If you make the acquaint-ance of one in winter, take her by the hand next door to the HAFNIA HOTEL's heated outdoor terrace. 'Neath a cuddly blanket, fortified by a steaming hot Gløgg, you're having all the best of Wonderful Copenhagen.

CLUB 10 (Badstuestraede 10) has for years been perhaps the most exclusive discothèque, known to few foreigners other than the King of Greece. Peep-hole. Somber, almost ugly stuffed-fish-in-glass-cases decor—reminiscent of Munich's P–1. Very pretty people. Similar but slightly more mature collection at AMBASSADEUR in the Palace Hotel. CLUB 6 (Jernbanegade 6) has much younger, more zealous blood—ten bars, up to one hundred single girls per bar per night, and plenty, yes plenty of competition, some of it with soul to burn. Sweet tooth? Chocolate bars and lollipops in the men's room, and pastel rubbers too.

LORRY (Allégade 7) is lovely, of course, the traditional Copenhagen volks nightclub, though not quite the happy hunting house it was just after the war. With any luck you'll encounter a small but hardy cross-section of working- and middle-class Danes here among the hordes of tourists. GROCK, under the same roof, is a late-night (noon to 5 A.M.) kind of Danish Sardi's—lots of actresses. Fear not that some names change—Copenhagen night haunts have longevity. Thus Pussy Cat remains a good eighteen-to-thirty "upper-middle-class" discothèque, but now it's called BONAPARTE (Gothersgade 15). Similar situation with Star Club, now called REVOLUTION (Aaboulevard 35). And the quaint, cozy railway station is as much a hippie home away from home as it was for the Beat Generation. MONTMARTRE (Store Regnegade 19) has long been the traditional jazz house, a favorite of the large colony of expatriate black American jazz musicians. Lots of Swedish girls are always paddling across the Kattegat for this reason. Those who prefer dancing with jazz like VINGAARDEN (Nikolaj Plads 21).

Middle-aged GIs may be saddened to find the infamous DIXI whore bar finally closed, but their sons may delight that it's been replaced by PRINZ HENRIKS discothèque (Lavendelstraede 15). (The whores have all retired to Valhalla.)

MAIDS' NIGHT OUT AND THE WIDOWS' BALL

Circle Wednesday night, "The Night of the Red Hands"—maids' night out in Copenhagen. Don't laugh—Denmark has some of the world's most beautiful chambermaids. Regard the floor girls of SAS's ROYAL HOTEL, for example. After that go up to the sauna, lie down and be quiet, close your eyes, relax, and enjoy the 18K "Lokal" or 26K "Universal" massage as executed by one of three lovely Japanese girls. You may be sure she will not take a bite out of your penis, though she may take a short stroll on your back. You'll emerge feeling wonderfully refreshed, perhaps even ready for the "Widows' Ball."

The *Inka Bel* has for over twenty years been a Thursday-night special of THREE MUSKETEERS (Nikolaj Plads 25), since 1936 a traditional meeting place of divorced or otherwise unattached thirty-to-fifty-year-old women—office-manager and executive-secretary types—and, understandably, many men who have admired them since that time. The city's many good old pubs are traditional contact points for adults of all ages, particularly HVIIDS VINSTUE (Kongens Nytorv 19, circa 1723), where, over an apéritif, an actress from the opposite Royal Theater may be glad to smoke your Tiparillo. If not, nip a leather cup of dice from among the gathered artists and writers and try next door at SKIND-BUKSEN ("Leather Trousers," but you'll be more welcome without them). And, of course, the elegant, rather *Death in Venice* terrace of the HOTEL D'ANGLETERRE is a likely place to cultivate Copenhagen's 400, and the international set.

Pubs

There are many all-night pub-restaurants, too, where student and other young girls think nothing of arriving alone at 4 A.M. for dinner. Try TOKANTEN (Vandkunsten 1), DEN RØDE PIMPERNEL (Kattesundet 4), LA FONTAINE (live jazz, cheap meals, horse-players, journalists, and girls who enjoy all that, till 8 A.M.; Kompagnistraede 11), or DROP-INN or PUK. If you like Italian boys, or Danish girls who like Italian boys, VIA VENETO (Fiolstraede 2) may please you. HULA BAR (Adelgaard 8) is a large, brash counterpart of an English workingman's pub. From 9 P.M. to 6 A.M. a rather tough, but no less amusing, rendezvous of sailors and their "ladies." Always lots of liberated women on the loose, but insure that her last partner has at least a double hernia or you may be called upon to fight for the right to adore her. High Society slums by once in a while.

Copenhagen has a drastic housing shortage (though lots of crash pads near the university) that makes consummation of chance liaisons rather difficult. Hotel clerks, however, may whimsically look the other way (generally to Malmö) at the arrival of unexpected guests. The nice Danish girl can often be found at CAFÉ LAURITS BETJENT (Ved Stranden 16, on the canal opposite the Royal Palace; ignore the sign that says "Café Royal"), an exceptional café where the young intelligentsia exchange the latest pop and folk tunes for the nostalgic sea chanteys of hardluck old sailors. Don't miss it! (And bring your instrument.) Best time, 2 A.M.

ODDS AND ENDS

Copenhagen literally means "merchant's harbor." Third syllable rhymes with the "A" in "maven," not "lager."

That Danes are down-to-earth, ingenuous, very democratic, but also civilized as regards fiduciary matters is dramatized by the local Rolls-Royce dealer who is also happy to sell you ten new Volkswagens.

The city is extremely safe, but should you require a policeman, dial o–o–o or holler (softly please) *"Politiet!"* For quick medical service, dial 0041.

If you're looking for hash, it might be available near certain Old Town bars and clubs near the university (founded 1479). From 7 to 10K a gram.

Like Amsterdam, the best way to see this comparatively small, virtually flat capital is on foot or by bicycle. Rent one from KØBENHAVNS CYKLEBORS (Gothersgade 157)—8K per weekend, 15K the week, 30K the month ($4.20). Demand is so heavy in tourist season that it is best to book a bike ahead (14–07–17). Nightlife may continue till noon but cabbies retire early, especially when it rains. Comparatively inexpensive (tip 10 to 15 percent); the vast majority are honest, very helpful, and speak surprisingly little English.

Should you or a friend require contraception, check the phonebook under *"Gummivarer."* Several pharmacies are open twenty-four hours (compare to New York or London!). Two are: Vesterbrogade 6C (31–82–66) and Amagerbrogade 158 (58–01–40). Old folks and thrifty flower children will be gratified to learn that the Danish Agricultural Marketing Board defines Danish Lurpak butter as "a favorite lubricant with a delicious viscosity."

According to Inge and Sten Hegeler, 95 percent of Danish girls have misplaced their virginities by their wedding day. This was ascertained for *The ABZ of Love* in 1961 and the situation has markedly improved since that time. Moreover, most of these girls speak very good English and require that you learn only three words of Danish—*"Tak," "Tak," "Tak,"* each of which means "Thank you." You don't have to use them up all at once.

Though the pretty girls behind the counter of the government Travel Association are happy to give you a list of Danish nudist camps, who needs it?

Full nudity is now in vogue on several nearby public *family* beaches.

Danny Kaye was quite right, Copenhagen is "Wonderful!" The Danes have been only imperceptibly spoiled by so many tourists bringing so much money. The way to end a perfect night or visit is to bike out to Langelinie and watch the sun rise over the Little Mermaid. Very romantic. Very Danish.

WHOOPS! THE COPS ARE COPING

In early 1972 the Copenhagen police closed 36 of 74 sex clubs and live shows. According to press reports, some of the enterprises were linked to the underworld. Several personnel have been involved in shootings, and there is talk of narcotics, smuggling, income-tax evasion, etc.

Fifty hotel porters have been accused of touting guests to some clubs and receiving rake-offs, according to press reports.

According to a February 7, 1972, report from a *New York Post* correspondent, Danes insist that they themselves never buy pornography, and that "the customers are ninety percent foreign tourists."

A London *Times* dispatch of February 9, 1972, reports that "many clubs have shown an amazing ability to survive, opening again the day after they are closed, under a new management board but the same name—a maneuver that makes it necessary for the police to obtain a new order to shut them."

Therefore, when you arrive in Wonderful Copenhagen consult *Ekstra Bladet* for the latest news.

NEWS

A spring 1972 visit revealed that the best live show in Copenhagen wasn't in Copenhagen, but rather in the nearby town of Espergaerde—EDEN CLUB (Strandvejen 390A; 03–23–16–42). The hottest central city situation is probably that of PARTY CLUB (Nansensgade 45; 12–40–26). Both of these are not cheap; count on a minimum 125K membership and 50–75K entrance fee. Less dear (35K all in) and looking it is CLUB MIDNAT (Teglgardsstraede 14), which advertises "Intercourse Man-Woman at 12 noon, 2, 5, 7, 9, and 11 P.M."

Rather than trying to fathom the complicated new membership formalities, put yourself into the hands of one of the several posh new porn shops located in the heart of the fashionable "walking street." PORNO HOUSE (Frederiksborggade 17; BY–1565) book "live shows all over the town" and have "sex all over the house." SEXY CENTER (36 Vimmelskaftet; 14–92–14) are equally reliable.

Nearby is the lavish, expensive (150K membership, 75K massages) INTERNATIONAL SAUNA CLUB-X (Nygade 3; 11–46–01), "an untraditional business meeting? Sauna party! . . . give us a call." Be careful your annual stockholders meeting doesn't get balled up with Club Intime's contact club which some-times holds small gatherings here.

SCANDINAVIAN ESCORTS (also in the walking street at Frederiksborggade 26; 14–91–93) may have the highest standards for beauty among its female escorts of any such service. You can select them from the photo album.

BAD NEWS

A clause in their contracts forbids them to sleep with clients. And the service charges 250K for an evening.

More bad news: You have to wear a tie to go upstairs (most action) at KAKADU. But . . . this bar remains perhaps the most frenetic example of its genre north of Spain.

GOOD NEWS

The recent police actions and the general allegations leveled at the live shows have left the learned sociologists *paucis verbis.* No erudite rectal zephyrs about how Danes do not exploit women, not for the moment at least.

Women's Lib, on the other hand, is beginning to make some noises, in spite of cruel ridicule in the local press. Calling themselves *Rødstrømper* ("red-stockings"), they have exercised squatters rights on a weary building (Aaben-raa 26, 28, 30; 12–56–60) in the old city which the town fathers had thought was going to be a museum. Here is a young but thriving Women's Lib commune and workshop which, according to a spokeswoman, sees Danish females as "exploited psychologically, sexually, and economically," and hopes all interested women who pass through town will stop by for discus-sions, *action* . . . or coffee.

"Live show? Yes, but you are not the audience! You will join in a marvelous intimate massage session with one of our attractive masseuses. Ask for any-thing . . . it costs nothing!" says the card for CLUB CAVALCADE (Enghavevej 6; 31–21–89). However, on visiting this dimly lit porn shop (cum-what?) you ascertain that the Portnoy's Compliant ("Swedish") comes off at 75K, the French Finesse retails at 125K, and the Royal Danish High Liver commands a cool 300K.

In the nineteenth century honeymooning Danish couples would hurry from the wedding ceremony in a closed white coach pulled by two white horses. Some fun. A certain Mister Duun has one (or more) of these in excellent condition and will rent it to you and your sweetheart if you call him at 97–02–22. (Kurt Nielsen of the National Travel Association of Denmark knows about the details.) Very romantic. Very Danish.

STOCKHOLM

SWEDEN

The basic unit of currency is the krona, which can be divided into 100 öre. At this writing you'll get about 4.78 kronor for each floating dollar. Thus each krona is worth about 20 U.S. cents. No more than 6,000 kronor in or out.

BOOZE, MYTHS, AND MISCONCEPTIONS

Stockholm is Philadelphia with women.

With some qualifications. Some years ago it was harder to find a drink after midnight than a girl. Wassailing—the only wickedly indulged Swedish sin—remains what fornication is to more sexually puritan cultures, but nightlife has come on of late, and the rigorous government liquor monopoly is more concerned with alcoholism than drinking per se (hard liquor prices are kept very high, but the finest Burgundy costs less here than in France). The females are somewhat more physically ravishing than you have heard (beautiful *and* plunderous as Huns in heat when *their* minds are made up); and somewhat less approachable strictly on your terms than you'd hoped, as the jet age has brought so many rutty foreign males to Sweden, the novelty of their alien spontaneity, politeness, and swarthiness lessens with each landing.

If you've come for girls, summertime is the worst time, because so many are on vacation (mostly to Latin countries) and there is so much competition (mostly from Latin countries, and deserted bachelors). Wait for the vigorous arid cold (little wind), when Stockholm and its women, more bijoued than warmed by the exotic blazing outdoor gas torches, are at their loneliest, most melancholy, and most achievable.

But whenever you come, be prepared for a very high cost of living.

Misconceptions and myths aside, a Swedish girl says "no" more firmly than the next girl, but rarely says "maybe," and often says "yes." This is nothing new. Trial marriages have been common for centuries; liberal abortion laws date from 1939; condoms are vended from streetcorner machines to anyone tall enough to reach them, by the RFSU—National Association for Sex Education, circa 1933; and petting is so foreign to Swedes that they use the English word for it. And when she does say "yes," with that gasping, breathy intake of the pasteurized air, it's the most gamic, inviting, unequivocal "yes" you've ever heard. This frequent inhaling of *"Ja"* (apparently no counterpart in English, which, not incidentally, is compulsory in all schools here), may account in part for good developments in breasts and the fact that if you negotiate a *pippa,* she's odds on to throw in a *slicka* and a *suga* with her *smeka* even if she's twelve and *trang* ("narrow"; she'll show you what the others mean). Swedish girls are perceptibly livelier than their men, whose speech, perhaps not coincidentally, sounds like a warped 78rpm record played backward at 33 1/3, under water; girl-talk recalls all the nightingales you've ever heard singing under showers.

Arriving in Stockholm your first time is as much a visit to another planet as a future century. The architecture is largely *fin-de-siècle*—some wonderful fifteenth-to-eighteenth-century Camelot things but mostly late-nineteenth-century *I Am Curious (Yellow)* yellow stolid piles and late-late-twentieth snow-white towers. Capitalism with a conscience has given Sweden perhaps the highest overall standard of living in the world, but not what you'd call ecstasy. Little affection is displayed on the streets, lovers to lovers, nor in the home, parents to children. Like the Swedes, their capital is grum, patrician, effortlessly elegant, and deficient in noise, temperament, mirth, and dirt. There are suggestions of good secrets, but this is more inhibition than the mystery of casbahs or even the kinky-kooky privacy of London. There is a fortuitous harmony with nature, small thanks to the inner-directed genius of Swedes—they soar in science, sculpture, demolition, construction, military defense, and sex; brood in painting, film, drama, literature, and love. At virtually every vista you have the fresh whim of the sea, for Stockholm is twelve islands connected by forty-two bridges situated in a sylvan archipelago that contains over twenty thousand piney islands. But central Stockholm is now called *Gropen* ("The Pit") rather than *Centrum:* for twenty years or more bumbling city planners have systematically destroyed—no exaggeration here—what journalist Jan Sjöby fondly recalls *was* "an almost-Parisian maze of narrow streets and alleys, a museum of three centuries of architectural fancy." In its place you now find a huge multi-block square hole of rubble.

WHERE THE GIRLS ARE BY DAY

A male visitor cannot ever really avoid thinking of females. Forget the suicide rates (several reporting countries have higher, not to mention some bashful ones that won't tell). Stockholm undoubtedly has more *beautiful* girls per capita (with environs, pop. 1,300,000) than any city on the planet. Make your own lunch-hour survey at any central city square; Hötorget, with its old "Haymarket" flower and produce stalls preserved amid the Buck Rogers towers, is a good starting point. Besides the girls, Sergels Torg, a twenty-first-century "superellipse" and underground piazza, has smart shops, a "free speakers stand," a "doodle plank" white board for graffiti, and TRÄFF ("Date"), where the authorities enjoy seeing all hash-hounds and car-radio thieves under one roof. But stoned youth perch like homeless pigeons all around this monument to Sweden's great sculptor, Johan Tobias Sergel, shoot heroin in the public toilets, peddle 8K grams or 30-to-40K matchboxes of hash near the Information Center. (One krona equals 20¢; 4.78 kronor to the dollar; 100 öre equal one krona.) Secretaries sun, skate, café-sit in Kungsträgården. Rousing revival meetings and band concerts too. In the nearby park behind the Opera House, GI refugees from Vietnam make pleasant body counts of country girls who adore them, old folks who abhor them.

Resembling a race of H. Rider Haggard Shes or some exquisite androids created by a satyristic scientist, these magnificent creatures should all be lunching at elegant RICHE or OPERA KÄLLAREN (whose baroque nudes made some *fin-de-siècle* scandal and were primly covered shortly after their unveiling). But no, a good Kungsgatan konditorei like OGO or VIVEL or MALMS (Sturegatan 4) will do (to get a waitress, call *"Fruken,"* which rhymes with "lookin' "); or the GRONA LINJEN vegetarian restaurant (Mäster Samuelsgatan 10, second floor); THYRA COOKING SCHOOL (Drottninggatan 53, third floor); or the indifferent food and service but delectable patrons of BÄCKAHÄSTEN (Hamngatan 2) and BRÄNDA TOMTEN (Stureplan 13) terrace cafés—but mind the Milanese competition; or BERNS (Näckströmsgatan 8), Europe's largest nightclub, serving up to two thousand office girls at lunch, cafeteria-style. All of the foregoing offer even better opportunities and far better odds by day than by night for improving foreign relations. And remember, if you can, that these are *ordinary* Swedish girls; some, of course, with careers that are the equivalent of those of professional men, but most are clerks, secretaries, shop assistants, students, waitresses, and maids. (Wednesday, second to Saturday as the big toot, is Stockholm's "Maids' Saturday.")

Much of the beauty pageant is a mere repetition of perfect features (if you can call this "mere"), but there are also some exotic combinations you've never dreamed of—almond-shaped, luminous lapis-lazuli and violaceous eyes staring boldly, appraisingly, at a man like . . . like a man stares at a woman! Wide, flat, curiously erotic noses with a certain carnal flair to the nostrils. And such hair! No rock opera, nor even a Swedish rhapsody, could sing it justice. The softest, silkiest shades of blond and buff, cinnamon and fawn, umber and amber . . . sheening in the quick stingy winter sun like spun fire, or the aurora borealis while we're here. If Francis Bacon hadn't some Swedish profile (though not body) in mind when he mused, "There is no excellent beauty that hath not some strangeness in the proportion," Hans Christian Andersen had when he described a classic Nordic fluff's complexion as of "milk and blood." What's more, like people who have magnificent houses and thus the incentive to keep them so, Swedes, men and women, are the best-groomed people on earth.

But if beauty has its spell, it has its little curses too. So spoiled are Swedish males (who physically are not so extraordinary) as schoolboys by the charms of their playmates that one can't blame the lads for wishing to try all the girls at least once, if not often, and as soon as possible. This is often *very* soon, for though the age of consent is fifteen, there is serious talk of lowering it to fourteen. Moreover, representative studies (like the Örebro) have determined that the average age at first menstruation is 12.75 years or less (coinciding with the theories of Dr. Clarence A. Mills, American climatologist, who rather discredited the widely held belief that Latins become lovers and ladies earlier when, in 1959, he found that Minneapolis first flowed at average age 12.8, New Orleans at 13.5, and Panama at 14.2).

Visitors are urged to read *Sex and Society in Sweden* by Birgitta Linnér (New York: Pantheon, 1967). It may not heat you up like some of the extraordinary Swedish porno, but it does tell what has happened here, though there are few insights into the emotional results. For that you must come and see for yourself. Of special interest is the appendix, excerpting elementary-education textbooks like the following Swedish Board of Education lesson for ages seven to nine:

"One day Mommy feels a pain, and then she and Daddy know that the baby is going to be born. . . . Then the baby comes out through the opening between Mommy's legs. . . . If it is a girl, she has a little opening between her legs like her mommy. Boy babies don't have an opening between their legs; instead they have something about as big as a finger that is called a penis."

If the tots have further questions, Professor Linnér suggests that the teacher may "give some such explanation as: 'The sperm can reach the egg after Daddy has put his penis into the opening between Mommy's legs.' " Evidently there are lots of questions, for a text used by ten-to-twelve-year-olds assumes, "You have certainly heard the word 'intercourse.' It means that a man's penis is inserted into a woman's vagina. . . . As a rule, intercourse results in a feeling of well-being called an orgasm. . . ."

SEX AND THE SINGLE TEEN-AGER

A healthy, optimistic touch, that last. Small wonder 79.5 percent of students at one typical church-affiliated college (students aged 17 to 23) had attained well-being by 1960, and 86.9 percent by 1965. Only 2 percent of the married population were virgins at their weddings, and nearly half the brides in Sweden were pregnant before their weddings, according to a study ordered by the Swedish Royal Commission on Sex Education.

Scholars have long been fascinated by the mating habits of Swedish youth. Donald S. Connery's *The Scandinavians* speaks of Stockholm's "teen-age demimonde":

"When parents are out of town and an apartment is free, the word is passed

. . . for another orgy. The well-publicized *raggare* are the most visible of all. They cruise in packs of unmuffled cars [*raggarbil*] . . . and pick up girls in a modern mating ritual worthy of serious anthropological attention. Minorleague versions of the same exercise can be seen in other Swedish cities. . . .

"Big, gaudy, secondhand Fords, Chevrolets, and Chryslers—'bedrooms on wheels' [*sangkammare*]—move slowly in parade down Kungsgatan, the Broadway of Stockholm, at about the time cinemas . . . and dance halls empty out. The sallow-looking young drivers and their friends, never smiling, never eager, look over the girls drifting along the sidewalk. A toe touches the accelerator. . . . A girl, or two or three girls, respond to the call by opening the rear door of the car and tumbling into the back seat."

And tumbling for real, parked in the lonely roads of Lill-Jansskogen, north of Valhallavägen, or Djurgården, once the royal deer preserve but now containing Skansen ("miniature Sweden,") and Grona Lund (amusement park and discothèques), both fine warm-weather daytime pickup areas; and Solliden, perhaps the most romantic view of the city. Author Connery might be interested to know that the *raggare* action has mostly shifted to Birger Jarlsgatan, *north* of Stureplan. If youth want to hold an indoor *ormgrop*, they make for a twenty-five room mansion thirteen miles northwest of the city which the authorities graciously—they really had no choice—have provided for sex parties. You should rent a car here, but you're liable to get smacked in the eye with a herring if you try to fashion that Hertz into a *raggarbil* unless, perhaps, you can pass for under twenty-one. Whatever, hang a ragged furpiece or necktie (the derivation of *"raggar"*) from your aerial, get a false black mustache, and join the parade.

HITCHHIKERS

Take heart, whatever your age. Though Stockholm at 3 A.M. is among the loneliest capitals for an insomniac, homosexual, or alcoholic, (and especially so for anyone who happens to be all three) few towns have more hometrudging and/or hitchhiking females at that hour—aged twelve to thirty-five or so —notwithstanding recent, and heretofore extremely rare, street disorders. Take advantage of the fact that when dancehalls and discothèques empty, from 1 to 3 A.M., the city provides little if any public transportation to the outlying suburbs (where most young people live). Your best route is back and forth (especially south) along Skeppsbron; or north on Birger Jarlsgatan. On a cold night count on three to six passengers, though take care not all at once. You might even get a family like that of Siv of Enskede who with her two "girlfriends" looked from twenty yards like three twenty-five-year-olds but, over delicious 5 A.M. coffee in their cozy flat, turned out to be mother (thirty-six), and daughters (seventeen and fifteen).

What happens depends, obviously, on whom you meet, how far she lives, and how badly she eventually wants to get home. You and the weather are not incidental factors. Surely a polite inquiry regarding sexual intercourse won't harm the relationship. It's rather like asking an American girl to dinner: either she's hungry or she's not. (But *don't* ask for a *pippa*. Keep to English if you can speak it; Swedes prefer it to Swedish.)

ADVANCED GYNECOCRACY

Even should you hit a quick jackpot (your chances increase the longer you stay) and her mother moves the twin beds together and presents you to Dad at breakfast, don't be surprised if your luscious new love breaks your heart and throws you out after two or three nights, no matter how good you think you are or in fact have been. She's simply a bit sexually bored, turning the sheets not only on her own but men from all over the world. Why should you be an exception? And *caveat:* foreign blondes do not have more fun in Sweden. In the kingdom of the blonde the black man is king, even the black-*haired* man. (And it doesn't hurt to shoepolish your pubes on the way in from Arlanda Airport—when in Stockholm do as the Romans do.) But even if you're sable and Trastevere-born, you'll agree: if Sweden isn't the world's most advanced gynecocracy, it'll do till Women's Lib gets the whole act together. Feminists, in fact, would do well to come here and make many notes.

Life described the idealistic yet practical marriage of Rune (forty) who quit his ad job to become *hemmaman* ("househusband") and nurse tiny Åsa and tend all the household chores. Far from it being Åsa's death, everyone is enormously pleased with the situation, especially the family's sole provider, pretty blond art director Ulla (twenty-seven).

But the very conception of formalized marriage is becoming obsolete here, whatever the roles of the respective partners. In 1966 there were more than 61,000 legal or certified marriages performed in Sweden. In 1971 the number had fallen by almost one-third to about 43,000. Although such a sharp decline is unique among modern Western nations, it does not necessarily indicate an upsurge of promiscuity, according to Elisabeth Wettergren of the Swedish Institute for Sexual Education. "People are simply living together without the formality of a legal marriage certificate," she plausibly suggests.

As to safety valves for those restless wives among the formally married: it is not unusual to encounter women married a decade or more keeping G.I. refugees or other American expatriates as "mastresses" in cozy Old Town *pieds-à-terre*.

GAMES SWEDES PLAY

Let's call him "Tag" because for half his twenty-four years he has been playing it. Moderately attractive, a promising law graduate from a successful family, with all the enormous social and economic advantages of the Swedish upper middle classes, he nonetheless speaks with at least some of the outsider's naïveté, for his parents emigrated from Poland:

"The Swedish men are cold because the Swedish women are mean"—Tag is not smiling—"you can do what you want to them, but if you marry them, you are mad. You know, the men are not waiting so long to marry *only* because the girls are so beautiful and so easy. Many men are afraid. So many girls want a man simply as beautiful jewelry, to be seen with in town. As a three-way *schmuck,* you know? Of course, money is everything here. If you do not earn, *she will!* And maybe then she leaves you . . . with the children."[1] (This is indeed a highly materialistic society. As far back as 1966 young Swedes spent $2.4 billion on clothes, cosmetics, autos, and other amusements; that was one-third of the year's total national budget, and more than the entire social-welfare-services outlay.)

"For three months I am in love with a girl," continues Tag. "Her husband takes fishing trips to the north and she and I are meanwhile fucking like Lapps in front of her three children. Finally it's too much for me. 'It's not natural,' I tell her. 'It is *you* who are not natural,' she says to me. . . . And how must the children be when they grow?

"Love? You cannot have it when she is chasing from one man to another. The Swedish girls say they want romance and temperament in a man. But they are going for the Negro, because even our most intelligent girls think there is more rhythm there. Or for the Latins, because they think there is more passion.

"Here you can take the girl and the mother . . . and the grandmother too if you want. You should see the old women in the hospitals. Ooooo, such a nice boy, *'putti, putti, putti'* . . . they will fuck even they are one hundred years old.[2]

"When you are away for military service, guarding our secret caves, if you have a girl back home you are going crazy. . . . They are slowly breaking down the men here. I am moving to France where people know who they are. . . ."

[1]If, indeed, there are any children. If Sweden's abortion laws are ultra-liberal, those of her Communist neighbor to the south are a Polish joke. *Kultura,* published in Warsaw, recently noted that "women from Sweden especially visit Poland for abortions." Considering that Poland has Europe's lowest birthrate, even lower than that of Sweden, it should come as no surprise that over 200,000 legal abortions were performed in Poland during 1971.

[2]Swedish females born in 1971 have the world's highest average life expectancy—76.5 years; males—71.9 years. Sweden also shows the lowest infant-mortality rates—12.9 deaths per thousand births. The U.S. rate of 21.7 deaths per thousand births ranks it twenty-first among other nations.

(In a spring 1971 case, a town of Solleftea court amazingly established that fourteen-year-old twins not only each have different fathers, but that their legal father may not have sired either; the frisky mother had intercourse with two lovers besides her husband at the time of her fertilization, apparently.)

A stranger's problem in Stockholm, then, is less where and how to find a girl than where to take her and how to keep her. Unless your room is a double, you may find the hotel clerk surprisingly cool to your new friend. Some quickie hotels are scattered near the Klara Kyrka area's porno shops—though there has been so much demolition near here that even the natives get lost—and in Södermalm and the Old Town, but none is distinguished. Cabbies (moderately expensive, exasperatingly unilingual) know. If you can afford it, start your Swedish romance in the romantic cellar of the OPERA restaurant—candlelight, thirty-six thousand bottles of wine, and the Heifetz of music boxes.

WHERE THE GIRLS ARE AT NIGHT

Nightlife is centered in Norrmalm (downtown), Gamla Stan (Old Town, site of the original 1255 settlement), and, of late, Södermalm (Southern Island), once grazing land, more recently home of the warmest Stockholmers, and fast becoming the most piquant, provocative part of the city. Higher prices have somewhat replaced the blue laws—one can at last drink standing up—but even in those *nattklubbs* licensed to 3 A.M. the well dries up at 2:30 and if you duck out after 1:15 to snatch some rowdy dolly girl (*tjejer* or *raggarbrudar*), you can't get back in. As in London there is much floating nightlife, characterized by private parties and illegal or private clubs. Rather than try to crash a covert mixed Old Town sauna, a stranger is advised to make for Strandvägen where boats frequently hired for overnight Baltic-bound office parties are docked. Among drinkers of the world Swedes are said to be second only to Yugoslavs in per-capita consumption, so a fifth of akvavit, or better yet Scotch, is your best boarding pass. After-hours *"Svarta-klubbs"* ("black clubs," often run by Yugoslavs) move nearly as fast as their peep-holes: Usually in Södermalm—cabbies know—a couple near Maria Torget, in the 1960s called "snow square" for the amount of hard drugs passed in its somber pre-Revolution-Moscow-like shadows. Nearby Slussen is the place for black-market *renat* (pure spirits); 35 to 40K for what you'd pay 16K in the State stores. Bring a brown paper bag.

This is not a town where you need make extensive rounds to find a girl. Comparatively few couples go out as such, and when they do, the girl often buys the gas. Any of the vast majority of females who prowl on their own or in pairs are fair game for a dance if you approach and invite them with a polite *"For jah loave?"* Remember, it's a conservative city, so wear a tie to all but the best discothèques, which are, incidentally, preferred by young people as less expensive than nightclubs or dancing restaurants, for most serve only wine or beer.

Swedes were at first confused by the nonstop discothèques, so accustomed are they to changing partners. They tend to marry late, divorce often, and in rural dancehalls as in many Finnish dancing places, one still encounters those painful pregnant pauses between every second set. (However with Finns it's more from shyness than fickleness.) Among Stockholm's best discothèques, all rather elegant as befits a city that thinks slumming is for the poor, are: ALEXANDRA'S (Biblioteksgatan 5, a street closed to motor vehicles), LORD NILSSON (Regeringsgatan 66, connecting to the very hot, traditional Ambassadeur), TOP FLOOR CLUB (Sturegatan 10), and MIA (Döbelnsgatan 3), a vivid example that Swedish young people really are somewhat less emotionally constipated than their parents. Mia, ignored by the guidebooks, is a very un-Swedish mélange of attractive straight people, and some homosexuals, and lesbians. Improvisational theater groups too. BERZELII TERRASEN, open-air in summer, draws a top-class girl, "wide in the brains, long in the legs." The classic divorcee and prowling-spouse dancehall is BALDAKINEN (Barnhusgatan 12). Medieval Old Town caves make superb discos. Try MANZANILLA (Bredgränd 4) for something under twenty-one; BOBBADILLA'S six sixteenth-century tombs still cater to the middle ages (eighteen to twenty-seven or so), at Svartmangatan 27, hard by the police station whose chief is Wahlgren. (Central police station is at Hornsgatan 36; phone 41-04-32.)

Many of the foreign males at AMBASSADEUR (Kungsgatan 18) are in town on business, but come here for pleasure: many many single girls and ladies. Visiting American executives find it a wonderful place to relieve tensions. Ditto BACCHI VAPEN (Järntorgsgatan 5, Old Town), whose so-so strip is often warmed up by black girls. Lots of lone twenty-five-to-thirty-five ladies in the discothèque. BERNS (Näckströmgatan 8) has good cabaret, few singles. (Hamburger Börs is gone: city "planning.") Most dancing places advertise daily, noting what age group's on for tonight, in newspapers *Expressen* or *Dagens Nyheter* under "*Dans,*" especially young people's haunts like DISCO 69, MAD DOG, VANILLA CLUB, and GYLLNE CIRKELN. LORRY usually has something on for people over thirty. From "Bal Palais"—women ask the men every other dance—to "*Grasanka,*" "grass-widow balls." So many people doff their wedding rings before coming here that the management often sells them to everyone (1K) at the door. FASCHING CLUB (Kungsgatan 63) "welcomes beautiful and ugly people from all countries." PLAYGIRL is a good Södermalm after-hours drinking club (Hornsgatan 62). KAOS, is a gentle, folk-singing winehouse (Stora Nygatan 21).

Suddenly Swedes have pubs. STAMPEN (Helga Lekamens Gränd 10, Old Town) is a warm, Greenwich Villagey room with live jazz groups, many jazzy girls, and no admission. Other good pickup pubs are TENNSTOPET (Dalagatan 50), TUDOR ARMS (Grevgatan 31), and the rather chic PLAYER's (Karlavägen 73). PRINSEN artists' and writers' restaurant (Mäster Samuelsgatan 4) is a gold mine for starving connoisseurs, who are free to sit at any girl's table here. One might even meet a writer. Or an artist. PIZZERIA PIAZZA OPERA (Gustav Adolfs Torg) lures the *jeunesse dorée* at apéritif time. Paris-copy DRUGSTORES (Birger Jarlsgatan 24, to 3 A.M.; Kungsgatan 4, to 1 A.M.) are fine for pulling teeny-birds.

NIGHT CRAWLERS

Stockholm has an unexpected number of dodgy, and some dangerous, characters prowling the forbidding streets till dawn, even in winter, simply because they've no place to go. Few, if any, get into SVARTA KATEN ("Black Cat," Regeringsgatan 16) after 2 A.M. but you might in a suit; lots of ladies of the theater. Hungry at 5 A.M.? Starve. You must prove you work at night to negotiate the very basic all-night snack bars RÖDA RUMMET (Norra Bantor-get) or MAGNETEN (Katarina Bangata 26, Södermalm). Nocturnal sociology is even less a qualification than prostitution, and if you are a homosexual engaged in either activity, you may go hungriest of all. Not for sex or trade, however, if you stick to the outdoor rendezvous, Humlegården Park, Engel-brektsplan area; Karlavägen between Sturegatan and Engelbrektsgatan; or the public toilets out front of the extravagant Grand Hotel.

HOMOSEXUALS

The Law and Youth

In theory, Swedish law and public education are far more advanced than other Western societies' in easing the legal as well as social burdens of homosexuals. The following is an excerpt from *Way to Maturity,* a 1966 textbook used in public schools by fourteen to seventeen-year-olds and also scripted as a radio and TV education series for ninth-graders:

"The word homosexual contains the Greek word *homo,* which means *like.* It has nothing to do with the Latin word *homo,* which means *man.* [Doubtless three-quarters of Italy's homosexuals don't know that.] . . . In Sweden, homosexuality was punishable by law until 1944. But . . . [it] is no longer subject to penalty unless it involves young persons under eighteen or minors in a dependent situation (e.g., a teacher with a pupil). . . . Many noted persons have been homosexual, among them Michelangelo, Tchaikovsky, Oscar Wilde, and Karin Boye.

"Although homosexuality is no longer a crime in Sweden, a good deal of stigma persists. Homosexuals are persecuted and derided, and are not accepted in professional or social circles, etc. This is especially true of male homosexuals. However, during recent years people have begun to realize that homosexuals have a right to live their lives in their own way.

"Many people wonder how homosexuals obtain sexual pleasure and gratification. The most common way is mutual caressing and kissing, in the manner of petting. Homosexuals may caress each other's sex organs until orgasm results. Occasionally, relations between homosexual men involve insertion of the penis into the anus. However, this is not common, although the practice has given rise to certain sobriquets for homosexuals."

Whether all that turns ninth-graders on or off, it should at least inspire a certain tolerance among them.

Sobriquets and enlightened textbooks aside, the traditional Swedish emotional conservatism and suspicion of any social behavior that deviates from the accepted "norm" (and this can range from disdain for anything from loud ties to loud fairies) has been as much responsible for the stigmatization as the Church of Sweden (Lutheran), which remains very intransigent indeed. Besides, argue many Swedes, what's our son need a midnight cowboy suit for when he's got all those pretty dolls to play with. The Swedes have had their revolution, silent and painless as it has been, and everybody will eat wild strawberries and cream, like it or not.

City Club

Peter Dunk, a handsome expatriate Dutchman, who looks like Dirk Bogarde, agrees that there has been some thawing in public attitudes and a significant temperance of police harassment. Surely Dunk's Mia Discothèque has broken down a few barriers as a thoroughly democratic mélange, especially Friday and Saturday when it's on to 6 A.M. With Bertil Safbom, Dunk also co-produces the vibrant discothèque and daytime restaurant of CITY CLUB (two thousand members, twelve thousand annual guests) at Döbelnsgatan 4. A refined but extremely loose place (but strangers should phone ahead, 11-27-28 or 10-88-90). Many homosexual boys bring their girlfriends as well as their male lovers here, and some their parents. And one his eighty-year-old grandmother who loves to waltz to 4 A.M. weekends amid the ingenious floating light shows. Periodic beauty contests. Cultural presentations (*Swan Lake* in drag). Probably the only club in town where men may enjoy close-contact dancing. Homo- and heterosexual transvestite groups also meet here, and City Club is apparently the most important lesbian rendezvous now that Diana Miller's celebrated Kungsgatan club has shut down. For years Diana's was *the* homosexual scene in Stockholm. Indeed, some studies have shown a greater incidence of female homosexuality than male among Swedes, contrary to many other cultures. The Örebro research, for example, found nearly

14 percent of girls as against 5 percent of boys studied reporting teen-age homosexual experiences.[3]

Stockholm will probably never have a significant number of gay rendez-vous. For years many homosexuals have made do with several otherwise straight places. For the pre-1944 mood, cruise SHANGHAI (Folkungagatan 146, Södermalm), a curious blue-collar, self-service beer café, anachronistically atmospheric in its listless, lackluster fashion. A varied menu, from "Schnitzel Moscow" to Egg Foo Yong at TIMMY'S RESTAURANT (Timmermansgatan 24, Södermalm) and they'll send out for kosher treats from the Yiddish food shop next door. Elegant and accomplished are the homosexual writers and theatrical luminaries at BERN'S BAR (only at the bar; Näckströmsgatan 8), but here they are lights unto themselves among their more numerous straight colleagues.

Hi-yo. SILVER BAR (Stureplan 6), says Stockholm nightlife is finally away. Opened in 1969, Silver has a pleasing 1940s Broadway Lindy's hip, and a stable of horse-player, show biz, tarty amateur, male homosexual, lesbian, off-duty masseuse, executive, shrewd spade . . . *types*; and good food, plenty of booze, roulette, noise, and, no doubt, your Uncle Fred. To 3 A.M.

Hold on to your wallet, and your Swedish meatballs too. Some of Europe's most beautiful and most ruthless gay whores prowl Humlegården. At Södra Mälarstrand, Slussen's pier, they're merely ruthless. Many Swedish male hustlers are as bisexual as they are bilingual: heterosexual they may be by preference, but homosexual they will be to beat the incredibly high cost of living. (Dying is cheaper: 25 öre up the elevator to the top of nearby Katarinahissen tower, a spectacular view and favorite suicide leap.)

Gay travelers requiring further attentions, perhaps sympathetic hotel accommodations or a tour of the specialty sex shops, should write RFSL (National Federation for Sexual Equality, Box 850, S-101-32, Stockholm 1), or, if victimized by a "queer bash" or police brutality (rare, but both occasionally occur), phone 84-31-18.

EROTIC AND EXOTIC MINORITIES

In 1964, Dr. (of medicine and philosophy) Lars Ullerstam's *The Erotic Minorities*[4] shocked even his countrymen. One should immediately qualify the "even," for Dr. Ullerstam's impassioned but no less incontrovertibly reasonable angst and wrath deplored the "astonishing fact that the comparatively intense public debate on sexual matters which has been raging in

[3]If you subscribe to the theory that male homosexuality is encouraged by those puritan societies which make little girls hard to get, Sweden's unique experience of the past twenty years, and these statistics, should add fodder to your position.
[4]An American edition was published by Grove Press in 1966.

Sweden these last few years is mostly concerned with . . . the right of the caste of the already sexually privileged to enjoy their sexual activities. I wonder why this horde of scribblers . . .have so obsessively concerned themselves only with the healthy, favored, heterosexual young."

Those who by age, physical or mental defect, incarceration—and these may include even mates of sexually fatigued spouses—or eccentricity, are deprived (not depraved) should, in Ullerstam's view, be attended at free, State-run, even mobile brothels, staffed by attractive young "erotic samaritans" of both sexes: "talented and cultivated people who understand the joy of giving." Indeed, what could be a better bridge over the troubled waters of the generation gap? In Ullerstam's utopia the state should establish sex-contact bureaus staffed by trained doctors and psychologists to pair sadists and masochists, scatologists and urophiles, etc.; maintain premises for exhibitionists to perform for voyeurs, "so scopophiles should not have to sit and suffer through hours of, say, *The Silence* and other depressing things."

Dr. Ullerstam's polemic is addressed as much to the world as to his native Sweden and, though nowhere have governments enacted his programs on a respectable scale, at least by their inertia or corruption in ignoring prohibitory statutes we may be progressing toward some fulfillment of his goals. In fact, several may already have been achieved.

With the great leaps in jet travel since 1964—and perhaps with some assistance from this book—necrophiles (still liable to swift "justice" in Sweden) may hie to Barcelona, perhaps forming a charter club with autoeroticists and the particularly advanced narcissists of the species who, Ullerstam observes, can perform only in halls of mirrors (how could one have neglected to parallel the Spaniards' narcissism and their *meublé* mirrors?), with stopovers for the Paris lovers' hotels. After noting certain eccentrics who can reach orgasm only by witnessing human disasters, traffic accidents, thunderstorms, etc.—these, of course, should immediately fly to join their fellows who champion the Vietnam War—Ullerstam cites "youths who could experience orgasm only when they kept the engine running." Surely they will find joy among Stockholm's *raggare*, not to mention youth of hundreds of other Western cities.

By implication, Ullerstam lamented the plight of Stockholm's then deprived scopophiles (voyeurs), who, at his 1964 writing, had to journey to Malmö (still a fairly hot town) to see striptease, and to Odin knows where to enjoy such banquets as staged by Peter the Great during which "dwarfs of both sexes" were "stripped naked and then baked into enormous pies" and "on agreed signal . . . burst forth from the pastries and danced about on the tables." (Fortunately, the airlines provide frequent connections to dozens of American cities where this arcane form of exhibitionism is regularly performed at so many Great American Lodge functions, though usually with bikinied females emerging from birthday cakes.) Since Ullerstam's polemic, Stockholm has blossomed, first with striptease, and now with bona-fide sex shows (but no officially sanctioned, live heterosexual intercourse at this writing); if not quite as strong as Copenhagen's (one hour by jet) the beauty of the Swedish or black performers nearly compensates; and pornography for all but children and particularly advanced sadists, for Sweden has long censored irrelevant violence from films as well as TV; and sex shops for all adults.

SEX-CONTACT CLUBS

Prior to 1944 statutory reforms, sexual intercourse with animals lay humans open to legal action (though no penalties accrued to the animals), but the social stigma remains. Let Swedish avisodomists safari to England, where the practice is more socially acceptable (especially among the better families), forming charter groups with algolagnists (aficionados of sexual violence and pain) who may enjoy stopover starters at The Hague or Hamburg. A boon for airlines too. Mercy flights of Roman pedophiles and blondophiles no longer need return half empty to the Eternal City if Swedish gerontophiles and literal pederasts form charter clubs.

Those who simply wish to cultivate new single or groups of *human* adults need venture no further than the *Brevklubbar* classifieds of some prominent Swedish daily newspapers. CLUB INTIME, which has been extensively described in "Copenhagen," includes thousands of attractive young people from all over Scandinavia—and perhaps some attractive samaritans among them—not to mention some deserving middle-aged and elderly ones. Write Box 35, S-101, 20 Stockholm 1. Enrollment, 35K.

Other clubs that welcome foreigners, promise lots of good things in the woods on summer camping expeditions, include: BREVFORUM, Box 8007, 720 08 Västerås 8; KONTAKT 70, Box 511, 701 07 Örebro (the town where they do all those sex surveys); and B.G.A. INSTITUTET, Box 130, 200 43 Malmö.

OLD TIMERS HERE ARE NOT FORGOTTEN

Just because of their incapacities, the aged and/or handicapped are invariably less affluent than the sexually privileged young and healthy. If we will not hire the handicapped, let us at least hire models and masseuses or masseurs for them. Sympathetic friends and family in Sweden can rejoice that while only six classified ads appeared under *Yrkesmoddeller* in a typical December, 1966, issue of *Dagens Nyheter*—a Stockholm daily whose undisputed power and prestige are as considerable here as *The New York Times's* is in America, and whose classifieds put *Screw* magazine's to shame for their high percentage of hetero female ads—no fewer than a hundred and four appeared on a summer day in 1970. And twenty-four more massage ads under *Hälso-o. kroppsvård*. Of course, not all ads yield sex, but a healthy percentage do. So get today's *Dagens Nyheter*, a street map (while new ads appear from time to time, certain neighborhoods and even streets sustain their character, and characters) and start telephoning. No doubt old grand dad has at least six pairs of slippers. What better birthday surprise, then, than a gift certificate for the visual treats to be got from one of the Gotlandsgatan advertisers; or a long, long look at Luntmakargatan's springing virgins; or perhaps someone in a Folkskolegatan flat is staging a private "69" show. And don't forget Grandma's golden wedding anniversary, particularly if she is widowed: several male models advertise too; and maybe your Uncle Jack is a homosexual.

PROSTITUTION

Prostitution per se is apparently no crime in Sweden, though persons "offending morality and decency" by overt solicitations (the few pros who work selected night clubs charge 100K and up) and those who promise or compensate persons of a sex other than their own under eighteen for temporary sexual liaisons, or members of the same sex under age twenty-one, may be arrested for "seduction of youth" and are liable to fines and six months or more in one of those model Swedish jails whose food and ambiance are infinitely more respectable than perhaps half the hash houses in New York City. (Some have conjugal visiting privileges as well.) So check the ID cards of the tough 200K teenyhookers hustling from dusk to 2:00 A.M., corner of Norlanndsgatan and Mäster Samuelsgatan, for years the traditional downtown beat. So fierce is the housing shortage that some young executives rent their midtown flats to *prostituerad* at 200K.

A "Brothel"

As a group Stockholm's good-time girls are pehaps less attractive than Paris's or Berlin's and expensive—some charge up to $28 for "massage," often double that for intercourse—but many are downright voracious in their sexual appetites, though considerably less than candid by phone. No need bantering with the answering service about "posing with some love" (60K); the resident nymphomaniacs of the fancy second-floor Ringwagen (Södermalm) flat will assure you in person that there is no greater love than the 150K special. You are met at the door of the apartment by a truly beautiful henna-rinsed brunette whose startling, shrewd orchestra-blue eyes (color of those World War II bandleader jackets) nearly immediately assess your preoccupation with the two huge bedrooms, large parlor, hand-tooled table in the waiting room. She leaves you to your inventory, whereupon emerges from the big bathtub a not unattractive blond amazon in sheer mininightie who, noting your reluctance, is yet so anxious for a *samlag* (lay) that she tries to ruse you onto the triple-size bed, pretending to believe that you have already paid the brunette!

Moonlight and Meatballs

Dishy and quite intelligent is a statuesque Swedish meatball who, like perhaps half the advertisers, speaks fine English and moonlights from an office job. "I think you call it masturbation. We are looking at a film together here in the flat. I take off all my clothes, you take off all your clothes, and I help you with my hand for eighty crowns, or with my mouth for one-hundred. . . . Come to Ringwagen——, walk through the garden to Bohusgatan——, and I am waiting for you with very long dark hair."

SEX SHOPS AND SHOWS, AND SOME MISCELLANY

Nearby at Renstiernas Gata 29, GALLERI EROTIC ART offers provocative sculpture and paintings, lesbian and other live sex shows, and a vast selection of internationally manufactured erotic utensils and pornography, laid out after the fashion of an East German trade fair. Admiring the young dental assistant purchasing a pair of rubber panties, to be worn inside out so that the attached phallus may be stuffed up her vagina, one recalls the exquisite, writhing agony of the Old Town's discothèque cave-dwellers. There are several other sex shops in vicinity of Södermalm's Renstiernas Gata. And sex shows as well, charging up to thirty "members" 15 to 20K for the folding chairs and one-hour film and live shows, usually consisiting of erotic, completely nude strip-tease and lesbian athletics.

While you're in Södermalm, don't fail to explore this "friendliest island in town." In spite of the incredible construction and land-moving, Södermalm is rather supplanting the Old Town as an "in" area, after the fashion of London's literati moving from Chelsea to Hampstead. Many writers and artists have restored the picturesque wooden cottages of livestock grazers, reminiscent of pre-Czarist Russian peasant dwellings, particularly in Åsögatan and Lotsgatan. "They knew how to deal with those feminists then," smiles a dour poet who lives in Katarina Kyrkobacke. His wife has left him for a Milanese film-cutter. "On this spot you stand, hundreds of neighborhood women were burned at the stake in the seventeenth-century witch trials." At the top of Fjällgatan you have a spectacularly romantic view of the city, perhaps surpassing even that of Solliden or Katarinahissen tower. Trudge up Mikaels Trappgrand—like several nearby streets, named for a local boy who, the little plaque informs, was city hangman from 1635 to 1650. Apocryphally, he offered expert technical advice at his own hanging (for murder).

Note: In contrast to, perhaps because of, Copenhagen police action against live shows there, Sweden has opened up its own live show market considerably, as regards quantity as well as quality. Finland and Norway may follow soon.

The Massage Is Medium

A 30K Japanese massage, executed by any of 32-74-84's four singing nightingales who perch in a Frejgatan walkup should restore your mind to pleasant thoughts. But remember, these girls and all *who advertise in Dagens Nyheter*, advise on the phone that there is nothing sexual about their services.

There is a great deal of activity on Östermalm, just north of the central city area, especially along Vastmangatan (they should call it "Old-timers-here-are-not-forgotten gatan), precariously close to the university. Cross to Kungsholmen island and district, but for heaven's sake leave Grandpappy in the hotel. If the view from the connecting bridge doesn't give him palpitations, surely his clock may come unsprung at the rigorous calisthenics offered by the big redhaired Finn and her pert blond native partner whose first-floor St. Eriksgatan (another hot street for ads) flat resembles nothing so much as a dingy porn movie set. Films, fellatio, fornication, 150K. Two girls, 300K.

Exhibitionism

It remains for the otherwise somber Swedes, almost all of them young ones, however, to introduce real puckishness to porn. Not to mention the world's most exquisite girls who relish this form of paid exhibitionism, available in an apparently never-ending supply, in a variety of posturings—often with produce: carrots, celery, chard, cucumbers, and cigars, cigarettes . . . Tiparillos? —reproduced in slick *Playboy*-quality magazines like *Ero* and *Private*, enhanced by some relatively literate and humorous four-language texts. Swedes produce little if any S/M or animal materials, though foreign editions are readily available under the porno shop counters, concentrating for the most part on heterosexual couplings of up to eight participants, often shot in the splendid solitude of the gentle Swedish countryside, and usually containing at least one black man for added color (though most all Swedish porn is shot in livid color), perhaps recruited from among Stockholm's Vietnam GI refugees.

For information on other more mundane employment, and immigration regulations—seven years' residence permitted before taking up citizenship— war refugees should contact the ex-soldiers' "THE CENTER," Gotlandsgatan 73, Skanstull district, Stockholm.

By recent law, sex shop window displays are comparatively tame—open crotches are covered by masking tape or flowers—but interiors like those in the central Klarra Norra area make Times Square's and Soho's look like Christian Science Reading Rooms. Porno shopowners the world over fight window-display restrictions primarily because cool windows encourage more hot browsing than buying. But Stockholm porn shops are veritable libraries. The Polish refugees who staff Klara Norra Kyrkogatan 24, and No. 22, and the shop around the corner at Gamla Brogatan 21, all offer gracious, shrewd counsel on your most esoteric porn needs. At K. N. Kyrkogatan 13 is PRIMO BUTIKERNA supermarket, the housewives' delight. No *Family Circle* for these ladies what with all the porn flakes by the cornflakes.

Several versatile masseuses live nearby. And the local rather ephemeral live sex film shows advertise daily on the sports and entertainment pages of the newspaper *Expressen*, as do those more permanent ones in the Old Town and Södermalm.

Sometimes you get a better free show hanging around the dressing rooms of SOHO SEX SHOP, a nearly elegant appliance and porn emporium whose connecting with-it leather-and-lace boutique is patronized by several transvestites and sadomasochists, but largely by tourists and pretty young girls. Lots of dating couples, for Soho is at Birger Jarlsgatan 15, in one of the city's smatest shopping areas. At Hötorget 4 is BLOOMOR OCH BIN ("The Birds and the Bees"), a kind of Biba of sex shops, operated by youth. One local guidebook speculates that it was created as a reaction against "the Swedish view of sex as being some sort of health activity." Here you may find giggling dolly birds trying on crotch-apertured see-through panties, considering new uses for portable vaginas (flowerpots? muffs?) and fluid-sacked phalluses (vinegar squirters? ketchup dispensers?).

For those Philadelphians still smarting at this chapter's perhaps too broad opening generalization, it should be said, by way of conclusion, that although Stockholm remains a kind of Philadelphia with women ("with some qualifications"), this in no way suggests that Philadelphia is Stockholm without women. There are many, many wonderful women in Philadelphia. And as if that were not enough, Philadelphia also has the Phillies.

LONDON

GREAT BRITAIN

The basic units of currency are the pound and new pence. Each pound is now (God save the Queen) divided into 100 new pence. One pound and twenty-five new pence is written thus: £1.25. At this writing one pound is roughly equivalent to $2.61 American. Thus each new pence is worth about 2.6 U.S. cents. No restrictions on import or export of currency.

Everything you ever wanted to know about sex, and a great deal you *never* wanted to know, exists in some form in London.

There are brothels of a sort and some lovers' hotels, though the former are generally short-staffed (by law) and both are of inferior ambiance; flagellation practitioners in abundance; call-girl rings, street whores, and nightclub hustlers; homosexual bars, clubs, hotels, and saunas; group-sex clubs (where, however, affairs may not be legally consummated on premise); porn shops; sex shows of a sort; retailers and custom craftsmen of flagellation and other "special" equipment; infibulation "surgeons" who do scrotum, nipple, penis, etc., piercings; some splendid opportunities for social contacts at London's several suburban nudist camps and hotels; and at least two mixed in-town saunas; massage parlors and masseuses of every persuasion. London has the lot, plus some very English specialties of its own. But the peculiar paradox of the English—as a nation, even as individuals, they can be at once priggish and prurient—often makes the finding of the thing a tedious game. But then, the English simply adore games.

THE ENGLISH GENTLEMAN, THE ENGLISH GIRL

Appropriately, this final city of our journey is the home of that most sexually arabesque of all Europeans—no, he is not at all a European, he is *The English Gentleman.* If you have encountered him in some corner of a foreign field, like a New York corporate office or a Majorcan beach, and found him rather prosaic, do not be fooled. The Englishman is a chameleon, adaptable on the surface to all strange climes. Moreover, he considers he holds world rights on secrecy and privacy, not to mention the High Hedge. Thus, it is only when you meet him on his home grounds that you *may* learn how nearly synonymous the words "Englishman" and "eccentric" are. More carnal than sensual, more sexual than romantic, he may be; but make no mistake, the Englishman, perhaps better than any man, knows exactly when and how to say the proper thing. And do it, when it suits him.

We are not speaking here of those young people, so many of them of working-class origins, whose lifestyles and appetites approximate those of their contemporaries in much of the Western world (indeed, in many instances modern "permissive" England has set the pattern); and surely not of those who have had such an influence in making London such a viable, exciting city where the overall quality of life is second to none. It is a hallmark of the English young that, unlike their elders, they freely share their eccentricities—the miniskirt is but one obvious example; or consider the eccentric genius of the Beatles who, if you take them as the entity they were, did more to influence the world's manners and mores than any single musician in history.

One can keep up on ephemeral with-it happenings through magazines like *Harper's-Queen, Nova,* and *Rolling Stone. What's On* saves any guidebook the trouble of listing pubs, discothèques, strip- and nightclubs. There are some promising ads in the personal columns of *Oz* and *It,* not to mention the *Times* and other less thunderous dailies. But by far the best "living guide to London" is *Time Out*: on theater and cinema, every sort of music and concert; museums, sport, revolution, sex, the occult, drugs and drag, etc. And the classifieds are among London's liveliest: several girls recently advertised for men to "help make a baby," for example. *Time Out* also provides some of the most perceptive and gutsy investigative journalism in the realm.

With publications like these, all written in a language nearly identical to your own, there should be no trouble finding or amusing a London girl (or man for that matter). A woman feels nearly as free as does a man to go prowling about on her own, London being perhaps the safest capital for her to do so (about 50 murders per year as opposed to over 1600 per year in New York. Similar comparison for forcible rape. New York has about 2400 a year, London about 75). If you must have a guide to "where the girls are," get the inexpensive *Good Girl Guide* or borrow someone's *New London Spy* and read the jokey but no less incisive chapter on "bird pulling." W. H. SMITH (Sloane Square, S.W.1) should have the book, and you might chat someone nice up before you buy it.

Of course, physical beauty is a subjective thing, but "in the opinion of the most varied aesthetic experts [including a pharmacist who's from Freehold, New Jersey, and a couple of fellows from Seattle who wouldn't give their occupations], the English race as a whole, not only the Englishwoman, carries off first prize for beauty among the nations of Europe," according to the randy early-twentieth-century German sexologist Iwan Bloch.[1] Even Lord Byron, who preferred Italian women, admitted that "among a hundred English women at least thirty would be pretty." That percentage surely still obtains in modern London, not only among the many native natural blondes and blue-eyed brunettes, but from thousands of girls drawn from the Continent to be *au pairs,* and other things.

This is not a nation of consumers or overindulgers; even the homes of the well-to-do are comparatively spartan. The quantity and quality of food have improved markedly over the past decade or so but have been such that the

[1]See his exhaustive and exhausting *Sexual Life in England*; Chapter I, "The English Woman."

archetype English girl remains delightfully slim, with excellent legs. Even when you encounter the classic combination of priggishness and coarse carnality, the English girl is as likely as any female anywhere to go quickly and sweetly to bed with a man she likes, however recently she has met him. Moreover, she knows next to nothing about current events, but can chatter agreeably about anything for hours. The legendary lusciousness of the island's complexions is probably attributable to the damp climate, which keeps the skin moist, though the lack of central heating may inhibit one from bathing as often as one might want to. With it all, one always presumes an English female to be a lady even if she is not, if only for the beautiful and/or inventive way she has with the language. (Oscar Levant said Moss Hart said, "They talk like that straight from the womb.")

ARABESQUES AND ECCENTRICS

But if all this is so . . . why the whips? If you want some insight into how florid and versatile the English Experience can be, read *Forum*—forerunner of the new Serious Sex Magazines; lectures and encounter-group sessions at the editorial offices, 2 Bramber Road, W. 14—especially the readers' letters:

•An Island of Jersey husband reports that his wife has achieved up to six orgasms per session and increased her bust measurement from thirty-six to thirty-nine inches because, prior to copulation, he attaches pumps to her breasts of the type used to extract milk from nursing mothers. "Could there be any danger?" he inquires, noting that he and his wife have thus had it off through sixteen years of marriage. "No danger in this practice," reassures *Forum*'s expert, "if ordinary common sense is used."

•A housewife has calculated the total footage of penage she has received during her marriage.

•A man has damaged himself on pips during his love affair with an orange. Another reader writes suggesting the "much more sophisticated choice of fruit . . . of the British soldier in Middle East Forces . . . the melon."

How does a stranger find such strange produce or, more to the point, such epicures? There are, of course, the personal advertisements on notice boards and in some newspapers and periodicals. A modern advertising agency specializing in *double-entendre* or simply kinky adverts—not to mention quite legitimate ones for marriage and/or simple companionship—could make millions. To avoid complications with the law, the English have evolved a method of advertising that is simultaneously evasive, informative, and witty. The visitor to England should be aware of this fact, and how it sets London apart from the Continental cities. Note, too, that the various purveyors of "the secret life" abhor publicity and appear to have all the custom they can handle from Englishmen, but are generally open to discreet newcomers. The English police are as fair and polite as any in the world, but they enforce the law strictly.

London can be a very wild goose chase: specific addresses have less longevity and are harder to ferret out than in other European cities. However, general locales, neighborhoods, and unusual practices, not to mention legal enterprises (but even these do not much appreciate notoriety) remain remarkably stable. The English, after all, worship tradition. *Thus you can know a great deal about what is happening in London if you know what has happened.*

THE GUARDSMEN'S BROTHEL

When next you are privileged to admire the stirring and excruciatingly precise pageantry of the Changing of the Guard or the Guards on Parade, temper your condolences that these fellows, so ascetic in their royally appointed rounds, lead similarly austere and abstinent private lives. Surely many do. However, brothels accommodating the special needs of a certain genre of Guards officer, active or retired, have thrived "since Julius Caesar was a pup." Such a fetish for secrecy in matters sexual have the English, and so sacrosanct remains the tradition of the "Guardsmen's Brothel," that a foreigner has great difficulty establishing its location, though any number of people are delighted to tantalize you with rich details of architecture, amenities, and personnel, as well as appropriate historical notes.

"Smartest knock-shop in London," says a publican.

"No set fee for the regulars," adds a chatty eavesdropper, "rather some sort of honorarium. Like a gentleman's club. Faded piss-elegant drawing room; sherry, tea, cakes—that sort of thing. Mountbatten-pink sheets."

A journalist is certain you're seeking a certain "Mrs. Featherston-Haugh, 'Ma Feathers,' that is. . . . An incredible string of blue films hidden under her floorboards. A fiver for about three quarters of an hour. Not your John Gilbert, 1927 on-the-couch thing, but real productions. Clever plots. I recall one in which this chap and his lady friend quarrel. He goes to sleep, but she's restless you see. Starts playing with herself, grabs his machine, has a quick gobble. Thinks he's dreaming, he does, then suddenly wakes up. They finish hanging from the chandeliers . . . get the cat in, and the postman too."

By now you've drawn a crowd in the little pub. One man recalls "this gigantic Victorian palace where for a fee one might partake of every known English fetish with real beauties, absolutely the bees' ["the bees' knees"]. . . . A covey of debs on call at an hour's notice. . . . Quite right, daughters of the best families, some very old blood's been spilled in *that* place. Though nowadays you can't tell a deb from a tart, the one dresses so much like the other. Mini-Minor and fifteen hundred a year. Do it for kicks, and the money too. They say one Guardsman found his sister there, another his fiancée, and him cunny-haunted seven months by her. . . ." Feeding this Englishman stout is like putting quarters into a jukebox.

". . . Of course, somebody's always trying to get at the Guards. Handsome devils, many of 'em. Honed sharp as a stone by breeding and discipline. And a bit hard-baked [constipated; strict, unyielding] as well. If it's not the Tommy Dodds [Cockney rhyming slang for "sods,"—sodomists], well-off poofers, and so forth suckin' 'round their pubs . . . it's the ladies, and not your ten-o'clock girls [cheap whores, in reference to that morning hour when they answer charges in court of unlawful soliciting], mind you. In the days when Guardsmen wore those high Wellington boots, many a duchess with horns to sell would drop a pound note right in: 'Meet you in the foliage for a quimming,' and that. Even nowadays your young Guardsman's very poorly paid, can always use an extra quid to take his dolly to the pictures. Now your Guards officer, he's middle or upper class. Likely graduated Sandhurst. When he's not seeing to the Queen—holding her safe from harm, that is—and marching about, you may find him at the Guards Club in Birdcage Walk, officers only. . . . But of course *any* well-set-up gentleman *with proper introductions* might pay his fiver and be welcome at a house like Ma Feathers'. And the majority of your Guards people are good family men."

"The Queen's Household Cavalry are drawn from Royal Horse and Life, and they're sent in rotation all round the world to stick a Wilkinson up some wog's bum [Westernized Oriental Gentleman], keep the peace. Though they may *look* like toy soldiers, they're the toughest fighting men in the world. And when they're sent back to London—well, you can rely on it—nobody's splittin' more whiskers. But no particular regiment patronizes a house like Ma Feathers'. It's traditionally a kind of retired gentleman's club, and also very much a part of a young Guardsman's education, so he won't go and make a mess of his wife."

Everyone Is Talking but No One Is Telling

But where is it![2]

Everyone has an anecdote, but no one an exact address. You've run a dozen snipe hunts, chasing down vague addresses in Launceston Place, Bourne

[2]Perhaps one's researches are inhibited by Scotland Yard, which, according to the newspapers, investigated an alleged great hutch of homosexuals—including many prominent figures—in connection with wild parties held at a certain Berkshire mansion, and in several Chelsea and Mayfair apartments. Five Guardsmen, since transferred to Germany, were alleged to have decorated the orgies. Members of Queen Elizabeth's Household Cavalry and the Welsh Guards were reported to be among those under investigation. Allegedly, two hundred-odd members of the Woman's Royal Army Corps have been under Army interrogation concerning lesbianism in London's Inglis Barracks. It should be noted that homosexual activities in groups and any homosexual behavior among members of the armed forces are still crimes in England, notwithstanding the comparatively recent law that has again legalized homosexual acts between consenting male adults. In modern times, tribadism among consenting females has been the subject of no legislation.

Street, Cadogan Place—all plausible for their proximity to Chelsea Barracks, Chelsea Bridge Road, where many (but not all) Guardsmen are quartered. (Here the mildest reply to your inquiries was "Go and eat coke and shit cinders.") Leaving no stones unturned, you've phoned all three Featherston-Haughs listed, and from the indignant responses, yours are not the first inquiries. Unequivocally, Ma Feathers has no connection with any Featherston-Haugh in the London phonebook. Not much better luck with the aged hall porters in Eaton Square—some of whom, you were touted, knew the place well—though two agree a trip to Elvaston Place might prove worthwhile. A similar consensus among several acquaintances made in S.W. 1 pubs frequented by Guards officers; among them THE ANTELOPE (22 Eaton Terrace), THE STAR (6 Belgrave Mews West; a bit of old Profumo perfume here), and THE GRENADIER (in Wilton Row off Wilton Crescent, behind Belgrave Square). The last-named is among the ever-increasing number of pubs where young girls arrive unescorted, a favorite of debutantes to whom it is known as "the Gren."

Three A.M.: chilly, lonely, ignorant, and foolish, you wander Elvaston Place, Kensington, S.W. 7 (a short, wide residential street of almost identical five-story Victorian townhouses, most of which appear to have been divided up into roomy flats), having been assured that this is *the* place by three apparently reliable sources. "Just opposite a structure which was once some sort of depot for U.S. Marines," the most garrulous had offered. "But I can't give you the exact street number. Wouldn't be sporting. It's on a corner, however." Elvaston Place, though merely the length of one crosstown New York City street has some sixteen corners, so bisected is it by mews. In London, even the mews have mews.

You spy a solitary figure strolling his dog. Whether he is intrigued by the hour and the nature of your inquiry, or is merely answering one eccentricity with another, he immediately responds by presenting his card and an invitation to chat the following afternoon.

"Yes, your Guardsman has entrée to so very much that's hidden and most secret among the upper classes, and I don't mean your swinging London rubbish. Among mature people he's very much in demand for weekend dos in the country," explains your new friend next afternoon amid the clutter of books and pamphlets in his study. He's a bookish sort, about fifty, attired in Sturdy Tweeds with hair to match, and no expert on brothels or Guardsmen. "But I've lived in the neighborhood many years. Now, then, come along. Let's have a look at it. It's just round the corner."

"Welcome to the Hotel Divan, 31 Elvaston Place, 589-6265. Your satisfaction is our pleasure. Singles from £4, doubles from £6. All with razor and TV points," promises the brochure. (£1 equals about $2.61; but rates are subject to change at a moment's notice.)

"Yes, this is what it's come to," sighs Sturdy Tweeds. "I'm afraid you've missed it, closed down some time ago. The current occupants are a solid second-class hotel, patronized by, among others, travelers from the Levant. They have no idea what went on here years ago, and of course the current management and patrons have nothing to do with such activities."

To the Turkish desk clerk: "My friend will shortly require accommodation for a period of three months for five of his aunts and three nephews arriving from the United States. Would you be good enough to lead us a tour of the entire premises.

"See there," whispers Tweeds, "that was the parlor . . . back*gam*mon, films, newspapers . . . sometimes the girls did a dress parade here. . . ." Second Floor: "Tatty Turkish modern, but look! Look there! See, they've partitioned the wall. This was the main ballroom. . . . Ahhhh, what this house has seen. . . ." Now to the desk clerk: "Tell me, my good man, what exactly *was* this place before you chaps converted it to a hotel?"

"Some kind of gentleman's club, I believe, sir."

Newspaper accounts confirm that a Mrs. Jessie Margaret Featherston-Haugh (pronounced Fanshawe, of course) was indeed twice convicted of keeping a brothel at portions of 31 Elvaston Place. But since 1955 the premises and new occupants have been thoroughly respectable and law-abiding.

Back at his flat, Tweeds moves to his telephone.

"Hallo, Irvin . . . Did you enjoy your chicken? Oh, very good!! What? Well, we'd had some stuffed calves' hearts and they were very nice. . . . Now then, do you recall that Featherston woman? The whore shop, remember it? . . . Very high class. Yes . . . and so she's long since retired, has she? But somebody must be carrying on the good work? I see. . . . I see. . . . Thanks awfully. Good-bye."

He scratches the springer spaniel's head, has a word with it. Then turns to you.

"Well, as you know, brothels are illegal in England. What is more, the law is now more strictly enforced than it was before the passage of the Street Offenses Act. Now that which constitutes a brothel is any flat which contains more than one girl for hire. Of course, there's a way round it: girls occupying different flats in the same premises. You'll find that sort of thing in Shepherd Market vicinity and in Soho. Small parlors operate for short periods here in Kensington and Victoria, serving the Guards and others as well, but they are generally not known for their creature comforts. You've nothing nowadays (at least nothing *officially*) on the order of Kate Merrick's club in Gerrard Street—not since the Prince of Wales became Edward VII. And nothing on the scale of Rosa Lewis's Cavendish Hotel in Jermyn Street. In the 1920s there was no finer house in the Empire. [All that has closed long since, of course.] Rosa was one of Edward VII's favorite mistresses when he was Prince of Wales. They say he bought the Cavendish for her.

"On the other hand you do have your caterers—procuresses. Sometimes they arrange lavish parties. There's a Frenchwoman in New Bond Street, or perhaps it's an Englishwoman with a French name. Very expensive merchandise. Hardly for a Guardsman, unless he's a peer as well. There's a great deal of freelance activity in Mayfair, but one mustn't be too specific about it. Even if one could, it moves about quite a bit."

A London prostitute has problems, notes a bobby and he is not speaking here of the law. "If a man is unattached, around forty or less, and in reasonably good health, he can knock off perhaps fifty birds a year. They do it almost as a matter of etiquette." Where does a man find such a girl in London? "You sort of find them on the tops of buses."

Never mind that London is a city of massive dimensions. (The public transportation system is comfortable, clean, efficient, and relatively inexpensive; however the Underground and most buses stop after 12:30 A.M., and taxis become rather scarce at late hours.) Your geographic areas of interest are well defined, close enough to one another, and for the most part nicely compact, being small cities or towns—which in fact they once were—within a great city.

If the unknown author of *My Secret Life* (hereafter referred to as "Walter") could relive it in London of the 1970s, the thrust of his interest would center on Mayfair, with more than occasional side trips to Soho, Shepherd's Bush, Notting Hill, Bayswater and other Paddington areas, and Earl's Court. But if he could somehow be persuaded to temper the pathological need to accomplish nearly all sexual connections by retail or wholesale purchase—by his own account the vast majority were made in this manner—he might spend up to half his time hovering about the boutique dressing rooms of the King's Road and Kensington High Street. Like so many men of his class and times, Walter's conquests were primarily the result of economic superiority, and he saw as neither immoral nor unsportsmanlike the sexual exploitation of the lower classes. He'd be surprised, then, to find so many of their descendants —perhaps not a few of his own progeny—independent enough economically (though the average London girl earns no more than £20 to £25 a week) and so emancipated socially as to be giving graciously what was stolen or hired in the Victorian era. Nor are the daughters of the middle and upper classes any more inhibited; if anything, less so. Money never hurts, but the new currency is youth, talent, humor, or illusions thereof. Hair helps.

Which is not to say that thousands of "secret lives" are not being led in London today. The nature of the Englishman has changed less than the pop songs and swinging travel posters would have you believe. And the older he gets, the more English he becomes.

PROSTITUTION: HISTORY AND LAW

A well-established tradition of culture and law guarantees an English-woman the right to "offer her body to indiscriminate lewdness for hire" as inalienable. That this may be a male Magna Carta protective of the English-man's superego and reflective of a traditional preoccupation with and abnormal fear of homosexuality will not be debated. (Unless the English can explain why penalties have always been stricter and the ratio of convictions far higher in cases of males offering themselves for sexual hire to other males, as opposed to females offering themselves to males.)

Modern English law has been concerned primarily with amenities—the civility of the solicitation; prostitution per se probably hasn't been illegal since Cromwell. The pompous hypocrisy of the basic Parliamentary Act of 1839 —that society must be protected from the annoyances of street tarts—is reflected in the current law. In fact, the 1839 Act remained in force until midnight August 15, 1959, when the celebrated (by ponces) Street Offenses Act took effect. The old law threatened a fine of 40 shillings to any prostitute who solicited to the "annoyance of the inhabitants or passengers . . . in any thoroughfare or public place."

That the Act was rarely enforced with much consistency or enthusiasm (and that no one should have been surprised by the discrepancies between Dickens' London and that of *My Secret Life*) is illustrated by the 1881 testimony of a London police officer before the House of Lords: ". . . from three o'clock in the afternoon, it is impossible for any respectable woman to walk from the top of the Haymarket to Wellington Street, Strand. From three or four o'clock in the afternoon Villiers Street and Charing Cross Station and the Strand are crowded with prostitutes, who are there openly soliciting prostitution in broad daylight. At half-past twelve at night a calculation was made . . . that there were five hundred prostitutes between Piccadilly Circus and the bottom of Waterloo Place. . . ."

According to the Wolfenden Report, issued in the mid-1950s, from which the passage is quoted, the situation did not much improve (or worsen, depending on your viewpoint) in subsequent years. In spite of periodic public outcries, by the early 1950s the heart of London—an area bounded by Oxford Street, Charing Cross Road, Piccadilly, and Park Lane, with extensions into the Bayswater Road and the Haymarket—was a solid fleshmarket. Airplanes were arriving with what would soon be millions of American tourists (more of whom visit England than any European country), among them Billy Graham, who saw London as one vast brothel. The public and press howled for a cleanup. Perhaps not coincidentally, the Wolfenden Committee had been appointed and subsequently submitted its famous report. As Geoffrey Fisher, Archbishop of Canterbury, noted, the report was particularly praiseworthy for drawing a clear distinction between crime and sin. More specifically, it concluded that "prostitution can be eradicated only through measures directed to a better understanding of the nature and obligations of sex relationships and to a raising of the social and moral outlook of society as a whole." As it has transpired, the current generation of English young has done more than its share in implementing the flatulent words of the Committee.

The Street Offenses Act of 1959, by making it an offense per se to loiter or solicit in public for purposes of prostitution—striking out any qualifications that an "annoyance" need be committed as well—facilitated arrests; fines were increased, prison terms made stiffer, the police were empowered to enforce the law strictly. Moralists hailed the new law, pointing to figures showing a drastic reduction in arrests for street offenses. But others knew better. Wrote former London vice squad chief John Gosling: "The remedy may well prove worse than the disease."

Prostitutes were driven indoors, or at least behind drawn shades. (And no posing in the windows à la Hamburg.) Carry on, but don't display the merchandise in public; nor state your business on brass nameplates at your doors like a surgeon or proper solicitor; nor advertise with the frankness demanded of other professionals. For all these could be deemed "soliciting in a public place."

"A three-pipe problem," Holmes would have called it.

To their credit, the doxies gave a Shavian interpretation to the Street Offenses Act: Her Majesty's Government really doesn't care what you do, as long as you don't call it by its proper name.

The Message Is "Massage"

Considering the comparatively low level of their education—but credit the indigenous flair for creative syntax and inventive euphemism, even among the lower classes—the former streetgirls responded with some of the most ingenious advertising copy the century has seen. The "adverts" began to appear on notice boards at tobacconists', newsdealers', and in daily newspapers as they had during certain other periods in English history for the past three hundred years or so. Hundreds of doorbells became suddenly illuminated, showing only a given female name, sometimes with the hint "Model" added. For a visitor translating the offerings of the coded cards and ads became as challenging as doing the *Times* crossword. Masochism, sadism, scatology, bondage, humiliation, fellatio, even sexual intercourse—the variety of interests catered to, the opportunities offered, are exceeded only by the nomenclature.

From among several boards in Soho, for example, one might obtain the following goods and services: "Full theatrical wardrobe for hire. Wigs, shoes, boots, chains, etc."; "Recaning of basket chairs"; "Student Teacher, English-

Hebrew . . . Seeks new position. No post too large, too small or too difficult"; "Large Italian chest of drawers for sale. Beautiful moulding"; "Stocks and bonds for rent"; "Young titled Lady will give lessons in speech correction and discipline. Phone Lady Penny–Candy Cane."

A great many advertisers have small flats in Paddington, Bayswater, and Notting Hill where, in addition to Victoria, Shepherd's Bush, and Soho, many boards are located. Fees range from £3 to £5; and up to £10 for services involving special equipment or more than one woman. Who can say what they look like? The advertisers give precious little information over the telephone. But many are near thirty or more and it is a fair axiom that the more complex the service, the older and less attractive its practitioner.

Bayswater: A Typical Beat

For a visit to a typical neighborhood, drive Oxford Street west past Marble Arch along the Bayswater Road (or take the Underground to Bayswater or Queensway stations). Turn into Queensway, Bayswater's bustling high street. No harm in a few all-night restaurants. God knows London has a dearth of them. In front of Barclay's Bank a busker, seventy or more, strums Debussy on a full-sized harp. But as he pauses there are *voce velata* wafting from the direction of Inverness Terrace, or is it Porchester Gardens? Could it be the hint of "Fly buttons sewn on and removed"? "French Polishing"? "Tongue Lashings"? "Erections and Demolitions"? Are the ads simply cute come-ons? Or is the "code" for the protection of the shopkeeper, who can avoid prosecution for "living off immoral earnings" by blandly maintaining that he presumed, in accepting such notices, that they were the legitimate advertisements of a tailor, a furniture cleaner, an elocution specialist, and a real estate developer?

Prostitutes have lived here in Bayswater since sometime before Edward VII fashioned a love nest for mistress Lillie Langtry in what is now the thoroughly respectable and law-abiding INVERNESS COURT HOTEL (1 Inverness Terrace, W.2; 229-1444).[3]

But there's more to this area than shady ladies and illuminated doorbells, and ex-royal residences. At the green baize table of a typical, small, private, ethnic gambling club, one of England's 150,000 Poles—all of whom apparently served with the RAF and are exiled aristocracy—pauses in mid-deal as his pretty daughter serves clear soup and great chunks of seedless rye bread to the poker players. "The bet is 25 pounds. Do you call the 25 pounds?"

"I will call . . . an ambulance."

Now that you've lost your shirt, remove the rest of your clothing and

[3]The leaded stained-glass windows and baroque Edwardian reception rooms make the Inverness Court a colorful choice for your wedding reception—about £3 a head. An excellent budget hotel, as well.

choose among QUEENSWAY HEALTH CLUB's charming masseuses (125 Queensway, W.2). But unlike in certain other massage situations, you are not permitted to do the masseuse. Three guineas, including use of sauna, gym, and plunge pool.

At BRUSH N' PALETTE (86 Queensway; BAY 2572) £1-£1.50 buys a meal of sorts and the opportunity to sketch or admire nude models who rotate every quarter hour. (Licensed to 3 A.M.) Materials are gratis. "We are basically a restaurant," explains an employee. "We have shown the pubic area since 1959, but not the *main* pubic hair. That is, she is not supposed to spread her legs." Art library. Children's classes Saturday mornings (landscapes only).

One of the best places in London to meet attractive girls of good albeit modest families is QUEENS ICE SKATING ARENA, in Queensway. They also have ice skating here.

There are some "business girls" in the neighborhood, especially along the Bayswater Road and in nearby Paddington, whose morbid nocturnal gloom is interrupted only by the shrill shrieks of steam locomotives echoing from the vast somber rail depot. Between whistles you may discern the delighted moans elicited by the openings of Paddington's full psychological umbrella: "Experienced organ grinder and instrument polisher. Also, organs bound, fastened securely"; "Domestic employment opportunities for gentlemen. Strict governess. Uniforms supplied"; "Large selection of rainwear and rubber articles. Machine tools. Miss Caine Mutiny"; "German Girl gives French or Swedish lessons to English gentlemen. Also speaks Hebrew. No coloured." Paddington also has many cheap, no-questions-asked bed-and-breakfast hotels, £3 to 4 for two. And many lonely young Irish and uplands girls—runaways who may sleep with strangers merely for a comfortable bed. The lack of transportation, the darkness and vastness of London, can make it a desperately lonely place to be in the wee hours.

Accustomed to being the major immigrant group in England, the Irish have had a measure of pressure removed by the West Indians. "Toasted Irishmen," they're called. Many live in Notting Hill and Shepherd's Bush, just west of Paddington. "Dusky Dolls for Sale," read some notices, and others "Shamrock Festival," "Four-Leaf Clovers for hire." The Notting Hill area is, along with Soho, a traditional center of narcotics distribution. As to centers of narcotics *use* in London—get stoned blind and shove a roach (they make them big as cigars here) in most any area of a map showing the West End. But while hash—spiked with anything from opium to Bovril—is readily available in some Soho coffee clubs and discothèques, good grass is harder to find than a good man.

By night the kerbs of Ladbroke Grove crawl with cars; £3-to-5 quickie tarts (the word was once no pejorative—the English have a great sweet tooth and to compare a girl with their beloved cakes and preserves was high praise indeed) commute from their rear seats to the cellars of after-hours drinking clubs. The law is so strict regarding pubs and clubs allowing their premises to be used by soliciting prostitutes that many publicans, like a group in Wolverhampton (and all Wimpy bars after 11 P.M.) refuse to serve unaccompanied women. But the Street Offenses Act has forced the girls to seek a variety of beats. Many Notting Hill clubs have been shut down, but several carry on, a couple with vending machines in the ladies' rooms dispensing contraceptives. Sometimes the whores hide their "French letters" inside their garter belts, an area where a suspicious policeman probably will not search for presumptive evidence of soliciting. (But a randy one might.)

A fair quota of illuminated doorbells and notice boards is found in the vicinity of Earl's Court, which nestles between Chelsea and Kensington, south of Notting Hill. ("Koala Bear for sale"; "Baby Wallaby has soft pouch for hire.") Dubbed "Kangaroo Walk," the Earl's Court Road features some lively coffee shops, all-night restaurants, friendly launderettes, and pubs catering to Australians, other members of the Commonwealth, and *au pair* girls. The following dialogue surely never took place (well, surely no more than a half dozen times), but is nonetheless illustrative of the reputed forthrightness of Australian girls:

IRISH BOY: Will you then?
AUSTRALIAN GIRL: I will do.
BOY: My flat or yours?
GIRL: Well, if you want to argue about it, forget it.

Not every illuminated doorbell in London rings sex for sale. (But if it adds "Model," don't expect the Queen Mother at the top of those narrow, rickety stairs.) *Nor are all adverts suspect.* Many *au pairs* really do seek charge of your progeny rather than your prong. And one is certain that all those ads in the *Times* for "high colonic irrigation" are perfectly legitimate. Neither the *Times*, the law, nor the Enema Mum is at all concerned that you may be an enema freak—that is, one who derives sexual satisfaction and release from "the pleasure and the anguish of the enema"—a quote attributed to Huxley by a *Forum* correspondent who described himself as "hooked" on the Higginson syringe.

But one can sympathize with a young Kensington mother of three who, after scanning the "Personals," sighed, "It's getting harder and harder to find a strict nanny these days, the poor dears are simply too terrified to advertise."

"Does it matter what she looks like?" asks the debby British Travel associate. "Well, of course it matters, damn it!" snorts her boss, a Cambridge man. "The fact a man cannot have any *choice*, they being off the streets and all . . . hiding behind these adverts . . . so you don't know what you're getting until you go in there . . . why it's pure *socialism!*"

Outdoor Venues

If one insists on paying for sex, then, he will pay dearly with time and money for the privilege of selection. In addition to street beats already noted, there are young runaways prowling Soho, especially Wardour Mews and Oxford Street (£3-5, but up to £10 if the punter is overripe), and many poodle-walkers prancing Mayfair, mostly on Park Lane. More in Curzon Street and Shepherd Market, particularly in the vicinity of Hertford Street and Pitt's Head Mews. Mayfair rates vary from £5 to £25, depending on the time involved, the quality of the girl, the services performed. (A particularly active, fancy dosshouse in Park Lane, the girls will show you where it is; £10 a time.)

Daylight venues include country lanes like Box Hill, Surrey, and the lovely fields between Lambourne End and Ongar in Essex. Until sundown one finds some of these scrubbers in Cable Street in the East End. But these are small potatoes. Since the Street Offenses Act, London prostitution has become a big-time indoor game, and prices have soared.

Hostesses and Clubs

In many West End supper clubs and cabarets, attractive and very companionable young hostesses and dancing partners *may*, after closing hours, "go case" with clients who can stand the expensive preliminaries. Consult the ads and listings in entertainment guides to ascertain which clubs are currently offering feminine companionship. From there on it's simply a process of trials, errors, and elimination of funds to see what can happen after hours. In addition to club membership fees (often reduced for overseas visitors), the cost of dinner, beverages for two (higher with a floor show), the hostess fee (generally £5), and the tip to the knowledgeable barman or waiter, you'll have invested £25 or more *on the chance* that she may accompany you after an early-morning closing. If she does, *her* £20-to-50 gratuity includes breakfast, an old English custom. Of course, the management of a club is not legally responsible for what a girl does on her own time, and few clubs extract a percentage of after-hours fees. Many, in fact, insist that they pay their hostesses no salary whatsoever, including that club which advertises a midnight closing "so the girls can get to bed early," and another where fornications could be charged on a well-known credit card. All of which rather begs the question of just how these girls do manage to make a living. But somehow, they manage.

Some clubs maintain bedrooms right on the premises; these are available solely in case a guest becomes a bit weary from too much food or drink. But in the history of modern London nightclubbery there has been not one single *documented* case of a fornication occurring between the sheets of one of these comfy beds. Rest assured.

Call Girls and Madams

Costs are lower, procedures less complex when dealing with call-girl rings or with the girls themselves, who during off-duty periods may grace the bars and lobbies of some of the better hotels—some rather near Park Lane. At any given period several madams offer models, film starlets, nymphomaniac debutantes, and other high-caliber merchandise. Prudent inquiries among that incestuous group of doormen, cabbies, waiters, hairdressers, and company chauffeurs, plus a well-placed fiver may put you through to some of London's better madams, and surely will afford a direct line to some of Mayfair's better call girls. (The definitive guide to London nightlife could be written from access to the little address books of the aforementioned gentlemen.) The more personal your introduction—say from the "social secretary" or a business associate from the branch office of your London firm—the better you'll fare. Otherwise, for all a procurer or madam knows, you could be a policeman or, worse, a journalist.

If you want some idea about the current state of affairs, a copy of Sunday's *News of the World* (largest single-issue circulation in the world) or *The People* may help. Though each paper takes a dim editorial view of London's whore life, they keep the police and other readers up on preferred neighborhoods, prices, and amenities (inadvertently, to be sure).

In the late 1960s, for example, the *News* sent forth a team of investigative reporters posing as punters to gather material for a feature subsequently headlined "London's Vice 'Madams.' " According to accounts:

Madam O (the full names are not pertinent here), an attractive and well-spoken brunette in her thirties, was found in her lavishly furnished, wall-to-wall-carpeted High Street flat in Marylebone, just above Mayfair. ("In the parish of Mary-le-bone only, 13 thousand ladies of pleasure reside," noted M. D'Archenholz in *A Picture of England*, London, 1789.) Among her alleged clients—"members of Parliament . . . Abdullahs . . .," a Kuwaiti oilman who "comes to me because I have the best and cleanest girls in London," Madam O told investigators, who "left when the girls began an obscene exhibition." Price: £40, of which £15 went to each young lady. "I can arrange anything," the *News* quoted Madam O: "Big parties . . ." for a group of 14, about "£150 plus the food and champagne."

Madam W, the most attractive of the madams interviewed and not above taking an "active part in the vice business herself," according to *News* researchers, operated from a Seymour Street flat just above Marble Arch. (Two madams and several independent call girls operate within three blocks of Seymour Street at this writing.) One, a film star, "holds some marvellous orgies at her country home." During the conversation a girl called Pam stripped to her bra and "leaf-patterned panties" and began shaking to a

Beatles record. When their services were declined, the two girls offered an "obscene exhibition" for £15 each, which was paid but reporters declined to watch, made excuses, and left. On another occasion reporters booked into a smart London hotel to await the arrival of "Lady Margaret," who emerged from a chauffeur-driven limousine wearing skin-tight black PVCs and a £15 pricetag.

Through a "spyhole" Madam B screened clients prior to admitting them to her smart Knightsbridge den, just a short distance from Harrods, where she has operated for ten years and "never had any trouble from the police." On hand was Judy, a beautiful nineteen-year-old blonde, moonlighting from her job in a West End boutique. "A lovely girl and a good worker," waxed Madam B, "she has been with one of my other girls to an embassy for a sex party which included a prince." Among her clients, she described a clergyman who "comes here once a week" and had assured her: "You will go to Heaven for pleasing me—I shall go to Hell." Speak of the devil and the doorbell rang. The priest had arrived, according to reporters, "complete with dog collar."

At this writing two extremely fetishy madam-practitioners, near Montpelier Street, do a very smart Knightsbridge trade.

Other *News of the World* investigators booked into a London hotel posing as businessmen on a spree. Judy and Jennifer, a twenty-two-year-old nanny to a society couple's children, arrived, undressed, and "began a display so perverted that it cannot be described here." All services were declined and Judy suggested, "I have many clients who like being whipped. I quite enjoy it and they pay very well—up to fifty pounds." The girls were paid £20 for their troubles. Mistaking the reporters' abstinence for jade, Madam B was exasperated but undaunted. "Well, what do you want?" she was quoted. "Would you like to watch an exhibition tonight? I have a Harley Street doctor and his nymphomaniac girlfriend coming round at ten o'clock. They are a really kinky couple and love someone to watch them."

When you deal with madams in exclusive Mayfair, Knightsbridge, and high-rent areas of Marylebone, you are paying a premium for real estate. Often equally attractive and even younger girls can be had from madams like J who, from her luxury flat in Inverness Terrace, Bayswater, was said to offer attractions like beautiful blond M of Warlock Road, Paddington, or A of Palace Gardens Terrace, Notting Hill—from £3 to £5. A Notting Hill madam offers "typists" for £10 of which £5 is the "agency fee." Inverness Terrace and environs are, at this writing, still hot, though prices have risen a bit since the late 1960s. (And the area is being overrun by tour coaches.)

Two prostitutes sharing a flat—even for company or safety—constitute a brothel as the law sees it and are thus in violation of the law; if a boyfriend moves in (however innocent the circumstances), he must prove that he has earned his share of the rent or be liable to charges of procuring or living off the immoral earnings of another. And, of course, any so-called "madam" may be liable under similar charges. However, convictions in this area are not easy to secure. Consider the story of J, the sensuous pop singer.

The Story of J

That a wealthy young industrialist, Mr. A, was willing to risk his reputation and marriage by admitting his own participation in what he alleged were sex orgies with a popular female pop singer, Miss J, and several other girls failed to sway a twelve-man jury, which found her not guilty of his charge of sexual blackmail. Names of blackmailees are always kept secret in such proceedings; of the dozens of women who fought for the three seats available to the public in the Old Bailey's tiny No. 8 courtroom, three admitted they'd come to see if Mr. A was their husband. "My wife doesn't know," he shuddered. "I've spent my time editing her newspapers."

Questioned closely by the Crown regarding her friendships with celebrities of the nobility and theater—including "Prince Farah . . . Sir Charles," and a retired naval commander—Miss J described them as "platonic." Why had she a list of phone numbers of the Mayfair, Dorchester, and other London hotels? "Because I meet friends from the north of England." (For those unfamiliar with London hotels it should be noted that a recent edition of the *Egon Ronay Guide,* Great Britain's *Guide Michelin,* rated the Dorchester second only to the Savoy as London's finest hotel, though it laments, "The penalty of continual use shows in bedrooms, which could do with touching up." The Mayfair, in Berkeley Street, is also highly touted, with rooms varying "from slick modern to opulent period styles.")

During the trial, police later claimed they had received an anonymous phonecall describing Miss J's flat: ". . . this is still a very thriving brothel. . . . Their motto is 'Have whips will travel' . . . contacts are made through clubs and hotels . . . among them X at the Cumberland." ("Massive, impersonal perhaps, but charged somehow with the undercurrent of excitement that you find at the great international airports," notes *Egon Ronay.*) Immediately following her blackmail acquittal, police charged Miss J with operating a "high-class brothel."

Again, Miss J was exonerated.

MAYFAIR

If you direct a business in Mayfair—embassies, hotels, saunas, gaming houses, supper and night clubs, advertising agencies, corporate headquarters, copulation or flagellation parlors—or if you live here—millionaires, aristocrats and/or their children, madams, governesses, and the best-kept freelance whores in England—you have one of London's most select addresses. Berkeley Square was a great fashion when laid out as open frontage for the pre-Buckingham Palace royal residence at Berkeley House, but lately the area has grown increasingly commercial—banks, auto showrooms, and those well-kept freelance ladies. Horace Walpole died at No. 11, Clive of India was a suicide at No. 45, and at No. 44 you can admire *the* exemplification of the Georgian Town House.

Annabel's

Inside 44 is ANNABEL'S (629-3558), a discothèque whose chic is exceeded only by its cheek. ("No, No. We are *not* a discothèque. We are a late-dining club.") Whatever it is, Princess Margaret loves it. (Her niece, Princess Anne, prefers RAFFLES in the King's Road, Chelsea.)

Annabel's has: no one but its extremely select membership and their guests, much of the peerage, the world's slimmest, handsomest plus-forty men, many beautiful women of all ages but few of their daughters, superb food, gentle pop sounds, and a gents loo where the glass plates of the urinals are slanted out so that one doesn't urinate on his John Lobbs (9 St. James's Street; crocodile and leopardskin for 76 guineas). Annabel's also has: a hidden bar off the two main ones for hiding pop and film stars and noisy, rich American people; a chatty lounge with latest issues of *Country Life, Punch,* and *The New Yorker;* a stock ticker, Onassis, Henry Ford, at least one Pole, and forty poles—only five of which are structural—that cleverly simulate privacy in the large, coffin-shaped main room. The decor is simple and elegant, though elements change—from displays of semiprecious stones to genteel erotic finger-paintings on the black glass walls. It can cost a pound to spend a penny with Mabel in the ladies'. Annabel's, then, is all one expects Mayfair to be and has simply everything . . . except, perhaps, you. It's certainly worth crashing, if you can somehow get past Jack, the receptionist. The simplest method is to sneak in through the ladies' cloakroom, which connects to the CLERMONT (Aspinall's). But the Clermont is probably even more difficult to crack than Annabel's for followed by nearby QUENT'S (Hill Street) and CURZON HOUSE (Curzon Street), it is the most discriminating gaming house in London. That is, they have the highest stakes and most refined play, and exercise microscopic scrutiny of your accounts and pedigree (if you have the former, the latter probably doesn't matter) before you are permitted to join and lose your £50,000. The 21 CLUB (8 Chesterfield Gardens, W.1), housed in the late Lord Chesterfield's splendid digs, offers an exciting evening of dining, dancing, and gambling, even to non-millionaires. COUNTER–REVOLUTION (14–19 Bruton Place; to 3 A.M.) is a workingman's discothèque set in the heart of Mayfair.

Poodle-Walkers and Other Call Girls

Occupying portions of other town houses in and around Berkeley Square are several call girls who let their poodles water the square's famed plane trees in the wee hours, often just after the various neighborhood gaming houses serve the closing breakfast. That they are walking their dogs assures that they never run afoul of The Law. (Provided, of course, the animal does not "foul the foot paths." Social note: A Pyrenean mountain dog, aided by council officials, officially opened the Royal Borough of Kensington and Chelsea's new dogs' lavatory at special ground-breaking ceremonies in mid-March, 1972. According to officials the new loo is part of an experiment to curtail what it calls "incidents" in the borough's lovely gardens.) If you look like you've had a big night at the tables, the tarts may drop a leash to attract you and, for £10 to 25 their panties as well. The later the hour or the nastier the weather, the lower the price. Business is even brisker along Park Lane and in little streets like Pitt's Head Mews and Stanhope Row. There are actual red lights in windows near Shepherd Street and Market Mews.

It is a custom among certain recent public (i.e., private) school graduates to order a call girl (if you know your Mayfair headwaiters, about as difficult as sending out for a pizza in Long Branch, New Jersey) with instructions for her to present herself at a chum's flat bearing a card reading "Surprise. Here's this darling fuck in commemoration of your birthday," or whatever is appropriate to the occasion.

The best Mayfair call girls are such snobs they charge in guineas, not pounds, sometimes 50 or more of them. So be prepared to spend "lots of shmoo."

Costly Corsets

"I am returning the book about mastery over women which
I ordered ten days ago. Unfortunately, my wife would not
let me keep it."
—Letter received by London bookseller (1968)

To describe Madame Medeq simply as a "corsetmaker" is to say no more of Sir Winston Churchill than that he was a civil servant. MEDEQ CORSETIÈRES LTD. (60 Duke Street Mansions, suite No. 10, midway between Grosvenor Square and Oxford Street; by appointment only, 499-6481) specializes in corsetry of the finest leather and workmanship, styled after the fashion of the eighteenth and nineteenth centuries. For the woman who has everything, including someone willing to lace it all up. For a really elaborate accordion-fold corselet—gold or silver lamé if you're bored with basic black—120 guineas should do nicely. All garments, even the 10-guinea panty belts, are custom-made on the premises and fitted to your most rigid requirements.

Madame Medeq, a soft-spoken, dignified lady in her mid-forties, who has perfected her art over twenty years, is as flexible a consultant and adviser as her garments are restrictive; her several male clients receive the same respect and attention as do her many female devotees.

A Sauna

Gentlemen who prefer the touch of an attractive masseuse to leather should walk a block west of Grosvenor Square into Park Street where, at No. 80, 5 guineas admits one to "London's most select sauna," and includes a massage in the "private treatment rooms." Reservations, 493-5111. Also has facilities for female clients.

Designed to physically resemble a fancy geisha house is the MAYFAIR SAUNA CLUB, 4-6 Deanery Street; appointments, MAY 7933/4/5. The staff of comely masseuses are mostly of Far Eastern origin, though one or two hail from no further east than that end of London. Tea or apéritifs are served with some sympathy and much ceremony in the Oriental lounge, where patrons can select their masseuses—all clad in appropriate native costume—and afterward discuss the treatments, perhaps plan the next one. All in all, among the most attractive and proficient masseuses amid the most pleasurable surroundings of any public sauna in London. Fifty guineas per year for company membership, transferable among three individuals; 10 guineas per year for residents living one hundred or more miles outside London. One-shot sauna and massage at 5 guineas, and "special facilities for overseas visitors."

Mayfair is comparatively quiet by day, but you may enjoy lunch at the GUINEA (30 Bruton Place, just behind Berkeley Square); because of its proximity to Norman Hartnell, dressmaker to the Queen, the place is wall-to-wall with fashion models at midday.

"Lovers' Hotels"—of Sorts

"Walter" spent a good deal of his "secret life" on the fringes of Mayfair, whoring along Regent and New Bond Streets. His favorite "accommodation house" (equivalent in function to some of the contemporary "lovers' hotels" of Paris) in "J***s St." may have been in either Jones Street, just off Berkeley Square, or nearby James Street—more likely the latter for its nearness to Oxford Circus and Regent Street according to the brief elapsed time between his many rendezvous thereabouts and subsequent consummations in "J***s St." It was the "best kept, best furnished, snuggest" accommodation house of his experience, where he had some "seventy or eighty women." Even in the mid-nineteenth century Mayfair was not cheap. A sovereign (£2, 18 shillings) for the best room in the house. Accommodation houses are no longer legal in England, nor are city pubs permitted to rent assignation beds, as so many did until the latter part of the nineteenth century. However, several modest hotels in the vicinity of King's Cross (W.C.1) are not at all fussy about the short time some couples occupy their rooms, nor that the registry books resemble cardiogram result sheets.

The SLOOP JOHN D, a floating discothèque-restaurant anchored in the Thames off Cadogan Pier (S.W.3; 223-3341) does have seven or eight private dining rooms containing velvet chaises and inside locks. Lunch and dinner are open to non-members.

In an ordinary hotel, if one has a suite, any female guest, however late the hour or shortness of notice of her arrival, is presumed to be a stenographer. If the girl is staying the night, simply register her as your wife, thereby absolving the hotel management of any responsibility of knowingly operating a "disorderly house." Short-time spur-of-the-moment visits can be risky, unless the appropriate nightman has his fiver. One young "masseuse" who regularly visits several Mayfair hotels reports: "It's more the getting *out* than the getting in that's the problem." This discussion may seem absurd in such a permissive age, in such a permissive city. But it is a fair axiom that the more exclusive the London hotel, often the more bold the escapades of its guests—and thus the more wary and guarded the management.

It's people like the Sultan of X who spoil things for the rest of us. According to the ANTI-SLAVERY SOCIETY, the Sultan "brought at least one girl slave with him" during a recent trip to London. "The young lady was apparently confined to the Dorchester, and the society added that 'There have been many other cases,' " reported *Queen* magazine. The Dorchester is surely not the only fine hotel in town that is alleged to have such sheik.

Curzon Street and Vicinity

When last seen, the reincarnated author of *My Secret Life* was wandering toward Curzon Street—and who could blame him? Curzon Street—fashionable after a fashion, but not quite so *riche* as Berkeley Square—a "street of whores and nobles," according to one longtime resident. Here are clubby restaurants like WHITE ELEPHANT (favorite of American movie producers), chic shops, and CURZON HOUSE (roulette, chemmy, gin rummy, kalooki, poker—all at high stakes), which is owned by the sixth Earl Howe, along with extensive chunks of the neighborhood. Close by is the lighted bell of one of England's busiest governesses, from whose parlor waiting room one has a good view into the sumptuous dining room of Curzon House.

Curzon Street and environs have a rich history. Nell Gwyn, Charles II's mistress, lived and loved in Carrington House, as did Lord Nelson somewhat later on. Here, it is said, he planned the Battle of Trafalgar and here, it is certain, he entertained his mistress, Lady Emma Hamilton, for she lived just around the corner at 11 Clarges Street. Earlier, with other beauties, she had posed as "the Rosy Goddess of Health" for the public lectures on sexual questions delivered by Dr. James Graham, whose nearby "Temple of Health" was among the more arcane eighteenth-century brothels. Those were surely the days, my friend, the prostitute's Age of Aquarius. Though most of the best houses were in St. James's, Curzon Street had its share, including that of Mrs. Banks, which had prostitutes of both sexes.

Eighteenth-century Mayfair was also known for its "Fleet Marriages": quick, no questions asked, no license or parental consent required. Dr. Alexander Keith operated from premises in Curzon Street (now Sutherland House, at No. 19, and in the nineteenth century the home of Disraeli) outside which he displayed the enbalmed body of his wife to attract passersby. Under the motto "Happy's the Wooing that's not long a'doing," he married more than seven thousand couples at a guinea a splice before the authorities closed down his "secret" chapel.

There is a great deal of contemporary secrecy about Leconfield House, if one can believe *The Espionage Establishment.* When the book, published in 1968, suggested the building is headquarters for MI-5, the British counter-espionage agency, there was a hell-fire of high-level embarrassment. Frank inquiries of the uniformed officer on duty behind the reception desk will be met, quick as a flea's leap, by a firm escort back out the front door, with a stern warning not to return. On the opposite side of Curzon Street, perhaps a block and a half east, at No. 39, is what appears to be a school for languages. In the street-level window near the corner of Trebeck Street, a red-neon sign, letters perhaps five inches high, reads: "PRIVATE TUITION IN FRENCH." An aging charlady-type serves as receptionist: "It's six pounds and you'll be usin' a Durex. It's for your protection you know." Through the parlor you glimpse the teacher having a last word with a pupil. She is indeed French, by her accent, about twenty-eight, in lounging robe; tall, slim, and not bad-looking. Though this sort of business is not exactly in MI-5's line—they prefer internal security, spies touring Britain, and other James Bondage—their alleged proximity to "Private Tuition in French" is no less delicious.

For well over a decade the sign has burned most every night till 5 A.M. and the man who originally paid the electric bill was "Uncle Eugene."

Uncle Eugene could be a gem from the pen of Eric Ambler. In fact, in matters of procuring and trafficking in women, real-life Uncle exploits recall those of Dimitrios Makropoulos, the protagonist of Eric Ambler's *Coffin for Dimitrios.* From the late 1930s until at least the early 1960s Eugene was the unchallenged king of London vice, in all languages including French.

Ironically, Eugene died on his wedding night in 1970.

• • •

Much of London's charm and style evolves from its traditions and sense of timelessness. At this writing, for example, French Lessons can still be obtained at 39 Curzon Street, an intensive, total-immersion crash course given from sundown to about 4 or 5 A.M. And an early-1950s visitor to Mayfair would be gratified to find at least a few of the same first names burning as brightly as ever on the doorbells of the 1970s.

Shepherd Market

But it is in Shepherd Market (among whose landlords, quite incidentally, are the Harrow School) that one is confronted by a virtual hardware convention of illuminated nameplates, doorknockers, and bells. Once the afternoon sluice of American antique freaks has gone, this becomes Macintosh Country. And some stalky Bowler Hats as well, their SWAINE, ADENEY, BRIGG & SONS LTD. brollies tucked up the armpit tight as a cavalry officer's riding crop. (Swaine, *et al.*, Whipmakers to the Queen, 185 Piccadilly, also have these latter, £30 with gold mountings.)

FLAGELLATION: "le vice anglais"

It is in Shepherd Market and vicinity that one finds specialties as germane to England's sexual cuisine as turbot, kippers, and kidney pie are to its table: whippings, beatings (one must be born in this country to appreciate the subtle dissimilarity), humiliations, as well as other more prosaic treats. This is not to say that all, or even a near majority, of the neighborhood residents deal in these or similar services. For example, there are some quite attractive, newly arrived French imports who offer straightforward coitus and fellatio hors d'oeuvres. A woman known as "Miss Cupboard-Love" copulates in a closet for £7, charges keyhole observers £3 each. Among the street scenes is a great pillowy blond affair of nineteen who looks a well-preserved forty. Usually turned out in chiffon and leather and eight-inch platform heels, she is very fond of extraordinary colors, particularly bright green, and wears a kind of ultra-Biba makeup. Gets fifteen quid a go for hand jobs. Saving herself for marriage, she says.

Of course the majority of the people around here don't want to know about it. Nor can one suggest that *every* illuminated Christian-named doorbell rings a sturdy lass with a swift true thong who can sense your threshold of pain across a crowded loo. But if you fancy a bit of caning, your chances are probably better around here than any other area of London. Though a bit more common than, for example, the alleged house in the vicinity of nearby Hill Street where "prosperous provincial grocers have a little kick on deprivation of oxygen or a bit of zoophilia with a goose" (so says a local publican), shopping in Shepherd Market is surely more reliable than answering most of the notice-board advertisers, not a few of whom are too young and inexperienced to properly attend the needs of the true connoisseur. Like so many advertisers in the American underground newspapers, some London whores use the kinky codes merely to appear "with-it" and are thus more abusive of the thrashing profession itself then their needy clients.

But certain ladies hereabouts have acquired their exceptional skills through years of observation, apprenticeship, and practical experience in the laboratory and the field. Several insist that they perform services as valuable as and not unlike those of psychiatrists or psychologists. It's not surprising that they attract a very good trade, and though they've not got as much of the peerage as has Annabel's, the neighborhood is traditionally a Tory's delight. Historically, of course, it is the English upper classes, of all the earth's billions, who have been most taken with this thing the French call *le vice anglais.*

Why do the English do this?

One could begin with some generalizations based on certain aspects of the English national character. Foremost is the eccentricity, or "spleen" as the upper classes like to call it, not inconsiderable numbers of whose males to this day consider the profession of Eccentric quite as valid and noble a life's calling as medicine or the law. And certainly, even in this heady decade, a man—or in rare instances a woman—to whom a daily four-o'clock flogging is as necessary as tea and biscuits stands out as something more than a mere individualist. (England is certainly a nation of these; perhaps one reason flagellation has been far more popular here than, say, in Germany.) The desire to inflict pain upon someone else for sexual gratification is, of course, a universal thing, though most people are not as candid about it as are the English. Generally speaking, the ability to bear pain and discomfort with stoicism is a much admired, nay required, trait in this country; hence the gift for understatement. They have what James Bond's chief, M, would call very high thresholds of pain, superior coefficients of toughness. Not to dwell on the exemplary courage and determination in the face of overwhelming hardship and odds during World War II, considering merely their traditional denial of the need for life's simplest amenities, a foreigner comes to believe the English enjoy even the most mundane discomforts.

Perhaps the English are what they are because of what they eat. Iwan Bloch, citing Taine's observations on the Anglo-Saxon diet, provides some historical food for thought: "Taine appears to attribute their excessive use of the rod to their way of life, above all to their over-indulgence in meat and alcohol . . . which certainly serves to encourage the use of a strong stimulant like flagellation. After drinking, and eating an incredible amount of meat, 'the coarse human animal finally satisfies itself with noise and sensuality.' "

Psychiatric theories? It is specious to insist that the English are exemplary of the well-established relationship between pleasure and pain. It is mere coincidence that the definitive work on the subject, *Pleasure and Pain,* was written by an Englishman, Havelock Ellis. Ellis does admit that "Those who possess a special knowledge of such matters declare that sexual flagellation is the most frequent of all sexual perversions in England." Then he hedges a bit: "This belief is, I know, shared by many people inside and outside England." And good Englishman that he was (1859-1939), Ellis attempts to shift some of the burden: "However this may be, the tendency is certainly common." ("Doesn't *everybody*?" is still the most frequent disclaimer one encounters when the subject is broached at cocktail parties between bites on those *super* chive-and-celery canapés.) "I doubt if it is any or at all less common in Germany, judging by the large number of books on the subject of flagellation which have been published in Germany," concludes Ellis.

Simply not so, says Iwan Bloch (1872-1922), sexologist and social "scientist" whose *Sexual Life in England, Past and Present* remains among the richest lodes in the field of English sexual manners and mores, if only for its unsurpassed compilation of original eighteenth- and nineteenth-century sources.[4] (The author apparently had access to the vast pornography library of Henry Spencer Ashbee, possible author of *My Secret Life*.) Indeed, the Arco edition's preface states: "No comprehensive history of English morals written in the English language has ever been published!" Bloch maintains that "the strongest evidence for the prevalence of flagellation mania in English education is the fact that far the greatest part of earlier literature on flagellation in Germany and France was compiled from translations and reproductions of English sources. . . . Neither France nor Germany has produced such a spate of erotic and non-erotic literature on the subject as the English."

Among hundreds (most of which are among the thousands of erotic books Henry Ashbee donated to the BRITISH MUSEUM; write J. L. Wood, Printed Book Dept, London W.C.1, for a visitor's card), there are: *Whipping Tom Brought to Light and Exposed to View* (London, 1681); *Venus School Mistress, or Birchen Sports* (1788); *The Convent School, or Early Experiences of a Young Flagellant* (1876); *The History of the Rod* (1868); *The Romance of Chastisement* (1870); *Lady Bumtickler's Revels, and The Experimental Lecture of Colonel Spanker* (1879); *With Rod and Bum: or Sport in the West End of London—a True Tale by a Young Governess* (1898).

Nor can one ignore more widely known examples such as the whipping scene in *Fanny Hill,* the flagellation-parlor description of the abbess in *My Secret Life,* the caning scene in the film *If. . . .* And, of course, the special proclivities of so many English celebrities are no secret. To name just three: biographer Lytton Strachey; poet Algernon Charles Swinburne, whose "The Flogging Block" (impishly signed "Rufus Rodworthy"), an erotic ode to whip-

[4]First published in German early this century; reprinted in England by Arco Publications Ltd. in 1958 and subsequently in paperback by Corgi Books, London.

ping penned between 1861 and 1881, is held in a private case in the British Museum; and Lord Byron, who penned these lines:

> O ye, who teach the ingenuous youth of nations,
> Holland, France, England, Germany, Spain.
> I pray ye flog them upon all occasions.
> It mends their morals, never mind the pain.

Subtler but no less significant preoccupations are to be noted throughout English literature: in Fielding's *Tom Jones,* Smollett's *Roderick Random,* Dickens' *Nicholas Nickleby,* and Kingsley's *Westward Ho!* And *Alice in Wonderland too:*

> Speak roughly to your little boy,
> And beat him when he sneezes:
> . . . . . .
> For he can thoroughly enjoy
> The pepper when he pleases.

And what of James *Bond?*

The English have shown a remarkable consistency in reviving or maintaining even the most esoteric sexual customs. For example, the magazine *Society* noted, in 1899, the fashion of nipple-piercing for the purpose of inserting what were called "breast rings"—usually of gold. There is a contemporary physician in Harley Street who does nipple, not to mention scrotum and foreskin, piercings, though apparently not under the National Health. (Inquire in some of the more twee gay pubs and restaurants, or ask Monique von Cleef in The Hague.) In the past decade Regency dress, Victorian argot, and modish sexual practices of both periods have had a vogue. Serving such revivals one cannot discount that the English are an exceptionally literate people—nearly always preferring the eroticism and whimsy of the spoken and written word to that of pictures or photographs. From the eighteenth century on, the comparative availability of euphemistic or bold pornography, pseudoserious "medical" texts—compare Spain, or the United States in the fifty years prior to the permissive 1960s—has assured a perpetuation of the old customs; has reassured readers, giving their so-called "aberrations" a kind of historical respectability; and has certainly served to inspire modern experimentations based on early practices and inventions.

Thus, since the 1836 reprint of *Venus School Mistress,* no Englishman with an inclination to chastisement need have suffered identity problems:

"The men who have a propensity for Flagellation may be divided into three classes:

"1. Those who like to receive a fustigation, more or less severe, from the hand of a fine woman, who is sufficiently robust to wield the rod with vigour and effect. [Just such a woman practices today in Shepherd Market.]

"2. Those who desire themselves to administer birch discipline on the white and plump buttocks of a female. [Several French prostitutes in the vicinity of Shepherd Market *may* oblige, but the price can run to £5 a stroke; they much prefer to provide simple sexual intercourse at approximately 20 new pence a stroke.]

"3. Those who neither wish to be passive recipients nor active administrators, but would derive sufficient excitement as mere spectators of the sport. [Those who are so inclined, will just have to make inquiries around the neighborhood; several governesses have regular clients who enjoy an attentive audience.]"

Certain standards are laid down for the profession: "Those women who give most satisfaction to the amateurs of discipline are called governesses, because they have, by experience, required a tact and *modus operandi*, which the generality do not possess. It is not the merely keeping a rod, and being willing to flog, that would cause a woman to be visited by the worshippers of the birch: she must have served her time to some other woman who understood her business, and be thoroughly accomplished."

Madam Berkley's "Horse"

Venus School Mistress reports "20 splendid establishments" were "supported entirely" by flagellants of the late eighteenth century. But it was during the early and mid-nineteenth century that the practice reached its zenith. According to Bloch and several other authorities, "without doubt the queen of flagellation was Mrs. Theresa Berkley, who kept a famous establishment at 28 Charlotte Street, Portland Place." (Her arsenal of pleasure has a modern counterpart near Montpelier Street, Knightsbridge.)

Madam Berkley's pre-eminence was due in no small part to her invention of the "Berkley Horse" or "Chevalet," "an adjustable ladder which could be extended to a considerable length, and on which the victim was securely strapped, openings being left for the head and genitals," according to *Venus*. Among several, there is a particular governess operating quite near MI-5 headquarters, Mayfair, who employs a similar, if more sophisticatedly constructed contraption. During a chat in her waiting room, she boasted of "at least £2500 worth of equipment" but declined to show it as at that moment she claimed no fewer than "five gentlemen hanging all over the house"—all of whom she referred to by numbers—including "one MP and a very well-known Harley Street physician." So successful has she been these past twenty-odd years that she has recently purchased a fine townhouse near Harley Street, the better to serve her distinguished following. (Anyhow her lease was up.) Of the hundreds of letters she has received over the years, not a few recall the following booking request to ride the "Berkley Horse."

To Madame T. Berkley
28 Charlotte Street, Portland Place   January, 1836
Honoured Lady,
I am an ill-behaved young man and quite incorrigible! The most celebrated tutors in London have chastised me but have been unable to correct my wilfulness. . . .
I herewith give you a list of my requirements:
1. It is necessary that I should be securely fastened to the Chevalet with chains which I will bring myself.
2. A pound sterling for the first blood drawn.
3. Two pounds sterling if the blood runs down to my heels.
4. Three pounds sterling if my heels are bathed in blood.
5. Four pounds sterling if the blood reaches the floor.
6. Five pounds sterling if you succeed in making me lose consciousness.

I am, honoured lady,
Your quite incorrigible, O.

After Madam Berkley's death her vaunted "Horse" was passed from peer to peer until, during the mid-1940s, it had come into the possession of Lord X, who as we shall see passed it on to his friend Hildebrand for safekeeping. But let Hildebrand himself proceed from here, for surely he is *the* craftsman-engineer, among all in Britain, whom Madame Berkley would retain (as indeed do several of Europe's leading governesses) were she alive today.

Hildebrand: Sex-Machine Inventor *Extraordinaire*

"As you are aware, there have been, in the past twenty-five years or so, two major scares that alleged that young Guardsmen from Chelsea Barracks were procured by titled gentlemen," chortles Hildebrand, a trim, ruddy-faced man of seventy. "Some MPs, a vicar, and a naval commander, among others. The first scare was just after the Second War, the second in late 1967. [See Bow Street Magistrate's Court Reports, December, 1967.] Now, several of my clients were mixed up in these. After the first, Lord X asked me to store some gear for him until the heat died down. Among this was Dame Berkley's Horse. He never recovered the gear, and so when I moved down from London to set up this workshop here in Kent, I brought it along. As nearly as I could ascertain it was indeed the real thing; surely the wood- and metalwork were of that period. On the bottom it read, 'J. Smith, Lisle Street, London, Soho.' I held onto it for over twenty years and, considering what happened again in 1967—His Lordship was a *devil* for young Guardsmen, used to pay 'em fifty pounds a time—I knew he'd never want it back. So I advertised it in the personal columns of *The Times* as 'Madam Berkley's Horse, Genuine Antique,' and finally sold it to a man from Toronto for thirty-five pounds.

Reinforced all the old hinges and metalwork first, of course. Damned bulky, that blinking gadget. Glad to have done with it. Resembled nothing so much as this one you see in this Danish sex magazine. [*Spanking Ritual,* previously described in the "Copenhagen" chapter.] But here, I'll sketch it for you as I remember it.

"Of course, we've made some improvements on the old design," grins Hildebrand as he modestly shrugs to acknowledge the libido-boggling contents of his twenty-one-by-thirty-two-foot carpeted, centrally heated laboratory-chalet, which, with its "torture" equipment, TV Showroom (transvestite, not BBC), toilet, shower, and kitchen is available as a gymnasium-playroom —when construction is not in progress—at £5 the afternoon or £15 for the weekend, "with meals supplied," according to his catalogue.

"Now, number eighteen in my catalogue ['Portable suspension frame, 8 feet high by 4 feet wide with ring fastenings for waist, wrists, and ankles; £40'] embodies the same principle as the Berkley Horse, but as you can see it's built of precision-engineered stainless-steel pipe, and it all folds down neatly with its own carrying handle to fit right into a golf bag. There are still a couple of chaps working in wood, but to get strength with wood you have got to have size. Too cumbersome. In design I aim for portability yet strength.

"A great deal of my stuff is sent abroad. As with number fourteen here ['knee irons with ankle brace and dildo bar; £30,' notes the catalogue] all the pipes are color-coded for easy assembly. Red to red. Blue to blue. I'm sending this one off to old Number Two One Two in Buenos Aires. As always, in two separate packages, mailed on different days, each package just a set of meaningless pipes to the nosy customs man. Because it comes from a farming community, it goes off as a pig-farrowing unit. When the client receives both packages, based on his previous instructions, well . . . a child could assemble it. Red to red. Blue to blue. Yellow to yellow. Rather decorative too. . . . In thirty years I've had, right up to now, exactly two thousand one hundred and twenty-five clients from all over the world. Male homosexuals, lesbians, and married couples. No names in these card files, just numbers. When I die, just a file of numbers. All letters are destroyed a week after they're received.

"Now let me show you the latest model of my most popular line ['Electric machine for simulating oral massage, penis enclosed in artificial vagina, £50,' reads the catalogue]. Variable speed, variable stroke with electronic control . . .*that's* the big new development! Series-wound, commutator motor, with a gear box. Up to one hundred fifty strokes a minute. When you get an orgasm with that one, you nearly go up through the roof! Except, however, you're in the face-down crab position with your legs and wrists securely strapped to the four pipe bases of the machine. I made the original for His Lordship twenty-six years ago. He's trading it in now on this variable-speed model.

Allowing him sixteen pounds on the old one. . . . I reckon Scotland Yard has got one of these from a client of mine.

"Now I'm also adapting that one for Her Ladyship. Of course it's a different engineering problem. Angle's different. She's had two fittings. . . . Or you can have two 'dildols' for the Lady, one up her 'vageena' whilst the other entertains her bottom. Should run about eighty pounds. I try to keep the prices as low as possible. . . . I'm too old to enjoy my sex now, so I enjoy myself helping other people to enjoy theirs."

Hildebrand laughs merrily, adjusts his sheer black tights.

"This one is still in the development stage," indicating a small sulky fitted with "vageena," and a huge white dildo with slapping testicles.

"This is a very popular model, the one over here in the corner. [Catalogue Number 36: 'Electric Obedience Control fitted with either metal dildo or scrotum clip with ankle electrodes, ensures instant obedience,' £40]. Sent three of these out to Beverly Hills last year—I've several good clients out there. The tool goes through here, screwed tight, balls clamped by this clip. This lead fastens to the ankle. When they're walking about on the end of this long lead . . . you just pick up the switch, give 'em a mild electric shock. Makes 'em mind, that one! Minor adjustment for the woman. Metal phallus up the 'vageena.' Safe as houses. But I never wire above the waist. Some of 'em want their nipples wired. Nothing doing. . . .

"Properly done by an expert, a beating before sexual intercourse is one of the most marvelous things you could ever have happen to you. And if you can get somebody to do it while you're actually having intercourse, then it is fan-tas-tic. It is *utterly fantastic!* And therefore I do sell quite a lot of flogging devices.[5]

"Infibulations?" responds Hildebrand like a druggist answering an inquiry for aspirin. "It's all right there in the catalogue. The piercing of scrotum, foreskin—a great many men are not circumcised in this country, you know— nipples is carried out with surgical precision at twenty-five pounds a piercing. That includes the stainless-steel 'keeper ring' inserted while it's healing. . . . One chap I know has got *everything* pierced. Even the septum of his nose. Wife leads him round with a ring through it. 'Course she does treat him something brutal . . . but he likes it. He has to do the housework in high heels, black silk stockings, and with that [an eight-ounce weight] hanging from his balls.

"I myself have had a kink for black tights since I was twelve years and three months old, at which time I became a lesbian's slave.

[5] Though apparently none but manual ones. However in the eighteenth century an Englishman, Chace Price, attempted to construct a machine that could whip forty people at once. London's *Society Magazine,* October 14, 1899, quotes American press reports of a corporal electric chair —a battery-operated "whipping chair" in use at a Denver vocational training school which, at the press of a button, automatically beat its inhabitant on the bottom.

"My birthday's at Christmas, and when I went back to school that year after the Easter, there was this new teacher. She was six foot tall, beautifully proportioned, Miss W, Furness Road Council School, Furness Road, N.W. 10. She was the one first got me. Well, she'd dress up in the old-fashioned English gym tunic—white blouse and short knickers, but it amounted to a short miniskirt. And she wore these black lisle stockings. She fastened the sole of a gym shoe to a wooden handle to give it length, and I had my wallopings. Well, sir, after the fourth one, me tucked up under her arm and she'd close her legs so I was imprisoned . . . rubbing up against her black lisle stockings, John come up and she'd got me. I was her slave until I was fourteen.

"She then passed me over to a man in Kilburn who ran what he called 'Doctor Johnson's Promise Boys.' They were boys who promised not to masturbate. But it was only a front for a homosexual boys' club. You can check all this out in past copies of the *Willesden Chronicle,* 1918–1919. Dr. Johnson passed me over to Mr. B, the manager of ——, the biscuit people, who had a penchant for young boys. He later kept two Italian boys permanently. They were twins. . . . B passed me over to a friend of his, Mr. J, of a magneto company, who later passed me on to the manager of an engineering company next door. . . .

"So I have been beaten and done since I was twelve years old. In between there have been a lot of exciting times, the most rewarding of which was my meeting with a man at Charing Cross who, besides doing me, took a fatherly interest in me sufficient to send me first to night school and, when I won a scholarship, paid all my expenses to Cambridge. . . . I must have been one of the biggest little whores in London. I used to buy a tuppenny ticket on the underground Inner Circle line and go round and round, stopping off at all stations to see whom I could meet in the toilets. No money. Never made a charge. Just did it for the joy of it. . . . And now, you might not believe this, but about four years ago I was at a party at a pub with some friends, and there was a beautiful legs competition and somebody said, 'C'mon, mate, have a go.' So I put on a pair of black tights and a pair of high-heel shoes. And I came in second in the competition. I was about sixty-six at the time and was competing with girls of nineteen."

In addition to his "chalet" just outside London, Hildebrand's little acreage contains a small factory equipped to manufacture "all types of equipment in steel, leather, and rubber." In one of the small sheds crammed with the rusted shells of long-forgotten contraptions, one instantly recognizes a minisub of the type seen propelling James Bond beneath the Caribbean in *Thunderball.*

Today in little Lisle Street, Soho, almost a century and a half since Madam Theresa Berkley stretched and flogged the dandies and daddies of the day on her famous Horse, quite close to the site of the shop where the contraption was probably designed and built, a porn shop peddles the latest English sex-contact magazines. Among the over seven hundred adverts of one publication (many with nude photographs of the eager "submissive male," "bored, vivacious young couple," "lovely young lady gives parties for generous execs, well-endowed coloured gents") is that of Hildebrand, The Magnificent Old Man with the Flying Machines. Drop him a line.

B.M. 3248, Holborn, England.

Discipline for Many Tastes

Meanwhile, off Queensway (W. 2), at this writing, a woman slips into a vest of porcupine quills; she's got two important clients coming this evening who like to wrestle. A neighboring practitioner keeps a pair of saddles, one "horizontal," another "upright," which clients ride while she whips them to the tune of £50 and her extensive stereo collection—Rossini, Wagner, Liszt's *Les Préludes,* and various English military marches are high on her equestrians' charts. Another governess, being a rather large woman, specializes in simple spankings, usually taking her patrons across her ample, dimpled knees.

Rates vary: £10 and more for a fairly substantial treatment, with surcharges for special equipment or if trained observers—usually much younger and more attractive than the governesses—are employed. For a simple licking, count on about a pound a stroke. Some ladies are on a retainer basis, clients paying a fixed monthly or weekly charge, *for in no area of "prostitution" are repeaters so common.* Should you wish to wield the cudgel yourself, there are frequent planes and trains to Paris. On premise this kind of job is usually subcontracted, there being a number of young French girls who, in addition to the odd English girl, have a taste, or at least tolerance, for it. But you may spend £50 to 100 for the privilege.

Modern developments in rubber apparel have, of course, made it possible to be whipped without ensuing bloodletting or scars. It was the French, apparently, who first saw such practical applications of rubber, having devised inflated rubber tubes for the purpose toward the end of the nineteenth century.

The greatest modern technological boons to punishment interests have been in the field of apparel, with English and American designers showing the way. In the late 1960s the publication *Rubber News* bid fair to become London's *Women's Wear Daily* of flagellation. But police raided its editorial offices—the firm of Arkinson Ltd., Middleton Buildings, Langham Street, Marylebone—and accused the editor under the Obscene Publications Act for conspiring to "corrupt people by offering for sale books, pictures, and equipment relating to masochistic practices and perversions." Also seized in the raid were "hoods, masks, gags, manacles, corsets and other clothing," according to *The People.* The demise of *Rubber News* was lamented by the governesses of Shepherd Market and Paddington and their clients. From a rundown of modern London rubbery in *It,* it is apparent that much of *Rubber News* was devoted to valuable interpolative comment on otherwise innocuous scenes. Thus one issue speculated as to whether it would be a "boots winter" and informed readers of particularly interesting window displays among London's better shoeshops.

Several of England's principal "seven or eight fetish suppliers" listed their wares in *Rubber News,* which, far from being a pedestrian slime sheet, acted as a kind of *Consumer's Report* in making objective evaluations of such items as an "imitation chastity belt," which, though described as "striking-looking," was felt because of defects in its leather straps and rubber crutchpiece to be "not entirely effective." Readers' comments were invited, like that of "Mr 466, London S.W.6," who, speaking for modern restrictives, suggested manufacturers bear in mind they must "achieve the highest possible degree of restriction without undue discomfort for the wearer"—the fetishist's classic Gordian knot. *Rubber News* also reviewed books of special interest like *The Rubber Family Robinson,* and had even begun its own book-of-the-month club. How curious, then, that such a serious, well-meant publication, honestly aimed at true aficionados, should have been suppressed by the authorities while brutal and frivolous successors, none of which approaches *Rubber News*'s integrity and missionary zeal, are permitted to thrive in Soho and Paddington porn shops.

But with all the complicated apparatus available, thanks to modern technology, some of the governesses' paraphernalia is no more esoteric than that found in the closets of one gracious Dame who, for £3, submitted to a quick inventory. This disclosed a wardrobe of aprons, granny caps, dustpans, brooms, cleaning fluids, and other household stuffs. "With customers like mine," she winked, "who needs a maid?"

Swinging, Scatology, and Savoury Treats

Swinging London? One woman has a small gallows (of the type noted in the "Secret Museum" section in the "Paris" chapter) from which she deftly hangs clients who can achieve orgasm under no other circumstances. She also has one of Hildebrand's old buggery machines.

In Shepherd Market, Paddington, and some stately English homes—for the governesses do on occasion make housecalls—there are opportunities for scatologic rites. Of course, these may also be had wherever the better dogs are walked.

The English also have this thing about food. One governess keeps an account with a fancy grocer that has one of the world's great selections of preserves. Two favorites, she reports, are Little Scarlet strawberry jam and Norwegian Heather honey, perhaps not coincidentally James Bond's preferences as well. These are applied to the governess' nipples or pudenda, then licked by the client as a "reward" after punishment.

Of course, everyone who saw it remembers the "eating scene" in the film *Tom Jones.* This was no hyperbole. In response to the question, "What is the most extraordinary situation you've ever encountered in the field of food and sex?" an official of British Travel gave a reply that simply boggles the palate.

"Ahh, well, during the bombings several of our neighbors joined for black-out parties at which they'd strip starkers and chuck buttered rolls at one another."

!

Young Boys' Punishment, Young Men's Sport

Though Eton no longer charges each boy's account half a guinea for birches at the beginning of term, public school new boys are still "randled" (to be punished as a schoolboy for breaking wind) by old boys; the practice of caning remains widespread in English schools and correction institutions, and the recipients' sexuality is generally at such an impressionable and formative stage that if the country is no longer "the promised land, the temple of flagellation" (see Eulenberg, *Sadism and Masochism,* Wiesbaden, 1902), it is at least the dosshouse. Current Home Office regulations require that canes be no longer than a yard and no thicker than three eighths of an inch. And students must not be made to drop their pants. But abuses are commonplace, some sanctioned by law. In the late 1960s, for example, the Liverpool City Council rejected by a vote of fifty-six to twenty-nine a proposal to abolish caning of crippled and psychologically unbalanced children. A Conservative Party spokesman defended the decision on the grounds that such children were perfectly capable of distinguishing right from wrong.

Citing historic precedent from as far back as the reign of Henry VI, the National Association of Head Teachers (this is not a society of professors of cunnilingus but a group that represents some fifteen thousand British school principals) overwhelmingly reasserted their discretionary "right" to use corporal punishments on students. At a recent convention, a prominent head-master characterized abolitionists as "long-haired woollies," and elicited delighted approval from his colleagues as he denigrated the thought that modern teachers abuse the privilege of the rod in hot pursuit of sexual gratification. At his age, the headmaster dryly noted, Brigitte Bardot would be hard put to get a rise out of him, much less the "grubby hands and trousered bottoms of antisocials."

The trousers reference begs a general question, for during the previous year a college headmaster got five years for requiring his boys to lie naked across beds while he severely and sometimes brutally beat them with sticks. A Surrey school for potential juvenile delinquents was closed after its headmaster and an associate were accused of caning boys "with excessive severity"; a seven-year-old girl was beaten "red and raw" for being "work-resistant"; two Southampton schoolboys received twenty-one lashes for incorrectly spelling the word "meringue"; and in mid-1970 a nineteen-year-old Isle of Man epileptic was caned as punishment for "trying to make a pass at a girl."

It was not until November, 1971, that caning was finally ordered banned from London elementary schools, the Inner London Education Authority overruling the majority of head teachers in London's nearly nine hundred primary schools, but giving them until January 1, 1973, to get their last licks in. Elsewhere, throughout the British Isles, the beat goes on . . . to assure yet another generation of clients for the governesses of Shepherd Market and Paddington. (To be fair, it should be noted that only three of the United States ban corporal punishment. But it should also be noted that until the late eighteenth century, America was a colony of England.)

INTERMISSION

At this point one might require a drink. Choose from several informative pubs in and around Shepherd Market. There is also a quaint café at whose terrace one can sometimes make some interesting liaisons. Many tourists enjoy SHEPHERD'S in Hertford Street for its ancient sedan chair that has been fashioned into a phonebooth. A better bet, if you seek local history and wish to keep up on current gen, is OLD CHESTERFIELD in Shepherd Street. You might prod one of the crabby retainers from nearby gentleman's clubs who drink here alongside their masters. Listen closely and you may hear more than just the river Tyburn flowing underneath.

Shepherd Market evolved from the fairground stalls of the famous May Fair, the raucous, bawdy festival of jugglers, hucksters, and whores which was held here from around 1272 until finally its "dangerous evils" were suppressed less than two hundred years ago. At the British Museum browse Ned Ward's *London Spy,* a 1704 guide to the raffish haunts of eighteenth-century London, which gives this account of the Fair:

"We now began to look about us, and take a view of the Spectators; but could not amongst the many thousands, find one Man that appear'd above the degree of a Gentlemans Valet, nor one Whore that could have the Impudence to ask above Six-pence wet and Six-pence dry, for an Hour of her Cursed Company. . . .

"I never, in my life, saw such a . . . Throng of Beggarly Stullish Strumpets who were a Scandal to the Creation, meer Antidotes against Leachery, and Enemies to Cleanliness."

Don't leave Mayfair without a visit to London's pioneer discothèque, the
SADDLE ROOM (1A Hamilton Mews, W.1, off Park Lane). Ringmistress Helène
Cordet is said to have brought the Twist to London; later the house became
"terribly keen on Zorba-type dances." Co-host Peter Davies is an accomplished horseman, which accounts for the decor comprising whips, crops,
bridles, boots, etc. Membership awfully Southampton (Long Island's, that is),
but younger than that at Annabel's. Three debs insist you hurry over to their
favorite antique dealer, "DENISA THE LADY NEWBOROUGH (1 Whitehorse
Street, Shepherd Market; 493-3954, business; 493-----, home," according to
the calling card).

It is a tinkly, tinsely little shop—fragile displays of cut glass, old snuffboxes,
antique jewelry—but the copper-haired Lady is not. Spicing any one of her
thirteen claimed languages with profanities of the other twelve, Denisa the
Lady Newborough (she is the widow of the fifth Baron) was, from the 1920s
to the 1940s, one of Europe's great sex symbols. Born Denisa Braun in
Subotica, Yugoslavia, she ran off with a circus at six and "bedded down with
a gypsy boy before I was old enough to know that gypsies had a word for
it." She had a silver Citroën in Paris, not to mention the Swedish match king,
Ivar Kreuger, and Kings Boris, Alfonso, and Carol. All this and assorted dukes
recounted in her autobiography, *Fire in My Blood.*

LONDON AND THE SINGLE GIRL

"Our scene is London . . ."
—BEN JONSON, *The Alchemist,* Prologue, 1610

As Paris is a man's city because its luxuries and chic attract so many
desirable women (or make them seem so desirable), so London (which attracts and produces some of the best men in the world) is very much *the*
woman's city of the 1970s—especially if she enjoys men. (But although
women comprise 38 percent of the work force and the Queen regent is, by
custom, never a man, England is no gynecocracy: compared to America,
women's salaries are pathetically low, career opportunities limited. Women's
Lib has a hard road ahead here: contact WOMEN'S LIBERATION WORKSHOP—
12 Little Newport Street, W.C. 2; 734-9541—an association of various independent groups which publishes the magazine *Shrew.)*

In no large city can a woman feel and be so free in public. In many areas
of the West End one can walk about all night. And not worry about rape. (But
don't trot Park Lane alone after dark, nor the Bayswater Road or Soho unless
you're *really* broke.) Oversimplifying: London is a city where the men, along
with most everyone else, are easy to encounter and rather hard to get to
know. New York, by comparison, is somewhat the reverse.

Men

If "the Englishman is far and away the most beautiful animal in the world," according to H. T. Finck (*Romantic Love and Personal Beauty*, Breslau, 1890; undoubtedly you've read it), beware those archetypes who seem ingenuous on the surface, but turn out to be knotty if not kinky at the core—and, worst of all, sometimes there's no core at all. Beware, too, that species of charming, witty Englishman who confides how boring he is so that you will think he isn't. "In England people actually try to be brilliant at breakfast," said Oscar Wilde, who himself was undoubtedly boring at breakfast—if he ever made it.

But never mind: "Most women in London, nowadays, seem to furnish their rooms with nothing but orchids, foreigners, and French novels." And today, even more than in Oscar Wilde's time, this is the most international of cities: an incredible variety of blokes—especially in Chelsea, where, as in Hemingway's Hong Kong of 1941, morale is high and morals are low—from American expatriates to Zambian students.

Somewhere the Right Honourable Mister Right might find you. But not at Trafalgar Square, the Tower, or the Tate on Sundays—not if he's English, that is. (By terms of the Treaty of the War of 1812 all Americans, and other foreigners, go to the Tate Gallery on Sundays, the English on Saturdays.) If you've done London before, try this year avoiding all the clichés. Almost impossible to miss, however, is the recent rise of the Great American Hamburger. Those at the GREAT AMERICAN DISASTER (335 Fulham Road; another in Beauchamp Place—pronounced "Beecham," of course) are the best this side of Southern California. PARSONS (spaghetti, red Ned, and saucy company) is another of several good rendezvous at the top of modish Fulham Road, as is nearby PIZZA EXPRESS, though not if you are a real connoisseur of this American delicacy. ASTERIX (at the "World's End" end of King's Road) is a new crêperie, fashionable with young "faces" (as some English designate their celebrities); classical music, batter specially imported from Brittany and filled with delicious savories. Nearby STAX has late hamburgers and Belinda. HARD ROCK CAFÉ, off Hyde Park Corner, is also good for late-night snacks, always a problem in Wimpyland. PIZZA RESISTANCE (2A Exhibition Road, S.W.7) is licensed until 2 A.M.

Pubs

At last girls on their own are welcome in many pubs. But some locals still invoke the "anti-soliciting statute"—remember that no lone women are permitted in any Wimpy after midnight, in spite of Women's Lib protests. And many pubs make you feel you're wandering into the midst of a Rugby scrum.

Not the previously noted "Gren" (GRENADIER, in Belgravia's Wilton Row, off Wilton Crescent). Mind the deb competition, but enough company directors (or their fathers) to go you a round. KING'S HEAD next to the Royal Court

Theatre in Sloane Square for theatricals. BUNCH OF GRAPES, Brompton Road nearly opposite the Brompton Oratory (lovers will enjoy the moody, evocative green at the rear of this famous church) has defrocked priests, extremely civil engineers, middle-echelon public school grads. A good health studio with tricky exercise apparati around the corner in Yeoman's Row is TOWN AND COUNTRY WOMAN'S HEALTH SALON. You'll be fit for FINCHES or QUEEN'S ELM pubs, both in the Fulham Road. Equally friendly is CHELSEA POTTER, King's Road; well touted, but nonetheless one of the great meet markets. TROUBADOR is one of London's rare Greenwich Village-like coffeehouses (265 Old Brompton Road). Every night in the Troubador's cellar, there's live jazz, films, or the city's oldest folk-music club.

At the bar of MR. CHOW in Knightsbridge (not the one in Montpelier Street), one of the twee David Bailey types may take you *upstairs* (treacherous spiral if you've heels) for the smartest fried seaweed in town. But Soho's DUMPLING INN (in shifty Gerrard Street) has the best of this reputed aphrodisiac (Roman Polanski likes the food here). If your man thinks Chinese food and romance are mutually exclusive, suggest CHINESE LANTERN, Thackeray Street behind Kensington Market. About £6.50 for two. Set menu, cooked at your table by authentically costumed attendants; rosey rosé wines in silvery buckets, velvety lighting to soften your most garish Biba (nearby) makeup. Otherwise, THE GOOD FRIENDS in the East End (Salmon Lane, E. 14) serves the best Chinese Food west of Suez and east of New York.

A likely place for a brief encounter by day is among the exotic varieties of Kensington Gardens—Russian and other diplomats sometimes stray from their nearby compounds along Kensington Palace Gardens walk. The VICTORIA AND ALBERT MUSEUM is vast but practical if you know what to look for and where to be found. English boys know that English girls enjoy the fascinating permanent exhibition of fashion through the ages—from original sixteenth-century gowns, shoes, cosmetics, right up to NORMAN HARTNELL's (26 Bruton Street, Mayfair) latest Queen gear . . . which indeed belongs in a museum.

Wine Bars

Wine bars are wonderful! None of the booziness, less of the inside male chat encountered at pubs. LOOSE BOX or LOOSE REIN wine bars: one in Cheval Place, Knightsbridge, best after 6 P.M. Chic yet friendly; many debs' delights. Inexpensive salad lunches; and convivial terrace, too. For weekday-shopping lunch hours it's LOOSE BOX in Wigmore Street, (off Oxford Street), an area blossoming with sidewalk terraces, a recent London phenomenon. Another LOOSE REIN in the King's Road just past Oakley Street; best Saturday afternoons—artists, writers, Chelsea people who've rather made it. Nearby restaurant 235 KING'S ROAD has good, moderately priced French cuisine, candlelit ambiance. Great for the lone female. Reserve a single at the big center communal table. "Pass the salt, Lot" is the cleverest opening you'll require. On your first date suggest he take you to Rome Away from Home: SAN FREDIANO (62 Fulham Road, S.W.3; 584-8375). Very *Joanna* atmosphere, very good Italian food, very reasonable (about £6-7 for two with wine).

If you didn't see Tom Courtenay at San Frediano, he and his lot gather some Sunday mornings in Putney-on-Thames for pick-up football. (Eccentrically, they play it with a soccer ball.) Expatriate Americans play softball in Hyde Park. Female spectators welcome at all Sunday-morning events. Afterward join the chaps at their pub, then perhaps Sunday lunch at DAISY (40 King's Road; 584-7346) or APRIL ASHLEY'S or ALVARO'S.

Friday nights the girls ask the boys at earthy HAMMERSMITH DANCE PALAIS. RONNIE SCOTT'S (47 Frith Street, Soho) is, some say, the world's best all-round jazz club. Perfect for the restless lone female after hours, when all London seems so shut up. SPEAKEASY (48 Margaret Street, W.1) is a good place to pull a pop star after midnight, but mind the groupies. TIDDY DOLL, Shepherd Market, Mayfair, has a non-membership disco and good food to 3 A.M.; some well-set-up single male diners. Perhaps owner John Campbell may invite you to one of his smashing parties.

Walking tours are advertised in the weekly guides and in the *Sunday Times;* a sensible way to meet a sensitive man.

Gear

Shopping is very much a social experience in London. Men really relish accompanying you on the Saturday-afternoon boutique safari. The stalls of KENSINGTON MARKET (Kensington High Street) stock everything under the Aquarian Sun. PLUTO'S PARADISE, for example (basement stall), have great quantities of milk-white chamois suede—a refreshing change from the common yellowish variety. Body shirts to your design, made to order, about $30; overnight to four-day service. Some say GURNEY SLADE'S upstairs stall has an even better selection of skins. Of the hundreds of other stalls: FORBIDDEN FRUIT have fabrics from around the world—from tie-dyes and Thai silks to Tart's delight Algerian synthetics. HOPE AND ELEANOR for art-nouveau buckles and brooches. Etc.

BIBA (124 Kensington High Street) is a living museum of feathers, hats, Beardsleyesque piperackery, Tom Jones foolery.

MR. FREEDOM boutique (Kensington Church Street) was an East Ender's D.C. comic-strip. Now the colorful founder has moved on. Still some fun. Worth a "butcher's" even if you're just trying things on. (East End Cockney rhyming slang: "Butcher's hook" rhymes with "look," *ergo* "butcher's" means "a look.") Lots of nubile if not noble young men hanging about, especially since Tommy gutted the normal-sized changing rooms and replaced them with impossibly tiny cubicles because he didn't "want the dears brooding in there by themselves. Let them come out into the shop. And mind you, it's good salesmanship." Many fun shops nearby: Bus Stop, Pant House, etc.

Of course, people have been wearing *anything*—make that everything—in London for some years. But the days of fine British-manufactured workmanship are gone with the London fog (pollution down perhaps 50 percent in the past ten years[6]). London is long in the Look, short in the stitching. That wonderful velveteen pants-suit copy of the Guards officer's uniform may wear out before it goes out.

Jean Machine in the King's Road has thousands of jeans (some with original jellybeans in back pockets), guaranteed used and prefaded at peace marches or debtors' prisons out in the Colonies. Great Gear Trading Corporation, King's Road, has somewhat overpriced freaky clobber. And a sex department: waterbeds, virility pills, sex manuals, personal vibrators. (But see "Sex Shops" section, or Amsterdam, Paris, or Copenhagen first.)

By the way, the amyl-nitrate (Great Gear does *not* sell it) orgasm ritual was "old as the itch" here even before *Time* magazine's April 15, 1966, "exposé" of "Swinging" London. Though the English still twit the piece, it did more for their tourist industry than all the Queen's Horses and all the Angry Young Men, and most of the situations indicated on *Time*'s "The Scene" map still exist.

Of course, nothing is duller than last year's discothèque. Aretusa, for example, is no longer a princess' delight. Directly across the King's Road, The Pheasantry is a special case. Though Charles II, Paul McCartney, and Laurence Olivier no longer drink here, some patrons can still remember the details, and there is probably no more amiable discothèque-club (liberal entrance policies) for the new girl in town. Nightly live groups in the cellar, too. Sandro's Cellar, next door, is fine for late dining.

Back to boutiques. Flashy Escalade (187A–191 Brompton Road, near Harrods) lures Americans, but even they reel from the prices. (Fabulous periodic sales, however.) But the ambiant, ingenuous, fashion shows on Saturday afternoons with coffee are delightful and free. Escalade's Long Island Expressway snack corral is a good rendezvous—much table-mixing and mix-ups at lunch. You might even eat something while you're waiting. By all means don't miss Way-Inn at Harrods. And even Julie Christie knows you rarely find two of a kind off the peg at Brown's (27 South Moulton Street). Half the shops in Bond Street seem to be by Royal Appointment. Among other things it is a good area to buy shoes. Or to meet a prince.

---

[6]And still "Falling Down." According to an early-1972 report from the Greater London Council, there was 80 percent less smoke in the London air in 1971 than in 1969, and 10 percent less sulfur dioxide.

Otherwise CHELSEA COBBLER (163 Draycott Avenue, S.W.3) has custom-made boots. Also GO GO's in Kensington Market, or DELISS at 38 Beauchamp Place. ROBERT WHITE and his sons (57 Neal Street, W.C. 2) hire out splendid fake jewelry. ROBINSON'S (theater props; 47 Monmouth Street, W.C.2) rent replicas of the Crown Jewels. GARRARD AND CO. (112 Regent Street, W.1) will give your poison ring (the one you bought at CAMDEN PASSAGE MARKET—from 9 A.M. Saturdays) the same attention they give Queen Elizabeth's worry beads. And INVISIBLE MENDERS (1 Hinde Street, W.1; 935-2487) do what you expect them to do.

CALMAN LINKS (33 Margaret Street, W.1) have minks from round the globe, and best bargains from their very own farms. Or hire one from TWENTIETH CENTURY FUR HIRERS (120 Wigmore Street, W.1). Or buy one from any of several street markets, or CHELSEA ANTIQUE MARKET (King's Road), or ALFRED KEMP, London's biggest second-hand clothier.

THE THEATER ZOO (28 New Row, off St. Martin's Lane, W.C.2), in addition to stage makeup, wigs, etc., sell marvelous "fashion masks" with Soozie sequins, plumes, tiaras. From £1. Black pussycat masks with whiskers, 10NP. PORTOBELLO ANTIQUE MARKET is obvious and fine for touring (Saturdays). ROYAL STANDARD ANTIQUES MARKET is better for buying, fewer tourists (52 bus to Blackheath, or boat to Westminster Pier or Charing Cross Pier and thence to Greenwich; Saturdays). PETTICOAT LANE (Middlesex Street, E.1) is for emotional haggling, but for a quieter Sunday try CUTLER STREET (Houndsditch; midway between Aldgate and Liverpool Street tube stops). A collection of ZaSu Pitts jewelry that would have given Miss Pitts fits; or make your own from among their thousands of old coins.

FEATHERS (45 Kensington High Street), THE SHOP (44 Sloane Street), and DEBORAH AND CLARE (29 Beauchamp Place) are too much for the poor people. And proud of it. And rightfully so. FENWICK's (63 New Bond Street, W.1) are for knickers; RIGBY AND PELLER (12 South Moulton Street, W.1) do the Queen's. THE RUSSIAN SHOP (278 High Holborn, W.C.1) have some pre-Kerensky shawls to keep the nip off or for visiting Karl Marx's Highgate Cemetery grave in; or Lenin's former residence, 16 Percy Circus, W.C.1.

Medium- or low-priced shoes seem no great bargain in London. But SHOOOOSISSIMA (Beauchamp Place again) has classic Italian design. That is . . . somewhat at the expense of function. However there's always old DOCTOR SCHOLL's FOOT COMFORT SERVICE (at 59 Brompton Road, or 254 Regent Street), £1.25 for a soothing, fetishy pedicure. RUSSELL AND BROMLEY (several stores) may be the best of the shoe chains. Among several quick shoe-repairers: the thirty-minute heel bar at South Kensington tube station and several in the Oxford Street shopping area and other tube stations.

Repair

Dry-cleaning can be a slow drag in London, but there's a ONE-HOUR MARTINIZING at 310 King's Road. Prince Philip prefers to send his to LILLIMAN AND COX (14 Princes Street, W.1), but JEEVES (8 Pont Street, S.W.1) are just as good, also have a professional packing service and a night-deposit hatch. HANDBAG SERVICES (Beauchamp Place; 589-4975) do quick repairs. DANISH EXPRESS LAUNDRY (16 Hinde Street, W.1) are very good, very quick; while you're waiting, the ROYAL ACADEMY (734-9052) or ST. MARTIN'S SCHOOL OF ART (109 Charing Cross Road, W.C.2; 437-0058) will pay you about $1.50 an hour to pose nude. You don't have to be gorgeous, just be still!

If, in Burns's Scotland, "A man's a man for a' that," in modern England, a woman's a woman for a hat. MALYARD (12 Ganton Street, W.1) are right for a Henley Regatta Straw, OTTO LUCAS (at Harrods) and SIMONE MIRMAN (9 Chesham Place, S.W.1) know what they're wearing at Ascot. Or go Old Hat at the various market stalls. Or go back to Biba's: Garbo cloches, pokey bonnets, plumeys, pithy helmets, snooty snoods, *alte* cockeds, Truman capotes. . . .

Sancta

Impossible-to-get-into-unless-you're-known places include, in addition to ANNABEL'S and TRAMP'S discothèque, the preposterously unpretentious-looking cell that is Muriel Belcher's COLONY CLUB in Dean Street, Soho. If your charm, whimsy, or whatever can't help you crash these, London has one of the world's great embassy party scenes. Just phone around 4 P.M. and ask what time the reception's beginning; it works, for females, an amazing percentage (about 30) of the time. THE FRENCH EMBASSY (11 Kensington Palace Gardens, W.8; 229–9411) is always good for a canapé. The ISRAELIS (2 Palace Green, W.8; 937–8091), for a *potch in tochis,* and the PERSIANS (16 Prince's Gate, S.W.7; 584–8101) also have a terrible London reputation in these delicate matters. The SOVIETS (18 Kensington Palace Gardens, W.8; 229–3628 or 727–6888) hold some very smart dos. But the Mao CHINESE (31 Portland Place, W.1; 636–5637) don't.

If all else fails, the Queen often has some sort of weekend effort at WINDSOR CASTLE. Phone Windsor 63–106 and try to get around the Palace Steward, Robert Smith. Be diplomatic, of course, but tenacious: Her Majesty is a Taurus.

Loos

Equally difficult to crash are *loos.* Outrageous that there are ample all-nighters for the lads, few if any (Hyde Park Corner? Kensington tube stop?) for the ladies. Complain to the GREATER LONDON COUNCIL (928–0303). Or perhaps THOMAS CRAPPER AND SONS, who make loos, can help. Surely the few all-night-garage ladies'—at CUMBERLAND GARAGE, Bryanston Street off Oxford St., W.1; MOONS garage in Davies Street, Mayfair; and the all-night petrol station in Park Lane—offer spartan comfort to a lady. If you haven't the price of a tank of petrol, there's always WEST LONDON AIR TERMINAL (Cromwell Road). Or VICTORIA STATION. Or the HILTON HOTEL.

By day, another story, bless Jonathan Routh and his very good *Good Loo Guide*. Baths and changing rooms at Victoria Station, platform 1. Psychiatrist's couch for a quick snooze in the LAW COURTS LOO, "opened" by Victoria in 1883. CAFÉ ROYAL has a machine that dispenses nylons at 15NP a pair. Silver hairbrushes at the ritzy RITZ HOTEL LOO, just as you'd hoped. One of London's most extensive loos is by the Serpentine in Hyde Park, beneath the cafeteria—hot-air dryers for your hair, nappy rooms too.

Abortion Holiday (or Honeymoon)

An abortion is never a picnic, but in London it can be a holiday. It may be legal now in New York, but with the low transatlantic fares, if you've time to plan yours (the section "Birth Control" is mostly for "quickies") and your man can accompany you, why not do it in style: boating on the Thames, quiet bistro dinners at spots like JASPER'S BUN ON THE GREEN (candlelight, toasty fire; just south of the Thames in Richmond, Surrey, on moody, lush Kew Green; 940–3987). Soothing walks in Regent's Park rose gardens. Concerts at ROYAL ALBERT HALL—no! no!, make that ROYAL FESTIVAL HALL; Albert is wonderful but very draughty. Or, if you're up to it, some postoperative gambling at CHARLIE CHESTER's raffish Soho club, which is open by day.

Get to bed early in the most romantic hotel (within a reasonable price range) in London. THE PORTOBELLO HOTEL (22 Stanley Gardens, W.11, near the stalls of Portobello Road Antique Markets; 727–2777) is housed in a well-preserved late Victorian terrace mansion. In the ground floor lounge and dining areas, French windows—framed by striking scarlet curtains cut from the same livery cloth used to fashion the full dress uniform of the Life Guards of the Household Cavalry—open onto the manicured beauty of the Portobello's classic English Garden. Take the lift (very important in your condition and not to be taken for granted in England) up to your bedroom which may have a round bed and a balcony overlooking the gardens, but which is certain to have private W.C., shower, color TV, well-stocked frig *with ice,* and a dispenser for making fresh tea or ground coffee. You'll admire Julie Hodgess's subtle blend of exquisite Victorian decor and late-20th-century conveniences — "a unique system of clear air heating pioneered in Scandinavia." Portobello Hotel, then, is rather a London version of Paris' L'Hôtel. Except on one count: Singles from £5.50, doubles from £7.50 (about $19.50), luxurious suites at £16 or £25. And, in case you bring your mother-in-law along, for £4.50 there are compact "Cabins" which offer the same conveniences as the larger bedrooms. All prices include service and continental breakfast served in your room.

Have dinner at nearby JULIE'S (135 Portland Road; 229–8331), which is affiliated with Portobello Hotel but qualifies on its own merit as one of the city's most romantic restaurants. The ambiance is so special—a series of caverned rooms that may once have been wine cellars, semi-private dining alcoves, candlelight, crackling fireplace in the cozy vestibule where you take coffee and brandy, and Beethoven on the stereo—that the food, which is not bad at £6 for two with mediocre carafe wine (the white is better than the red) seems quite ordinary by comparison.

Hair

Hair dye and rouge were found in early Celtic graves, tweezers among the early Anglo-Saxons. The English are traditionally skillful at applying rouge, or is it the moist climate? ELIZABETH ARDEN (20 New Bond Street, W.1; 629–8211) of course. Or THE FACE PLACE (26 Cale Street, S.W.3; 589–4226). YARDLEY (33 Old Bond Street, W.1; 629–9341) for that rose-petals-floating-in-double-cream English-Girl Look. HARRODS will install the world's largest cosmetics department and move its bank to accomplish it.

Among the three best hairdressers, MICHAELJOHN (Albemarle Street, W.1) has the most interesting phone number: MAYfair 6969. They also do a wash, set, and manicure for the equivalent of only about $8. Trevor has a nice sense of style, knows what looks best for you. Michael does Princess Anne, but he's much too busy to attend her at the Palace regularly as she had requested. LEONARD (6 Upper Grosvenor Street, W.1; 629–5757) is big with duchesses. It's unisex too, as is trendier CRIMPERS (80A Baker Street, W.1; 486–4522; strong on gossip). Like many good salons, they do tea with those succulent watercress (again!) sandwiches the English have such a genius for. Try for Laurence. And hasn't VIDAL SASSOON come a long way (171 New Bond Street, W.1; 629–0813) from shampoo boy for "Professor" Adolph Cohen (Whitechapel Road, in the East End)? ESCALADE salon is more fun than smart, but very practical for a fast wash and set. Big staff will usually take you on short notice. Also full sauna, massage, relaxing room, soft music, tea, health-food cafeteria. Great off-the-plane first stop. (A short bus ride from the West London Air Terminal.)

Tea

Your first London tea should be taken among the flamingo and fishponds of DERRY AND TOM'S exotic roof garden; perfect after doing the Kensington High Street boutiques or the ANTIQUE HYPERMARKET. Little GLORIETTE has a tiny terrace opposite Harrods if the latter's fourth-floor BUTTERY is packed out; fine for displaying yourself to some of the best catches in Knightsbridge.

SEARCY'S gourmet food shop tearoom (across Montpelier Street in Brompton Road) is an ideal place to tea-and-tattle with your Auntie Samantha or wait out the quick-mend East End expatriate tailor nearby. Nearby RICHOUX has some attractive Harrods personnel, usually about 10:30 A.M. THE DOCTOR'S (19 New Cavendish Street, W.1) is a likely place to await pregnancy-test results, it being close by Harley Street.

There's more tea in the STRANGERS' CAFETERIA, House of Commons, or on the terrace at the invitation of an MP. (Write one.) CRANKS (10 Ganton Street, W.1, behind the Carnaby boutiques; also several branches) has kooky teas. But health foods are their specialty. Tea with knobs on: at the Ritz, Dorchester, or Claridge's Hotel; or The Savoy overlooking the Thames. Historic Tea with the ghosts of Oscar Wilde and Frank Harris at CAFÉ ROYAL (great Sunday brunch, too). Four A.M. tea at OPERA TEA BAR, corner Henrietta and Southampton Streets, Covent Garden. Tea with journalists, MICK'S CAFÉ, Fleet Street. With barristers, OLD BAILEY CAFETERIA. With crumpets, GROSVENOR HOUSE HOTEL. With strumpets, several all-nighters near Berwick Street, Soho, or perhaps in Oxford Street. Tea with Polish Aristocrats (guaranteed), some Czarists too, at DAQUISE CAFÉ (20 Thurlow Street, S.W.7, near South Kensington tube station; a very lively crossroads). Ask for Serge. Tea with dancing and mature singles, CAFÉ DE PARIS (3 Coventry Street, W.1; from 3 P.M., Wednesday through Sunday). Tea with Harold Wilson? Try the LABOUR PARTY (Smith Square, S.W.1; 834-9434).

Sympathy and "Help!"

"Tea-blow"? This is not what you may be thinking—though it could turn out to be—but rather refers to the little sheds at certain taxicab ranks (a sweet one, corner of Lupus Street and St. George's Square, S.W. 1) where the drivers enjoy tea and cakes among themselves, and may share them with you. If you're feeling really "f*cked and far from home" (See Eric Partridge, *Dictionary of Slang and Unconventional English,* New York, 1961), ring the social service unit of ST. MARTINS-IN-THE-FIELDS (5 St. Martin's Place, W.C.2; 930-1732). If your roommate's fud is on FIRE!, or you need an AMBULANCE, or you simply want to chat up a handsome POLICEMAN, dial 999. Emergency hospitals include CHARING CROSS (Agar Street, Strand, W.C.2; 836-7788), ST. GEORGE'S (Hyde Park Corner, S.W. 1; 235-4343), and MIDDLESEX (Mortimer Street, W.1; 636-8333). Like all of the foregoing, including the "tea-blow," BOOTS the Chemist (Piccadilly Circus, W.1; 930-4761) and ST. GEORGE'S HOSPITAL (Tooting Grove, S.W. 17; 672-1255; for emergency dental problems) are open twenty-four hours.

THE SAMARITANS can be reached in the Crypt of ST. STEPHEN'S CHURCH, Walbrook, E.C. 4 (626-2277), 24 hours. If you are particularly depressed, even feeling suicidal, they're the folks to call. You can visit from 9 A.M. to 9

P.M. LEND-A-HAND (20 Cambridge Park, E. 11; 989–9044) is an association of good people, mostly under thirty, who will comfort you and discuss literally any problem—sexual, physical, emotional. They deal with loneliness too.

If your problems are more mundane, dial 246–8091 for the weather; 123 and you've got the time; and 246–8021 for motoring information within fifty miles of London.

Paradise

"England is the paradise of women, the purgatory of men, and the hell of horses," wrote John Florio over three centuries ago. And today, if a woman reads her tarot cards right, most all the best things can be hers, very often free. And we don't mean the clap, Luv. (If such is the case, however, and the clinics aren't your scene, remember that medical specialists are rarer here than in the States. Many Belgravia GPs also specialize in everything from bursitis to cystitis.) Begin with the promise—or warning, if you prefer—that those 11 P.M. pub-closings make London a very fast town indeed: after dinner there's often no place to go but his or hers. Or yours.

Next morning play "Postman's Knock" around Hyde Park's Round Pond (but mind the kite-flyers) or "Knock-Shops" in Kew Flower Gardens. Reincarnate a Thomas Hardy heroine on Hampstead Heath. Please don't feed the swans in Green Park, or pull the peacocks' tails in Holland Park. Float along the Serpentine (sailboats and rowboats) or along Regent's Canal. Antonioni made those evocative shots for *Blow Up* at Charlton, near Woolwich; especially nice, here, are the smaller Maryon and Maryon Wilson parks. The maze of hedges at Hampton Court gardens is excellent for "Kiss Chase." Waterlow Park (N.6; Northern Line tube to Archway stop, then a short bus ride) is little known to tourists, has idyllic ponds, gardens, an aviary, a grass theater, and a mynah bird that says "Love!" (or a word to that effect).

Downs? These are hills—not drugs—which produce wonderful "ups." Hop a Green Line bus 708 or 709 to Caterham, whose North Downs rise to 1000 feet. *Digs?* COUNCIL OF BRITISH ARCHAEOLOGY (8 Andrews Place, N.W.1; 486–1527) need help. *Waterfall?* Streatham Common, S.W.16, has one; also summer theater. *Forest?* Go along to Hainault (via Central line tube) whose ESSEX FOREST HAS 1100 acres; or take the same line to Loughton and walk down Forest Road to EPPING FOREST, 6000 acres. Back in town have a candlelight dinner by the fire at GASWORKS II, 342 King's Road, S.W.3; 352–2218. *Horse Riding?* In Hyde Park. From dawn till dusk: 32a Grosvenor Crescent Mews (Hyde Park Corner), S.W.1. Ring 235–6846.

"The British cook is a foolish woman—who should be turned for her iniquities into a pillar of salt which she never knows how to use," said Oscar Wilde, who might be pleased that the modern British (read "immigrant") cook has improved in direct proportion to the Lion's decline as a world power (some correlation here?). There are now hundreds of atmospheric candlelit bistros and intimate restaurants where two can dine well for £4 or more, all in, sometimes even less. Random choices: try LUBA's Russian Bistro (Yeoman's Row, S.W. 3, next to the ikon gallery); or FIVE-FIVE-FIVE (555 Battersea Park Road, S.W. 11; 228–7011)—the chef is Polish, the prices prewar, the tables (only five) oilclothed, and Princess Margaret and Tony like it. And "Swinging" London old standbys like TRATTORIA TERRAZZA (19 Romilly Street, Soho; 437–8991), ALVARO's (124 King's Road, S.W.3; KEN 6296), and NICK's DINER (88 Ifield Road, S.W. 10; 352–5641) still serve beautiful food to the beautiful people at £3 or more per head. PARKE's (4 Beauchamp Place, S.W.3; 589–1390) may be the best restaurant in London. DRONES (1 Pont Street, S.W. 1) has David Niven, Jr., Prince Charles, Rex Harrison, and hamburgers.

Gentlemen snooping at this section over the Single Girl's shoulder should immediately dispatch her a hand-delivered rose from UNIROSE (727–3922), £1. Or see Gaston at MILWARDS (21 Cheval Place, S.W.7; 584–7268).

The Proper Affaire

Of course, if one really wants to lay it on, few cities offer better facilities. A recent article, "Doing It in Style," by Donald Wiedenman in *Queen* (which has since merged with the British *Harper's Bazaar*), superbly demonstrates that "perhaps more than any other city in the world" London "is the ideal place for a truly Proper Affaire." And in the bargain Mr. Wiedenman sketches an archetype English Lady and Gentleman whom one may aspire to emulate, if not cultivate.

Unlike the infamous "Dirty Weekend, and its counterpart the One-Night Stand," the Proper Affaire must be planned far ahead "as that adds Carnal Anticipation. . . ."

The Lady spends Thursday morning at Arden's having a massage, facial, and "an ultraviolet treatment; in the nude, of course, so she will be rosy all over." There has been a great deal of shopping for Very Special Things, but "She will not take any scent, as a Lady *never* takes or buys her own scent."

Meanwhile, the Gentleman is booking a double room for three nights—"a suite is too vulgar and not nearly as intimate and it takes absolutely *huge* quantities of incense. . . ." After lunch with an Ex-Girlfriend ("she will be kind and understanding, and amused to think he is taking the Lady to the same places he once took her") he will get the Lady's favorite scent, and then proceed to organizing: theater and restaurant bookings, car hire, etc. In the evening he goes to his gym, David Morgan's in Hanover Square, of course, where he will have someone named "Trevor . . . prepare him for the impending weekend. . . . He emerges relaxed and refreshed, and most important, Able to Cope."

According to Donald Wiedenman, "Without a doubt, there is only one hotel to stay in for a really old-fashioned, slightly camp Proper Affaire, and that is the Ritz. [Piccadilly, W.1; 493–8181.] Amidst mirrors, gilt, and fading elegance, the Ritz offers the best service, most discreet staff, the biggest bathtubs, and the most intriguing atmosphere—you can still actually meet behind the aspidistra. . . ."

The Gentleman has booked ahead under a "Completely Fictitious Name. . . . For the married participants, this is an obvious must, but even for single ones it lends a certain air of adventure. . . . Do not use a foreign name, as the clerk might ask for your passports. The Gentleman, if he has been to the Ritz before, must use the same name he used the last time, as the staff have particularly good memories in this department. They will, however, turn a blind eye to the fact that you are not with the same Lady."

Friday "the Gentleman checks into the Ritz at 11:30, inspects the room . . . moves the beds together—there are, alas, very few double beds at the Ritz. . . ."

The Lady and Gentleman meet in the lobby, but instead of going directly up to the room ("this casts the shadow of a Very Callous Motive") they "walk down Jermyn Street to Jules Bar . . . because the vodka martinis are the best in London. . . . An alternative Quiet Place might be . . . Martinez in Swallow Street . . . where *no one* goes, or the Roof Bar at the Hilton . . . where *everyone* goes, but no one that a Lady or Gentleman would know."

At last in their room—after a long lunch, lingering kisses, and light fondling —and when they are both "Very Ready and the Gentleman's Ardour is Displayed . . . the Lady lights the incense and the candle" and they get into one of the twin beds.

"Later (much later) [nothing cut here] and after a short nap, the Lady . . . runs the bath, using twice as much Badedas as the directions call for. The Gentleman . . . rings Room Service for a bottle of Champagne, but requests tumblers instead of the usual long-stemmed glasses. . . . The Gentleman sips his Champagne, and then, using the tumbler as a boat, pushes it to her through the Badedas foam. The Lady in turn reciprocates, and this is called Bubble Boats." [Or perhaps "Rules Britannia."]

After a nap it's off for a nip to the Rivoli Bar: ". . . the best Champagne Cocktails in London." The barman, whose name is Edward, "has a delicate touch indeed." So does the Gentleman, apparently, for at a performance of *Hair* (which they have both seen before, of course) "during the nude scene it is even permissible (*Hair* being what it is) for the Gentleman to slide his hand up the Lady's leg until it will go no further."

Saturday afternoon the Gentleman takes the Lady to his favorite salacious bookshop in Soho where the proprietor, whom he knows by name, shows them into the room marked "PRIVATE."

"The Lady giggles all the way" back to the Ritz "because she is convinced they will be arrested any minute." In their room the Gentleman "provides them each with a Very Special Cigarette" and during "yet another bath together, the Lady—blushing but enjoying every minute of it—is made to read aloud the heavily illustrated book, which is called *The Ups and Downs of a Boy Named Paul,* while they splash about the water and see strange things in the room."

After Sunday Brunch at the Café Royal several friends—mostly couples—drop by the Ritz for Mouton Rothschild 1962, fish, incense, and chips. Leaving the other couples to the bath, the Gentleman surprises "the Lady in the act of picking up a discarded wrapper from a cod fillet," and he does what any proper Gentleman might do in the event: "gently wrestles with her on the floor and for the next hour they enjoy Much Activity."

Monday Morning, concludes Donald Wiedenman, "the Lady, saying adieu to the Ritz and all that it stands for," taxis to Victoria Station, where her husband meets her train and takes her to lunch. Meanwhile the Gentleman, if married, takes a taxi to Heathrow "where his chauffeur (who is also his wife's secret lover) meets him, thus solidifying his alibi beyond the smallest shadow of a doubt."

But even that is not the end of it. For the remainder of Monday, and Tuesday as well, Mr. Wiedenman assures us, the Lady and the Gentleman "will spend a great deal of time savouring the Meaningful Memories from a Proper Affaire in London."

BETTER GRAY THAN GAY

History and Law

"Since English women are so beautiful and the enjoyment of them is so general, the revulsion of these Islanders against pâederasty passes all bounds," wrote J. W. von Archenholtz in the late eighteenth century. And to this day few peoples seem more chary of what the English call "queers," but none is more fascinated by them. Thus nothing is so odd about the status of homosexuals in England as the paradox presented by repressive public attitudes and law enforcement on the one hand and permissive practice in the bushes. Or behind the high hedges.

For a "love that dares not speak its name," it has enjoyed an inordinate popularity among the genteel folk, if not since King William Rufus (son of the Conqueror, reigned 1087–1100), surely since Nicholas Udall—author of *Ralph Royster-Doyster,* the first English comedy—who, before his 1557 death, was dismissed as an Eton master for his sadistic administrations of corporal punishment, and as a reward appointed Director of Westminster School by King Edward VI. Most English candidly acknowledge pederasty's causative relationship to their gentleman's clubs and public schools, but nobody's sure which begat which. But if the thing has had such favor among an influential elite, why have the penalties been so severe? Surely it's more complex than a mere case of predilection being the father of supression.

And what of the working classes? Granted, they've probably had no more "Nancy boys," "Margeries," "pooffs" among them than a cross-section of the AFL–CIO. All the queerer, then, that weekly or even nightly drag shows in *neighborhood* pubs are no more unusual here than are the equally commonplace drag routines on TV soap operas and comedy series. A curious sort of voyeurism for a workingman (and often Mum and the kids too), or is he secretly, even subconsciously, mocking upper-class foppishness?

Flagellation was disproportionately championed—even for the English—in the abundance of nineteenth-century popular literature. This *"vice anglais,"* in fact, often a euphemism for the socially less acceptable homosexuality, was rarely extolled, if mentioned at all, in public writings of the period. At least so goes the quite plausible theory of Professor Stephen Marcus in *The Other Victorians.* Yet for over a century London's gay life was far more open and vibrant than it is today, perhaps beginning with the Mollies' Club, described in Ned Ward's 1708 *London Spy.* By the end of that century Clare Market near Covent Garden had become notorious for the strange fruits to be picked at the Bunch of Grapes; and an 1813 account describes a pederasts' club in nearby Clements Lane where role-playing patrons "were caught in the act of nursing and feeding some of their suffering 'sisters' lying in 'childbed'! the newborn babies being represented by big dolls." According to its records, the Old Bailey of that day was kept busy with complaints against boys' brothels (though some judges saw no harm in visiting them by night) and the infamous Vere Street, Clare Market, White Swan house had not only an upstairs male bordello but a "chapel" for marriage ceremonies, as well as wedding-banquet rooms and "bridal suites."

But although male homosexuals could be sentenced to death until 1861 (1889 in Scotland)—and until 1836 many were—before 1885 English law was obsessed only with "sodomous" or "indecent" behavior committed *in public.* Then came the revelations of the Stead Commission in 1885: debauchery of the female working classes had become such an accepted Establishment game or sport (depending on the quarry) that young teen-age girls were regularly kidnapped from the West and East Ends, many to be "certified" as *"virgo intacta"* by Harley Street physicians, thus increasing their "market value." What has this activity—rarely considered "indecent" until exposed in the *Pall Mall Gazette*—to do with homosexuality? Precisely. However, when legislation was proposed curtailing it, spiteful heterosexual MPs angrily attached a completely irrelevant rider: the "blackmailer's charter," which for the next eighty-two years made it an offense punishable by two years in prison and a lifetime of social disgrace ("broad arrow," as they say here) for males, even adults, to commit together "acts of gross indecency," even in private. Even if such acts were not proved until many years after their commission.

The 1967 homosexual "reforms," the result of the Wolfenden Committee's Report, which again dealt irrelevantly with prostitution as well, by no means reflect a great public or official change of heart. Or spleen. Nor would there have been much change in the preposterous event that Britain had members of Parliament or other high officials who were homosexual. Such men would, like all British homosexuals, be wise to keep their affairs to themselves; and surely never dare use their high office to lobby for civil rights and social justice equal to that enjoyed by heterosexuals. Thus the foreign homophile seeking to penetrate, as it were, London's gray gay scene for the first time requires not only a guide, he may need a solicitor and barrister as well!

Though the law is more liberal in England—but not in Scotland and Northern Ireland where homosexual acts between men of *any* age, even in private, are still forbidden—than in the vast majority of the United States, the gay scene, even in London, is far less flamboyant than in New York or San Francisco, for example. As a rule, it is far more difficult to ascertain, by dress or mannerism, just who, among Britain's estimated 2 million homosexuals and bisexuals, is. Even that little cupboard queen who smears OXO where it counts and keeps a jack russell lapdog, and *especially* that elderly distinguished-looking Man of Integrity at the next table teaching the pretty young Lambeth bloke to use chopsticks.

Caveats: though two males over twenty-one may again, in England and Wales, commit their "indecencies" in private, three's a culpable crowd, and homosexual "offenses" against a boy under sixteen may subject the accused adult to life imprisonment; against a boy sixteen to twenty-one, up to five years. Acts of "public indecency," such as simple snogging, liable adult males to two years, but heterosexual smoochers would probably receive no more than a month for even advanced polework in front of Buckingham Palace. (When the girl in seat 19A spied a man she fancied in seat 25A and promptly moved to 25B, thereupon to copulate with him somewhere over Hawaii on BOAC's New York–Sydney flight 591 recently, the couple received no more than a polite request from the crew that they "stop molesting one another.") Recently a publication was convicted of "conspiring to corrupt public morals and outrage public decency" for running homosexual contact ads of the type heteros have been placing with impunity for hundreds of years.

No such prohibitions apply to lesbians. Apochryphally, Queen Victoria refused to extend the 1885 prohibitions to them simply because she couldn't imagine women charvering one another.

Restaurants

The "sympathetic" restaurant was a rather peculiarly English institution. Born of necessity to provide a certain discreet ambiance that most pre-Wolfenden pubs apparently lacked, some of these restaurants have survived in name if not in concept. But in contrast to many gay pubs and clubs, most "special" restaurants are at best mélanges *(as are all the following)*.

APRIL AND DESMOND AT AD8, for example, is probably at least 60-percent straight, "the most bisexual restaurant in the world," according to Desmond, an extremely friendly (*to all,* strangers included) host. For the price, £6-£7 for two all in, with good carafe wine, one of the very best restaurants in London. Near-Parisian ambiance; smart as a carrot, *extremely varied* clientele: on a good night the three romantic alcoves may contain a heterosexual couple, a homosexual pair, and two lesbians (each in a different booth, of course), with a mélange of "faces" scattered throughout the house and "Bet" Davis records on the gramophone. The cuisine is outshone only by some of the choice cuts hanging on the "meat-rack" divans opposite the bar. Thanks to modern science, Liverpool has lost a merchant seaman and London has gained a beautiful, gracious, charming hostess—April Ashley. 8 Egerton Garden Mews, S.W.3. Reservations imperative, 584–9576. Sunday brunch is especially merry.

If AD8's waiters (a surprising number are straight) aren't the most beautiful boys in London outside the male mannequins in Harrods windows (their live help isn't so bad either, though with not quite so much chest and armpit hair as the dummies have), LA POPOTE's are (3 Walton Street, S.W.3; 589–9178). Rococo cuisine and ambiance. Clientele are drawn from all sorts of London scenes, comparatively few are gay. So don't despair if you can't tell who's who here, or most anywhere in London outside a very, very "queer" pub. The better English boys leave off their dressing-up after Eton. However Jilly Cooper, who writes an eclectic biweekly *Sunday Times* column that ranges from the snooty to the snotty, recently went to a "Hampstead drag show in a hired bus with 45 queers" and thereby became an authority on sleuthing them out:

"You can sometimes detect it in the deadness of the eyes. . . . Another indicator is the upper lip, or rather the flesh between the nose and the upper lip, which is fuller, broader, and more petulant in homosexuals.

"Often too they walk in a special way, leaning backwards at 100 degrees to the ground, and, when there are two of them, one walks slightly in front, so the back of his shoulder brushes the front of his companion's."

Unfortunately this method apparently works only for women using it, and even for them it won't do at all in certain establishments near Covent Garden or its promising environs, one stockbroker looking pretty much like another, even in the company of successful theatrical types. In "Belgravia the golden, with mink and money blest . . ." try LE MATELOT (49 Elizabeth Street, S.W.1) or COLLAGE (46 Churton Street, S.W.1; 828–6295; dinner 7 P.M.–1 A.M., dancing in the club 10 P.M.–2 A.M.). Still hungry? LA CASSEROLE (338 King's Road, S.W.3; 352–2351), MASQUERADE (310 Earl's Court Road, S.W.5; 373–3480; drag shows every Wednesday midnight) and "? RESTAURANT" (294 Fulham Road, S.W.10; 352–1625), which has dancing until 2 A.M.

Membership Clubs (Names indicate personnel, managers, or owners)

Among the membership clubs—these are even more essential to serious homosexuals than they are to St. James's surviving Colonel Blimps—THE ROCKINGHAM (9 Archer Street, W.1, Soho; Toby Rowe, 437–4872) and Victoria's SPARTAN CLUB (62 Tachbrook Street, S.W.1; TAT 9581) have perhaps the most interesting selection of successful Gentlemen, albeit those least interested in strangers. Divorce rates are low among toffs. ARTS AND BATTLE-DRESS (27 Wardour Street, Soho, entrance in Rupert Court) with its basically younger crowd has some overlapping membership with Rockingham and Spartan. Far better cruising opportunities at TOUCAN (13 Gerrard Street, W.1) and APOLLO (31 Wardour Street, W.1) if the saucy porridge of the very young and the very old is any indication.

All the foregoing are licensed to sell alcohol, close by 11 P.M. (However a newcomer, DISCOTEK, 2A Lowndes Court off Carnaby Street, is licensed from 10 P.M. to 1 A.M.) Open later and offering dancing and drag acts are ESCORT CLUB (89A Pimlico Road, S.W.1; Archie, 730–3224) and the cheekier CABAL (64 Frith Street, W.1; often a midnight drag show. Phone 437–0795). And MANDY'S (30 Henrietta Street, W.C.2; 836–0267), a glittering, spirited discothèque that stocks the choicest produce in Covent Garden. Were it in most any other capital there'd be an even higher quota of epicenes and straights. Everyone does get a free salad, however. That old steamers' standby PAINT BOX (29 Foley Street, W.1) has had a mild sex–change operation. Chinese fortune cookies, and lively cabaret (9:30 P.M. to 1 A.M.). Younger, less vain, more with-it than ahead-of-it is the cellar of 142 Kensington High Street, W.8; don't phone, simply queue. Some nights it just falls short of adding "I'll show you . . . if you'll show me . . ." to its apt name: YOURS OR MINE. While contact dancing between males is apparently not expressly proscribed by law, most if not all the foregoing membership clubs play safe and forbid it, if only because they are licensed and thus subject to visits by the police on virtually any provocation. But unlicensed "coffee" clubs, open "very, very late," can be spotchecked only for cause and it appears that the police have a fair threshold of tolerance for GIGOLO (338 King's Road, S.W.3), the previously noted COLLAGE (46 Churton Street, S.W.1), and THE CATACOMB (279A Old Brompton Road, S.W.5), Sunday-matinee drag shows. And LOS

CHICOS (312 Old Brompton Road). They actually seem afraid to enter LE DUCE (22 D'Arblay Street, W.1, Soho), which admits no one over twenty-five.

Drag in the Pubs

There are perhaps forty public houses in and around London that offer regularly scheduled drag acts (a decade ago perhaps three or four), and some eighty full-time performers, when they are not pushing lorries or tugboats, or even raising families. The queerest thing about the following rather *ordinary* otherwise very straight pubs is the spectators, the vast majority of them the same ordinary neighborhood people whose locals these were long before drag enlivened the scene; but watch out for skinheads on "queer bashes," particularly south of the river: ADAM AND EVE (14 Peckham High Street, S.E.15; 703–9868); BLACK CAP (171 Camden High Street, N.W.1; 485–1742); CITY ARMS (1 West Ferry Road, E.14, East End); DUKE OF FIFE (35 Katherine Road, E.7; 472–0963); CRICKETERS (317 Battersea Park Road, S.W.11); DORSET ARMS (124 Clapham Road, S.W.9; 735–3427); ELEPHANT AND CASTLE (2 South Lambeth Place, S.W.8; 735–1001); GREAT NORTHERN RAILWAY TAVERN (67 High Street, N.8; 340–6969); UNION TAVERN (146 Camberwell New Road, S.E.5; 735–3605); VAUXHALL TAVERN (372 Kennington Lane, S.E.11; 735–7359); And WINDSOR CASTLE—not *that* one, the one with London's only lunchtime drag shows; it's at 309 Harrow Road (W.9). Ring the pubs or consult *Time Out*'s weekly listing for when (usually from 9:00 P.M.) and who.

The Stars

Among others, try to catch Bermondsey's own Lauri Lee, who once impersonated a merchant seaman but now does a passable Mae West. Kabell and Carr do more changes (fifteen) in one hour than the Palace Guards in a week. Terry Durham has the best boobs in the business (great tassel dance), Barry Scott the best legs, and Gilbert Oakley a wife and a grown daughter. Having written some sixty books on human behavior, Mr. Oakley, a psychologist, does *femme-fatale* and striptease sendups as "Linda." "Honey" (Jeremy Garner) is the tallest. Sandy Graham, the Menamimes (Jack makes "instruments," Alan is a tailor), and Alvis and O'Dell are among the funniest. Chatt and Gardener are nostalgic character comedians, recalling the old music halls to which modern drag owes so much. Skip the Tower before you miss Billy Carroll's impressions of Sophie Tucker.

Of course Danny La Rue is Britain's, perhaps the world's, premier female impersonator, but his versatility and raw talent as an actor transcend mere drag. Named Show Business Personality of 1970 by the Variety Club of Great Britain, he is a great favorite of Princess Margaret and her husband, who were so moved by one of Danny's performances at his Hanover Square club that they went backstage to congratulate him. Sadly, the club closed in March,

1972, due to neighborhood re-development, but you can usually catch Danny's super act at a West End theater like the PALACE (Shaftesbury Avenue, W.1; 437–6834).

Balls

For gluttons there are balls galore, and beauty contests too. Elephant and Castle pub climaxes its winter competitions with the Spring Ball by hiring the Battersea Town Hall, and similarly in Paddington's Porchester Hall Mr. Jean Fredericks, a jolly fat Canadian who plays trombone and goes by the name of "Mrs. Shufflewick," holds periodic balls and beauty competitions attended by up to one thousand connoisseurs. Not a few simple transvestites, too.

Pubs and Parks

PIG AND WHISTLE'S (14 Little Chester Street, S.W.1) Sunday lunchtime is *the* London scene of its kind (but *only* Sunday morning). However, with luck you'll fill up for the whole week on the brilliant peacockery, some of which wings in all the way from Islington—a few people arrive in slippers to suggest that they live here in oofy Belgravia. The odd Guardsman, and some quite ordinary ones as well, have their Sunday-morning (*only* Sunday morning) dress parade at HORSE AND GROOM in nearby Groom Place. These are among the most astonishing gatherings in London, particularly Pig and Whistle, if only for the numbers—a cast of literally hundreds. Field Marshal Lord Kitchener of Khartoum, General "Chinese" Gordon, and Cecil Rhodes would have felt good here.

But even more so, in their younger days, at THE COLHERNE (follow the revving to 261 Old Brompton Road, S.W.5), enough leather and bike-chain male to fit out a regiment. Classic of its type, as is THE BOLTONS, across the road: "best upstairs, downstairs they're married. And outside . . . nothing but 'pooffs in boots.' " THE SALISBURY (90 St. Martin's Lane, W.C.2), is beloved of American tourists and Off-Broadway actresses for its Edwardian decor. By all means drop in, whatever your proclivities; and that goes, of course, for any place mentioned in this section.

"It was a spring day, a day, a day for a lay, when the air/Smelled like a locker-room, a day to blow or get blown. . . ." Perhaps in Air Street, Soho, or Warlock Road, W.9., and certainly in Queensway, but more than likely it was heady Hampstead Heath that the poet had in mind, either the public path that runs between Jack Straw's Castle and Bull and Bush pub, (but *only* on the path) or at The Pond, Parliament Hill Fields. Afterward choose carefully among the clever young mélange at WILLIAM IV (Hampstead High Street, N.W.3), for not all of them are going your way. Or cruise the Serpentine and its Lido in Hyde Park, adjourning to CHAMPION (1 Wellington Terrace, Bayswater Road, W.2).

Wherever you gambol in the Gay Outdoors be warned that "Police entrapment is being increased to frightening proportions" lately, according to *Alternative London,* whose chapter on homosexuals was written by GLF. Of the Hampstead Heath oases, Kenwood Pond is described as a "women's pond. Partly gay." Highgate Ponds have "men's nude sun-bathing. Partly gay." Wimbledon Common, Queensmere: "Very dangerous. Leather." Sundown is traditional for meeting new friends.

Seek refuge, of sorts, in a Soho pub like THE GOLDEN LION (51 Dean Street) or ADMIRAL DUNCAN (54 Old Compton Street), but if you'd rather *real* sailors go down to the East End. On second thought, don't. A reporter for *Incognito Guide* confides that bands of "queer-bashing" skinheads lune about outside some of the traditional pubs.

Hotels

Exhausted? Or spunky? In either case you'll want a hotel. For years the most guarded, but well worth the effort, was the debby little house at 18 Walpole Street, S.W.3, mysteriously called "HOTEL." Always fully booked far in advance, perhaps for its sentimental Chelsea location near the house at 34 Tite Street where Oscar Wilde lived for eleven years until his tragic 1895 trial. Dennis Scott has moved "Hotel" to larger premises at 10 Queen's Gate Terrace, S.W.7; 584–9600. More basic among hotels that do not make homosexuals feel unwelcome *(nor anyone else),* but surely adequate with bed and breakfast for £2 is THE WEMBAR (19 Warwick Road, S.W.5; 373–9950). Recently renovated.

Of the several discreet rural retreats scattered about the south coast, LA PETITE MAISON (203 Havant Road, Drayton Cosham, near Portsmouth, Hants; COsham 76556) is exemplary. Under the direction of an ex-Royal Navy officer, this guest house, "exclusively for MALE PERSONS ONLY," provides the "strictest privacy in seclusion and tranquillity," at £2 for bed and breakfast, and from £12.75 weekly, lunch and dinner taken separately at 50 New Pence per head. Rooms accommodate from one to four persons. A young masseur is always in attendance, and massage treatment is given by the director or his young assistant, an invigorating spa bath thrown in for £1.50. Good beefcake photos on the walls of the bar, admired by Show Biz and Establishment clientele. "Some of them household names," so Hugh keeps things on a first-name-only basis. Only two hours by train from Waterloo Station to Cosham, where their private car will meet you.

Miscellany

If you like to look at nude boys, get a copy of *Male International,* an extraordinary magazine published by DON BUSBY STUDIOS (10 Dryden Chambers, 119 Oxford Street, W.1). But "as regards erections," says Mr. Busby, "they would most certainly be illegal."

A lavatory attendant at a Soho cinema has described Victoria's BIOGRAPH (47 Wilton Road, S.W.1) as a "gropey cinema," but it is absolutely untrue that they admit one-armed gentlemen at half-price. He's probably jealous; the Biograph is the oldest functioning film house in the country, built in 1905 by an American, George Washington Grant and this fact is the sole reason this cinema is cited.

Information and Social Services

A Gay Liberation Front has been mounted only recently and thus far does not compare in intensity with that of the United States. Historically it has not been exactly fashionable, nor terribly English for homosexuals to lobby their own cause, the brunt of those reforms that have been effected being the work of well-meaning if not "guilty" (according to the more militant of the GLF) heterosexuals. General meetings every Wednesday at 7:30 P.M. in All Saints Church Hall, Powis Gardens, W.11. Gay Lib phone is 837–7174. Legal, social, even extremely personal queries should be addressed to the ALBANY TRUST, 32 Shaftesbury Avenue, W.1; or "CHE," Committee For Homosexual Equality, BCM/Box 859, London, W.C.1.

The INCOGNITO DIRECTORY, a quantitative listing of European and British rendezvous, can be purchased directly (£1) from its London office, PRIVATE SWEDISH BOOK SERVICE, 283 Camden High Street, N.W.1. The proprietor here is himself a knowledgeable guide to the gay (and others) scene. He even writes a bit of the erotica on sale, under W. C. Fieldsian pseudonyms like "Desmond Montmorency." In London only Victor Heppel, a colleague of Montmorency's who edits the magazine *The Drag Queens,* knows more about the gay scene than Monty himself. Interestingly, neither man is gay.

"Bless Thee, Bottom, bless Thee!"—*A Midsummer Night's Dream*

The *"Bad Loo Guide"* wants writing. Earl's Court, Cheyne Walk (S.W.3), Piccadilly, Chalk Farm, Mason's Yard, etc., etc. But the law being ever more vigilant, street hustlers, male and female, grow scarcer each year. Currently, a curious coed gathering in Half Moon Street, Mayfair, centering on its intersection with Curzon Street and overspilling into Shepherd Market, usually after midnight.

Love

As to true love, the beauty of London is that lightning may strike in the most unlikely places: Saturday mornings in the materials department of Harrods or along the Portobello Road. Sunday brunch at Claridge's Hotel. After midnight in Earl's Court or Park Lane. Sotheby's or Christie's afternoon auctions. The ballet at Covent Garden. Strangers' Cafeteria at the House of Commons. Or anywhere else on a fine day in London town.

But why bother now (since summer, 1971) that London, and Britain, has its first GAY INTRODUCTION BUREAU (30 Baker Street, W.1; 402–6702)? It's operated with all the security of MI-5 but, happily, no computers. Registration fee and form £3. According to how you've completed it GIB will send a *description* of a client they think you'd find compatible. Only if you're satisfied, and if he or she (for GIB serves female as well as male homosexuals) also fancies your description, are you sent each other's names and addresses.

"GAY GIRLS"

There are no lesbians in dark-as-a-pocket Lesbia Road (E.5), but thousands of every background and lifestyle belong to the GATEWAYS, a largish jukebox discothèque licensed to 11 P.M., which though it may have seen better days during the war—according to the murals, recently overpainted—remains Britain's leading club of its genre. Up to five hundred "gay girls" (they dislike "lesbian") a night (the Albany Trust claims one in twenty British women are), particularly Wednesday, Friday, and Saturday. A wide range of young fluffs, some butch, a few bull dikes. The girls are far more cliquish within their social and economic groups than heteros or even male homosexuals, and they dance quite close, "even in the fast dances!" Unknown men won't get past the firm lady at the door, though Gateways does have its few house gay boys. New female membership welcomed, after some scrutiny and £1. Though it appeared in the film *The Killing of Sister George,* few Londoners can tell you that the Gateways is at 239 King's Road, S.W.3, in the heart of Chelsea, entrance at the green door in Bramerton Street; 352–0118. And fewer still know WHITE RAVEN (12 Monmouth Road, W.2; 229–8351) or ROBIN HOOD CLUB (11 Westbourne Gardens, W.2; 229–0972).

The girls also coexist with male homosexuals at such clubs as Mandy's and MASQUERADE (310 Earl's Court Road, S.W.5), a discothèque that also has a pretty fair French restaurant. Masquerade is open from 8 P.M. until 2:30 A.M. every night.

From Babylonian sculptures and the plays of Aristophanes we know that dildoes—since called variously *"consolateurs," "bijoux indiscrets," "gode-michés," "Cazzi," "parapilla,"* etc.—have been used since ancient times. *Satan's Harvest Home* (London, 1794) noted that the "game of flats"[7] was "as common in Twickenham as in Turkey," and several nineteenth-century

---

[7]But Iwan Bloch or his source may be in error here. Eric Partridge says "flats" has been in use to denote "playing cards" since at least 1812.

observers remarked on the shop of a certain Mrs. Phillips in Leicester Square which specialized in "dil-dols." Iwan Bloch says they cost about £2/10 during the 1840s, were made of India rubber, and were of several varieties: "one that can be used by two women at the same time, another with appliances for several *orificia corporis,* a third with an attachment for the chin, etc." (More up-to-date models can be had from PELLEN PERSONAL PRODUCTS LTD., 1A West Green Road, N.15; 340–7692.) Perhaps because "no seed is lost," as Dr. Albert Ellis has observed of lesbianism generally, the law in England, and most Western nations, has usually ignored homosexuality between women. But the social stigma, the resulting psychological pressures accruing to women, may be even greater than those felt by men.

If English law has not taken lesbians seriously enough to prohibit their sexual relationships, it has also done little to protect their rights as human beings. By its own admission the *Times* is one of all but three national newspapers who refuse ads for a quite innocuous Peter Pannish magazine, *Arena 3.* The Church Commissioners continue to refuse permission for lesbians to sign joint leases, even couples who have lived together for many years. A dying lesbian was permitted visits only from her "immediate family" (who had long since disowned her), but forbidden by her priest and doctor to have a last word with her lover of sixteen years. In the face of such public contempt you have the MINORITIES RESEARCH "TRUST" (reserves £30) whose Esme Langeley, a mother of two, publishes *Arena 3* (write BCM/SEAHORSE, London W.C.1), which carries news, advice, love stories, considerable correspondence. Many of its mostly youthful subscribers (£1 for six months) wear seahorses as a sort of Masonic handshake. KENRIC members hold bimonthly meetings at the Gateways or designated pubs, gather frequently in members' homes for discussions—office prejudice, what to tell the children (for many members are formerly married to males), etc.—and social evenings. Write Cynthia Reid, BM/KENRIC, London W.C.1. Better yet send her and Esme a donation.

There is, of course, a very active women's branch of Gay Liberation which, in addition to participating in the Wednesday night general meetings in All Saints Church Hall, Powis Gardens, W.11, gathers on its own Friday evenings. Further details in the general GLF monthly magazine *Come Together,* 5 NP per copy.

LONDON FROM A TO ZED

(The following information is meant to be taken in the English Spirit with which it was given—that is, Quite Literally. There is no suggestion of anything immoral or illegal.)

avisodomy   Considering how the English feel about their animals, see a good Safari travel agent. If you're incurable, see zoophilia.

birds   Britain has some of the world's most promiscuous ones, according to Leicester University studies, particularly the reed bunting, described as "an incorrigible trigamist." The word has also connoted a young female human, since about 1880. (See Partridge's *Dictionary of Slang,* etc., New York, 1961.) Or see RENTABIRD. Ring 935–0149. RENTAGENT too.

birth control   Has been a fashion in England since Dr. Conton (if he did indeed exist) purportedly gave his name to those seventeenth-century devices fashioned of lamb or fish bladders which Casanova referred to as "the little shields which the English have invented to keep the fair sex from worrying." Late-nineteenth-century Leicester Square shops sold them decorated with caricatures of Gladstone, Disraeli, and the Duke of Wellington. Today you'll find them even in the ladies' rooms of petrol stations.

At this writing over 2 million women are on the Pill, including the two-year-old daughter of Dr. Malcolm Potts, medical secretary of the International Planned Parenthood Association. (By the time this is read, it is presumed the young lady has gone off the Pill.) Under the National Health a six-month supply costs £1.75 to £3, a "Dutch Cap" (diaphragm), including cream and pessaries £1 (about $2.60). No girl at the age of consent (sixteen) can be legally denied contraception by her GP. BROOK ADVISORY CENTER (233 Tottenham Court Road, W.1; 580–2991) give birth-control advice to unmarried sixteen-to-twenty-five-year-olds. MARIE STOPES CENTRE (108 Whitfield Street, W.1) do likewise for all ages.

The abortion act of 1967—which requires that two doctors recommend abortion if they believe that the potential mother's general health, or that of her existing children, is endangered—is much abused and has made London the abortion capital of Europe. (But in early 1972 the authorities saw the situation as getting out of hand and closed several private clinics.) A good Harley Street man charges around £175, a bad one up to £300. Stay far away from airport cabbies who work as touts and the "pregnancy advisory clinics" they pimp for. Rather, read the excellent chapter on abortion in *Alternative London* by Nicholas Saunders (a 30NP bargain at selected newsdealers or 65 Edith Grove, S.W.10), then go to LONDON YOUTH ADVISORY CENTRE (31 Nottingham Place, W.1); RELEASE (50A Princedale Road, W.11; 727–8636, an organization especially helpful in rehabilitating drug-users); or PREGNANCY ADVISORY SERVICE (40 Margaret Street, W.1; 629–9575). With all that, about one fourth the babies born in the Royal Borough of Kensington and Chelsea are illegitimate, the highest rate in the country.

There were 137,463 legal abortions performed in Britain in 1971 (compared with 83,849 in 1970). Of these, 30,134 were carried out on foreign women—13,315 from West Germany and 11,529 from France.

blue films   "Clubs" in Tottenham Court Road and Old Compton Street (see *Time Out*'s weekly "cinema voyeur" listings and reviews), but censorship is more rigid than in the United States, where so many of the films are made. (Even the shady Soho doorway touts can lead you to nothing like what's publicly shown in Stockholm or Copenhagen.) However, domestic programs at Soho cinemas like the DILLY or the CLASSIC can be instructive and very funny. Try to catch *Naughty Knickers* if you can.

buggery   Illegal between man and wife (*life* imprisonment), but not between members of the same sex. A priest near Trevor Square marries homosexuals, but these unions are not recognized by Church or State. Thus two adult males may commit buggery so long as they do not marry. Which makes the whole thing quite confusing.

buskers   There's Ronnie Ross who begins as Chaplin, finishes as a snake. A man who may be Trotsky tootles the flageolet in Sloane Square, also by Harrods and sometimes outside Derry and Toms in Kensington High Street. Daily exhibitions of flagellation and bondage techniques near the outdoor soft-drink stands by the Tower of London. (By all means bring your camera.) But by far the most spectacular of London's street entertainers is the sprightly old mummer who performs for Leicester Square cinema queues. Placing an ordinary matchbox on the pavement with great care, he paces off thirty yards or so, then motions the crowd for absolute silence. Now he waits, allowing tension to build. Then with a spat to his hands and a slap to his cap he's off in a hoary burst of rickety-split, wheezing along at amazing speed toward that matchbox . . . *and he jumps clear over it!*

clairvoyant   is MADAME BETTY, who specializes in coffee readings, but also does tea. These can be accomplished in her flat (No. 11 at 43 Leinster Gardens, W.2) or "clients can be visited." Ring 723-2206.

colonic irrigation   Where better than in Tooting Bec! PATRICIA VEAL (13B Upper Tooting Road, S.W.17) does a very nice enema, if that's your bag, at £3.50, thank you, or full colonic at £5.50. Ring 672-4021 for a vivid delineation. ANNE COULT's purges include "relaxing remedies of the 1890s," range from £3.50 to £8 in the privacy of her home, behind the black door at 98A Bedford Mansions, Bedford Avenue, W.C.1; 637-1195. Very handy for a post-British Museum catharsis. "Super enemas by Super Nurses" at ALLAN CLINIC, 3 Vincent Court, Seymour Place, W.1; 262-9306—£3 to £5.

Colony Club   Up a flight of seedy Soho stairs. Up you go now, into a room that is so nondescript it is almost vulgarly so. "Out you go!" bellows Belcher, or hisses, depending on the mood of the day. "Nasty little piece of work, wasn't she?" observes Muriel Belcher, whatever your sex or gender, for she refers to everyone she doesn't know or doesn't like in the third person feminine. You'll have better luck crashing MI-5 in Curzon Street than the Colony Room. The membership includes some of the best-read lorry drivers and worst-dressed millionaires on the planet. And several bad painters (but also Francis Bacon), working-class film producers, homosexuals, bookmakers, lesbians, priests, and J. B. Priestley, and Frank Norman, the prose laureate of Soho. The *Millionaire's Diary* ($18) recommends six London clubs, including White's, Boodle's, and Miss Belcher's sanctum. Best time: a rainy Wednesday afternoon in March. Best drink: just say "Make mine Baby Cham" to Muriel or Ian Board, her associate. Though the Colony is undoubtedly the most discriminating club in London, some of its atmosphere and many of its components may be relished by the rest of us in the nearby YORKMINISTER (or "French" pub), also in Dean Street, Soho; De Gaulle took a lot of meals here during the war.

cuddling   Is cool between members of the opposite sex (one from each) but in February, 1970, police claimed to have seen a former Young Liberals Association chairman "cuddling another man" in Hyde Park, and though the accused pleaded not guilty to "committing an act of gross indecency," he was fined £100.

discreet private club   THE OFFICE, 16-17 Avery Row, W.1, Mayfair; 629-4327.

discipline and corrective equipment   As you might expect, several British firms deal in these necessaries. But none exceeds the craftsmanship and ingenuity, nor all of them combined the inventory, of PAMELA SPECIALIST MAILSERVICE, INTERNATIONAL. "There is virtually nothing in leather, metal, wood or any combination of these that cannot be provided to suit your particular requirements" by Pamela and her workshop, notes the *Connoisseurs Catalogue*. If you don't find exactly what you want, send along your own drawings or specifications. "No offense will be taken on account of your explicit description, *but* deliberately salacious writings (pure filth) will be ignored." The following items, all listed in a recent catalogue, may serve to inspire you.
    •Under the heading "Punishment Canes" the catalogue takes great pains to warn that, although lengths can range from twenty-four to thirty-six inches as required, "the Home Office has made an Order that the dimensions of

Canes (used for Punishment) shall not be more than thirty-six inches in length and ⅜ of an inch in diameter. Whilst I do sell Canes of other dimensions it must be on the strict understanding that they are not to be used for Chastisement." Heard and understood. And understood to apply to any and all of the following home furnishings and hardware:

•Come on, own up. Isn't that cast-iron pink flamingo out on your front lawn rather passé? Why not replace it with a "Free-Standing Kneeling Pillory/-Stocks Combined," complete with wrist chains and knee straps, only £28 "carriage mainland." (Pamela has customers drawn "from all over the world" and will gladly advise you as to additional shipping costs wherever you live.) Another "ideal conversation-piece . . . utterly dignified and secure in use" is the £25 "Whipping Bench." Now you can throw out that old coffee table that you cleverly fashioned from a door, but no longer amuses your wife's bridge club.

•Your neighbor will fall out of his hammock with envy when he sees you've exchanged yours for a Limb Separator, "an extremely uncomplicated device for keeping the legs (or arms) apart during discipline. . . . Ideal for taking on Holiday or when visiting, when more bulky apparatus would be in the way. . . . Discreet-Effective-Popular." Only £5.75 for the de-luxe model, "padded with foam sponge and covered in Suede Leather."

•Only a bloody fool would continue to make do with a simple chaise longue when he could have, for a mere £37, the "Fully Functioning Medieval Type Rack," eight feet long, folding to only four feet, and thus quite convenient for outings, beach parties, clambakes, etc.

•The "Juvenile Punishment Chair Harness" does not necessarily belong in the nursery. "Although named 'Juvenile' since it was originally designed by us at the request of a one-armed customer who, being a Widower, required something to assist in his administering discipline to his five children without difficulty due to his particular disability, the Harness is eminently suitable for ladies, gentlemen or anyone for whom a 'third' hand might be necessary. Adjustable to any size from two to twenty stone," the J. P. harness "can be tucked away unobtrusively in a drawer or cupboard when not in use and can be carried anywhere in a ladies' large hand-bag." £10; £12.25 with collar harness.

•Other home furnishings include Table-Top Portable Pillories, Convertible Reclining Chairs, Bed Conversion Racks, Gibbets, Flogging Horses, Whipping Benches, Lined Wooden Coffins, etc. If you're this far into it, why not redo a spare room: "Fitting out complete rooms, understair cupboards, cellars, attics, etc., is of course carried out under my personal supervision by trusted Staff. . . . a Quotation places you under no obligation whatsoever. . . ." The Wife of Bath travels "anywhere in the world to discuss Customers' requirements and to arrange for installations. . . ." Special consideration to "Professional Users, Widely Practising Amateurs of note (this is obviously subject to establishment of bona fides), and educational and penal establishments."

•The Connoisseurs Catalogue draws a distinction between the two kinds of Chastity Belts. . .those "designed for 'decoration' or 'conversation pieces' . . .and those Garments tailor made to fulfill their proper function." Described as "fully functional" is the leather and wrought steel "Semper Fideles" model, locking at the front with two built-in locks. (Keys supplied.) Unlined, £15.50; Suede-lined, £15.75.

•If you prefer something that is both "highly decorative" and "extremely strict" and "absolutely effective. . . (as are all our real Chastity Belts)" the Medieval is "the last word in Prevention." Surely more than an ounce of it, for the Medieval is "composed of beaten, shaped, and wrought . . . steel." A suede-lined bargain at £19.25. All Chastity Belt prices (the Germanic capitalization of nouns is infectious) are for ladies' belts. "Where required for male use, please add 50 New Pence."

•The catalogue stresses that its "leather Security Corsetry Restrictive Equipment . . . are NOT 'Fashion' Garments and are not really suitable for wearing as foundation garments." Available are four-, five-, and six-buckle corsets; matching accessories for wrists, ankles, biceps, thighs, collars (state neck size); most items are trimmed and fully lined with red, blue, or brown suede. These are apparently favorite English old-school-tie colors.

•How's your mother-in-law fixed for "Executioners/Torturers Leather Hood-Masks"? . . . "In best Black Garment Leather these are designed to Historically accurate patterns." The complete set—which includes "Medieval-pattern Leather Apron & Studded Cuffs"—at £22.50 makes a lovely gift.

•Quotations are available on hinged steel waistbands, "iron" boots and "iron" gloves. And you'll be comforted to learn that "iron maidens" in either wrought steel or resin-bonded fiberglass come with either "toy" plastic spikes or authentic steel ones. If your finished basement has run low on manacles, they've a nice line of "Antique type wrought steel dungeon shackles" thoughtfully lined throughout with suede. With hinged collar on detachable three-foot chain, £8.50. Including the brass padlock. ("Give neck measurement when ordering.")

•A kind of adult womb is the "Total Enclosure Leather Bag, a totally enclosing 'suit' with interior pockets for arms and legs. . . ." The unit "provides exactly the right warm dark situation, with the most delightful aroma of leather. . . . For 'Suspension' purposes a leather harness is available which secures the whole body safely, at top of head, sole of feet and waist, in a stout cradle of secure harness-leather straps which are tested to hold a body well in excess of 300 lbs. in any conceivable position." At £48, this is womb-service deluxe.

•The catalogue lists a great many more items, including "Second-Hand and Clearance" specials, and "If you have any interesting items (NOT Rubber or Plastic please) you wish to dispose of," let Pamela know about it, "together with price required." A bit off the subject, perhaps, is the "Ladies *Mobile* Personal Battery Vibrator/Massager. The last word in luxury" and the first for the Junior Prom. "Operated by *remote control* from batteries in the handbag," or your friend's pocket, "the vibrator is enclosed in a super-supple leather harness to keep it in precisely the required position whether still or moving about. No one but you will know it's there, and it can be switched on and off at will. Devised by our R. & D. team and obtainable nowhere else in the world. . . . Single model complete with harness, £10.25. Double model (two vibrators) £15.50."

•If you'd like a private consultation with the "R. & D. team," the trip to Bath—a sinister-looking but no less fascinating, almost purely Georgian city rich in Roman history—takes no more than two hours from London by train, three by auto. Met in their workrooms at the rear of their dress shop—which is admittedly little more than a front—Pam and John are an engaging and sympathetic couple for whom no request is too difficult. Except one:

"One gentleman demanded that we design and construct a pair of pants which would be absolutely, unequivocally impossible for him to get out of. . . . Unless he wanted to!"

Visitations are "*Strictly by confirmed appointment only!*" Write "Pamela, P.O. Box 53, Oldfield Park, Bath-Somerset."

Should you have no time for a trip to Bath, note a recent London development: Used discipline and corrective equipment may be purchased at several outdoor markets—Portobello Road is likely. The venders' patter can be colorful and instructive. Best time, Saturday afternoons.

Monique von Cleef has found "the best craftsman in London" in Kensington, S.E. 11, near the Imperial War Museum. Ask her for his address.

dolphins   LONDON DOLPHINARIUM (65 Oxford Street, W.1) claims to have the only dolphin pantomime in the world. Plus playful penguins, Pebbles the Sea Lion, and lovely aquamaids. Shows at 11 A.M., and 12:30, 2, 3:30, 5, 6:30, 8, and 9:30 P.M. Adults 70p, children 35p. This is one of the best things in London that you can do with your girlfriend; if you have no children the CHILD POVERTY ACTION GROUP (1 Macklin Street, W.C.2; 405-5942) or INTERNATIONAL VOLUNTARY SERVICE (same address; 405-8331) can probably put you in touch with an orphanage or other social service group who know some children who need to see these dolphins—and need someone like you to take them along.

drugs   You're better off with the dolphins. For a visitor, just to *be* . . . alive and aware and in London can be the ultimate high. (And, of course, for so many natives too, which makes London such an enjoyable place.) If you don't agree, at least take this advice: Don't bring anything in. Don't take anything out. Get the paperback *Alternative London* (only 30p at selected newsdealers; $1 by ship mail to the U.S. or $2 air mail, from author Nicholas Saunders, 65 Edith Grove, S.W.10) and commit to memory two chapters (there are 30 in all): "The Law" and "Drugs."

Alternative London tells you where to get it, how much, how not to get busted, and reviews the new (1971) Misuses of Drugs Act: "1. Drugs are now classified according to their danger. 2. There is only one act. 3. Dealers and people who carry a lot can now get fourteen years and not just ten."

From the book we learn that Chinese heroin is currently available at from £3 to £5 a grain in Gerrard Street, W.1. Opium is selling at £15 to £18 an ounce, methadone at £4.50 a grain, cocaine £150 an ounce. Price of an LSD journey ranges from 25p to £2, but it is suggested that morning glory seeds contain lysergic acid amide. You can purchase 10p packets containing about 60 seeds (no insecticide; each seed may contain about a microgram of LSD). In any event one can purchase morning glory seeds from CARTERS, 80 Victoria Street, S.W.1, among other better seed shops. Needless to say, you needn't inform them what you plan to harvest. Mr. Saunders' book also cites nutmeg for those who would like to experience "euphoria, drowsiness, and intense nausea," and lettuce, "whose milky sap is said to be similar to opium." He doesn't say where to buy lettuce or nutmeg, but Covent Garden is probably as groovy a place as any to get it, or perhaps one of London's many greengrocers. Many London restaurants also serve lettuce in salads.

As to marijuana, or what the British call "Cannabis," if you are American the chances are good you know a lot about this. Spring, 1972 prices for hash: about £120 per pound, £12–£13 per ounce, about £1.25 for anything from a twelfth to a twentieth of an ounce. (As has been noted, British roaches tend to be massive, perhaps because the dope is often of such inferior quality one mixes anything handy that might spice it up—Scottish heather, licorice, pubic hair, etc.)

For those few visitors who have heard that the British system of treating and caring for addicts is more enlightened and humane than that of the United States, and thus presume that the British authorities will be lenient with drug carriers, users, or purveyors . . . forget it. If you're caught, you're in trouble. And you're thousands of miles from home.

escort agencies and services   Galore. Among the fanciest and most experienced, NORMAN COURTNEY LTD. (37 Old Bond Street, W.1; 493-5073) are highly recommended; a near Duke or guaranteed Deb (if you give them some notice) who'll do you proud at anything from a Queen's reception to an

East End drag ball. £10.50 the evening. They also do *au pairs* (493-7866).

The best all-round service is undoubtedly GLAMOUR INTERNATIONAL V.I.P. (61/63 Beak Street,W.1; 437–5815). Like several other firms V.I.P. enables one to select his companion from albums of color photos—with informative résumés detailing education, career, hobbies, interests, age, vital statistics, etc.—but no other service allows you to audition your choices on fifteen-second color video taped "commercials" as this one does. Indeed, V.I.P., which bills itself as "the world's largest escort agency," is a veritable mini-Playboy Club, with the important difference that you can take the young lady away with you (£12). And if one takes a "V.I.P. card" at £5 per annum he enters a world of "Glamour, Private Parties, Premieres and Gala Nights, Charter Flights," not to mention free use of the large, nearly lavish lounges, conference rooms, and color TV room. And, at supplementary fees, the club offers a full-range secretarial service and use of a silver Rolls-Royce limousine complete with cocktail bar, radio-telephone, stereo, and pretty chauffeuse. Sounds slightly hokey but many London executives are satisfied members and some of the "Glamour Girls" are very attractive and, not incidentally, quite intelligent and knowledgeable about London. The club is well financed and so it is able to advertise heavily and thus attract many escort applicants. From there, Darwin's theory of natural selection takes over. "Many call, few [about 200] are chosen."

For those who may be wondering, stop. No escort situation cited in this book employs "whores," to put things bluntly, and right. Prostitution may be legal in England, but soliciting is not. Thus for a girl to exchange ultimate sexual services for money (or even a Winnie the Pooh bear) would violate the agency's rules and practices. (If this should occur, please don't tell them.) On the other hand, theoretically anything might happen, once you and the young lady are alone (perhaps you'll make arrangements for a "Dutch" tea date the next day, for example); and not a few men have married their escorts.

Bear in mind that thousands of lovely young ladies (and hundreds of attractive young and some middle-aged men) have listed themselves with the escort services—secretaries, actresses, models, students, musicians, buskers, cricket players—people from literally all of life's walks (other than the street). In London this is a perfectly respectable way to earn some extra cash and, not incidentally, enjoy a pleasant evening on the town. (In fact, if you are pressed for cash and feel you could handle the job, there's no harm in offering your services as an escort at any of the agencies listed in this section.)

Because this is such a popular institution—particularly advantageous to the visitor who is spending only a short time in the city—you will often find phone lines busy. Thus, a fairly extensive listing follows. As with all situations, this book cannot be responsible for any numbers which do not answer (this being an ephemeral world at best), but all the following appeared to be thriving at press time. (Use the weekly *Where to Go* as a supplement.)

ALPHA is a good bet for businessmen and budgeteers alike; moderate prices for a girl (£7), or a full night out from £12 to £20, which includes "girl, dinner, show, dancing," and a free carafe of wine. (When you consider that a Miami Beach agency has recently advertised afternoons which consist of a wicked two- or three-hour auto ride up and down Collins Avenue with a "pretty girl" for from fifty to one hundred dollars, you may agree that London does have certain advantages.) Ring Alpha at 437-6116 or drop round to 22 Great Windmill Street, W.1.

"Selected, refined male and female social partners available for any of your special occasions," say the folks reached at 935-7460, who, not incidentally, welcome credit cards.

CHELSEA GIRL ESCORTS (584-6513 or 584-2749) promise "select girls for all occasions." And a prudent call to ANINA SPITZER, a Mayfair agency established in 1968, "will provide you with the perfect companion—beautiful girls with charm and personality" (140 Piccadilly; 493-6960).

"Girls, girls, girls. Young and lovely" can be arranged for if you ring 437-9556.

ON THE TOWN, which has a veddy St. James's address (10 Park Place, S.W.1; 493-7860), has "a personal invitation for you. We have the most beautiful girls in London to escort you around town daytime or evening." Their motto is "Discretion is our motto."

ANNABELLE'S MAYFAIR ESCORT AGENCY (3 Cork Street, W.1; 734-3114) "have a High Standard of Attractive Girls." THE ELIZABETHAN international escort/guide service is for discerning ladies and gentlemen, who should immediately phone 437-7285 to find out more; and add 01 (London code) on overseas calls. Why not have one greet you at the plane with a sonnet?

Are you getting bored, then? A rose is a rose, you say, even an English one. But not if it's MISS PETAL, for she supplies "escorts for Paris or London Weekends"! "Inclusive prices for Ladies or Gentlemen to have an elegant companion at your side." This is surely a better way to see Paris than with your Aunt Grace or your Uncle Jack (who, if he has any sense at all, remained in Stockholm). This operation also promises, "Hotel massage service for ladies and gentlemen by Tony or Miss Petal; 834-3211."

HIGH SOCIETY ESCORTS offer not only escorts, guides, general tourist services, but babysitters as well (52 Shaftesbury Avenue, W.1; 734-7086).

Women should be advised that men are available from MALE ESCORTS AND GUIDES on 24-hour call; and "comfortable cars when required," should you need to go anywhere. Ring 937-3228/1673.

Ornithologists should not forget RENTABIRD (935-0149 or 935-6206).

Lucy has JOLLY DOLLIES "for your leisure pleasure." Ring 229-2974 between 10 A.M. and 7 P.M., typical office hours although some agencies stay open until 8 or 9 P.M.; at most agencies a girl can usually be secured, with an hour's notice. Allow more time if your requirements (age, hair color, type of figure, education, cultural interests, etc.) are quite specific.

Dial DIANA for "Duchesses, Debs and Delectable Dollies," 670-6235. "Actors, actresses, and models to help you enjoy London" may be auditioned by calling PREMIERE ESCORTS at 580-4790.

EROS BUREAU, established 1948, has "the right partner for dinner, dancing, theaters, clubs, and all social occasions" and what is more, "American Express and Diners' Club cards are accepted" (213 and 214 Piccadilly, W.1; 734-0167).

gggggghosts   The GHOST CLUB (c/o P. Underwood, Esq., The Savage Club, 86 St. James's Street, S.W.1; 839-5595) visits haunted houses, investigates psychic phenomena. Founded 1862. Conan Doyle and W. B. Yeats among the illustrious membership.

governesses   In the case of London's better practitioners, none of whom advertises on the tobacconists' message boards and few in the kinky contact magazines, it would be imprudent here to give addresses. Though what they do to consenting adults is probably legal under English law (the police generally refuse to discuss the matter), these women might be liable to vague charges of "corrupting or disturbing public morals," or some such rubbish. Except among their chosen circle, for the English governess public notoriety would be as much anathema as a daily enema might be for a diarrhetic. Certainly those with a serious mission to find these ladies will do so. One should be reminded that the best Continental practitioners—Monique von Cleef, The Hague; Jaky Duprey, Paris; *et al.*—have a wide acquaintance with their English counterparts. They're surely more appropriate than the Yellow Pages if your inquiries cannot locate "MADAM MOONGODDESS" of Shepherd Market; "LADY SYBILSADDLE," near Dolphin Square; "LADY A, the Countess of Zippity Zap; the good Knightsbridge houses. Or MADAM E, now of Marylebone, late of Mayfair (though there are two new ones there). She has a fine house near Harley Street.

The current rage among the peerage is MADAM P of Edgeware. A handsome, properly severe lady of about thirty-eight is she. Her forte is versatility, but not simply because she happens to be bisexual. P can be an "extremely nasty piece of work" if that's what you're after or, if the price *and chemistry* are right, she'll go to any lengths to please. For the whole of one recent week, for example, she entertained an "operation freak," having spent the previous fortnight converting her large mansion flat into a "hospital."

When His Lordship checked in, his "illness" was promptly diagnosed, charts were prepared and hung from his crank-operated bed, which had been specially rented for the occasion, and he was given several alcohol rubs and baths by Madam P's lesbian "houseboy." Three High-Class Whores were called in as consultants, all dressed as nurses, of course. In the days to follow they starved the client, kept his bedpan empty, did urine analyses, checked pressures, pulses, twitches, etc., and twice brought him to orgasm by introducing his rectum to a stethoscope.

After numerous enemas and even a try at intravenous feeding, the Big Day (the fourth) finally arrived. The patient, advised he had a fifty-fifty chance of survival, was wheeled about the flat on an old coffee table, given a delirious dose of sodium amytal, then scalpeled across the buttocks (Madam P acting as surgeon). This was quickly and expertly sutured by one of the nurses. Three days later, having enjoyed his Miraculous Recovery nearly as much as his terror over the Life-or-Death Operation, His Lordship emerged into the bright Maida Vale sunshine "fit as a fiddle," and far richer for his experience, albeit he might have got much the same effect at half the £500 fee had he checked into Paddington Hospital, where, incidentally, one of Madam P's assistants had actually briefly trained as a nurse.

"group (discreet)   welcomes couples. Details SAE/phone: Mrs. C. Jones, 38 Crawford Street, W.1." (Postal drop—*no callers.*)

hair (pubic)   Yoko Ono advises us to smoke it. A man in Pimlico is building a model of the Victoria and Albert Museum out of it. Perhaps Mary Quant (3 Ives Street, S.W.3; 584-8781) may fashion your lady's into the shape of a heart—or, if you prefer, a club, as in the ace, king, queen, jack, or trey of Clubs—as her husband has done hers. (The suggestion is made solely on the basis that Miss Quant has suggested this cut as a fashion wave of the future; don't scoff, remember what she did for the mini-skirt.) *As long as you don't tell them from whence it came, and as long as they don't suspect,* INTERSKILL LTD., (P.O. Box 65, Cambridge) just might freeze a lock of your girlfriend's in a solid crystal-clear slim block, with her Name and Deb Ball in italic script.

incest   Not allowed. Perhaps since given a bad name by Sawney Bean, who, by vigorous incest, produced a family of six daughters, eight sons, fourteen granddaughters, and eighteen grandsons. Together they ate up nearly everyone in Galloway, hung the odd limbs from their cave. All the Beans were finally bagged by James I of Scotland, who had them delimbed or burned alive.

"... And I myself don't much fancy my sister," wheezed the crusty solicitor who related the tale at Old Wine Shades (6 Martin Lane, E.C.4),

London's most venerable winehouse, perhaps the only City tavern to survive the Great Fire of 1666. "In fact, I feel rather sorry for her husband."

Italy   "Go go" there. "Sunbathe all day and earn £40 plus p.w. 1st class Italian Night Clubs. Fares paid. Attractive female dancers required. . . . Dance Partners/Hostesses" also "urgently required for 1st class European Night Clubs. Tel: 764-7946."

kiss   The world's record of one hour, thirty-five minutes, forty seconds was recently claimed by a Miss J. Winmill, 19, and a Mr. D. Atkinson, of London, according to 1968 wire service reports. However, according to a New York City copy editor, two men held an unbroken kiss for the better part of a day—over twelve hours—before a crowd of witnesses in Central Park during the Gay Pride Week of 1971 (or 1970?). Undaunted, a certain young gentleman from Paterson, New Jersey, claims that he and a certain young lady from Islington (whom he met while walking his dog—Fred—in Pickle Herring Street, S.E. 1) subsequently set the world's record, July 28, 1971, underneath Hyde Park's romantic ALBERT MEMORIAL: thirteen hours, twenty-two minutes, and twenty-two seconds. The Guinness people really ought to step in here and settle this matter.

In March, 1972, a UPI story datelined St. Albans, England, reported that George Apter is looking for two handsome young men and four women to kiss all his women customers and male customers respectively in order to promote the opening of his new service station. He was offering $52 for eighteen hours' work.

Not all the news is good, however. Also in March, 1972, the World Health Organization reported from Geneva that "kissing disease" (which, says WHO, is otherwise known as mononucleosis) is on the rise in Britain: reported cases of kissing disease rose from 2852 in 1961 to 7479 in 1971. The *New York Times* account of the epidemic noted that "the study did not say if the increase was due to more kissing or better reporting."

Kisser (Jack the)   is loose in London. By spring, 1972, he had struck six times. According to Scotland Yard, he functions "just like the prince in *Sleeping Beauty*" except that prior to or after the stolen kiss he robs his victims—all women thus far. The latest was a seventeen-year-old hosiery firm employee who was rudely awakened in her Loughborough bedroom, but managed to bite the intruder before he fled. Police say they are "looking for a man with a badly damaged lower lip."

leather couture   Johnny Sutcliffe of ATOMAGE is by far the best. Virtually anything can be accomplished in fine leathers or "patent vinyl" ("a layer of foam PVC spread upon and bonded to a knitted jersey cloth base"), but no ready-to-wear. "So if you have a 'dreamsuit' . . . helmet . . . battle dress . . . built-on boots . . . a design, a rough sketch, an idea of your own or would like our Design Service to produce something according to your personal instructions—why not come and talk with us" (10A Dryden Street, Drury Lane, W.C. 2; 836-0150). Practitioners, couples no less welcome than thespians. Built-on boots from £30. Battle dress from £80. Boudoir suits, £120 to £200.

Lloyd George   Far more than G. Washington, this man was a true father of his country. One of England's great liberal statesmen—fifty-four years an MP, Prime Minister (1916–22), and one of the 1919 "Big Four"—he also found time for at least seventeen enduring love affairs during his marriage, not to mention uncounted quick ones with wives of Cabinet ministers and MPs as well as charladies and their daughters, consummated everywhere from 10 Downing Street to the hard back benches of Parliament. Whatever you may think of his politics, "The Goat" was one hell of a goat.

love potions   Have enjoyed great favor among all classes for centuries. Lady Elizabeth Grey was arraigned before Parliament, on the accusation of Richard II, for having seduced King Edward IV into marriage with cantharides (Spanish flys). Iwan Bloch considered the "excessive consumption of meat" as exercising a particularly "stimulating effect upon the *vita sexualis.*" (In the 1880s, for example, a French soldier on active service got a meat ration of 350 grams daily, an English soldier 670 grams daily.)

Nowadays ground rhinoceros horn and other hot treats may be had at some West End barbershops. The Indian government says its rare one-horned rhino is nearly extinct "because poachers are killing them, selling the horns as aphrodisiacs for about $1200 each," the AP reports.

" 'Yellow Emperor' was the rarest and costliest remedy" for "lost vital physical vigor," according to the current British suppliers, Apothecary Cathay. "Because one of the major ingredients lost its efficacy soon after harvesting, it could not be sent by normal trade routes. The method of dispatch was one of the most expensive ever devised. Relays of horsemen carrying heavily sealed satchels over their shoulders galloped night and day from the foothills of the Himalayas to Peking with a swordsman riding swiftly at each flank. And when they arrived, utterly exhausted, waiting merchants sold the consignments for twenty times their weight in fine gold." Originally known as "the Emperor Hu'ang Ti's Prerogative," it is now everyone's, at £3 a try, thanks to PELLEN PERSONAL PRODUCTS, (1A West Green Road, N. 15; 340-7692). Also box of one hundred high-grade Ginseng tablets, £2.30; and many more.

Try HARRODS food stalls for truffles.

macintoshes   For the man who has everything. And wants to flash it. Stuff your Aquascutum and Burberry, CHAS. MACINTOSH (28 Saville Row; 734-4030) are directly descended from the man who in 1824 originated the rubber-vulcanizing process. They're out of the raincoat trade now but may advise where you can purchase a breakaway flying front model. Then position yourself before the Little Girls' (maximum age fifteen) loo opposite Lancaster Gate, Kensington Gardens, or the Little Boys' (to age thirteen). For a more mature, discriminating audience ride the Piccadilly Line tube between Earl's Court and Piccadilly Circus, being especially ready at the randy South Kensington and knobby Knightsbridge stops.

marriage and introduction bureaux   England is surely the birthplace of the modern marriage advertisement, the first said to have appeared in *Houghton's Collection for Improvement of Husbandry and Trade,* July 19, 1695: "A gentleman, thirty years old, who says he has a very considerable fortune, would like to marry a young gentlewoman, who has a fortune of about £3000, and he is willing to make a proper contract on the matter."

In the eighteenth century women were regularly sold at the Smithfield Cattle Market, except perhaps the week of July 22, 1797, when a notice in *The Times* apologized: "By an oversight we are not in a position to quote this week the price of women. The increasing value of the fairer sex is considered by various celebrated writers to be a sure sign of increasing civilization. On these grounds Smithfield may raise a claim to rank as a place of special advancement, for at its Market the price of women has lately risen from a half a guinea to three guineas and a half."

Marriage clubs and agencies were established as early as 1700, the most resourceful of the eighteenth century being the "Marriage Bazaar" at 2 Dover Street, St. James's.

Continuing in the tradition, the most successful is IVY GIBSON (41 Oxford Street, W.1; 437-4471), which claims some forty-three thousand marriages (many of them Anglo-American, for which there is a special department) in its quarter-century career, runs dozens of highly descriptive, entertaining ads for clients in each issue of the *London Weekly Advertiser.* In that paper's center pages are also many individually placed ads. HEATHER JENNER, runs her 124 New Bond Street spouse shop (629-9634) with wit and flair, has some titled clients, and a special Jewish branch. MAYFAIR INTRODUCTION SERVICE (suite 2, 60 Neal Street, W.C.2) are good too.

English computer-dating forms are so precise and frank, as to both your own characteristics and those desired in a partner, and so beautifully anonymous, of course, that this method is probably the odds-on best of a bad lot for a quick candid liaison. Two or three pounds for three or more dates. To save time, have them meet your plane. Write COM-PAT (213 Piccadilly; 437-4025) or DATELINE (23 Abington Road, W.8; 937-0102).

CONTACTS UNLIMITED (2 Great Marlborough Street, W. 1) can be reached by phone (437-7121) all day, all night, all week.

The most zealous social contact group is PHONATACT, whose extremely varied programs include frequent gatherings in members' homes, outings, picnics, pub crawls, etc. Each member (£6.50 a year) receives a frequently updated list of everyone's phone number and address, broken down by postal districts. About 55-percent female membership, mostly aged twenty-five to thirty-five. New members interviewed (with vigor and candor) Tuesday to Thursday evenings, Grosvenor Hotel, Buckingham Palace Road, S. W.1. First contact Bryan Snellgrove (37B Lilyville Road, S.W.6; 736-5594). All of these marriage and intro bureaus, computer dating firms, and Phonatact are, of course, strictly legitimate, wholesome organizations and neither practice nor tolerate any kind of funny business. Nor do any firms which advertise in the *London Weekly Advertiser.* Nor those in *Time Out*'s "lonely hearts" column.

massage and sauna   As every English schoolchild knows, the stews and bagnios of London were established next to the Southwark bear-baiting gardens during the reign of Henry II (1154–1189) *by act of Parliament,* in contrast to the baths in Germany and France which degenerated to licentiousness through the laws of nature: "No single woman to take money to lye with any man, but she lye with him all night 'till the morrow." The eighteen houses were at first under the charge of the good Bishop of Winchester, and in 1380 passed to William Walworth, fish merchant and Mayor of London, who let them to procuresses. By the eighteenth century venue had shifted to Covent Garden. In the classifieds of the journal *Society* (issue of July, 1900), ads like the following were common: "Rheumatism and Neuralgia, Nerve and Insomnia Treatment. School of Modern Discipline. By August Montgomery, Edgeware Road, Oxford Street, W."

In 1970 the *Times* admitted that "some masseuses operating from establishments" and some girls who advertise (in the *Times*'s classifieds) massage treatment at homes or hotels "were prepared to give clients sexual pleasure for extra payment." Though the *Times* says it is assiduously vetting, they admit the problem is vexing, not only to newspapers but also the Westminster City Council, which alone "controls" as best it can 290 establishments and practitioners. Though virtually any type of massage is apparently permitted in private premises (yours) by invitation, sexual extras are forbidden by law in public establishments. But it is nearly as difficult for the various London councils to control what's happening in those private cubicles as it is for the managements concerned.

Thus the following (and those in the regular text) are cited *solely* because all have been found to offer attractive young female masseuses who give expert, therapeutic massages from £2 to £5. *There is no suggestion that any illegal or immoral practices take place.*

Six skilled wenches at MAYFAIR CLINIC (1 Chesterfield Street, W.1; 499-1868), from £3. A few Oriental blossoms among the bouquets at MISS LOTUS'S 13A Pall Mall parlor, convenient to several Pall Mall clubs. "Attractive maidens in mini kimonos" at KUMIKO MASSAGE (20 Lisle Street, off Leicester Square; 734-7982). GEORGE STREET CLINIC (2 Cumberland Mansions, George Street, W.1; 723-2048) are strong on technique and apparatus. And "hotel visits a specialty. Early or late." After a Rotten Row canter in Hyde Park, put your body in the hands of ULTRA TAN's nubiles (143 Knightsbridge, S.W.1; 584-7212). All five "Miss World-type" masseuses at the twenty-four-hour LONDON SAUNA (47 Bedford Street, W.C.2; 836-6019) specialize in the "Wertheim Massage. . . . It would take me as long to describe it as to give it, sir." About an hour and a half.

As you'd hope, Soho has nearly as many rubbers in the saunas as scrubbers in the streets. WINDMILL SAUNA (Great Windmill Street; 437-8552) goes from 10:30 A.M. to 10:30 P.M. GRECIAN URN (25 Rupert Street; 734-0246) has petitioned the Westminster City Council to allow couples and mixed singles in its saunas. No decision yet. Next door at WAY-A-HED (437-1055), Joanna-in-Hot-Pants commences your Special Hangover Cure by bonging a nasty bell. Next a mug of high-vitamin fructose, whereupon she lathers you in the shower, plies you with "Formula-9" (dissolves alcohol in the blood), mints, whiffs of oxygen, and finally a "sympathetic massage," with emphasis on the spinal column and back of the neck. After forty-five minutes of this and a strong cuppa tea "even a blind drunk will sober up" according to proprietor Connor Walsh. The WESTSIDE HEALTH CLUB (201-207 Kensington High Street, W.8; 937-7979) is ideal after shopping in the nearby dolly boutiques, provides separate facilities for men and women, but only masseuses. Stonehenge Council law apparently considers it improper for the ladies to be worked over by men.

Thus, apparently, any sauna that provides only masseurs caters only to men. Young males, adore KING SAUNA. Five thousand members but only "twenty-four beds," according to an admitting attendant, who warns that the King discourages "tourists."

"But I thought this was a sauna, not a hotel! What are the beds for?"

"God only knows," says a man behind the desk.

Yearly membership £3, four-week transient membership £1.50. Members' guests 50NP. Open daily from 2 P.M. to 8:30 A.M. Special night rate from midnight to morning, £1.60. King Sauna, 11 Abingdon Road, W.8, off Kensington High Street; 937-6868.

London's largest exclusively male sauna is PREMIER (10 Upper St. Martin's

Lane, W.C.2; 240-2141). Sauna £1.25. Massage £1.25. STRAND is also very busy (396 Strand, W.C.2; 240-1766). And of course so are the SAVOY TURKISH BATHS (91 Jermyn Street, S.W.1; 930-9552). Perhaps one of their twelve masseurs can direct you to WEST HAM BATHS, Romford Road, Finsbury. All saunas cited as for males are just that: for any men, whatever their politics or proclivities. And all are thoroughly respectable and law-abiding.

Police say thirteen men committed "acts of gross indecency" while officers —experts in these matters—kept a close watch in the steam room of the ROMAN COURT HOTEL's sauna (77 Inverness Terrace, W.2; 229-4639). Sounds implausible, for some months after the alleged acts took place the basement facilities remain available.

massage (visiting)   Why not enjoy the luxury and convenience of having a lovely young masseuse administer to you in the privacy of your hotel room, your home or wherever it is you are staying? The following offer such amenities (unless otherwise noted, i.e. masseurs), and all of these situations are thoroughly law-abiding. The laws governing visiting services are, however, somewhat different from regulations applying to those which the client visits. As with the escort services (and there is some overlapping here, for some of the visiting services, where noted, also supply escorts) the phones are apt to be very busy, hence the following extensive listing.

"Let's face it. When you're staying at one of the best hotels, flats or houses in London, you tend to be a bit choosy about the kind of Masseuse you have to visit you. . . . She should be a cultured intelligent girl, kind and considerate, attractive and well-dressed. . . . We insist all our Masseuses should fit that description. . . . Most of our young ladies are more than just professional masseuses—they're fully qualified physiotherapists. Nationalities? English, Japanese, Scottish, German, South African, Jewish [with chicken fat?], Russian, Persian. All races, all colours—but all cultured, all very very good. . . . 9 A.M. to any reasonable time in the late evening. Please give us at least one hour's notice, and a little longer if possible." ROEDEAN MASSAGE, London's High-Class Visiting Service, 373-0052. With all that, you wonder, why no Scandinavians?

EVE MARIE (602-2832) has 'em. "Swedish massage by an attractive masseuse who will visit you." And SWEDISH THERAPY MASSAGE (352-1510) advertises that "an attractive and qualified masseuse will be delighted to visit you at your home or hotel." SUOMI (Finland) have masseuses and masseurs "for ladies and gentlemen at your home or hotel." Ring 370-2425.

PLAYGIRLS suggest you call 629-0906 any time and they "will reserve a beautiful masseuse who will be at your home or hotel in twenty minutes. London's most reliable service." Escorts too. The massage is £6.50 plus fares, typical rates for most services.

ANN not only has beautiful girls but attractive masseurs as well. Book for a visiting massage by phoning 272-8033 any time from noon to midnight (and see "photography" in this A to Zed).

"Gentlemen! Be pampered in the old oriental fashion with attention for bathing and massage from two [count 'em!] attractive masseuses or if you prefer, you may have only one. Our massage is not only the best in London, it is unique. . . . An attractive qualified masseuse will visit your hotel or home for a genuine therapeutic massage at £7.50 for a 1-hour massage (including spirit rub)." PRIVATE MASSAGE, 402-4544.

Things must be very crowded by now in that little hotel room of yours, so take a quick run over to VIVIEN DANIEL, who says she is "apart from the rest of them." (Indeed she really should have been listed under the on-premise massage establishments.) Anyway she is "private in an unrushed, unbusinesslike, comfortable and *totally private* atmosphere." There you "receive a highly expert massage, not just to my routine, but to your choice; also no fussy time limit to negate your enjoyment. Be bathed in invigorating Badedas. For appointment please telephone only between 10 A.M. and 2 P.M., 727-8962 (Bayswater area), individual care always."

Back to the traveling girls. POMPADOR "offer you well groomed intelligent young lady masseuses to give professional massage and courtesy to gentlemen in their hotel suites; 493-5111." "Beautiful" are TIDDY'S MASSEUSES who invite you to ring 492-5763 "anytime." THE CONNOISSEUR (and by now you should be), visiting massage and escorts services, can be contacted by telephoning 370-5935. MISS IRENE JAMES (727-9390) wants to hear from all "professional people who require top quality massage by a fully qualified young lady therapist."

"We're here," say RELAXATION PLUS (492-0749), "beautiful young masseuses will visit your home or hotel anytime including Sundays." And in London, the part about the Sundays is quite something.

There are always some nice ads in the classifieds of the magazine *Time Out*. In a March, 1972, issue, for example, someone called White tells us that he is a "masseur, male, middle aged and knows how to handle women, will visit; 289-2467." Then there is "Super Masseur" who "gives beautiful massages, females only. Private visits. Tel: 351-0273."

Let us close on a note of versatility. GIRLS ALL-PURPOSE EMPLOYMENT AGENCY "for staff and clients" have "escorts, sauna, visiting masseuse, models, massage, home or hotel." Get the details at 140 Marylebone Road, N.W.1, or phone 935-4002, 486-2218, or 240-2748. Or 836-6019.

museums   According to an Englishman who should know, Alfred Hitchcock, "Our preoccupation with crime, especially murder, is concerned with the Englishman's aura of outward respectablity. But underneath that immaculate exterior—that's quite another story. Heaven knows what pent-up emotions are panting to escape." Not surprising, then, that the legendary BLACK MUSEUM of SCOTLAND YARD is basically asexual and definitely awhimsical compared with its Paris counterpart (write the Commissioner, New Scotland Yard, Broadway, S.W.1; 230-1212, ext. 278, but don't say you're compiling a lusty guide to Europe) and has little to offer other than memorabilia of crimes of violence. "All confiscated pornography is supposed to be destroyed," according to one official, though some of the choicer confiscated apparatus and pictures are held for private showings in several inspectors' offices—for instance, a gramophone designed to piston any of a set of twelve iron phalluses up the vagina of the engineer-inventor's insatiable mistress. Also one of Hildebrand's old buggery machines. And a sexual gallows. (See the British Museum's copy of *Bon Ton Magazine*, No. 31, September, 1793, for a discussion of "The Pleasurable Effects of Temporary Strangulation.")

Apparently to qualify for display in "The Black," an article may not simply be "pornographic" in its own right but, to lend respectability, must have association with a particularly violent crime. Thus, they'll proudly show off a tobacco tin containing four lots of female pubic hair that John Reginald Halliday Christie harvested from among his six (known) sex-murder victims at 10 Rillington Place (now Rustyn Close, W.11, for history-lovers). Also exhibited is the riding crop with which Neville George Clevely Heath horribly mutilated the vaginal passages of his comely victims after first lashing them brutally and biting off their nipples. (A surgeon at ST. MARY'S HOSPITAL, Praed Street, W.2, Paddington—whose VD clinic is kept unusually busy by London prostitutes—reports "bit paps" are a common occupational hazard among streetgirls.)

Some English fancy their own nipples. Take the jabbernowl who, in his wisdom, wired his to a battery. When it at last had run down, he switched to the mains. After scalpeling them off, the pathologist presented them to the MUSEUM OF THE WOOD STREET POLICE STATION, where they float in a bottle next to the intestines of "this bloke who used to stand on a stepladder with a broomhandle up his backside." One day he fell off. He was still alive when his wife pulled out part of the broom handle—"There! You see the remainder of it," observes your guide—but he died on the way to hospital. In the same large glass display case are tops of skulls battered by iron bars, a concentration-camp-numbered piece of skin, a shotgun-blasted heart, assorted genitalia, and various semiaborted wombs, one with catgut, another with knitting needles intact.

"You all right?" solicitously inquires Police Constable Donald Rumbelow, a handsome, articulate young man who began collecting in 1966, opened the museum in June, 1971. All adults are welcome without charge, particularly small parties up to about fifteen, provided they first write "The Chief Superintendent, Wood Street Police Station, London E.C.2," for to Constable Rumbe-low "the secret of a museum of this type—indeed any museum—is to make visitors see what is not there . . . *to make it come alive again*, and somehow I put it over best for groups rather than individuals. Perhaps it's the ham in me."

Here at Wood Street are the only publicly displayed photos of Jack the Ripper's victims, including a full frontal nude shot of Catherine Eddowes showing the zipperlike "Ripper's Rip" as she experienced it in the little alley between Mitre Square and Duke Street. (Other Ripper venues in the East End included Duval Street, Gunthorpe Street, Castle Alley, and Swallow Gardens.) Dare you shut your eyes tightly as Donald Rumbelow, his rich Cambridge accent melding to low Cockney, lays on an eerie reading from two of the Ripper's notes. The first, to one Mr. Lusk of the Whitechapel Vigilante Com-mittee, was sent "From Hell":

> "Mr. Lusk
> "Sir, I send you half the kidney I took from one woman. 'Tother piece I fried and ate. It was very nice. I may send you the bloody knife that took it out if only you wait a while longer. [*Horrible rasping whisper*] Catch me if you can Mister Lusk."

Another letter was sent to the pathologist:

> "Old Boss
> "You was right, it was the left kidney. I was going to operate again close to your 'ospital. Just as I was going to draw me knife along of her bloomin' throat them cusses of coppers spoiled the game but I guess I will be on the job soon and will send you another bit of innards.
> > Jack the Ripper."

The Wood Street Police Museum is also a wonderful repository of nine-teenth-century police history. What must be one of the earliest mug-shot files extant contains 1850s daguerreotypes portraying dozens of Dickensian petty criminals, most of them, like one "Mary Ann Welch," street or shop thieves, and a Mister Andrew Howell, convicted of that classic crime: "robbing a drunken sailor." There are also death masks of hanged men, mementoes of public executions that were held outside Newgate Prison until 1868, and an early police inspector's coat; the high collar has a leather stock to prevent garrotting. (See *Frenzy?*)

nightclubs   Among London's many, many "membership" nightclubs (see *What's On*), none gives better value for your money than Harry Meadows' CHURCHILL'S (160 New Bond Street, W.1; 493–2626). And the PLAYBOY CLUB (45 Park Lane, W.1; 629–9211) is to the PENTHOUSE CLUB (11 Whitehorse Street, W.1; 493–1977) what *Playboy Magazine* is to *Penthouse Magazine*.

penis (Napoleon's)   CHRISTIE'S FINE ART AUCTIONEERS (8 King Street, S.W.1) has had it. Removed from the Emperor by his confessor-priest. The catalogue described it as "a small dried-up object." "Looks like a seahorse," said a night porter. Phone Christie's at 839–9060 if you want it. It is rather surprising that the thing was "withdrawn" (the auctioneer's own phrase) at a recent sale, even considering the £13,300 price and one-inch length—Napoleon suffered a rare disease that makes the phrase "Not tonight Josephine" no idle maxim—for Christie's backs right on to the Eccentric Club.

"I don't care a twopenny damn what becomes of the ashes of Napoleon Bonaparte," said the Duke of Wellington. Nonetheless, at the WELLINGTON MUSEUM OF APSLEY HOUSE, Hyde Park Corner, you can see the most ludicrous statue in London, a fifteen-foot-high nude prepostrocity of the Emperor with luxuriant pubic hair but *sans* privates (covered by an enormous fig leaf).

photography (portraits)   "ATTRACTIVE FEMALE PHOTOGRAPHER will photograph you any way you pose." But you mustn't move, of course, or the photograph will blur. "Comfortable and quiet North London studio. Details 272–8033 after 2 p.m. Twenty Shots £10."

pornography   The law and practice are pretty clear on this one, if recent precedents can be relied upon: if you maintain a seedy bookshop in Soho, or better yet in Paddington, particularly in vicinity of Paddington Station and display *in the front windows,* so that all pedestrians, including children just old enough to toddle, can see material on necrophilia, bondage, flagellation, etc., and if you stock in your "looking for something a bit stronger, sir" back rooms (which several clerks laughingly admit are absolutely against the law for what they contain) the most graphic and the most crude photographs and booklets for sale or exchange—from £2 to £7 for what you'd pay a quarter the price in Amsterdam or Copenhagen—the authorities don't care a fig about your enterprise.

If, however, you edit a protest magazine that attacks the Establishment and its conventions as does *OZ,* whose erotic articles, drawings, and illustrations are made to resemble the *Tales of Benjamin Bunny* when placed alongside what's available in even the front rooms of some Paddington shops (at least two of whose clerks estimate that up to 50 percent of their trade is in flagellation "literature") . . . if you edit such a magazine as *OZ* No. 28, the judge may flip his learned wig and sentence you to up to fifteen months in prison. And the police will cut your hair.

Next case.

pubs   There are about 6000 in or near London. Or maybe 7000. Hours are staggered in hopes patrons won't be (and in order to give the pubs time to "breathe" and to clean them). Most pubs open at 11 A.M., close at 3 P.M., reopen at 5:30, and close at 11 P.M. Sunday from noon until 2 P.M. is a big scene, and then from 7 to 10:30 or 11 P.M.

There are Polish pubs (POLISH HEARTH, 55 Princes Gate, S.W.7), pubs with polish (RED LION, 1 Waverton Street, W.1), with a balcony (THE GRAPES, Narrow Street, E. 14), with pilots and stewardesses (THE GOAT, 3 Stafford Street, W. 1), with wine (BULL'S HEAD, Leadenhall Street, Aldgate, E.C.3), with waterfall inside (COACH AND HORSES, 29 High Road, W.4), with doctors (DEVONSHIRE ARMS, 21a Devonshire Street, W.1), lawyers (ESSEX HEAD, 40 Essex Street, W.C.2), dead monks (MONKS' TAVERN, Craven Street, W.C.2), live satirists (PUNCH TAVERN, 99 Fleet Street, E.C.4), television commentators (GROSVENOR ARMS, 2 Grosvenor Street, W.1), TITS! (FEATHERS, 20 Broadway, S.W.1; also has discothèque), top of the pops (TRAFALGAR, 200 King's Road, S.W.3), jazz (BULL'S HEAD, 373 Lonsdale Road, S.W.13), country and western music (NASHVILLE ROOM, 171 North End Road, W. 14), old-time music hall and river view too (THE OLD SWAN, 116 Battersea Church Road, S.W.11), champagne (THE CASK AND GLASS, Palace Street, in Victoria, S.W.1), and caviar? (EMPRESS OF RUSSIA, 362 St. John Street, E.C.1), American girls (CHESHIRE CHEESE, 145 Fleet Street, E.C.4), English girls in a courtyard (BRITANNIA, 1 Allen Street, W.8, off Kensington High Street), poetic girls (HENEKEYS, Westbourne Grove, W.11), East End girls (PEARLY QUEEN and the BLIND BEGGAR, both in Whitechapel Road, E.1; best time, Friday and Saturday nights), Australian girls (SURREY, 9 Surrey Street, W.C.2), French girls (BAR NORMANDIE, 22 Portman Square, W.1; first floor), German girls (BIERKELLER, 103 Queensway, W.2), opera-singing girls (OPERA TAVERN, Drury Lane, W.C.2), Scandinavian girls (HORSE SHOE, Tottenham Court Road, W. 1), boxers (BUTCHERS ARMS, 256 York Way, N.7; gym in same building), butchers (NEWMARKET, 26 Smithfield Street, E.C.1; here's rum in your tea at 6 a.m.), more boxers and another gym (THOMAS A BECKET, 320 Old Kent Road, S.E.1), ambassadors (PLUMBER'S ARMS, 14 Lower Belgrave Street, S.W.1), plumbers (very hard to find in London), thespians (NAGS HEAD, Floral Street, W.C.2), thrifty drinkers (ADMIRAL CODRINGTON, 17 Mossop Street, S.W.3; remarkably low prices), M.P.'s (ST. STEPHEN'S, 10 Bridge Street, S.W.1), pensioners (ROSE AND CROWN, Turk's Row, S.W.1), stevedores and bosuns (ROUND HOUSE, 19 Manor Way, E.16), songwriters and songpluggers (ROYAL GEORGE, Charing Cross Road, W.C.2), radicals, "but not your hippie types, mind you" (ROSSLYN, Rosslyn Hill, N.W.3 in Hampstead).

There are pubs for romantics, many along the river such as BOULTERS LOCK, Maidenhead, Berks (phone Maidenhead, 21–291) which has candlelight, dancing, and a splendid terrace to propose on. CITY BARGE (27 Strand on the Green, W.4) occupies a 1484 pub site and features a hearty, roaring hearth.

There are also pubs where people go to drink. Try THE BARLEY MOW (8 Dorset Street, W.1) or BILLY'S BOOZER (Coventry Street, W.1).

Pubs are people. Go to a place like the versatile KINGS ARMS (98 Kennington Lane, S.E.11) or move off the King's Road in Chelsea and explore the convivial pubs in and off Lawrence Street, S.W.3, and you will see why London has so many pubs and so comparatively few psychiatrists.

If you still can't find a pub to suit you, visit THE PUB INFORMATION CENTER, operated by St. George's Taverns (333 Vauxhall Bridge Road, S.W.1), Monday through Friday between 11 A.M. and 3 P.M. They will arrange a personal introduction to one of their 381 pubs. Or phone their 24-hour "DIAL-A-PUB" service at 828-3261.

rubber apparel   KASTLEY LIMITED are to Latex, Starsheen, and Glamatex garments what Johnny Sutcliffe is to leather—the best in the kingdom. Made-to-measure or off-the-peg capes, hooded suits, corsets, Italian or French knickers, panty bloomers, bras, jockstraps, sleeping bags, eyeshields, chin supporters, "Balaclava Style Hoods," and thus and so—in colors of the empire or the rainbow, from mango and mimosa to mink, lynx-green, and ice-pink. Write Kastley Limited, P.O. Box 24, Blackburn, Lancs., for an illustrated catalogue and some feely swatches; or phone Accrington 37591 and request a plant tour (Altham Industrial Estate, Burnley Road, Altham, Lancs).

sex change (and communes)   Yes, it can be had under the National Health, at cost to the taxpayer of about £300, including three weeks in hospital. Foreigners will, of course, pay more. There are a couple of physicians in Harley Street who know about this.

This is not the kind of thing one undergoes merely on the advice of a friend who says, "Try it. You'll like it!" You might first send one dollar to 196 Main Road, Romford, Essex, for a copy of *Two in One,* a magazine linked with GRAIL (Gender Research Association International Liaison). And perhaps you'd like to visit THE TRANS SEX TRIP, a commune of transsexuals. They welcome transsexual, sex-change, transvestite visitors, "and also kinky people (R & B tightlacers) and Commune Movement people," according to *Alternative London.* To secure their address write to The Secretary, THE COMMUNE MOVEMENT, 12 Mill Road, Cambridge, an organization which has no special affiliation with The Trans Sex Trip commune, but rather is devoted to aiding and forwarding mail to dozens of communes in the London area.

If you aren't interested in having your sex changed but are interested in communes in general, send one dollar, or equivalent, to The Commune Movement and they will forward their directory of communes of every variety.

sex shops   There's a certain musty Edwardian ambiance about those seedy barbershops and "ethical suppliers" dispensing sex aids, but by and large you'd best save your custom for Germany, Denmark, and Holland.

Ann Summers' sex supermarket in the Edgeware Road was a bland copy of Beate Uhse's German operation, from whom many of the Summers products were imported. Several of the best-selling stimulants (strong on caffein) and coitus-prolongers (simple local-anesthetics ointments) that she sold are available at your friendly neighborhood chemist's at one third her prices. Miss Summers, a pretty, pleasantly plump blonde, admitted that she was a mere front for the place and recently left the organization—but not before trying out "all these products myself first"—shortly before the shop closed "for lack of custom."

The SANDRA X leatherwear, rubberwear boutique (52 Shepherd Market, W.1), whose show window contains nothing but a very English sign proclaiming "certain articles are not displayed as they may offend some members of the public," has been called "an absolute disgrace" by the chairman of the Shepherd Market Association, which protects what it calls the neighborhood's "traditional character." Even some of the neighborhood practitioners have attacked Sandra X as "unesthetic," perhaps because the quality and selection of wet-look underwear, slave chains, chastity belts, whips, cushion vaginas, zip-front pussy-fur G-strings, and Welsh ticklers are mediocre at best.

PELLEN CENTRE (for the last time!) is long on male prosthetics, contraceptives, clitoral and vaginal stimulators, technique manuals; resident psychologists hear confessions, give "sound advice" in private cubicles. There's a trendy little sex boutique somewhere amid the stalls of Kensington Market (Kensington High Street, W.8) and another in GREAT GEAR TRADING CORPORATION, 85 King's Road, S.W.3. And a couple of others near Tottenham Court Road.

The nicest shop for couples to visit, or young ladies on their own, is probably LOVECRAFT (13 Tottenham Court Road, W.1; 580–7814), "the walkaround shop for lovers." Soft lighting, soft music, and "an atmosphere of friendliness and helpfulness . . . even the most reserved individuals can feel at ease. Our staff are experts in the business of the shop and can answer all your queries." Moreover, you are most welcome to browse and inspect, even if you don't purchase any of the wide variety of family planning products, sex aids, books and films. Open 9 A.M. to midnight, Monday to Saturday.

shower (assisted)   Even in the best hotels or the most elegant homes a shower can be hard to come by in England. (You could always provoke some Gentleman coming out of a St. James's club to throw a glass of water in your face, but this is liable to get your clothing wet.) The bathtub, however luxurious, is not always practical for the time-pressed traveler. Rejoice, then, that

AQUARIUS SAUNA AND MASSAGE SALON not only has showers—not to mention "sauna, massage, manicure . . . and a fully qualified female staff at your service"—but something they advertise as "Assisted Shower" as well. Located at 278 Gray's Inn Road, W.C.1, Aquarius is convenient after visiting the law courts or Fleet Street. Open all week, 10 A.M. to midnight; 278–1691.

Should you feel the urge to sing during the assisted shower, but find yourself at a loss for words, here, first from Sir Winston Churchill and then from John Osborne, are some.

"Let us therefore brace ourselves . . . and so bear ourselves that if the British Empire and its Commonwealth last for a thousand years, men will still say:"

"Yes, this was our finest shower."

slavery   The ANTI-SLAVERY SOCIETY (membership £3 a year; 296 Vauxhall Bridge Road, S.W.1; 834–6065) keeps tabs on those polygamous sheiks in some of the better Mayfair hotels, reports that Saudi Arabia remains the center of world slave trade, and insists that "the problem of European girls in harems should be looked into." Secretary, Col. J. R. P. Montgomery, M.C., has evidence of a number of cases in which English girls of "good families" have either been enticed or kidnapped and disappeared without a trace. Lock up your daughters.

"striptease" (professional and amateur)   The original proper English strippers were probably the "posture girls" who first appeared in Great Russell Street around 1750, close by where now stands the British Museum; therein you can browse a copy of the 1766 *Midnight Spy,* which describes their art:

"Behold an object which rouses at once our disgust and our pity. A beautiful woman lies stretched on the floor and offers to the view just those parts of her body that, were she not without all shame, she would most zealously seek to conceal. As she is given to drink, she arrives usually half drunk, and after two or three glasses of Madeira exposes herself to men in this unseemly manner. Look, she is on all fours now, like an animal. She is ridiculed, and men gloat over such prostitution of incomparable beauty."

And still they gloat, in certain seedy Soho cellars, the act having changed little in such clubs for donkey's years but for the addition of a scratchy gramophone record. If you haven't the 50NP-to-£1 admission, not to worry: the girls are nearly as exciting observed dashing the streets from one club to the next, for many work six or more cellars from noon to 2 A.M. Most strippers are young, tough, and pretty enough. If you get sufficiently hotted up by the salty banter exchanged with Midlands gents up to London on a tear, at the push of certain Berwick or Wardour Street or other Soho doorbells you can interfere with a "French Model" for £3 including the "French letter." However, the amenities fall considerably short of those afforded the noble and royal patrons of England's first "French-style" brothel, established 1750 by Mrs. Goadby right here in Berwick Street, "to refine our various amusements." Indeed it did, providing a selection of beautiful girls of many nations —to rival a modern Mecca Miss World contest—as skilled with the lute and embroidery needle as with their snappers, surrounded by costly laces and silks, imbibing nothing stronger than almond milk, mind you.

Don't play "knocking down ginger" with the busy doorbells near Wardour Mews marked "Model." One of the ponces may cosh you proper. "Make 'em cry, they'll piss the less," snarls a young tearaway of his teen-age charges who work the alleys after the doorbells go dark around 1 A.M. In the eighteenth century they might have stocked the brothel of one Mrs. Nelson, at nearby Wardour and Hollen Streets, who took a position as girls' school governess to insure her clients a constant transfusion of virgin blood.

Though PAUL RAYMOND REVUEBAR insists that it is "the world center of Erotic Entertainment" (Brewer Street, W.1; 734–1593), perhaps the most esthetic environment for watching people take off their clothing is wherever LONDON HEALTH AND SAUNA CLUB is staging its mixed naturist meetings.

amateurs

Currently L. H. and S. C. are at the Queensway Health Club (125 Queensway, W.2), having recently moved from pishposh Knightsbridge. More relaxed than even the very progressive Berlin saunas, London H & S even have mixed locker rooms, affording an unparalleled opportunity to watch a stunning variety of English people getting undressed: from vivacious young debs and dolly birds to haughty Belgravia matrons; handsome Guards officers too, and mischievous old warhorses with fascinating battle scars. A slow, if not tantalizing peel, considering they chatter a lot along the way prior to storming the very convivial capacity-fifteen sauna. Wondrous sights at the cccccconveyer bbbbbelt exercisers. For further details contact London Health and Sauna Club: The Secretary, Vikki Sheppard, Kent House, 87 Regent Street, W.1; 205–9251. They meet Monday, Wednesday, and Thursday from 8:30 to 11:30 P.M. £1.50 admission charge per couple, single ladies 50NP. Yearly membership £2. About six hundred members, tending to under-thirty-fives. "Naked as the truth," as the English say, but *this is strictly a health* club (and has no affiliation with Queensway Health Club).

At this writing the club hopes the local council clarifies its exemption from licensing bylaws, which apparently discourage mixed facilities, or alternatively will grant a permit for a mixed sauna and health club. To aid its case, there must be as close a balance of the sexes as possible, and so male members unaccompanied by a female are charged £2 per session. Prospective new male members may be denied admission on nights when there is already an imbalance, unless they are with a female. A single man could always chat up an unaccompanied female member on her way in, or perhaps pluck a partner from a lively Queensway café. Also, in accordance with council bylaws, apparently males can be massaged only by males, females by females. If the club receives its exemption, this restriction will no longer apply.

Unisex saunas, herb baths at SWISS COTTAGE SAUNA, from 9:30 A.M. to 4 A.M., at 2 New College Parade, Finchley Road, N.W. 3; 586-4422.

Perhaps the most exciting starkers club is Mark Wilson's very relaxed EUREKA CLUB in Pennis Woods near Fawkham, Kent (Longfield 4418). With over one thousand members (many females, all admitted free) Mr. Wilson—who as "Mark Langtry" was jailed for eighteen months in 1955 for running a call-girl bureau and later operated Jane's strip house—claims it to be the fastest-growing nudist club in England. (But he is absolutely out of the call-girl business or any other funny business.) Jolly dress-up parties: "Everyone wears paper hats." Sign at the gate reads "Trespassers welcome." Phone Mark or his wife, Maureen, at home (Gravesend 64-207). If you can't catch them there, ring the office and they may invite you over for color films and coffee.

The nearby NORTH KENT SPORTS, SOCIAL, SWIMMING AND SUNBATHING CLUB (Sheepcote Lane, Orpington, Kent; only sixteen miles from London) claims to be Europe's largest; over fifteen hundred members, nearly six hundred of them children under eighteen. Fifty acres of excellent facilities; family oriented.

QUEEN'S HOUSE is a misnomer for this very heterosexual naturist hotel, comprising a splendid 1809 Georgian mansion and seven acres of romantic garden and woods. Single bed and breakfast £2.50. Double-bedded rooms £25 per week per guest, singles £25 the week. Write Box 5, Dept. NR, Deal, Kent, or phone Deal 3565.

Bill Richardson's NATURIST PROJECTS may have a certain appeal to singles aged twenty-one to forty or so. Write his FIVEACRES CLUB, The Bungalow, 8 Nascot Wood Road, Watford, Herts; phone 47 (Garston) 73-073.

swingers' club   "CLUB SYLVANO, London's club for the swinging set. A modern club with modern ideas [though not a few Ancient Romans may have had similar ones]." For details, and "screening interview" appointment, write the Membership Secretary, 60 The Chase, S.W.4. Enclose S.A.E. The chase is on every Friday and Saturday night, beginning around 8:30 P.M. *Go early,* because people tend to move fast here and the nice ones are often gone by 9:30. You're sure to be chatted up, down, and sideways by "like-minded" couples, but this being a typical English club—it's in *Clapham,* not Paris!—nothing but conversation (very friendly, albeit to-the-point) occurs; on premise, that is.

topless   A UPI dispatch from Doncaster (a Yorkshire city of about 86,000) alleges that in the early spring of 1972 three male bath attendants were discharged from the municipal swimming pool "for drilling a peep hole from the men's to the women's dressing room." Coincidentally, England has recently gone topless heavy.

In London CLUB BELLES DE NUIT (14 Rupert Street, W.1; 437–6001) has topless barmaids and "completely see-thru waitresses. Top and bottom!" Open to 3:30 a.m. CRAZY HORSE (2 Allsop Place, N.W.1; 486–1873) has topless waitresses, striptease until its 1 A.M. closing and, like Belles de Nuit, 25p drinks. More topless in Mayfair at THE BACCHUS (23 Woodstock Street; 629–0906). At 23 Gerrard Street is EL PASO, topless restaurant. (At No. 43 lived poet John Dryden. "Sex to the last," said he.)

transvestites   Cross-dressers, not necessarily homosexuals, are uncommonly common in England. The frivolous may be found Saturday mornings in the King's Road; midnight to 5 A.M. in the Earl's Court Road; the serious in some of the better public schools or weekending it in Cromwell Road *pieds-à-terre.* If you are what author Dr. Harry Benjamin calls a "true transvestite," the BEAUMONT SOCIETY (BM/Box 3084, London W.C.1) will advise you and perhaps find you good company. Write Sylvia Carter, Secretary.

Behind the façade of a most ordinary, working-class shoeshop in Westbourne Grove (Bayswater, W.2) is the showroom of a most extraordinary couturier—COVER GIRL, "Specialist Outfitters for Stage, Film, and T.V." For over thirty years Cover Girl (and her father for 25 years more) has played Chanel to transvestites—"Today I have not a few peers, some prominent physicians and executives, several doctors, a famous wrestler, even a Covent Garden porter among my many customers. You find cross-dressing at all levels of society. Why, I even have a blind man who visits me to buy clothes."

Everything is either made to order or carefully selected "as to the individual's special needs" from the "Falsies . . . £1.50, add 50 New Pence if nipples required" to "Bishop, halter, polo or deep cleavage . . . evening gowns, from £30." "Three very clever dressmakers" are on staff who will copy any design. They also do underwear, corsets, negligees, etc. Cover Girl herself consults closely with all callers, giving as much attention to the dustman's quandary over how wide should be his "Victorian black velvet neckband" (with pearl drop on front, £2) as to the rigorous needs of the many professional drag "artistes" who swear by her. (Only Virginia P. of the United States has a comparable reputation in this field, the Continent aside.) She also does an extensive mail-order trade: "Of course we advertise in the national press, but with discretion. Quite ordinary adverts for shoes, you see. But comparing the sizes and heel lengths tells you who we are. . . ." Indeed, the ads offer a wide range of mules, pumps, etc. with spiked heels up to seven inches, sizes "tiny 4 to large 12."

Drop in at Desmond Montmorency's book shop (283 Camden High Street, N.W.1) and ask him to contact his friend Victor Heppel. Mr. Heppel will, in turn, secure your appointment with Cover Girl.

VD   Some of the best English people have had it, including King Edward VII. Up 79 percent in the past nine years. Good checkup and cure facilities at JAMES PRINGLE CLINIC, corner Charlotte and Tottenham Streets, W.1; *call first:* 636–8333, ext. 664. UNIVERSITY COLLEGE HOSPITAL (Gower Street, W.C.2; 387–9300) is nearly as friendly and equally discreet. Both are good places to snatch groupies, particularly Monday mornings. Dr. R.D. Catteral, head of the Pringle Clinic, says that in large cities like London, New York, and Paris, more than half the infectious syphilis seen in clinics occurs among homosexual men.

vampires   Armed with a crucifix and sharp stake one recent summer midnight, Allan F—— was ferreting for them in ST. MICHAEL'S CHURCHYARD, HIGHGATE CEMETERY, N.6, undoubtedly the best venue in town. GEORGE ALEXANDER, Jeweller of the Occult (63 Queen's Gardens, W.2; write him) will fashion a silver bullet, wooden stake, talisman, wand. Or what? ARCANE SCHOOL (235 Finchley Road, N.W.3; 794–5788) meets every full moon.

virgins   "Tying down for the purpose of rape is not at all unusual in Half Moon Street," declared an 1885 issue of the *Pall Mall Gazette,* Iwan Bloch's primary source (and everyone's else's) for his exhaustive chapter on the English "Defloration Mania." The "systematically organized traffic" in virgins and "patched-up" virgins was so well organized that the procurers even had their own physicians who, upon duly examining a child, provided her custodian a certificate guaranteeing the merchandise as *"virgo intacta"* and thus worth the asking price . . . varying, according to supply and demand from £5 to 20. Editor William T. Stead of the *Gazette* offered documents like the following in evidence to the rather reluctant government investigating commission, some of whom knew more about the business than they cared to admit:

—— St.,London,W.
17th June, 1885

I hereby state that I have to-day examined D., sixteen years old, and confirmed her virginity.

Dr. ——

In attempting to explain why the "defloration mania should have reached such epidemic dimensions," Bloch observed that "for the Englishman, only the best is good enough. He must have something which can only once, and by only one person, be possessed, and of which he can boast before others. This is the case as regards the virginity of a girl, which attracts the Englishman primarily as something select and unique."

Well, of course, one might say much the same for the Englishman's taste for bespoke tailoring. And considering that since Victorian times, he's lost his bent for neither, a visitor is bound to find precious few attractive girls in London at or above the age of consent (sixteen, but there is some talk of lowering it to fourteen) who'd pass muster in the Harley Street stirrups. However, don't despair. In addition to the thousands who come up to London each year from the provinces, many *au pair* and "student" girls arrive from the Continent with the expressed purpose of gaining a fair command of the language, savoring the London way of life, and losing their innocence in the bargain, away from prying family and neighbors.

They have their favorite "ethnic" discothèques—like RHEINGOLD (361 Oxford Street, W.1; German and Austrian girls); LE KILT (60 Greek Street, W.1; French girls); or DIE FLEDERMAUS (7 Carlisle Street, W.1; Scandinavian girls)— but are as likely to be found at any of the places of the moment in the West End, Chelsea, South Kensington, Fulham, etc. Not a few hang around the King's Road's only "international" terrace café, the PICASSO. Several are courted daily by Marcel Chagall, a round little Jacques Tati character who affects Panama hats and gold-knobbed walking sticks, and has been barred from the PHEASANTRY discothèque for urinating in its venerable fountain. M. Chagall, who says he is a nephew of the great painter, enjoys sketching the neighborhood beauties, then presents the portraits to the girls and the girls to his *amis*. If you prefer to work without such a lure as M. Chagall, just amble along the King's Road some Saturday morning, or Kensington High Street, managing to look young (it is some help, but not mandatory, if you really are), very sympathetic, gentle, and at the same time "old dog."

If all this fails, punt. The best place to do this is in a stream up at Cambridge or Oxford, according to 1972 virginity surveys conducted by the undergraduate publications *Isis* and *Varsity*. "Then worms shall try/That long preserved virginity" (see Andrew Marvell) at Cambridge where fifty-five percent of female students and forty-seven percent of males were found to be stainless as steel. At Oxford, where, perhaps, "the virgins are as soft as the roses they twine" (sorry, Byron), forty-seven percent of the female undergraduates and forty percent of the males were "as chaste as ice, as pure as snow" (see Shakespeare). Perhaps in response to this lugubrious state of affaires (see virginity studies in "Stockholm" and "Copenhagen" chapters), "a growing number of school teachers—'at present about one hundred'—are in favor of specially furnished rooms in schools where pupils can make love," according to London journalist John Ezard's appraisal of Bruce Kemble's book *Give Your Child a Chance.*

witches   ALEX SAUNDERS and other better witches cast spells (but not at virgins) at CRAFT WORKSHOP, 15A Glenricade Gardens, W.2; 229–6861.

yellow Rolls-Royce   Attend Ascot, propose marriage (or divorce), or simply debark the aircraft with pomp and circumstance in a 1930 Laundaulette 20/25 Rolls Limousine whose rear roof folds down for "royal waving." Equipped with Fortnum & Mason hamper, Taittinger champagne, H. Uppman cigars, Biba-ed blond chauffeur-guide (or appropriate male): £50 the day, or £32 without the accessories. From HORSELESS CARRIAGE HIRE (59 Eccleston Square Mews, S.W.1; 834–9922), who promise virtually any make and color car in twenty-four hours—Maserati Ghibli, Jensen FF, etc. Ferraris £4 the hour, including the blonde. *(As chauffeur.)*

zoophilia   HARRODS fourth-floor zoo (Knightsbridge, S.W.1; 730–1234) qualifies as an avisodomist's dream, but only on the grounds that they can supply virtually anything from an emu to a zebu to a kinkajou (dearth of rocs, however). One can meet, shake paws with the animal before purchasing, perhaps even take him off on approval for the weekend, then bring him back for exchange. As noted, this is merely a dream, for Harrods, being even more English than the next store, would, if they knew what one had in mind, absolutely refuse to sell the animal for such use. Indeed, an incredulous attendant nearly wept with rage when told what would be required of one of his monkeys, and of course refused to part with the little chap at any price. But then there is always Covent Garden. Or the Regent's Park Zoo if you're quick about it.

This is hardly an appropriate note on which to leave London, but no zed words come to mind that alphabetically follow "zoophilia." Too bad "kiss" doesn't begin with "Z." Yes, Sir Max Beerbohm's "Zuleika, on a desert island, would have spent most of her time in looking for a man's footprint." But "she was hardly more affable than a cameo." Perhaps it is most appropriate to seek the assistance of that man who is the zenithal authority on sex, love, and romance among the English, not to mention the rest of the human race.

"Zounds!   I was never so bethump'd with words."

—WILLIAM SHAKESPEARE, *King John*, II, i, 466